SOCIAL INSTINCT

KRISTAL STITTLE

SEVERED PRESS

SOCIAL INSTINCT

For Phyllis & Doug, Barb & Ken, and Doug & Pam

Each of whom saved me from disaster at one point or another.

SECTION 1:
HUNGER

1: EVANS
5 DAYS AFTER THE BOMBING

Moe plodded along the side of the road, his hooves kicking up little puffs of dust. The old grey horse seemed to appreciate that he no longer needed to carry riders, only supplies. Evans barely had to lead him, the reins slack as the pair moved at the same sedate pace.

"How much longer?" Gerald complained, following anxiously behind them.

"Days," Evans replied. "Even longer if your whining causes anything to take notice of us."

Gerald huffed. He was not a good travel companion, but Evans had promised to bring the teenager to some place that would accept him for who he was. While it wasn't exactly a common belief, he wasn't the first person to think the zombies should be treated as something other than a threat. Evans had met all kinds of people during his travels.

"How many days?" Gerald whispered, unable to keep quiet for more than a couple of minutes.

"Depends."

"On what?"

"On who and what we come across. And whether my injuries get infected." Evans had been glad to help the people in the shipping container yard, to make up for the pointless attack he had allowed his party to wage, but he hadn't escaped the task unharmed. During their rush across farm fields to set off a bomb that would collapse an underground facility full of hostiles, they had been seen. Most of the enemy there had been distracted by the arrival of a submarine—which began hurling zombie offal at them with a pair of trebuchet-type devices mounted on top—but not all of them. Thankfully, the hostiles who had spotted the little gang of outsiders had come up from below ground, unready and relatively unarmed. Evans' Scottish broadsword had come in handy at that point, as he was able to fend off the blades of others, keeping safe Rose, the one-handed woman who carried the detonator. He had received several minor cuts during the encounter, and a particularly bad one along the back of his left forearm that caused some concern.

After the explosion, a deafening crack that had caused the ground to buck and sent great plumes of dust and debris hurtling through the air, the invasion team had had to about-face and run the other way. The confusion and chaos had provided some cover, but they had finally been spotted by men with rifles. Bullets whizzed past as they had run for the fence. Everyone had made it over and back to the building where they had stashed their gear, but they weren't all in great condition. Rose was the best off, as they had protected her on the way in. She had sustained only one bad gash on her arm with the amputated hand during their escape. Canary's older leg wound had reopened, and Doyle had received a fairly bad gash along his side. James had taken at least one round, maybe more, to his foot. Pure adrenaline had managed to keep him running on it. Jamal was the worst off, having had to be slung between Rose and James as they crossed the field. He might not have survived. Evans had no idea, because he had separated from them at that point, going back to where Moe and Gerald were supposed to be waiting. It wasn't until Evans was safely among the trees with no sign of pursuit, that he had stopped for a breather and discovered a bullet hole through his pants. He had been very lucky that the shot hadn't been just slightly more to the right where it would have caught his leg as well.

"You should have gone to get medical attention," Gerald continued to whisper. "They could have given you antibiotics."

Evans didn't bother with a response. This ground had been covered before. If he had gone back with them, he wasn't sure when he'd get the chance to leave again. Gerald wouldn't have waited, and Evans didn't trust the teen to take care of Moe properly. Instead, he had stitched up his arm himself—not the first time he had needed to administer his own aid—and then carefully wrapped it, using supplies the container yard folk had sent with him. A few of his other wounds he had bandaged as well, in order to keep them clean, but he wasn't all that worried about them. He had survived worse.

"What happens if you die?"

Evans sighed. "Then I imagine you'll take some rope and turn me into a pet." The comment bought a blessed ten minutes of silence.

"I can't stop thinking about them."

"About who?" Evans knew he'd end up getting the answer to that question even if he didn't ask.

"All those people I killed who were attacking the container yard."

"You mean the giant zombie horde? They weren't people; they were already dead."

"But how do you *know*?"

"Because people want to do more than just eat my face."

"But what if they could be helped? Maybe if people just tried to communicate, they wouldn't be like that."

"Trust me, if there was more to them than that, someone would have figured it out by now, and I would have heard about it."

"Right, 'cause you're the great traveller. I heard you didn't know about the mega horde before those runners showed up," Gerald sneered.

"Shut up."

"What, have I hurt your feelings?"

"Shut up!" Evans hissed back at him as he brought Moe to a stop. "I heard something."

The colour drained from Gerald's face as he scuttled closer to Evans, turning his back to Moe and searching the area with eyes wide. Evans watched the horse, as well as their surroundings, trusting the beast's greater senses of hearing and smell. When Moe suddenly raised his head with a snort, and focused his ears ahead and across the road, Evans faced in that direction. He placed one hand on the hilt of his sword, and the other on his shotgun. Unfortunately, he had no ammunition for the latter and could only use it as a prop with which to scare people. The ruse had worked before, but it was unreliable and risky.

A single zombie came stumbling out of the trees. Evans waited, expecting more, since they usually roamed in packs, but no others came. It was a lone dead thing, and a slow one at that, so Evans relaxed.

"Here's your chance to try communicating," Evans told Gerald, nodding toward the zombie that was making its way toward them.

"I'm not an idiot," Gerald glared at him. "You have to spend time with them, like you would a wild animal."

"Either way, it's your turn."

"My turn?"

"To kill it. I've been taking care of all of them so far. I know you fought the mega horde, but with the way you think, I can't trust you to watch my back until I witness it for myself. You have a knife, go put it down."

Evans was glad to see that Gerald didn't hesitate. He walked straight up to the shambling corpse, side-stepped as it lunged, and drove his knife into the side of its head. As the thing collapsed to the pavement, Gerald turned with his arms out, as if inviting Evans to give him another challenge. Evans just tugged lightly on Moe's reins to get him walking again.

"Happy?" Gerald said as he returned to Evans' side.

"I'd be happy if you would stop talking. But yes, it's good to know that you won't hesitate to take them out. We're coming up on another population centre."

The fear Evans was used to seeing in Gerald's posture and expression returned. Lately, they had been travelling through what had once been farmland, as well as forests and bogs where no one had bothered to build.

"Does anyone still live there?" Gerald's voice dropped into a low whisper again.

"I've never passed through the town up ahead, so I can't say. It's unlikely. Small towns tend to be pretty empty, but it is possible for someone to have set up shop there. And the dead are always present where the living used to be."

"Can we go around?"

"We can. It'll add at least another day's worth of travelling, maybe two depending on the terrain. Like I said, I've never been in this particular area before. It's your call." Evans had run into trouble in towns before, but he had also run into trouble outside of them. Going through the place would be quicker, whereas going around tended to provide more options for running with its open spaces.

"We'll go through," Gerald decided, a little unexpectedly. "Maybe we'll be able to find some more supplies."

Evans highly doubted that, but didn't say anything. If something were easy to find, it certainly would have been found by then, and they weren't going to be stopping anywhere long enough to do a thorough search.

The town came upon them gradually. The wild spaces that flanked the road slowly gave way to more and more structures until Evans and Gerald found themselves surrounded by shops and houses on all sides. They had been following a road through the town for several minutes before Evans realized that something was wrong and brought Moe to another stop. Gerald crowded up close behind him, listening intently.

"I don't hear anything," he finally whispered in Evans' ear.

"That's the problem. We need to turn back."

"Why?"

"I should have noticed it earlier. There's no trash. No leaves in the gutters. This breeze isn't moving anything. I should have seen it right away. Abandoned towns trap litter everywhere, and there's always broken shit creaking in the wind. Someone's cleaned this place up. We have to go back."

"Why would someone clean up a town like this?"

"Noise draws the dead, so if something makes a noise, you get rid of it. Right now, *we're* making noise, Moe especially. We're turning around."

Evans guided Moe in a tight circle, the horse's hooves clopping on the pavement that they hadn't been able to avoid. Their footfalls echoed between the silent buildings. Evans cursed himself for not having been more observant, for not seeing what wasn't there. Now that he had noticed it, the difference was quite obvious. It had been too long since Evans had travelled so alone, not surrounded by a party that he could rely on.

Before they could reach open space again, a figure walked out from between two buildings. The individual was dressed in a formless heap of rags that matched the drab shades of the town, and made it impossible to identify gender. The long rifle in the person's hands was unmistakable.

Evans brought Moe to a halt once more and raised his hands.

"You're not going to threaten them?" Gerald whispered.

"They've been watching us. They know exactly what I have on me. If they decided to come out, it's because they know they can take us. Now put your hands up."

Gerald raised his arms.

"We don't mean you any harm!" Evans called out to the individual, betting that there were more hiding, and that they were listening. "We're just travellers moving north, and came across your territory here by accident. We're happy to leave and go around."

The shrouded person in their path made no move. Beside Evans, Gerald kept shifting his weight back and forth. His jaw twitched as if he wanted to say something but wasn't sure what.

Moe let out a soft whinny and snorted, suddenly half turning with his ears twisted in the direction they had been headed originally. Evans looked back over his shoulder and saw a similarly attired person close behind them, holding a dark blade. The eerie part was that Evans hadn't heard a sound from either of them. These were silent people.

"Perhaps you'd be willing to make a trade? We could make a toll payment." Although what with, Evans had no idea. They weren't carrying anything that they could do without. Then again, exchanging anything for his life would be worth it.

"There's another one to the left," Gerald whispered.

Evans glanced over to confirm this for himself and saw another blade as well. "Keep your eyes on as many as possible. We don't want them getting closer." Trying to watch every direction at once wasn't easy, but at least with the two of them, it wasn't impossible.

Here and there, more of the clothing heaps appeared at the edges of the buildings and on rooftops. They were being watched by many eyes. But Evans again looked for what was missing and saw that only the first person carried a rifle. What would such silent people want with a gun anyway? Guns were noisy, and guaranteed to bring the dead.

"I have a plan," Evans whispered to Gerald over his shoulder. "But you're not going to like it."

"I'll take anything that'll get us out of here."

"You're going to jump on Moe and ride hard at the first person who showed up."

"You're right, I really don't like this plan."

"They're not going to shoot. These are silent people; guns are too loud. They probably don't even have any bullets."

"It's the probably that worries me. And what are you going to do?"

"Run after you."

"Run? As in on foot?"

"I don't see any horses among them, and I don't want to put too much strain on Moe by having him run with both of us and our supplies on his back."

"You're crazy."

"I'm open to saner suggestions."

One of the silent watchers took a step closer in full view of Evans.

"They're getting bolder."

"All right, fine. We'll go with your insane idea."

There was no sense in waiting, so Gerald quickly clambered up onto Moe's back. Evans gave the horse a hearty smack to his rump to get him running, and then took off after them. He drew his sword as he ran. The old horse immediately outpaced him. The silent one with the rifle stepped aside as the large beast bore down, and remained at a distance as Evans rushed past. There was something unnerving about it. As his breath puffed in and out, Evans risked a glance over his shoulder. No one was coming after them. Half just stood there, watching, while the other half faded back into the gaps from which they had appeared. Who were they? What had they wanted? And most importantly, why were they letting them just leave?

***

"What the hell was that?" Gerald asked after they had backtracked a fair distance and stopped to take a break in an overgrown field. Evans had removed the supplies and saddle from Moe's back, swapping his reins for his lead so that the horse could take a proper breather and munch on the greenery.

"I'm not sure. The only time I've ever run into silent ones like that before, was far to the north, but they didn't act like that."

"Why did they surround us like that only to let us leave?"

"I don't know. Maybe they just wanted to make sure we felt threatened enough that we wouldn't think of returning."

"We told them that we were travellers just passing through."

"Says the known liar."

Gerald bristled, hating it whenever Evans said something along those lines. Having first met the eighteen-year-old during his trial, Evans learned that Gerald

5

would immediately resort to lies if he thought they would get him out of a situation. It was one of the reasons why a travelling rule of theirs was that Evans would do all the talking whenever they came across living people. The other reason was that Evans simply had more experience at it.

The pair lapsed into silence as they nibbled on a light lunch.

"Which way do you think we should go around the town?" Evans eventually asked. He had been pondering the decision ever since they had been driven out.

"What's the fastest route?"

"I'm not sure. I can only guess the size of the town based on that overgrown population sign we passed on the way in, and that tells me nothing about the shape of the place. As far as I know, it's the same either way."

"We'll go that way then," Gerald pointed to their right.

"Why that way?"

Gerald just shrugged, apparently choosing the direction on a whim, not bothering to attempt to study the terrain. Still, it was a decision.

"East it is then."

Evans first checked on his injuries, unwrapping the bandages that ran up his arms. They didn't look great, but none of them looked infected. He took the cleanest of the bandages, and rewrapped the deep one on his left forearm. The others had actually closed over a while ago, and should be fine as long as he didn't reopen any of them.

"All right, let's get going," Evans said with a sigh. He liked the field in which they had stopped. Despite having to keep an eye out for snakes, and other dangers that might be crawling through the scrub, the place had great sight lines for anything bigger. With the strange way those silent ones had acted, being able to see around themselves felt important.

As Evans loaded up Moe again, the horse gave a disgruntled snort. He liked the field too, it seemed. They didn't bother returning to the road to the west of them, opting instead for the quicker route crossing the open terrain. Gerald led the way, sweeping the ground ahead of him with a long stick that he had found to clear off any snakes. A rattler bite was about as good as a zombie's when travelling. Hell, ever since the virus went airborne, the victims all turned unless someone took care of them after they died.

At the far end of the field, they came to a forested, yet marshy, area. The ground seemed solid enough, and neither Evans nor Gerald minded getting their feet wet. Evans took the lead once more, guiding them through the muck. He wanted that town as far to their backs as possible by the time they stopped for the night.

Evans' only warning was a moment of stubbornness from Moe. The horse stopped walking, although he gave no indication that he was afraid. Evans tugged sharply on his reins to get him moving again, only to manage just a few more steps. The mossy ground ahead wasn't nearly as stable as it had been everywhere else. Evans quickly found himself sinking hip deep into thick mud, unable to warn Gerald in time. The teenager also became trapped a few feet to his left and about a step behind him.

"Come on, Moe, you can do it," Evans quietly encouraged the disgruntled horse. "Pull me out."

"You're going to throw me a rope, right?" Gerald asked, struggling in vain to free his legs.

"Keep your voice down," Evans hissed at him. "This mud isn't natural."

Gerald paled and froze in place.

Evans had traversed plenty of terrain, including marshes, bogs, and swamps. He knew where water would gather, where mud like this would form, and it wasn't here, especially considering how abruptly they had come upon it. Someone had made this mud, and placed a weak carpet of moss overtop as camouflage.

"Come on, Moe," Evans continued to whisper, patting the big horse. "Get yourself out." Based on the tree roots ahead, the muck was in a narrow band, and they wouldn't have to go far before reaching more solid ground.

Moe pulled one leg free and took a step, his leg sinking back into the mire. Then he took another. But his progress soon halted as the horse snorted and tossed its mane.

"Uh, Evans? They're back," Gerald whimpered.

Evans looked around and confirmed that Gerald was telling the unfortunate truth. The silent ones were appearing from behind trees, gathering around the mud hole. One came forward, stopping at the edge of the mire in front of Evans. She pulled back the fabric from around her face, revealing an impassive gaze behind dirty camouflage markings. She held out her hand to Evans, but he didn't know what to do. She wasn't offering to help him; she was still too far away for that.

"Toss me the horse's reins or you shall never get out," she spoke in a breathy whisper.

Evans twisted to take in all those who had surrounded them. They truly were trapped this time. If the silent ones decided that he and Gerald weren't going anywhere, then they weren't. With a sigh, he threw Moe's reins to the woman. She didn't encourage the horse, or click her tongue, she simply leaned back as though to pull the horse out. Moe snorted in protest, but took another slow step.

"Go on," Evans patted his side again.

Moe strained against the suction of the mud, but at last freed himself. The woman handed his reins over to another silent one, who proceeded to walk Moe off through the trees, supplies and all.

"I take it you're stealing our stuff," Evans commented. "Pretty good trap you set up here."

The woman's face twitched with what seemed like her version of a smile.

"So are you going to leave us to try escaping on our own, or what?"

"Weapons," she whispered, pointing to the sword across Evans' back, and then to the shotgun at his hip.

The shotgun had to be pulled up out of the mud, but he tossed it over. "It's empty," Evans told the woman. "Gerald, give them your weapon," he instructed as he removed his sword, sheath and all.

"I can't," Gerald sulked. "My knife is in my boot."

The woman stayed still for a moment as two more silent ones whisked away Evans' things. She then made a gesture, and within seconds, two ropes had plopped down on top of the mud beside both Evans and Gerald. Evans grabbed hold of the one nearest him, but Gerald hesitated.

"We don't have a choice," Evans told him.

Gerald huffed and snatched up the rope. With a couple of silent ones hauling on each, Evans and Gerald were soon free of the sucking mud. Instantly, one of them fell upon Gerald's boot, finding his trench knife and relieving him of it.

"For future reference, that's a stupid place to keep it. Not easy to get to in a hurry," Evans told him.

"I think we have bigger problems than where I keep my knife right now," Gerald replied, lying on his back with his hands held partly up, splayed in a posture of harmlessness. All around the two of them, the silent ones stood with blades pointed inward.

Evans looked about until he found the one who had spoken. Her face was still the only one uncovered. "Anything else we can do for you?"

Her face twitched again, that possible smile. Then, in one swift motion, she had placed a rag over Evans' face. He responded quickly, which unfortunately meant that he also inhaled deeply. He scrambled up onto his feet and away from the rag, but it was already too late. The world spun around him, as the foul taste of some sort of ether danced across his tongue. With a thump, he dropped back down to his knees. As arms reached around him, jamming another rag across his mouth, Evans saw that Gerald was already passed out on the ground, another silent one administering to him. But then everything became watery, and went black. Evans didn't feel the ground when he hit it.

2: MISHA
3 DAYS AFTER THE BOMBING

There was no way to tell what time it was. All Misha knew was that he was hot and sweaty upon waking up. The hole in the roof of his container, the one once plugged by a plastic bottle filled with water and bleach to act as a light bulb, remained dark. Because of the rats, the hole had to be blocked off. A heavy log was currently up there, protecting his container home and those of his neighbours by lying across the openings. The rats also meant he had to keep his doors closed, preventing both light and airflow from entering. It took Misha several seconds to recall that he had been sleeping in the middle of the day, taking a nap instead of eating lunch rations again. It should be sometime in the afternoon, which explained the heat inside his metal box.

"Rifle?" Misha whispered, unable to recall if the dog had decided to lie with him or not. He flailed about to either side, but encountered no fur. All of his dogs were probably still out hunting rats, which was admittedly better for them than lying in this sweatbox. It had been three days since they set off the bombs in the Black Box, more since the attack of the mega-sized zombie horde, and still they were dealing with a bunch of infected rats. Boss said they came with the horde, that the little bastards lived on and in the zombies, the packed corpses making a travelling nest of food for the colony. His team had neglected to mention this fact when they had come to warn the shipping container yard of the mega horde's approach.

Pulling himself upright, Misha felt around for his boots, which he always left beside the mattress on which he slept. His sweater was a different matter. It should have been hanging nearby, but lately Misha had been letting it fall wherever he took it off before sleeping. Groping in the dark, his fingers finally located the thin fabric, but he didn't put it on as he had his boots. It was too hot for that. Continuing to conserve his various lights, Misha made his way to the doors of the container by feel, and pushed one of them open. Sunlight momentarily blinded him, and while the air felt good as it washed over his sweaty flesh, the smell didn't improve.

Once Misha's eyes adjusted, he looked about at the work still going on near his home. People were all over the place with buckets of sea water, rags, and mops, doing their best to clean off the slime the mega horde had left behind. The body burns were nearly complete. The ashes and remaining bones were being shovelled into the river that flanked one side of the container yard, but there were still bits and pieces of the dead things clinging to a lot of surfaces. It was unfortunate that they had been hit by a storm before the attack, as opposed to afterward. In fact, they were hoping for rain to bolster their fresh water stores.

Following the shadows of the containers in order to keep his shirt off and cool down, Misha made his way to the end of the 'street' where his container was situated. With all of the Black Box residents now moved in, as well as the travelling party members that had joined them, they had needed to come up with a system to help people navigate quickly. Each row of containers now had a name based on the colour and symbol painted on the end of it. Misha lived on

Green Plus, which sounded too much like pus for his liking, but he hadn't been given a choice in the matter.

"Misha! Hey, Misha!"

The voice calling after him was that of Riley, so Misha came to an instant stop. He knew she couldn't move very fast these days. Her chest was still healing from her surgery. As he turned to face her, he was again momentarily jarred by the flatness of her chest, still adjusting to the fact that she had had her breasts removed due to the likelihood of cancer.

At her side was Rifle, whose tail set to swinging when Misha smiled at him. The old German shepherd had taken to sticking by Riley's side whenever Misha wasn't around. Her hindered pace agreed with his own.

"Do you have any more extra boots or shoes?" Riley asked once they got close. Misha knelt down to rub Rifle's cheeks and ears.

"No, I've already given them all away." Misha had a tendency to collect footwear. After spending a good portion of the Day without any, his feet had become battered and scarred, an experience best not repeated. But several people from the Black Box hadn't been prepared for their forced exodus and so hadn't been able to get anything on their feet. Misha, knowing exactly what they would have gone through during their walk through the woods to the submarine, had donated his stockpile to their cause.

"Damn," Riley muttered. Convalescing was not something that Riley was good at, and therefore had been using her time assisting people with their needs as opposed to her own. She had helped create a list of the dead, and tracked down which containers were now empty so that other people could move into them. She tallied supplies, tested people's blood for infection, and now, it seemed, located needed items.

"Have you tried Idris?" Misha suggested. "He tends to have a lot, although it'll be harder to get him to give them up."

"Trust me, he's not going to have a choice in the matter. By the way, has Crichton found you yet?"

"No, I've been asleep."

"Well, he's looking for you."

"I gathered. Where can I find him?"

"Most likely the community centre."

"Guess I should go see what he wants." Misha was betting it wasn't anything good. It rarely was whenever one of the group's leaders issued a personal summons.

"I don't suppose you know where Idris might be?"

Misha shrugged. "Sorry."

"It's all right. I'm sure I'll find him."

When Riley and Misha went their separate ways, Rifle followed Misha. As he walked to the community centre, pulling on his shirt along the way, a few of his other dogs spotted him. They all ran over to receive scratches, and petting, and hardy pats on their sides, depending on what they liked best. The majority of them then went running off again. For the dogs, the past few days had been very exciting. They sensed the nervous energy emanating from the people, but they had also been working a lot more. The dogs were used to hunt rats, as well as performing sniff checks to determine if someone was infected and avoiding getting tested. The bigger ones even helped haul around smaller items that needed to be transported. On top of all this, there were the many newcomers whom the dogs had never met. As long as no one showed them hostility, the dogs loved meeting them. The only pooch who didn't run off back to work was Bullet. Like Rifle, the Australian shepherd stuck to Misha's side upon reuniting with him. Usually, when they walked at Rifle's preferred pace, Bullet would dash ahead and then loop back around to Misha's side, but today he was sticking close.

"What's up?" Misha asked the dog, whose eyes were the same ghostly pale blue as his own.

Bullet glanced up at the sound of his voice, his tail and ears then pricking up higher when he realized that Misha was looking at him.

"Is there something going on today that has you worried?" Misha wondered.

Bullet's tail swished back and forth, not understanding the words beyond the fact that they were directed at him. Maybe he had just missed Misha while he had slept, and that was why the dog was staying so close. That was the least concerning reason that Misha could think of, and therefore the one he most hoped was correct.

The community centre was a hive of activity. People flowed in and out through the doors, picking up or dropping off supplies, grabbing something to eat, running messages, or asking what job currently needed another set of hands. There was no point in trying to keep the main doors closed with all the traffic moving in and out, so a badger named Root was tied up just outside of them. He was a fierce creature, especially when it came to rats. Even if he were dead asleep, he'd wake up in a second should the scent of a rat reach him. The rest of the community centre was protected by dogs patrolling its other sides, as well as the cats who roamed everywhere.

Inside, there were still a number of injured jammed together on cots in a corner, with at least one doctor always tending to them. Opposite, sat the ration distribution, where there was constant disappointment at the meagre amount of food doled out. Meals were now always cold, as just about everything that was safely combustible had gone toward incinerating the dead. Misha knew that he wasn't the only person skipping lunch in order to stretch out the time before they ran out of food entirely. If things didn't improve soon, lunch was going to be cut off for everyone.

"Misha, there you are!" Crichton called out over the din. He broke away from the people whose concerns he had been managing and took hold of Misha's arm, guiding him back outside.

This couldn't be good.

"I have a mission for you."

Misha sighed. Yup, it wasn't good.

"I'm sending a team over to see what's left of the Black Box and to test for radiation leaks. I want you and your dogs to join them."

"Why? The dogs are doing an important job here helping with the rats."

"I haven't seen or heard of a rat in nearly twenty-four hours, have you?"

Misha had to admit that he hadn't, but he also spent a lot of his time sleeping. Cat owners were the best judges of the remaining rat population, since the rodents that weren't eaten were generally brought to them as gifts.

"I don't like being away from Rifle for more than a day," Misha told Crichton.

"Bring him along."

"I don't think he can walk that far."

"He won't have to walk. The team I'm sending over is being given a cart so that they can gather any supplies, especially crops, that may have survived."

"Why not send the sub over for this?"

"Because we're currently using it to distill fresh water, and I'm not about to risk that."

Misha knew this; he was just trying to delay the inevitable. He knew that there was no way out of going on this mission beyond outright refusing, and he wasn't about to do that.

"When do we leave?" he finally asked.

"Tomorrow. I'm hoping to have the team moving out around sun up."

"Alright, I'll make sure the dogs are ready to go by then."

"Thank you." Crichton then turned back toward the community centre and waded into the masses, instantly being swamped by people with concerns, questions, and suggestions about what they should be doing.

Misha knelt down in front of Bullet and Rifle. "What do you think, guys? Do you want to take a trip?"

Bullet wagged his tail, while Rifle nudged him with his nose.

"I hope that's a yes."

***

Misha got up before sunrise the next morning. He used a flashlight in order to light a large candle, and by its light, he packed a bag. Not much went into it, just his stash of emergency food and water, one of the dogs' balls, a small knife, some rope, and his gas mask for which he hadn't had filters in years. He wore his most comfortable clothing, even if it wasn't all that clean, and adjusted the machete on his hip. The bolt action rifle he tended to sling over one shoulder, he strapped to the side of his bag, despite the lack of bullets for it.

Eyes shone in the semi-darkness: all nine of his dogs were watching him. Rifle was lying on the bed that Misha shared with him. The others were on the mattresses near the door.

"Come on, *bratishka*," Misha waved at Rifle, who got up and off the bed. Some days, the old dog couldn't do that on his own, but today he seemed to know something was going on and it made him dig out an extra nugget of effort. Misha hated any time he had to acknowledge Rifle's age. He had taken to calling the German shepherd his brother in his native Russian a long time ago, because that's what Rifle quickly became to him. They weren't owner and dog; they were pack mates.

With Rifle on his feet, the other dogs hastily stood up as well, knowing this meant that they were about to go outside. Misha grabbed one last bundle of items before opening the doors, things he didn't take out often: collars. For each of his dogs, he had over the years woven tough, paracord collars. They weren't

12

like traditional collars, in that there was no ring for a leash, but he had done his best to train each of his dogs to understand that while they were wearing them, they should stay close. Even Bullet had one that he wore along with Rifle's old harness. Not wanting to put them on now, Misha simply carried them for the time being as he opened a door and let all the dogs walk out before him. His other reason for having made the collars was one he hoped would never be needed. While all the dogs had spent some time beyond the community's walls, they had never really left the actual container yard since Misha had started taking care of them. Out there, they might run into people who might think the dogs were feral. Feral dogs were dangerous, and could easily elicit a hostile response. Misha had taken care to use only paracord of a colour that would stand out against each dog's fur tone, in hopes that if any strangers came across one, they would see the collar and understand that the dog had an owner. These theoretical strangers still might hurt Misha's dogs anyway, but there was nothing he could do about assholes or the badly frightened.

Walking at Rifle's pace, Misha headed for the wall made of large shipping containers that protected them. His pack members were curious about what was going on, but a few tried to wander off elsewhere anyway. Misha wouldn't let them, always drawing them back with a sharp call. He had trained all his dogs in a variety of skills, but coming when he called was the one he had reinforced the most.

The sky was grey when Misha reached his destination. He was surprised to see just how many people there were lingering around the area. It also looked like every single horse was being carefully encouraged over the wall, using massive, temporary ramps made out of the sides of hacked-up containers. It had been a long time since they used the cumbersome and somewhat dangerous ramps, but the cranes they had been using instead still hadn't been returned to their normal state—they were still makeshift trebuchets on the side of the submarine.

"Danny!" Misha called out, spotting the closest thing he had to a human brother.

"Hey!" Danny jogged over to him, his bag bouncing on his back. He was forced to stop a bit short as Misha's dogs all crowded up to him, seeking attention. "You going out, too?"

"Crichton's sending me to check out the Black Box, but there's no way he's sending all these people. What's going on?"

"You didn't hear? Some of us are being sent out on scavenger runs, but others are being sent to make contact with other communities."

"Communities?"

"Yeah, Evans' people know of a bunch of communities, and so does Boss. They know which ones are safe to make contact with, so we figured it was time to reach out. Maybe we'll be able to do some trading, and I know a lot of people would be happy to know that there's somewhere to go if they decide this isn't the place for them."

"Are you going to one of these communities?" Misha generally distrusted strangers, and didn't like the idea of Danny going to meet a bunch.

"No, I'm on a scavenger team. Jon, Larson, Bryce, and I are going to do our thing. Rose is coming with us, too."

"No Lenny or Shaidi?" Usually when Danny went out, those two were with him.

"No, they're in one of the contact parties."

Misha nodded. He wondered how many communities they were planning on reaching out to.

"Well, I better get going. We all plan to move out as one, but we're supposed to gather with our groups." Danny hiked a thumb in the direction of his waiting team.

Misha raised his hand toward them in acknowledgement, getting the same in return. He couldn't help but notice that Bryce still hadn't healed from his beating. And he made note of Larson's missing finger and Rose's more prominently missing hand. She still wore a bandage from her more recent injury sustained during the Black Box's destruction, and Danny's shoulder still wasn't completely healed from the bullet that had grazed him. The container yard was truly desperate if they were sending out all of these potentially ill-formed parties. He was glad he hadn't refused to take on the task that Crichton had assigned to him.

"You're bringing Trigger?"

Misha turned to find Cameron frowning at him. The veterinarian had confirmed shortly before the zombie horde had attacked them that Trigger, the golden retriever-lab mix, was pregnant.

"She could whelp her puppies while you're out there, you know that?" Cameron continued.

"I'm aware," Misha nodded. "It just doesn't seem right to leave her here by herself without the rest of the dogs. Besides, I want to be with her when her puppies are born."

Cameron sighed. "I guessed as much. That's why I brought you this." She thrust a large sack into his arms.

Peeking inside, Misha found nothing but tightly packed fabric.

"So you can build a nest for her," Cameron quickly explained. "Just make sure there's always room on your cart."

"Are you being sent anywhere?" Misha wondered.

"No, the health of our farm animals is more important than ever, so I'm staying right here."

Misha nodded, glad to hear it. If everyone he was close with were to be sent out, he'd probably get too stressed worrying about them to do his job effectively. "By the way, do you know where I'm supposed to be? I wasn't given much information about this whole part of the process."

"You're not the only one. I think a lot of information didn't make it to the people who are supposed to have it. This was put together way too fast. But I found out you're going to the Black Box with a cart, so you can probably find your team already on the other side of the wall."

"Thanks."

Cameron petted all the dogs who had been seeking her attention. Misha watched as she performed a few basic tests on the sly, like trying to look into their ears and at their teeth, while holding her hand flat against their chests to feel for their various heart beats. When she was done, she waved toward the ramp.

"Okay, enough of that. You better get going and I better get back to work."

"Make sure Riley doesn't work too hard," Misha said, at the same time doubting the woman's twin sister needed to hear it.

"Definitely. And you all come back in one piece, without puppies if possible. Having them born here would be better than out there."

Misha nodded and turned back toward the ramp. He whistled sharply to make sure he had his dogs' attention, and then walked toward it, with the sack Cameron had given him cradled in his arms. All nine of his pack stayed close.

After joining the group of people lined up to cross over the wall, they patiently awaited their turn. The ramps could only take so much weight, and so the organizers were limiting how many people could walk up at one time. When it finally came to Misha and his dogs, they climbed without the accompaniment of any other people.

The metal ramp was a little slick. Even though it was corrugated and therefore looked like a tightly packed staircase, it wasn't easy to walk up. A couple of ropes had been draped down the ramp's length, but they weren't helpful for the dogs, who were cautious and untrusting of this ascent. Spring, the little terrier mix, was fine, bounding up the ramp in an instant, while the rest plodded their way along, always making sure they had good footing. Misha had to encourage several of them to keep climbing, but they eventually all made it to the top.

"Good boy! Good girl!" Misha scratched and petted all of his dogs in turn. "Now we have to go down the other side."

Rifle looked over the edge and whined. If he were younger, this would be easy for him, but his old bones were less co-operative.

"I know, *bratishka*. It'll be all right. In fact, I'm going to help you."

Taking himself out of the descent line, Misha brought his dogs to one side. He removed the harness from Bullet and put it back on Rifle. Bullet shook his fur out, having grown used to wearing the harness. He then sniffed Rifle all over, as though checking to make sure the old man had it on right. When Misha brought all the dogs back to the top of the ramp, a few of them seemed disappointed. Even the big dogs, Powder and Guard, seemed to prefer the method of being carried up and down ladders.

"Okay, here we go." Misha let the fabric bag tumble down the ramp so that he could have his hands free. He kept one firmly wrapped around a rope, while the other held tightly to Rifle's harness. As he had while walking, he paced himself with the old dog. Spring, once again, showed everyone up by zipping straight down without a problem. Barrel ended up being the only one to have issues. The dog that looked like a Doberman with stumpier legs and a much thicker body, was the lowest member of the pack, despite Misha's equal treatment of him. Near the bottom, his back legs suddenly went sideways on him. The dog spun around when his front legs managed to find a bolt to hold onto. He whined pathetically.

"It's okay, Barrel. You're all right," Misha comforted the dog. But Barrel refused to move; his eye, ear, and tail postures ones of stress. He had always been somewhat clumsy for a dog.

After getting Rifle to the bottom, Misha climbed the short distance back up to Barrel. He stood over the dog, and placed his hands on either side.

"Here we go," Misha soothed the dog. "Here we go. Just going to step backward now. We're almost there. Just a little farther. There we are."

Once Barrel's feet were on the flat pavement, he shook himself, and then went to stand at Rifle's side, the only dog who never tried to establish dominance over him. Probably because he felt no need to. The other dogs all knew who came after Misha in the pack order, and they accepted it without challenge.

Glad that that was done with, Misha grabbed his sack of fabrics and went to check which of the carts he was supposed to be with. The first person he asked directed him over to a large, flat bed cart hitched to two horses. Misha recognized them as Thumper and Potato, who usually went out with scavenger teams. The only people waiting with them were Harry, and a man Misha recognized as having come with Evans' party but whose name he didn't know.

"Harry, I'm surprised they're sending you," Misha commented as he reached the cart. He threw the sack of fabric into the back, then knelt down to put each of the dogs' collars on. He also moved the harness back onto Bullet.

"There could be some salvageable equipment from the things we left outside. Also, Crichton really wants to make sure the Geiger counter is in proper working order, and so needs someone who should be able to fix it if it starts misbehaving."

"Still, I figured they would need you here to fix the cranes, or build new ones, or something."

Harry shrugged. "Enough people helped me with them that I think they can put them back on their own. By the way, Misha, have you met Ki-Nam?" He gestured to the quiet man.

"Not directly. Hi." Misha waved from where he was still kneeling on the pavement, not much of one for shaking hands.

Ki-Nam nodded, his silver hair waving with the movement. He either had ancestors from somewhere in eastern Asia, or had come from there himself at some point.

After all the collars had been clipped on, Misha climbed into the back of the cart and started to build a nest for Trigger. Harry looked on with curiosity.

"There's a possibility of puppies being born on this trip," Misha explained. "I figured I might as well get this part out of the way, just in case." He also lifted Rifle up onto the board that served as the driver's seat, so that he could accompany whoever took the reins.

While they waited, Misha spotted a few people he knew joining different parties with empty carts outside the wall. There were more grouped together without carts, but it was impossible to tell who was going out to scavenge and who was going to investigate new places. Misha could only guess a few based on the amount of supplies they carried.

In the end, they were joined by two more people: Angela, who had lived in the Black Box before Misha had even known of its existence, and, surprisingly, Crichton himself.

"Everyone ready?" he asked the assembled group.

They all nodded or verbalized that they were.

"Excellent. Let's get going then. Misha, I want you and your dogs to take point."

Of course he did. Misha whistled sharply again to make sure he had his dogs' attention, and then started to lead them through the remainder of the container yard. Behind him, he heard the cart start to roll across the pavement, quieter than one would have expected. They made sure all of their carts were well oiled and outfitted with rubber tires for just that reason, although there wasn't much they could do about the actual sounds of friction, or the horses' hooves.

"Is anyone going to be checking out these containers?" Angela asked of the stacked metal beasts on either side of them.

"Bronislav might arrange for a team to open up and look inside the ones we can get to, but he has to wait to see just who's left, and some of the contents of these containers aren't so easily determined."

Misha's job, before the double shot of attacks, had often been to help clear out the containers, and so he knew exactly what Crichton was talking about. Sometimes it was easy, as there were boxes labelled in clear English, but sometimes the writing was in a language no one knew how to read, and the disassembled products inside were equally as mystifying.

They didn't get far before they reached the edge of the cleaned up area. The lower containers and pavement ahead were all slimed with zombie debris. Pus, and guts, and hunks of skin coated everything, just like it had their home after the attack. Dark, poisoned blood was everywhere. At least the container maze had already been cleared of any moving zombies that had remained, somehow getting caught on the latches of various boxes. Still, the dogs had paused and looked back at Misha, silently asking if they really had to walk through the slop.

"I'm putting some of the dogs on the cart," Misha told Crichton. "We don't need all of them walking through this stuff and getting it on them."

Crichton agreed.

Misha helped Trigger, Spring, Barrel, and Stock up onto the back. Bullet seemed determined to stay by Misha's side. Powder, the Great Dane whose narrow face suggested some greyhound mix in her genes, and Guard, the Newfoundlander that was probably part mastiff, were both very big dogs, and so Misha kept them on their feet. The last dog, Slide, was pure, unidentifiable mutt, and although she was no bigger than Trigger, she had the best nose for identifying mobile zombies at a distance, and so Misha kept her walking ahead with the others.

It was disgusting moving forward. As he had loaded his dogs onto the cart, Misha had withdrawn his mask from his pack and put it on. The strong scent of rubber helped cover the rancid smell, but couldn't get rid of it completely. It also could do nothing for the sight of the mess, nor the slick feeling underfoot.

Although the sun had dried the surface into a sort of crust, underneath it was still damp. Misha had to walk very carefully. Occasionally one of his feet would almost kick out from underneath him as he stepped on some particularly slimy offal. His group happened to be the first to leave. With the other groups passing behind them, the pavement would become clearer, somewhat like slushy snow, making it easier for those at the back. Misha wished he were with them instead of at the front. On top of dealing with the gore, everyone would have to maintain a vigilant watch for rats.

Other than being incredibly gross, the walk between the containers was uneventful. The dogs kept their distance from the sides and clearly found the pavement as distasteful as Misha did, what with the way they lifted their paws higher than usual. Powder and the others had walked over carpets of corpses after the mega horde's attack was over, but that didn't mean any of them liked it.

Past the containers was where an old warehouse once stood. Now, half the battered structure had collapsed. Misha and those following him paused for a moment to look at it, for they hadn't known that that had happened. The sheer force of the zombies' passage had taken out the weakest parts of the structure.

"It's a good thing you and your people decided to join us as opposed to hiding in there," Crichton mentioned to Ki-Nam, who nodded in silent agreement.

The zombie debris continued beyond the very end of the container yard, but at least now they weren't so hemmed in. It was likely they would have to continue walking through it until they reached the bridge that would allow them to cross the river to the north. And even then, that was only if the zombies hadn't come across the same bridge. No one had thought to ask the runners, who had warned them, what route the mega horde had taken to reach them. Or at least, no one had told Misha if they had.

It was unsettling, seeing all the damage that had been done. Windows that had survived eleven years' worth of storms since the outbreak, were now shattered. Cars, long dead, on flat tires, had been pushed far from where they had once sat. Some had even been partly crushed, the zombies having crawled over them. Even without the zombies' insatiable, infectious hunger, the mega horde had been dangerous simply due to its sheer mass. Misha was glad he hadn't known its true size before they had had to fight it off.

When they finally came to the much smaller shipping container yard that was near the bridge, the dogs suddenly came to a stop. Misha halted the others with hand gestures. Moving forward, he stood between the two large dogs and carefully watched Slide. The mutt's posture was one of studious intent. She had caught a whiff of something, and, with her, that usually meant a walking corpse. Her tail and ears stood straight up as she focused on what had caught her attention. The other two dogs swung their heads slightly with their noses up, scenting the air. Misha couldn't be certain whether that was because they had caught something as well, or because they knew Slide had.

But then Slide lowered her head, her ears twisted back, and her tail tucked firmly between her legs. Silently, she backed up until she bumped into Misha. Only one thing would make her react that way. Zombies. *Lots* of them.

3: ONIDA
APPROXIMATELY ONE YEAR AGO

It was hard to keep running. Onida's lungs were burning, and her muscles begged for a rest. She needed to stop, but was too terrified. Who knew how close her pursuers were? She was panicked, she knew, more than she should be, but if it put distance between herself and them, then so be it. Panic had its usefulness.

Right up until her footing failed her, and she went sprawling into the underbrush and a carpet of dead leaves. She was able to use her gloved hands to break her fall, but that meant she couldn't use them to defend her face against the prickly bushes that scraped it. The wind was knocked out of her by an ill-placed root, and after all her collapsing motions came to a stop, she just lay there. Her body wanted to rest, and so now she was finally obliging.

This had been going on for too long. She couldn't keep running like this. She couldn't keep *living* like this. For nearly a week now, her life had been consumed by fear. Every day, something startled her into running. Every night, she barely slept; the smallest sound jolted her into wakefulness. Now, she was also out of food. In addition to putting distance behind her, she was also going to have to find time to feed herself. They were well into fall, not a great time to have to forage. Even if she could hunt down chipmunks, killing and eating them along with their caches of nuts, winter would hit next. She needed to go south, but didn't know how. Some places in that direction were irradiated from melted reactors, and would kill her slowly and painfully. The sickness would be the only thing to let her know that she had gone the wrong way.

Whatever she eventually did, she couldn't keep lying on the ground, crumpled and uncomfortable. She pushed herself up into a kneeling position, grateful that nothing felt broken or sprained. A crow took off from a nearby tree, the snap of its wings causing Onida to flinch.

"A bird," she whispered to herself at a barely audible level. "It was only a bird."

She stood up and started walking, looking over her shoulder almost as often as she looked ahead.

It didn't take long before she was running again.

***

Another night was spent crunched up in a human ball, this time wedged into the bottom of a hollowed-out tree. When Onida crawled out in the morning, every joint was stiff. At least she had slept a little more deeply that night, not waking up as often. It was probably her body rebelling against its recent treatment, forcing her to sleep even when she didn't really want to.

Spending next to no time shaking herself loose or getting her bearings, Onida set off once more. Her stomach was a constant chasm. She ate everything she came across that was edible, even if it didn't provide much in the way of nutrients, just to ease that feeling of having a hole in the middle of her gut. The previous night, she had almost caught an unaware pheasant, but it had escaped at the last moment in a flurry of feathers. Maybe she would do better today. At least she had found what she assumed was a deer trail to follow. The narrow path was much easier to walk along than hiking over the rocks and bushes had been.

The soft crunch of leaves ahead caused her to pause. Sounds behind her were always frightening, but ahead, they gave her hope for a meal. She proceeded slowly, walking on light feet as she had been taught. That was the lesson that had truly stuck with her the most.

Just past a small rise, she spotted a raccoon nosing about in the leaves. What it was doing out during the daytime, Onida didn't care. She only cared that it looked like it would provide a decent meal.

The wind was against her, however. It carried her scent directly to the creature, who turned and gazed up at her. She expected the raccoon to run away, but it didn't. Instead, it did the exact opposite. With only a dash of caution, the raccoon came toward her. Onida held her breath. The animal was curious, and she didn't want to frighten it. The closer it came to her, the better the chance she had of grabbing it.

The raccoon came up to her feet, staring into her face. As she watched, it reached forward and touched her battered moccasin, as if confirming that she were real. When it stopped looking at her face in order to give her feet a thorough sniffing, Onida reached down and snatched up the raccoon by its scruff. The raccoon cried out in indignation, and uselessly flailed its limbs. With her free hand, Onida grabbed the knife out of the sheath on her belt.

"Put him down!" came the most terrified and hoarse screech Onida had ever heard. Instead of putting the raccoon down, she dropped it in fright.

Out of the woods, down a skinny trail she hadn't seen due to the distraction of the raccoon, came a man dressed all in leather. Onida's first thought was that she had been caught, that her pursuers had closed the gap between her and them when she had stopped to let the raccoon walk over to her. She was about to take off running, but actually managed to keep still. This man was clearly not one of those pursuing her. His leathers were inferior to hers and those of her pursuers, and his face was covered in a large, ratty beard instead of being clean-shaven. He bent down to the raccoon that had run over to him, gently cradling it in his arms and mumbling soothing words.

"I'm sorry," Onida told the wild man. "I'm so sorry. I didn't know he was someone's pet."

The man startled, as if he had forgotten that she was there. His eyes turned into coals of hatred.

"What are you doing here?" he barked, so rapid fire that it was almost difficult to understand.

"I'm sorry. I'm sorry. I didn't know anyone lived this way. I'll just go now and leave you alone." She turned to walk off the path, to head across rough terrain again, directly away from this strange man.

"Stop!" he shouted, causing her to freeze in place. "What do you have in that pack?"

Onida turned back around to face the man. He had put down the raccoon—that was now scurrying up a tree—and had taken a bow and arrow off a strange rig he wore on his back.

"Nothing," she told him. "I have nothing in there except for maybe a blanket and an empty water bottle. I swear, I have nothing. I would have left your raccoon alone if I had any food."

"Don't-" he shouted and cut himself off. His face twisted as he tried to hold back some awful emotion. "Don't talk about eating him." He had to force the words out, and his eyes had become shiny with tears.

"I'm sorry." Onida had never apologized so much before. Looking at this man, it was clear to her that something was off about him, which meant she had to tread very carefully.

"How..." He had to swallow a lump in his throat before he could continue. "How old are you?"

"Sixteen," she told him truthfully.

His eyes wandered and lips silently moved as he seemed to try to work something out. "How old were you when the dead came?"

Was he that incapable of math, or had he lost track of the years?

"I was six," she told him.

He thought some more. "You have nothing in your pack?"

Onida couldn't quite tell if he was asking a question or stating an affirmation, but she decided to go with the former and answer. "That's right."

The man looked around him. "Are you alone? Why are you alone?"

"Yes, I'm alone. Are you alone?" Onida ignored the second question.

"I'm not alone," the man shook his head, baffled by her question. "I have Mask." He gestured up the tree beside him, where the raccoon was watching the proceedings in safety.

"Mask, of course. He's very cute."

The man beamed. "Yes, yes he is, isn't he?"

So the raccoon was a good topic provided he wasn't referred to as a potential meal. "Is he as smart as he looks?"

"Even smarter." The man seemed very proud of this fact.

"My name is Onida, by the way." Maybe he would be less likely to hurt her if he knew her name.

"Onida. Onida," he tested the shape of it.

"What's your name?"

There was a pause, the man frowning at nothing. It seemed he had forgotten his name, but it came back to him with a sudden raising of his eyebrows. "Shawn. My name is Shawn."

"It's nice to meet you, Shawn."

His eyebrows descended again as he scrutinized Onida. "You're..." He hesitated to say this next thing out loud. "You're real?"

"Yes, I'm real." Onida wondered just how long this man had been on his own.

"May... May I?" After putting away his arrow, he reached out and then withdrew his hand, a gesture similar to the way Mask had touched her foot.

"We can shake hands." Onida held hers out.

Shawn took it tentatively. He didn't really shake her hand so much as he caressed her glove and felt the shape of her knuckles beneath it. When he

21

brought his hand back to his chest, his eyes were distant, as he became lost in thought.

"You should come visit my cabin," he muttered, his eyes still far away.

"Um, okay. But I can't stay very long." Onida was hoping that maybe this man would feed her. A good meal could carry her far if the distance she had travelled already was any indication.

"What?" Shawn looked at her without understanding.

"You said I should visit your cabin. I said okay."

Shawn nodded, his head bobbing up and down on a neck that was invisible behind his wild beard. Onida was thinking that maybe she should repeat herself again, that he still didn't get it, when he suddenly turned and started walking away down the path.

Onida followed him, getting a good look at his strange pack. On one side was a quiver full of arrows: some the graphite kind found in stores, others clearly homemade. On the other side was a strange setup made out of numerous materials that had probably once been trash. It looked to Onida like some form of quick release holster for his compound bow. The bottom portion of the pack was a large pocket with a battered zipper, not unlike the worn and faded backpack that Onida carried. Above the pocket, however, was a sort of cloth bucket she didn't understand, and beneath everything hung several long strips of leather. She learned the purpose for these when Mask came waddling along after them. Without Shawn breaking stride, Mask was able to grab the leather strips and climb up to the bag. Gripping the fabric, the raccoon hauled himself up to the fabric bucket, and plopped inside. After some shuffling, the raccoon made himself comfortable, his face peering out over the top at Onida. His nose kept wiggling as he picked up her scent.

"How long have you had Mask?" Onida wondered.

Shawn flinched and glanced over his shoulder at her as though he had forgotten that she was there. Maybe he had. "A long time," he answered.

Onida had figured out that much on her own based on how comfortable they both were with that rig. "How old is he?" she tried again, guessing that Shawn had probably raised Mask from a baby.

Shawn just shook his head, and Onida got the sense that he didn't know. He had definitely lost track of time.

Onida attempted to think of another question to ask him, not wanting her existence to be forgotten and that bow to be drawn upon her again. But as she tried to come up with something, they reached the end of the path, entering the clearing that held Shawn's cabin. It was certainly not what Onida had been picturing. She thought she would be brought to some small place made of logs, not all that different from most of the homes where she had lived, but this was very different.

Before her, a large deck loomed, at least a storey up in the air with railings draped in old camouflage netting. On top, what she could see of it, stood a small but solid cabin, the glint of solar panels just visible on its roof. Beneath the deck, filling in a large portion of what would be the overhang, was a massive slab of concrete, with perfectly smooth sides. A matching cement block stood not far away, although this one had no deck, and no cabin on top. Onida couldn't see what it might be for; there didn't appear to be anything on top of it, and no openings along the sides that she could see. Beyond the cabin, she spotted the cool waters of a lake. It had been a while since she had had anything to drink, and the sight of all that fresh water served only to remind her of that fact.

"Your cabin is very impressive," Onida managed to say.

"Thank you," Shawn replied without looking at her.

"Would you mind if I went down to the lake? I'm very thirsty."

"I wouldn't recommend it. There are polar bears."

"Polar bears?"

"Did I say something else?"

"No, I just didn't think about them, is all." Onida was glad she hadn't run into one during her flight. They would be foraging for all sorts of food at this time of year, and Onida would definitely be food.

"I have boiled water inside. Come on."

Onida wasn't sure that she wanted to go inside the fortress in front of her, but she needed water so badly now that she followed along. By tracing the edge of the deck overhead, they reached a jagged section with no railing. Onida guessed that there used to be a staircase there, but that it had been destroyed at some point. She wasn't about to ask about it.

Shawn stopped and reached one of his hands over his shoulder, wiggling his fingers at Mask. The raccoon didn't seem all that interested in coming out of his pouch, but he did. Shawn carefully held his fluffy body and lifted him up to where some netting hung down. Mask reached up until his little hands could grip it, and then hauled himself up the rest of the way, climbing the netting until he disappeared over the edge of the deck. Shawn then stood there, waiting.

Onida didn't like waiting, even if it was for less than a minute. She looked all about her, arms held tightly against her chest, a posture she had adopted a lot lately as she tried to make herself smaller. She felt exposed away from the sheltering trees, for the clearing's growth of ferns around her legs wouldn't hide her for long should she need to duck down. The shadows of the forest seemed sharper, now that she was out of them.

A clattering caused her to jump, to flinch away from the source of the sound. When she turned, her eyes wide, she saw it was only a rope ladder unfurling itself from the break in the railing. Mask's little face was peering down at them from the top of it, his big, dark nose jiggling as he scented the air.

Shawn turned to look at Onida, his face beaming. "I taught him to do that," he said, pointing up the ladder at Mask.

"Very clever," Onida smiled weakly back at him, her heart still hammering in her throat.

Shawn scrambled up the ladder with ease. Only once he had disappeared over the edge, did Onida take hold of the swinging rope and wood. It was all very soft and worn, previously used many times. A few slats appeared newer than others, replaced over the years. Shawn had been here a very long time, perhaps since the infection spread. But had he always been alone?

The ladder swung as Onida climbed it, as the bottom wasn't anchored to anything. It was difficult. She had never had to climb a ladder like this before, and Shawn wasn't offering any advice. When she reached the top, however, he grabbed the straps of her pack and helped pull her up. And then he kept pulling, sliding the bag up and over her head, off her arms.

"Stop!" For a second she thought it was an accident, which gave him enough time to steal her backpack completely.

"I need to see what you have. I need to know you're not a liar."

As Onida pushed herself upright on the deck, Shawn scuttled away and searched through her bag. There wasn't much to search through; it had only two pockets, and she hadn't been lying about what she was carrying. He pulled out the empty water canister, and then the blanket, which he shook. There was nothing else but some dirt, a few flakes of pinecone, and the cap off an acorn.

"Satisfied?" Onida asked, as Shawn felt along the fabric of the backpack, making sure there were no secret pockets. "Can I have my stuff back now?"

Shawn nodded and dropped her bag. As Onida went over to it to put her blanket and water container back inside, Shawn switched places with her to draw up the rope ladder. He carefully rolled it and settled it above the opening in the railing, using a small wire to make sure it wouldn't unroll accidentally. Onida guessed that getting back down must involve jumping in order to keep the ladder rolled up.

Now that she was level with it, Onida got a better look at the cabin. The deck stretched all the way around the squat building. Along with the solar panels, one edge of the roof peak had a small windmill protruding up from it, barely turning in the calm air. The door she saw was unusual: it was a metal hatch she imagined would be more at home on a submarine than here in the woods. Then she realized she couldn't see any windows. The wood planking that made up the siding appeared quite sturdy, but remembering the other security measures she had seen, Onida wondered if there was something even stronger beneath it.

"Would you like to come inside?" Shawn asked her, stepping toward the door. Mask was already sitting in front of it, waiting patiently.

Onida hesitated. The cabin seemed like the kind of place in which she could become trapped. No windows, and so far, no other doors, meant no alternative exit. But then Shawn had offered her water, and it was the first time she had felt even remotely safe from her pursuers. She stepped toward Shawn and the door.

Through the metal hatch, they entered some sort of mudroom. Heavy winter gear hung along one side on hooks above some boots. All of it was dirty, some of it was torn, but most was still in surprisingly good condition. Onida figured he wore the leathers in order to save the outerwear for the coldest days. It's what she would do. Shawn took off his leather boots, so Onida followed suit with her moccasins.

Before closing the door to the outside and cutting off the light, Shawn opened the inner door. Onida was immediately drawn by the electric glow she saw. Ignoring the space that was a kitchen on one side and a living room on the other, she went straight to the stone fireplace. Beside it was a bin of dirt with green shoots of various sizes thrusting up. Above them, glowed a sunlamp.

Onida was enraptured by the light. It had been a long time since her family had given up on electricity, and even longer since the bright lights of her childhood.

"Those are my potatoes," Shawn said, mistaking what had drawn her over there.

When Onida gave them a bit more attention, she saw that he had cleverly planted several at various different times, so that there were always some nearly ready to harvest. She also saw the dangerous looking wire configuration that attached the solar panels and windmill to some sort of battery, and from there, to the light. She moved away, distrusting it.

"Come sit down, I'll make you something to eat," Shawn said, as he revealed the only window in the place: a porthole in the kitchen that had been covered by a hatch.

Onida didn't need to be asked twice.

***

The meal was eaten in silence. They had a potato each, some blackberries, a bit of dried squirrel meat, a few acorns that weren't very good, and some maple syrup that was. Shawn kept glancing across the table at Onida, as if she might disappear. Mask also ate on the table, munching his way through a small bowl of the same food they had, minus the potato. Onida drank two large glasses of water with her meal.

"That was very good, thank you," Onida finally spoke again once she finished. "It was very nice to meet you and Mask, but I should get going."

"You're leaving?" The hurt in Shawn's voice was clear. "I have an extra bed here. You can have your own room, and stay as long as you like." His voice cracked. Here was a man so desperate for company, he was willing to offer his home to a complete stranger.

"That sounds very nice, but I can't stay." A bed *did* sound very nice, especially if it was the kind topped by a mattress as she imagined it would be. A place like this was definitely built before the infection.

"Of course you can stay," Shawn insisted.

Onida shook her head. "I can't. For your own safety, I have to leave. There are people after me."

"People? What kind of people? Why are they after you?"

"The people I used to live with. I stole something."

Shawn's eyes jolted up and down, realizing that he hadn't checked her person.

"I don't have it anymore," Onida shook her head. "But that doesn't matter to them. They're coming for me, and they'll hurt you for helping. I need to go so that you'll be safe here."

"You can be safe here, too," Shawn told her. "I can keep you safe. I know how to set traps, traps for people. If they come here, I can kill them for you."

Onida could tell that he meant it. She shook her head again. "They would see your traps. They're very good at that. They're excellent hunters; you wouldn't be able to take them all out on your own."

"At least stay one night. Rest. One night can't hurt, can it?" Shawn was very insistent. "I can pack some food for you to take with you, but you have to stay the night if I'm going to do that."

Food in exchange for providing some company did sound like a fairly good deal. And there was a bed to boot. "Just stay the one night?"

"We can play cards. You can tell me about where you're from."

"Okay, I guess. But don't expect any more than that. We're not going to have sex or anything like that."

Shawn scrunched up his face. "Don't be gross, you're only sixteen. I'm not like that, okay? I'm not that kind of guy." He was genuinely offended.

"Sorry, I just needed to make sure we were clear on that part."

He continued to be upset by what she had felt the need to say while he removed the dishes from the table and washed them in a bucket of water with homemade soap. Mask walked over to Onida, curious about the new human in his midst. She let him give her a good sniff, and then he let her run her fingers through his fur.

"I still have plenty to do before nightfall," Shawn said once the dishes were on a drying rack. "I would like you to accompany me."

"Okay." She figured she was being invited along more so that Shawn could make sure she wasn't going to take his stuff and leave, rather than for company. She didn't mind; it meant she would be out in the open should her pursuers show up.

Leaving the cabin, Onida's theory about Shawn dropping himself off the deck was proven correct. He let her climb down the ladder first, however, when he saw her reticence after he told her to jump. When he rolled it back up, the ladder was probably stored without the metal wire holding it, so that Mask could easily unroll it when they got back. On the other hand, maybe the raccoon was clever enough to know how to work the wire.

Onida followed Shawn around as he checked traps for animals, gathered mushrooms in a nearby cave, and picked berries. Whenever a critter revealed itself, Shawn's bow and an arrow were in his hands in a heartbeat. Only once did he actually take the shot, felling a rabbit.

"Dinner," he smiled back at Onida.

Most of the time, Shawn barely acknowledged that she was trailing along behind him. Occasionally he would glance back at her, making sure she was still there, but he whispered more to Mask than spoke to her. He didn't even ask her to help pick mushrooms, and she wasn't going to volunteer. Shawn seemed very choosy about the ones he plucked, and not knowing the reason for that, Onida wasn't going to risk upsetting him.

It wasn't until water was to be hauled from the lake to the cabin that Onida actually helped out. That was also when she finally spoke, a question digging away at her.

"Is that an airplane?" she asked, referring to what appeared to be one smashed and tangled into some trees at one end of the long oblong of water.

Shawn glanced from her to the plane as if he had forgotten it was there. "Used to be," he answered.

"Looks like a rough landing."

"It was."

"Were you in it when it crashed?"

"I was flying. I wasn't as good at landing on this lake as I thought, not in that plane."

"Ouch. Was anyone with you?"

Shawn shook his head. "I was all alone by then."

"I'm sorry."

"Why?"

Onida shrugged, not really sure how she wanted to answer that.

They dropped off the first of the water buckets under the edge of the deck—later they would hoist them all up—and walked back down to the lake for more.

"What did you steal?" Shawn asked. His tone had zero accusation in it, merely curiosity.

Onida shook her head as he had done earlier. "It doesn't matter."

"I had a dog once." This seemed like a strange change in topic. He paused so long before speaking again, that Onida almost asked him about it. "My sister stole it."

"Your sister stole your dog?"

Shawn nodded. "She and her friends. They abandoned me."

This time Onida resisted saying she was sorry, given his confusion last time. "Why'd they steal your dog?" she asked instead.

"I don't know."

It seemed pointless to ask any more questions. The dog, Shawn's sister, and all his sister's friends could very well be dead by now.

They finished hauling buckets to the deck, and then lifted them up with a rope. It was a job that must have taken Shawn a lot longer to do on his own, but with Onida there to tie the buckets on whenever the rope was lowered, it didn't take much time at all. After the last bucket left the ground, she joined Shawn up top and helped carry them all inside. The rest of the chores Shawn had to do that day were things about the cabin. Onida boiled the water, one bucket at a time, using a big pot over the fire she built, while Shawn prepped the rabbit in the kitchen. He was skilled at the task, very efficiently gutting and skinning the animal, separating the parts into their various uses. The meat was cooked over the fire Onida had built, along with some mushrooms that made it extra good.

They didn't play cards for long, or even talk all that much. Shawn just seemed happy to have another human body in the cabin. Once the sun had gone down, he unplugged the dangerous wiring for the sunlamp, causing the fire-cast shadows to deepen. They played a single game of cards after that before Shawn had to go back to doing chores. Onida could tell he got anxious when not doing them. She didn't mind though, getting to relax while he busied himself with drying mushrooms, preserving some blackberries, tending the potatoes, and beginning the tanning process for the rabbit pelt.

"You should go to bed," Shawn told Onida after seeing her yawn several times.

"So should you."

"Soon. I have some more chores to do. You don't need to stay up; you can sleep in there." He pointed to one of the doors that led off the main space. Earlier, Onida had learned that one of them led to a bathroom without running water, but the toilet could be flushed by pouring some water from a bucket. It was probably Onida's favourite thing about deciding to stay there for the night, other than the food. Of course, it had some stiff competition when she went into the bedroom and climbed into bed. The mattress was so soft, and pillow so squishy, despite being somewhat dusty. Onida left the door open a crack so that she could have a tiny bit of light in the windowless room from the living room's fire. Also because Mask had followed her in to explore and she didn't want him becoming trapped.

Onida didn't plan on sleeping until after Shawn had finished his chores and gone to bed. She didn't think she could sleep with a stranger moving about out there. But her body won the fight, plunging her into the world of dreams.

***

"Wake up," a soft voice hissed in her ear, barely penetrating through Onida's sleep. "Stay quiet." A hand clamped over her mouth before she could ask what was going on. There was a subdued anger in the voice that badly frightened her. "Your friends are here. Come with me."

Onida nodded in the pitch black. The only thing that terrified Onida more than the idea of her host turning against her, was the thought of her pursuers catching up.

Shawn took her hand and led her out of the room, pressing her moccasins into her other hand at the same time. She could see nothing, and the only thing she could hear was the soft scrabbling of Mask's nails against the floor as he accompanied them. Onida guessed she had been brought to the kitchen. When Shawn momentarily let go of her hand, it made Onida tremble, being alone in the dark like that. She flinched at the soft creak that sounded close by, wondering if it had been Shawn or the others. But then Shawn took her hand again and guided it toward the floor. He had her feel an opening, some hatch he must have lifted. Onida brought her other hand forward, patting around the edges until they located a firm ladder.

A crack followed by a kind of *foosh* made them both freeze. Shawn moved away from Onida so that she couldn't tell where he was anymore. She stayed put and pulled on her moccasins while she waited.

Light came into the cabin as Shawn opened up the cover over the porthole window. To Onida's horror, it was firelight. If Shaun had disbelieved her about the people who were after her, he couldn't now. Without even knowing who might be living in the cabin, her pursuers had begun to burn it. In that light from outside, Onida could see the pure rage on Shawn's face.

"You can't fight them," Onida risked whispering.

"I know," he whispered back. Not bothering to close the porthole again, he rejoined her by the hatch. Without a word, he gestured for her to climb down. She silently obeyed, having no choice but to trust him.

It was much colder down below. It was also deeper than Onida had expected. The hard packed earth beneath her feet was considerably lower than that of the ground outside. In the dim light that made it down from above, she could just make out the edges of shelving units crowding the space.

Shawn spent a few more seconds above, making Onida wonder if she was to hide down here alone. When his body finally blocked the light, which was growing brighter as the flames grew higher, he had his rig back on, with Mask nestled inside the pouch. As soon as his feet touched the ground, Shawn took Onida's hand and led her into the dark.

They crossed to a wall, Shawn placing Onida's hand against it. He then drew her down to her knees, and had her feel another opening: this one horizontal. Onida didn't need to be told to crawl. She simply slid inside and scrambled forward, having no idea where she was going. She froze up only once in that dark, tight space, and that was when a hammering on the metal door reached its way down to her ears. Her pursuers were giving up their silence as they found ways up onto the deck and discovered no way into the cabin. A gentle tap on her foot from Shawn got her moving forward once more.

There was moonlight at the far end of the tunnel. When she emerged, Onida could see some of the firelight flickering along the edges of rotten beams overhead. Whatever had once stood on this cement block had been gone for some time, allowing the elements to rot away what was left. A couple of hulking pieces of machinery sat piled in one corner, while the rest of the space was occupied by old fire pits and pots for boiling sap into syrup, stretchers for large animal hides of various shapes and sizes, and a mound of soft dirt and unusable animal organs that Onida thought might be fertilizer for the potatoes. Shawn emerged from the hole behind her. He gestured for her to follow him over to the machinery, where he withdrew from the shadows two large hiking packs. One of them had a bow and arrow rig set up on its sides, and Shawn quickly transferred his weaponry over to it. There was another soft pouch for Mask to climb into: this one hung from the chest straps, so that the raccoon was against Shawn's belly once he put it on.

Onida put her arms through the straps of the bag she had been given, feeling the full weight as she stood up with it on. This was the kind of bag of supplies she should have run with the first time. Still, she grabbed her backpack that she had dragged along with her and wore it on her front. Seeing this, Shawn grabbed some pelts he had stored there, along with a few small tools, and rapidly stuffed them inside her bag. He then pointed up the machinery: they were going to climb it. Onida swallowed hard, not certain she could while burdened by all that weight, but she would have to try. Her pursuers had begun to whoop and howl, an attempt to intimidate and frighten whoever they thought might be inside into coming out.

Shawn climbed first, clearly having done this before. Onida watched him carefully as she followed, placing her hands and feet in the same spots that he had. At the top, Mask crawled out so that Shawn could slide on his belly onto a section of old flooring that continued to hold steady. Onida wasn't sure if she could make that last little bit of distance on her own, but Shawn was able to reach her and helped haul her up. They crawled to the side of the cement block and peered over the edge. It seemed Onida's pursuers had made the mistake of ignoring this place, believing it was a completely separate entity, as Onida had upon first seeing it. There was nothing but earth and shadow below.

With no hesitation, Shawn slid over the edge, hanging by his hands for just a second before dropping down onto his feet. Mask jumped after him, completely trusting Shawn to catch him. Not trusting Shawn to wait for her,

Onida scrambled over the edge. She pretty much fell over the side, unable to hold on with her hands for any length of time. She hit the ground hard, her legs collapsing beneath her so that she ended up on her side. Luckily, there was no pain, just the shooting tingle of a hard impact. Shawn was still there and helped her back up onto her feet.

They crept off into the forest together, with Shawn leading the way. He circled around a bit, not going in a straight line. Onida wanted to tell him to stop, or to run off in a different direction, directly away from the cabin. Through the trees she could see that the flames had become quite substantial. The roof, with its solar panels and mini windmill, was also burning now. In the bright light that was cast, dancing figures could be seen on the ground below. It turned Onida's stomach to think that people would dance at her death.

It turned out that Shawn knew exactly where he was going and had a good reason for it. He took them to the pursuers' horses: their means of hunting Onida down as relentlessly as they had, her reason for running almost constantly. There was a guard, but Shawn dispatched him with an arrow. Like a lot of things he did, Shawn killed the man without seeming to think about it. Clean headshot. A couple of horses tossed their heads and snorted at the sudden scent of blood, but they remained relatively calm, used to the stench of death. Shawn retrieved his arrow and wiped the worst of the blood off on some nearby fronds, pointing to Onida and then a horse as he did so. Onida understood, untying the horse's reins from a tree branch, and then scrambling up onto the beast's back. She waited as Shawn moved among the horses, unable to see what he was doing.

Just as Onida considered bolting, Shawn popped up on a horse beside her. He held a finger to his lips, needlessly reminding her to be silent. She nodded.

When Shawn started his horse along the trail, Onida discovered what he had done. Several other horses were strung in a line behind his, each one tied to the saddle of the one before it. Twisting around, the shifting weight of her pack nearly pulling her off with the motion, she saw he had created a second train behind her horse. Once the line that Shawn led had passed, Onida kicked her horse to follow them down the narrow trail. It seemed that Shawn had decided if Onida's pursuers were going to burn down his home, he was going to take their transportation, as well as all the supplies the horses carried.

As they walked quietly out into the night, with the fire roaring behind them, Onida couldn't help but grin.

4: CLAIRE
4 DAYS AFTER THE BOMBING

"Wait, wait, wait," Claire urged, scrambling up the ramp before they could start removing it. She paused only once in her haste to get over the wall, when she saw the damage done to the container doors that had been struck by a grenade. It was the one breach along the upper level. There was no time to think about that, however, since Claire needed to get down the far ramp before it was hauled back inside, which was going to happen at any moment. She grabbed a rope and hurried down, her virtually empty pack flopping against her back as she hadn't had time to properly adjust the straps yet.

"Thanks guys," she said to the men preparing to move the ramp, because they had stopped working in order to let her down. Claire then took off running, soon passing through the container aisles that formed a sort of maze. All the groups had left, but not very long ago, and it wouldn't take much for her to catch up. Reaching where the zombie slime still coated everything caused her a minor misstep, but she had known she was going to come across it and so kept going. She was on a mission, after all.

"Excuse me. Pardon me. Excuse me, sorry." She made her way past a few teams, careful not to touch any of the slick walls. Her shoe slipped on the gunk once, as it was deeper outside of the path where people and horses were walking, but she kept her balance. Even if she hadn't, a friendly hand had grabbed her shoulder to catch her. "Thank you," she said, before continuing on her way.

There were fair sized gaps between each team so that if the group ahead needed to suddenly turn and flee, they had some space to do so. Through those open spots, Claire moved as quickly as she dared, planting her feet wherever she saw the most pavement.

"Do you think we should go over that way and help them?" a familiar voice spoke from around the next corner.

"A bunch of teams went that way; I'm sure they can handle it. Another messenger will find us if we're needed."

"Needed for what?" Claire asked as she turned the corner and came upon the team she had been looking for.

"Claire? What are you doing here?" Jon was the first to ask.

"Maybe she's the second messenger," Larson suggested.

Claire shook her head. "I'm not a messenger. I'm coming with you guys."

"With us? Scavenging?" Jon raised his eyebrows.

"And why can't she come scavengin'?" Rose immediately challenged him. "I'd love to have Claire join us." She draped her arm across Claire's shoulders. "We need another woman."

"I noticed on the board that your team only consisted of five people," Claire quickly explained. "From my understanding, scavenger teams are usually six people, so I added myself to the roster."

"That's when we have a cart, not on foot," Danny pointed out. "But there's nothing wrong with having another set of hands to help and another bag to fill."

Jon didn't look so sure, but Claire had known he would be like this before she had left. Even though it was only post-zombie adoption that made them siblings, Jon still looked out for her like any big brother. Ever since he had driven her to the hospital on the back of his dirt bike on the Day, weaving through a city of chaos, he had watched over her, so, of course, having her outside the walls would make him uncomfortable. But Claire wasn't a terrified little girl anymore, and she was more than capable of helping out in this way, and so she was going to.

"So what was that you were talking about before I got here?" Claire asked as they continued walking. "Something about a messenger?" She hadn't been the only one dashing about between groups. Several runners had been delivering last minute messages concerning various details. With the speed this operation had been put together, some information had been left out.

"We heard that the groups who are going to cross the bridge have run into a substantial pack of zombies," Bryce filled her in. "There hasn't been a call for back-up though."

"We might run into a bunch of them too," Larson added. "All those zombies that Boss and them lured away with the fireworks could still be hanging around somewhere."

"We'll just have to wait and see," Rose said with a wide grin.

It wasn't much longer before they had exited the container maze. They passed the old warehouse that had been half flattened, following the groups who weren't headed toward the bridge. The farther away they got from their home in the shipping container yard, the more alone they became, as various teams split up to head in different directions. They passed a few dead zombies, slain by those ahead of them, but had yet to come across one still moving.

"So where is it we're going?" Claire finally asked. She suspected her presence had disrupted the usual easy camaraderie of the group. Rose hadn't joined the boys before either. She had lived at the Black Box with Claire, but she used to be a scavenger back on board the Diana, before she lost her hand, and therefore knew how to fit in with them. For Claire, this was the first time she had been allowed out like this.

Jon slid off his pack and grabbed a map out of a side pocket. It was battered and covered in various colours and markings that Claire didn't understand.

"This is home," Jon told her, pointing it out on the map. "This is where we're going." He pointed a fair distance away, where there were no coloured markings. "If we get separated somehow, go south-east. You'll hit the sea and can follow it all the way back home. Don't try to find us unless you're certain you know where we are. The meeting point is always back home, understood?"

"I got it," Claire nodded.

"Do you have a compass?"

"No, they ran out, but I don't need one."

"I'm going to give you mine anyway, just in case." After Jon returned the map to his bag, he took out a sturdy brass compass and pressed it into Claire's hand. She put it into one of the side pockets of her pants, doing her best not to feel offended or that she was a drag on the team.

It wasn't much later when they came across a zombie that was still mobile.

"Dibs," Rose called out, walking toward the slow moving thing while pulling her hammer off her belt.

As she watched Rose approach the zombie that was stumbling its way up out of a drainage ditch, Claire decided she would call dibs on the next one. It would help show the guys that she was capable, which was probably why Rose wanted to take out this one. Living at the Black Box together, Claire had seen how Rose always felt a need to prove herself capable despite her missing hand. Maybe she was just trying to prove it to herself; Claire couldn't be sure.

Rose raised her hammer, and was just about to bash the zombie's skull in, when she suddenly screamed and toppled over backward. Claire started to run to her aid along with the others, but stopped dead when they all received a shot of ice into their veins.

"Gator!" Rose screamed needlessly. The beast had reared up out of the drainage ditch in an attempt to make a meal out of her, narrowly missing. Fortunately, it battered the zombie in the process, knocking the dead thing away from her. Rose kicked at the pavement, pushing her way back from the alligator. It was momentarily distracted by the zombie getting back up, but it soon returned its attention to Rose.

No one had any bullets, but Jon stepped forward anyway. He drew his long katana, and slashed at the gator's nose. It hissed and turned its attention toward him. Rose continued to scramble backward until Bryce and Larson grabbed her shoulders and dragged her a short distance away before setting her on her feet again.

Jon faced down the alligator, which was clearly infected by the same virus that turned people into zombies. The disease reacted differently in the gators. The large reptiles stayed alive, but they became a lot more aggressive, like the rats. They were far more prone to leaving their territorial waters as well, often spotted walking about on dry land.

The alligator hissed and roared and snapped at Jon, who continued to take it on. Dancing out of the way, he slashed and stabbed at the beast. His sword was sharp, but the gator's scales were thick and tough. Jon was clearly aiming for weaker points, like the eyes and throat, but couldn't land a successful blow.

Claire remembered the zombie while everyone else was distracted by the battle taking place. She pulled out her knife and went after the dead thing, which took her dangerously close to the alligator. It looked like the shuffler was going after Jon, who couldn't afford to lose focus. Claire drove her knife through the zombie's eye socket. Blackened and gooey blood leaked out along with the greyish mass that had been its eyeball before the zombie dropped to the ground.

A hissing alerted Claire to the alligator taking offence to her proximity. She didn't bother to look at how close it might be; she just rapidly sprang farther away. The hollow *wap* of its closing jaws was far too close for comfort.

When Claire finally did turn around, she saw the alligator spinning away from her, back toward Jon. He had used her distraction to slash at the side of its belly, delivering a nasty cut, but not a killing blow. The gator charged Jon, who narrowly stepped out of the way in time. When the alligator's jaws next made that flat *wap,* they managed to snag a few teeth on the fabric of Jon's pants.

Jon shouted in surprise and fell to the ground as his leg was yanked out from under him. The alligator shook its head, and therefore most of Jon, who was barely managing to keep a hold on his sword. If the large reptile decided to change its hold, then Jon's leg was in danger.

Danny jumped into action. He threw himself onto the alligator's back. With one arm, he pressed its muzzle down to the pavement, while with the other, he did his best to cover the gator's eyes. The alligator thrashed some more, trying to buck Danny off, but at least Jon's leg was safe for it couldn't open its jaws.

Larson threw himself on top of the alligator behind Danny, and Bryce approached the side of its head.

"Move your leg," he instructed Danny.

The moment Danny lifted his leg out of the way, Bryce thrust at the side of the animal's throat with his spear. Its efforts to thrash off the other two increased with the pain, but as it began to bleed out, the gator weakened. Once it had stopped moving altogether, Danny and Larson climbed off. Jon grabbed the top of its mouth in order to open it, quickly freeing his torn pants before letting the upper jaw drop back down.

"That was some Steve Irwin shit right there," Rose commented to Danny.

"You pick that up watching the Discovery channel with Emma?" Jon asked as he got to his feet.

"Yeah, probably," Danny said quietly, a look of distress momentarily crossing his features.

"Damn it. Sorry, man, I forgot that you were with her when…" Jon didn't bother to finish his sentence.

Danny shrugged. "Its okay. It was a long time ago now, right?"

Claire wasn't sure what they were going on about, only that Jon gave her a weird look.

"That zombie might have gotten you if I hadn't stepped in," she told him, misunderstanding the thoughts behind his expression.

"It could have," Jon nodded, surprising her by agreeing. "Thanks."

Claire shuffled her feet, momentarily confused, for she hadn't expected gratitude. "Well, you're welcome, then."

"So how do we drag this thing back to the container yard?" Bryce asked.

"Why would we bring it to the container yard?" Larson wondered.

"Food," Danny simply replied.

"It's got an active infection," Jon pointed out.

"There are ways to cook infected meat so that it's safe," Rose mentioned.

"Yeah, but no one really trusts those methods, and so they don't eat it," Jon reminded her.

"People will eat it," Claire told them. "I mean, we're out here to find food because people are starving, right? They'll cook the meat properly and they'll eat it."

"I agree," Danny nodded.

"Are we taking a vote?" Jon looked around the group.

"Claire's got a point. Our whole reason for being out here is to get food," Bryce sided with her and Danny. "If we don't bring it back, then what are we out here for?"

Rose stepped alongside the dead alligator and grabbed one of its limbs with her good arm. "Come on, boys. I can't carry this bitch by myself, grab hold. If we get movin' now, we can make it back to the container yard before dark."

With Jon lifting the tail, Danny, Bryce, Rose, and Larson each hoisting up a leg, and Claire holding its long jaws, they were able to carry it between them. It was awkward for Claire at first, because she wasn't sure of the best way to hold it and still walk comfortably facing forward. Eventually, Danny helped her out by hooking its upper teeth through a strap that hung off her bag, allowing the weight of its head to rest on her shoulders while leaving her hands free.

As they passed people who were still outbound from the container yard, they received a lot of attention. A couple skittered fearfully out of the way, as though the alligator might still be alive. A small handful clapped and cheered for them. Claire found herself both proud and uncomfortable with the attention.

By the time they reached the container yard once more, all the parties sent out were long gone, and all evidence of the ramps had been removed. The sky was a dull orange, the last remnants of the sun's passage.

"Hello, up there!" Jon called out once they were near the wall.

A head poked out through the opening created by the blasted doors. "What is *that*?"

"Food," Danny replied.

"We killed an alligator," Bryce elaborated.

"Can we get a ladder?" Jon asked.

Once the ladder was in place, it took a lot of manoeuvring to get the gator's dead body up. Getting it down the far side was a lot easier: they dropped it.

Groaning from the continuing effort, the team picked up their designated gator part once more. They muscled the thing through the container yard to the community centre.

Claire couldn't help but notice how empty the shipping container yard was. Even at that time of night, she'd always seen a number of people walking about, but now she had to actively search in order to spot anyone. It was eerie.

"Do you think our leaders did the right thing in sending so many people out?" Claire wondered.

"You were originally listed to stay," Jon reminded her. It seemed that despite her help with the zombie, he'd still rather have her remain behind.

"I think it's the right thing," Rose responded to Claire's question, ignoring Jon's remark. "We had too many people to feed. This way, those who can fend for themselves outside are doin' just that, while also workin' toward improvin' our future by reachin' out to other groups. Killin' two birds with one stone."

"You don't think they should have left more people behind to defend this place?" Danny asked.

"From what?" Larson questioned him. "The people at the Black Box? Crichton himself is going over there to see if there's any of them left. No zombies are going to be coming by anytime soon, not with all the parties that just went out clearing away any that are nearby. What's there to defend us from?"

"I wouldn't go that far," Bryce shook his head at his cousin-turned-brother. "We don't know just what kind of threats could be out there. I don't know whether it was a good idea to send out so many people at once or not. Yeah, it helps with the food situation, but it does also make this place more vulnerable."

Their conversation ended when they entered the community centre and were suddenly swarmed by the remaining trio of cooks who had been cleaning up. They took the alligator and hauled it over to where it would be diced up into thin slices and thrown over a low fire that was using what little fuel remained after all the body burns. The infection would be sizzled out of it.

"It's too late to head out again," Jon decided. "We'll meet by the wall again at sunrise." With that, he walked off, probably to find Mark. The runners who had come to warn them of the coming zombie horde hadn't yet decided what they wanted to do. Their purpose in life for the last decade or so had been to follow around the mega horde and warn people of its coming, at the same time trying to find an opening in which to take down the intelligent zombie that controlled it. Now that the intelligent zombie was dead, along with a good-sized portion of the horde, they didn't know what to do with themselves. They had been offered the chance to stay, but none of them had made that decision yet. Not even Mark, who had been best friends with Jon before the Day, and had lived in the same apartment building as Claire. She didn't talk to him much, but she was glad to see that he had survived. Seeing him reminded her too much of their apartment's swimming pool, and everything that had happened to her there.

The team quickly disseminated, leaving Claire unsure what to do with herself. She wasn't tired yet, and hadn't planned on being at the container yard another night.

"How'd you like to help me with somethin'?" Rose suddenly asked, sidling up behind Claire and draping an arm across her shoulders.

"Sure. What do you need?"

"An accomplice."

***

Back outside the wall, Claire was feeling particularly energized. She and Rose had done a fair bit of bonding the night before by playing harmless pranks on the kids who had had no choice but to remain behind. It was also exciting to know that no other groups were near them anymore, for now they all had a full day's head start. No more messages were being run between teams. If something happened, they were completely on their own.

Without the other teams so closely ahead of them, they were able to pick up their pace. They passed the site of the alligator attack earlier than the previous day. It was clearly marked by the gator's blood on the pavement, and the unmoving zombie corpse.

Rose approached the ditch in which the alligator had lain. She cautiously looked down into it, wondering if another might have taken its place, but none had.

"We should just keep lookin' for gators," she had suggested a few times. "A lot of meat, and we know how to kill them now."

"How? By having me jump on them?" Danny replied. "Not an ideal method in my opinion."

"We'll take turns jumpin' on 'em."

No one outright refused Rose's plan to hunt alligators. She was right about the meat they provided, and finding food was their first priority.

The three cooks who had taken the alligator from them had stayed up most of the night. They sliced up and fried all the meat, making sure it was prepared and safe to eat for breakfast in the morning. Apparently, one of the elderly residents who'd been injured and was sleeping on a cot in the community centre had volunteered to try the meat first. She said that if anyone was going to croak because of it, it might as well be her. But the meat proved safe. Doctors had checked the woman's blood every few hours, but the dormant virus they all carried hadn't woken up. A few people still refused to eat the meat in the morning, but the majority were willing to try some. Most of the strips had been turned into jerky, and a few had been given to Claire and her team members to take with them. It was the only reward they could be given.

It was a good thing they had been given that little bit of extra food to carry with them, because every time they came to an area that was known to grow some wild edibles, they found it already picked over by the groups ahead of them. It wasn't until nightfall that they came across some tubers to pick. They had spotted a number of rabbits, squirrels, and birds throughout the day, but without bullets, no one had been able to take any of them down. Jon, Danny, Bryce, and Larson had all been taught how to sling stones, but, so far, none of them had proven themselves as adept at it as Freya. Although they had all made valiant attempts, not a single stone had hit its target.

"That looks like a good place to spend the night." Danny pointed to a building across a small parking lot. The windows they could see were still intact, so hopefully the place was secure.

Claire, Rose, and Larson all waited outside, while Danny, Jon, and Bryce went to check out the interior. It didn't take them long, and so they were soon all inside, laying out their bedrolls. In the darkness, they whispered their goodnights and tried to sleep. Claire found it difficult to close her eyes. This was her first time sleeping outside the safety of the walls, and it made her pretty wired. Ever since the Day, she had been kept in relative safety. Her first few nights were spent holed up in a motel, surrounded by army personnel, police officers, and everyone else who had been evacuated from the hospital. After leaving that place, she ended up on the Diana, and the cruise ship became her home for several years. When it was sunk, they had made it to the Black Box, eventually expanding to the shipping container yard, which was her home now that the Black Box had been taken over and destroyed. While there were many terrifying days during these events, whenever she had had to close her eyes, she knew she was protected. Out here, that wasn't the case. There were only six of them to watch each other's backs, and the walls could prove to be not as strong as they hoped.

Perhaps Jon sensed her distress, or maybe he understood what she was going through. After Claire had been lying there for what must have been an hour, thinking she was alone in her conscious state, he got up and moved his bedding beside hers. It was dark where they had decided to make camp. The only light came from the moon and stars, and they had to shine through dirty windowpanes that had security gates drawn across them. Still, Claire's vision had adapted enough to make out the word Jon said to her in sign language.

Scared.

He didn't add the additional modifier to make it a question. Claire didn't know if that was because he wasn't sure she'd see it, or because he didn't need to ask and just knew. Either way, she nodded. Jon nodded back, and then opened up his arms, inviting her to snuggle into them. It had been a long time since Jon had comforted Claire that way, but she didn't refuse the offer. Jon had been one of her greatest protectors since the Day, and so she always felt safest around him. Curled up in his arms, she thought she might be able to sleep. At least, she was able to close her eyes.

* * *

Claire was uncertain how long she had managed to sleep, only that she was awoken by a hand gently clamping down across her mouth. It was a frightening way to wake up, but she understood rather rapidly that she wasn't being threatened. The hand belonged to Jon, and he was making sure she stayed silent. Why he was doing that wasn't, at first, clearly evident to Claire.

On the nearest sleeping mat, Rose had watched as Claire came awake. Her eyes flicked up to Jon and she nodded slightly, letting him know. Jon's hand then slipped away from Claire's mouth.

Moving as little as possible, Claire used her hands and expression to ask Rose what was going on. They were fortunate to have had someone who could teach them sign language after reaching the Diana, as it had proven to be invaluable at times like this for many people.

Possessing only one hand, Rose couldn't fully sign back. All that was needed, however, was a pointing finger.

Claire's eyes slid down toward her feet. They had all slept with their heads against the far wall, across the room from the window. As Claire realized that there were silhouettes in the shape of humans beyond the dirty glass, her body froze solid. The yellow light beyond them told her that it was morning, but not whether the forms outside were living or not. The layer of grime coated more of the bottom of the windows than the top, but it was enough to obscure the figures.

The longer Claire lay there, the more she was certain that they were zombies outside. They weren't moving, just standing there, perfectly still. People would have moved by now. If it was an intimidation trick, there was no reason to keep it going for so long.

But if they were zombies, then what the hell were they doing out there? There was no reason for them to be drawn to that window, and if there had been, then why weren't they trying to break in?

Claire knew she was breathing more rapidly than she should. Closing her eyes tight, she forced herself to take a slow, deep inhalation. When she opened her eyes once more, Rose was looking at Jon and pointing toward a little hallway that led deeper into the building. Claire felt Jon shrug in response. When he had entered the building with the others the previous night, they had only checked that the one room was secure, not the whole structure. The building was situated close enough to the container yard that it would have been searched for useful things years ago, so they hadn't planned to do a sweep of it. The place was just meant to be a stopover for one night.

They waited several more minutes, and still the figures outside remained motionless. Claire had no idea what they were going to do.

5: JAMES
4 DAYS AFTER THE BOMBING

It was hard not to worry about what had happened to the people whose route took them across the nearest bridge. James had wanted to go and help them, but was under instructions not to stop. The path chosen for him and his partner didn't take them across the bridge. In fact, the two of them were to travel much farther than anyone else. Evans had told them about many camps that were likely to be friendly. They couldn't get to all of them and so had to narrow them down. Out of those selected, James and his partner, Katrina, were to travel to the one that was the farthest.

For the moment, they joined a larger group headed for another colony along their route because there was safety in numbers. James sat on the back of an old horse named Soot, who was almost completely deaf. He felt bad riding when so many others were walking, but his left foot was still healing. He wasn't exactly sure what had happened to it. It could have been a bullet, or it might be that the man with the hatchet whom he had fought managed to connect a blow. There was also the possibility that it came about from the upheaval of land when the bombs went off. James didn't know, since he had been surging with adrenaline at the time and, honestly, barely remembered the events at the Black Box. He hadn't realized that something had happened to his foot until after he had climbed over the fence and landed on the other side. With all the running and then hobbling he had done on the foot, not even the doctors who looked at it could say for certain what had happened. All James knew was that the end result was two missing toes, and a lot of time spent keeping weight off his foot, while wearing bandages instead of boots. Even now, as he rode on Soot's back, his wounded foot was exposed.

Soot was an old horse, but James thought he was perfect for their present job. He was what they called a push-button horse. Even little kids who had no idea how to ride, found it easy to get Soot to go where they wanted. Just a slight tug on the reins would get him to turn, and even a fairly weak kick with one heel would cause him to either start walking, or pick up his speed. Perfect for James' current condition.

Walking beside him was a much different kind of horse. The young, highly spirited Spark took a lot more effort to control, although for the moment, he was plodding along at the same pace as everyone else. Katrina didn't need to ride like James did, but since they were going so far, Crichton insisted they both take horses. For now, Katrina had Spark carrying her gear, as well as some belonging to the people with whom they were travelling. She held Spark's lead as they wandered down the streets, her rifle slung over one shoulder. Katrina was one of the few people who had been given the last of their remaining bullets. She had proven herself to be a phenomenal sharpshooter, but more importantly, she never fired in a panic, or when it wasn't necessary. James was glad to have her with him, as he knew there were many other groups that didn't have a single bullet among them.

Up ahead, White raised his hand to call for the group behind him to stop. He had been walking about a block ahead, making sure the way was safe for the dozen people travelling together. James wanted to urge Soot forward, to see whatever it was White was seeing from his position on the hill ahead, but a horse's hooves were loud and could put the others in danger. James silently cursed his injury, which would have become a mantra were he not always coming up with creative new terms.

The group stood together for a tense minute. Katrina slid her rifle off her shoulder and handed off Spark's lead. Glancing down at her, James could see that she wanted to move out of the street, over to the partial shelter of the one building they were near.

When White signalled everyone forward, the relief could be felt as a wave washing through them. James remained fairly tense, though, for White wasn't moving. Whatever he saw up on the hill, he wanted everyone else to see before proceeding.

Astride Soot, James had a higher vantage point than anyone else, and so saw what lay ahead seconds before the others.

"Are those...?" someone beside James started to say before her voice died out.

James found himself nodding. "Lions."

Up ahead, basking in the sunlight, lounged a large pride of lions. James was glad that he and the others were downwind of the big cats. Still, the hefty male had spotted them, his golden eyes watching what they would do next. There was enough distance between the humans and the lions that the animals didn't feel threatened. At least not yet.

"What are we going to do?" White asked without turning his head, addressing everyone within hearing.

"We find a way around," James answered.

"Is no one else wondering what the fuck African lions are doing in Texas?" someone behind them asked, with a voice steeped in incredulity.

"They escaped or were released from the zoo," someone else put simply. "Without a lot of us humans around anymore, it looks like they're thriving here."

"Wonderful." James could practically hear the eye roll that accompanied that sarcasm.

"I like lions," Katrina thought aloud. "Never thought I'd get to see one again."

"Good for you, sweetheart. You'll get a real good look when they're eating your face," the sarcastic guy told her.

"Want to know how I got so good at shooting?" Katrina asked him, in a perfectly calm voice. "Because before the Day I went to a rifle range a lot. I was practising to shoot the nuts off a guy who wouldn't stop calling me things like baby, and honey, and *sweetheart*. I wouldn't waste a bullet on you though: a knife will do fine."

"Okay," James interjected before the conversation could descend any further. "So do we head around them to the north, or to the south?" he asked, trying to get the group back on track and thinking about what was important.

"The north is the direction we're eventually heading," White pointed out.

"Yeah, but we'll eventually hit the river going that way, limiting our options if we need to make another course change," Katrina mentioned.

"I doubt we'll need to," said the man who had been so sarcastic earlier. James finally turned on his horse to see that it was Skip, putting a name to the voice. "I mean, what do you think will happen? More lions?"

"The river's not that much of a barrier," said someone who James thought was named Aaron. "Even if we can't find a bridge across exactly when we need one, we can all swim, can't we?" He had been a member of Evans' party, and was thinking about maybe staying at the colony his team was going to contact. He had never actually been there; he was making the decision based on what he had heard about the place. Katrina had earlier introduced herself to everyone in the group, which James now felt he should have done instead of double-checking the horses and their packs. He'd ask Katrina later if he had the name right.

"Whichever way we go, I recommend we first walk backward," suggested Lindsay, pointing to the lions. "That big guy doesn't look too happy about us all standing around up here."

James returned his attention to the lions and saw that she was right. The adult male was now standing as he stared at them, and so were a few of the females.

"All right everyone, back down the hill," James ordered, turning Soot in a wide circle as if to shepherd them. He twisted around on the horse's back in order to keep an eye on the lions for as long as possible. He was pleased to see one of the females lie back down, although it would have been much more comforting if it had been the male who had done that.

At the bottom of the hill, a quick vote was taken, and they decided to go north. They were too far west to take the bridge that several other groups were taking, so James wouldn't be able to find out what had happened with the zombie horde there. He wouldn't be able to find out until he got back. Not knowing anything about what was happening to anyone until he returned from this mission caused more anxiety than he expected. He had been on plenty of missions outside the Black Box's fences, but this one felt very different. Maybe it was because the last time he had left for a few days, he had returned to find his home occupied by an enemy. While there was no reason to think anything like that could happen again, there had also been no reason to think something like that could happen in the first place. Not as fast as it had occurred, anyway.

As they moved north down a different street, James couldn't help but look over his shoulder several times. The thought that the lions might follow them was one he shared with several others in the group, because he wasn't the only person obsessively monitoring their tail.

"You're going to get whiplash," Katrina commented beside him.

"Better whiplash than a lion's jaws around my throat."

"If the lions felt like attacking us, they would probably come at us from the sides, or hide and wait for us up ahead."

"That sounds more like wolves."

"You don't think lions are capable of intelligent pack hunting?"

"I honestly don't know that much about lions, which is why I'm worried."

"The only thing you need to know is that you can't outrun them."

"Great," James sighed sarcastically.

"No, it's useful information. It means you have to stand your ground and fight them. There's no sense in trying to run away; you'll only end up tired before you die."

"I'd feel better about the whole standing your ground thing if I had more than just a knife to fight them off with."

"Yeah, human bodies are pretty terrible at self-defence, aren't they?"

James found himself nodding. "We're certainly ill-equipped without our tools. Which oddly enough reminds me..." James bent over to keep everyone else from overhearing. "Before I make a fool out of myself later, what's the name of the guy who was beside Skip when you threatened to cut his nuts off? Is that Aaron?"

"Yeah, that's Aaron," Katrina confirmed. She then went on to tell James everyone's names just in case there was someone else he was unsure of.

"Would you really cut off Skip's nuts?" James wondered.

"If he keeps being an annoying pig, yeah, I would."

"Have you ever done that to a guy before?"

"Almost, but no. I wasn't lying when I said why I went to the rifle range. I was going to shoot the nuts off my abusive husband. The zombies came and got him first though. I never was able to decide whether that was more satisfying or not."

"Why shoot his nuts off? That seems..."

"Excessive?"

"Sure, let's go with that."

"It felt like a suitable punishment, and I didn't have to be near him, which meant there was a chance I could get away with it. Yeah, I could have been caught and gone to jail, but at that point, I would have been willing to. It seemed worth it."

"I'll make sure to stay on your good side then."

"It's not that hard to do: just don't be a prick."

James rode in silence for a minute before speaking to her again. "You don't think you should apologize to Skip for threatening him?"

"Not in the slightest," Katrina instantly answered.

"It's not like he knew what kind of effect those words would have on you."

"And now he does. If I apologize, then I'm telling him that his behaviour was okay, and that the problem was with me. I'm not going to do that. Maybe now he'll think before he opens his mouth. I mean, he's now an envoy for god's sake; he needs to be diplomatic."

James could see that there was no way he could change Katrina's mind on the subject, and he wasn't even sure he should. As long as she didn't actually try to hurt anybody, he thought it would be okay.

They planned to walk until nightfall, at some point reaching the river and following it west. They could have crossed any of a handful of bridges, but they knew that the main line of the river eventually swung north, and their destination lay on the western side of that. They ended up travelling a couple of blocks south again, out of sight of the river, where there was a greater chance of finding overgrown home gardens.

It wasn't until they started to look for a place to spend the night, that they had to deal with the lions again.

"We're being followed," said Belle, who had been bringing up the rear.

A few people were at first hopeful that she was just talking about some lone wanderer, but instantly grouped together once she clarified that it was lions. They knew when the big cats had drawn even closer by Spark's agitation. Those near him had to be mindful of his nervously dancing hooves. Even Soot must have caught their scent, for he tossed his head uncharacteristically.

"We need to find somewhere to shelter from them," White voiced what they all were thinking.

"Stay together," James told everyone. "Keep your weapon in your hand. Don't present an opening."

They grouped around Spark, which actually calmed the horse somewhat. Forming a sort of ring around him, they could watch for the lions in all directions. Those facing backward linked arms to make sure they kept pace. Only James was outside the circle, as there wasn't enough room for him and Soot within it. He stayed at the front, leading them as he stood in Soot's stirrups for a higher vantage point. It caused his foot to hurt, but right now he had to ignore that.

"Why aren't we just ducking into one of these houses?" Aaron wondered.

"We can't be sure the lions haven't learned to break through windows," James told him.

"Well there aren't any shops around here," Belle pointed out. "I don't think we're going to find a place with bars over the glass anytime soon."

She was right, but James wasn't sure what else to do. These lions had survived in this urban layout for who knew how long. They may have developed some tricks and knowledge about the place that the group was unaware of. As James looked to one side, he thought he caught a glimpse of one of the golden cats crouched just beyond the peak of a bungalow's roof. How it might have gotten up there, he couldn't say.

"We need to get into a garage," Lindsay suggested.

James mentally smacked his own forehead for not thinking of that sooner.

"Is anyone familiar with these houses? Do we know if they have doors inside that connect into the garages?"

"I can't say I've been in any of these houses specifically," Aaron spoke up. He had probably travelled more than the rest of them. "But I'm going to say that there isn't. In similar areas I've been to, there's only been the garage doors in front, and a regular door that leads outside in the back."

"Meaning we'll have to find one that's unlocked," James translated. If there had been a door from inside the house, they could have gone through a window to get to it.

"Back door or front?" White asked.

"Front," James recommended. "We don't want to be going down the narrow spaces between the houses." Especially if he really had seen a lion on a roof.

Moving together, they made their way up the nearest driveway and pulled on the garage door.

"Locked, move on," White ordered.

They checked two more garages with the same result.

"The lions are getting bolder," Samson pointed out.

They were revealing their positions more and more. After the group checked the fourth locked garage, one lion started to follow them right out in the open.

"They're probably going to start probing for weaknesses soon," warned Katrina.

They tried another garage, and had a brief moment of hope when it started to lift, but then the blasted thing jammed on them. Although they tried, it was impossible to open it any more than a couple of inches.

Watching the door partly rise had momentarily caused James to lower his eyes to the ground. The distraction had just about caused him to be scalped. It was only Soot's startled reaction that had saved him from the lion's swiping paw. It turned out he *had* seen one on a roof earlier, and that it wasn't the only roof they knew how to reach.

Marissa, who carried a fairly long spear, stabbed up at the lion. She managed to draw blood and a pained yowl from the animal. It quickly turned and retreated over to the far side of the roof.

"Thanks," James said, his heart racing in his throat.

From then on, Marissa and Samson kept their eyes on the roofs of the houses they approached, for they both had spears long enough to reach the eaves. James kept himself and Soot a few steps farther away from them.

After another two houses, the lion that had been boldly following them decided to test the strength of their group.

"Here she comes!" Belle shouted.

"Hold together, and watch out for any others that may try to flank us!" White reminded everyone.

Samson and Marissa had been standing on either side of the ring. As the lioness trotted toward the group, they all carefully shuffled so that the two spear bearers were together and facing her.

The lioness growled as the sharpened points waved and jabbed at her face. She swiped at them, but Marissa and Samson held firm. They were unable to land a proper blow, as the lioness kept just outside of their range. As the animal moved left around the ring, they shuffled again in order to keep the spears pointed at her. James kept himself and Soot moving as well, always on the far side of the ring. In the middle, Spark whinnied nervously, and stomped his feet. Eventually, the lioness retreated.

"Let's hurry. She's probably going to have company next time," Katrina warned. Her rifle was constantly held at the ready, always pointed toward the nearest lion, but she'd rather not waste a bullet if she didn't need to.

The next garage was locked, and James was starting to lose hope that this plan would work. As they moved on, he spotted the big male standing between two houses. He made sure to point him out to the others.

They approached the next garage, with Marissa and Samson holding their spears up, and Katrina facing across the street with her rifle. This time, there was a satisfying rattle as the garage door opened. They had finally found one.

"It's going to be a tight fit for the horses," White warned.

James didn't care. He rode Soot through the opening, squeezing the big horse between some tool benches and a large workbench that held an incomplete cabinet lying on its back. James had to duck down, lying across Soot's neck. Spark didn't seem too happy about following, but the young horse wasn't about to let the old one leave him behind. He crowded in right against Soot's rump. James twisted himself over the cabinet to watch through the open garage door. Everyone squeezed in, spears and assorted blades all pointed outward. On the street, a trio of lions had gathered together and were pacing around one another. The male lion was walking over to join them. Then the garage door was yanked down and everything became darkness.

***

The night was spent very uncomfortably in the packed garage. People had crawled into every available space they could find. James found himself lying on the cabinet, grateful that at least the door on one side was complete, providing him with a surface to lie on. Also, the handles hadn't been installed, so it was only the carved bevelling of the design he hadn't been able to make out in the dark that caused him discomfort. Beside him, Soot made the occasional complaint. Being almost deaf made him like the total darkness even less. James spent most of the time that he was awake petting his steed's neck. Somewhere on the tool bench, White was doing the same for Spark. If Spark bit Soot's rump out of agitation, Soot might then start kicking, which was dangerous for everyone. Neither of the horses were comfortable with their cramped confinement, but fortunately they had had practice lately, having had to spend their nights in chock-full containers with the new horses that had come with Evans' party, thanks to the rats. Still, James thought it would be nice if they had some sedatives for the animals.

Thump.

"Sorry," Katrina whispered.

"It's okay, I wasn't asleep," James whispered back.

Katrina was spending the night curled up in the cabinet's largest opening. She said that she was fine not having room to stretch out, but she still bumped into the sides or the door under James every now and again. Other members of the group were underneath the workbench and the tool bench, on the floor up against the garage door, curled around heaps of various junk at the back, and Belle, the smallest of them, was wedged into a tiny space between another cabinet and the ceiling. There had been a lot of crashing and banging as they moved about to find themselves space, and no one was comfortable. James wondered if all the noise would have drawn the dead, and if it had, would they have scared off the lions?

When morning came, James could see the faint light coming through a heavily clouded window set in the door at the rear of the garage. He got the sense that he wasn't the only one lying exhausted yet awake. It felt like the morning after an all night party, where everyone knew that as soon as one person got up, they were all getting up, and no one wanted to be the first.

A young man named Jack was the one to finally break the morning silence.

"I really have to take a piss," he whispered into the dim light, which seemed bright only when compared to the all-consuming darkness that had been their night. He was lying under the tool bench, beneath White. "Do you think the lions are still out there?"

"Only one way to find out," James whispered back. "We'll go together."

It didn't take long for a pair of flashlights to blink into being. They weren't very bright, as they were the kind you had to shake to build up a charge, but they provided ample light for everyone's dark-adjusted eyes.

Over his wounded foot, James pulled on a boot he had found that was a few sizes too big, and so could accommodate his bandages, as well as a pair of padded insoles he had found in one of the containers. It wasn't ideal, but it helped protect the injury during the times he *had* to put weight on it.

Leaving the horses alone didn't feel right, but everyone needed to empty their bladder and it was safer if they all went together. Scrambling over the layers of junk, they all made their way toward the rear door. There was much groaning and complaining, since everyone was stiff. James heard a number of joints pop, and several of them weren't his.

Lucy went out first, as she was the closest to the door. She opened it slowly, ready to shut it the moment she saw even a hint of tawny fur. When nothing attacked her, she stepped outside, closely followed by Marissa and Samson with their spears.

Soot snorted as the light and a puff of fresh air reached him.

"You'll be out soon. Just be good for a few more minutes," James whispered to the horse before following the others out. He grabbed a chunk of two-by-four before exiting, placing it as a door jamb. The door had a pneumatic hinge and he didn't want it to somehow lock behind them, but even more so, he wanted the horses to get that little bit of light and air that crept through the opening.

The moment James stepped outside, he breathed deeply. The garage air had gotten both stale and rank. The horses had no choice but to relieve themselves where they stood, which was more than unpleasant for everybody. Outside, the only smells that James could pick out were created by the greenery.

Huddled together, the group made their way to the middle of the large backyard, stepping high through the long grass. James winced with every step, his foot flaring with pain. He shouldn't be walking on it yet, the doctors had said so, but they understood that sometimes there was no choice. James figured that when he got old—if he got old—there would be plenty of other people with whom he could commiserate about bad joints and improperly healed injuries.

Out in the open, the group broke into two. The girls took one side, the guys took the other. Watching each other's backs, they all emptied their bladders while giving each other just that tiny amount of privacy. James figured you could tell who had spent the most time outside of communities based on how comfortable they were with urinating—or even more so with shifting their bowels—among other people.

After everyone finished, they retreated back toward the house. So far, no lions had been spotted. James and Katrina went back into the garage to prepare the horses, while the others walked around the side to the front in order to reach the roll up door. For just a few seconds, James worried about them being attacked out there, about them discovering that the lions weren't gone, only waiting. If that happened, he and Katrina would be trapped inside that cramped space with Soot and Spark for what could amount to days. But then the door slid open, allowing the garage to be flooded with an abundance of light and air. There were no lions behind them.

James bent over flat on Soot's back again, grateful to be off his foot. Once Katrina had guided Spark out, he gently pulled back on Soot's reins, guiding the old horse toward its freedom. Of course, the moment they were outside, the reins were taken from James. The horses needed to eat, so Soot's bit had to be taken out. Everyone breakfasted on the driveway except James and Katrina. James ate while remaining seated on Soot's back, and Katrina fed herself while standing. She stayed near Spark as he cropped the grass of the unmown lawn, just in case they suddenly needed to move in a hurry.

While James had fully expected to discover that the lions weren't gone, that they had waited, not one was spotted the entire time they ate their breakfast. The beasts must have left in search of another animal, one that wouldn't jab at them with spears or hide behind doors.

When it was time to leave, the group walked a little closer together than they originally had. White didn't go as far ahead, and everyone looked over their shoulder more frequently.

It was around lunchtime when they all finally started to relax a little, to believe that the lions were gone. James made sure to write down in his notebook the various street names that he saw, specifically indicating where they had encountered the lions. The container yard didn't have nearly enough maps for everyone, including James, but he thought that when he next saw one, he could start trying to figure out the lions' territory. They were awfully close to the container yard, and James worried about future scavenger teams. There was even the possibility that, once they had the capability again, they would need to kill the lions. The thought of killing a species that had been, and possibly still was, at some level of endangered didn't sit well with James, but he knew they couldn't expose the container yard inhabitants to the risk. He wondered what things were like in Africa, for both the lions and the humans still living there. He wondered if they'd ever manage to re-establish contact that far away during his lifetime.

James believed that they had gone far enough to swing north again and cross the river. He was just about to call ahead to White to ask his opinion on the matter, when the lioness came streaking out of some bushes and leapt at the scout.

6: DAKOTA
4 DAYS AFTER THE BOMBING

At first, being trusted to finally cross Bitch Bridge completely on her own was great; the novelty of it quickly wore off. Dakota was tired of spending most of her time on Animal Island. She just wanted to sleep in her own bed. But Cameron said it wasn't safe yet. Their container wasn't secure enough from the rats for her to let Dakota spend the night there. Dakota wondered if that was actually true, or if Cameron just said that so she and Brunt could keep fucking. That's what the fifteen-year-old assumed they were doing. It's what she was certain they did whenever she slept over at Hope's, especially when Cameron insisted that she spend the night.

Cameron was pretty cool though. She had been taking care of Dakota for something like five years now, ever since her last caretaker hadn't made it off the cruise ship. Dakota had had a handful of caretakers after the Day, or at least she thought she had. She couldn't keep them all straight in her memory. She couldn't remember which face was her actual mother. But Cameron was cool. She hadn't shied away from telling Dakota about all the intricacies surrounding sex, even before she had gotten her first period. If it weren't for Cameron, Dakota would have been terrified to find blood on the toilet paper that first time, but because of the vet, she knew what to do and had been able to deal with it ever since. It was annoying, but survivable.

On Animal Island, Dakota had seen a number of the farm beasts going at it. Many of the younger children were confused by what was happening, and when they asked their parents or caretakers, they were told lies. Dakota didn't think that was right, so she told them the truth later, when nearly all the adults had returned to the container yard for the day. All the kids liked Dakota for her honesty. Or at least, that was why Dakota thought they liked her. It might have just been the cowboy hat she wore all the time.

"What are you doing?" Hope asked, walking up behind Dakota.

"Nothing," Dakota told her, which was pretty much true. All she was doing was poking at some rocks with a stick she had found along the shoreline.

Hope sat down beside her. "I'm bored too."

"What are the others up to?" The others referred to Peter, Adam, and Becky, who were Hope's best friends. They were Dakota's friends too, but being older made her a bit more of an outsider. Dakota knew a lot of people, especially among the younger groups, and a fair number of them she'd call her friends, but she couldn't say she had a *best* friend. There wasn't one person she liked to be around more than any of the others. Hope was definitely the closest merely due to the fact that they were often forced to spend time together because of Cameron being Hope's mom's twin sister. They were basically cousins.

Hope shrugged in response to Dakota's question. "They're bored too. Peter is taking a nap, and Becky is helping with the chickens today." All the kids were to take turns helping with the chickens at some point. All it meant was keeping track of which hens had laid eggs, and taking the eggs from the bigger pen that didn't also have a rooster in it. "I don't know where Adam is. He's probably over in the container yard somewhere, since he said bye to his dad over there."

"Where's that new girl you've been hanging around lately?"

"Emma? I don't know. Her parents took her with them to do something, but I don't know what."

Emma had come with the group of people who had tried to attack them. Some of the kids thought it was really weird that they were now living together, especially Adam. He thought that they should all be driven out, and encouraged others to think the same way. Despite his efforts, even he was becoming fast friends with Emma, who had a myriad of stories to tell them about her travels.

"Took her where?" Dakota didn't think any kids had left the container yard, but maybe she was wrong.

"Somewhere over there," Hope answered, gesturing across the water. So she hadn't left.

"Did you try this morning's toast?" Dakota asked. The cooks had been experimenting with unusual ingredients in an attempt to stretch their supplies.

"I couldn't really taste anything beyond all the charring."

"Yeah, it was really burnt."

"I can't wait till we start having proper food again."

"Me, too."

Right now they were mostly eating rationed preservatives, both their own and what the new people had been carrying with them. The only fresh food they had were eggs, but there weren't nearly enough to go around every day, and so they drew lots. Those who won got to eat an egg that day, but then they weren't allowed to draw a lot again until everyone had won once. Dakota hadn't gotten an egg yet.

"Do you want to go find Adam? See what he's up to?" Dakota eventually suggested.

"Sure. I'm going to ask Peter if he wants to come."

Dakota walked with Hope over to the cluster of colourful tents that had been erected around the shack that housed the island's one permanent veterinarian. Just beyond the camping tents that housed the young who had been left behind, were tarps and lean-tos that adults, mostly parents, spent their nights beneath. Not everyone had a container to call home yet, or one that was safe enough. With the influx of people from the Black Box and the travellers, they needed to find spaces for all the new residents. They had managed to create a list of people who had died during the zombie attack, but were still tracking down where all those people had lived. Even finding an empty bed wasn't always enough, because if the dead person had shared their container with someone still living, that living person wasn't necessarily going to let a stranger into their home. It was all very complicated.

In a bright green tent that he shared with Adam and a boy Dakota's age named Mike, Peter lay curled up on a sleeping mat.

"Peter, you awake?" Hope whispered through the screen.

Peter raised his head to look at them and nodded.

"We're going over to the container yard to see what Adam is up to. Do you want to come?"

Peter nodded again and rolled upright. Dakota had always thought that Peter was a bit weird. He was very quiet, and actually liked doing math, which, to her, was the strangest thing for someone to enjoy. She guessed that he was bored a lot, now that he didn't live in the Black Box and have a computer to do math problems on, but it was impossible to tell with him.

Threading their way back around the tents, Dakota led the other two to Bitch Bridge. Several people had put in a lot of effort over the last few days to make it less wobbly and dangerous. Along with a few more boards to help keep the old lifeboats, dock floats, and empty drums from shifting too much with the waves, they had also finally finished the rope railing that lined one side. In single file, Dakota, Hope, and Peter crossed the bridge. Having heard all about people breaking a leg or twisting an ankle while crossing, they took their time. Each of them held the rope tightly, and made sure their feet were firmly planted on the boards at all times. It took a while to cross by being so cautious, but if someone saw them being reckless and reported it to their caretakers, they could lose the privilege of being allowed to cross at all. Waiting for a boat to bring them over would take way longer.

Finally on the other side, the trio decided to go down to the dock first where the submarine was secured. Sometimes Adam could be found there hanging around, watching whatever his adoptive dad was doing. Although, now that his dad was on the team going to inspect the Black Box, Adam might not have any reason to be anywhere near the sub.

At the end of the dock, they didn't find Adam, just a few people sitting around, using the hotplates hooked up to it to distil water. There wasn't even anyone trying to dismantle the cranes so that they could be moved back to the walls, however some of the metal plating they had added was now gone.

"Do you want to go inside?" Dakota asked the others. A couple of submariners had taken to living in the submarine, so there was always someone watching over it, and Dakota thought they wouldn't mind giving her a tour. They probably didn't get to show off all the neater bits around the submarine very often.

"No," Hope said, while Peter shook his head beside her.

They had both gotten to ride in the sub after the forced evacuation of the Black Box. Dakota had never been inside herself, and despite hearing the stories of how cramped and scared everybody had been, she remained curious. Maybe another time, when she was alone again, she'd get a chance to check it out.

They wandered over to the community centre next. The badger was no longer asleep outside. It had been taken by the zookeeper on a contact mission. Dakota had never seen the place so empty. It was between meals, and with so many adults gone over the wall, there weren't even people just hanging around. Some cooks were cleaning the plates and utensils from that day's lunch, and there was one doctor sitting on a chair among the handful of injured still recuperating on their cots. A few teens around Dakota's age were sitting together huddled in a corner, holding a whispered conversation, but, when asked, they said they hadn't seen Adam anywhere.

"Let's do a perimeter walk," Dakota suggested, and the others agreed.

Following along the inside of the wall, they found more people there than anywhere else. The wall guards continued to maintain their numbers, which was probably why not much else was getting done. Dakota spotted Brunt up there, but didn't bother to say hi.

"We outnumber them," Hope suddenly said.

"What?" Dakota had no idea what she was talking about.

"Us. Kids and teenagers. All the ones they decided are too young to go on any of the missions. I think we outnumber the adults who stayed behind. We *definitely* do if you don't count the people currently guarding the walls."

"We outnumber them," Peter agreed.

"Huh." Dakota didn't know what to do with that information but it certainly was interesting. She started to notice a lot more people her age and younger walking around than she did adults. Virtually all of the adults were parents and caretakers, but not even all of them had stayed behind. Like Adam's parents, a few pairs had split up in order to get the jobs done that needed doing outside the wall. Dakota wondered if there were enough people left to do those jobs that still needed doing inside. Mostly there seemed to be wall guards, cooks, doctors, and vets. Who was there to finish repairing the containers that needed repairs? Who was preparing more containers for habitation? No wonder the cranes were still in place. And there was certainly no one left to investigate what was in the containers that remained outside the wall. This also meant that no new empty containers were going to be moved over to the part of the wall that was still only one container high. They were basically at a standstill. After that morning's bustle, it felt especially quiet.

Adam was finally located over by the logs that were used to roll containers around. Well, the ones that weren't currently on top of some containers to block the holes in them. They had gotten a lot of use lately, first moving some containers into strategic positions before the zombies came, and then moving them back out of the way again.

"What are you doing?" Hope asked in the exact same tone of voice she had used when asking Dakota the same question.

"Thinking," Adam told her. He seemed to be studying the logs.

"Thinking about what?" Hope wondered.

"If we get enough of our friends together, we might be able to move a container," he said, pointing to the rolling logs.

"Why would we want to do that?" Dakota asked.

Adam shrugged. "To help, I guess. The containers that are over there aren't yet properly modified enough for people to live in, but we could start making a row of them. It would make things easier for my dad when he gets back."

"We don't have a crane to lift the containers with, dummy," Hope pointed out. "How are we supposed to get them on the logs?"

"Oh yeah," Adam sighed. "And don't call me a dummy. At least I wanted to *do* something for someone."

Hope's faced pinched with anger, but she couldn't think of a comeback.

"We could set up the cranes," Peter spoke up.

Everyone turned to look at him like he was crazy.

"You've seen them tons of times, right?" Peter went on. "You know what they're supposed to look like, and the math isn't all that hard to do."

Only Peter could make a statement like that.

"There's no way anyone would let us do that," Hope told him. "No one's going to let a bunch of kids mess around with the cranes. They're too important."

Peter shrugged.

"Well, I mean, there's only one person we'd have to convince," Dakota realized. "Crichton's gone to the Black Box, and Boyle is out with a scavenger team right now. Bronislav is the only one in charge."

"You think we could convince Bronislav to let us try setting the cranes back up?" Adam nearly laughed.

"It's a thought. Or we could just go back to doing nothing," Dakota brought up her own reason for being interested in the project. With literally nothing else for them to do, why not try? "Besides, it's not like we'll get in trouble just for asking."

"Okay. We'll ask," Hope agreed.

Peter had no objections, and Adam nodded after a few seconds of thought.

"Maybe we should ask Becky and Emma and some others if they'd be interested in helping first," Adam suggested.

"That's a good idea," Dakota agreed. "If we can present Bronislav with a number of names of kids interested, he'll probably be more likely to agree."

"Let's go find some others then," Hope declared.

They could have covered more ground if they had split up, yet the four stuck together so as to waste more time and prevent asking the same people more than once.

Dakota was a little bit surprised by just how many kids wanted to help out. Word spread quickly, and some started to seek them out in order to volunteer. By the time they crossed Bitch Bridge again, the whole island knew and was excited about the plan. Dakota knew they were going to have to disappoint some of the kids. Not everyone would be able to help out, as there just wouldn't be enough work for that many hands. At least not until they got to the container-moving portion of the project, when they would need all the strength they could get, even from the youngest ones.

"I think we've talked to everyone," Adam said, flopping down onto the ground. They had done a lot of walking.

"Way more people are interested in this idea than I thought," Hope admitted.

"Everyone is just as bored as we are," Peter pointed out. "They also want something to do while waiting for everyone to come home."

"What's the next step?" asked Becky, who had weaselled her way out of chicken duty, passing it on to another kid in order to join them.

"Next, we have to find Bronislav," Dakota told them. "We have to convince him that letting us do this is for the best."

Adam frowned. "I don't remember seeing him anywhere."

"He must be in the submarine," Dakota perked up, excited to have an excuse to go inside. Even though Hope and Peter weren't keen on it, neither Adam nor Becky had been in the sub and should be easily convinced to join her.

"Or he's right there," Becky said, pointing.

Everyone looked over to see Bronislav crossing Bitch Bridge. His eyes seemed to be on them as well.

"He must have heard," Dakota sighed. She thought that springing their idea on him would have gone better.

"Can anyone tell if he's angry?" Adam wondered.

No one spoke up, but a few shook their heads, uncertain. As far as Dakota could tell, his face was impassive, neither showing displeasure nor joy at their plan. She couldn't tell if that was a good thing or not.

No one moved, waiting for Bronislav to cross the bridge and then follow the shoreline along to where they were sitting. One of his arms was in a sling, still recovering from a bullet it had taken while he had aided in the bombing of the Black Box. Dakota generally found it easier to look at his arm than his face whenever he was around, since he still had stitches on his head, holding together a nasty scalp wound. The thought of having thread holding someone together always made Dakota feel a little wiggly. It was why she wasn't fond of shadowing Cameron as a veterinarian anymore. While the animals rarely needed stitches, the vets did help out the doctors with simple procedures like that. Dakota figured that if she didn't like looking at it, she couldn't do it, and so Cameron had been sending her around, trying to find a different job she could shadow.

"I heard you kids are looking for something to do," Bronislav said as he got close.

"Yes, sir," Dakota answered for them. They were all about to get to their feet when the Russian submarine captain waved them back down with his good arm. He joined them in sitting along the shoreline.

"You want to move the cranes back to the wall?"

"Yes, sir. We believe we can do it. We know what they're supposed to look like, especially Adam," his dad had designed them in the first place, "and Peter knows how to do all the math to make sure it's right."

"And why are you so eager to move the cranes?"

"So we can move some containers," Adam spoke up this time. "We thought we could move the incomplete housing containers into a new row. That way they're ready to go as soon as the modifications are done. People could move into them even before they're done if they want."

Bronislav nodded, understanding, but his face was so neutral that Dakota wasn't sure she trusted him. "You understand that right now there's something we need more than housing?"

"Yes, sir," Hope answered this time. "Food. But how are we supposed to help with that? The chickens don't need *all* of us checking for eggs, the goats and cows can only be milked at certain times, and we're not allowed to go hunting or foraging outside the walls." She didn't even bother to mention that they only had two butter churns.

"And why aren't you allowed to hunt or forage?"

They all knew that Bronislav knew, and so were confused that he would ask.

"Because we're not capable of defending ourselves yet," Becky said after a few seconds.

"You've been taught how to use knives, haven't you? And I can see that at least a few of you have taken to carrying around slingshots."

"We're too young," Dakota told him.

"Says who?"

"Our parents, for one," she said, feeling like he was challenging them, testing them in some way. "You and the other leaders, for another."

"And if we all changed our minds, would you go outside the wall?"

"Why? To hunt? None of us have ever been trained to, so we'd probably be pretty terrible at it."

Was that twitch a repressed smile? "So what you need is training."

"I guess," Dakota shrugged. The others nodded in agreement with her.

"Okay then, I guess we know what we need to do."

"What?" Dakota frowned. "Train us?"

"Yes."

The answer actually surprised everyone, since it wasn't what they had expected.

"Maybe not to hunt," Bronislav continued. "We already have people out there doing that, but to defend yourself outside of the wall. What we need, is a place to grow things. We shouldn't have allowed the container yard to depend so much on the Black Box's fields. We need to make a place to grow things here."

"And there's no room inside the wall," Dakota realized.

Bronislav nodded.

"So we're going to make a field outside of it?" Becky asked for clarification.

"Yes, which means you'll need to be able to take care of yourselves out there. I want you to go to all the other kids and teenagers you talked to today, all the ones who wanted to help. Tell them to gather in front of the community centre tomorrow morning, after breakfast. If their parents agree, and I *will* be asking around about permission for everyone, we'll get you ready to go outside. If anyone has both their parents out on missions right now, they need to ask whoever is currently keeping an eye on them, as well as me personally."

Dakota felt her stomach flutter. She couldn't tell if it was from being nervous, excited, or terrified. Maybe it was all three.

***

Cameron spent a long time deciding whether to give her permission or not. Dakota had waited as patiently as she could, knowing that being overeager wouldn't help her. She watched as Cameron had discussed the matter with Brunt, and then with Riley. At least Dakota knew that Hope was in the same boat while the twins were talking. Still, Dakota was almost embarrassed at having to wait so long. There were kids younger than her who had received permission the moment they asked. Emma's parents thought it was a great idea, especially since she had already been getting some inconsistent training while travelling. She was only nine, the youngest out of Hope's group. Dakota was fifteen, only one year away from mandatory training, and yet Cameron had to mull it over.

It became a restless night for Dakota. Cameron had said she'd give her an answer in the morning. At least Dakota was finally back in her own bed. She liked to think that was because Cameron thought it silly keeping her out on Animal Island when she was being considered for training to go outside the wall, but really, it was just because their container had been fully repaired, and was now rat-proof once more. The mattress of her upper bunk wasn't helping Dakota sleep, because she had gotten used to the sleeping mat in her tent. She wondered how long it would be before all the containers were repaired and all the kids could sleep in their own beds. Only a handful of people were working on the repairs between their other jobs. Dakota wondered if she should have had the kids volunteer to do that first.

When the morning finally came, Dakota watched the pop bottle light bulb grow steadily brighter. She had slept in spurts, her mind skimming the surface between thoughts and dreams.

Brunt got up with a soft groan, sliding off the lower, queen-sized bunk without shaking the whole thing too much. He got dressed quickly. The only sound was a soft rustling of fabric. As always, he picked up his boots and carried them to the door, intending to put them on outside. With fewer people available, the ones whose official duty had always been to guard the wall, had been taking longer shifts so as to train those who were new to it. A slice of sunlight pierced the container for a few seconds as Brunt slipped out.

"Dakota?" Cameron spoke from where she still lay on the bed below. She didn't even whisper. "I know you're awake. You always roll over when Brunt gets up unless you're already awake."

"Have you made your decision?" Dakota asked, glad that she wasn't facing Cameron in case it wasn't the news she wanted.

"Yes. I've decided that you can go and train with the others."

Dakota's heart began to race with fear, which was in complete contrast to the smile that spread across her features. "Thank you, Cameron."

"You should be thanking Bronislav. He's the one who ultimately convinced me. He said they need the older kids like you to help give the younger ones more confidence."

This surprised Dakota, as she hadn't realized that Bronislav and Cameron had talked. It seemed that once the captain had decided to go ahead with this idea, he was fully onboard and committed to it.

"How about we eat breakfast together this morning?" Cameron suggested.

"Okay. I have to pee first though."

"So do I."

As Dakota climbed down from the top bunk, Cameron rolled away from her spot against the wall to the side of the bed. They both got dressed in the dim light, not needing more than what was coming through the bottle and not wanting to waste a candle.

"It's weird not seeing Misha's dogs everywhere," Dakota commented as they walked toward the wooden stalls bolted to the cement pad that lined the river: the structures that served as their toilets.

"They'll be back sooner than most of the others," Cameron commented.

"If they're okay."

"Yes, if that. But they're with Misha and are quite capable of handling themselves if any unexpected events occur." Cameron never lied to Dakota—as far as she knew—and wasn't afraid to share information with her. So while her words weren't the typical kind for comforting, they did make Dakota feel better. She really liked all the dogs, and she had to admit that she thought Misha was pretty cool too. Weird, but cool.

The line for the toilets was long that day; it seemed every kid had gotten up with the sun. There were nervous caretakers and parents standing all about, yet the general air was one of excitement. Dakota wondered if they all felt the same worry deep in their guts that she did.

Because it was a big day for many of them, Dakota had subconsciously thought that they would get more rations for breakfast, and was therefore disappointed when she received the exact same discouraging meal that she always did. She didn't even get a chance to try the alligator meat as it was only for adults, due to the slight chance it wasn't cooked properly and still carried an infection. She sat at a table with Cameron, Hope, and Riley. The doc wore a baggy T-shirt; Dakota knew that Riley still had stitches and bandages and things around her chest. She tried not to think about it, but every now and then her friend's mom would wince and carefully change her posture. Ever since her double mastectomy because of a cancer scare, it had become a lot easier for everyone to tell the identical twins apart, but Dakota could already do that, and didn't like the reminder that the same thing could happen to Cameron.

"Do you know who's going to be teaching us?" Dakota asked during breakfast.

"I'm not sure," Cameron replied. "Bronislav didn't give us any details. I think he was still putting everything together."

"I don't like how last minute all of this is," Riley added.

"Mom, we'll be fine," Hope sighed.

"I don't mind you receiving training; it's going outside the wall that I don't like."

"I doubt he would send us out alone," Dakota did her best to soothe the adults. "And it's not like we'd be going very far. He just wants to use us to make a field ready for planting. We'll probably be right beside the wall, and the guards up there will also watch over us."

"I understand," Riley nodded. "But I still don't like it. There are times you're going to find yourself in the same position, having to do things you know are right but that you'd rather not do."

Coming from a woman who had voluntarily had her breasts surgically removed, the words carried more weight. Dakota really hoped she wouldn't have to make *that* sort of decision.

After they had finished breakfast and placed their dishes on the washing pile, Cameron and Riley accompanied Dakota and Hope outside. They immediately found where they were supposed to meet with Bronislav, where a pile of kids and a handful of guardians were lingering around, but Bronislav himself was currently nowhere in sight.

"Will you be okay if I leave you?" Cameron asked Dakota. "I have rounds to make."

"I'll be fine." Dakota wanted her to go, in fact.

Riley also left, so Hope and Dakota were free to wander about the group. They located Adam and Becky, who were on their own, and stood with them. Peter was lingering at the edge of the group with one of his caretakers, Lauren. She was basically his mom, having raised him since he was just a year old. Dakota wondered what it would be like to have spent her life with the same couple raising her. Emma also stood with her parents to one side.

When Bronislav finally did arrive, he wasn't alone. He had brought Freya with him, which caused Dakota's heart to instantly speed up. Dakota knew that Freya was a fierce warrior. She was surprised that the Jamaican woman wasn't out scavenging, although maybe she preferred to stay put because she was a mute. Learning sign language was a must for everybody because it allowed them to safely communicate in silence, but it also let them speak with Freya. A disease of some kind had paralyzed her vocal cords, which meant she couldn't call out any kind of a warning. If you weren't looking at her, she couldn't talk to you.

"All right, we've got a good grouping here," Bronislav said. "Parents, guardians, if you don't mind, I believe you all have your own jobs to do. Your kids will be well taken care of, and they won't be going over the wall today."

Many of the adults still hanging about were hesitant to leave, but they obeyed. Peter and Emma were soon both standing with Dakota and the others, as the whole group of kids gathered close to Bronislav so that he wouldn't have to shout.

"So who's ready to learn how to defend themselves outside the wall?" Bronislav asked.

Dakota raised her hand along with most of the others. As Freya's hard gaze swept over her, she prayed that she was actually ready for this.

I: THE SKY

Randall sat on the floor, listening to the conversation going on in the next room. He wished he could join in, that he could laugh at whatever jokes they were telling one another. But he was old, and learning more than a few words and phrases of their language had proven impossible, despite the immersion. He was all but alone; only one other man could speak his language, and he had not taken a liking to Randall.

Standing up, Randall walked over to the floor-to-ceiling windows to stand amongst his plants. They were going to need watering soon. Water was the most precious resource, carefully rationed and jealously guarded. A lot of men and women had died to build the pumps, and still more had perished in the maintenance of them.

Leaning against the glass, Randall looked down. Despite how often he did this, a thrill of fear still fluttered its way through his belly. The ground was so far below, that the walking dead were mere specks, even harder to distinguish because of the sand that covered both them and the streets. Randall wasn't even supposed to be here when the virus broke out. When he retired, he had originally wanted to go to Hawaii. But just before it was time to plan his first trip since his twenties, Randall happened to watch a *Mission Impossible* movie. Tom Cruise scrambling around outside the Burj Kalafi had enamoured Randall with the building. He decided that Dubai would be the first stop on his trip, and then he'd pop around to a few other countries before finally landing in Hawaii. He had worked hard for many years, and deserved to see the places he wanted to see.

The virus broke out in Canada as he was on the plane. Three days after he had checked in, the massive hotel closed its doors, refusing to let anyone in or out. They said it was for public safety, and Randall had no reason to disbelieve them. Unfortunately, an infected individual, who had checked into the Burj Kalafi the day after Randall, attacked a small part of the populace out on the streets and spread the disease. The hundreds of people within the one hundred sixty-three storey hotel were kept safe from Dubai's outbreak, but they could only survive inside for so long before resources became scarce, and people began to die either getting them or fighting over them. Randall didn't like to think about those times. His limp made it difficult to forget.

Randall's room—not the one he had originally booked—didn't have a view of the ocean. Instead, he faced outward toward the desert and so he could monitor the progress of the coming sandstorm. Sandstorms were both a blessing and a curse. The bad ones shredded the dead, sometimes burying them for a few hours, so that it was safer for people to exit the building. But the sand also wreaked havoc with their water system, forcing people to go outside.

The coming storm didn't look too bad. Randall moved away from the window and limped over to his bed. He picked up his e-reader and carried it pressed to his chest as he circled his room. Filled with books he wanted to read, the device had eventually run out of batteries, leaving them inaccessible. Randall wasn't sure why he continued to cling to the hunk of plastic. Maybe it was because it was the only thing he had left from home. All the rest of his luggage had been stolen one night.

Following a worn path in his carpet, Randall exercised his legs. Others jogged out in the hallways, but Randall hadn't been able to manage a fast pace since even before he had injured his leg.

Another burst of laughter came from the room next door. He could hear it clearly, as both doors were propped open. It was the best way to get light into the halls, and people got nervous whenever someone shut themselves away for too long, even someone who could barely communicate with everyone else.

When he finished his walking, Randall sat on his chair and waited. He had become very good at waiting. It was not a skill his profession had taught him, but one he had been forced to learn over the years due to long periods with nothing to occupy his mind but his thoughts. Some people hadn't been able to learn how to wait. They tended to make use of their belts in such a way that they'd never have to wait for anything ever again. But Randall could wait. His belt remained on his hips, holding up a pair of pants that might have fit him before his forced diet.

A man, whose name was unknown to Randall but whose face was recognizable, stepped through Randall's door. This was a man who often looked at him with pity, which was better than those who looked at him with disgust, anger, or annoyance. The words he spoke were ones that Randall knew and had been expecting. In his mind, they translated to *your turn to pump.*

Randall walked to the room in which the pump had been placed, after climbing down several flights of stairs to get there. The stairs were always so dark despite the propped open doors, and Randall hurried down them. He didn't know how the people who went outside tolerated the long climbs. He knew they took rests on the way back up, but he couldn't tolerate the dark for even five flights, let alone the dozens and dozens they mounted.

The pump room was easy to find. Randall walked alongside the line of people, all of them waiting for their ration. Randall always got his in the morning. There was always a set time of day when everyone got theirs, yet they lined up anyway, day and night. Randall did too.

The woman currently pumping was glad to see him. Not only did it mean she no longer had to pump anymore, but she got an extra water ration as she went off duty. Randall would get the same, which he would feed to his plants. But first, the pumping.

Sitting on the stool, Randall wrapped his hands around the metal handle that had been worn smooth with constant use. He began to pump. His arms were far stronger than they used to be, and his hands bore tough calluses. Still, if it weren't for other pumpers stationed all along the line, some even set up in different buildings, there would be no way that Randall could move the lever. It was a long way up, after all.

Each pump sloshed more water into a trough below the nozzle. If they were on a lower floor, another pipe would be sucking it up from the trough, carrying the water through holes that had been drilled through both floors and ceilings. But Randall lived at the top, the highest point to which they carried the water. As he sat there, pumping, he listened to conversations he couldn't understand. He watched as one person after another dipped their ration cups into the trough, every single one making sure that their cup was completely full to the brim before departing. Randall silently identified the people whose names he knew. There were more whom he didn't know, but he recognized their faces, and thought of the memory he most associated with each one. Some memories were bad, some were pleasant, but most were completely benign. No one tried to talk to him, since they knew he wouldn't understand whatever language they spoke.

Randall worked the pump. Every time he pressed on the lever, he prayed that it would feel right, that there wouldn't be the loose sensation of no water, which happened whenever a problem along the line caused the trough to empty below the last pipe. Up and down, up and down, the lever went, making use of the fact that nature hates a void.

Up there in the desert sky, water was life, and Randall still wanted to live. Despite everything, he still wanted to live. He worked the pump.

SECTION 2:
HUMAN

7: MISHA
4 DAYS AFTER THE BOMBING

Misha gripped his machete tightly as his breath started to fog up his mask. He didn't mind the faint blur this overlaid the world with, since he preferred not to see too many details of what was coming. All too fresh in his memory were the images of wave after wave of zombies coming toward him.

They had waited for the others to catch up, the groups that had planned to cross the bridge. Many suggestions were vocalized, including just sneaking past the dead. But with the close proximity of the container yard, that idea was quickly shut down. Another suggestion had been to block in the zombies, to trap them in the smaller yard until they could be dealt with using their full force. Whilst this idea was very popular, no one knew how to actually trap them, not even Harry, not without wasting hours upon hours, and risking the dead things hearing them work, anyway.

Misha shifted his feet from side to side, and back and forth, making a somewhat clear patch in the slime so that his boots could better grip the pavement beneath. At that moment he couldn't see any zombies, but based on what he could hear, others elsewhere were already encountering them.

"Ready?" Crichton asked, standing at Misha's side.

Misha nodded.

Raising a machete of his own, one that didn't have jagged saw blades along its back like Misha's, Crichton started pounding the butt of it against the nearest container. The ringing clang seemed to echo around the entire small yard, but in fact, it was others doing the same. The plan was to split the zombies up into the smallest possible groups in order to make them more manageable. They had spent maybe an hour or more waiting for everyone to get into position, encircling the place. By having everyone not currently engaged in taking out the zombies make a lot of noise, the pack should be broken up as they moved toward different sound sources. They were to hit the largest metal object, start shouting, or blow on a whistle until zombies came their way, even if they had just finished killing a dozen. The hope was that if those killing the zombies did so as silently as possible, the chains the dead occasionally formed—of one following the corpse ahead of it as if it knew where it was going—could be broken up and redirected. This would make it so that one team wasn't forced to take out considerably more zombies than the rest.

"Here they come," Misha said to Crichton, his voice muffled by the rubber of his gas mask.

Crichton pulled up the bandanna that had been around his neck so that it covered his nose and mouth. His eyes were protected by a pair of close fitting sunglasses. As he stood alongside Misha, he kept tapping the tip of his blade against the nearest container, making sure the zombies heading toward them weren't going to suddenly peel off. Misha thought that he should probably be doing the same on his side, but couldn't bring his body to move out of a ready stance. When the zombies were just a few feet from striking distance, Crichton finally mirrored Misha's pose.

The nearest of the dead lunged at Misha, who sank his blade through its partly decayed skull, and the battle had officially begun.

It didn't take long for Misha's arms to get tired. His legs, too, felt rubbery from kicking zombies off his blade. It was a feeling he knew he could power through, having learned how from defending his home. This assault was different than that one, however. Here, there was no one to call changes to the line; there were no lines. In that narrow alley, it was just Misha and Crichton, each of them having to cover a little more area than they would have liked. There was no one to take Misha's place when he got tired. He just had to hope that they got a break when the dead were called elsewhere. The biggest difference, he found, was that at any moment he was free to run away. If he and Crichton began to feel overwhelmed, they were to retreat and regroup elsewhere. Misha wasn't boxed in this time. Only his desire to get the job done, to not let Crichton down, kept him fighting. It made the task surprisingly more difficult.

The next time there was a break in the zombies, Misha held out his hand, asking Crichton to wait a minute before he went banging on the container again.

"What is it? Are you all right?" Crichton's voice was flooded with concern.

Misha nodded. "I just need a breather."

"Pull your mask up for a minute."

Misha shook his head. He pointed to the pile of bodies at his feet by way of explanation. There was no way he was going to take his mask off with so much contaminated flesh around. His gloves, also, were coated in the thick, black gunk that was once human blood, and he wasn't about to risk accidentally touching his face.

"Hate to tell you, but it looks like the dead aren't going to give you a break," Crichton said, pointing down the container alley.

Through the haze of his foggy mask, Misha could see the shapes stumbling toward them. He brought his machete back up, prepared to cleave more bones. He cracked another skull, and then another. And then something strange seemed to happen. Misha started to see faces beyond the rot. Eyes weren't clouded over, noses hadn't been broken or chewed off, lips hadn't been peeled back. These human faces were even more terrifying. Of course, Misha didn't realize that with his mask fogged up he shouldn't be able to see such details. To him, he was being attacked by zombies who hadn't been dead for long. He was being attacked by people who weren't dead at all.

"Misha! Misha!" Crichton was shouting beside him.

Misha hadn't realized that he was screaming, and swinging at air for there was nothing but stilled corpses at his feet. When Crichton tried to grab him, the man narrowly avoided having the blade buried in him. But he had proper military training and was able to step within Misha's guard, grab his wrist, and twist so that the machete was forced free of his grip. Spinning Misha around, Crichton pinned him to his chest with his arms, and then quickly used one hand to rip the mask off Misha's face.

"Breathe. Breathe," Crichton urged in Misha's ear.

The inhalation was more like the ragged gasp of a dying man.

"Slowly. Slowly."

Misha obeyed, taking in slow, deep breaths. The air smelled foul, but it was much cooler than what he had been breathing.

"We're falling back. Come on," Crichton released Misha and picked up his fallen blade for him. With a hand on his back, he guided Misha away from the containers.

As he walked, Misha pulled off one of his gloves so that he could wipe the sweat off his face.

"What happened back there?" Crichton demanded once they were a safe distance back, closer to where the carts had been left with a light guard.

"I don't know," Misha admitted, shaking his head. He couldn't think. He searched around for a place to sit, but everywhere the ground was coated in zombie slime.

"You lost it back there," Crichton insisted.

"I think it was the mask," Misha told him. "It got too hot. I couldn't breathe right. I don't think the air valve was working correctly."

Crichton looked at the mask he still held in one hand. "Are you sure that's all?"

Misha nodded. All he wanted right then was a glass of water and a place to sit. "Is it all right if I go back to the carts? I'll send one of the guards there to replace me."

It was impossible to tell what Crichton was thinking beneath his bandanna and mirrored sunglasses, but Misha got the distinct impression that he was being stared at. Studied. Evaluated.

"All right, go get some water. And maybe think about using something different next time," Crichton said as he handed back Misha's mask and then his machete.

Misha nodded as he turned away to head back to the carts. Crichton would remain at the fall back position until Misha's replacement met up with him.

It was obvious to Misha when he neared the carts, because he could hear the horses snorting with displeasure. They didn't like being forced to stand around on the zombie slime trail, and were irritated. Once they were in view, a single bark alerted the people standing around as guards that he was coming. Misha was pleased to see his dogs, all of them standing on the flatbed cart, watching him approach with tails wagging. If they hadn't been tied to the cart as a precaution with bits of rope, all of them would have run over to greet him.

It didn't take long to find a guard willing to replace him. It seemed some of them were eager to crack a few skulls, or at least do something more active than what they had been. Misha had worked sentry duty on the wall before, and knew how tedious it could become. Also how paranoid one could get, especially out here when you knew there were zombies nearby.

Climbing onto the cart in order to retrieve the water from his pack, Misha was thoroughly sniffed by the dog pack. They knew better than to lick him; while they wouldn't be infected by the blood on him, one could assume it wasn't a pleasant taste. After taking a long swallow of water, Misha stripped out of his soiled shirt and hung it over the cart's side with his gloves. Since they were carrying equipment that would allow them to desalinate water, and they were following the bay, Misha wasn't afraid to splash some over his head, and also wipe down his neck and forearms and anywhere else he thought the zombie bits might have reached his skin. Because of the way his dogs watched with interest, he put some water in a couple of pots and let them have a drink. He then fished a clean shirt out of his bag. His pants he didn't bother to change, for the hems would pick up bits of the slime trail anyway, and he didn't mind as much if they dried into a crust. Besides, he hadn't even brought an extra pair of pants.

Satisfied with his cursory cleaning, Misha sat on the cart's driving bench. He had a nice vantage point from there to watch the surrounding area, and could pull back on the horses' reins should they decide to start walking on their own. Most of the guards had opted to sit somewhere on the carts, with only Angela actually walking a tight perimeter around the little cluster of carts, horses, and gear.

Sitting with Rifle on one side and Bullet on the other, Misha tried to sort out what had happened to him. His first thought was to wonder if he had hit his head recently. He thought of Nicky, who had managed to get them through the Black Box's entrance despite the various mental and memory problems she had after receiving multiple blows to the head. Thinking through the past few days, Misha couldn't remember getting any injuries besides muscle strain, especially not head injuries. He next contemplated the mask, but he had worn it before without issue. He tested the valve that let air in and out, usually covered by a filter, and it seemed to be working fine. Could it have been the heat? He didn't want to believe it was just stress that had made him see what he had. Perhaps it was a combination of elements. Whatever it was, Misha decided to stop thinking about it and forget that it ever happened. If he could.

After more than an hour had passed, Misha began to worry. Surely it shouldn't have taken this long. Were there really that many zombies in the small container yard? He could still hear the occasional whistle or shout, but most of the sound was hidden by distance and a building they had decided to keep between the horses and the fighting. Was everyone still okay? Had there been mass casualties and those few sounds he could make out were from the survivors who didn't yet know that they were the last?

As Misha tried to convince himself that he was just being paranoid, he could see that the other guards were also growing restless with concern. Why was this taking so long?

Beside him, Rifle whined, then shifted so that he could put his head on Misha's lap. He was picking up on the nervous tension. All the dogs were. Bullet sat very alert, and Misha could hear the others snuffling behind him. They were wondering if there was danger somewhere that they were failing to pick up on. They trusted the humans to know what they were doing, even when they didn't.

Misha had just been in the middle of telling himself that he would give them five more minutes when a handful of people returned. A minute after them came a few more, and then a few more, each of them trickling back in batches depending on how long they had decided to search the small container yard for straggler zombies. It was no surprise to Misha that Crichton was with the last group.

"How are you feeling?" Crichton asked Misha, who felt it should have been the other way around.

"I'm fine," Misha insisted. "Once I had some water, I felt much better."

"Good."

Everyone hung around for a bit, exhausted. Several people took some time to sit on the carts before locating their packs and having to start walking again. Misha spent the short break untying his dogs, letting all of them off the cart for a bit in case they needed to relieve themselves. Once it seemed time to go, Powder, Guard, and Slide stayed off as before. Misha's small team made sure the packs belonging to people going elsewhere were off their cart, and then they left first. Harry had removed a jacket he had worn to keep the blood off himself, but Crichton and Ki-Nam remained soiled, neither of them having yet bothered to change their shirts.

Crossing the bridge was an unpleasant affair. The zombies had been funnelled across it, following the intelligent Dean who somehow passed onto them that they should avoid the water. The slime they had left behind was thicker, which also made it more slippery. Misha had to be careful walking across, moving slowly. He had seen this bridge before and knew that there were more cars abandoned upon it before the zombies came. A few must have been pushed over the sides, which was telling of just how large a mass the horde had been. The remaining vehicles had all been flattened, except for one tanker truck, too tall for the zombies to clamber over easily. Ki-Nam studied the ladder at the back of the truck, debating climbing it to take a quick scout ahead from an elevated position, but the ladder was gooey, and using it could prove to be dangerous. A slip and a fall into the gunk could easily prove fatal. One open wound, or one splash into the mouth, would result in an active infection.

When they finally reached the far side of the bridge, they found more zombies. It seemed not all of them had been smart enough to avoid the water, and had become trapped in the mud on either side. They appeared to be thoroughly stuck, either up to their knees or their waists. Misha spotted one zombie that had managed to tear its own legs off trying to get free, but didn't make it far before its arms were trapped up to the shoulders. A rope of intestines still connected the two halves.

"Keep walking," Crichton ordered. "They shouldn't become a threat to the container yard anytime soon, and we can take them out on our way back."

Misha had no idea how Crichton planned to take them out. The mud would trap them just as readily. There was no way to get near them, and no way to take them out from a distance, not without using all of Harry's arrows.

Across the river, they turned east, which took them away from the slime trail. The zombies had come from the north-west on this side, and Misha felt sorry for anyone heading in that direction. Once again on dry pavement, he shook out his feet. His three dogs did the same. Even the horses swung their legs a little more, kicking off the gunk. No one wanted the stuff drying on them. The other dogs were let off the back of the cart to walk around, but they stuck close, rarely more then twenty feet from Misha or the cart.

"We need to start looking for a place to spend the night," Ki-Nam said, gesturing to the sky that had begun to change its tint with the lowering sun. He was the most experienced with travelling, and so they trusted his judgement.

Crichton didn't seem too happy about it, but he didn't complain. They were supposed to be much farther along than this, but the zombies had eaten a good chunk out of their day. If they had been ferried across the river instead of walking, they could've reached this spot in an hour, maybe less.

"There," Harry pointed to a building with a slash of red paint sprayed across the front of it. Before building up their flotilla of canoes and kayaks, people had to walk between the container yard and the Black Box, and so had marked buildings proven to be safe. But just because the building had been safe back then, didn't mean it still was. Misha brought his dogs over to check it out.

The building had once been a bar with an outdoor patio. As part of its semi-industrial style, the place had installed a garage door as its entrance to the patio, which would allow Ki-Nam to walk the horses and the cart inside once it was proven safe. The tables and chairs had been moved away long ago, since their cart wasn't the first.

Misha walked around the place, checking out the kitchen and the bathrooms, but neither he nor his dogs found anything of interest. Ki-Nam and Harry unhitched the horses and walked with them outside for a bit, letting them eat before confining them indoors for the night. Crichton set their packs down on the bar and poked around, double-checking that all the cupboards were indeed bare. The booze had likely been stolen long before anyone from their group came across the place. Alcohol had been one of the first things to go, leaving only the nasty stuff they occasionally distilled themselves when someone wanted a drink.

There wasn't much housekeeping to perform before they were ready to bed down for the night. Harry, Ki-Nam, Angela, and Crichton all set up behind the bar, but Misha chose to sleep on top of the cart. His dogs could all join him there without bothering the others. Misha listened to the breathing of his pack until he fell asleep.

* * *

The whining of a dog combined with the application of a cold nose to his cheek brought Misha back to consciousness. He sat up immediately, wondering what was wrong. There was the faint light of morning coming through the windows in the bar's doors, but that was the only change from the night before. Most of the dogs were looking at him, and based on the way his blanket was all twisted about his legs, he thought that maybe he had been having a nightmare. He couldn't remember one, but evidence suggested otherwise.

"Come on," he whispered to the dogs. "Let's go see if anything's outside."

The dogs were more than happy to go, immediately forgetting their concern for him. While all of them but Rifle hopped down off the cart, Misha put his pants back on, regretting that he hadn't packed a second pair. The goop was now dry and not much of a threat, but he still did his best to touch them as little as possible. He then put on his boots, holstered his machete, and lifted Rifle down off the cart.

As Misha neared the door, he saw Crichton's head poke out from around the side of the bar, his features suggesting that he had just woken up and was still half-asleep. Misha quickly signed to him that he was just going out to walk the dogs. Crichton nodded, and withdrew back out of sight.

Outside, it appeared it was going to be another clear, sunny day. Misha wished he could see just one cloud in the sky, but it seemed that it wasn't meant to be. He wanted rain, even if it made for miserable travelling.

The street remained the same as it had the night before. Misha walked at Rifle's pace toward the end of the block, intending to circle the strip of shops and restaurants around the bar. The rest of the pack wandered ahead, or behind, or to the sides, sniffing everything, and peeing on much of it. When one of them took a shit, Misha ignored it; society no longer cared if anyone picked up after their dogs or not. Hell, along here, there was still evidence of the many times horses had passed through. Manure that had become trapped in the gutters by debris, now simply appeared to be dirt. They were likely to start seeing stuff that was relatively fresh as well, because they were following the same route that Evans had taken when he left to deliver the detonator.

As Misha walked along with his dogs, he tried to picture what the street used to look like, back before the Day. He figured with all the shops, restaurants, bars, and salons it had been a fairly busy place. Maybe the bar they had slept in was a hot spot, a place where people gathered after a long day at work. Or the area could have been a dead zone, where stores came and went with the years, each place hoping to do better than the last. It was impossible to say. It was difficult for Misha to imagine the street without the weeds pushing through the cracks, or the buildup of leaves along the gutters and edges of the buildings. The trees would have been nicely pruned, the branches that had fallen off in storms taken away. The downed wires would have been repaired, broken windows replaced, and the cars wouldn't have been abandoned for so long that they were sinking into the pavement. Misha always wondered about the cars and how they got there. On major roads, there were always quite a few, having been abandoned where they had stopped. Had they run out of gas? Was it engine trouble? Did the owners just give up, or were they attacked and forced to run? This area had had some forewarning, and had attempted to evacuate people to a shelter, so there weren't too many obvious traffic snarls. Did the cars parked on streets like this one belong to people who ignored the order? Or had they come here after the various quarantines had failed? Perhaps survivors like themselves, ones who had come from far away, had driven here. So many questions that would never have answers, but they gave Misha something with which to occupy his mind.

As he rounded the end of the block, Misha brought his dog pack down the alley that ran behind the bar and its neighbours. The poorly paved strip was littered with old garbage, the smell long since dissipated. Even though his dogs would warn him, Misha kept his distance from the large trash bins that could hide anything from rats to hostile humans.

At his side, Rifle chuffed.

"What's the matter, old man? You getting tired already?" Misha looked down at his friend, concerned for his joints. The German shepherd had been very active during the attacks on the container yard, straining his old muscles, and causing his touch of arthritis to flare up.

But when Misha looked down, Rifle wasn't looking back at him, which he would have been if he wanted to take a break. The old dog kept lifting his head toward the rooftops. Turning to study his other dogs, Misha thought a few of them had heard or seen something up there as well. If they had smelled something, it wasn't anything they thought was dangerous.

Not knowing what might be above him, Misha kept walking, keeping a close eye on the roofline. He couldn't think of many things that could be up there. He hadn't seen any ladders on the outsides of the buildings, which meant if it were someone living, they had found a route up from the inside, or had climbing gear that allowed them to scale the walls. Other than a bird, Misha didn't think any animals would be up there. Rats and mice were likely too small for even the dogs to notice at that distance, and besides, his pack knew how to recognize rodents and always responded accordingly.

By the time he reached the end of the alleyway, Misha hadn't seen or heard anything. His dogs hadn't either, and became disinterested in the roof long before he did. While it had likely just been a bird or maybe even a squirrel, Misha continued to worry. Rifle wasn't the type to draw his attention to birds. Of course, Misha had to remind himself that Rifle was partly blind now, and could have easily been overreacting. No matter what excuses he thought of, concern continued to gnaw at Misha's gut as he made his way back to the bar's front entrance.

Back inside, Crichton, Harry, Angela, and Ki-Nam were up and getting ready to go.

"I set aside some breakfast for you," Crichton told Misha as he pointed it out. There wasn't much, but at least it was something.

"We've decided to follow the edge of the bay more closely," Harry informed him. "We all have clothing we'd like to rinse off, plus it'd be good to refill our water supplies, and we might be able to catch some fish."

Misha nodded, although he doubted they would catch any fish. They didn't have the proper gear for it, as it was all with fishing teams that had gone out even earlier than everyone else, and there was certainly nothing they had that could be used as bait. Besides, they had probably already over-fished the bay.

"We'll just graze the horses and then head out," Crichton informed them all.

"We should actually wait, and graze the horses a little later," Misha advised. He told them about his walk, and how there was a possibility that something was on the roof. While it was unlikely a threat, no one wanted to take chances, so they agreed to hook up the horses and leave right away. Misha ate while the horses were made ready, giving a little bit of his food to Rifle even though he didn't really have enough for sharing. The other dogs could hunt quite well for themselves, and weren't against eating infected rats, but Rifle wasn't as quick as they were. Misha couldn't bring himself to eat while his brother went hungry, and so neither of them got enough.

After bringing the dogs back outside, Misha watched the roof while Ki-Nam drove the cart out. There was no sign of anything up there, and the dogs didn't act unusual in any way. As they began walking, with Misha and his dog pack taking the lead, he couldn't help but glance over his shoulder a few times. There was something that kept making the little hairs on the back of his neck stand up.

8: EVANS
5 DAYS AFTER THE BOMBING

The ether didn't last very long. When Evans came to, he was still being dragged to wherever it was they were taking him. His head pounded, and it was difficult to focus either his mind or his vision. He could hear Moe walking nearby, and he guessed the other rattling of leaves was Gerald being dragged in the same manner that he was. It was hard to tell just how many silent ones had hold of Evans' arms, and he had no way of knowing how many were walking around him.

As his lower legs passed over the sharp edge of a rock, it was impossible not to grunt. His forward motion was immediately stopped, and another rag was pressed to his face. The darkness came creeping back.

***

Evans woke two more times to find himself still being dragged, and each time he was knocked out again by a rag placed over his mouth. When finally he awoke to discover that he wasn't moving, he was left in peace.

As he opened his eyes, Evans had a terrifying moment when he thought that the ether had made him go blind. After a few heart-pounding seconds, he came to the conclusion that he was just in a place without light. It seemed the silent ones hadn't been dragging him to the edge of their territory to dump him, but had, in fact, kidnapped him.

Trying to sit up, Evans instantly learned that it was a bad idea. His head was still swimming, compounded by the disorienting and all-consuming blackness that surrounded him. After a single attempt, he lay flat on his back once more. The fact that he could lie flat was something. The stillness of the air informed him that he wasn't outside, and the dense, dry scent of concrete made him guess it was a basement, but at least it wasn't one with an earthen floor. By slowly sweeping his hands along his sides to his head, he could feel no imperfections, nor did it feel like the floor wasn't level, although that wasn't easy to determine what with the lingering effects of the ether. If pressed, Evans would guess that he was in a basement, in a house somewhere in town.

His right hand touched something near the apex of its arc. With only the tips of his fingers, he couldn't quite make it out. Gritting his teeth, Evans rolled slowly onto his stomach, turning in the general direction of what he had felt. As he did so, he noticed that his boots were loose. It seemed the silent ones had decided to let him keep his footwear, but not after what was undoubtedly a most thorough search.

What he ended up grasping was another boot. Based on the weight, there was a foot in it.

"Gerald," Evans whispered, partly because of the dark and partly because his throat burned. "Gerald, wake up." He shook the boot.

A low moan came from the body.

Evans pulled his hand away so that he wouldn't be accidentally kicked. "Gerald, it's Evans." He didn't know if the teenager would be able to recognize his voice in its current state. His throat felt like crumpled up sandpaper.

"Evans?" Gerald croaked, confirming that it was indeed him and not some other person. "Where are we?"

"I don't know, I just woke up."

"My head is killing me."

"I know. Don't try to sit up; it only makes it worse. I'm going to crawl around a bit, see if I can learn anything."

"See? I can't see anything."

"Neither can I. Just stay where you are so that we don't crash into one another."

"Sounds easy enough." Gerald's throat rasped as badly as Evans'.

Evans picked a random direction and started crawling, cracking the dried mud caked to his clothes. He moved slowly, sliding one hand over the floor as far as it would reach, and then waving the other about to make sure there was nothing held up off the floor in some way that could collide with his face. Moving was hard, both because of the spinning and because his legs were killing him. The silent ones hadn't cared at all about what they dragged Evans over, resulting in multiple contusions. The wound on his forearm was also throbbing again, and his shoulders ached from having the weight of his body hanging from them.

After crossing a short distance, Evans' hand found a wall. He got close and swept both hands all over it, making sure it wasn't just some object he was mistaking for a wall. It wasn't.

"I'm at a wall," he reported to Gerald. "It's concrete, like the floor. I'm going to follow it around. Don't be alarmed if I brush against you."

"Understood," Gerald croaked.

Working his way around, Evans didn't bump against Gerald, but he guessed that he came close. It unnerved him a little bit, making him wonder if there was something else in the middle of the room that he hadn't yet come across. No, not a room, a cell. As he followed a wall, his way forward was impeded by a set of bars built into a metal frame that was flush with the concrete. The bars were thick, and spaced far too closely together for him to attempt squeezing through. He followed them as he had the wall. Periodically he stuck his arm out through the bars to confirm that there was still nothing but more floor beyond them. At one point, he came across what must be the door. Rattling it proved the lock was secure. He reported all of this to Gerald, his throat feeling a tiny bit better.

Once he believed he had completed his circuit of the cage, Evans carefully propped himself up against the wall. His head had started to swim less and less as he had explored. He figured that if he sat for a little while, it should return to normal, and then he'd be able to stand and investigate the door more thoroughly.

"What do they want with us? Why are my boots untied?" Gerald wondered.

"I don't know, and they most likely took your boots off to search them." Having been reminded of his own boots, Evans thought he might as well tie them back up. It wasn't that easy to do in the dark; the dried mud added another layer of difficulty.

"I'm coming toward you," Gerald said.

Evans listened to the scraping on the concrete as Gerald crawled, sliding his own leg back and forth so that he could track the sound to him. Gerald grabbed his leg, causing an involuntary flinch, and then made his way to the wall where he proceeded to sit beside Evans.

"So what do we do now?" Gerald asked once he was settled.

"I suppose we wait. I don't think they would put us in here just to let us die. If they wanted us dead, they had plenty of opportunities to kill us."

"How long do you think they'll make us wait?"

"I have no idea. We might not see them until tomorrow."

"Tomorrow?" Gerald's voice took on its whiny tone. Evans didn't bother to say any more.

It turned out that it wasn't tomorrow when they received visitors. Evans was guessing that only twenty or so minutes had passed when a light finally appeared. There was a brief sliver that washed across the room, from a doorway at the top of a set of stairs opening and closing, and then a shrouded figure carrying a lamp descended. The lamp was dim, yet it was still hard to look at. That might have been caused by sitting in the dark for so long, or it might have been another after-effect of the ether. Evans studied what the light revealed of the room. It did appear to be the basement of a house. The bars crossed the space, as Evans had determined, preventing him and Gerald from reaching the dormant furnace and fuse box, the stairs, or any of the high, covered windows. The far side of the room had some wooden framework. Whoever had once lived here had been in the process of fastidiously finishing the space, but hadn't gotten much farther than smoothing out any rough patches in the floor.

Gerald managed to keep his mouth shut as the figure stepped up to the bars, definitely a newer construction than the wooden framing.

"Are you the one I spoke to earlier?" Evans asked, unable to tell from the heap of rags. If it was, she had covered her face once more.

There was no response, merely an unseen stare, for the figure's eyes were cast in shadow.

"I'm guessing you don't plan on killing us," Evans continued. "If you did, we'd be dead already. Whatever you want us for, or want us to do, we'd be better at it after a drink of water. That ether of yours packs an unpleasant punch to the back of the throat."

After a few seconds passed without any response, Gerald leaned over to Evans and whispered, "I don't think they're listening to you." He then added some sarcasm. "Maybe you're not being polite enough."

Evans didn't bother to whisper back, figuring the silent person had heard Gerald just fine. "I never say please to anyone who's drugged me and put me in a cage."

The figure suddenly turned and walked away, heading back toward the stairs.

"No, he didn't mean that!" Gerald called after them, moving away from the wall to half-crawl toward the bars. "I'll say please! Please, leave the light! Please!"

But the lamp was carried away, disappearing into the brighter beam that flashed across the room from the door at the top of the stairs.

"Look what you did," Gerald seethed once they were plunged back into darkness.

"I didn't do anything. They were going to leave anyway." Evans got up carefully, using the wall to support himself. While his mouth and throat still didn't feel great, his head wasn't spinning nearly as much as it had been.

"What are you doing?" Gerald whined, suddenly afraid again.

"Looking for anything I missed the first time." He didn't bother to elaborate further. He had now seen the room, so he did another circuit in order to feel it. All the walls were solid, unlike another prison where he had once found himself. There would be no escaping this one in the same manner. The locks, too, were of good construction. Three heavy bolts held the door closed: one near the bottom just above where he had explored earlier, one in the middle, and one at the top. All three bolts were kept shut with heavy-duty padlocks. On the other side of the door, the hinges matched the placement of the bolts. They were on the outside, so the door must swing outward. This was advantageous for them should they try to rush the door when it was opened, but Evans got the sense that the silent ones would have a method for subduing any such attack. The hinges were as thick around as the bolts, and there was no way to get the pins out. The pins had rounded tops, and hung down lower than the hinges. Those lower sections had holes bored through them, from which hung more padlocks, albeit smaller ones. They seemed unnecessary to Evans, since without any tools, the pins were likely impossible to remove.

By the end of his study, Evans' hands were slick. All the moving parts on the cage door had been either oiled or greased. While not much noise would ever escape this basement, the silent ones were thorough. He wiped off what he could on his shirt, which had less mud than his pants and got in better around his nails. He then sat back down, unable to think of anything else to do.

"What do you think people like them would want with people like us?" Gerald asked.

"I honestly can't say." He didn't think the silent ones were cannibals, keeping them temporarily alive as a way to store the meat for a little while, but it was a possibility. It would mean that their captors had succumbed to some sort of group madness, possibly a damned religion, as this area of the south tended to provide enough food for those who looked for it. And the silent ones were definitely smart enough to find it.

The door above eventually opened again. A brighter lantern accompanied three people down the stairs. One of them carried a tray with food and water glasses on it. So these people weren't starving. The other two were guards, with weapons held at the ready.

The tray was placed on the floor, out of reach. The silent one who had carried it sat down beside it. Evans moved himself to sit as close as he could. Gerald lingered farther back, away from the light casting barred shadows across him. The silent one gestured for him to come closer. Gerald didn't move, continuing to eye the guards.

"Just come sit down," Evans told Gerald, motioning to a spot beside him.

Gerald didn't take the spot Evans had suggested, however, he did sit. He refused to place himself against the bars, and instead chose a patch of floor just behind Evans' right shoulder. The silent one deemed this acceptable. He, or perhaps she, picked up one of the two plastic water cups and held it out. Evans reached through the bars and took it, passing it back to Gerald. He was then given the second cup, which he emptied in one go. There were two more cups on the tray, and there was no reason to assume that they weren't also for him and Gerald. Before more water came, the food was passed through. It consisted of an apple, a tomato, a small block of cheese, a slice of tough bread, and a strip of meat; all food groups were covered. There was one apiece for each of them, and Evans was pleased to find that the meat was beef. He had worried that it was a strip off of Moe when he'd been handed it, but long ago he learned to tell the difference between most meats. After both he and Gerald finished eating their offerings, they were handed the last two cups of water. Evans' throat was feeling much better.

"Thank you," he said, raising his second cup slightly.

"So you won't say please but you'll say thank you?" Gerald said snidely behind him.

"When appropriate," Evans told him without taking his eyes off the silent one. "So what is it you have us in here for?" he cut to the chase. "We have no reason not to co-operate with whatever it is."

The silent one on the floor turned to one of the guards and made some gestures. That guard turned away to go back upstairs.

"I think he said something about getting a notebook," Gerald said.

Evans had forgotten that everyone at the container yard knew sign language, including Gerald. Had he remembered, he would have had the teenager teach him while they travelled, for it was a useful skill in dangerous situations. And, apparently, for somewhat startling silent ones.

"What notebook?" Evans asked their host.

The host pointed to him. Evans didn't need a translator to understand.

"Do you need me to help you read it?" Evans wondered. His notebook wasn't a traditional journal like so many others he had come across, but consisted mostly of bullet point notations. It contained lists of people he had travelled with, supplies he'd had, trades he'd made, points of interest about various camps he'd visited, and any other useful tidbits he had picked up along the way. Some of his notes involved a bit of shorthand notation he had developed, and with the way information was sometimes jumbled together, it could easily be confusing for other people attempting to read it.

The silent one said and did nothing in response to his question, merely waited.

"You have a notebook?" Gerald asked instead.

Evans gave Gerald the same answer that their host had given him.

The second guard promptly returned, with Evans' leather bound notebook in hand. He gave it to their host, and then resumed his protective stance. Their host flipped to a particular page, then held it toward Evans while pointing at a section.

Curious as to what these people were specifically interested in, Evans took the notebook and read through the section.

"What about this camp?" Evans wondered. It wasn't too far away, somewhat farther than the camp to which he was taking Gerald.

With hooded face pointed toward Gerald, their host signed something. If this person could speak, they were choosing not to, now knowing that they didn't need to.

"He said *go there*," Gerald translated.

"You want us to go there?" Evans wondered.

"Pretty sure that was *we want to go there*," Gerald translated the next batch of signs.

"You? As in your group? Why would you want to go here?" Evans pointed to the page. They seemed to be doing just fine on their own where they were, and the camp they wished to visit had nothing special about it.

There were a number of signs after that.

"Hard to get a direct translation," Gerald admitted. "Their sign is a little different than ours, and usually we rely on facial expressions and mouthed words to help us out. But I think I understood the gist of it. It's not the whole group that wants to go there, just some of them. They've never travelled before though, and are afraid. They want a guide, basically you, to take them there."

"Sounds easy enough. I don't know why you didn't just ask earlier, before going through the whole rigmarole of drugging and kidnapping us."

Their host looked back at one of the guards, the one that hadn't retrieved the notebook. That silent one nodded, giving permission for something. Their host scooted forward, coming right up to the bars.

"We're not supposed to leave," came a soft whisper through the rags.

"I understand," Evans nodded to each of the silent ones in turn. It was possible they weren't even supposed to be down here with him. His notebook had likely been stolen from whoever was in charge of this place. "Can you do it?"

Their host nodded.

"Do what?" Gerald asked, not figuring it out for himself.

"They're going to have to break us out of here," Evans told him.

***

It was impossible to mark the passage of time down in that cell.

"Are you still bringing me to the place you said you would?" Gerald asked.

"Yes, it's only somewhat out of the way of a direct route from here to where they want to go. I'd probably stop there anyway for supplies and news, so don't worry, you'll get there."

Gerald had asked questions incessantly that Evans couldn't answer, like how their host was going to get them out, why had the others caged them, and were they going to get their supplies back. He had asked pointless questions, like what would they do if they were followed, or if one of the silent ones who came with them turned out to be a spy. Evans simply told him that everything would be dealt with as needed.

His notebook had been left with him. He got the impression that their host wasn't sure if their supplies could be returned to them or not. By letting Evans keep the notebook, they would at least have that. Evans also suspected that if whoever was in charge realized the notebook was missing, the cell was unlikely to be one of the first places they'd look for it.

Gerald eventually fell asleep, based on his even breathing and the fact that the questions had stopped. Evans found the ensuing silence somewhat unnerving. The passage of air entering and exiting their lungs was all he could make out. No pipes rattled, no floorboards creaked overhead, no shouted orders drifted through the covered windows from outside. There was no ticking clock, no electric hum, or even a wind in a hollow. The place was a crypt, somewhere only the fully dead belonged. The total silence brought him back to the time before his father had killed his mother. It had been silent then too. A winter storm had blanketed the earth and killed the power. It felt as though everything in the world except for thirteen-year-old Evans had been asleep in that moment. But then he heard his mother softly weeping in the kitchen. And his father slammed their bedroom door and began to stomp down the hallway toward her. Whenever Evans found himself in such a silence, he found himself becoming tense. He was always waiting for that soft weeping, for that slamming door.

When a door finally did open, it barely made a sound. If Evans' ears hadn't been straining for any sound at all, he wouldn't have heard the soft click of the mechanism as the handle turned. There was no beam of light this time. Whatever had been causing it above, either the sun or something artificial, it was gone now. Evans worried that someone other than their host might be coming down, and gently shook Gerald awake, who grunted as he came to.

A pencil thin beam from a tiny flashlight momentarily highlighted the stairs, and then went out. Evans strained his hearing to listen to the silent one come down. It was hard to track the sound across the concrete floor, but he could tell when whoever it was got close. The little light blinked on again, just on the other side of the door.

"It's time," came the soft whisper.

Evans thought it was their host, but he couldn't be certain.

Keys were produced, each one individually wrapped in leather. Gerald stood close to Evans, with a hand on his shoulder, as they waited. The thin light illuminated one lock at a time. Each key was unwrapped and inserted slowly and with precision, producing as little sound as possible. The locks all opened with a soft click, and were placed gently on the floor. Gerald was clearly impatient with this process, but he managed to hold his tongue. Finally, the bolts were drawn back and the door was opened. The light located Evans' face, and the silent one stepped right up to him, first taking hold of his arm and then his neck. Evans bent so that the silent one could reach his ear.

"No sound now. You must be one of us."

Evans nodded his understanding. When the silent one let go of him, Evans turned to Gerald and whispered the instructions to him in a terser tone and emphasizing that he shouldn't speak a word.

Gerald kept his hand on Evans' shoulder, and Evans placed his own on the shoulder of the silent one. They were led slowly through the dark, being careful to lift their feet high so as to prevent their boots from scuffing. Every footstep was taken one at a time, and every motion was exaggerated to prevent their clothes from ruffling.

At the steps, the silent one briefly shone the light along the railing. They ascended one at a time.

The stairs led into a kitchen illuminated by the light of the moon and stars coming through the windows near the sink. With their eyes adjusted to the dark, this was more than enough to see quite well. Two other silent ones joined the first. They had a bundle of rags on the table, which they proceeded to drape and wrap around Evans and Gerald. They even strapped thick furs to the bottom of their boots. While this would cause a serious lack of traction should they need to run, it would silence their footsteps a lot more.

Once they were ready, Evans and Gerald were led outside. They moved in a line, with one silent one ahead, leading the way, and two behind.

It was likely the middle of the night, yet they didn't conceal themselves at all. Their small group walked boldly down the middle of the residential street, heading toward the shops and offices. It seemed it wasn't unusual for bands of silent ones to be out and about so late. They passed a few others, mostly in pairs, a few alone, but not one tried to stop them. Evans felt very conspicuous. At six feet, four inches in height, he was taller than most. These people could likely recognize one another beneath their rags in the daytime, but even at night, Evans likely stood out. He tried to walk with a slight hunch, and kept his knees somewhat bent at all times, reducing his height as much as he could without it being too obvious.

They walked through a large portion of the town, never once being accosted. Evans could see a few people on the roofs every now and again. They appeared to be working, not guarding, and ignored those below. Based on the watering cans and spades he spotted in a few hands, he guessed that it was up there where they grew all their food, out of sight of anyone passing through. Evans bet that if he had arrived with a party the size of the one he had left at the container yard, the silent ones would have stayed hidden and he would have passed through the town without even knowing about the community that lived there.

At the far edge of town, Evans and Gerald were guided through a parking lot, toward the loading entrance of a large grocery store. The leader of their little band walked up to the one person-sized door, which had an opaque window set within it. The little light was once more produced and pressed against the glass. The door immediately opened; someone had been waiting for them.

There was no light other than the flashlight's narrow beam, but they didn't linger long. Within the grocery store's warehouse space, a second large room with plywood sides had been constructed. As they walked through a thick door set into it, Evans could see the soundproofing material built into the walls of the new room. Inside, the room was fairly evenly lit by lanterns, but they all burned low to preserve everyone's night vision. And there were far more people than Evans had imagined there would be. With the addition of the three who had accompanied Evans and Gerald, the room contained eleven silent ones. It was a hostile looking room, with pointed foam cones covering the walls: more sound suppression material. And it was needed. With the people were Moe and a herd of six camels. Evans understood that while camel feet were a lot quieter than a horse's hooves, their vocalizations could be rather loud.

It was revealed to Evans and Gerald that not only was Moe perfectly well, but their packs had been loaded up on him. Moe looked rather pleased to pick up the scent of his companions, and whickered softly when Evans approached to stroke his muzzle. The horse had been decked out in a manner similar to Evans and Gerald, with dark coloured rags draped over his grey coat, and hanging in strips from his tack. He looked like he belonged to an interpretation of *Sleepy Hallow*, minus the headless rider. The horse's feet had also been wrapped in furs to silence them, to which Moe was clearly still adjusting, based on the way he kept lifting and shaking his feet.

"Are you all ready to leave?" Evans whispered.

Heads nodded all around the excessively warm and smelly room.

"Lead the way to the closest edge of your community then. We'll reorient ourselves once we're out."

Pins were removed from a section of wall, allowing it to be lifted and placed elsewhere. The camels were already up and prepared to go, burdened with packs, but Evans hadn't spent nearly enough time around such animals to know how to read their body language. He had no idea if they were going to be stubborn or not. As they were moved into the gap between the inner room and the doors to the outside, Evans saw he had originally miscounted the number of camels. There was a seventh, although it was a baby calf and carried no gear. A silent one led the young animal; they were followed by the adult camels. Evans led Moe behind them, wondering what the horse had thought of the camels when he had first been shacked up with them. Camels made for even uglier horses than Moe.

The section of wall was returned, blocking off the lamplight within. A silent one remained in the room to replace the pins and to snuff out the lanterns. They weren't in the dark for long. A roll up door was raised on greasy tracks. The silent ones were trying very hard to reduce the amount of noise it made. A ramp was retrieved from somewhere in the room and set in place. The camels and Moe were walked down it. Like Moe, the camels were draped in rags to hide their pale fur, which had the added advantage of allowing Moe to better blend in with them. It seemed that while the camels could be taken, the horse was supposed to stay put. The silent ones urged Evans to walk him in the middle of the camels, which they carefully guided in a clump as opposed to the line they wanted to form.

Evans had lost track of which figure was Gerald. He tried to spot a pair of feet wearing furs like his own, but it was impossible with all the camel legs around him. He just had to trust that Gerald knew where he was, and wasn't going to do anything stupid that would get them caught.

They were travelling through town for far longer than Evans would have liked. He had hoped that the camels had been housed near the edge of their territory, but this was not so. Even after they left the town, they kept walking a considerable distance. When finally the camels were allowed to form a line, Evans figured that they were safe. He noticed then that not all of the silent ones were with them. They must have split up to reduce the size of the group while travelling where others would see them. As he looked around at those who were with him and the camels, he realized that he hadn't been able to spot Gerald earlier, as he wasn't among them. He must have ended up following, or being brought along, by a different group. Evans hoped to hell that he kept his mouth shut until they reached wherever the rendezvous point was.

9: JAMES
5 DAYS AFTER THE BOMBING

White had hit the pavement hard when the lioness attacked him.

"Katrina!" James shouted, calling on the only person with bullets. The rest of the group had quickly reformed their defensive circle, terrified about where the rest of the lions might be.

Katrina had appeared at James' side in a flash, but she was taking her time aiming.

"Why aren't you shooting?" James demanded.

"Because White is already dead," Katrina told him calmly, focused on her task. "I want to make sure I use only one bullet to repay the favour to this kitty."

James looked forward once more and knew that Katrina was right. White was most certainly dead; his head was so battered and crushed by the lioness' jaws that they didn't even have to worry about him turning. As the lioness grabbed hold of White's body and began to drag him away, Katrina's rifle finally cracked the still air. It was a perfect shot, straight through the lion's eye, dropping her instantly.

Human shouting and an angry yowl had James twisting in his saddle once more. A second lioness had chosen to take a run at the group, but the spears were thrust forward once more, drawing blood.

"Move together," James ordered. "We have to keep moving forward!"

The second lioness had retreated, disappearing beneath a porch. The group shuffled along in a ring. White's absence resulted in wider gaps between people. The lions were definitely around them: people called out when they spotted flashes of tawny fur.

When they reached the bodies of White and the lioness, James had them halt. Not wanting to order anyone else to do it, James climbed down off Soot's back to salvage what he could of White's gear. This included stripping off his boots, socks, and pants, which were mostly untouched by his blood. The lioness had focused all of her attention on his head and neck, cutting up strips of scalp. Even though the backpack was fairly diced up and soaked in blood, James removed it and slung it over Soot's rump, much to the horse's displeasure. He would go through the contents later.

"Anyone with gear on Spark, remove it now," James ordered.

Katrina had her pack on the younger horse, as did Skip and Belle.

"Throw the lion corpse over the saddle," James ordered next.

"Are you sure?" Katrina asked. "Spark's not going to like that."

"The lions might like the smell of their dead even less. Anyway, it would be a hell of a waste of food." James didn't like the idea of eating the lion that had just killed his friend, but food was food, even if White had had to die for it.

The body of the lioness was hoisted up by a trio of people and some rope, and draped over Spark's saddle. Katrina was right that the horse really didn't like it, but once his emergency blinders were retrieved and put on, he settled enough to be controlled.

"What about White?" asked Vin, clearly distressed about the idea of leaving his friend behind.

"We have no time to bury him. He'll slow down the other lions for us." James hated to say it, but it was true. Grieving would have to come later; for now they needed to keep moving.

As they left their companion behind to be eaten, James could hear someone weeping behind him, but refused to turn to find out who. As long as they continued to press forward, they could cry as much as they wanted.

James guided them toward the river, which thankfully took them along the nearest cross street and placed a building between them and White before the lions could have their meal. Unfortunately, White's corpse wouldn't slow the animals for long. There wasn't enough of him for the lions' bellies to be satisfied, and now that they had taken one down, they might become bolder about attacking the rest.

Their progress was slow, and by the time they saw the water, they were seeing the lions again too.

"I'm not seeing a bridge," Katrina complained.

They weren't as far west as James had thought. They were just far enough to be past where the majority of the river swung north, but unfortunately there were no bridges in that area. James could see the three directions of flowing water, but not a way to cross. The closest bridge to their position was a wooden footbridge that had collapsed in a storm. The next nearest was in the wrong direction.

"We're going to swim."

"What?"

"We're going to swim!" James called to the group. "Get out your ropes and take the saddles off the horses."

"You're crazy, you know that right?" Katrina told him. "Lions can swim too."

"Well, let's just hope they remember Africa, and worry about there being crocodiles and hippos."

"They're zoo animals; they've never been in Africa," Katrina reminded him. "And while there may be no crocodiles, there could certainly be alligators."

"Would you rather deal with possible alligators, or definite lions?" James directed this question to the whole group, and wanted an actual answer. They decided on the possible alligators.

Because the broken bridge was upstream, plenty of its boards had washed up either singly or in chunks still nailed together along the shore where they gathered. While the rest of the group watched their backs, James and Lindsay determined which pieces were most buoyant. These, they strapped to the horses' saddles, and the dead lioness. It was nerve wracking being down by the water, since they couldn't see where the lions were unless the animals decided to come to the edge of the road built along a ridge at the end of the river rocks.

"Why are we bringing the dead lion again?" Lindsay wondered as they worked.

"I don't know about you, but I'd certainly like a good dinner tonight."

"What if it draws the alligators to us? Or a shark?" The river bend was where the salt water met fresh water, and while there were unlikely to be any sharks, James understood the concern.

"Because Katrina's such a good shot, there's very little blood. We'll be fine." James projected a confidence he did not feel.

The group members rotated their guard positions, taking turns to remove their shoes and boots. The plan was for three people to swim with each saddle, and three with the dead lion. Any wood that hadn't already been lashed to these items was passed around to be used as personal flotation devices. The horses would have to swim, with one bareback rider each. Luckily, both horses came from the container yard, and not the travelling party. James knew that both Soot and Spark had been taught to swim with riders. Still, he worried about the river. While it appeared slow, he wasn't sure just how deep it was, and deeper water could move faster. He also didn't know if there was a steep, underwater drop that could frighten the horses, or any large rocks they might bump into. He was especially concerned about the width of the river, which was going to exhaust both people and horses alike.

"Get in the water and go," James commanded the moment everyone looked ready. "If you have to ditch something to survive, then ditch it."

He scrambled up onto Moe's bare back. Katrina climbed onto Spark beside him.

"Can you handle this? Have you ridden a horse in the water before?"

Katrina nodded. Not the most confidence inducing response, but it would have to do. She may not have been the most experienced rider, but Katrina had insisted that taking care of Spark was her duty, which meant being the one to ride him across the river. James felt the same way about Soot, and tried to recall everything he had learned during his one experience with riding a horse in water. That time had been long ago, back when vacations were still a thing.

Everyone got into the river and began swimming. James wanted to give them a head start, to make sure the lions weren't going to follow them. The horses could run if the lions showed up, but the rocks wouldn't provide great footing. At least they had the spears, that they had temporarily traded for the rifle and bullets.

"There's the big boy," Katrina commented, pointing up toward the road.

The male lion stood with his front paws on the guard rail, looking down on his escaping prey. His golden eyes swept over to where James and Katrina sat on the horses, his muzzle red with White's blood.

"You think they're far enough out?" James asked, not taking his eyes off the big lion.

Katrina kept twisting about, watching both the swimmers and the rest of the road for more of the beasts. "I have no idea."

Soot and Spark were both agitated, terrified of the lions. They knew their protection was currently swimming away.

"It'll have to be. Let's go." James kicked his heels into Soot's side. One foot was bare, the other wrapped in bandages he would need to change after they crossed.

Soot wasn't too eager to go into the water. He walked slowly, not trusting the rocks. Beside him, Spark was bolder. The younger horse splashed his way in, kicking up plumes of water. Once it reached his belly, however, he slowed.

James let Soot enter at his own pace, turning to watch the road. There were several lions gathered up there now. A couple of the lionesses had even moved beyond the guard rails and were pacing back and forth at the top of the rocks.

Just as Soot got deep enough to start swimming, one of the lionesses charged. She rushed down over the rocks, her large paws kicking up the smaller pebbles. As her lithe body hit the water, Soot started to kick harder. James didn't want him to. He wanted his horse to swim at his normal pace. To try changing rhythms now could cause the horse to exhaust itself and drown, but there was little James could do. Instead, he wrapped one hand around Soot's mane, and twisted around with the spear in the other.

The lioness was very close, her wide paws pushing her swiftly through the water. James raised the spear. The big cat hissed at him, and raised one of her front paws as she attempted to grab Soot's tail. James jabbed at the lioness with the spear. He missed the eye he had been aiming for, and nearly got swept off Soot's back in the process. Instead, the spear slid across the lioness's skull, leaving a jagged wound that ran from above her left eye, over to the base of her right ear. It was enough to drive her back. The lioness turned in the water, quickly retreating back to shore, snorting water out of her nose. The rest of the lions had gathered at the water's edge, but thankfully none of them had decided to pursue the swimmers.

"It's all right Soot, she's gone." James turned around to stroke Soot's neck, and find his seat again. "Just keep swimming buddy, you're doing great. Swim nice and easy." He was careful not to tug Soot's reins and risk having the animal's nose dip below the water, which would frighten him further.

The horses had been encouraged to swim between the container yard and Animal Island, although it wasn't a common occurrence. If they had to move horses across any bodies of water, they tended to put them in boats. Still, it was times like this when James was grateful that someone had had a forward thinking idea. He didn't know who had taught the horses to swim with riders, he had been at the Black Box at the time, but resolved to thank them when he got back home. However far into the future that might be.

Glancing over his shoulder, James checked to make sure there weren't any more lions coming after them. He saw none in the water, and most of those along the shoreline had disappeared. While James wanted to hope that they had given up, he admitted that, for all he knew, they were just heading off to an intact bridge and would meet up with them again on the far side.

***

There was no choice but to take a long break when they reached the far shore. The horses didn't have the energy to climb up the bank, and the humans weren't looking forward to it either. Those who had had to swim were exhausted, but they had managed to hold onto all their gear: saddles and dead lioness included.

James fussed over Soot. Everyone else dried out what they could. Katrina made sure her rifle and bullets had crossed safe and dry in their plastic tarp and bag. James worried that the old horse could still keel over from exhaustion. He made sure Soot stood where he could drink from the river, and scrambled up and down the bank to bring him long grass to eat. It aggravated the hell out of his foot wound.

"No, no, don't lie down," James told Soot when it looked like he was going to. "This is not a good spot. Look at these rocks. They wouldn't be comfortable at all." He had no idea if his words made any difference, as they fell on mostly deaf ears, but Soot did remain standing. He closed his eyes, however, potentially catching a quick nap.

James hobbled over to the group. A lot of socks were laid out on the rocks, drying in the sun.

"Someone needs to go find a place where we can make camp," he told them.

"We haven't gotten very far today," Skip pointed out, looking up at the location of the sun.

"I know, but the horses need a place where they can lie down for a little bit. And I'm sure everyone would like a chance to dry themselves out." He then added in a lower voice, with a head jerk toward Belle, who was crying. "I also think we need some time to grieve White."

Samson agreed. "I'll go. We should also replenish our water supplies and turn that lioness into meat we can carry."

"I'll come with you," volunteered Katrina.

Jack and Lucy also volunteered to go. A team of four felt safe, especially as they didn't plan to move far from the river. The other seven remained behind with the horses.

James checked on Spark, but he seemed to be doing much better than Soot. He had already climbed part way up the bank, chowing down on the grass and weeds that had managed to take root between the rocks. The sun was drying off both horses well enough that James didn't feel a need to rub either of them down with the tattered towel he had brought. He had finally started wringing out the clothes he was wearing when the four came back.

It hadn't taken them long to find a place to camp. On this side of the river was a sparsely wooded area, with a footpath that followed the backs of townhouses. Since the townhouses had been built on a bit of a hill, they had walk-out basements, and the team of four had picked one with a large set of doors the horses could comfortably fit through.

Everyone reluctantly gathered up their gear. In order to give the horses a break, they had to carry the saddles and the dead lioness up the bank. James was excused from helping with this task because of his injury, but he took it upon himself to lead Soot and Spark. Soot was still quite reluctant to climb, but he managed, albeit slowly. James learned that the best way to get him to move, was to keep Spark a certain distance ahead. The old horse didn't want the young horse to leave him behind, and James had to be careful not to let Soot push himself too hard. He was glad when he finally had both horses through the tall, wooden fence.

The grass in the yard was long, and Samson said they had already checked for snakes and rats and had deemed it safe. Spark began to mow it eagerly, but

Soot went straight into the shade of the finished walk-out basement, and lay down on the carpet. James sat down nearby to monitor the horse and take care of his foot. There had been some seepage through the stitched up holes, but nothing too concerning. He applied fresh bandages from a plastic bag that had kept them dry. James was more worried about Soot, knowing that the big animal couldn't lie down for too long, or else his own weight could damage his blood flow, making it impossible for him to get up again. James didn't think they'd be able to do anything if that happened, so he intended to wake Soot up before it could.

It wasn't long before everyone had laid out their gear to dry all over the uppermost floor. There was a little balcony that stuck out the back, where a lot of clothing had been draped over the railing. Katrina stood up there with her rifle, using the high vantage point to watch for danger. She also occasionally switched whose gear got the most direct sunlight.

Wood was gathered, and a fire was started on the small stone patio. Anyone who had the energy, carried water up from the river so that they could boil it and capture the steam with the equipment they had brought. It was actually unfortunate that the river hadn't been salt water at that point, otherwise they could have used the salt residue to cure any meat they might have left over.

It turned out that James didn't need to worry about Soot sleeping too long. Once Marissa began cutting into the lioness, he was awake and up on his feet. The scent of blood had reached him through his dreams and frightened him.

"It's okay," James told Soot, getting up to pat his neck and sides. "Let's go outside."

Soot seemed calmer once he was with Spark across the yard from the butchering.

After knowing so many who had already died, mourning had become a strange affair. The atmosphere at the townhouse was generally light, practically a party, with everyone happy to have survived. Occasionally someone would fall quiet, and become introspective, but never for long. James knew that if his previous self had been suddenly placed here, he would have been confused, not believing this to be a funeral, or perhaps even finding it disrespectful. But times had changed, and everything had changed along with it, including their capacity to grieve.

The lioness's hide was scraped and cleaned, and draped over a couch to dry. Without enough time to properly stretch and tan the hide, it wouldn't be soft and was more likely to degrade, but the hope was that they could find a way to treat it, either at the camp to which they were heading, or maybe once back home. The hide was presented to Katrina, as she was the one who had killed it. As for the lioness's teeth and claws, everyone claimed various bits, making simple necklaces and bracelets, or just planning to carry them like totems. James took only one piece, but it was one of the big fangs that had killed White. He located a thin, tough piece of leather he had brought in case one of his shoelaces broke, and used that to hang the tooth around his neck.

Getting to eat until they were full was the most joyous part of their stay.

The most solemn time came shortly before nightfall, when they went through White's gear. They sorted everything they had taken from his ravaged body, sharing the most important items—food, water canisters, and weapons—between them. His spare clothing went to those it would fit, and his personal items were given to whoever wanted them. James got his spare shoelaces, replacing the leather he had used to hang the tooth. Even the tattered pack was kept. The top was full of holes, but the body of it could still hold things. After cleaning it as best they could, they put the pack with Spark's tack. It would become a saddlebag when they were ready to leave.

After finishing the gruesome task, they organized a guard schedule. One person would always be on the balcony, and another would stay awake by the open basement doors. That way, the horses could stay outside if they liked, and always had two people watching over them. They could also be brought inside in a hurry if need be.

James took the first watch in the basement, opting to sit just outside on a couch cushion he placed on the stone patio. While watching over the horses, he kept the embers of the fire glowing.

***

No one slept well. They were constantly afraid that they would be attacked by lions in the night. But other than a pair of slow zombies who showed up outside the back gate, they were left completely alone. James hoped that meant that they had crossed outside of the lions' territory, but considering the fact they also thought the lions had gone just before White was attacked, it was a very cautious hope.

Everyone packed up quietly. Another zombie stumbled up to the front of the house just before they left, and Vin dispatched it even though it wasn't going to cause any problems. There was no way for the horses to get out through the front of the house, so they would have to follow the river side path until they reached the end of the block of townhouses.

James mounted Soot, grateful that the horse had survived its ordeal crossing the river. Katrina rolled up her lion hide and put it in Spark's new saddlebag. The young horse didn't seem to mind that his new bag had come off a dead man, or that the skin of the animal that had killed him was placed inside.

While walking, everyone remained extra vigilant. They didn't group together as tightly as they did when they knew that the lions were near, but they did stay in a tighter bunch than when they had first started. Marissa took over the duties as their forward scout. James would have liked to do it, but Soot and Spark wouldn't want to be that far apart from one another, and there was no way James' foot could tolerate that much walking.

As the day progressed, they came across more and more zombies. None of them were in a herd—the most they saw at once was five, and usually they were in twos or threes—but it was still disconcerting. They were still within the range that the scavenger teams would occasionally cover, but they kept running into unexpected problems. First the lions, and now a higher concentration of the dead. Both were likely related to the mega horde. The lions had likely been driven away from their previous territory due to its arrival, and the zombies they were coming across now could easily have been stragglers that got separated from the main mass. It made James wonder what else could have changed that they didn't know about, or were ill prepared to face.

10: CLAIRE
6 DAYS AFTER THE BOMBING

Moving was agony, both physically and psychologically. Every motion was slow and deliberate. Claire had to hold herself in a kind of plank position for fairly long stretches of time. When she got tired, she lowered herself to her stomach and took a break. Rose was having an even harder time due to her missing hand.

If they could have stood up, everyone would have been able to move more quickly and easily, but they couldn't be sure how well whoever or whatever was outside could see through the windows.

Their first priority was to move farther away from the clouded glass to reach the back hall. Packing their sleeping gear had taken a long time, especially the sleeping bags that were made out of a slick, waterproof material, that tended to make a lot of whisking sounds whenever it brushed against anything. There were many moments of held breaths and bitten tongues.

During their slow creep across the floor, Claire winced every time her pack shifted. It was more empty than full, ready to receive food and other useful items they might come across. This meant that what was inside had space to slide about: a potential source of noise as well as the capacity to throw her off balance.

One by one, they crept over to the hallway and then down the length of it. They gathered at its end to give their trembling muscles a break. A counter prevented them from seeing the windows, but there was no reason to believe that the shadows had moved off. Claire prayed that they were just zombies who had come to a standstill at that particular spot for reasons she couldn't fathom. She had had a number of dreams about the men and women who had invaded the Black Box, and understood that anyone standing there for that long a time wasn't going to be friendly.

Jon was the first to stand up. There were two doors at the end of the hallway: one was labelled as a washroom, the other was unmarked. Based on the size of the storefront, the assumption was that this place was some sort of pick up, or made to order location. A few items had been displayed out front—long since stripped by scavengers—but the main service happened in the back. The hope was that the back room had some sort of loading entrance that they could use to escape. Unfortunately, it also had a lock on the door: one that was still intact.

There was no keyhole. Instead it was a dead electronic number pad. There were no tumblers on which to use their lock picks. Jon signed down at Danny, asking for a flat head screwdriver he was carrying. Danny carefully retrieved it from a side pocket on his pack. While they waited for him, Larson asked if Jon could see anything of the windows, now that he was standing. He responded that he could, and that the shadows were still there. Claire guessed that it had been at least an hour by then, likely closer to two.

After receiving the screwdriver, Jon pried off the plastic cover. He looked past the buttons at the mess of useless wires, then looked down at Danny and shook his head. Whatever he had been hoping was possible, was not. Bryce pointed to the hinges, his eyebrows raised. Jon shook his head again. The hinges were on the inside of the door, so there was no way to dismantle them from the outside. Rose then asked the obvious question: *is it even locked?*

Jon turned the handle and, much to his embarrassment, it was not. They all slithered their way inside and let the door close behind them. It was pitch black in the back room.

What they found when Larson turned on his solar-charged lantern was neither a large storage room nor a workspace. The room was fairly small, containing a number of shelves for storage, with a few mouldy cardboard boxes still sitting on them. It looked like an employee break room and office. There were no other doors, to the outside or elsewhere. Whatever this place had once been, it was a tiny operation. And this room was a dead end.

Everyone sat on the floor in a circle, with the lantern in the middle. Silent arguments were held: a flurry of expressions and arm and hand motions. Rose was clearly frustrated, unable to sign as quickly as the others, forced to spell out certain words due to her inability to use their proper signs. It often resulted in others 'talking' over her. Larson's injured hand also tired quickly, compensating for the missing finger that restricted some of what he could say.

Claire didn't follow much of the debate, which was generally between staying put or fighting their way out. She was ready to do either, and accepted that she had the least amount of experience in the group. She looked at the mouldy boxes and wondered if she should look inside them. They were the only things left, so they probably contained nothing but the most useless of items. Whatever scavengers had been there earlier, whether another team from their own community or complete strangers, they had been very thorough. Claire wasn't sure why her eyes eventually drifted upward, but it was good for everyone that they did.

Snatching the lantern from the middle of the ring caused all eyes to turn immediately to Claire. She ignored them as she rotated the light in order to see the ceiling better. There, in the corner, mostly hidden by a shelf with an old box on it, was what appeared to be an attic access hatch. Having followed Claire's gaze, everyone else saw it too. After looking around at one another and shrugging, they decided to investigate. It was likely just another dead end, but it was something.

Because they were unsure of the strength or stability of the shelving unit, Claire was sent up first, being the lightest and having plenty of experience with climbing. Back at the Black Box, she often scaled the crane they used as a lookout point, spending hours strapped into one of the seats they had installed along its arm. Compared to that, the shelf was nothing.

Half the box under the hatch all but disintegrated when Claire attempted to push it sideways. More of what was in her way ended up flattened as opposed to being moved aside. Crunching herself up on the highest shelf, Claire used her whole body to push up on the panel of wood that covered the attic access. For a few seconds, she thought that it was sealed in some way, that it would be impossible to find out what was beyond it, but then the panel gave way with a sudden *pop* that nearly caused her to lose her balance.

Everyone stood perfectly still, wondering if those out front had heard anything. After a couple of seconds without the glass being shattered, Claire placed the piece of plywood down to one side, and then Danny handed her a flashlight.

Shining the weak beam of light around the space, Claire saw there wasn't much. The underside of the roof was low. Insulation puffed up between the rafters of the break room's ceiling. She could make out the walls that made up the corner she was in, but the rest were beyond sight. Claire crouched back down and relayed what little she had seen. More silent discussions were had, although this time they were short-lived. They wanted Claire to explore more of the space if she were willing.

By wearing gloves and tying a scarf around her neck and lower face, Claire should be able to avoid touching the insulation. She hauled herself up into the attic, keeping the flashlight close at hand, and set out. She knew to keep her weight on the rafters, and not trust the strength of whatever was between them. In a manner that wasn't too dissimilar to the way she had crawled down the hallway, she explored the narrow area she had found. At least this time she didn't have a pack to worry about: her gear was left behind with the others.

Much of her exploration was proving unhelpful. The building stood by itself, so there wasn't another to sneak into. The ceiling above her was the roof, and there weren't any more hatches that she could see.

It was creepy up there. Only small patches were revealed by the weak flashlight, leaving the rest in darkness. It was all too easy to imagine that she wasn't alone up there. Every time she came across a particularly large puff of insulation, she kept expecting to find something on the far side of it. What that something might be, she was never very sure, but even if it were an innocent sheet of forgotten paper, it would probably freak her out enough to cause a hasty retreat back to the break room. But there was never anything. It seemed that no one had been up there since the place's construction, and none of the workers had forgotten any tools or other items.

Claire was thinking of giving up. She was frightened, and so far this was looking like just a lot of wasted effort. But then her light caught something along the wall she was following. A faint metal flash had her wiggling forward a little faster. There was some sort of panel along the wall, and when she pushed at it, slats creaked open a tiny amount, letting in small slivers of sunlight. It was some sort of ventilation grate. Claire jabbed harder at the slats, which hadn't been moved in a very long time. They protested, but eventually opened further, allowing in even more light. Pressing her eye up to one of the gaps, Claire could see a little bit of the outside.

Mentally mapping her progress through the ceiling space, Claire figured she was along the side wall, opposite the one the break room was situated against. Studying the size of the vent, she thought she might be able to fit through the opening once it was removed. She couldn't remember who had told her, but she had heard that if your head could fit through something, the rest of you could too. Of course, that could require some painful twisting, crunching, and compression in order to fit, but Claire thought the opening would be a little larger than her head, leaving her enough space for minimal squeezing.

Claire looked behind her, desperately wanting to go straight back to the break room, but she knew she should explore the rest of the ceiling space first. If there was something even better than the ventilation grate, she needed to know about it. Setting off again, she found her situation less terrifying. The knowledge that she had located something of interest, and that touch of sunlight—as weak as it was—had eased her thoughts.

Eventually, after finding nothing else up there, Claire happily made her way back to the break room. After sliding back out of the opening and crouching down on the shelf, she saw that the others had eaten a light breakfast while she had been gone.

Danny? she asked, noticing his absence.

Bathroom, was Jon's simple answer.

There was unlikely to be anything of interest or use in there, so he was probably using the bathroom for its intended purpose. Some of the others had likely gone too, meaning it would not smell very pleasant. Claire was glad that her own bladder had gone dormant from the stress. While they waited for Danny to return, Claire was handed her portion of the breakfast they had decided on, and ate it sitting on top of the shelving unit. She was informed that the shadows were still outside the windows.

Once the team was all present and accounted for, Claire told them about what she had found, including the fact that she might be able to fit through and get outside if the grate were removed. Jon asked if she thought the rest of them could fit through, but Claire had to admit that she doubted it. Maybe Rose could, but it was unlikely any of the guys would be able to get through, not even Larson who was the lankiest of them. It was decided that Claire and Rose had to try to get out, to see what was lingering in front of the store.

Claire waited, surrounded by the insulation, as Rose clambered up, followed by Larson. Even though Claire was quite certain he wouldn't fit, they needed someone to relay messages should it prove impossible for Claire and Rose to get back inside. All three of them had been given what tools the group had brought, which were now dispersed among their pockets for carrying.

Back at the ventilation grate, the three of them set to work. Removing the inner plate proved fairly easy, since it was held on by some nuts, for which they had the correct size of wrench. The outer plate was more difficult. They could get at the back of the bolts holding it on easily enough, but the heads of them were out of reach, the slats too narrow for more than a pinky finger to be wedged between them. Of the four bolts, only one was easy to remove. Rose simply pushed it out, using a screwdriver to poke it the rest of the way once it was within the wall. They heard it clatter down on the pavement below, all three of them wincing. They waited, but no footsteps or shuffling groans came to investigate. The rest of the bolts took more work. They were wiggled and turned back and forth in an effort to loosen the wood's hold on them. Claire even tried chipping at the wood a bit, but it was thick and it would take a long time to cut out the bolts. Larson eventually crawled back to the break room to get some sticky blue tack he thought Bryce had packed. He had, and by sticking a gob on the end of a screwdriver, they were able to unscrew the bolts, albeit painfully slowly.

A second bolt, and then a third clattered to the pavement below. Each time, the three up in the attic space paused to listen. The last bolt, along the bottom, they left on. It turned out they could use it to hold the outer plate after they had popped it out of the opening. If the grate had fallen, it would've been a lot louder than the bolts. All three of them took turns peering out at the section of parking lot that was below and at the other nearby buildings. Larson tested to see if he could fit, but decided the opening was too small, that it would be far too painful to try to get through it.

It was decided that Claire would exit first. She had to remove her belt in order for her waist to wriggle through the opening. Larson held her arms, lowering her as much as he was able. With his arms filling the opening, and his head jammed up against the wall, he couldn't see Claire and had to trust that she was ready to be dropped when he let go.

Claire landed lightly on her feet, the slight crunch of leaves and pebbles putting her on the alert. After a speedy scan of the area, she reached up to receive her belt and, more importantly, her knife.

Rose took a little more time getting through the opening, as her hips were slightly wider. Claire waited, knife in hand. Once Rose was on her feet, and her hammer passed down to her, the two young women headed toward the front of the building. They stuck close to the wall, pausing as they reached the corner.

Claire looked back at Rose, who nodded that she was ready. Holding her breath, Claire peered around the corner. The air in her lungs escaped with a whoosh as she immediately became confused. She stepped around the corner. Rose followed her, fearing the worst.

"Mannequins?" Rose spoke as soon as she registered the same thing that Claire was seeing. "Why…?"

"Go tell Larson. I'll let the others know."

Rose didn't leave right away, she walked with Claire to the door and made sure that all the figures were indeed mannequins and not just someone posing as one. The lack of clothing on all of them made it pretty obvious, but both Claire and Rose were unnerved.

Claire stepped in through the door.

"Hey, guys," she called, knowing she didn't have to raise her voice very much. "It's safe."

"What the fuck?" Jon shouted once he was outside and saw the mannequins for himself.

"Someone must have seen us go in there last night and decided to be funny," Bryce suggested.

"Do you know how much time we've wasted?" Jon was pissed. He lashed out at one of the mannequins, booting it in the stomach. It sailed out into the road where it landed with a clatter, its head and arms popping off on impact.

After how silent they had been all morning, this felt like entirely too much noise.

"They might still be watching us," Larson pointed out, clearly trying to get Jon to calm down.

Instead of shouting again, he raised both of his middle fingers and pointed them in all directions for the benefit of anyone watching.

"No one we know would do this. There must be strangers in the area," Danny observed. "Should we head back to the container yard and warn them?"

That was a serious question. Heading back again, this time without food, would feel like an even greater loss of time. And while setting up the mannequins had been a cruel joke, it wasn't as if they had been attacked or were in any danger. If they were still being watched, they could have all been shot by now, but hadn't been. This whole thing might have been to study their reaction, or a way to keep them inside while the person or people who set up the mannequins moved out of the area.

"Rose and Claire should go back while the rest of us go on," Jon said.

"What? Hell no," Rose told him. "We'll all keep goin' together. They might want one of us to head back to camp so that they can follow us."

"And if we split up, both parties are in more danger," Bryce sided with her. "This was annoying, but they didn't try to harm the six of us. In smaller teams, that might not remain true."

Jon pushed over another mannequin, annoyed with the whole situation.

"Come on, let's stop wasting more time with these things and get going." Danny started walking, prompting everyone else to follow. "Besides, a few of the dead have been drawn to the noise." There were only two zombies coming, and they were both so mutilated that they could barely walk.

Rose and Claire slung their packs onto their backs; Danny had brought them out. The zombies in their way were easily dispatched.

***

They had travelled the rest of the day, but couldn't make up for the time wasted that morning, and so hadn't quite reached the area they were to search. The only time they stopped, was to go behind a house where it was known that a small vegetable garden once grew. It had been a planned stop, for the garden had gone wild, and sometimes edibles could be found there. They took only what was ripe, leaving the rest to grow again the following year.

"This time we pick a place that we know has two exits," Jon said as the sky turned from pink to purple.

They agreed upon a particular bungalow. Not only were there front and back doors, but the bedroom windows could all be opened and were large enough for everyone to be able to escape. They could also see clearly through the glass should it turn out that they were followed by the mischief maker. Unless the place was completely surrounded by hostile forces in the night, they would be all right.

They set up their sleeping rolls in the hallway, where they were out of sight from all windows and had quick access to several rooms. They also set up a watch rotation, which they should have done the night before, but had been too arrogant, figuring that the light sleepers would have been woken up by anything coming in or banging on the glass. Each of them was to spend an hour and twenty minutes watching over the others during the night, covering an eight hour window. Claire took the first watch, too alert to sleep.

It was strange being the only one awake. She sat at the end of the hallway that opened up to the living room, where there was the most light coming in from the moon and stars. They had closed all the doorways along the length of the hall, so that the sleepers beside her were in darkness. It was a very lonely feeling. She was glad that Bryce was the one nearest to her, because he breathed quite audibly in his sleep. It wasn't quite a snore, but it let her know that he was alive and close at hand. It also helped cover the ticking of their shared pocket watch, which threatened to drive her mad.

It was hard not to peek around the corner and out the living room window every five seconds. Claire glanced out on occasion, sometimes leaning even farther to see through the kitchen entrance, and out the sliding glass door at the back of it, but mostly she resisted. If the dead were to shuffle by, she didn't want to be spotted by them.

With nothing to do, the hour dragged by, and the twenty minutes seemed to pass even slower. As nothing continued to happen, Claire began to find herself growing sleepy, the day's exertions catching up with her. She stayed awake though, pinching her skin any time she thought there was even the remotest chance of nodding off.

When her time was up, Claire carefully stepped past her sleeping friends to where her bedroll was positioned at the end of the hall. She gently shook Jon's shoulder, waking him up for the next guard rotation and handing him the watch. He groaned softly, clearly still tired, but he got up to do his job.

As Claire settled down to sleep, she was glad he had taken the time slot after hers. Knowing that he was watching over everyone made it easier for Claire to fall asleep. It wasn't as deep a rest as she hoped to get, however.

All night, every time the guard was changed, Claire woke up for a moment or two. Her senses remained alert, so that nearby noise, even someone trying to quietly get up or lie down, caused her to waken. Jon rolling over at one point beside her, also caused her to wake up for a few seconds. She guessed this was why those with experience hadn't wanted to set up a guard rotation the night before. No one slept well.

When morning finally came, Bryce, who had taken the last shift, didn't wake anyone up, but let them sleep as long as they wanted. It wasn't for much longer than his time slot. The sunlight highlighted the early hour whenever they partially awoke. Once Larson decided to get up, they all did.

"Is there a water source near where we'll be searchin'?" Rose asked as they packed up their gear.

Jon said that there was.

"We'll need to boil more water once we settle on a base camp."

Their equipment wasn't as sophisticated as the setup used in the container yard, meaning steam would be wasted and it would take longer to refill their containers. They would also need to find firewood, but that shouldn't be too hard. Many buildings had things to burn if you didn't care about keeping them intact.

They searched the house before leaving, as it seemed this place hadn't been picked clean. Claire and Larson each took a small pile of towels from the linen closet, and everyone took a pillowcase to use as an overflow sack. Food was the priority, but there were other things the container yard could use more of. Had they a cart, they would have taken all the linens, including the dusty bedspreads. Whatever fabric wasn't used for its intended purpose, could be turned into clothing or used as patches. Jon made sure to note the location of this place so that another team could return in the future.

The house contained no food, batteries, guns, or bullets. Someone had been through the place in the early days and had taken those things. All Claire and her friends found in the way of food was something that had rotted away long ago in the fridge, and a few rusty cans whose contents couldn't be trusted. There was also an empty gun rack, and in a drawer was a ripped open plastic package for batteries. They did find rolls of duct tape, though, as well as some string, thread, yarn, and a fair number of tools. Danny packed up the pliers, and the drill bits and socket heads that had proven most useful to them over the years, as well as the rechargeable battery packs from the power tools. The rest, they took the time to hide beneath couches, the fridge, and any other place where only the most thorough scavenger would look, so that there was a greater chance of them still being there when they returned. Jon packed up a pair of work boots he found, and Bryce removed all the shoelaces from a couple of pairs of sneakers. Rose found an excessive number of belts, most of them more fancy than useful, but grabbed all of them. Larson located a bunch of cold weather gear in a storeroom, suggesting that the couple who had once lived there also once lived in a chillier climate, or perhaps vacationed there relatively often. He took all the gloves, and Claire took a wool knit hat with a pom-pom that she adored. She hadn't seen snow in a very long time.

With the house searched, it was time to go. Jon believed they could reach their search grid in plenty of time to locate a good place to make their camp and begin boiling water. Claire wore her new hat perched precariously upon her head, for it was far too hot to pull it down over her ears. Rose told her that it was cute.

As well as a few zombies, they finally managed to kill a rabbit while they walked. Bryce was the first to hit something with a sling stone at last, and while it wasn't a powerful enough shot to kill it, the rabbit was stunned long enough for them to get close with a knife. They planned to make a stew out of it for dinner.

The area in which they were to search was a mix of residential and business. There were houses, an apartment building, a row of shops, and a few small offices.

"I vote for the apartment building," Bryce said. "We should probably search it first, and it's the tallest structure in the area, making it easy to find if someone gets turned around out here."

"I second that decision," Larson chimed in. "The river is also fairly close."

"Then if no one has any objections, the apartment building it is." Jon led them to the front door, which had been pried open.

They scoured the first floor and the basement, often needing flashlights and lanterns to see due to the lack of windows. The office had been rifled through, and the laundry, storage, and utilities rooms were covered in a heavy layer of dust. There was a door to a parking garage, and another to a small convenience store that had been cleared out. All the glass remained intact in the store, with security bars over the windows, so they decided to make their camp there.

"Claire, you and I will go get some water," Jon decided, putting down his pack to retrieve the pot he carried. The others removed their water canisters and handed them over, so that they'd be able to carry back as much water as possible.

"Bryce, Larson, how about you two get us some firewood?" Danny suggested. "Rose and I will get to work making this place more comfortable and secure."

The teams and tasks were agreed upon. Claire and Jon headed out, Claire's pack holding all the water canisters while Jon left his pack behind, carrying only the pot in his hands.

"Give me an idea of what tomorrow will be like," Claire said as they walked down the street toward the river.

"Well, we'll be in smaller teams like we are right now; no one is to ever be alone."

"So it's good that I came. Even numbers."

Jon ignored her remark. "One pair will always stay near home base. They'll handle boiling water, as well as do their best to hunt and forage in the immediate surroundings. Basically, they guard our stuff."

"Who has to do that duty?" Claire was expecting that Jon was going to make her do it, to try to protect her again by making her stay put.

"In this instance, we'll rotate the job, since we're all on foot."

Claire was surprised and pleased to hear it. Maybe Jon had accepted her as a full member of the team after the mannequin incident.

"The other four will be searching every inch of our grid, which is smaller than usual. We bring everything of use to home base, even if we can't carry it all back to the container yard in one go. We can always stash it, and come back with a cart later."

"Where will the search start?"

"The parking garage, most likely. It should be pretty empty of vehicles, and I noticed it had a door covering its car entrance outside, so there shouldn't be any big surprises lurking down there. I also think-" Jon abruptly stopped mid-sentence, and mid-stride.

Claire's hand fell to the hilt of her knife, wondering what Jon had seen. She followed his gaze down the street they had been crossing. She had been checking the other direction for threats, and hadn't seen what occupied Jon's side of the street.

More mannequins. A group of them were standing around outside one of the shops, in a similar fashion to how Claire had found them the other morning.

"Same person?" Claire whispered.

"Most likely," Jon whispered back.

"Could there be someone in there, trapped by fear like we had been?"

"Impossible to say. They could have been set up there days ago."

"They can't be the same mannequins, right?"

Jon shook his head. "I don't know. Whoever set them up could have passed us during the night, or while we were searching that house this morning."

"Do you think they followed us?"

"If they had, I think those mannequins would be set up outside the apartment building, not here."

"I think they're the same mannequins."

"Why?"

"Because otherwise it means someone is out there carting around enough mannequins to be able to leave a bunch behind and still have plenty to scare a different group of people."

"If you're right, that shop might be occupied."

Claire realized that. "Anyone from home have a travel path through this area?"

"I don't know. I don't think so. We're not far from the river. Let's get the water and get back to the others. We'll explain what we've seen and decide what to do then."

Claire nodded. They continued on to the river, which was narrow and fast flowing. While Claire filled the canisters, Jon watched her back, his hand never leaving his sword, ready to draw it in an instant. By the time Claire filled up the pot, she knew she was in for another night of little sleep.

11: DAKOTA
5 DAYS AFTER THE BOMBING

When the sun sank beneath the horizon, it was a relief. Not only was it cooler, but it meant that Dakota was free of Freya for the time being. As one of the oldest kids in the group, Dakota was driven by Freya harder than the others. Never before had she had to run so much. Hope, Peter, Adam, Emma, and Becky were all pushed hard too, but their age group was allowed to take more breaks, and received more encouragement.

"I think I'm going to puke," Dakota mumbled, her face buried in her arms as she and her friends sat around a table.

"Does that mean you're not going to eat that?" Adam asked.

Dakota raised her head and smacked his hand away before it could reach her dinner plate. She wrapped an arm around her food and drew it closer to her, although it meant she could no longer put her head back down. Her exhaustion-induced nausea made the thought of eating repulsive, but she also knew that it had to be done, that she needed to restore the energy she had burned off. She started with one tiny bite.

Most of their training so far had just been exercising. Dakota prayed that it would be more than that tomorrow, that she would actually learn something new. She already knew how to run.

As time passed, Dakota was able to eat bigger bites and more frequently, until she was eating normally by the time the food on her plate was gone. Although she didn't feel hungry after finishing, she also didn't feel full.

"How long do you think it will take before we get to eat a normal sized meal again?" Dakota wondered out loud when there was a lull in the conversation.

"It's going to take a long time," Becky answered.

"Not if we find a community willing to trade," Hope told her.

"Trade what?" Becky retorted. "What could we possibly give them that we don't need?"

"They can bring us food, and we can charge their batteries using the sub in exchange," Peter said. The way in which he said it made it sound as though he had overheard an adult in charge telling this to someone else. Maybe he had. Maybe that was what was being offered by those going out to meet the other groups: give us food and we'll give you electricity.

"We wouldn't have this problem if we hadn't let all those people who attacked us stick around," Adam complained rather loudly. "Except for you, Emma," he quickly added in a quieter voice. "You and your parents are cool."

Emma didn't say anything. She never did when Adam complained about the new people.

The topic of conversation was soon about other things, such as when the fertilized chicken eggs were going to hatch. All the children had a bet going, with the island vet keeping track of it for them. They had all guessed when they thought the chickens would hatch, and whoever was closest to each egg, got to name the new chicken. Dakota was hoping for Mega Bok Bok.

They had all finished eating, and decided to either go to bed, or do whatever chores they were usually given. They all walked to the toilets together. Dakota and Hope then accompanied Peter, Becky, and Adam to Bitch Bridge, since they were still sleeping on Animal Island, but they didn't cross with them. The two girls then each went to their own containers. Now that they had begun to identify the rows of containers, it wasn't as easy to make a wrong turn. Still, Dakota wished that her row wasn't the red circle. She didn't like the colour red, and the circle looked like a target.

Approaching the container, Dakota could see that neither Cameron nor Brunt were home yet. Their solar charged lights were still clustered outside the doors, several of them glowing as they were set to turn on automatically when the sun left. Dakota brought all the lights inside with her, turning on those that were off once the doors were closed. She moved about the container placing the lights in their usual spots. There wasn't much to clean or tidy, yet she picked up and put away a few wayward items before she changed into her pajamas and brushed her teeth and hair. Climbing up onto the top bunk, she ended up lying there with her eyes open. Though her body was tired, her mind was not yet ready to sleep. She wished she had a book to read, but didn't have anything new, and of the ones currently in the container, none were interesting enough to read again. Instead, she picked up a piece of paracord draped over her headboard and practised the knots Brunt had taught her.

"You're still up," Cameron commented when she finally came in. She had opened the door slowly in case Dakota was asleep. "From what I saw, I expected Freya to have completely wiped you out."

"Trust me, my body is pretty much sleeping without me right now."

"How was it?" Cameron began going through her own nightly routine.

"Hard."

"It should be. Are you going to continue tomorrow?"

"Of course. Where's Brunt?"

"He should be back soon."

Dakota silently watched her move about the container, checking again on their stocks of various supplies.

"Why aren't we religious?" Dakota suddenly asked, clearly surprising Cameron with her question.

"I'm not religious because I don't believe in any sort of higher power. Why? Do you think that you do?"

"No, I just thought it would be nice to get time off, like the Muslims do during their prayer times, and the Christians on Sunday mornings."

Cameron laughed. It was obvious that she had thought this was going to be a much more serious discussion. "That's not a good reason to join a religion. And besides, they don't see that as time off. That time is spent devoted to their respective Gods."

"Peter used to go to church with Abby and Lauren. He said that he just sat there, counting how many people showed up, or how many times certain words were said." One of the containers acted as a church for all the religions that needed one. Their various accoutrements of religious ritual were packed in boxes. The leaders of each sect took them out and put them away depending on whose turn it was. Brunt once referred to it as a religious timeshare.

"Because Peter's not a believer, which is also why he no longer attends."

"I bet there's other people who don't believe but still go through the motions."

"I'm sure there are too. I'll also bet that some people struggle with their beliefs, and are completely devoted some days, and not at all on others. There's likely even some who have never believed, but enjoy the bond it forms between people, or, as you said, gives them time off. If you ask me, I'd rather keep working than have to pretend while putting up with potential boredom."

"Me too," Dakota agreed.

"If you ever do decide to believe in a god, don't be afraid to tell me just because I don't," Cameron said, looking directly at Dakota. "I may not understand it, but I'd try, and could introduce you to the various religious leaders if you'd like."

"Okay." Dakota didn't think she'd ever believe. She liked the idea of heaven, but whenever she thought about it, she wondered about the zombies. Had those people's souls moved on? Or were they trapped in the rotting corpses? Dakota preferred to believe that you were just your thoughts, and when they stopped, you weren't alive anymore. It meant there was no afterlife, and that the zombies weren't people anymore, only machines for a virus.

Brunt came in, and Dakota showed him some of the knots she could make. He complimented them, and then showed her a few new ones before getting ready for bed. While Cameron didn't usually mind changing in front of Dakota, Brunt always went behind a privacy screen they had set up in a corner. Despite this, Dakota knew what a naked man looked like. Cameron had taught her all about the human body, using books that had visual aids. She had also flipped through the few art books they had, which contained nudes, like Michelangelo's *David*. She had a few sparse memories of when she was little around the time of the Day, when a man's mind had broken and he had taken all his clothes off for no reason. And then there were several naked zombies who had once been male, but nobody counted them because nothing ever looked right. Only the fresh ones appeared normal, and they tended to still have clothes.

"Bright light, or dim light?" Brunt asked Dakota once they were all ready to sleep.

"Dim light," she told him. Usually she wanted the dim light, requesting the brighter nightlight only if she was really scared something might happen. They always kept one of the lights on, placed on the far side of the privacy screen, next to a bucket they used as a toilet when someone needed to go before morning.

Dakota returned her paracord to where it usually hung over her headboard and rolled to face the wall. Her bed rocked a little as Cameron and Brunt shuffled about, getting comfortable beside one another, and then it went still. It wasn't until Dakota could hear Brunt's heavy breathing a moment later, a sure sign that he was asleep, that she closed her eyes to do the same.

***

Dakota lay on her belly in the shade of a container, watching Robin's cat, Splatter. He was licking the side of his paw and rubbing it over his face, giving it a good wash. He was so calm and nonchalant, that it infuriated Dakota. For the last hour, she had been trying to catch the cat. If Freya had given her the task of scooping up one of the container yard's other cats, it would have been no problem. All those cats knew her, and were friendly with her. Splatter, on the other hand, had lived at the Black Box. He didn't know Dakota, and was wary of strangers, so he ran away whenever she attempted to approach him. Lying on the pavement, Dakota was attempting to devise another plan, because running after the cat was clearly not working.

Splatter finished his wash and flopped over in the sun, rolling about a bit on the pavement. He was perfectly aware of Dakota's presence and was taunting her. To him, this had become a game.

A soft footstep behind her caused Dakota to turn her head. Freya was standing there. She had managed to come up behind Dakota without her noticing. The sound of her last footstep was caused deliberately to get the teenager's attention. It was the kind of silence she was trying to teach some of the kids.

No luck? Freya asked in sign language. She still carried around a piece of chalk in a little container that hung from a necklace, but she had lost the small chalkboard that went with it when forced to leave the Black Box. This meant that the woman was restricted to sign until another could be found to replace it. Dakota didn't mind signing. She liked the practice, but it did make teaching the new children difficult at times. Dakota had never learned why Freya was mute. She overheard someone once talking about an illness, but that could have just been a rumour, and there was no way she was ever going to ask.

Dakota shook her head in response to Freya's question.

Freya sat beside her, prompting Dakota to sit up. She suspected she was about to receive a lesson and was right.

The cat is aware of you, Freya told her. *You will not be able to catch him with your hands. He is too fast and clever.*

"I wasn't supposed to be able to catch him, was I?" Dakota had realized.

Freya smiled, as good as a yes. She went on to explain how humans needed to use their brains to catch animals. Traps were best, even the kind that simply drove the creature into a corner from which it could not escape. Co-operation between humans made it even easier. You use the animal's fear of one human, to drive it toward another.

"Is that how wolves hunt?" Dakota wondered.

Freya didn't know much about wolves, and so couldn't say for certain. Dakota liked to think that she was right. That she could one day be a wolf.

She thought about asking Freya to help her catch the cat so that she could learn how the woman would go about it, but when she looked toward the sunlight, Splatter was gone. It probably wouldn't have been a good lesson anyway, as Freya had lived at the Black Box, so odds were that the cat knew her and was less likely to flee.

Besides, it turned out that Freya had a different lesson planned.

Dakota and a few of the others around her age had been gathered together near the wall, beside a big plastic bin. A short distance away from them, stood a line of tables, with empty jugs and cans on top. Freya had to go find one other student for this lesson, leaving Dakota to stand around with the others.

"Looks like a shooting range," Mike commented with a gesture toward the table.

"There's not enough bullets to teach us how to shoot," Dakota reminded him.

"Maybe we'll be using our slingshots," suggested Maui.

That was probably it, although everyone was already fairly accurate with their slingshots. They had practised plenty of times before on various set-ups not too dissimilar to what they were standing beside. Maybe Freya wanted to see how good they were. Although they were all curious about what was in the bin, they all managed to resist looking inside. Part of their lessons earlier had been about the dangers of curiosity, so they thought it possible that the bin was a sort of test.

As they waited, Bronislav went by with a group of younger kids. He was quizzing them on various things that they should know about, while having them walk at a brisk pace. Based on the exhaustion Dakota saw on their faces, they had been doing this for a while, or were perhaps jogging earlier. She had done all her physical exercise in the morning, running around the container yard like Misha usually did, followed by a series of push ups, sit ups, lunges, and yoga stretches. Lunch had been a wonderful break after that.

When Freya returned, the group of students became six. When she asked to see their slingshots, they handed them over; all but Josephine who was new to the container yard and didn't have one. Freya inspected each one, testing its durability and elasticity. When she was done, she didn't hand them back, but instead gave them all strips of leather.

"What's this for?" Mike wondered.

"We're not going to be blindfolded, are we?" worried Maui.

"I think they're slings. Like Freya uses," Dakota guessed. She had seen the ones given to Danny, Larson, and Bryce.

"What do we need slings for?" Mike asked, gesturing to the slingshots that Freya had placed on the ground.

Dakota translated for Josephine as Freya explained that their slingshots weren't actually very good. They didn't have much power, and had been built in such a way that they would either break, or lose all their elasticity over time. Slings were better, for they were of simple construction, and like their slingshots in that ammunition was easy to find once you knew what you were looking for. Also, strangers weren't likely to realize a sling was a weapon, meaning that they could be put at ease, not realizing the trainees were armed.

"These worked great for hurling grenades over the wall and all," Mike said, "but you can't kill a zombie with them."

Freya asked him to pick a target on the table. He chose a tin can. Dakota was excited to watch, for though she had heard what Freya could do with a sling, she had never gotten a chance to witness it.

After plucking a stone from her pouch, Freya dropped it into the thicker part of her sling and almost immediately had it spinning in a tight whirl. When she released, the stone whipped across the distance, smashing the tin can off the table with a clang. She then had Mike go retrieve the stone and the can.

"Holy shit!" he commented as he picked up the tin. He held it up so the others could see how it had become deformed.

Freya went on to explain that skulls were very hard, so a sling stone was unlikely to take down a fresh zombie. The older dead, however, the ones that had softened over time, could be destroyed. If ever they needed to use their sling against a human, a headshot with that kind of force behind it, could easily kill them by shaking up their brain in their skull. They could also break bones by aiming elsewhere, or stun a person with a weaker shot to the head, and so the teens were instructed to treat them like guns. They were never to start a stone swinging if someone they didn't want to hit was within their line of fire, not even as a joke. If there was even one accident, or someone reported them not treating the weapon with respect, the teenager's sling would be taken away. Freya had only six new slings made to start with, and chose the six teenagers based on how responsible they seemed. Dakota was rather proud to have been picked.

The six chosen students very quickly learned that slings were a lot harder to use than slingshots. The plastic bucket had been opened, revealing a pile of rocks that Freya had been gathering ever since the zombie attack. Apparently, she had been planning on teaching some adults her skills, but Bronislav had convinced her to teach some of the older kids instead. Just getting the stone to go forward took quite a bit of practice, and a handful of times the teenagers had to scatter as someone accidentally launched one straight up. Freya could see that they were honestly trying, however, and so never scolded them. She was far more encouraging than when it came to their physical training, and offered plenty of advice.

They spent hours hurling stones, going through the whole bucket more than once. Gathering them up after their pathetic attempts had become its own sort of training, with Freya timing how long it took them. By the end, Dakota and the other five could at least always get their stones to go in the right direction every time, even if there wasn't much strength behind the shots. Hitting the tables or anything on them was pure chance.

After refilling the bucket one last time, Freya called a halt to their training. Dakota was glad, because her arms hurt. Everyone had used both their left and right arms, to see if one was better than the other, but also because Freya insisted they be able to use both. She wanted them to be able to hurl stones even if they injured an arm.

You have one last task, Freya told them. *You're to bring dinner to the guards on the wall.*

This was a big deal for three of the teenagers who had never really been up there before. Dakota and Maui had both delivered meals to the watch guards in the past, and Josephine was still too new to realize how rare it was for anyone not on guard duty to go up there. Freya wanted them to be comfortable with what the terrain looked like beyond the wall.

"Can I eat my dinner up there?" Dakota asked.

Only if a guard says it's all right for you to sit with them, Freya responded. *And don't stay up there after dark.*

Dakota bet that Brunt was on duty right then, so she was pretty much guaranteed to find someone to sit with.

Walking toward the community centre with their new slings tied around their waists, Dakota and the others discussed who would deliver meals to what part of the wall. When Dakota entered the centre, Hope and her friends were already there at a table. Hope waved to Dakota, gesturing to the empty seat beside her.

"I won't be eating dinner in here today," Dakota told her friends once she had walked over. "I have to deliver food to the wall guards, and I was told I'm allowed to eat up there with them."

"I wanted to ask you about the sling," Hope pouted. Their group had gone by a second time while Dakota had been practising.

"I'll tell you everything at breakfast tomorrow." Dakota hurried back over to the meal line. She wanted as much time as she could get on the wall before the sun disappeared completely past the horizon.

The rations for those on guard duty were already packed into stackable containers, and it was easy for Dakota to balance her own on top. With five of them making the deliveries that night, she didn't have to carry very many.

Heading to the ladder nearest the community centre, Dakota climbed up and down several times in order to get the food up safely. She then walked along the wall toward her designated sector, knowing she wasn't taking the fastest route by walking around up there.

None of the people to whom she handed dinner was Brunt. As she approached the last guard, her stomach flopped over. She didn't know his name, only that he had come with the new group, and that he was gorgeous. To be on the wall and carry a gun, he had to be older than sixteen, but beyond that, Dakota knew next to nothing about him. She had been too shy to talk to him, and there was definitely no way she would ask Brunt about him.

"Ah, dinner," he commented as he glanced over and spotted Dakota coming. "Best part about this job is probably the service." He smiled and it was lovely.

Dakota found she could think of nothing to respond with beyond a smile of her own, which she immediately thought must look ridiculous. After handing over the last container, she looked past him, trying to locate where Brunt might be.

"I think Idris was already given a meal," the guard told her, thinking she must be looking for the next person down the line.

"Oh, no, this is my dinner," she awkwardly explained. "I was trying to see where Brunt is."

"Is it important? Do you want me to radio him?"

"No, no, it's nothing. I was told that I would be allowed to eat my dinner up here as long as a guard agreed to let me sit with them. Brunt is sort of my step-foster-dad." Dakota told herself to shut up.

"I wouldn't mind the company if you'd like to sit with me."

Dakota hoped her face didn't turn as red as she felt it must be. "Okay."

"I'm Elijah, by the way." He held out his hand.

"Dakota."

"I like your hat."

"Thank you." Dakota felt her ears grow terribly hot.

Elijah sat down in the opening between the two upper containers and gestured for Dakota to sit as well. She was mostly glad that he kept his eyes pointed outward, watching the uninhabited part of the container yard as opposed to her. Mostly glad, but not entirely.

"I saw you training with a sling earlier," he commented.

Dakota realized that they were essentially right beside where the table was set up. "Um, yeah, Freya decided it would be a good idea to teach a bunch of us. Usually we're only given complete weapons' training once we're sixteen."

"How old are you now?"

"Fifteen." Dakota spoke the word toward her food. "I would have received gun training soon, if we had enough bullets."

"Well, I must say that I'm very glad to have been given some of the few that were left." He had a rifle slung over one shoulder, as did everyone on the wall. None of them had more than what the gun could hold, however, and some didn't even have full magazines.

"How old are you?" Dakota asked hesitantly, hoping she didn't sound too obvious.

"Eighteen."

That was only a difference of three years between them, which surprised the hell out of Dakota. "I thought you were twenty-something," she blurted out.

"I get that a lot," Elijah shrugged. "I'm told I'm mature for my age. Evans certainly trusted me to help him manage the party."

"Bronislav and the others must trust you a lot here, too," Dakota told him. "You're new, and yet they've already put you on guard duty."

"I don't think they had much of a choice given how many people left to contact other groups and find food. Besides, a bunch of people living here now are from my party, and I want to defend them just as much as you guys want to defend your own."

Dakota thought that maybe she had hurt his feelings or something, and mentally beat herself up.

"So why did this Freya person decide to teach you how to use a sling?" Elijah asked.

"She's really good with hers, and thinks it's a good weapon for us to learn how to use."

A soft laugh escaped from Elijah. "I meant why did she decide to teach you now, when you normally wouldn't receive weapons' training until you're sixteen."

Dakota was pretty certain she could have died of embarrassment right then. "I convinced Bronislav that we needed something to do." She almost referred to herself as a kid, and would definitely have died if she had. "He decided that we'd be most useful getting a field ready for planting out there."

"And you need training to go over the wall," Elijah nodded. "Makes sense, to keep the younger ones inside. I would have started your training earlier, personally."

"We were given basic knife safety lessons, and taught the softest parts of a zombie's skull should something happen." Dakota found herself wanting to defend the rules set down by her elders, even though she didn't always agree with them.

Elijah shrugged, and Dakota had no idea what it meant.

This conversation was going terribly. She shovelled more food into her mouth, the perfect excuse to not say anything else embarrassing.

Elijah opened his mouth as if he were about to say something else, but quickly closed it again as his posture became rigid. He moved his food container off his lap and unslung his rifle; he never took his eyes off the distant shipping containers. Dakota turned her head to look as he brought his scope to his eye.

"What is it?" Dakota couldn't see anything right away, but then she spotted the figure coming around the end of a container. The distance made it impossible for her to make out any features.

"Possible contact," Elijah whispered into his walkie-talkie, and followed it up with his location code on the wall.

"Zombie?" came a whispered reply.

"Can't quite tell yet. Could just be someone with an injury."

"Call out to them."

Elijah stood up, nearly kicking over his food container. Dakota pulled it out of the way.

"Halt!" Elijah shouted in a strong voice. "Identify yourself!"

There was no response from the figure.

"If you can understand me, raise your arms!" Elijah shouted next.

To Dakota, it looked like the figure did nothing.

"No response," Elijah whispered into his walkie. "It's still coming."

"Likely a zombie," came the reply. "Keep an eye on it. If it's alone, just wait for it to reach the wall and use a spear."

"Copy." Elijah sat back down, but kept his rifle in a firm grip, frequently checking on the figure through the scope.

"Is it really that hard to tell the difference between a zombie and a human at a distance?" Dakota wondered.

"Fresh zombies can look pretty human, and injured humans can look a lot like zombies, so yeah."

"How do you tell the difference then?" Dakota didn't like the idea of sounding dumb in front of Elijah, but she also understood how important it was to know the answer to her question.

"It can be difficult. The first step is to look for any injuries that no one could possibly walk with: ankles that are completely sideways, bones sticking out of legs, guts dragging behind them, that kind of thing. If there are other injuries, look at the blood. Is it still bright red and flowing? Then it's much more likely to be a human. The longer a zombie's been dead, the darker and thicker the blood gets, until it becomes that blackish goop we had to clean up. Sometimes the eyes will give a zombie away, but that's unreliable. In a fresh zombie, they can still look pretty lively. And of course, the very last way of knowing, is that if they try to bite you, they're a zombie."

"Sounds like you have to wait until they're fairly close for that method."

"That's why everyone likes the long dead better than the freshies." Elijah looked through his scope again. When he next lowered it, he carefully removed the scope from the rifle and held it out to Dakota. "Here, take a look."

Dakota accepted the optical device and held it up to her eye. She had gotten to use binoculars plenty of times before, but never a rifle scope. It took her a few seconds to locate the figure within her field of view. She studied the features Elijah had mentioned. She assumed that he had determined that it was a zombie—or else why give her the scope?—and attempted to see the same thing that he had.

Ragged clothes, dirty stringy hair, an awkward shuffling gait. Dakota was fairly certain it was a woman's body, and she would instinctively assume it was a zombie, but she could see how it might be just an injured person who had been through a lot. As the woman continued to come forward, Dakota struggled to pinpoint one thing that said she was a zombie and not the living. She was about to give up, to ask Elijah to tell her, when the woman stumbled. As her body twisted to the left, her arm and part of her shirt fell out of the way to reveal that a substantial chunk of her side was actually missing. When she started coming toward them again, Dakota could see how the arm and tattered shirt perfectly hid it from their distance and angle.

"She's a zombie," Dakota reported, lowering the scope. "It looks like part of her side has been carved out." She handed the device back to Elijah, who proceeded to reattach it to the rifle.

"Good job. Learn this lesson well. You don't want to make a mistake."

"It sounds like you've had experience."

"We all have," Elijah glanced back at her. "Didn't anyone ever tell you why my party attempted the attack?"

"No," Dakota shook her head, feeling stupid and ignorant. She overheard a lot, but the attack was something no one discussed. Probably because those people were now living with them, and they wanted to make sure everyone continued to get along.

"One of your scavengers accidentally killed one of our men. Wycheck had gone off on his own and was somehow injured, and then one of yours mistook him for a zombie. We had had some trouble lately with our own scavengers being killed by cowards with knives, and so my people overreacted. I'm ashamed to say that I'm the one who found your friends, allowing my party to attack and kidnap several of them." And he really did look ashamed about it.

Dakota had no idea what to say or do, and so she said and did nothing.

When Elijah next spoke, it was to confirm for the other people on the wall that the figure was indeed a zombie and that he would take care of it. Slinging his rifle back over his shoulder, he stood up and opened one of the upper containers next to him, and drew from it a long spear. Dakota watched as the zombie approached. Whenever it looked remotely like it was about to stagger off into another direction, Elijah tapped the butt of the spear on the container beside him, the sound luring the dead back in his direction.

"Have you ever killed a zombie?" Elijah asked as it got near.

"No," Dakota admitted. "I've never really been close enough, and only those who've completed their weapons' training are taken out by their teachers to kill one."

"Here." Elijah held out the spear to her. "If you ask me, this is the safest way to do it for the first time. There's only one, it can't reach you, and you don't need to waste any bullets or make much sound. Hell, you can even drop the spear, because we have more."

Dakota tried to keep her jaw from dropping as she accepted the weapon. She wasn't certain she should be doing this, not without permission from Cameron, or Brunt, or Freya, or Bronislav. It felt like it was against the rules, but then the rules had been changing over the past few days. She had a sling now, and was being trained to go over the wall. Elijah was right: it would be better to kill her first zombie from up here rather than when she was down there. Down there, she was in more danger, and if she froze up, someone would have to save her. Here, she could freeze and still be safe.

"Okay, turn the spear over so that its point is down," Elijah instructed. The dead woman was just about to reach the wall.

The spear was large and a little cumbersome, but Dakota managed to turn it over without dropping it or hitting anything.

"It helps to lean it against your shoulder," Elijah advised. "The skull on this one is likely still pretty solid, so you're going to need to put some strength behind it, although the weight of the spear will help. She's likely to look up once she reaches the wall if her neck still functions, so aim for an eye. The orbital socket will actually help guide the point of the spear where it needs to go."

Some of the advice Dakota already knew, but she was glad to hear it again. Her heart was hammering in her chest, and it wasn't easy to think straight. As she stood on the edge of the container, she felt Elijah's hand wrap itself around the back of her sling belt; slowly so as not to startle her. He was making sure she didn't fall forward.

"Whenever you're ready," Elijah told her.

Dakota stared down, meeting the eyes of the zombie woman below. It was much easier to tell that she was dead up close. Her skin had begun to grey, her veins blacken. Her eyes were partly cloudy now, but they had once been brown. Dakota focused on where Elijah's knuckles pressed against her back through her T-shirt.

Moving the point of the spear so that it hovered over the zombie's eye, Dakota took a deep breath. She held the air in her lungs for a few seconds, and then, in one swift, smooth motion, lifted the spear and then plunged it down. Her aim wasn't completely true. The point of the spear struck the bridge of the woman's nose, but it skidded sideways and found an eye. Elijah was right about the orbital socket helping to guide the spear, but it was so strange to feel.

When the zombie slumped, the spear was nearly pulled out of Dakota's hands. Why she thought it would just simply slide right out again, she had no idea, but the dead woman canted sideways, and if it weren't for Elijah holding onto her, Dakota might have gone right off the wall in an attempt to hold onto the spear.

"I gotcha," Elijah said, as he reached around her with his free hand to help her steady the spear. "I should have warned you about pulling the spear back as quickly as possible. Have you got it now?"

"I got it." Dakota was acutely aware of Elijah's arm alongside hers, his shoulder against her scapula.

"Okay, try to pull the spear up." Elijah let go of it, but he kept his arm hovering next to her own in case she needed help.

She did not, and yanked the spear up and out of the zombie's head, allowing the corpse to collapse completely to the pavement. Elijah then stepped back from her, gently pulling on her sling belt so that she'd step away from the edge as well. When he let go and Dakota turned around, she couldn't help having a huge smile on her face, even if it might look ridiculous.

"You did it!" Elijah cheered, partly throwing up his hands for her.

"I did," she realized. Dakota put down the spear and cautiously peered back over the edge. A zombie lay dead at the base of the container wall and she had been the one to kill it.

She knew it would be the first of many.

12: ONIDA
APPROXIMATELY ONE YEAR AGO

Shawn must have taken many overnight trips to know the terrain as far away from his cabin as he did. Even when they reached a mound of sharp rocks and razor cliffs, he knew a way to get the horses safely down. It wasn't much farther, however, when even Shawn ceased to know what was ahead, and their progress slowed.

Before then, they had ridden the horses all night and all of the following day after Shawn's cabin had been attacked. Onida felt sore in a dozen places, unused to being in a saddle for such an extended period of time. At least she didn't have to control her horse much, as it seemed content to follow the train of horses behind Shawn's. This allowed Onida to wiggle around somewhat, and change the position of her legs a little bit. Still, whenever she got off the horse to pee, she just about fell over. By the time they stopped the next night to rest, Onida could barely walk.

It seemed that Shawn was also unused to riding horses for such a long time, but he powered through whatever pain he felt. While Onida sat on the ground, rubbing her sore spots, he took care of each of the horses, bringing them by twos to a nearby stream to drink. Mask was delighted to be able to run around again.

"How well do you know horses?" Shawn asked her that night.

"Okay, I guess," Onida shrugged. "Depends on what you want to know."

"Can you tell which two horses are the ones who like the lead the most?"

Although Onida hadn't been allowed to ride the horses very often, she had taken care of them many times and knew them fairly well. "I would say that one, and that one," she pointed.

Onida had slept while Shawn had worked. By the time she got up, he had modified the tack on every horse but the two Onida had picked out. All the saddles had been carved up. The straps and saddlebags remained, but the seats and horns were gone. The reins had been cut into long leads, and the bits removed for the comfort of the horses. Shawn had even taken their backpacks and attached them to the backs of a couple of horses using the saddle straps that remained. The leather that used to hold the stirrups had been saved and bundled up.

"We're just going to leave all this stuff here?" Onida had asked of the saddle remains.

"If they're still following, and they make it this far, then they don't need confirmation that they're going the right way. It won't matter if they find this stuff."

That day was spent in the saddle again. The packhorses appeared more comfortable with the greater space the longer leads allowed them. Shawn called for a midday stop, and then another stop that night, so the ride wasn't as brutal.

It had been the day after that when they descended the cliffs and entered unknown territory.

"Where are we going?" Onida asked when they stopped for lunch.

"South."

"Yeah, but where south? Do you have a destination in mind?"

"Do you?"

"I don't know where anything is."

"I don't know what it's going to be like to the south. All I know is that we aren't going to find shelter from the winter weather up here."

"What *is* to the south, anyway?"

"Death."

"That doesn't sound like a place I want to go."

"We won't be. We have to go around. We have to avoid the irradiated areas."

"Can we do that?"

"I have a Geiger counter in my pack. But it's possible there isn't a way around. We'll just have to find out."

Onida didn't like the sound of that. "And what if we don't find a way around?"

Shawn's only answer was silence.

They travelled through the woods for days. Sometimes they would make camp around noon, and Shawn would go hunting, but every morning was spent riding the horses. There were fifteen of the animals with them, seven males and eight females. Onida knew most of their names, and for those she couldn't remember, she made up new ones. Shawn didn't seem to care about them as individuals, only as a collective for riding and carrying supplies. He was always more concerned about Mask's wellbeing, even more so than Onida's. She supposed that was fair. It had been her fault that his home was burned down, after all. While Shawn was good at finding water for the horses and making sure there was greenery that they could eat, Onida more often took over the job of caring for their wellbeing. Whenever he went hunting, she would remove a horse's gear and give him or her a good brushing down with the supplies she had found in a few of the saddle bags. There were too many horses to brush down in one go, but she created an order in her head, always knowing which horse's turn was next.

Rain was the worst. Whether it was a drizzle or a deluge, Shawn had them press on, occasionally having to backtrack as the path he chose was either a dead end or began to hook north for too long. Onida didn't have any spare clothes to change into; she always had to hang her wet stuff in the tent when they stopped, hoping they wouldn't be too damp when she next put them on. She was never comfortable lying naked in her sleeping bag, awfully close to Shawn in the small tent. He never made any sort of comment or advance though. Shawn just seemed to see her as another set of hands to help him, never as a woman.

There was very little conversation between the two of them. Because they rode their horses single file, with each of them leading half the train, they were never near one another while on horseback. When they stopped, they both had the jobs they had assigned themselves, which often took them apart. Even on stormy nights, when they ate cold meals in the tent, with the rain making it sound like they were in a river, the two of them didn't speak. What words they did pass, always related to their predicament: which way to go next, how the horses were holding up, what their supplies were like, did either of them feel ill, and so on. Most of Shawn's words were saved for a whispered and one-sided conversation with Mask. Sometimes this bothered Onida, who, on occasion, wished to discuss other things, like the way the trees sparkled after it had stopped raining, or the way the sunlight slanted through a particular section of leaves, or even their different childhoods. But most of the time she knew to keep quiet, not wanting Shawn to press her about why she was being pursued.

Perhaps it was their lack of horses, but the people hunting Onida hadn't been seen or heard from since the night of the fire. If they were still following her, they must have fallen a fair distance behind, hindered with all their resources gone. It was even possible that they had simply given up, but Onida wouldn't let her heart believe this. She feared that the moment she did, that was when they would reappear.

Onida hadn't been counting, but it had certainly been over a week when she finally saw another human construction. This time it was a road: a strip of sun-faded asphalt that carved its way through the forest. Winter after winter had cracked the surface like a broken windshield, and without anyone coming to fix it, weeds had taken hold within those cracks. Young trees and long grass had sprouted from the gravel shoulder, all of it at its last peak of greenery before the cold nights truly hit.

"Is it safe to follow the road?" Onida asked. Once they started along it, she was finally able to ride abreast of Shawn.

"How should I know?" he asked her in turn. "I haven't seen a road in eleven years. Have you?"

"Yes. But my people protect them. I don't believe this road is within their range, however."

"What did they protect the roads from?"

"I don't know. Zombies, I suppose. Raiders, maybe, although we know all the tribes in the area and are in good standing with them. And I've never heard of a stranger coming to our lands."

"We should be safe enough."

It was the *should* that worried Onida. Shawn had his bow and arrows, and was good with them, yet Onida had nothing but her knife. If it turned out that they weren't safe on the road, she would be in more trouble than him.

They followed the asphalt—Onida twitching at every sudden sound—until they came to a rest stop. It wasn't much, just an overgrown gravel parking lot, some rotting picnic tables, and a relatively simple structure to house both toilets and a little information centre, but it made a good place to spend the night. Shawn went inside the building to investigate, while Onida prepped the horses for the night. They were very good at sticking together overnight, so she only needed to put a long lead on one horse that she tied to a rusted flagpole on the side of the building. The rest of the horses just wore their hobbles. That was when she noticed something wrong with the horse she had named Askuwheteau.

"What's wrong with it?" Shawn asked when he returned, noting that she was giving the horse special attention.

"I'm not sure," Onida admitted. "I can't see anything wrong, but he's favouring his foreleg."

"When we head out tomorrow, put it at the back of a line and we'll distribute its packs among the others."

"If we stop for more than a night, it could get better."

"You're the one those people are after; do you think it's a good idea to stop?"

Onida felt the anxiety seize her throat. "No, I suppose we shouldn't."

"I'm going hunting. There's enough space inside that we don't need to set up the tent."

"Understood."

Shawn took only his bow and arrows and disappeared into the nearest stand of trees. Mask stayed behind, exploring the area in which they had made their camp. Onida switched the long lead to Askuwheteau, figuring that it would be better for his leg if he weren't hobbled.

"What do you think of all this travelling?" Onida asked the raccoon.

He looked over at her when he heard her voice, but then went back to sniffing around a picnic table.

"Must be strange for you. Riding on great beasts all day, and spending every night in a different place. I wonder if you still know the way back to your home."

Mask waddled over to her, and placed his paws on her leg. He probably thought she had something for him, as she had occasionally slipped him a little treat from their supplies.

"Maybe you don't care," Onida continued, bending to pet his head. "You have Shawn, your family, and that's all you need."

Thinking of her own family caused her guts to twist into knots.

When Shawn returned, Onida had a low, smokeless fire going that they could use for cooking. It had just become dark, and the occasional mosquito fluttered over to harass Onida, but thankfully the lateness of the year reduced the biting insects to more tolerable levels than during the height of summer. Shawn walked over with two dead rabbits, a pheasant, and a porcupine. He had a good hunt. While Shawn skinned, gutted, and cooked the rabbits for dinner, Onida prepared the pheasant and porcupine for tomorrow's breakfast and lunch, as well as other ensuing meals. As she plucked the quills, she laid them out on a rag beside her, intent on keeping them despite not having an immediate use. Any feathers that might be good for arrows, she also set aside. The pheasant's long tail feathers she wove onto the side of Shawn's quiver as decoration. He didn't seem to mind.

Meal complete, and the rabbit skins taut in small stretching frames, Onida, Shawn, and Mask went into the visitor's centre to sleep. It was dark and musty inside. There was probably a large number of spiders, but Onida had never been bothered by arachnids all that much. Mask had explored the place earlier, when Onida had laid out the sleeping bags, but he gave the room they were staying in another once over, sticking his nose into all the corners and getting covered in dust.

Onida curled up inside her sleeping bag, grateful that it hadn't rained, and that she could keep on whichever articles of clothing she wished. She had gotten rather good at falling asleep despite being afraid, but on that night, she lay awake

114

for longer than usual. The old structure was strange to her, after she had spent so many nights in the tent, but she didn't think it was that. She was more afraid of the dark than usual. Something nagged at her. Some of her elders had told her that this could be a sign of the spirits trying to warn her, but she wasn't so sure. The spirits were unlikely to want anything to do with Onida. She closed her eyes and willed sleep to come.

***

A most mournful, haunting, and dangerous sound had both Shawn and Onida sitting bolt upright. Onida could hear her companion breathing rapidly in the dark.

"Wolves," Onida said as the sound came again. It was not as far away as she would have liked, and there was more than one voice calling.

"We have to bring the horses inside." Shawn's voice trembled with fear. Other than bears, Onida had thought he wasn't afraid of anything. It turned out that she was wrong, that he had an even greater fear of wolves than he did the mighty polar bears.

"Is there room for the horses?" Onida asked, scrambling out of her sleeping bag.

"We have to bring the horses inside," Shawn repeated, as though he hadn't understood her question.

Onida went over to the metal door and pushed it open, letting in the moonlight so that they could see. Shawn hadn't moved from his sleeping bag; he continued to sit there, staring with wide eyes. He had Mask cradled in his arms.

"Are you going to help or not?" Onida asked him.

He neither answered nor moved.

Annoyed, Onida placed a rock to hold open the door for her. It would be a tight fit for the horses to get through, but the bathrooms inside were fairly large and should be able to accommodate them all.

The horses were all agitated. They had heard the wolves too, and were afraid. Had they not been hobbled, they might have attempted to run off, even if it meant leaving Askuwheteau behind. Onida went to the most spirited horse first, and grabbed hold of his lead in order to bring him inside. She removed his hobble first, although she intended to put it back on once he was safe.

"Could you at least get up and move our gear out of the way?" Onida asked, practically begging, as she returned to the door and found Shawn still frozen with fear.

Mask's wiggling finally allowed him to escape out of his arms, which seemed to bring Shawn around.

"Can you make a light for me?"

Shawn finally helped, taking out a weird little lantern that he rarely used. It had a crank on the side, which had to be continuously turned for the light to work, and Shawn didn't like the noise much. This was an emergency, however, and neither they nor the horses would be too keen on a fire indoors.

As the gear was moved out of the way, Onida coaxed the first horse through the doorway. They hadn't yet heard the wolves a third time, but that only made Onida more fearful. They could be hunting, moving through the shadows, surrounding them.

The light wasn't a very strong one, but it was enough to navigate by. Shawn kept turning the crank, while Onida led the horse around the annoyingly tight turns of the female bathroom entrance.

There were several toilet stalls, and they were wider than Onida had thought they'd be. She walked the horse down to the end of the row, and tied his lead to the dead toilet's piping. Getting back out required crawling under the side of the stall, but Onida figured that having the partial walls between the horses' heads would prevent them from nipping at each other in irritation or fright. Now she had to get the rest of them.

Each time Onida walked a horse inside, Shawn worked the light. Outside, he didn't help with the horses, but instead put together hastily built fires along their perimeter. The picnic tables were dragged about and set alight in an attempt to keep the wolves at bay before they even appeared. Onida worried about the woods catching fire despite the recent rains, but she didn't say so to Shawn. Considering how frantically he worked at his fires, often muttering curses at his flint and steel, she didn't think anything she might say could get him to stop.

As Onida took hold of the second to last horse, the only one still wearing its hobble, the first wolf made its appearance. A luminous pair of yellow eyes flashed in the firelight. It was only for a moment, but Shawn had seen it and it was enough for him. Abandoning his latest fire along with Onida and the two remaining horses, he dashed inside and pulled shut the door, kicking away the rock with which Onida had propped it open.

"Fucker," Onida muttered.

Both Askuwheteau and Sokw, the horse Onida was currently holding, had become very agitated. Onida was barely able to keep her hold on Sokw's lead now that she had removed the hobble. And what of Askuwheteau? She couldn't just leave him tied up out here, alone, while she got Sokw inside. She didn't trust the fires to do their job of keeping the wolves back.

"Shawn!" she called, nearing the door. "Shawn! I need you! Get out here!"

Was that a slinking form between those trees?

"Shawn! Open the door!"

Frustrated, she knew she was going to have to do something she didn't want to in order to force him to help. Walking Sokw over to the flagpole, Onida tied her lead alongside Askuwheteau's. She needed to leave the two horses, but just for a moment, and hoped that the two of them could defend themselves should the wolves move in.

Running back to the door, Onida ripped it open. The firelight behind her revealed Shawn curled up in a terrified ball at the far side of the space, but that was all right. What Onida needed was much closer.

Mask wasn't at all afraid when Onida walked quickly toward him, although he cried out when she roughly scooped him up. Without a word, she carried Mask to the door.

Shawn screamed wordlessly. Onida didn't even look at him; she just walked straight outside with the raccoon. It was cruel, but if the possible threat to Mask could get Shawn to move, then so be it.

Onida waited outside near the horses, holding Mask in her arms. He seemed to sense the danger and went still, curling up in a tight ball, trusting her to protect him. Shawn's wailing continued, and Onida hoped the sound was more likely to frighten the wolves away than to draw them in as a wounded animal might. She watched the trees and the overgrowth, searching for any sign of movement. The dancing firelight made this difficult, and Onida wasn't always sure if what she saw was a circling wolf, or just a trick of her mind.

Finally, Shawn appeared in the doorway. He was a trembling mass of terror, his whole being drawn up into a tightly coiled beanpole. Tears glittered in his eyes, on his cheeks, and in his beard.

"Please," he begged, holding the door open but not taking that last step to exit the building. "Please. Bring him back. Bring him inside. Please. Please don't hurt him."

"I don't want to hurt him," Onida confessed. "I also don't want any of our horses to get hurt either and I need your help to ensure that."

Was that wood popping in the fire behind her, or a branch breaking? Onida wheeled around but saw nothing. She turned back to Shawn.

"I'm going to bring Sokw over to you. When I hand over her lead, I'll put Mask down so that he can go inside. You bring Sokw into the men's washroom while I get Askuwheteau, all right?"

"Yes, yes, just give me Mask back!"

Onida continued to cradle Mask in the crook of her arm, while she used her other hand to untie Sokw's lead. Once more, she walked the horse over toward the door.

"Come get it," Onida said, holding out the lead and insisting that Shawn take at least a few steps outside of the structure.

Shawn hesitated, still shaking like the flames of the fires around them. But then his eyes looked at Mask in Onida's arm and he found the courage to leave the safety of the rest stop. Once he took hold of Sokw's lead, Onida handed over Mask. The raccoon was most willing to be given back to his person, his little clawed hands gripping tightly to Shawn's shoulder.

While Shawn quickly retreated back through the door, coaxing Sokw to follow after him, Onida returned to Askuwheteau. He was highly agitated now. He could smell the wolves, and the flames weren't making him any calmer. The horse danced about, his hooves churning up the grass and dirt.

"Easy. Easy," Onida whispered as she approached.

Past the horse she could see a wolf. It stood just at the edge of the firelight, its eyes glowing. It was staring straight at Onida and Askuwheteau, as its upper lip trembled and revealed its vicious teeth. The smaller fires were already beginning to die down; only the picnic tables still burned brightly.

"Easy. Easy," Onida continued, although she drew her knife and now kept her eyes on the wolf. "Easy."

As she untied the long lead, a new sound drifted over that of the crackling flames. A low moan, almost unheard by Onida's ears, but definitely picked up by both Askuwheteau and the wolf. The wolf's head shot up, its eyes and ears instantly alerted in the direction from which the moan had come. Askuwheteau whinnied loudly and tossed his head. Onida was only saved from being picked up and thrown by the motion thanks to the length of the lead he was wearing.

The wolf turned and disappeared into the foliage, its head and tail tucked low. A second wolf ran past, through the open area, fearing something more than the fires. Onida turned to face those fears.

A zombie staggered into the light from the direction of the road. Just one wouldn't have chased off the wolves though, and so Onida knew that there must be plenty more behind it. Another loud groan only served to confirm this.

Onida pulled Askuwheteau toward the door. He wasn't keen on going, since it took him a few steps closer to the walking corpse, but Onida pulled hard and insistently. She locked eyes with the dead thing coming toward her and the horse, and held her knife at the ready. She hoped that Askuwheteau didn't bolt, as the tight grip she had on his lead would cause her to be dragged.

The sound of something ripping through the air by her ear startled Onida. The zombie went down, an arrow now protruding from its face.

"Hurry!" Shawn called from the doorway. His fear of the walking corpses was less than that of his fear of the wolves. As Onida approached with the horse, Shawn stepped outside so that he could continue to guard them with his bow while they entered.

Upon stepping into the structure, Onida saw that Shawn hadn't bothered to bring Sokw into one of the bathrooms, that she stood within the small area where their gear was still littered about, threatening to walk all over it. Mask couldn't be seen. Askuwheteau crowded up behind Onida and blocked off the light. The horse was eager to follow her through the tight doorway, preferring to move in any direction that took him away from the zombies.

"We're in!" Onida called out once she confirmed that Askuwheteau was completely through the opening.

Shawn slipped back inside and pulled the door shut, closing them up in darkness. The building was a good place to hide from the dead, since there were no windows that they could break through, and the walls were a solid brick.

"Work this," Shawn told Onida, thrusting a device into her hands. She wondered how he knew exactly where she had been standing.

Feeling the box, she realized that it was the crank light. She turned the handle, which was more difficult than she expected, and brought the thing to life.

"Point it at the door," Shawn instructed. He was far calmer now.

Onida did as he directed. She continued to turn the crank, and watched as Shawn tied a rope around the door's inner crash bar, and then the other end around an electrical pipe that connected a large light switch box to the other electrical piping along the ceiling. If one of the zombies out there was smart enough to know how to pull open a door, it still wouldn't be able to.

Shortly after Shawn finished his work, one of the dead smashed into the door, with a metallic and hollow bong.

"Let's get the horses settled," Shawn said, as though there wasn't something currently trying to get in. He took the light from Onida so that they could move Sokw and then Askuwheteau into the bathrooms.

Mask climbed up onto Shawn's shoulders while they worked, clearly missing his carry pouch.

***

Onida was surprised that she could sleep at all with the zombies outside, but the next day she found herself rising up out of a dreamless slumber. It was strangely silent, as nothing was banging on the door anymore. She wondered what time it was. A bird singing somewhere beyond the walls suggested that it was at least daylight.

Whether she woke Shawn, or Shawn woke her, there was no way of knowing, but they were both up at relatively the same time. Shawn used his light so that they could check on the horses, and then go investigate the door. When knocking on it received no response, Shawn untied the rope so that they could push it open. Bright sunlight flooded into the rest stop.

Walking outside, they looked about the area. A single corpse lay on the gravel with an arrow still sticking out of it. The picnic table fires were now just black spots among the grass, a few still smoking a little. An area of torn up grass suggested where Askuwheteau had been. Only these three things and nothing more hinted at what had actually happened last night.

Shawn walked over to the dead and pulled his arrow out of it.

"Let's eat breakfast and then get the horses outside. We should get moving."

Onida was inclined to agree.

II: Underground

Were the other bunkers like this? It was a thought that often crossed Mariah's mind. Sometimes she was thinking about the governmental bunkers that must exist elsewhere beneath her country, at other times she was thinking about those in foreign countries. Royalty, presidents, other important heads of various states: it was likely that they had all been brought to such places when things got bad.

None of those important people were in her bunker. She probably shouldn't have been in there herself; she was just a lowly aide who got swept up in the evacuation. Today was a day when she couldn't remember who she had aided. Maybe they had been important. Maybe there used to be an important person down there with her. Her memory wasn't so good anymore. Sometimes she thought she had early onset Alzheimer's, but if she did, it was *really* early onset. Besides, she always remembered that it took her thirty-two steps to reach the bathroom from her bunk. There were six concrete slab tiles that made up the ceiling of the operations room. It was good to swap out the air-filters whenever the orange light came on, and clean the dirty ones. She must *never* go into the north end. These were all good things to remember.

Mariah's days were simple enough. Check for orange lights, cook the day's meals, exercise, see if her plants were growing, and try three passwords in the operations room. At least, Mariah thought these were her days. She didn't actually know when one day became the next. She couldn't get into the operations computers to see what was going on, and there were no clocks: none where she was anyway. Maybe there was a clock in the north end. She would never know. She must never go into the north end.

"Hello," she greeted Sheiffer on her way to the kitchen. Sheiffer never greeted her back. He—or maybe she?—was a skeleton in a military uniform with the name Sheiffer on it. Mariah sometimes got confused by Sheiffer. A real skeleton? A fake one? Not a skeleton at all? Sheiffer sometimes made her sad, but he was her only company. She never remembered cleaning the flesh off his bones, and so assumed someone else must have done it. Someone in the north end. She must never go into the north end.

The kitchen was very well stocked. Mariah had never counted the supplies, but there were years' and years' worth. She didn't think she would ever go hungry. Her main concern was the hydro generator. Its turbines were pushed by the raging, underground river that passed along the east side of the place. Mariah liked to listen to the river through the walls. If something ever happened to the hydro generator, she could access it through a room on that side, but to get there, she would have to go through part of the north end. And she must never go into the north end. Never. It didn't matter that that's where the door to the surface lay. The surface could be a toxic wasteland for all she knew. Until she got into the operations room computers, she'd have no idea. So without knowing, it was best to never go into the north end. That's where the bad things happened. The bad things that Mariah didn't like to think about. The things she hid from, both physically when they had occurred, and mentally now that they had been over for years. The door to the north end remained sealed, her only company on this side being Sheiffer. She remembered closing the door. She remembered a woman—an aide like her?—running and screaming for her to wait. Mariah had not waited. She couldn't wait. She didn't know the woman. Maybe she was on the side of those doing the bad things. It was better to be safe than to be executed.

In Mariah's mind, it was better to be safe than anything else. Not even her all consuming loneliness or boredom could put a dent in that mentality. Safety was everything. Safety was life. Routine was safety. What would happen if she finally figured out the code to turn on the computers?

SECTION 3:
HELP

13: MISHA
5 DAYS AFTER THE BOMBING

Despite the lack of any real threats, only the stray zombie here and there, Misha couldn't shake the feeling that something was wrong. At random times throughout the day, he would turn around, looking past Angela, even though she was doing the job of guarding their rear just as well as Misha could. His dogs never alerted him to anything that would explain why he felt the way he did. Despite all this, he remained jumpy, alert for any possible danger, or even just something that seemed off.

When they reached the bay, they made a stop to refill their water canisters and wash the shirts and pants they had worn while dealing with the zombies in the small container yard. Misha knelt in the shallow water, scrubbing himself and watching his dog pack hunt for something to eat. He also watched the nearby buildings, picking up on every small movement, which always turned out to be either the wind or a bird. No one was successful in catching any fish, but once they got moving again, Crichton walked down near the water, holding a long stick; it trailed a line with a hook and lure attached to the end that he had made himself.

They travelled a good distance that day, doing their best to make up for the delay caused by the container yard zombies. They might have been able to make it to the Black Box that day had that problem not occurred, but as it stood, they would definitely reach it the following afternoon. It would be better than arriving in the evening anyway.

As night fell, they found themselves settling into a laundromat, its double doors missing, leaving a large enough hole for the horses and cart. The plan was to partly block the opening with some of the washing machines when they went to sleep, as clearly others had done before based on the shifted machines and scrapes covering the floor.

"You've been jittery all day," Crichton commented to Misha as the two of them accompanied the horses to graze, with the dogs roaming nearby.

"I can't shake the feeling that something's wrong," Misha admitted. "Ever since Rifle reacted to something in that alley, it's felt like... I don't know."

"Like we're being watched?"

"Maybe. Do you feel that way?"

"No. But we're moving toward potentially hostile territory, so I suppose it's only natural you'd be extra wary."

Crichton's words made sense, but Misha didn't think that was it. He would have felt like this earlier if that were true. Was it because of the zombie attack? Misha remembered the suffocating feeling in his mask, wondering if it was somehow related. Was it possible that he was finally cracking up? That he had finally reached the point where his mind was breaking down? He didn't want to believe that it was true, but it had happened to others, and at calmer times than this. The skin on Misha's back crawled at the idea that maybe he could no longer trust his own senses, his own mind.

Because they couldn't completely block the entrance, they organized a watch detail for the night. Ki-Nam had the first post, but Misha found himself restless and unable to sleep. He could see his feeling of anxiety was affecting his dog pack, who also struggled to find comfortable spots, often getting up and circling another area of the laundromat. Eventually, Misha gave up on sleep and went to sit with Ki-Nam where they could both see outside. He had the second watch anyway.

"I've been mildly curious about something," Ki-Nam whispered in the dark. "Are you one of the Russians who came across in the submarine? I detect a similar accent."

"I'm not," Misha told him. He knew that over the years his accent had changed, becoming less pronounced, but the Russian still clung to certain syllables. "I am from Russia though. I was attending college in Leighton when the Day happened."

Ki-Nam nodded, satisfied with his answer.

"Where are you from?" Misha decided to ask. "You also have an accent that's different."

"I'm from North Korea originally."

"Were you here before the Day, or did you find your way across an ocean afterward?"

Ki-Nam didn't answer, so Misha didn't pry.

"Angela, she is Texan?" Ki-Nam eventually asked instead.

"I guess so." Misha never really thought much about where people had originally come from before joining their group. "She was living in the Black Box when we found her, and I guess her accent is Texan."

"Harry is from Leighton like you are," it wasn't a question this time; it seemed Ki-Nam already knew. "And while Crichton was living there when what you call the Day happened, he has lived in many places around the world."

Misha had no response to that. Ki-Nam was generally a quiet individual, however he clearly had an interest in people's origins, and had asked a few questions regarding the topic.

"You have a large variety of people living at your container yard," Ki-Nam eventually spoke again. "They come from many places."

"The subs had a lot to do with that," Misha said. "Especially the German sub. It picked up a bunch of people in Europe before meeting up with us."

"That's when you lived on the cruise ship, correct?"

"Yeah."

"Which came from Canada. The world has lost its borders."

"I guess," Misha shrugged. "You could make the argument that our wall of shipping containers is a border."

This seemed to please Ki-Nam. "Yes, I suppose you could."

They lapsed back into silence, and this time neither of them chose to break it. Not until Ki-Nam's shift ended, and he went off to bed with a quiet goodnight.

Misha didn't like keeping watch alone. He had enjoyed sitting beside Ki-Nam, because his calm presence kept Misha calm. Now, it was just him and his nerves, and a slight distrust of his senses. What if he saw something? What if he *thought* he saw something? Misha didn't want to overreact and wake up the others for nothing, but then he also didn't want to let something slip by in an attempt to overcompensate for his fear. It was a tough predicament.

Eventually, Misha briefly left his post in order to wake up Bullet. Having the dog sitting with him helped to put him at ease. If there was something to really worry about, Bullet would know. Unless it was a sniper. There was never anything anyone could do about a sniper who decided to fire. Not for the first shot, at least.

Misha found himself wishing that Alec was still around. It had been five years since the bomb in their room aboard the Diana had killed him. A former military sniper, he always had an air of confidence about him. Even while in his wheelchair, Alec always seemed to know what to do. Misha often had no idea what to do in most situations, always relying on his instincts to get him through. It had worked so far, but such luck could change in an instant.

Bullet had been lying with his head on Misha's lap, more asleep than awake, when he suddenly lifted it up. His ears perked up, as they and his muzzle pointed toward a nail salon that was across the street and a few doors over. Misha felt his spine solidify, but he didn't move. He watched the nail salon: both its dark interior and the roofline. When Bullet got up on his feet, his attention still completely focused on the building, Misha knew there was definitely something over there. But what was it? Something he needed to wake up the others for, or something he could handle on his own?

"Stay," Misha whispered into Bullet's ear, reinforcing the command with hand gestures.

Bullet stayed put. The dog hadn't lowered his head or tail, but Misha wasn't sure which of two things that might mean; Bullet had not yet identified what had drawn his attention, or he had determined that it wasn't a threat. Misha felt compelled to find out, but told the dog to stay where he was in order to protect his sleeping friends.

As he was crossing the street in a swift crouch, Misha pulled his machete out of its sheath. He pressed himself up against the building, hoping there weren't a pair of eyes watching him. Wondering if maybe this was the stupidest thing he had ever decided to do, Misha made his way toward the nail salon. Before reaching its cracked window, he glanced back at Bullet. The dog was standing in the same position with the same posture as when Misha had left. Was that a good sign, or a bad one?

Holding his breath, Misha crouched down and peered through the corner of the window, trying to present as small a target as possible. The moon didn't provide much light, and the row of chairs and the reception desk cast even more shadows. Waiting until he was forced to exhale, Misha saw no signs of movement. Either it was something on the roof that Bullet had noticed, or Misha would have to go inside to find the culprit.

Looking back at the Australian shepherd, Misha saw that he had sat down, but remained alert. It was possible he was just watching Misha now, however. If only the animals could talk, situations like this would be a lot easier to deal with.

Keeping his eyes on the shadows within, Misha kept low, and did an awkward side-scuttle toward the door. He noticed there was a pile of old leaves and dirt where the building met the sidewalk, including along the base of the door. If the door had been opened, then that pile would have been disturbed. If someone *were* inside, then they hadn't entered through the front door.

Looking through the glass in the door, which gave him a different angle of the interior, Misha still couldn't see any movement, or unusual shapes. The nail salon didn't seem like the kind of place to have a rear exit, but he couldn't be certain. He wasn't about to go check the back of the strip of shops by himself, and he didn't want to go through the front without knowing what might be in there.

Deciding the nail salon wasn't worth it, Misha hurried back over to the laundromat and his guard post. Bullet was pleased when he sat back down beside him, especially when Misha scratched his ears. For the rest of his shift, Misha paid particular attention to the roof across the street.

"Hey," Harry whispered, having woken himself for the next block of guard duty. He sat down on the other side of Bullet. "Anything happen?"

"Not sure," Misha admitted, whispering at the same volume as Harry. "Bullet became alert to something near that nail salon over there. I went over and looked inside, but couldn't see anything, and it doesn't look like the door's been opened for some time. I don't know if there's a back door, and though I haven't seen anything, there might be something on the roof."

"Didn't you think there might have been something on the roof of the bar as well?"

"Rifle alerted me that time."

"Do you think we're being followed?"

Misha didn't want to answer that question. If he said no, then what would Harry think was actually going on? And if he said yes, and there was nothing, then Misha was paranoid. And he certainly felt paranoid. No one else had seen or heard anything. Misha himself hadn't; it was entirely his interpretation of how his dogs reacted to an unknown entity. Maybe Crichton was right. Maybe Misha was just super nervous knowing they were heading toward a place where they last knew hostiles to be.

When he laid down on his bedroll, and Rifle partly woke up in order to flop over against his back, Misha found his body was exceptionally tired. His mind still wouldn't shut up, however, constantly running through various scenarios that might explain recent events. He was trying to convince himself that he wasn't crazy, while also fearing that he was.

***

No one else reported anything strange in the night. Misha was exhausted and definitely looked it, so Crichton had him drive the cart. Misha didn't know horses nearly as well as he knew dogs, however, Thumper and Potato required very little guidance. Rifle was very happy to have Misha up on the driver's bench with him. The rest of the dogs seemed annoyed that they couldn't ride on the cart as well.

Because the horses required such little guidance from Misha, he ended up watching his dogs more than them. He kept expecting one of them to react to some stimulus that was unseen and unheard by the humans. He was just waiting for them to become curious about a roofline, but it never happened.

When they came to a massive tree that had fallen across the road, their journey was once more delayed. Misha wanted to go around, but Crichton insisted that they cut it up. The container yard needed firewood after all. It was hard work with only hand tools, but it managed to keep Misha distracted as he sawed away with the back of his machete. The task consumed the rest of the day, so they set up camp in a spacious dance studio. Despite being exhausted, Misha still struggled to sleep, so the next morning, Crichton stuck him on the cart again. It had been more than a day since his dogs had alerted him to anything, but Misha just couldn't shake the feeling of something being wrong. After loading up several large pieces of wood on the cart and stashing the rest for later pickup, they continued on their way to the Black Box with aching limbs.

They soon reached the two bridges that weren't far from their destination. One supported a road, the other a rail line. Because of the cart, they had to cross the road bridge. Burnt out vehicles were dotted about and needed to be avoided, yet Misha spent half the time twisted around, watching the end of the bridge behind them.

"Think we're being followed?" Angela asked him as she walked alongside the cart.

"I don't know. Just making sure."

"Could be one of those bastards that attacked us. They might have travelled that far and are now following us back."

"You would know what they're capable of better than I would." Misha thought that they seemed like the kind of people who would have attacked already, and not spooked them like this.

"I *hope* there's still a few kicking around. I'd love the chance to personally kill one of the bastards."

Misha wondered if that was true, or just a show of bravado. He didn't know Angela very well and couldn't be certain.

At the far end of the bridge, they entered a wooded area. Misha took one last look back the way they had come. Had that been movement that he'd seen across the way? Or just a trick of the mind? It could have just as easily been a leaf or an old piece of trash catching the breeze. Misha faced forward once more and gripped the reins even tighter. He didn't like feeling this way, but he couldn't get his brain to stop. It was like being afraid of his own fear.

It didn't help matters when Harry began to periodically turn on the Geiger counter. They walked in a somewhat tighter group, accompanied by the sound of a crackling tick. Every time the ticks increased, no matter how minutely and only ever for a second or two, the little hairs on Misha's arms stood up. While there had been no confirmation of a radiation leak, he found that he was becoming increasingly itchy as they neared the Black Box. At least this time he knew it was just his body reacting to his worries, and it gave him something to fret about that wasn't a ghost on their tail.

Before the border of the Black Box community came into sight, Crichton had them stop between some buildings.

"Angela, I want you to stay here with the cart and horses," Crichton told her.

"What? No. I need to see what's left!"

"And you will. But I don't want to risk the horses. I need Harry and Misha with me, and I'm not sure I totally trust Ki-Nam not to leave without us." Crichton turned to the man in question. "No offence."

Ki-Nam gave a sort of shrug and nod, a gesture that suggested he understood and wasn't offended in the slightest.

"As soon as we know it's safe, I'll come get you."

"This better not be because I'm a woman," Angela growled.

"You know that it's not."

Misha reluctantly climbed down off the driver's bench so that Angela could take his place.

"Do you want me to leave any of the dogs with you?" he asked.

"No, I'll be fine." She was still sour about being left behind, but was allowing it to happen.

Misha gathered his dog pack to him, clustering them around the four people who would be continuing onward. Harry's Geiger counter was constantly on now. Misha was glad that the dogs didn't know what it was, and therefore could concentrate on listening for other sounds. All Misha could really hear was the ticking. His heart was beating a faster rhythm than the counter as they moved out.

They went slowly, wary of what they might find. It worked out for Rifle, who kept close to Misha's side. Where the other dogs tended to sniff about, he kept his head up and ears alert. Bullet attempted to imitate him, but he was more easily distracted, especially when it seemed that another dog had found a good scent.

When the fence first came into view, everything appeared normal. Harry handed the Geiger counter over to Crichton, freeing up his hands so that he could have an arrow at the ready. Misha wished his gun had some bullets in it, that it was more useful than a club. Maybe he should hold it in his hands? At least make it look like he was capable of shooting someone?

When they reached the fence, they were able to see the surface of the earth above the area where the Black Box had once been. The fields in which their crops had grown were in total turmoil. Chunks of concrete and rebar had pierced the surface. Dirt and stones had been completely turned over, burying the greenery beneath them.

"Let's take a closer look." Crichton guided them along the fence toward the nearest opening. It wasn't the usual spot people had used to pass through the fence, but new holes had formed when the ground beneath some fence posts had given way. They trod cautiously over the debris, unsure of where there might still be sinkholes.

Crichton led them along the edge of the territory to start with, since the ground tended to be safest there, even untouched in various spots. As they studied the devastation in worse areas, Misha thought about how lucky the team had been that had set off the bombs. They could have easily been sucked downward, or buried by falling debris.

The Geiger counter continued to click at safe levels, and so far, no one had seen any signs of a living hostile.

"The crops that survived have been picked over," Harry pointed out.

"Probably by the survivors who were already above ground," Crichton theorized. "If I were them, I would have taken what I could carry and gotten the hell out of this place."

"Then let's hope they're like you."

The dogs were curious about what had happened here. They stepped carefully, noses to the ground. Powder snapped up an unsuspecting rat, so the team kept an extra eye out for them, but the dogs weren't acting like there were many in the area.

When the four humans decided to pick their way to the centre of where the Black Box's many spider web levels had overlapped the most, they didn't get far. A vast, sunken pit had taken over the site, which had then filled with water to form a new, small lake.

Crichton touched the water and tasted his fingers. "Salt water."

"Must be from the river," Harry pointed toward the barge dock that remained intact. "The internal water filtration system must have blown, allowing the river to flow down into any voids left behind." Before moving to the container yard, Harry had studied all the Black Box systems, putting his engineer's mind to good use as he taught people how they worked, just in case one should break down.

"It doesn't leave much for us to look at," Crichton commented.

"Yes, but it will help contain the nuclear material buried underneath all this slag." Harry had been taking readings continuously, and found they were perfectly safe.

"Well, I think it's safe to say that this place has been cleared out of the attacking force. Misha, go get Angela and the cart. Let's see if we can save any of these plants to bring home with us."

Although it had been proven safe, Misha was glad to be leaving the new lake. The thought of those waters possibly touching nuclear material made him view it as poisoned, despite the fact that it didn't work that way. Only the water next to the nuclear source would be dangerous, and that was considerably farther down.

Misha instructed most of his dogs to stay behind, in case more rats poked their noses out. The churned-up soil and twisted debris piles on the surface would make good burrows for the dangerous critters. Misha took only Rifle, Bullet, and Trigger to go get Angela and the horses.

After getting back outside the fence, Misha stopped for a moment to check on Trigger. She still felt quite pregnant, but, so far, hadn't started searching for nesting to suggest she'd be giving birth soon. She also appeared to be all right despite all the travelling. There were no injuries that Misha could see, and she wasn't walking in a way that suggested she was in much discomfort. Rifle, on the other hand, had already tired from their exploration of the Black Box.

"You can lie on the cart again real soon," Misha promised him.

He scrutinized the buildings as they walked between them, fully expecting one of the dogs to react to some unseen stimulus. But none of them did, which brought a little relief mixed with a little disappointment. Misha still hoped that they weren't being followed by anything, but at the same time, he'd feel better about himself if it turned out that they were.

Angela was sitting bolt upright on the cart, hyper alert. She didn't even relax when she saw Misha coming.

"What's the matter?" Misha wondered, immediately thinking she had seen or heard some phantom.

"Are they all dead?"

"Who? Crichton, Harry, and Ki-Nam? They're fine."

"No, the assholes who stole the Black Box from us."

"Oh. We didn't see any. Not even signs that they may have been there recently. Did you see something?"

"No." She sounded disappointed.

"Come on. There's not much to salvage, but there may be a few plants we can bring back with us."

Misha lifted Rifle up onto the driver's bench before they headed out. The German shepherd promptly lay down with a satisfied huff.

Back at the Black Box, which was now more of a crater than anything else, it took them a while to find a safe spot for the cart and horses to cross the fence. Plenty of ground outside of it was safe, but they thought it would be more prudent to have them inside should any zombies arrive. Travelling around beyond the fence, they came across a few of the undead that had been killed and left to rot. It was likely they had been enticed to the site by the explosion, and subsequently killed by the survivors. Eventually Crichton cut a hole in the fence with some wire cutters, allowing the cart to be driven into the most stable section of land. Angela immediately went back out to search for any more signs of the men and women who had taken her home from her, and where they might have gone.

Misha explored a little more, making his way toward the barge dock. It was still covered in the zombie slop they had launched from the submarine. Arms, legs, heads, and unidentifiable innards had made for an excellent distraction. Misha had been part of one of the teams hauling on ropes to launch their makeshift trebuchets. It was interesting to see his work from the other side. They had made one hell of a mess, even before the explosives had gone off.

On his way back up the hill, Misha came across the crane that had once been used as a lookout. Part of the ground beneath it had given way, so that the whole structure was now lying at a severe angle. The arm at the top had smashed into the ground, preventing the whole thing from falling flat. The angle where the two massive sets of struts met was still higher than anything else in the area. It could again be used as a lookout, provided it was secure. Misha decided to climb up to the apex, taking his time in case it proved to be unstable.

Sitting on the highest section of the downed crane, Misha found himself over the edge of the lake that was closest to the river. From up there, he could see just about all of the devastation at once. Even better, he had a fairly clear view of the area that lay beyond the fences. There was no one sneaking around out there. The only movement he saw was Angela returning to help explore the interior.

They spent all day crawling about the crater and its surrounding land. They discovered a few ripe crops that had been overlooked, and picked them clean. Those that weren't yet ripe, were carefully dug up in order to be transplanted back at the container yard. Where they would transplant them, they didn't know yet, for the container yard was mostly concrete, and Animal Island didn't have room. Perhaps they could use Quarantine Island, since it had been a long time since they had needed to use it. Or they could just keep them in the piles of dirt they ended up filling most of their cart with.

"Find anything interesting outside the fences?" Harry asked Angela when they had all gathered together for dinner. They had decided to spend the night in the area, figuring the fence, the dogs, and everyone taking a guard shift would be enough to protect them. They used a bit of rope to temporarily hold the hole they had cut in the fence for the cart, closed.

"Mostly just dead zombies, but I did come across some graves," Angela told them.

"Graves?" Crichton raised his head from the water he had been boiling. He intended to top up their canisters with water from the lake, which Misha wasn't too enthused about.

"Yeah. I couldn't tell how fresh. Best guess, some of those fuckers weren't completely buried, or got so badly hurt that they didn't survive. Those that did, buried them instead of burning them. The graves weren't even that deep; they were pretty shallow."

"And how do you know how deep the graves were?" Crichton asked.

Misha couldn't picture Angela digging up graves, not even with her furious anger. Piss and spit, and maybe even shit on them, sure, but not dig them up.

"Either one of them went zombie, or an animal dug it up," Angela explained, not offended in the slightest at the suggestion that maybe she had disturbed the graves. "I didn't see a body, just a divot where the grave should be, and a slightly bigger hole at one end. Hell, one of the bodies I assumed was a dead zombie, could have been the grave corpse for all I know. I'm just happy to see that some of them died."

"A whole lot of them died," Harry muttered. "We've been moving around on top of them all day."

Misha looked at the ground. Because they were camped out on a spot that had remained level, untouched by the blast, they weren't currently on top of the mass grave, but they were beside it. Misha had never believed in ghosts, but given his current state of mind, he became unsettled by the idea of so many buried corpses so close. For all he knew, there was someone still alive down there, trapped in a pocket that had gone untouched by either the explosion or the flooding. Misha shuddered, imagining what it would be like to be trapped in the dark, with little to no food and no hope of getting out. While he hated what those people had done, he didn't wish that fate on anybody. If someone had become trapped, he hoped they had the means of killing themselves before it got too bad.

Everyone bedded down around the cart. Misha, Angela, and Crichton all slept underneath it, while Ki-Nam chose to sleep on the driver's bench. The horses had been hobbled, just in case, but otherwise were free to shuffle about the area. Harry had the first nightshift. Misha told him how to keep Spring awake and engaged, so that the little dog could take out any rats the sleeping dogs might not sense. The plan was for at least one dog to stay awake with whoever was on guard duty.

That night, Misha fell asleep quite quickly. He was exhausted from his previous lack of sleep, and from the exertions that came with crawling around the blast site.

It felt like no time at all before Angela was shaking him awake. It was his turn to guard, and she had nothing to report. She took Misha's bedding just as Harry had taken hers when she went on shift. When Misha rotated off, he'd take over Crichton's spot beneath the cart.

Stock was the dog currently awake, but Misha got him to curl up and rest. He woke up Bullet to accompany him. Still half asleep, Misha walked around the area in order to become more alert. At times like this, he missed coffee. He checked on the horses first, both of which were content with where they were. Some damaged crops made for good fodder.

It was when Misha decided to check on all of his dogs that he realized something was wrong. He found the lumps of their bodies sleeping in a variety of places, but there weren't enough. He searched and searched, but one was missing.

"Rifle," he hissed in the night air. "Rifle, come here. Come here, *bratishka.*"

Panic started to grip Misha's throat, belly, and balls. Where was Rifle? Why wasn't he here? He wasn't the sort of dog to just go exploring on his own.

What if he had walked off to die?

Misha shoved the thought away the moment it had formed. No, Rifle was not dying. He had shown no signs of anything seriously wrong with him. And besides, he'd come to Misha. He wouldn't go off alone; that wasn't like him.

"Bullet, where's Rifle?" Misha turned to the Australian shepherd. "Where's Rifle? Find him. Find him, boy. Find Rifle."

Bullet understood, as Misha had trained him more than any of the other dogs. He was especially good at finding Rifle, because Misha had used the German shepherd in training Bullet the find command.

Almost instantly, Bullet was off. He would run a little way ahead, and then stop and look back to make sure Misha was following.

When Bullet crawled through an opening in the fence, Misha's heart dropped into his stomach.

14: JAMES
6 DAYS AFTER THE BOMBING

James watched Marissa impale another zombie on her spear, and then deftly kick it off. As the forward scout, she was dealing with more of the things than the rest of the group were. While they had to put up with those staggering in from the sides, she met with anything already in their path.

"Someone should join Marissa," James decided. "Or we should rotate the position of forward scout, so that she won't tire quicker than the rest of us."

"I'll join her," Lucy volunteered. She trotted forward until she was walking beside Marissa, blade in hand, prepared for the next zombie they met.

James was uneasy about all of the undead. They weren't killing all of them: that would take too much time and energy. Only the shuffling corpses that could reach them had their skulls bashed in or sharp objects driven into their brains. Those that they didn't bother with, the ones that couldn't catch them, were left behind to trail along in their wake. They would start to build up into a horde, and while the group could outpace the zombies during the day, they would eventually need to sleep. There was also the return trip to worry about. James didn't want to run into a horde of his own creation on his way home, which could happen even if he planned a different route to avoid the lions. During that hard-to-imagine future, there was a good chance that it would just be him and Katrina, with the two horses.

The group eventually reached farm country, and the end of where any scavenger teams had travelled before. Everyone grew nervous. Thinking of the lions, they were afraid of the long grass, and the long distances between structures in which they could shelter. Even the structures they did pass weren't always comforting, as some of them had started to rot and decay even before their inhabitants had gone.

"That's some nice looking wood," Samson commented on one of the dilapidated barns.

"I ain't going to help you haul any of it," Skip promptly informed him.

"I don't plan to take any of it." The eye roll was evident in Samson's voice. "I was just commenting that I liked the look of that wood."

"Maybe when things become less dangerous, a team could take the trip back out here to gather some of it," Belle suggested.

"What would you do with it?" Jack was genuinely curious.

"Might be nice to build a little house, instead of living in a container," Samson told him. "Do you plan to live in a container the rest of your life?"

"I never think about the future," Lindsay informed the group. "Spend too much time thinking about the future and you'll never live long enough to see it."

"That's bleak," Vin responded. "You have to think of the future at least a little bit. Or else what are you living for? What are your goals? What do you hope to do with the life you're so preciously clinging on to?"

"Shh," James ordered, halting the philosophical discussion. Ahead, Marissa and Lucy had come to a stop. Lucy had also signalled that those trailing a safe distance behind the pair should stop as well.

James strained his ears. He figured they must have heard something that he had missed over the sounds of voices and hooves. They weren't near any hills, bends in the road, or large obstructions that would allow the women to see anything that James couldn't from his position astride Soot. He scanned the area anyway. There was a barn a little way ahead and back from the road a bit, but not much else. Mostly there was just grass, weeds, and wildflowers. There might be some crops that managed to grow back each year hidden among the greenery, and a few shrubs and young trees attempting to claim a space, but these were all things they had walked past before.

A wave of wind washed over the land, rustling all the plant life. It came off the field to their right, and gusted past the group. On that wind, Soot and Spark both caught the scent of something they didn't like. With a toss of his head, Soot shied away from the field. Spark danced in place. The fact that neither of them whinnied was especially disconcerting.

Lucy had been watching the group, and saw the horses' reactions. She and Marissa turned to come back, to increase their numbers and talk about what was going on.

"Do you think it's lions?" James asked in a whisper once they had returned.

"Worse," Marissa whispered back.

"What could be worse than lions?" Aaron's voice rose a little louder than James would have liked.

Lucy answered him. "I think we've got a pig problem."

James swallowed hard as a prolonged silence enveloped the group. Pigs *were* worse than lions. They reacted to the virus the same way that humans did: total zombification. Finding uninfected pigs in the wild these days was incredibly rare. The shipping container community bred their own from pigs that had been found near the start of the outbreak. They assumed the handful of non-infected pigs the scavengers had snared over the years, had been bred by people who had kept them safely in captivity and that they had merely escaped. While coming across a healthy pig was a major boon, coming across an infected pig was the complete opposite. Zombie pigs were different from zombie humans in that they retained the ability to run far more often. And they could run fast.

"Group together, same way as we did with the lions," James ordered. "We don't yet have confirmation that it's pigs. You didn't see anything, right?" James asked Marissa and Lucy.

Both women shook their heads and Marissa said, "I'm fairly certain I heard a squeal."

Because zombie pigs were so dangerous, even the slightest possibility that they could be in the area meant the group had to take every precaution.

"Based on the way the horses reacted, we know there's at least something on the right," James continued. "But that doesn't mean there might not be something on the left as well. You all know what to do, so let's get moving."

Back in their defensive circle once more, they followed the road that would one day disappear. Weeds had found plenty of places to grab hold along the cracked pavement. Some of them were tall enough to brush along Soot's belly. James would have felt better if the road had remained intact. Not a lot better, but it would have been nice to have at least somewhat of a clear space in which to operate, like they had had in the suburbs.

From his elevated position, James spotted some rustling a distance off to the right. He brought the group to a halt. While both were dangerous, the main difference between lions and zombified pigs, was that if the pigs knew you were there, they would definitely attack. Even if shelter were within easy reach, if the pigs saw them go inside, they would wait forever for the humans to come back out. There was a slim chance that they could sneak past the pigs, but standing their ground and fighting them off was likely to be their only option.

When there was no follow-up movement, James had them start walking forward again. Of course, there was the possibility that there were no pigs there, that Marissa had been mistaken about hearing a squeal.

But she hadn't been mistaken. This time they all heard it, as the high-pitched sound cut through the air. In its wake, all the insects fell momentarily silent, as though they too had something to fear. And that sound had definitely not come from a healthy pig. There was a tearing, shrieking quality to it, that James had never heard himself, but had had described to him many times, back when they had lived aboard the Diana, and he had organized the scavenger teams. He had heard all the reports of when those teams had come across infected boars on the islands. Being told what they sounded like, and hearing the death squealing for himself, were completely different experiences.

Another rustling, this time to the left and closer to their position. James brought them to another halt. The worst thing about zombie pigs is that they are rarely ever alone.

A bird, some sort of grouse, burst up from the grass in a flurry of feathers and beating wings. The whole group startled, a squeak escaping one of them. Soot snorted loudly.

And then, when their focus had been drawn to the left, a pig came charging at them from the right.

Jack screamed as it lunged straight at him. He panicked and tried to back up into the middle of the circle, only to crash into Spark's flank. Jack had only a knife, and no real experience with pigs. He slashed ineffectually at its rotting snout, and then it had him. Jack's scream jumped an octave as the teeth of the pig latched onto his knee.

Spark was frightened, pushing over Katrina and Skip as he bullied his way out from the center of the quickly collapsing ring. Katrina curled up into a tight ball around her rifle, as afraid of the hooves passing over her as she was of the pig so close by. Skip was less fortunate: his left hand got caught and crunched beneath Spark's rear hoof. The weight of the horse instantly snapped his bones, drawing out Skip's screams to harmonize with Jack's.

A second pig came at them from the right. Samson was ready for it, bracing himself with his spear and allowing the animal to impale itself.

Under James, Soot was terrified and nearly bolted. By the time James got him back under a modicum of control and turned him around, it was too late for Jack. The first pig had got him on the ground and had moved from his knee to his balls. Even if he didn't bleed out, his system was being flooded with active infection.

Marissa and Belle attacked the first pig, finally killing it before it could decide that it was done with Jack.

A third pig burst out of the field on their left. Aaron wasn't fast enough to react, but when the pig grabbed his ankle, he did manage to keep to his feet. Unfortunately, the pig's lowered head protected it from the hatchet Aaron wielded in terror, hacking at the thing's shoulders.

A fourth pig arriving on the scene drew the attention of Lindsay, Lucy, and Vin, who focused their counter-attack efforts against it.

James kicked at Soot's flanks. The horse wanted to run, no matter the direction in which James had pointed him. Nearly trampling Katrina and Skip a second time, the horse thundered past them, straight at the pig who had Aaron. Massive hooves crashed through the rotted flesh, snapping the bones beneath. Aaron stumbled backward, his ankle suddenly freed. James brought Soot around in a tight circle. The horse now understood that it could fight back, even more so since the pig could barely move with its spine already shattered. Soot stomped, and bounced, slamming his front hooves down on the pig, over and over again, until it was a pulpy smear on the road. James had to hold on tightly to keep from falling.

Belle put Jack out of his misery and prevented him from turning, while Marissa and Samson went to Aaron.

"Wait, wait, wait, wait," Aaron kept urging as Samson held him down and Marissa rolled up his pant leg.

Lindsay and Vin soon joined to help, while Lucy went over to Skip and Katrina to check on them. It seemed that there were no more pigs.

"Wait, wait, wait, wait!" Aaron's voice took on a higher pitch as a clean blade was produced. His words were suddenly muffled by a strap of thick leather that was jammed between his teeth.

James got Soot back under control and helped Katrina retrieve Spark from where he had trotted a short distance away into one of the fields. Once Katrina mounted up, the two of them rode in circles around the wounded group, on the lookout for any pigs that had lagged behind the other four.

Aaron eventually passed out during the amputation of his leg. It was the only way to save him from the zombie infection. Whether he would die anyway from shock, blood loss, or a different infection altogether, they would have to wait and see.

"We need to get inside somewhere," Lindsay barked once the procedure was complete.

Samson produced a small, folding stretcher from his gear. They couldn't trust Aaron to stay on a horse unconscious without lashing him to it, so they thought it might be safer to just carry him. With Vin holding up one end, and Samson the other, Aaron was brought along on the stretcher. Marissa carried his pack for him, and Lucy grabbed what could be salvaged from Jack. It seemed another night of mourning was in order, and this time they didn't have lion meat to help ease their loss.

Skip groaned and whined as they walked, his injured hand cradled to his chest. Katrina remained mounted, hyper alert to any other possible threats that might be hiding nearby.

At the very next farmhouse they came to, they broke in and made themselves at home. The injured were hustled upstairs, where whatever administrations could be done were carried out. A fire was hastily built in a bathtub up there so that Aaron's leg could be cauterized, hopefully before he woke up again. It was debated whether Skip's hand should be amputated as well.

James stayed downstairs. He could hear everyone upstairs rushing around, their hurried footfalls thumping through the ceiling. The horses wouldn't easily fit through the front door, but they were all right standing within the screened-in porch for a time. James limped around with his bad foot, making sure the house they had chosen was secure. Katrina remained with the horses, trying to calm them down enough to convince them to pass through the narrower door, while Vin investigated the cellar.

As the adrenaline started to wear off, James collapsed into an overstuffed chair in the living room. A large dust cloud puffed out of it and set him to coughing. Katrina managed to get the horses through the door and into the safety of the living room after removing their tack. They stood there, looking wholly out of place, as she started to brush them down. The ruckus upstairs had quieted. Some of the group came down, while others decided to remain up there. James was told that, for the moment, Skip was to keep his hand. It was to be monitored closely and might still be amputated at a later date. Despite Skip being told that waiting could result in part, or even all, of his arm having to come off with the hand, he insisted on waiting.

When Vin returned from the cellar, he reported finding a pile of preservatives and pickles in jars.

"Don't eat any of it," James warned.

"Why? It doesn't look so bad. The thing hasn't bubbled." Vin had brought up what looked like a jar of jam, and tapped the top of the lid.

"That stuff is only good for about two years. Anything pickled lasts even less. Based on the level of dust and spider webs around this place, I'd say it's been a lot longer."

"Eaten a lot of bad jams, have you?"

"Yes, I have." Occasionally James had tested for himself the foods brought back to the Diana. While people like Cameron and Riley Bishop knew how long various foods lasted, the scavengers often decided to find out for themselves. More than once, James regretted that decision.

"The contents may be no good, but those are some good jars," Lindsay pointed out. "I'm thinking we should dump out what we can, and then wash them the next time we come across a water source."

Everyone else in the living room agreed. James remained seated, his foot bothering him, and Katrina continued to brush down the horses, but the others from the living room returned to the cellar to gather the jars.

"I bet you one of them tastes something," Katrina said.

"I wouldn't take that bet," James replied. The thing about hunger was that people didn't always listen when they were told not to eat something that looked like food.

Vin was the one who ended up tasting a jam, and he agreed that it shouldn't be eaten. No one tried any of the pickles, or the pickled fruits. Three jars per person were selected and emptied out back.

"I'm disappointed that there was no wine down there," Lindsay sighed.

"With our luck, it'd have turned to vinegar," Vin grumbled, clearly still disappointed that the preservatives hadn't worked out.

Knowing they'd be at the farmhouse for a while, a foraging team headed outside. They didn't go far, fearing there may be one last pig out there, but the field they were in was rather bountiful. Some berry bushes were located, as well as some tubers. A groundhog was almost caught, but managed to escape down its hole. James watched the brief excavation attempt through the living room window.

He worried about the water if they had to stay there very long.

***

Two nights were spent in the farmhouse. Food wasn't an issue, especially once they set up snares for the groundhogs and rabbits, but they hadn't been able to locate a water source. Even though the berries were extremely juicy, and they conserved their water as much as possible, they couldn't stay put. Knowing there was a predator out there, something that had dragged off Jack's body, didn't help.

"We'll have to carry him," James said to Katrina on the second morning, as the two of them sat on the steps that led up to the screened-in porch.

"We could strap him to a horse." Katrina didn't need to be told who they were talking about. Aaron had been the topic of many conversations lately. The man had developed a fever and was delirious much of the time. There was nothing they could do for his pain, and he occasionally had fits of screaming.

"And if the horse decides to bolt?"

"You expect us all to take turns carrying him on the stretcher?" Katrina shook her head. "No, we're not going to do that. If we get attacked again, we'll need all hands on deck."

"You know, if we hadn't had so many delays, we would likely have reached the first community by now." The people in their group were to make contact with a total of three communities. The first one, they would arrive at together, where they could hopefully bolster their supplies and receive more information on the others. One small group would head off toward the second community, with James and Katrina accompanying them about half way there. They were to split up then, and the two of them would ride the horses to the third community. All of these places felt so very far away when James thought about how much they had already gone through.

"I know." Katrina nodded. "And we have to strap Aaron to a horse and get him there. He needs medicine that we don't have. Maybe they do."

James sighed. Katrina was right, of course. "All right, we'll strap him to a horse. One last foraging team will head out, gathering what they can, and then we'll leave this place."

Katrina shot up onto her feet and headed inside to convince the others. James looked at the dead zombie about twenty feet away from him, its upper half tangled within the bush it had fallen upon. Aaron's screams had been luring the zombies toward the farmhouse, and while he could occasionally be muffled, they risked suffocating him every time they did. At least the zombies had been showing up alone or in pairs so far, and it proved that there were no more pigs in the area.

James got up and went back inside. His foot was having a relatively good day, but he chose not to join the foragers, and instead led the horses outside. They had gotten used to passing through a small doorway of the house and the larger doorway of the porch, for they had been brought in and out through them many times since arriving at the farmhouse. Outside there was food for them, but inside it was safe, and so they had gone back and forth depending on the threat level. Water for the horses needed to be found especially soon.

Just getting Aaron out of his bed and downstairs was an ordeal. They allowed the man to take a break on the couch before bringing him outside to the horses.

"Are we growing things?" he mumbled, his face pale and covered with sweat. He was staring at some of the horse shit that now perfumed the living room in the worst way. No one bothered to explain.

Aaron screamed as they manhandled him up onto the horse, and again when they tied down his amputated leg. It had been cut off at the knee, not leaving much for them to get a proper knot around, and so they had to focus mainly on his hips. The packs of the two dead men, as well as his own, were tied down in positions that offered him some support. If he needed to slump forward, the pack with the lion hide in it would provide a small modicum of comfort. Spark seemed a little confused, as he understood a human was now on his back, but that person was giving no orders, providing no directions.

When they headed out, James rode on Soot as close to Aaron's side as he could safely get. Sweat was pouring off the man, but he managed to stay conscious, his eyes up and staring between Spark's ears. He mumbled occasionally, which sometimes carried the tone of a question, but he was never loud enough for James to make out the words. And it seemed he was never expected to. Whoever Aaron was talking to, it wasn't him.

In the early afternoon, they finally came across a small, muddy stream. While not ideal for filling their containers, they did wash out the jars to prevent flies from being drawn to them. The horses drank greedily. Soot got a short break when James hopped off his back, but Spark had to remain burdened.

They didn't stop for long, and were back on the road in no time. James hoped they left farm country soon. It usually provided more food to be foraged, but he felt too exposed in the open lands. Anything could be watching them from the undergrowth. James himself couldn't do much watching, since he had to concern himself with Aaron. He needed to lean over, a little precariously at times, to make sure the injured man drank some water. Everyone else had limited their water intake as much as they were able in order to allow Aaron to consume what he needed. They were sacrificing their own health in the hopes of keeping him alive. James knew that if this continued, they would grow to resent Aaron. Some of them might even start campaigning to leave him behind if he didn't begin to show some improvement soon.

Before nightfall, they reached an intersection of roads that must have seen a fair bit of traffic, for a number of buildings had been built in a cluster around it. To everyone's relief, the only dangers they came across getting there were a few easily dispatched zombies. A pair of coyotes had been spotted in the distance at one point, but the animals never came closer and weren't seen a second time.

"What building should we camp out in?" Katrina asked, having waited for the rest of the group to catch up with her and Skip. They had been taking a turn scouting ahead, Skip's hand held to his chest by a strap.

The decision came down to a garage adjacent to a gas station, or a post office.

"Garage has a better door for the horses to get in and out, but the post office has windows," Samson pointed out. "We'll be able to see if anything invades the streets while we sleep."

"Garage has more space," Lucy commented.

"Post office has thicker walls and security bars across the door," Lindsay came back with.

"The garage might have some tools in it," Vin suggested.

"I vote for the post office," James chimed in. "There's a chance there's carpeting in there, which would be better for Aaron to lie down on."

"Both of those points don't matter unless we look inside," Katrina said. "So why don't we do that? We're clearly not in a hurry to decide, so we'll scope out both places first."

This was agreed upon, and a small team was quickly formed to investigate both buildings. James did his best to check Aaron's temperature while they waited. He was still hot. They needed to get him off the horse and take another good look at his leg.

James watched with interest as the team, having checked out both locations, went on to investigate a third, and even stick their heads inside a fourth and fifth.

"There's nothing," Katrina reported when they returned.

"What do you mean 'nothing?'" James asked her.

"I mean there's nothing. This whole place has been stripped completely bare. Even the shelves are gone."

"Check all the buildings." James felt his heart kick up a notch, and all his senses became more alert.

"What's wrong?" Skip wondered.

"No one would strip a place completely bare unless they lived close by and had a use for everything. There might be someone here, so we have to check everywhere."

"We better do it fast then, because it'll be dark soon," Katrina pointed out.

Everyone was quickly divided into four teams of two, each team to check a quadrant of structures. James had to remain outside with the horses and Aaron, but he kept alert and offered advice.

"No need for a thorough search," he told them. "If someone is living there, they'll have likely made a barricade of some kind. Just test the doors. If you enter a building that doesn't look like it's been looted, take extra precaution, because you may have just entered their space. Make special note of basements. Don't bother to be quiet. Let any zombies inside come to you, and you don't want to scare any residents. Talk while you explore; let anyone living know your intentions. We don't want to hurt them, we just need a place to stay for the night, and would like to ask them a few questions about the area."

James was anxious as he monitored the teams. He had Soot trot from one corner to another as he watched the pairs enter buildings. He mentally checked off each one in his head as it was cleared. Every team signalled to him when they found nothing before moving on to the next place. There was only one house in the area, so most of the buildings didn't have very many rooms to investigate. Windows flashed and glowed, as the sinking sun required the use of lights indoors, allowing the progress of the teams to be monitored even more closely.

After it had become fully dark, the last team finished with the last structure, and returned to where the group had gathered in the intersection. Belle shrugged as she joined the larger circle of light cast by the gathering.

"Nothing," she said. "There's nothing here."

James looked up all three of the streets they hadn't travelled. Someone must live on one of them, but which one? And how far away were they? Before the sun had set, he hadn't been able to see any other structures in which a person might take shelter, not even another farmhouse.

"Let's get inside." Katrina turned and headed for the post office. Decision made.

Aaron groaned as Spark began walking. The horse had stood still for so long, that he had managed to fall asleep in the saddle for a little bit. The movement jarred him awake once more.

Outside the post office, they had to untie Aaron in order to get him inside. His scream was weaker this time, as he was dragged off the horse and lowered to the stretcher. Once Aaron had been hustled into the building, James dismounted in order to lead Soot through the small door. Although he had been getting used to riding, his legs were still sore whenever he got out of the saddle.

In discussing where to stay, they should have given more weight to the fact that the garage was larger. The horses stood together, filling the space before the front desk. Everyone else clustered behind it. At least there weren't any shelves to contend with, thanks to whoever had stripped the place clean. The cramped quarters also required less light to illuminate it. By the time James had entered and gotten Soot settled, Aaron's leg had already been inspected, and the bandages changed. He didn't bother to ask what it looked like. He would only get a false answer, seeing as how Aaron would hear it as well. James could see the truth on people's faces, anyway, and smell the stink of disease in the air. The prognosis wasn't good.

After laying out his bedding, James nibbled on a few berries he had picked from beside the muddy stream. His fear all but negated his hunger, but he figured having some food in his stomach would help him sleep. It did not.

For a few hours, James just lay there on his bedding, eyes closed. He wasn't totally conscious, but drifting through the realm of half-sleep where every little noise brought him fully awake again. After one such disturbance, he realized he had to pee.

James carefully made his way around the counter, and past the horses. The beasts were likely to relieve themselves inside. James didn't feel comfortable doing that. He paused at the front windows and peered out. The moonlit crossroads were as empty as when they had first arrived. Looking up at the sky, James could see that a few wisps of cloud were starting to move in from the east, blocking out parts of the explosion of stars overhead. Maybe they would get some rain on their travels. Even just a short break from the relentless sun sounded great, whether it brought rain or not, so hopefully the wisps turned into actual clouds by morning.

After waiting a minute without seeing or hearing anything outside, James slipped out through the door. He limped over to the corner of the building. If someone else woke up, they should be able to see him through the window without seeing his junk. It was the most privacy James would allow himself. Had he needed to empty his bowels, he wasn't sure exactly where he'd do it, and was glad that it was a non-issue for the time being.

After pissing onto the dust and leaves that had accumulated at the base of the building, James zipped up and located the nearest, non-poisonous plant on which to wipe his hands. As he stood back upright, James heard a slight scraping sound behind him, like a boot on the pavement.

Instead of wheeling around, James threw back his elbow. If it had been a zombie, he would have likely knocked it over. But it was not a zombie. A human had been behind him, a very fast and intelligent one who seemed to be expecting the blow. James' elbow was caught at the same moment his bad foot was kicked out from under him. He opened his mouth to scream, to warn the others, but instead got a taste of fabric as a rag was shoved between his jaws. James screamed anyway, hoping someone might hear the muffled sound. Since he was off balance, it was easy for his attacker to bring him all the way down to the ground, his stomach meeting the road. Before James could fight to get the knees off his back, he felt the cold muzzle of a pistol placed against the back of his head. James went still, and held his hands out in submission. Perhaps this was someone who could be reasoned with. They could've just shot him outright, after all.

15: DAKOTA
6 DAYS AFTER THE BOMBING

Dakota would have liked to spend more time on the wall with Elijah, but the sun had set. She was told that she wasn't allowed to stay up there once it got dark, and she wasn't about to risk disobeying and losing her newly given privileges. If Freya decided that Dakota wasn't responsible enough to use a sling, then it would be given to someone else.

"Thanks for the company," Elijah said after Dakota explained that she had to go.

"Thanks for the zombie killing lesson." Immediately, she thought she should have said something else, but there was no way to take her words back.

"See you around."

"Yeah, see you." Dakota carried his food container along with her plate, figuring she might as well bring it back to the community centre now, so that he wouldn't have to when his shift was over.

Back down on the ground, she felt buoyant, like she might start skipping at any moment. Skipping sounded incredibly lame though, so she resisted the urge. Still, she had gotten to talk to Elijah! She had learned his name and that he was only three years older than her! Three years wasn't that much, was it? She knew adults who were together who had far greater age gaps between them. Becky's foster parents for instance, were separated by more than ten years, as far as Dakota could tell.

Stupid, get your head out of the clouds, Dakota chastised herself. Elijah wouldn't be interested in a ridiculous fifteen-year-old like her. The difference between fifteen and eighteen was greater than that between forty and fifty. And besides, Dakota was awkward, and had a weird smile, and practically no boobs compared to the other girls around her age. She wasn't attractive like Josephine, or funny like Terry. She was just Dakota, the girl with the cowboy hat.

Upon reaching the community centre, she returned the dishes. By the time she walked back outside, she didn't know what to do with herself. She was too wired to go to bed, and she didn't feel like tidying up her container again, especially if Cameron was already there, for she would ask questions that Dakota didn't want to answer.

"Dakota?"

She startled, thinking Cameron had found her anyway. But when she turned, it was only Riley.

"Sorry," she apologized for startling her. "You were pretty lost in thought, I guess."

"It's okay. I was just trying to think of something to do. I'm not ready to sleep yet."

"I was about to inventory another box of medical supplies if you'd like to help."

Dakota shrugged. "Sure, why not." She followed the doctor back into the community centre.

Riley explained that she had been inventorying one box a night, when she had a bit of time and there wasn't really anyone in the community centre to get in the way.

"My stitches tend to get itchy around this time," she said as she chose that night's box and they found seats. "I like to have something to occupy my hands and mind."

Dakota couldn't help but feel sorry for Riley, and not just because of her recent surgery. Although the teenager knew in the conscious levels of her mind that it wasn't her fault, her subconscious still wanted to take the blame for Riley's husband's death. The night the Diana sank, Dakota, Hope, and Peter had been separated from their minders and ended up alone in a room instead of going to the evacuation points. They could have been burned to death that night, or at least died of smoke inhalation, if it weren't for Mathias locating them. In order to rescue the children, he had to throw them all over the side of the ship, into the sea, and then jumped in after them. When a life raft was finally picking them up, Mathias was taken by a shark. Dakota didn't see it. All she knew was that one minute he was about to get into the raft, and the next he was gone. No matter what anyone said, not even Dakota to herself, she kept thinking that if she had just taken charge, if she had just led Hope and Peter to one of the evacuation points, none of that would have happened. Hope would still have her dad and Riley would still have her husband. It wasn't often that the guilt twisted itself around her guts, but it had been happening more frequently ever since Riley had had her surgery. She was forced to go through that without Mathias to comfort her. And if Riley had died, Hope would then have no parents.

"So what has you so deep in thought?" Riley finally asked.

Dakota shrugged. "Just stuff."

"Stuff, huh? Any of this stuff something you need to talk about with someone who isn't Cameron or Brunt?"

"No."

"I see you have one of Freya's slings," she changed topics. "Are you enjoying your lessons with her?"

This was the kind of question Dakota had expected to be asked by Cameron, and was exactly why she hadn't gone home yet. "I guess," she answered, trying not to sigh about her ill luck.

But Riley was different from Cameron in that she stopped pushing for answers when she saw Dakota didn't want to talk. That didn't mean that she wasn't going to tell her twin, however, and Dakota would have to have a similar conversation later.

It didn't take long to inventory the box of supplies. When they finished, Riley thanked her for her help, and went to check on the few patients who still slept on cots in the community centre.

Back outside, Dakota made her way through the moonlight. She took a circuitous route back to her container, avoiding as many people as she could. It had been a very strange day, and she attempted to organize her thoughts. It wasn't as easy as organizing the medical supplies had been when placing them back in their box. Her thoughts and feelings about how well her meeting with

Elijah had gone were especially conflicted. She didn't really want to bring herself down, but she also couldn't let herself get her hopes up too high.

She thought about Elijah's shoulder against the back of her own, his arm practically around her as he helped hold the spear. His skin had been very warm.

Entering her home, Dakota found that Cameron wasn't back yet, but Brunt was.

"I hear you killed your first zombie today," he said by way of greeting.

"Yeah." Dakota didn't really want to talk about it with him. She didn't want to bring up Elijah for fear that Brunt would somehow pick up on her feelings for the eighteen-year-old.

"Great job." Brunt was smiling. "I'm proud of you."

His words shocked Dakota somewhat. She hadn't been expecting them. She couldn't remember anyone ever telling her before that she had made them feel proud.

"Thanks," Dakota said, not knowing how else to respond.

"How do you feel about it?"

"I don't know," Dakota shrugged. "Fine, I guess."

"You grew up with zombies, so I suppose it's different for you. You understand what you're doing, that the woman was already dead."

"Yeah."

"I know a lot of people who didn't get to have that comforting knowledge beforehand." Brunt had never really talked to Dakota much about the Day, especially not in personal terms.

"I guess it was a lot harder for you guys, huh?"

"Some. I mean, I worked for Keystone so I had some idea about what was going on. Still, it wasn't exactly normalized like it is now. No matter what you tell yourself, you're still seeing a person at that point, ya know?"

"I guess so." Dakota thought it must have been a little like her guilt. It didn't matter what thoughts the logical side of the brain produced, the emotional side was going to feel what it was going to feel.

"But yeah, I'm proud of you," Brunt told her again as he snapped out of his own reverie. "You weren't too scared, were you?"

"No. I was safe on the wall, and had a guard with me."

"Yeah, Elijah mentioned that you were pretty cool about the whole thing."

Elijah said I was pretty cool? Dakota's brain nearly stalled out.

"He said that you'd probably make a good wall guard if that's what you wanted to do."

"I don't know." Dakota hoped her voice didn't betray her humming nerves. "I have to finish training before deciding anything like that. Bronislav has a plan for us."

"Between you, me, and the walls, I'm not sure how much of a plan it is. I think he just wants to make sure all you kids are ready should something else bad come our way while we're split up and weakened like this."

"Maybe." But Dakota didn't believe that. She felt certain that Bronislav was going to continue to put them to use even after a planting field was made ready. "I'm pretty tired. I should get to bed."

"Right, of course. You have another day of training tomorrow."

Dakota changed behind the privacy screen. While she was climbing onto the top bunk, Cameron returned. She was exhausted; apparently it had been sheep shearing day, and the sheep had been very uncooperative. It meant that she didn't want to talk to anyone, just sleep, which suited Dakota just fine.

Her mind chased itself in circles around the day's events until it couldn't remain conscious any longer.

***

Freya and Bronislav kept Dakota very busy. She had to jog before breakfast, and then practice her knife technique afterward. Her blade glinted in the sunlight. She had been trusted with the sharp implement several years ago, but this was the first time she had ever been given permission to stab something. Sure, it was only an old plastic buoy, one that had become so cracked as to be useless for anything else, but it was something.

Lunch was eaten with all the other trainees, gathered together in a cluster before the one blackboard in the community centre that wasn't covered in names, tasks, and locations. Bronislav walked them through various scenarios that could occur outside the wall, and how they should attempt to respond to each one. It was interesting that he himself used the word attempt, for he understood that they were unlikely to end up in such neatly organized situations, and that emotions sometimes made it difficult to remember lessons taught in such a calm environment. Freya translated everything Bronislav said into sign language. It was a nice refresher for Dakota, and probably helped the new kids learn.

After what was the closest thing they got to a school lesson lately, Freya took Dakota and the other chosen teens to practice with their slings. They were getting better, but to Dakota, it still seemed like they hit things more by luck than skill. At least the majority of the stones had all gone in the right direction: fewer than a handful released way too early, way too late, or gone off ridiculously far to either side. Dakota had looked for Elijah up on the wall when they approached their practice area, as well as every time they had to gather their stones and when Freya stopped them all to give an individual a piece of advice. She never saw him though.

Of course not, he has to watch outward, not inward, Dakota told herself. Or alternatively, *why would he care what* you're *doing?* And sometimes she simply thought, *maybe he's stationed at a different part of the wall today.* She tried to keep these thoughts from interfering with learning how to sling stones, but that was something easier said than done.

After the slinging lessons, Freya had them practice their co-operative hunting skills. She herself was the target, and all the group had to do was touch her with just one hand. Even though there were six of them, this seemed like an impossible task. Freya was fast, and even when they managed to surround her, she slipped past their fingers as though repelled from them by magnets. She also had a lot more stamina, or was otherwise much better at hiding her exhaustion. After she had called a halt to the game, and gathered her pursuers to her, she explained all the things they had done wrong. Dakota was embarrassed by some of their missteps, especially the ones committed by her personally.

Dinner went the same way as it had the previous night. Dakota was given a stack of food containers to deliver to the guards along the wall. She chose the same spot as last time, hoping to get to sit with Elijah again. But it was not to be. He wasn't anywhere along the same stretch as before, but Brunt was. He was the second person she came across, and so, after delivering the rest of the meals, she returned to eat with him.

"You look like you're about ready to drop dead," Brunt commented. "What did Bronislav have you doing today?"

"A group of us had to try to catch Freya." Dakota took her hat off in the shade of the containers cast by the lowering sun. Both she and the hat were quite sweaty. Was that good or bad for her pimples? She couldn't remember.

"So you were given an impossible task, huh?" Brunt chuckled.

"Pretty much. There were six of us, and yet we still couldn't tag her even once."

"Don't feel bad about it. I don't think even Misha's dogs could catch that woman."

"Where do you think they are right now?"

"The dogs? I don't know. Enough time has passed for them to have reached the Black Box by now. They could already be on their way back, depending on what it's like over there, and what kind of obstacles they may have run into along the way. You worried?"

"No, just curious."

"They could be back any day now, if everything went smoothly."

"Do you think things went smoothly?"

"I'm not going to lie; they very likely came across a number of things that could slow them down. We don't know what that mega horde has done to the landscape out there."

"When will people start worrying about them?"

"There are some people who are worried about them already. Cameron, for one. She's been worried since the moment they all left."

"Yeah, but I mean, when will people start worrying that too much time has passed? When should we start thinking that something really bad happened to them?"

"Not for a while yet. The group that went over to the Black Box is very capable. They can handle just about anything that comes their way." Brunt placed his hand on Dakota's shoulder in an attempt at a comforting gesture.

They didn't talk much after that, just watched the space between the wall and the unchecked containers. There were no zombies that night.

The next morning started the same as the previous, with Dakota and the others running laps around the container yard. Freya kept ahead of the group, setting the pace, while Bronislav hung back to monitor and encourage the youngest ones who couldn't keep up. The only difference was the tendrils of gauzy clouds that occasionally blocked some of the sunlight. By breakfast, however, plans had to change.

The only man who knew how to read the weather signs well enough to predict anything ahead of time, had gone with one of the envoy groups. As such, they had no warning before the wall of dark clouds was spotted on the horizon, and no way of knowing how bad such a storm might be. Rain was often a blessing, but it could also mean their death if they weren't prepared. If they were ever directly hit by a hurricane, they could all be easily washed away. It was generally thought that the last storm that hit, the one that came before all the attacks, was the edge of a major storm that had made landfall elsewhere. If they were lucky, this would skirt around them as well.

"All right, kids," Bronislav's voice boomed as he walked over to his blackboard. Those who hadn't yet finished their breakfast were quick to shovel it down. "Today you're to be given your first assignment, and it's a very important one. You're all going to help button this place down before the storm hits us. You up for it?"

There was a lot of enthusiastic nodding as some replied "yes, sir!"

"Excellent. Here's what we need to do."

Dakota's first task was to gather some rebar from a stockpile they kept in one of the containers that made up the second layer of the wall. As she went up there, she noticed there were far fewer guards on duty than usual. Bronislav had pulled some of them to help with other tasks that needed doing before the storm came.

There was no guard at the container Dakota went to, so she had to open the doors herself. She felt exposed, being alone in the opening. Looking outward, there was nothing to see that she hadn't seen before, but it was still unnerving. Maybe because she knew that on a normal day, teams would be out there, opening the containers that could be reached and identifying the contents, but none of the days lately had been normal. Dakota ended up opening the container doors on either side, blocking off her view of the outside world, so that no one out there could see her. The doors would have to be closed again later, but gathering the rebar was going to take a few trips anyway.

The rebar was very long, longer than the spear she had used to kill her first zombie. It was awkward, and heavy, and she could carry only three at a time if she didn't want to drag any of it. Not having been told what it was going to be used for, she opted not to drag it. At least the length made it easy to get down off the container wall, as she could easily prop them up against the inner side before climbing down.

The first load she carried over to the end of the first row of containers, which consisted of the container streets Blue Square on one side, and Green Plus on the other. A pair of wall guards were waiting for her.

During her training, Dakota had seen some people using hand tools to burrow holes into the massive cement pad that made up the container yard's ground. She had been curious when she saw people doing that, wondering what they were up to, but hadn't bothered to ask. It was clearly a task that had been organized by Bronislav, Boyle, and even Crichton, as the work had started before anyone had left. As she watched now, one piece of rebar was lifted up and slotted into the hole, which was as close to the row of containers as they could make it. It didn't slot into the rough hole all that well. Based on the hammer and ladder nearby, the guards knew this would be the case. She imagined that once they got enough of the rebar in, one would climb up onto the container and hammer it the rest of the way home.

One of the guards saw that Dakota was just standing there. "Go on," he said. "Go get the rest. We need one for every hole."

Dakota saw that there were four holes along the ground, two beside each container. When she looked up, she saw another team of two waiting beside the next row. She ran off to get more rebar.

It turned out that it didn't matter if one end was dragged along the ground, so Dakota did just that in order to haul more along at once. The work quickly tired her out, and she wished Freya and Bronislav hadn't made her run that morning. It wasn't their fault; they didn't know a storm was coming, but still. Based on what Dakota overheard as she went back and forth, the storm was slow moving, but still coming straight toward them. Even on the wall, she had yet to see it. A spotter, lying flat on top of the wall's second layer, was monitoring its progress through a pair of high-powered binoculars.

Once Dakota had outpaced the teams waiting for the rebar, she allowed herself to slow down a little. She dragged four at a time, laying them down at the end of each row, so that once one of the three teams installing them had finished with their current task, the next was ready for them. Her legs felt like lead, making climbing up and down the ladder especially difficult. She eventually figured out how many were needed in total, as more were to go in at the far end of the rows as well, and propped them all up along the inner side of the wall. She had once complained that math seemed like a useless skill, and yet she had just used some to save her having to climb the ladder needlessly. She knew a couple of people who would be amused by that fact.

One of the pieces of rebar was badly rusted, and snapped as Dakota was dragging it. She screamed, tired and frustrated and knowing it meant getting another piece down from the wall. She would get that one last. The broken piece she just left where it had snapped off, dropping the other half to join it. Another kid had been given the job of gathering up loose items like them and putting them somewhere secure. The next time she picked up a load, she checked all the rebar for rust, and set aside three that looked like they might also snap. That meant grabbing four more from above: a whole load.

By the time Dakota finished her task, it was well past her usual lunchtime, and she was starving. Dragging her feet, her arms hanging dead at her sides, she made her way to the community centre. More clouds had appeared overhead: not the black clouds of the storm, but more white wisps that were being pushed along ahead of it. She had just been able to make out the storm clouds as she grabbed the last load from the top of the wall, and understood why everyone had become so worried.

None of her friends were in the community centre, so Dakota found a table where she could eat alone. She wasn't alone for very long, however.

"Mind if I sit here?"

Dakota told herself to remain calm about Elijah's sudden appearance. "No, go ahead." Her exhaustion made it easier.

"Thanks. So what do they have you doing?"

"I was carrying rebar. I just finished though, so I don't know what I'm supposed to do next yet."

"The rebar they're hammering in beside the containers?"

"Yeah."

"Are they that worried the storm might move them?"

Dakota shrugged. "The end containers were actually bolted down in place, so I don't know why they think the rebar is needed as well. What have you been doing?"

"Paddling a chicken kayak. They're moving the chickens to one of the containers, so I'm helping them come across."

"Sounds like not so fun."

"I'll say." Elijah pulled up his sleeves to show her where a few of the chickens had scratched and pecked at him. "My ankles are worse. They did not like being put in the bottom of the kayak."

"I didn't expect they would."

"At least their poop was contained down there, although it still smelled like you wouldn't believe."

Dakota laughed when he did. "Are they moving all the animals off the island?"

"I think so. Does that normally happen?"

"No. They must be really worried about this storm."

"Have you been hit by bad ones before?"

"Pretty bad." Dakota shrugged, not really knowing what he considered a bad one. "I know that people worry about a hurricane hitting us directly."

"Hurricane?"

"Yeah, they hit along the coast from time to time. We've never taken a direct hit, but we've gotten a ton of rain from the edges of them."

"I've never seen the ocean before. I don't know much about hurricanes."

"Really? You've never seen the ocean before?" As someone who had lived for five years with the horizon all around, it was strange for Dakota to think that some people had never seen it.

"I grew up inland. It wasn't until two years ago that I had to move, and eventually joined up with Evans' party."

Dakota wondered why he had to move, but resisted asking. The details didn't really matter, did they? All asking would likely do was dredge up pain. "After the storm, you should go down to the shore and see it. The ocean, I mean. I mean, technically, yeah, our bay is a part of the ocean, but it's not the same as seeing it stretch all the way away." Dakota stared down at her food, feeling like a moron after saying all that.

"Maybe I will," Elijah said, his tone neither suggesting it was a good idea nor a bad one, leaving Dakota to torment herself about it.

They lapsed back into silence. Dakota thought that maybe he was thinking about his reasons for having to move. She shouldn't have questioned him about having never seen the ocean. That was stupid of her. Eating a little faster, she hoped to get back to work sooner and forget that this awkward moment had ever happened.

"Can I comment on something I noticed while living here?" Elijah asked before Dakota could finish her meal.

"I guess."

"You all talk with your hands a lot." He mimed sign language as he spoke.

"Sorry." Dakota noticed she signed the word as she said it. Hopefully he just thought it was a joke. "We all know sign language, more or less. I don't know about everyone, but my age group was taught by signing while we speak, so it became a bit of a habit. I think we also keep doing it because it helps to keep those who don't get out and use it much from losing the language."

Elijah nodded. "I've been getting lessons, but I don't know much more than numbers and a few letters right now."

"They always start with numbers and letters. That way you can at least spell out whatever you mean, if you need to."

"If only my spelling weren't so atrocious, then that might be useful." Elijah grinned to indicate that this was a joke, so Dakota laughed.

"Well, I'm done eating," Dakota observed. "I should go find out what they want me to do next."

"See you later."

"Yeah, see you."

Her meeting with Elijah had thrown her into an emotional turmoil again, so Dakota was looking forward to her next assignment to provide some distraction. No one in the community centre had a job for her, but they did tell Dakota that Bronislav could be found over by the submarine, so she headed that way. The clouds overhead had thickened while she had eaten. The sun and sky were now completely hidden by a layer of grey, that got darker toward the direction of the sea.

"Dakota, finish your task?" Bronislav asked as he spotted her walking down the dock. On the submarine, men worked to remove the plates of metal that had been used as a sort of armour for the deck. They weren't even trying to save the bullet-riddled hulks of scrap. One dropped off with a great splash as it was cut free, and then swiftly sank. The cranes were already gone.

"All the rebar's been delivered." As Dakota walked, she noticed that large spools of heavy ropes and chains had been rolled out of storage. It looked like they intended to attach one end to the rebar, and maybe wrap the ropes around the fronts of the containers or over the tops, she couldn't say.

"I've already asked your foster mother this, and she said it's okay, but feel free to reject the next task I have for you."

Dakota immediately stood up straighter. What task could Bronislav give her that she was allowed to say no to? Something dangerous?

"This dock is not a good one for the submarine to be tied alongside when the storm hits," Bronislav explained. "We're going to sail her out to sea, where she can hopefully dive beneath the storm and ride it out, safe from harm. Enough crew were left behind here to pilot her, but I'm asking for a few more hands to join us should we suddenly need them. We're unlikely to, but I would feel better about it. How would you like to be my personal assistant on board?"

"Me?" Dakota wasn't sure she had heard right.

"I've asked some of the more mature young ones already. They'll be assisting some others on board. Shadowing them, if you will. It could come in handy, having some more people know a thing or two about the submarine."

Dakota stared at the sub. "And Cameron said that it's okay?"

"You'll likely be much safer on the submarine than you will be on land."

"Yes. Yes, I want to assist you on the submarine."

"Excellent. We're still getting her ready to go, but stick close to me. I may need you to run a few messages before we depart."

Dakota forgot all about her conversation with Elijah in an instant. This was definitely the most exciting part of the day. She was finally going to get to ride in the submarine!

16: EVANS
6 DAYS AFTER THE BOMBING

Waiting at the rendezvous point had been nerve wracking. Every time a silent one showed up, Evans wondered if it was someone from their group, or some spy that was infiltrating their numbers. At least he knew when Gerald arrived. The teenager was accompanied by two others, who were leading him with hands on his shoulders.

"Evans," he hissed, a little more loudly than anyone would have liked.

"I'm right here," Evans whispered back.

"Jesus, I thought they were leading me away to kill me or something."

"You kept your mouth shut, though?"

"Yeah, yeah, I kept quiet. Pretty sure someone would have stabbed me if I hadn't."

"Good."

Evans had spent the time waiting figuring out where they were, and which way would be the best to get to their destination. Thankfully, they were closer than when Evans and Gerald had first run into the silent ones, and they didn't need to go around their territory.

"Everyone is here," the silent one who had come to get Evans and Gerald told them once a final straggler had arrived.

"All right, let's get going then. I want to be as far away from here as possible by the time the sun comes up." And that was only a few hours away, as far as Evans could tell.

Evans led the way with Moe, the camels formed a neat line behind them, and the silent ones flanked the animals. Gerald stuck close to Evans, clearly not liking the idea of splitting up again.

They all walked in silence. Only Moe and the camels made the occasional noise, but nothing too loud. Evans had them follow a road for a short distance, then went overland for a while until they reached a different road. They didn't stay on that one long, turning at the next intersection. Evans didn't want to make it easy for anyone who might try to track them down come daylight. He deliberately took an odd route, one that didn't lead straight toward where they wanted to go. At least not during those early hours. Once he knew that they weren't being followed, he would choose the quickest path.

As the coming dawn began to turn the eastern horizon grey, Evans started to search for a place where they could stop and rest for a little while. He also had a few questions for the silent ones.

"What about there?" Gerald pointed ahead and a little to the west. He had been watching Evans and recognized when he started to look for a rest stop.

"It'll do, provided the weather holds." The place Gerald had pointed out was a rather drafty looking barn, but it was large enough to hold everyone, as well as the camels and Moe.

Evans led them across a field that had become dry and dusty. Without tilling and irrigation, it had reverted back to a patch of land that was inhospitable to most plants. Although weeds still managed to find several places to grow.

The barn was old and ill built. The boards that made up its sides weren't flush together, and there were holes in the roof. When the sun finished rising, it would be fairly well lit. Rotten hay sat in piles in a couple of corners.

"Watch for mice, rats, and snakes," Evans warned as they all entered. "We'll stop here for a few hours, and then move on. I suggest you nap if you can."

Many of the silent ones took bedrolls off the camels and lay them out on the earthen floor. A few decided to explore the barn a little, stabbing at the hay to make sure there was nothing living in it. Evans noticed that out of the eleven silent ones, three were children. Other than that, he couldn't distinguish one from another. Considering how clean the streets were that they had lived on, Evans was a little surprised to see just how comfortable they were with the condition of the barn.

Evans himself didn't feel very tired, and after the ether, he wasn't sure he'd want to sleep even if he were. It wasn't often he willingly stayed up all night and the following day, but this particular situation called for the rare exception. Gerald was perfectly happy to take a nap, but one of the other silent ones stayed awake. He couldn't be certain, but Evans thought it might have been one of the guards who had accompanied their host. Whoever was beneath that heap of rags, they were continuing to keep an eye on Evans and Gerald. Evans didn't mind. He would have done the same if their positions were switched.

Moe had still not adjusted to the rags on his feet, which had become dirty and torn during their walk. Seeing that he would remain uncomfortable with them, Evans took the time to remove them. He left the other rags hanging from the horse's tack, and intended to keep his own on. It was decent camouflage. However, once the horse's feet were freed, he took the fur off from around his boots. His footfalls wouldn't be as quiet, but he'd rather have traction.

The rags taken care of, Evans went on to search through the gear that had been loaded onto Moe. He was most glad to discover that his sword had been returned to him. He didn't feel comfortable without it slung across his back. Gerald's knife was also among their packs, which he would be happy about. Still, Evans debated withholding it from him until the kid became more comfortable with the silent ones. Even now, despite feeling comfortable enough to sleep, Gerald had set up his bedding as far away from the others as he could.

The hours passed slowly, but at least it wasn't as silent as the cell had been. Evans listened to the birds outside sing their morning songs. A gentle breeze ruffled the weeds, and softly whistled through a few of the cracks in the barn. Moe and the camels kept moving about in the small space they had been allotted, scuffing the dirt with every footfall. Their breathing was heavier, more audible, than that of the sleeping humans. Evans stayed put after checking the gear, knowing his own footfalls might wake up the sound-sensitive silent ones, but the other person who was awake did not. He or she moved about, maintaining a constant patrol in case some critter came crawling out of the hay. Evans watched the way the silent one moved, trying to learn the secret of their stealth. The tattered rags made this difficult, since they hid and distorted the human body's natural lines and curves, including some of the ways they moved.

"All right, it's time to get up," Evans eventually spoke.

The silent ones all woke up right away, some even startling upright, fearing an attack. Gerald had to be lightly shaken.

"We'll eat, and then we'll head out," Evans told the group.

He watched as the silent ones picked out food from their gear upon the camels. When it looked like they were serving themselves fair to large sized portions, Evans intervened.

"Eat less," he advised them. "It will be hard, but you want to conserve your food. You never know what kinds of delays you may come across, and you can't always count on foraging to fill in the gaps. Eat only what you must, and save the rest."

The inexperienced travellers obeyed, allowing Evans to show them what a good meal size might be.

"I have a request for all of you," Evans told the silent ones as they ate, their hoods still hiding them in shadows. "I need to see all your faces, and I need names. I won't travel with strangers."

A flurry of sign language ruffled the rags, as the silent ones seemed to argue amongst themselves about this point. Gerald was eating his own meal on the other side of the barn, and didn't offer to translate any of it.

"Okay," one of the silent ones eventually whispered once their conversation had finished. There was still a hesitant pause before that one pulled down his hood. "My name is Ang."

"It's good to meet you, Ang. I'm Evans." He offered his hand to the silent one, who shook it.

One by one, the silent ones removed their hoods, and pulled down any scarves that were still up. Evans found out that he was wrong about there being three children. There were, in fact, only two. The third turned out to be a woman with dwarfism. Evans introduced himself to everyone, always offering his hand and not being offended when some of them didn't accept it.

"That's Gerald over there," Evans said by way of introduction. He noticed that the majority of the silent ones travelling with him were either quite young in appearance, or very old. Only two looked like they fell between thirty and seventy. One of them was Ang, and the other Evans felt certain was the one he had thought of as his host, the one who had introduced himself as Burt.

"Thank you for agreeing to do this," Burt said. All the silent ones continued to whisper, despite Evans speaking at a relatively normal volume. It was a habit for them, one that would likely be hard to break. Two of the silent ones hadn't yet spoken at all; their names had been given by one of the others.

"No need to thank me. We're making a fair trade. I get you to where you want to go in exchange for you letting me out of that cage."

Ang and Burt both nodded.

"Now, let's get some ground rules out of the way," Evans addressed the group. "When I speak, I highly suggest you listen. You waited until I could bring you before leaving because you wanted someone with travel experience to guide the way. Listen to that experience. If you see anything you think might pose a threat, you let the group know. Better to be over cautious than surprised by something deadly. Also, point out food and water sources if you think I haven't noticed them. Don't eat anything you don't recognize. In fact, even if you do think you recognize it, it's probably best to ask me first. In the past, I've mistaken one plant for another, and let me tell you that you don't want to do that. Until I get to know you all better, I want you to keep your scarves off."

A ripple of discomfort went through the silent ones.

"I know." Evans nodded his head. "You're not used to your faces being visible. But I can't yet tell you apart when they're hidden, so I need you to keep them off. You can keep your hoods up while we're walking. In fact, I advise it to protect you from the sun." Evans himself had gotten more sunburns over the years than he cared to think about. He assumed that if something else didn't get him first, skin cancer would be the thing that ultimately took him down. "I believe that about covers it for now. If you have any questions, don't hesitate to ask. There are no stupid questions." Evans waited a moment to see if there were any right off the bat, but no one spoke up. "All right, finish your breakfast and then let's get going."

While the silent ones finished up, Evans walked over to Gerald. The teenager had already packed up all his stuff and was ready to head out.

"You should try talking to some of them," Evans advised.

"Why?"

"Because it's a lot better knowing the people you're travelling with. Several of them look like they're not too far off your own age. I'm sure they'd feel more comfortable not thinking of you as a stranger."

Gerald rolled his eyes. "Still seems pointless. Once you take me to that community, it's not like I'll ever see any of them again."

"Trust me, it's good to have contacts in other communities."

"Sure, whatever you say."

Evans hoped that he had used sarcasm just to be annoying, and not because he wasn't going to heed Evans' advice.

Once everyone was ready to go, Evans led them out of the barn. He handed Moe's reins to Gerald, and requested that Ang and Burt walk with him. They seemed the most likely to talk, and Evans still wanted a bit more information.

"Do you think we'll be pursued?" Evans asked in a low voice. He wasn't sure how much the silent ones wanted the two kids to know.

"Hard to say," Burt whispered back.

"But what do you think?"

"I think so, but not for long," Ang answered. "Having us walk all night, and again now, we will probably be far enough away by the time the sun sets that the others won't bother to come after us."

"Why did you want to leave so badly?"

Neither of the two men answered.

"Look, I need to know so that I can tell people to avoid that area if it's for a reason they disagree with. You clearly read my notebook. I'm assuming you chose the community you have, because it's the closest place without anything about it that makes you uncomfortable." Evans knew that the container yard might be a little bit closer, but he hadn't yet written about it in his notebook. He didn't want Gerald stealing it and finding his way back there, so he had planned to write about it after dropping the kid off.

Burt sighed. "It is a breeding place."

"A breeding place for what?"

Ang gestured to himself and then all the others.

"People?" Evans guessed.

"Yes," Burt nodded. "They think we need many more people to take back what we lost to the dead."

"Do they rape the women?" Evans felt his hand turn into a fist. He couldn't stand places that allowed that. He once helped set up an escape system for dozens of women who had found themselves in just that kind of trouble.

"No." Ang shook his head. "No, it's not that bad. The women have the right to chose, although they are pressured into having children. We all are. It made things very difficult for people like Burt and myself."

Evans looked from one to the other. He couldn't see why it would be particularly hard for them.

Burt caught the confused look on his face. "Ang and I are gay," he told Evans, somewhat hesitantly. He probably hadn't said that out loud in a long time.

"I understand. And the others? Did they just disagree with what was going on?"

"The old folk were worried about being put to death. They're still strong, but they know if they show any signs of weakening, of not being useful, they will be disposed of." Ang glanced over his shoulder, confirming that they were too far ahead for anyone to hear their whispers. "It's happened before. The weak are removed to make room for the strong."

"And the other three?"

"Each has a different reason." Burt shrugged. "Patterson is gay like we are, and also the mother of the two children. She didn't want her kids to grow up feeling trapped like she did. Blue had her tongue cut out for being too loud. Patrick has had the same treatment, by the way."

Evans knew that Patrick was one of the old folk.

"As for Dev, he never wanted to be there to begin with, but was caught like you and decided that assimilating was his safest bet. Kathy's always worried she'd be seen as a defect, and that she'd be completely removed from the gene pool."

Kathy was the one with dwarfism.

"So Gerald and I were caught to be assimilated?"

"You, definitely," Ang told him. "Even if you didn't want to join, you'd be forced to breed."

"I thought you said there wasn't rape?"

"The women aren't raped," Burt clarified. "They get to chose. Sometimes the men they pick don't get a say in the matter."

"Is there anyone else caged up there?" Evans was thinking that he might have to make his way back after seeing these people to safety.

"No. People haven't been caught in a long time."

"What would have happened to Gerald if he didn't assimilate?"

"He'd have been killed," Burt put simply.

Evans was definitely going to warn people away from the area. He would get the word spreading through the connected communities, so that no one else was snatched up.

"Is there anyone else who wanted to leave but couldn't come with you for any reason?" Evans asked.

Ang shook his head. "None that we could find. We had to be very careful in our planning, you understand."

"I understand." Perhaps Evans would gather a large, well-armed group and return to that place. He would challenge the silent ones to come out, and then invite anyone who wanted to leave to go with them.

He thought of the woman who had spoken to him while he had been trapped in the mud. The one with that twitch for a smile. Evans bet that she was the one who wanted to claim his genetics for herself.

"Thank you for telling me all of this," Evans eventually said.

"It's strange to have spoken of it," Burt admitted in his whisper voice. "We've kept it inside for so long."

"It's a relief to finally let an outsider know," Ang added.

Burt agreed with him.

The two men stopped speaking after that. It was probably the most they had said out loud in a very long time, and Evans doubted he would have gotten as many answers had they not shared the burden between them. He still had a few more questions, mostly about the size of the place and how they sustained themselves, but decided that those questions could wait.

Whenever zombies came, Evans had all his new travelling companions prove that they could kill them. Only the children were exempt from this, because at seven and five years of age, they couldn't be trusted to do the right thing even if they knew what that was. Evans was a little concerned when Kathy's turn came, as her low stature meant she couldn't reach a zombie's skull as easily as everyone else. She carried a javelin, however, which she could both throw with great accuracy, and use like a spear. After seeing how proficient she was with it, Evans saw there was no need for him to worry about her.

By nightfall, they reached the edge of another town, one that wasn't so suspiciously clean. An old clothing store, picked over by scavengers, became their camp. Evans had his new party pile up all the remaining racks and mannequins against the windows, and then set a watch schedule. Everyone was wiped. The silent ones had taken turns riding some of their camels, as they were unused to walking so much. The children even spent some time on Moe's back, learning the basics of horsemanship. Evans was used to walking, and did so all day despite his injuries. He needed to appear strong for the silent ones. When he finally got to lie down, he breathed a sigh of relief.

Gerald claimed a sleeping spot beside him, while the silent ones kept to themselves a little distance away.

"So did you try talking to any of them today?" Evans asked Gerald.

"A bit. They weren't really interested in talking."

"Did you try sign? They seem more open to using sign language."

"That's how I was trying. No one really wanted to have a conversation with me."

"Did any of them tell you anything?"

"Blue commented on the weather, and Elmore asked me my age. That was it."

"Did you see them talking to each other at all?"

"That Patterson woman sometimes signed with her kids. I couldn't catch it all, but it just generally seemed to be mom stuff. Asking how they were, warning them against doing stupid stuff, that kind of thing."

"Keep spending time with them."

"I still don't get why you want me to. If they're not interested in knowing me, then what's the point?"

"Maybe I'm telling you to do it for their sake."

"That makes no sense."

"Doesn't it? These people haven't had to interact with anyone outside of their own for a long time. What do you think is going to happen when I bring them to the community they want to join? If they're not willing to get to know new people, they won't be able to stay very long. Communities tend to toss out those they don't trust."

"Then tell them that."

"I want to see if they're willing to open up on their own, first."

"You have weird ideas," Gerald eventually sighed as he rolled onto his back.

Evans would agree with that, but his weird ideas had so far kept him alive in multiple environments, and among many different people.

"Wait." Gerald frowned up at the ceiling before turning his head to face Evans again. "Do you want me to try to get to know them to prove that I'll be able to get along with the community you're bringing *me* to?"

Evans didn't bother to respond. It seemed the kid wasn't totally stupid. Instead, he closed his eyes, and almost immediately fell asleep.

***

The next day, Evans didn't push the party as hard. He trusted Ang and Burt when they believed that the other silent ones wouldn't pursue them as far as they had already gone, so he set an easier pace and allowed for longer rest stops.

While Evans himself wasn't big on talking, he made an effort to chat up the new travellers. He tried to avoid topics about where they used to live, saving all his questions about that place for Ang and Burt. With Patterson, he asked simple things about her kids, and he found Dev knew a fair amount about the camels. Both Elmore and Janet were comfortable talking about their lives before the zombies, and seeing as how they were seventy-two and seventy-five, they had a lot of life to talk about. Kathy was a tougher nut to crack. Evans had yet to find a good topic with which to draw her out of her silence. He couldn't talk to either Blue or Patrick without an interpreter. Throughout the day, all his conversations happened in short snippets. Evans would chat with one person until they seemed to run out of steam, and then move on to the next party member. He eventually worked his way back to the first person, and would pick up where they had left off as if hours hadn't passed in between. He noticed that Gerald was studying him, and hoped the kid actually learned something.

When they bedded down the next night in a farmhouse, the silent ones spread out a little more, not minding being closer to Evans and Gerald. They also whispered to one another sometimes as opposed to strictly using sign. Evans didn't care if they never chose to speak at normal volumes, but he wanted them to get used to talking before joining what would, to them, be a very noisy group.

The following day was much the same, although this time Gerald did his best to communicate with Blue and Patrick. He both signed and spoke to them, occasionally having to ask for clarification when their finger languages differed. Both he and Evans continued wearing the rags of the silent ones, for they were comfortable, airy, and the hoods kept the sun off their faces. Evans also thought it was a good idea for them to be dressed uniformly, or else he and Gerald might stand out as targets should they be ambushed by bandits.

They bypassed a town, as Evans had passed through it before and didn't like the place. The people who had been there were undoubtedly gone by now, but he still went around on principle. Besides, they had been finding some good foraging along the edges of the old farm fields lately. By avoiding the town, it meant they had to decide to spend the night in an old barn again. Evans went in first to check if it was clear.

While just as drafty, this barn differed from the first in that it was larger and clearly once held animals. Evans began to walk down the length of the place, verifying that all the pens lining the left side were empty. The boards beneath his feet creaked, which was a little concerning. If they had been built directly onto the ground, then they shouldn't be able to creak, not like they were. He should have paid them more mind than he did.

His next step did not produce a creak, but rather a *crack*. Evans stopped moving, but it was too late. The floor gave way beneath him.

Evans hit the earthen floor beneath with a thump, letting his knees collapse to absorb the shock. It was too dark to see anything down there; the fading sunlight coming through the gaps above was unable to reach inside the hole. But Evans' ears were just fine. He lay perfectly still, not wanting to disturb the rattlesnakes any more than he already had. The buzz of their quivering tails was a sound he knew better than he would have liked. Never bitten himself, he had nevertheless watched a former party member die from their venom. There were no longer hospitals to rush to, no more vials of anti-venom. Depending on the snake, and where he was bitten, a man of Evans' size might be able to survive. Or he might have to lose a limb, the same as if a zombie had gotten him. The best option was to just not get bitten in the first place.

Afraid to call out, Evans simply stared up at the hole above him. He figured someone would come to check on him. His continuing lack of movement allowed the rattlers to settle. One even slid over his ankle. Evans was glad that he always tucked his pants into his boots.

Ang was the one to come and find out what had happened. It didn't take long. Evans guessed that his sensitive ears had heard the wood give way, as well as Evans' resulting fall. Before even seeing Ang's face, Evans could tell it was a silent one coming to investigate, since the floor above creaked far less for him than it had for Evans.

"Are you all right?" Ang whispered.

"There are rattlesnakes," Evans whispered back.

Ang nodded. "Are you hurt? Have you been bitten?"

"Not that I'm aware of."

"What do you need?"

"Light. And a rope with a loop on the end of it. I should be able to reach the opening once I stand, but I'm still going to need something to brace my foot against."

Ang nodded, then disappeared to retrieve the items.

Evans continued to lie still. He wasn't going to move until he could see exactly where the snakes were around him.

When Ang returned, he wasn't alone. Burt and Gerald both accompanied him, but they kept further back from the hole, concerned it might break open more, and Evans only knew that they were there because he heard their whispered voices.

"I'm lowering the rope," Ang informed Evans. "I've wrapped it around one of the beams up here."

Evans hoped the beam was stronger than the floor.

When the rope came down, a lantern had been tied to the end of it so that Evans could finally see. He told Ang to stop once it was low enough.

Moving his head as slowly as he could, Evans first looked toward the wall on his right. Nothing but stony dirt and wooden beams lay that way. Turning his head to then look left, he locked eyes with a rattler that was only three feet away. It lay there, coiled, its tail still. Moving his eyes, Evans located a few other snakes, but they weren't nearly as close. A few even retreated further into the darkness where a bunch of pipes glinted against the far wall.

Keeping his eyes glued to the nearest rattlesnake, Evans moved his arms in toward his body, placing his hands on either side of his hips. As he started to rise, exerting a tremendous amount of strength from his core, the snake's tail buzzed. Evans froze, his muscles locked yet slightly quivering.

"Do you need something else?" Ang asked from above. He could see and hear the snake. "Should I get Kathy and her javelin?"

"No," Evans whispered back. He didn't want to risk agitating any of the others any more than they already were.

After the tail had stopped for a few seconds, Evans continued to haul himself upright. Once he was in a sitting position, he took a short break. The rattler was no longer looking him dead in the face. Twisting in place, Evans made sure that there were no other snakes nearby which he had failed to see earlier. The only new one he spotted, was a rather large rattler that had had its head crushed by part of the falling rotted wood. Pinching its tail, Evans carefully drew the corpse toward him. Why waste meat?

As he drew his legs in, the rattlesnake buzzed again, its head pulling more tightly into its coils. Evans wished it would just retreat like its friends had, but apparently this was a stubborn snake. But patience would win out, and Evans had a lot of patience. Once the snake appeared to relax a little, Evans tucked his legs underneath him. He stood up fast, drawing forth a hiss this time, as well as a rattle from several snakes. Evans reached up and grabbed a floor beam at the edge of the hole. Ang had disappeared once he stood.

Glancing around the hole, Evans spotted a snake coming toward him. It was big, and it looked like it was on a mission as it travelled along the wall toward him. Not wanting to learn what that mission was, Evans jammed his foot into the loop and used it as a step while hauling with his arms. The foot in the loop suddenly rose up with him, as Gerald, Ang, and Burt hauled on the other end of the rope, and Evans popped up out of the hole. It was probably just his imagination, but he thought he heard a pair of small jaws snap behind him.

"I suggest we find a different place to sleep tonight," Gerald recommended and the others agreed. After gathering up the rope and lantern, they retreated back outside, being careful where they stepped.

They travelled through the dark until they found a good farmhouse in which to camp. Evans cooked up the dead snake, and shared the small scraps of meat with everyone. He noticed that Gerald and Blue were 'talking' an awful lot.

The next morning, they were all up with the sun and moving once more. They weren't far from their first stop, but as the day wore on, Evans didn't like the look of the storm clouds rolling in. He did not want to get caught out in whatever weather they were bringing.

"Zombie," seven-year-old Iris said from her position atop a camel. It was the loudest Evans had ever heard one of the silent ones speak.

"I'll take care of it," Dev whispered as he drew a machete.

"Wait," Evans held out his arm to stop him.

The zombie was on the other side of a chest high rail fence, which had been reinforced. Its gaps were filled with chain link, chicken wire, and scraps of sheet metal. When the zombie reached the fence, it bumped into the barricade and snapped its jaws, but couldn't get at them.

"Why are its hands tied to its waist?" Burt asked.

"So that it can't climb over the fence," Evans told him and everyone else who was listening. "We've reached the corral. See how its ear has been tagged?"

A bright piece of yellow plastic had been pierced through the rotting flesh. Some faded letters were scribbled on it in black marker.

"The corral?" Gerald wondered.

"It's where they put the zombies of their loved ones. I'm a little surprised we haven't come across a guard yet, although I suppose they're all preparing for the storm. Come on, we have to keep moving. The zombies in the corral can't hurt you, but feel free to kill any outside of it before we reach town."

Evans wasn't too keen on this community, mainly because of the smell, but as he glanced back at the dark mass consuming the sky, he was certainly glad to have made it.

17: CLAIRE
7 DAYS AFTER THE BOMBING

Bryce and Larson had opted to stay at their newly established base camp in the small convenience store in the apartment building, so that the others wouldn't have to carry their packs. Rose had strapped on her homemade prosthetic, which she could use to push back any zombies that got too close. She didn't wear it often because it was cumbersome, especially with a pack on. Claire walked with her knife in her hand, prepared for the worst.

The mannequins were just as Claire and Jon had seen them before. They were standing around in front of a store whose name didn't at all help Claire identify what it might have once sold. The whole street consisted of various shops and restaurants, creating a sort of boundary between the residential and business sectors. As the group approached in a diamond shaped formation, they closely studied the storefronts they passed for any signs of movement within. Danny took the point position, with Jon covering their rear, leaving Claire and Rose in the middle and closest to the shops. They tried not to walk too near to one another, just in case this was some sort of trap.

When Danny reached the mannequins, he studied them all closely, making sure that they were all what they appeared to be from a distance. Satisfied, he wove between them to approach the store. Claire went around to the far side of the mannequins, watching Danny from where she pressed herself up against some brick siding that separated the unknown place from its mattress selling neighbour. Danny boldly approached the glass and peered inside.

"Hello?" he called out, tapping gently on the glass. "Is there anyone in there? We don't mean you any harm. We saw the mannequins outside and decided to come take a look."

Across the street, Jon stood within an alcove created by a recessed doorway, his eyes darting every which way.

"I can't see anyone," Danny eventually said. "I'm going in to take a look around." He was talking louder than normal, not wanting to startle anyone who might be hiding.

Claire peeled away from her position and followed Danny to the door. Rose and Jon were going to remain outside, watching the street.

The door was unlocked, and opened relatively easily on its squeaking hinges. Based on the dust and dirt patterns around the entryway, someone had been in there before them. But how long ago?

"If there's anyone in here, it's better for both of us if you make yourself known," Danny called out. "We don't want any accidents. I have no plans to harm you or take your gear; I just want to know if anyone living is in the area."

Only silence greeted his request.

Claire went one way through the small store while Danny went the other. The shelving units were low enough that they could easily see one another over the tops of them. The place was full of useless knick-knacks, and one wall was lined with greeting cards. There might have been clothes there once, but those hooks were empty now. Claire and Danny kept pace with one another as they moved toward the back of the store, checking between the rows of shelves together. A few items littered the floor. Most looked like they had been knocked down when the clothing had been taken. Just when exactly that had happened, Claire couldn't tell.

At the back of the store, was a counter with a register sitting on top. The register was open, and there were no signs of damage, so it was probably the store owner or an employee who thought to take the cash before the healthy were evacuated. A tray for lottery scratch tickets also stood empty. Beyond the counter was a door. Danny stepped through it, while Claire checked back over her shoulder. Despite knowing that they were mannequins and even though she was able to see them clearly, the plastic figures still freaked her out.

Squeezing in behind Danny, Claire soon found that there wasn't much to report. A single tiny bathroom which was cleared with a single sweep of a flashlight, and a little storeroom containing a single box of snow globes were all that were back there. Claire and Danny beat a hasty retreat back outside, regrouping with Jon and Rose a little way up the street.

"Place was empty," Danny reported. "I didn't even find anything that suggested recent habitation."

"I noticed something," Claire spoke up. It had just dawned on her. "The mannequins. They could be seen quite clearly from inside. There was no way someone would mistake them for anything else the way we did. Not unless it was a really dark night."

"So why are they there then?" Jon wondered out loud.

"Whatever the reason, we should probably head back to camp," Rose recommended. "Those things could've just been abandoned there, and we got a job to do."

"I also think that we don't want to be out here once it gets dark," Danny added. "We'll finish setting up camp, and then check on the mannequins in the morning. If they're still there, then great."

"And if they've been moved?" Claire asked.

"Then we watch each others' backs a lot more closely," Jon answered.

In the same formation in which they approached the mannequins, they returned to the apartment building and their temporary camp. Bryce and Larson had no new ideas about the mysterious mannequins after being filled in on what was found.

By working together, they were able to quickly secure the convenience store, and make it almost comfortable. Knowing they'd be there for a while, they could leave some of their gear unpacked, as well as the items taken from the house. Claire was happy she wouldn't have to hunt through her bag each morning for the bar of soap she used as deodorant. Her hair was kept in a braid, but she had brought her brush in the hopes that maybe there'd be time to bathe. With the river not terribly far, the chances seemed good. Even the boys would want to clean themselves up eventually.

Not having to worry about water for the time being, they drank as much as they wanted, which helped offset the lack of food. Another round of guard duty was assigned, although they thought if nothing happened the first night, then maybe they wouldn't need guards the second. They had secured the shop's door to the apartment building so that it could only be opened from their side, and anyone trying to get in from outside, would have to push past a wire rack; there was no way to do that silently. They had tested it. Broken windows they would also hear, and the bars over them meant no one was coming in that way. Really, the only reasons they decided on guard duty that first night was for peace of mind, and to watch for anyone who might be creeping around in the dark with some mannequins. Claire took the first shift, and saw nothing. No people, no zombies, not even a bat fluttering through the darkness. Her exhaustion afterward made her fall asleep surprisingly quickly. It was a light sleep that had her waking up with every shift change.

***

Bryce and Larson had agreed to stay at the base camp again and get breakfast ready, while the other four went to check on the mannequins.

"Are there fewer today than there were yesterday?" Rose wondered as they looked at the figures.

"I can't tell. I didn't count them yesterday," Danny admitted. It seemed no one had.

"I don't see any obvious gaps," Claire pointed out.

"Someone hand me a knife," Rose demanded.

Claire was closest, so she handed over hers. Rose went up to the nearest mannequin and attacked its head with the knife. She carved a deep number one into the back of it. Satisfied, she then moved on to carve a number two into the next one. Getting the point, Danny and Jon moved in to help. With her knife in Rose's hand, Claire didn't have anything with which to help, so she simply stood guard.

"There's twenty-five of the cunts," Rose growled when they had finished. "A nice easy number to remember."

The carved marks were jagged and not always easy to read, but that was fine. The point was that they could now tell if any of them went missing.

After returning to the apartment building, they had breakfast and decided on the teams. Rose and Danny were going to stay put, watching over their stuff, getting more water, and attempting to hunt, while the other four were going to start searching the parking garage.

"Take everything out of your pack," Jon advised Claire. "I doubt we'll find much, but just in case, we want as much room for carrying as possible."

Claire did as she was told.

"Too bad we don't have any shopping carts," Bryce lamented as they got ready.

"Would you really want to haul one up the stairs?" Larson retorted.

"It's just one set of stairs; we can use the car ramps the rest of the time."

"We'll properly investigate the laundry room and storage room first," Jon decided. "There might be something in there that we can use."

There wasn't much in the laundry room, but they took all they could, disturbing the dust as they searched inside and underneath all the machines. The best find was a netted laundry bag, but they also came across several lost dryer sheets, some coins, a couple of paper clips and rubber bands, one sheet of laminated paper, and one thumbtack. Some items were useful just as they were. Others could be modified or melted down for different purposes.

They stopped at the office before going to the storage room, hoping to find keys. They had no such luck, but they did find some more stationery which they brought back to pile in a corner of the convenience store. They also found a small, foldable dolly tucked away in a corner.

"Excellent!" Bryce was very pleased with the find. "We can use this to move car batteries."

The storage room came next. Someone had been there before them; they had managed to pry down the corners of some of the metal wire doors. For one reason or another, they had given up after breaking into only three of the cages that held people's extra belongings. Jon, Bryce, and Larson had a better way of getting into the cages: a bolt cutter.

"Stay close," Jon said to Claire. "I'm sure you know the kind of stuff we want to bring back, but if you're confused about anything, let me know."

It was strange, going through other people's things. In the first cage that Claire was assigned, the space was dominated by a large couch. Why was there a couch in there? Why wasn't it in the apartment? Was it too big? But then why would they have bought it? Had they been forced to downsize from a larger place? Claire couldn't help but wonder about the couch. When she came across a snowboard, it made sense to her that it would be stashed down here. Snowboards weren't often needed in Texas, at least not around these parts. But a couch had plenty of purposes. Surely the owners could have found a buyer for it if they no longer wanted it. To Claire's mind, in which a paperclip was also a bookmark, a hair clip, wiring for a simple light, and even a small aerial booster, the abandonment of a whole couch was ludicrous.

"Grab the cushions," Jon told her, when she spoke aloud her bafflement. "We can sleep on them, and maybe use the covers as bags when we leave."

Claire removed the couch's cushions and placed them by the stairs.

The whole storage room was a treasure-trove of materials. Larson, however, found the best stash, surrounded by a bunch of gardening supplies: a dresser drawer full of seed packets. The seeds could very well be dead, and many of them were flowers instead of vegetables. They wouldn't know if they were still viable until they planted them.

It took the rest of the morning to go through the cluttered storage room. They found another dolly, one with a fixed frame this time, and immediately put it to use. A stolen shopping cart was also located but the wheels barely turned, and squealed horribly when they did, so they left it. Everything that was of immediate use, or that might come home with them, was brought up to the convenience store. They moved supplies they might return for into the cages closest to the doors, including the stationery. Totally useless items were heaped in the farthest cages.

"I don't like the look of those clouds," Danny commented when Claire and the others stopped at camp for a late lunch. Rose had gotten lucky and snagged an armadillo that they cooked up.

They couldn't see the storm clouds from inside—the windows faced the wrong way—but Claire had stepped out to take a look. She found herself instantly agreeing with Danny. The black mass taking over the southern sky felt threatening.

"We'll be all right," Jon told her. "We're in a secure building that was built to withstand some pretty brutal storms."

"It's the container yard I'm worried about," Claire admitted.

"They'll be okay. We've ridden out some pretty serious storms there. And remember, they shouldn't be totally exposed to the storm surge. Do you remember when we first arrived there on the boats? There was a long chunk of land we went around before entering the bay. I think that land tends to take the power out of the storm surge, which is really the most dangerous part."

Claire knew all of this, but it was good to hear it again. Despite his lack of evidence, Jon sounded totally confident that everything would be fine. Claire needed to be that confident, to not have to worry so that she could focus solely on the task at hand.

"We should start with the lowest levels of the garage, just in case there's a bit of flooding," Bryce recommended.

The others agreed, in particular because it would give them a chance to make sure the whole place was clear of zombies before they started checking out the cars.

It was dark down in the parking garage. In the storage room, with the door held open at the top of the singular staircase, they had gotten a tiny amount of bounced light from elsewhere on the first floor. There was no such light in the parking garage. It was pitch black with the lights out.

"Hello?" Jon called as they walked around the first level, searching for the ramp down to the lower ones.

Bryce dragged the butt of his spear along the pavement. It rattled and scraped and echoed off the low ceiling. In addition to the smothering darkness, it had also been as silent as a tomb before they started making noise. They were probably the first people to bring sound and light to this place in years. If there were any zombies inside, the dead would be drawn to them like a trained dog to the word 'treat'.

Claire was glad that she was holding a lantern as opposed to a flashlight. She liked being within a pool of light instead of just following along behind a beam. It was also less obvious that her hands had developed a slight tremor. She felt a strange sensation, as though the world didn't exist outside of what she saw. Every time a car appeared at the edge of the light, its shine visible before anything else, her chest tightened. Why that happened, she couldn't say. It was always just a vehicle, and she knew that, but her anxiety acted up anyway.

They located the ramp to the surface first. Jon went up and tested the door, making sure that it was indeed secure. They didn't want anything coming down behind them. The ramp to the lower level was right beside it, so they walked down. It turned out that all the ramps were right beside one another, like a stairwell for cars. They could've gone straight down to the bottom, but instead opted to search each level for movement first. They made their way back to the stairwell, which descended to every level, and made sure that the door wasn't jammed.

The parking garage turned out to be made up of four, relatively small levels. A lot of the parking spaces were empty. The vehicles were likely driven away during the area's evacuation. The cars that remained wore a coat of dust.

"Okay, it looks like it's time to get to work," Jon said once they successfully reached the bottom without running into anything that moved.

Bryce used the butt of his spear to smash the driver's side window of the sedan farthest from the ramps. A short, sharp scream escaped Claire's throat at the sudden explosion of sound. A wash of embarrassment undoubtedly turned her face a bright red, but none of the guys commented on her startled response.

Going through the car was quicker and easier than the storage rooms had been. Claire was assigned the back seat, Bryce searched the front, Jon investigated the trunk, and Larson checked under the hood. They had a device with them to test the charge of the car's battery, but even if it was dead, the submarine could be used to recharge it. They had plenty of car batteries back at the container yard, but they could always use more. Before moving to the next vehicle, they also checked the car for any fluids that could be drained from it. Oil, gas, washer fluid, brake fluid, everything. Even the stuff that had gone bad some people could find a use for, and so they drained it all into various containers they had located throughout the day.

The next vehicle in line was a blocky SUV. This time Claire was more prepared for the explosive shattering of safety glass, and so managed to keep her own sound inside. She still flinched though.

There was never much to find in the back seats of the cars. Some had long forgotten bits of trash or a water bottle. One had a blanket in the back, and another had several toys scattered around a child's car seat. Twice there were maps, and three held tissue boxes. The glove boxes and the trunks always held the best finds. Napkins could be used as toilet paper, and so every single one was to come with them. All the car jacks and tire irons were taken, with the intention of putting them in the storage room for a possible future pick up. Only one was kept with them.

"Here," Jon said, handing the tire iron to Claire. It had a socket wrench for wheel nuts on one end and a pry bar on the other. "I've always felt you needed more than just a knife. This pry bar is a little sharper than the others we've come across, and should go through a zombie's skull quite easily."

"Thanks." Claire didn't yet have a method for carrying the weapon in a way that would allow it to be drawn easily, so she held it in her hand for the time being. It was pretty good for smashing windows, she found out when Bryce let her break into the next vehicle. The sound wasn't so startling when she was the one causing it.

Everything they intended to take to camp with them was piled either on one of the dollies, or inside one of their packs. Everything else they planned to take to the storage room, they clustered by the stairwell doors for later pick up.

The last vehicle to check on the third level was a panel van. It had no windows along its sides other than those at the front. The windows at the very back were covered in some sort of black paper or film, so they couldn't see in that way either.

Jon pressed his ear to the vehicle's metal skin. He tapped on the side with the butt of his sword, listening for any movement. Bryce shone his flashlight in through the front.

"There's some sort of barrier between the front and rear," he reported. "I can't see anything back there."

Larson pulled on the handle of the passenger side door, expecting the resistance of a lock. When the door swung open, he was taken completely off guard and nearly fell to the ground as he stumbled.

"Door's open," he needlessly reported.

"Driver side, too," Bryce added, having gone around to that side.

Claire went to the rear doors and was a little surprised to find that they were unlocked as well. She held her tire iron at the ready, in case something popped out, even though Jon hadn't heard anything. Nothing came out of the rear compartment, but Claire's jaw still dropped.

"Um," she whispered, and then cleared her throat. "Um, guys?"

"What is it?" Jon walked around to join her behind the van. "Oh. Um. Yeah."

Inside the van were several chains bolted to the walls with leather straps attached to the ends of them.

"Oh wow," Bryce breathed as he came to look.

"Oh shit!" Larson said, a little too enthusiastically as he joined them as well. "Did we just find a serial killer's van?"

"We did not just find a serial killer's van," Jon admonished him, refusing to believe it. "This person was probably just a dog walker or something. Picked up the dogs in the van, and then transported them to the park to be walked." He didn't sound as confident in his assessment as he usually did.

"Then wouldn't there be leashes and not chains?" Larson questioned him.

"Could have been a dog catcher," Bryce suggested. "Dealt with strays."

"Animal control always has labels on the sides," Larson reminded him. "And they tend to have a lot more equipment than this. We've found some good stuff in the animal control vehicles."

"It's not a serial killer's van," Jon insisted. "There's got to be some other reason for this that we just don't know about."

"Whatever they were, I'm sure the owner is dead," Claire finally chimed in. "And whatever those chains were used for, they can still be useful to us."

"Yup," Jon nodded. "Come on, let's get back to work."

Larson and Bryce headed back to the front of the van; Claire and Jon climbed into the back.

"Well, I don't see any stains, so that's good," Claire commented.

Jon, who had seen plenty of old bloodstains during his time scavenging, nodded his head in agreement.

Claire held the light while Jon worked at the nuts and bolts with the tools he had brought. He didn't have the right sized wrench for the job, but was able to make do with some pliers. Whenever a chain came free of the wall, the slack fell to the bottom of the van with a rattling thump. Claire was not a fan of that sound. It was worse than the smashing windows.

"Last one," Jon said, moving to the final bolt.

Bryce and Larson had finished with the front, and had drained the liquids. They had gathered up the chains that were already free, and were carrying them over to the stairwell.

"Have you ever come across anything like this before?" Claire finally asked the question that had been percolating in the back of her mind.

"A van full of chains and restraints? Not really."

"No, I mean... something criminal."

"We've found plenty of formally illegal drugs hidden in people's homes, and once we came across a decent sized stash in a warehouse." Jon referred to them as formally illegal, because nowadays they had to use the stuff for medical purposes. Recreational use was still frowned upon, and addicts were dealt with on a case by case basis, but it wasn't like there was enough of the stuff for that kind of thing to happen often. Marijuana was only grown in tiny batches by individuals, and even alcohol wasn't distilled all that often—at least, not the kind that was safe to drink. Claire had tried both booze and pot, but found that neither was for her. When her mind wasn't sharp, she got scared. She suspected that that was true for a lot of people, and so that was why neither was produced in much abundance.

"What about other stuff?" Claire asked.

"You're referring to kidnapping and murder scenes?"

"Yeah."

"No, I've never come across anything like that. Not that I know of, anyway. There've been a few times on the islands when I've come across places that looked like a mass execution occurred. I've always chosen to believe that that was one of their attempts at dealing with the sick."

Claire was glad to hear it.

"You know what I have stumbled across a few times?" Jon continued, his voice taking on a lighter tone. "BDSM stuff."

"What?"

"Yeah, hidden away in people's closets or basements you can sometimes find some super kinky shit. Masks, and whips, and ball gags, all that junk."

Claire chuckled, trying to picture what it must have been like the first time they came across such a collection.

"It's always startling to find a dildo," Jon went on. "You never know where one of those might be kept."

Claire was full on laughing now, which kept her from being bothered by the sound of the final chain falling to the van floor.

"Did we miss a good joke?" Bryce asked, appearing at the back of the van.

"I was just telling Claire about what it's like to find dildos," Jon told him.

"Fucking dildos!" Larson lamented, as though it were as awful as finding a snake. "Those things are everywhere! I found one at that house we were in earlier."

"Did you tell Rose about it?" Jon asked.

"No, why?"

"You've never had to scavenge with her before. She likes to throw dildos at guys when she finds them."

"Good to know," Bryce nodded.

Claire couldn't help but giggle.

"If you start doing that as well, so help me God," Jon told her, with a serious finger point that just made the situation seem all that much funnier to Claire.

Since there weren't that many chains left, they opted to carry them up to the next level and leave them by the stairwell up there. Jon and Claire led the way, leaving Larson and Bryce to push the dollies along behind them. The guys were telling Claire about other humorous items they had come across, trying to keep her laughing as they reached the next ramp.

"Son of a bitch!" Jon startled everyone by yelling halfway up to level two, the chains slung over his shoulder crashing to the ground.

The group instantly fell silent, and weapons were drawn, as all the lights converged on the top of the ramp.

There, standing in the center of the opening, was a mannequin. It had one hand raised as if in greeting. Eyes and a grotesque smile had been drawn on its face with some sort of black paint. Someone had come into the parking garage behind them. Someone with a very perverse way of saying hello.

18: ONIDA
APPROXIMATELY 1 YEAR AGO

They were making their way around a patch of radiation when the first heavy frost hit them. Onida had woken up to discover that the ground both glittered and crunched. She didn't like it. The frost would kill some plants and cause the others to go into hibernation. It would be harder to forage. And after the frost would come the snow.

Onida listened as the grass crinkled and cracked beneath its covering of ice as she walked over to the horses. Askuwheteau's leg wasn't getting any better. He could still keep up, but he couldn't carry anything and it was hard to get him moving. Onida worried about him having some sort of infection that she couldn't see. She worried about Shawn deciding that he was no longer worth the trouble. Onida knew what would happen at that point: Shawn had said as much. The only reason the horse was still being kept around, was as an emergency supply of meat. Shawn had likely had that plan all along, and it was why he refused to use the horses' names, and why he let Onida always be the one to take care of them. He wasn't going to form any attachments to an animal he would later slaughter for food.

"I think we'll get around the worst of the radiation today," Shawn said as he built a small cook fire for their breakfast. He believed that most of the radiation had been in a sort of belt, in the places where people didn't have enough time to prepare, or didn't believe they could be overrun. But for all either of them knew, the south was an irradiated wasteland.

After breakfast, they mounted up and got moving again. Onida had no idea where they were. She generally knew which way they were going, but she wouldn't be able to point out where she was on a map. But then, it's not like either of them needed to know. They had no destination in mind, only a general direction.

Onida shifted around in her saddle. Her ass and legs would never be the same after this journey. She sometimes imagined being an old woman, walking around with her legs bowed out to the sides as if there were still a horse between them. It was an amusing image, one that scattered like dry leaves in the wind whenever she reminded herself that she might not live to be an old woman. Life expectancy rates had taken a nosedive over the last decade.

It was in the afternoon when Shawn brought them to an unexpected stop. Night came early this time of year, but not this early. Onida kept quiet as Shawn listened. He had taken a radiation reading not long ago, and they were still okay, so she didn't think it was that. Had he seen something? Heard something?

"Stay here with the horses," Shawn whispered as he dismounted.

Onida held his reins and worried as Shawn walked off the road they had been following. Had he spotted an animal that was too good to pass up? Was he hunting?

After ten minutes dragged by without any new sights or sounds, Onida hopped off her mount to stretch her legs. The horses were getting a little anxious too. They didn't understand why they had stopped, or why, having stopped, they remained tied together. Both trains were no longer in straight lines, but rather a wiggly shape as some horses bunched together, and others attempted to reach the more abundant foliage at the side of the road. Onida took a quick look to make sure none of them were getting tangled together.

After another ten minutes passed, Onida had to free the horses from each other before they got nippy. She hung a long rope across the road, and tied a few of the horses to that. The others shouldn't be tempted to leave without them, and those that looked like they were about to wander a little farther away than Onida liked, she would round up and bring back.

How long was she supposed to wait? Onida thought about what it would be like to travel south on her own and shivered. She didn't know how the Geiger counter worked, and she realized now that she should have asked. She also should have gotten Shawn to teach her more about hunting. Even if she could hunt as well as him, how could she do both that and care for the horses at the same time? She'd end up killing and eating the horses one by one. That's what would happen.

Just when Onida was seriously considering moving on, to go looking for some shelter for the night, Shawn came back out of the forest. Onida was relieved to see him, and not just because Mask, whom she had grown very fond of, was also with him.

"Where did you go?" Onida had to restrain herself from yelling. She was pretty sure he hadn't been hunting, for he brought back no meat, and it looked like he had the same number of arrows.

"I found the Amish."

"The Amish?"

"I think we should go meet them."

Onida fidgeted with the reins of the horse she was holding as Shawn started to move the others back into the train formation. "What good will come from meeting the Amish?" The idea of meeting any new people made Onida squeamish.

"If we like them, and they like us, we could ride out the winter with them. Maybe we can just stay there even after winter has passed."

"I thought we were heading south?"

"We were heading south so that we could find a place to survive. We could survive with the Amish."

"I don't want to."

"What? Survive?"

"Stay with the Amish."

"Why not?"

"We're too close." Onida finally moved to help with the horses.

"Too close?"

"To where I'm from."

"We're miles and miles away. Are you really still afraid that they're still after you?"

Onida didn't answer him. She thought that doing so would make her look paranoid. Her silence had the same effect, however. Shawn stopped tying the horses together and stared at her.

"Tell me what you did."

"I told you." Onida wouldn't meet his gaze; she focused entirely on the horses.

"All you said was that you stole something. Something you no longer had. Tell me everything, or I'm going to leave you. I'll take half the horses and half the gear, and Mask and I will go join the Amish."

Onida sighed. She had naively thought that she would never have to tell Shawn the truth. That she would never have to tell anyone.

"Tell me what you stole." Shawn's voice raised in pitch, and Onida remembered just how good he was at killing things, and just how alone he had been when she first met him.

"A soul."

"A soul?"

"I stole a soul."

"You killed someone."

"Yes, although it's not like that."

"Tell me then. Tell me what happened."

Onida sighed again. She turned to the next horse so that she could keep her hands busy and not have to look at Shawn while she spoke. "It was my grandfather. He was sick. It doesn't matter that he wanted me to do it, that he wanted me to take his life to the point that he told me how best to use the knife. Everyone must pass on their own terms for the soul to be free. To take someone's life is to take their soul. It's completely forbidden no matter the circumstances."

"When you say sick, was he going to turn into a zombie?"

"No, nothing like that. He would have been too well guarded, his passing too closely monitored if that were the case. I wouldn't have been able to get near him. I think it was cancer that was killing him, but we had no way of determining that for sure. All I know is that he was in a lot of pain." Tears forced their way out of Onida's eyes and ran down her face as she remembered how frail her grandfather had looked. How his hands had become twisted claws as he grabbed at anything that might help him.

"And your grandfather, he was important?"

"Yes. He was very well respected. Everyone listened to him."

"Did he know that you would be pursued for doing what he asked you to do?"

"Only if I got caught. He didn't think I would be. Neither of us realized how the aftermath would paralyze me." Onida could practically smell the inside of the tent as she remembered the deed. After she had killed her grandfather with a knife through his eye, she had found it impossible to move. She just knelt there, staring. When her little brother came to see what she was up to, he found Onida still kneeling beside their dead grandfather. His own horror made him slow to raise the alarm, giving Onida time to start running. And she had been running ever since. "If you want to leave me to go live with the Amish, I understand."

Shawn was silent. He was silent for so long that Onida worried he had walked off. But no, he was still there, with his own set of tears glittering in his beard.

"Shawn? Are you okay?" Onida wiped at her face.

"I'm fine." He turned rapidly, and set to work on the horses once more. "I don't think we'll stay with the Amish. We should stop there, but we won't stay."

"We? You'll still come south with me?"

Shawn grunted, and moved his head in what Onida hoped was a curt nod.

Once the horses were ready, they mounted back up. Shawn led them along the road to the Amish.

It was almost a relief to have told Shawn what she had done. She was still afraid that he would leave her, but now it was something that was out of her hands. For all she knew, Shawn would give her to the Amish in exchange for sanctuary, and they would then use her as a bargaining chip with her own people. She could probably be traded for a lot of supplies, since her people generally got along quite well with the Amish, even if this particular community didn't yet have contact with hers. Onida would just have to follow Shawn and find out what would happen.

Based on how long Shawn had been gone, Onida thought it would take some time before she saw any signs of the Amish. It didn't take much time at all, however, before they reached a literal sign, an old one, welcoming people to Amish country. Not far past that, a large fence had been erected, much newer than the sign. A gate barred their entrance, but on horseback, Onida could see over it. There were farm fields that had already been harvested just on the other side, and wooden structures whose roofs were barely visible among some hills in the distance. White smoke curled up from the structures, and Onida could hear a handsaw at work. She also thought she might be able to hear voices, but couldn't be positive.

They weren't standing at the gate for long before a horse and rider appeared. A man dressed in the simple blacks of the Amish rode toward them on a beautiful chestnut mare. Onida thought their own horses looked rather drab in comparison.

"Hello, there," the Amish man greeted them with a friendly smile.

Out of the corner of her eyes, Onida saw Shawn shifting uncomfortably in his saddle. She got the sense that his time with her made him think that socializing with other people would be easy, and was being proven wrong.

"Hello," she answered for the two of them. "We're looking for a place to rest up."

"For the winter?" the man's brows pinched slightly together. They were probably not the first to seek shelter through the hard season.

"No, just a few nights. Maybe three, four?" She looked over at Shawn, hoping he would contribute.

"Three. Three nights." He had mumbled, giving more weight to Onida's theory.

"We just want somewhere safe to give our horses a break, and maybe trade for some supplies." Although Onida didn't know what they had to trade. Other than herself, that was.

The Amish nodded his understanding. "May I have your names, please? And where are you coming from?"

"Peter," Shawn said with a hand to his chest. He gave the man a false name like it was nothing.

"Numees," Onida gave the name of her aunt before Shawn could bestow some white person's name upon her.

"We're travelling down from the north-east," Shawn told the Amish man.

"Why?" The man was eyeing their horses, but mostly Shawn. He likely recognized that all of the horses' gear was made by Native American hands, which Shawn was most definitely not. While many folk, of all races, had been accepted into Onida's tribe after the zombies came, Shawn's wild man looks and the packs he had brought from his cabin, did not match the rest of their gear. Onida was afraid that maybe word had spread, that communities such as this had been told to keep an eye out for Onida and all the horses. Was that why Shawn had encouraged her to lie about her name by lying first? It was unlikely he was in danger of being recognized, since no one had seen him the night his cabin burned down.

"We both lost our homes a little while ago." Shawn gestured to himself and Onida. He was becoming a little more confidant with the Amish man, speaking at a more normal volume. "Numees was lucky to have saved so many horses, and I was lucky to have come across her."

"We were both lucky to have come across each other," Onida added, hoping it sounded genuine.

"What happened to your homes?"

"Zombies." Shawn told the easiest lie of all. "A large horde swept through both our lands, managing to take us by surprise."

The Amish man nodded, finding nothing to question about that.

"May I ask your name?" Onida asked.

"Jacob. If the two of you will wait here for a minute, I'll go discuss your request with the others."

"Please don't take too long. We'd like to be sheltered before dark." Onida often thought of the wolves. They never slept in the tent anymore, preferring to find a building in which to stop. When they couldn't fit the horses inside, they took shifts keeping fires lit and watching over them. Those long nights were the most exhausting, but no wolves had been seen since that first pack.

Jacob nodded again, understanding Onida's request, and rode off toward the roofs just beyond a small hill. Onida looked behind her, checking to see how the horses were doing. She then turned to Shawn.

"What do we have to offer?" she wondered.

"Depends on what they need," Shawn replied.

"We don't have much."

"We'll trade in labour if we have to."

"That doesn't sound very restful."

Shawn grunted in agreement.

When Jacob returned, he was on foot and accompanied by three other men, who carried simple rifles. They didn't introduce themselves, but they opened the gate.

"You are free to camp on our grounds for at least one night," Jacob told them. "We will discuss what you have to offer, and see if more nights in proper beds can be agreed upon."

Onida felt a weight lift off her as she rode past the fence. While still fearful of somehow being recognized by the Amish, or of Shawn betraying her, being within a guarded boundary after living out in the open for so long was wonderful.

They rode slowly, allowing the four men to keep pace. Jacob and another man walked on either side of her and Shawn, while the two others shut the gate and followed behind their horse trains. She suspected those two men were eyeing their supply bags, although they likely couldn't tell how empty most were.

At the top of the hill, the paved road came to an abrupt end. A well-trodden dirt path led them down the far side and into a clearing between several large buildings, all of which were made of wood. More hills dotted the area, and Onida could spot more modest sized dwellings among them. The clearing itself was full of people. She wondered whether they had already been there, or if they had just come to meet Shawn and Onida.

"Welcome," a man who looked like Jacob, but with grey hair and deeper wrinkles, spread his arms as Shawn and Onida approached. "I've been told you're here to trade."

Shawn nodded, his eyes darting about. He did not like having all these people around. Onida guessed, based on certain faces, haircuts, and articles of clothing, that not everyone there had chosen to join the Amish for their religious practices, but rather out of necessity. She was grateful not to spy any faces like her own.

"Why don't you come inside?" the man who looked like Jacob suggested. "Your horses and gear will remain untouched, you have my word."

Onida didn't climb down off her horse until Shawn did. Mask grunted and wriggled about as Shawn picked him up out of the saddlebag where he tended to spend his days. Some of the younger people giggled and whispered at the sight of the raccoon. There were no children present, but Onida suspected they were safely hidden away somewhere until it was ascertained that neither she nor Shawn presented them any threat.

"I'm Paul," the man told them as he guided them to the nearest building. "Your names are Peter and Numees, correct?"

"Yes," Onida answered after a second or two when Shawn didn't. He walked with Mask cradled in his arms, fearful of the people gathered around. Onida suspected that Paul had noticed the way Shawn looked at the people and had opted to bring them inside for his comfort. Onida didn't know what the building was that they were led to, only that it wasn't the church.

Inside, there was a large room, with many chairs, and a little platform stage against the far wall. Perhaps it was where they held their town meetings, or maybe even held dances, based on the way several chairs had been cleared away from a central space. Paul brought them to the nearest seats, allowing them to be arranged however they liked. Jacob had followed them in, and so had a handful of others, but most of the Amish stayed outside.

"So, you'd like to stay for three nights?" Paul cut straight to the chase. "And I assume you'd also like some supplies before you head out? What do you have to offer in exchange?"

Onida looked to Shawn, worried he wouldn't be able to speak to this small group. But by petting Mask, and looking down at the animal's huddled form on his lap, it seemed he was able.

"We can give you a horse," Shawn started with.

Onida frowned. He had said nothing of the sort to her.

"Which horse?" Jacob asked.

"The one without any gear on it."

"You mean the lame one," an unnamed man grunted.

"He's not lame," Onida defended Askuwheteau. "He just needs to rest. We haven't been able to stop for more than a night since we started."

"Do you know what's wrong with him?" Jacob asked. It wasn't a hostile question, merely interest.

Onida didn't answer, because she didn't actually know.

"We'll take the horse," Paul said, causing several heads to turn his way. "That will get you three nights in a bed, plus meals for you and the rest of your horses."

"You're not going to eat him, are you?" Onida asked, a touch of fear entering her voice.

"No, we won't eat him," Paul reassured her. "Not until he has lived a full life at least. We will assess his leg, but even if he does turn out to be lame, we can use him as a teaching aid for the young ones. We could also use some fresh genes for breeding with our own horses, and if his hair is good, we can trim his mane and tail when we need it." The other Amish looked annoyed at how freely Paul told them these things, and how easily he accepted the horse in exchange for beds and meals.

"I can also offer the hair off the rest of our horses," Shawn added.

Onida shot him a look that he ignored. Horses had manes and tails for a reason.

"We can also trade labour for supplies," Onida said. She figured that with beds and meals, working for the Amish shouldn't be too awful. "And we have a lot of extra horse gear: brushes, hoof picks, and the like. We also have some extra blankets we can offer in trade."

Jacob leaned down and whispered something in his father's ear. Paul nodded and raised his hand, the gesture combining with his expression to state that he already knew or realized whatever it was that Jacob had said. Although it was one of the unnamed men who spoke next.

"Convenient that when you had to flee your home the horses were all loaded up to go." There was clearly an accusation in his voice.

"A hunting party was preparing to head out, one last long outing before winter." Onida had to think on her feet, hoping the lies didn't show plainly on her face. "I was left to watch over the horses while they said goodbye to their families and gathered a few last minute items. When the screaming started, the horses began to move on their own, including the one I was holding, and I was too stunned and scared to stop them. I could only climb up into the saddle."

Was that believable? Did it make sense? Was she about to be bombarded with questions about an event that never happened? She tried to imagine what that sort of zombie attack would be like, her mind racing to sketch in details.

"The raccoon, what's his name?" asked a woman, turning the attention away from Onida. Well, most of the attention. The man who had questioned her was clearly still suspicious. Had they known to be on the lookout for Onida, however, then she would have been caught already. They must not have had contact with her people since she ran.

"Mask," Shawn told the woman, there being no point in giving him a false name.

"He wouldn't be up for offer, would he?" the woman asked, her voice completely innocent. She had no idea that Onida had nearly been killed because of Shawn's bond with the raccoon.

Shawn's eyes finally raised and locked onto the woman. "No." There was menace in that simple word, and the darkness in his eyes made the Amish woman squirm in her seat. She clearly regretted having asked as her face flushed and she stared down at her own, empty lap.

Shawn's arms had subconsciously gripped Mask tighter. Mask was not a fan of this and began wriggling around to find a better position. His movements brought Shawn's gaze back down to him, and the murder left his eyes.

"I don't suppose you'd be willing to trade any of your other horses?" Paul asked, clearly ignoring the dark expression he just saw. He continued to smile pleasantly.

"No."

Onida was glad to hear Shawn give that answer, and even more so to hear that the threat had left his voice.

"We need all our other horses."

"Well, we'll take a look at your excess horse gear, although I doubt we'll need any of it. Blankets too. We'll come to a work arrangement. Come, dinner will be served soon, and we should get your animals all settled beforehand."

Settling the horses also involved showing their wares to the Amish. The horses were all brought to an open-sided stable that could temporarily house even more than their herd of fifteen. Five stalls remained empty after they filled the others, and Onida figured this was where visiting horses were always kept. While Askuwheteau was housed alongside them, he was immediately beset by the Amish, who inspected his quality and cleaned him up more than Onida had been capable of doing on the road. Everything they had that they were willing to trade was removed from their packs and put on display. The extra blankets were hung on a rack along one side of the stables, and everything else was placed on long shelves that ran along the backs of them. While they stayed there, the Amish could walk over and inspect their offerings, and propose whatever sort of trade they thought was fair. The Amish came across as trustworthy enough that neither Shawn nor Onida worried that any of their things would be stolen while they were away from them.

Dinner was a communal affair, thanks to the visitors. Long tables had been set up not far from the stables, and food was laid out for all. It had become dark by then, but a plethora of candles kept everything well lit, whilst also providing a touch more warmth. Onida wondered if the hall where they had spoken was used for such meals when it was raining, or when the earth was covered with snow. She saw a couple of people, mostly older folk, who clearly wished they were already inside, as they wrapped blankets around their shoulders.

Paul sat at the head of the table, with Shawn and Onida to his right, and Jacob and Jacob's wife to his left. Onida wondered if that was the usual arrangement, or if Paul was being considerate of Shawn's dislike of crowds by putting him on the end instead of in the middle somewhere. Throughout dinner, Shawn and Onida told Paul the kinds of things they could do, what skills they had to offer. They were also introduced to a number of families, for while there was to be another big meal just before they left, all their meals in between would be taken in different homes. Onida hoped they all tasted as good as this one. The mashed potatoes were especially yummy. Mask was even more skittish of the strangers than Shawn was, perhaps deciding that, unlike the time Onida had appeared, there were just too many of them. He seemed content to sit on Shawn's lap, however, his little hands stealing food from Shawn's plate, much to the amusement of Jacob's wife.

"Father?" Jacob said in a low voice, and tilted his head toward two young men who had appeared behind him.

"Yes, yes," Paul nodded. "Come here."

The two young men shuffled up beside Paul. They were likely even younger than Onida was.

"You haven't yet said where in the south you are going," Paul mentioned as he turned to Shawn and Onida. "It's all right, you don't have to say, but we were hoping you could do us a favour. These two young men came up here to deliver news and packages from a neighbouring community to the south. Unfortunately, when they tried to get back home, they discovered the way had become too dangerous."

"In what way, dangerous?" Shawn grumbled. He seemed to know what was going to be asked.

"Bandits. We were hoping that you could accompany them home. There aren't many bandits from my understanding, and they may have even moved off since we last checked. You said you're quite capable with a bow, did you not? And if we build straw men to sit on your horses, to make it appear as though there were more of you, the bandits should leave you alone. Afterward, the straw and clothing we make the false men out of will be yours to keep, as well as some supplies. You'll probably still want to do some work around here for more, but it would be a start."

Shawn's brows furrowed with thought. He contemplated the request. Onida kept her mouth shut. She didn't have much experience outside her village, especially not when it came to dealing with bandits. Then again, she knew that Shawn had lived in his cabin for a long time. He might know how to deal with bandits raiding on his land, but road bandits? He would have as much experience as Onida did.

"We'll do it," Shawn decided. "Provided you show me the route on a map and I like the look of it."

Paul beamed. "Excellent. Excellent."

Onida shovelled in a mouthful of mashed potatoes. They didn't taste as delicious as they had a minute ago.

III: MOUNTAIN LIFE

Owen sat on the porch he had built for himself and watched the storm approach in between the peaks. He was worried about the wall. As people often pointed out, he was *always* worried about the wall. When it came to storms, however, he had a very good reason to worry. When he had first begun building the thing, gathering bricks and mortar from the nearest town, he had only been thinking about the dead, about keeping out those walking corpses. The pass had been perfect: a narrow slot that was the only entrance to the high valley. Unless someone had climbing gear, they couldn't get in any other way, and while some of the zombies were smart, they weren't climbing gear smart.

People had arrived before the wall was done. Some of them had just moved into the valley without offering any assistance, leeching off his hard work, but he let them. Others had asked first, and helped with the bricking. The wall was now about thirty feet tall, and maybe three feet thick. But it wasn't strong enough to last forever.

Owen knew there would be problems with the wall after that first rain up there in the mountains. The valley was where the water naturally gathered, and the slot was where it escaped. With every brick they laid, they prevented that natural exit. Despite having drilled some deliberate holes in their wall, Owen knew that every time the rain fell, the wall would weaken. The rushing water was wearing down the brick, especially with the mud it picked up along the way. If the storm was particularly bad, the valley flooded, and someone would have to clear out all the debris that ended up heaped along the bottom of the wall. On their side of the wall a pile of mud and rocks had collected that no one knew what to do with, and so they had just left it. The caves they lived in were up the sides of the valley and kept dry, even during the worst flooding, but on multiple occasions their crops had been washed away.

"Owen, get inside before the snow gets here," urged his sister-in-law. It was for her and her children that he had built that wall. After his brother had died during the evacuation, he knew he needed to watch over them. He knew he needed to do better by them than he had in the past.

"I'm worried about the wall," he told her, getting up from his rickety lawn chair.

"I know you are. But come inside. At this time of year, it's going to snow, not rain."

"Snow melts," Owen pointed out.

"If the wall holds, it holds, and if it doesn't, it doesn't."

"But what if it doesn't?" Owen grumbled as he allowed himself to be led inside.

"Well, we won't need to worry about the walking corpses, because they'll all be washed away too."

Any zombies that found their way up the pass always ended up getting washed away with the next storm, sometimes after they were frozen in place through the winter. No one ever had to go near them.

"Yes, but they'll come back," Owen pointed out.

"And by that time, we'll have built a new wall. A better wall, that will have good drainage, and that you won't have to worry about so much. You can do that, can't you?"

She was trying to coddle him again, just like she used to. Just like she still did most of the time. Owen hadn't been able to handle the city where they used to live. Everything there had been too bright, and too loud, and too full of people. Here, there were only twenty-five people, twenty-six once Marsha and Bradley had their baby. Owen liked it up in the mountains much better, where there was a lot for him to do with his hands. Still, as he was led into the cave, he looked back at the storm and worried about the wall.

SECTION 4:
HURRICANE

19: MISHA
7 DAYS AFTER THE BOMBING

He wasn't thinking. He shouldn't have gone squirming through the opening of the fence on his own. He should have woken up the others. Of course, Misha wasn't entirely alone: Bullet was leading him. Leading him to Rifle.

They passed a corpse, totally dead, and Misha's whole body trembled. What if Rifle had been attacked? What if he were the next corpse?

Bullet was so confident in the direction he was leading Misha, that he only dropped his nose to sniff a few times while waiting for Misha to catch up. They were headed toward a building. It had been a large textile factory, full of machinery that was stripped for parts as needed. Misha did not want to go in there. He hadn't brought a source of light, and the windows wouldn't let in much of the moonlight. Inside, there were hundreds of hiding places.

But Bullet didn't go to the main door. He turned and headed for the loading docks along one side. Was that better or worse? Misha didn't know if there were any openings along the outside of the building that Rifle could get into. *Why* he would want to get in there was another, more pressing matter.

Bullet slowed as he neared the corner. The loading docks were just around the other side. His ears pricked forward, picking up some sound that Misha hadn't. The dog's posture wasn't one of fear; he was merely alert. Placing his hand on his machete, Misha followed closely behind the Australian shepherd as the two of them rounded the corner.

They found Rifle, but not in any situation for which Misha had mentally prepared himself. His brother was sitting on the pavement beside one of the loading ramps. A living person was with him, feeding him something that Rifle was enjoying. He couldn't make out the features of the person very well in the dark. He was guessing it was either a short, scrawny man, or a woman. Whoever they were, the moment they noticed Misha and Bullet, they took off. Or tried to. Apparently this individual was attempting to steal Rifle and had tied some sort of rope to the German shepherd's collar. When the stranger tried to flee, Rifle stubbornly refused to move, and the improvised leash nearly yanked over the unprepared, would-be thief.

Misha ran at the stranger, worried about what they had been feeding Rifle. The leash was abandoned, and the shrouded individual took off running like a startled rabbit. Bullet loved chasing rabbits. By the time Misha reached Rifle, Bullet had latched onto the escapee's sleeve. He growled and tugged, pulling the person off their feet and onto the ground.

Rifle wagged his tail at Misha, but Misha couldn't stop to pet him and look him over. The quickest way to find out what the dog had eaten, was to ask the one who had been feeding him.

Bullet hadn't gotten any skin, just a mouthful of sweatshirt, but he worried and tore at the fabric every time his prisoner attempted to get up. His growling intensified too, which would make anyone afraid. When Misha reached them, he drew his machete and pointed it at the stranger.

"Bullet, release," he commanded.

The dog let go, but continued to stand guard.

"Stay still," Misha next commanded the stranger.

Using the tip of his machete, he pushed up the bill of the person's baseball cap. The person's facial features still didn't help Misha identify the gender. The face was soft and hairless, so either a young man or a woman.

"What did you feed Rifle?" Misha demanded.

"What?"

"My dog! What did you feed him?" His shouting caused his captive to flinch.

"Some meat. Just some meat. Venison. Deer. I had killed one a while ago and knew the last of it needed to be eaten before it went bad." The voice was that of a woman attempting to pitch her tone lower, but her fear made it inconsistent.

"Why were you trying to steal my dog?"

"I'm sorry. I'm sorry. I shouldn't have done that. It's just that your dogs are so well trained, and the way you worked with them, I wanted that for myself."

"So train your own dog. Wait... have you been following us?" Was it possible that Misha hadn't just been paranoid? That this woman had actually been tailing them?

"Yes. I'm sorry. I just wanted to know if you were safe to approach."

"And you couldn't determine that over a few days, but you could decide to take my dog? Is there anyone else?"

"With me? No. No, there's just me."

"Get up." Misha took a step back to give her some room. "The others will want to talk to you."

"Crichton, right? That's his name? The one who's in charge?" This statement nearly brought Misha's blade back to her face. It was creepy, knowing she had been following them. How much had she heard and learned?

"You clearly know the way. Start walking," Misha gestured back toward the campsite. "Don't try to run or Bullet will just take you down again. What's your name, anyway?" While her back was turned, Misha quickly untied the rope from Rifle's collar and pocketed it, making sure to pat the dog's head afterward. He wanted to thoroughly check Rifle over right then and there, but knew he had to wait until his prisoner was secure.

"Sherlock," she answered his question.

"That's not your name." Misha couldn't imagine anyone naming their baby girl Sherlock, especially not since she was old enough to have been born before the Day.

"A name is just what people call you, right? People call me Sherlock." The fear was leaving her as they walked, her voice smoothing out in that lowered pitch she adopted.

When they reached the fence, Misha whistled loudly. All his dogs were immediately up on their feet. The humans also jolted awake, with Harry cursing loudly as he banged his head on the cart. They were all over at the fence and helping to hold it open within seconds.

"I found this one by the textile factory," Misha explained. "She says her name is Sherlock, and she was trying to kidnap Rifle."

"*He*," Sherlock snapped at him, a sudden flash of anger. "I'm a male."

"You're a male?" Angela questioned. "You don't seem like one."

"Fuck you," Sherlock snapped at her next.

"If you have a penis dangling between your legs, then I'm the Second Coming of Jesus," Angela snapped right back.

"It's not about what's between your legs, you piss head," Sherlock growled at her, and then Misha understood. She, or rather he, was transgender. It explained the odd voice pitch. Sherlock wouldn't be able to get any hormone therapy, or vocal training, or gender confirmation surgery, and so he had to make do with what he could on his own. Misha had known a transgender woman at college, a friend of one of his roommates.

"What did you call me?" Angela challenged.

"Step back, Angela," Crichton told her as he stepped between the two. "Sherlock, you're in no position right now to be throwing insults. I suggest you reassess your situation and priorities."

Even in the dark, Misha could tell that Sherlock flushed a bright red as his eyes darted about those who surrounded him.

"Ki-Nam, why don't you start a fire?" Crichton suggested. "It would be better if all of us could see one another clearly, and I wouldn't mind some more warmth."

When the fire was lit, and they were seated, Misha started examining Rifle while the rest of his dogs investigated Sherlock with their noses. He didn't seem to mind the dogs' attention, occasionally giving one a scratch behind the ear. Sherlock had put his hat back on when Misha marched him to the camp, but he took it off now so that everyone could clearly see his face. His hair had been butchered, cut short in uneven clumps. He had likely done it himself.

"I'm Crichton," he introduced himself. "This is Ki-Nam, Angela, Harry, and Misha."

"I know," Sherlock told him, as he was almost knocked sideways by Powder bumping her large head against him.

"He's been following us," Misha told everyone. The dogs all appeared to like Sherlock, and while that normally put Misha at ease, this time it had the opposite effect. He didn't like that they weren't cautious. He really didn't like that Rifle had been somehow lured off.

Crichton nodded his head at Misha's statement. "How long have you been following us?"

Sherlock shrugged. "A while. Since you left that trail of slime. There were a bunch of you, all breaking off into smaller groups. I chose to follow yours because of the dogs."

Most of the dogs were now starting to investigate Rifle because Misha was.

"Why did you follow us?" Crichton asked next.

"Because I wanted to learn about you. And I liked the dogs."

"How did you get them to trust you?" Misha interjected before Crichton could ask anything else. It really bothered him.

"While you were sleeping, I rubbed against stuff in the area, or rubbed trash against my body that I then put in places where you wouldn't notice but they would. I left some food out too, although I didn't have much to share. They got used to knowing I was around, and that I was a source of food. Dogs are very food driven."

Misha knew that was true, and hated that this guy had found a way to manipulate that fact.

"You're very quiet," Crichton commented. "We didn't know you were there."

"He almost caught me," Sherlock pointed to Misha.

"How did you get on the roof?" This time it was Harry who was asking.

"I'm good at climbing. Most of the stuff in my pack is climbing gear."

"Were you ever going to make contact with us?" Crichton wondered.

"No, I had decided not to. I just thought I'd take one of the dogs for company and then go somewhere else. But I was unlucky. I couldn't get close enough to this place to hear what your guard schedule was going to be. If Misha's was later on at night, I would have been gone before he noticed that Rifle was missing."

"Rifle wouldn't have gone much further away with you," Misha told him, his voice carrying ice.

"He might have."

"No. He wouldn't."

"I would have tried for one of the other dogs then," Sherlock said, as if it were no big deal. "Rifle was the only one awake who wasn't on patrol, but I think I could've woken up another without alerting any of you."

Misha remembered how many times in the past he had gotten up in the middle of the night to let Rifle out of the container so that the dog could pee. He must have been relieving himself when Sherlock had offered him food from beyond the fence.

"Why did you decide not to make contact?" Crichton's voice continued to remain level, absorbing Sherlock's comments without any sort of reaction. Beside him, Angela fumed, but was successfully managing to keep her mouth shut.

"Because you're afraid of someone. Most people tend to call out when they think they're being followed by a stranger. At least, people who aren't that afraid of zombies, which you clearly aren't based on what I've seen. You think there's some other threat in the area."

"We used to live here," Crichton explained. "A large group of raiders took it over. We did this in response," he gestured to the crater behind them, hidden in the dark beyond the firelight. "We don't know how many survived."

"And you're worried I'm a surviving raider," Sherlock figured. "Let me tell ya, hearing that you blew up an entire group of people doesn't make me feel all warm and fuzzy toward you guys."

"We never said we blew them up," Angela growled, highly suspicious.

"I have eyes that can see," Sherlock retorted. "The crater, the debris. There're all the signs of a large, underground explosion. This area doesn't seem like the kind for caves, so I'm guessing you were in some sort of bunker. Did the raiders ask to be let in, and you turned them away?"

Angela opened her mouth, ready to snap off another insult, but Crichton cut her off. "A child showed up, starving and weak. We took him in, not knowing he was a plant for the raiders. He somehow got word out to them about the layout of our place. They came in during the night, captured several people, beat some, killed a few, and then ordered us out of our home without any supplies."

"Why are you telling this asshole everything?" Angela grumbled to Crichton. "*She* could be one of them."

Sherlock bristled.

"Angela, there's no need to mis-gender him," Crichton told her, his voice just as calm as when he spoke to Sherlock. "If he is one of them, then he would know this already."

"You're a bitch," Sherlock told Angela.

Angela looked like she was about to get up and lunge across the fire at Sherlock, but Harry placed a firm hand on her shoulder, and whispered something in her ear.

"I take it these raiders didn't know that you had another place to go." Sherlock turned back to Crichton. "It must have been attacked by one massive herd of zombies. That slime trail is the largest I've ever seen. Probably why you sent out a bunch of groups. I'm guessing where you live is hurting."

"We're talking an awful lot about ourselves," Misha finally spoke up again. "Why don't you tell us where you're from? What you're doing in the area? Where you planned to go after you kidnapped one of my dogs?" That last question was unnecessary, but Misha was still feeling rather prickly.

Sherlock shrugged. The gesture was so nonchalant that it was irritating. "I lived in a community farther west and a ways north. They were of the same mindset as that one." He pointed to Angela. "I decided it was better for me to leave. I wandered around for a while, trying to find a good place to fit in. Some communities were pretty good, but when I didn't like it there, I moved on. When I came across all the zombie debris, I decided to see where it led. Better to know where the herd was so that I could avoid it in the future. Then I saw all your groups heading out, and I figured you had been hit by the dead. I already told you why I decided to follow you. As for where I would go afterward, I don't know. The real question is, what are you going to do with me now?"

"That is the question," Crichton agreed.

"I say we tie rocks to *his* ankles and chuck *him* in the lake," Angela suggested. When she had used the male pronouns, she looked at Crichton to show that she was complying with what he had said. A bit of her hostility was now directed at the commander.

"There's no need for that," Harry told her. "He hasn't done anything to us."

"Speak for yourself," Misha muttered. They hadn't felt the paranoia that he had, or wondered if they were losing their minds. They hadn't been nearly paralyzed by fear, discovering that Rifle was off beyond the fence.

"What would you like to do?" Ki-Nam unexpectedly asked Misha. "You are the most aggrieved party here. It is your dogs Sherlock intended to steal."

Misha shifted uncomfortably under the gaze of the others. Even Crichton was looking at him, wondering what his answer would be. Misha didn't know what he wanted done. He hadn't thought about it. His plan had ended with bringing Sherlock to Crichton, and doing whatever the man decided needed to be done.

Turning his head, Misha met Sherlock's gaze. Sherlock was clearly trying to appear impassive like Crichton, even disinterested, yet there was fear within Sherlock's rigid posture. Misha, returning his attention to Rifle who was lying comfortably with his head on his lap, knew that Sherlock hadn't harmed his friend in any way. He had had no intention to cause harm, which Misha supposed should count for something.

"Do people really call you Sherlock, or is that a name you gave yourself?" Misha asked. It was a stall tactic as he worked through the various options he could think up.

"People did actually call me Sherlock. I like the name."

"Why did they call you that?"

"Because I'm observant. I have a good memory and can put things together based on what I see." He had shown them a bit of that with his deductions about them.

"Are you sure it's not because you're self-centred?" Misha didn't realize he was speaking aloud until after the words were out.

Sherlock shifted in place. "That might be why some of them used the moniker," he admitted.

"We should tie him up and decide what to do in the morning," Misha finally suggested. He was exhausted, too tired to come up with any real solution to their predicament.

"Very well," Crichton agreed.

"Come on, now, it's not exactly easy to sleep while tied up," Sherlock complained, as the others began to move.

"Good," Angela grumbled, kicking dirt onto the low fire.

Ki-Nam grabbed Sherlock's large bag and proceeded to yank it off his shoulders.

"Easy! Easy." Sherlock pulled his arms in, letting the pack slip off. They were then pulled behind his back as Misha tied his wrists together. He then hauled Sherlock upright and patted him down. Sherlock flinched a few times, as Misha was very thorough. He wasn't going to take any chances, and this wasn't the time to be polite. Sherlock kept his mouth shut, perhaps understanding that Misha's intentions weren't actually meant to be hostile, and definitely weren't sexual.

The search produced a climbing axe on his belt and a knife in his boot which was removed during the process, then Misha frogmarched Sherlock over to the cart. There, he was made to sit beside it. His ankles were tied up, and the bindings around his wrists were tied to a wheel axle. He had enough slack to either sit up or lie down, but not much else.

"Am I at least allowed to have something for a pillow?" Sherlock wondered.

"You tried to kidnap my dog," was the only reply Misha gave him.

It was still his turn to keep watch. Misha settled his dogs, making sure they were all close this time. He even fed them all a little bit, hoping that would convince them not to wander off. He worried that maybe Sherlock hadn't been alone, and that someone else was going to try the same trick.

He kept awake by walking circles around the camp, staggering his speed and how widely he walked a circuit. By the time he switched with Crichton, it appeared that Sherlock had managed to fall asleep. Still, Misha watched him as he crawled under the cart. Other than shifting a little bit, with the changing of the guard, their prisoner didn't move or say anything.

Misha would have liked to keep an eye on him all night, but his exhaustion got the better of him and weighed down his eyelids.

***

Misha picked through the debris with his whole dog pack. He was searching for anything of interest that they might have missed on the far side of the new lake. With Crichton leading Sherlock around, the prisoner was safe from Angela's hostilities, and Misha wanted some time to himself to think about their options. Or rather his options. In the morning, Crichton hadn't changed his mind, and seemed to insist that Misha decide what to do with the would-be thief. There had to be something they could do that would satisfy Misha, without disappointing Crichton or setting off Angela's fury. It had become sort of a diplomatic situation, and Misha had always hated diplomacy. Sometimes he thought back to the Day, when it was just him and Rifle, and he didn't have to worry about what anyone else wanted. Of course, those hours were filled with pain, terror, and confusion, so he never really missed them. He sometimes missed Riley's cabin, though. Had that tree never fallen on the greenhouse, they could've made a good go of it, especially if Shawn had never shown up. Mathias, Alec, and Tobias would probably all still be alive. But if Shawn had never come, then Riley would never have been reunited with Cameron, and Abby would never have known that Lauren was still alive. Josh's rivalry with Mathias would have gotten worse with time, Danny would never be around people his own age, and Hope wouldn't have been born in a place stocked with medical gear—safer if something went wrong.

Beside Misha, Rifle chuffed. The dog was looking up at him with concern. Misha had been standing still, lost in his thoughts.

"Sorry, *bratishka*." He gave Rifle's ears a scratch. Bullet and a few of the other dogs saw this and wanted in too, so Misha gave them various scratches, pats, and rubs as well. Spring was not one of the dogs to come over, which was strange. Misha instantly feared that she had been taken, but that fear didn't last long. She wasn't far, sniffing intently at the ground. Had she found a rat's nest?

Misha walked over to Spring, calling to her as he got close. She raised her head at the sound of her name, but her ears and tail remained drooped with concern. Misha was just near enough to hear her whine, and so sped up when she lowered her head once more.

It was not a rat's nest that Spring had found. Sticking up through some of the Black Box debris was a hand. An animal must have been at it at some point, as much of the flesh had been stripped away. Ants were working on the rest.

The dogs all took turns sniffing it while Misha found some rocks small enough for him to lift, but large enough to cover the hand. It must have been a raider, the rest of him buried beneath the surface, but Misha thought that he nevertheless deserved a better burial. The ants would still be able to get at the hand, and likely more, but there was nothing Misha could do about that.

The raider's hand had given him an idea about what to do with Sherlock, however.

After rounding up his dog pack, Misha began to make his way back around the lake. He noticed a sort of irritation in his dogs that he hadn't picked up on before due to his wandering mind. It was the same nervous nature they got when they thought a bad storm was coming. Misha didn't know whether that meant they would be hit by one or not. Often they were right, but a few times they had been wrong, and the storm simply passed them by.

Misha found Crichton sitting with Sherlock at the cart. Sherlock's hands were still tied, in front of him now, and his ankles were free. The rope that had tied him to the cart axle remained attached, but now the other end was in Crichton's hands. It was somewhat satisfying to see Sherlock leashed the way he had leashed Rifle.

"Where's Angela?" Misha asked.

Crichton pointed. "Why do you need her?"

"I want her to hear what I've decided to do with Sherlock."

Sherlock had been attempting to relax against the cart until that point. Now, he stood up straight, his fingers nervously scratching at the rope that bound his wrists. His brown eyes, so much darker than Misha's ghostly pale blue ones, studied his face, trying to read Misha's intent. It made Misha uncomfortable, but he understood that he would do the same if their positions were reversed.

Crichton looked up to study the sky. "Should be lunch time soon. We'll wait until everyone's together." Then his face pinched, his usual placid expression turning momentarily into a frown.

"What's wrong?" Misha looked up, trying to see what he was seeing.

"There's a storm coming," Sherlock answered instead. "A bad one."

"I think he might be right," Crichton agreed as he studied the cloud patterns.

"The dogs think so," Misha admitted.

"Does that affect your decision?" Crichton asked him.

"Maybe." Misha shrugged, deciding not to elaborate further for the time being.

When Ki-Nam eventually came over to join them, he was certain a storm was coming. He had climbed the fallen crane as Misha had yesterday, and had gotten high enough to see the storm clouds. He was rather concerned about them.

"I don't think we're staying here much longer," Crichton informed him, with a glance at Misha because he didn't know Misha's plan. "We'll find a safe place to shelter."

Harry and Angela returned to the cart not much later. Once everyone had piled their finds onto yesterday's gatherings, the cart became rather full. Crichton handed out equal portions of food for their lunch, including to

Sherlock. He also gave Misha a second portion to distribute to his dogs, which was a little surprising. It wasn't much once divided nine ways, but maybe after what had happened the night before, Crichton had decided that they should be fed a little better.

"So what's this plan you've come up with?" Angela asked while they ate. Crichton had mentioned that Misha had an idea while he handed out the food.

"You said you're observant," Misha turned to Sherlock. "That means you should be good at tracking, right?"

"Yes." Sherlock's eyes never left Misha's face.

"Are you good enough to track the raiders who left here?"

Sherlock shrugged. "Depends on what's left. After the coming storm, it's not going to be much, if anything."

Misha turned back to the group. "We're worried about where they went, right? Sherlock can show us. We're not likely to find them, not with the storm coming, but we can at least get a good idea of which way they went."

Was that a smile that pulled ever so slightly at Crichton's lips?

"And what do we do with this turd afterward?" Angela gestured at Sherlock with her chin.

"Let him go. No one was hurt. Helping us ease our fears about the remaining raiders will be payment for what he tried to do." It seemed like a good trade to Misha: cause a fear, alleviate a fear. As long as the raiders weren't heading for the container yard, that was.

"Will I get my stuff back?" Sherlock gestured to his bag, which was sitting on the cart's driving board.

"You will," Harry spoke up, firm in his words so that the others knew he would fight them if they wanted to decide differently. "We're not thieves."

"We should get going then. We want to use all the time we have to move before the storm comes," Ki-Nam told them.

It didn't take long to get going. The horses, Potato and Thumper, were hooked up to the cart while the fence opening was widened again. Most of their stuff was still packed, and it didn't take Misha long to gather up what hadn't been. Harry and Angela scanned the area around their camp one last time to make sure nothing was forgotten. While all this was going on, Crichton had taken Sherlock out into the fields to find the start of the trail. It took a little while, because the raiders had apparently moved about outside the fences quite a bit, but Sherlock eventually led them away from the Black Box. Misha doubted he would ever see the place again.

They started by heading north-east, away from the direction of the container yard, which was a good sign. When they reached streets, Sherlock guided them straight north.

"How will you know if they turned down one of these side streets?" Harry asked, curious.

"I might not be able to tell," Sherlock admitted. "It's harder to track across paved areas. I look for footsteps in the areas where dirt's accumulated, weeds and grasses that have been flattened, dead zombies left in their wake, buildings that have been recently broken into, that kind of stuff. These raiders of yours are interesting."

"In what way?" Harry was holding Sherlock's leash, with Misha and Angela following closely behind. Crichton had chosen to guard the rear, and Ki-Nam drove the cart.

"They left in two groups. A small one, I'm thinking three people, and a larger one that's over a dozen."

"Which group are we following?" Angela immediately asked, glancing back over her shoulder, doubting that they were heading the right way.

"Both."

"So the three are scouts," Harry determined.

"Sort of. They're weird scouts, though."

"In what way?" This time Misha asked.

"They're a little gooey."

"Gooey?" Both Misha and Harry spoke at the same time.

"I obviously can't say for certain, but I think they disguised themselves as corpses. Wouldn't be the first time I'd seen someone do that."

"Gross," Angela wrinkled her nose. "Why would anyone do that? To hide from the zombies?"

"No," Sherlock shook his head. "The dead still know. I've seen people do it as a way to hide from other people. At a distance, most can't tell the difference."

"And a zombie at a distance can go by ignored," Harry added. "The humans won't bother hiding if they don't think the dead have seen them."

"Right. I'll bet your raiders first scoped out your place with people disguised as the dead before they sent that kid to you. Makes them easier to track though." Sherlock pointed to a tiny stain, which Misha wasn't going to admit he couldn't really identify as anything. "To keep up appearances, the ones I've seen before tend to kill zombies fairly regularly. They use the corpses to keep up their shiny glisten. If they look fresh, they can walk more normally, because the dry ones tend to be slower and stagger about."

Misha had never spent that much time studying the zombies, and couldn't say he had noticed. If it was near him, he killed it, and that was that.

Harry was very interested in Sherlock's tracking methods. Sherlock seemed to like the chance to show off, and so he freely told Harry all the objects he was looking at, even the things that weren't tied to the raiders. Misha had to admit that Sherlock was seeing a lot more than he could. Hopefully the guy wasn't bullshitting them all. His 'signs' could all be made up. He might be leading them in a random direction of his choosing, or worse, guiding them into a trap. The raiders had proven themselves capable of such deceit already.

They passed an intersection, and Sherlock came to a stop.

"What's wrong?" Harry asked.

"I lost the trail," Sherlock said. He wandered back and forth across the street with Harry, like a dog searching for a scent. "They must have turned," he decided.

The east was checked first, partly due to the raiders' original north-east course, and partly due to the fact that they hoped that that was the direction they had taken. But no signs were found. Sherlock looked to the west, and nodded.

"You're positive?" Misha asked.

"Yeah. See, here's another drip. And there, further along, there's a footprint in those leaves."

Angela's jaw clenched. She hated the raiders most of all, and was very unhappy to discover that they were headed in the direction needed to reach the container yard.

They didn't get very far to the west before Crichton called them all to a stop.

"We have to get inside," he said, as he jogged up from the rear. "We have to find good shelter, now." He spoke with an urgency that brokered no argument.

The sky was getting darker by the second, and the wind was picking up as they searched for the best location. All the dogs stuck close to Misha, save Rifle who was on the cart with Ki-Nam. Every now and again, he heard one of his dogs issue a low whine.

"There's a bank!" Angela called out from down a side street.

Misha ran over to investigate the interior with her. The dogs made short work of the place, spreading out quickly and checking each office with a fast once over. It was a large bank, old, made out of a lot of stone and not boasting many windows. They were able to get the horses and the cart through a set of grand double doors just as the rain descended upon them. They located the vault, which was open and empty, but didn't go inside. No one liked the idea of somehow becoming trapped within it. Instead, they set up camp at the top of the stairs that led down to the basement in which the vault was housed. If they needed to escape, they could run back to the front doors, or one of the other fire exits. If the place started to collapse, then they would move what they could into the vault, which was even more solidly built than the stone building.

The wind outside howled, as the rain lashed at everything. Sherlock was set loose, for there was nowhere for him to go, and they wanted to use all their ropes to secure the doors, which couldn't be locked without a key. Outside, it had become as dark as night. Misha's flashlight, when pressed to the glass, revealed that the street outside had already become a shallow river. Thankfully, the old style bank had the majority of its teller windows and offices up above street level. After finishing with the doors, Misha scrambled up the wide, marble steps. It had been a bitch to get the horses and the cart up, but they had persisted. Misha crossed the grand floor with its high ceiling, and returned to the camp tucked away in the hallway that was normally for employees only. Even hidden away inside all that stone, Misha could hear the storm. As he sat down, all of his dogs gathered to him. They were frightened, and Misha thought that they had good reason to be. The light cast from the group's collection of flashlights and lanterns, revealed matching worried expressions on the faces of all the humans. Angela didn't even seem to mind that she was sitting right beside Sherlock. They should have reduced their lights to just one, but no one was ready to cede ground to the dark yet.

No one spoke, at least no words that could be heard above the wind and rain. Ki-Nam was standing with the horses, calming them, and while Misha could see his lips moving, he couldn't hear anything of what was being said. He, too, was constantly leaning over and whispering soothing words to his dogs.

Despite the ropes, the doors rattled. Somewhere inside there must have been a leak, since Misha could hear running water, but the sound-reflecting nature of the stone made it impossible to pin down which direction it was coming from. Hopefully the vast basement beneath the bank would hold any floodwaters. They had checked the stairs and found there was only one more floor above the one where they were crouched. It would be very difficult to get the horses up there, and impossible for the cart, because the stairwell was narrow and contained a sharp bend, so everyone hoped they wouldn't have to move.

And then Trigger whined. It was a different sound than usual. Misha pointed his light at the golden dog. She had gotten up and was sniffing around. She was looking for a place to nest.

Not now, Misha groaned internally. Of all the times for the puppies to come, now was quite possibly the very worst.

20: DAKOTA
8 DAYS AFTER THE BOMBING

By the time she had climbed into the submarine, the wind had picked up and the sky had gone quite dark. While eager to check out the sub, Dakota was also a little scared. Storms always put her somewhat on edge, but this time was different. She was going to be riding this out in a different place, without all the people she knew. What if something happened to the submarine while she was on board? What if something happened to those left behind on shore?

As Bronislav led her through the close confines, receiving word from the various stations that they were ready to get underway, Dakota looked at the others who had been brought on board to study different positions. Most of them were a lot older than she was, often their twenties. The only person she really knew was Peter, and though he was younger than her, it wasn't surprising that he was there. The kid was a math whiz. There was certain to be some job on the sub that he would pick up faster than anybody.

"Dakota?" Bronislav said, startling her. "Pay attention, please."

"Sorry, sir."

"You've never been on a submarine before, is that correct?"

"Yes, sir, that's correct."

"I'll show you everything in more detail later then. For now, we have to get moving."

The hatch within the conning tower was sealed. All the wires that had been run from the sub's generator to the surface, for people outside to connect to the power supply, had been disconnected and coiled up out of the way. The engines rumbled to life, and Dakota tried to pay attention to what Bronislav was doing and saying, but she didn't understand all of it. He used submariner jargon, even slipping into his native Russian at times, but he tended to repeat himself in English when he did that. The submarine was German, and so were several of the sailors on board. Dakota couldn't read any of the labels. She wondered how Bronislav knew what everything was. Had his sub been that similar? Or had Captain Karsten taken him through it all sometime before he died? Was Dakota expected to learn everything? She couldn't imagine doing it. There was no way anyone could learn it all during one outing, but she didn't think she could learn it all even after a hundred outings. A thousand! It seemed an impossible task.

The submarine pulled away from the dock and they got underway. They could have gone up river—it was deep enough—but Bronislav felt safer in more open waters, given that they didn't know the exact severity of the storm. This meant that they were actually heading toward it, and Dakota had to trust that the captain knew what he was doing. She also had to trust that they had left soon enough to reach the open sea before the worst part of the hurricane hit them.

The submarine rode the waves, and Dakota could hear the water sloshing against them, all around.

"Have you ever gotten motion sickness? Sea sick?" Bronislav asked her as he hovered near the men who, Dakota assumed, were doing the actual driving. How did they know where they were going without being able to see outside?

"No," she answered him.

"If you start to feel queazy at all, let me know. You won't be able to get out of the sub, and there's not much we can do for you besides give you a place to lie down and a bucket to throw up in, but don't try to look tough. We don't want vomit on any of the instruments."

"I'll be okay." Dakota had no idea if she'd be okay. She had no idea if anyone would be okay by the time this storm went through.

"Do you have any questions right now?" Bronislav asked her.

"Yeah, how come you don't use the periscope?" She didn't even know what part of the bridge *was* the periscope. There was so much stuff lining the walls and ceiling, and even down by the floor. Pipes and wires and consoles and people. All of it labelled in German.

"We don't need to," Bronislav told her. "Our instruments tell us all we need to know in this situation. Besides, you wouldn't be able to see much. The sky is getting steadily darker, and the chop is also increasing."

"Chop?"

"Waves. We move with the waves, periscope included, which means anything stationary, such as the land, could be difficult to make out." He patted a large vertical pipe, which Dakota took to be the periscope. Low down on it, she could see handles folded up and an eyepiece. She figured that they lifted higher when the periscope was raised.

Bronislav had no more time for questions, as he and the other sailors began tossing more jargon back and forth. There was even a phone to speak with people in other parts of the submarine. Dakota did her best to keep out of the way. She was lucky the brim of her hat occasionally warned her just before she was about to bash her head into something low.

The submarine rose and fell with the large waves. Even after Bronislav ordered the men to dive, causing a brief alarm to sound to warn everyone, the motion didn't cease all together.

"We're underwater, so why does it feel like we're not?"

"Waves are like icebergs: they're not just on the surface," Bronislav gave her the quick explanation for he was apparently still quite busy. Dakota wanted to go find out what Peter was doing, but she didn't dare leave Bronislav's side. The deal had been for her to shadow him. She also didn't completely trust her balance if she were to walk somewhere. She eventually found a place to stand where she didn't appear to be in anyone's way, and where there was a bar she could safely hold onto should the *chop* get any worse.

What's happening at the container yard? Dakota wondered. Were they being hammered? Was everyone safely inside? She found herself worrying the most for Cameron, Brunt, Hope, Riley, and Elijah. Had Elijah ever been through a storm like this one? If he had never seen the sea, then it seemed unlikely. Of course, he may have dealt with a tornado in his past, or a massive snowstorm in the mountains. If she remembered, and if everyone survived, perhaps Dakota would ask him next time she saw him. The thought of actually having something to talk about made her stomach flutter. Or was that just the motion of the submarine?

Dakota had no idea where they were in relation to anything else. She had never learned how fast the submarine could move, and didn't really know the distance between the container yard and the open sea. Every few minutes, Bronislav ordered them a little bit deeper. How deep could the submarine go? Deep enough that they stopped rolling with the chop altogether, apparently. Dakota could still feel some movement, however. Maybe it was the pull of the currents or the deep thrum of the engines. She didn't know what the currents were like here, or how the engines worked. Subs were supposed to be silent, right? Or was that some misinformation she was remembering from a long time ago?

"All right, ladies and gentlemen, we can go no deeper without putting ourselves at an unnecessary risk," Bronislav eventually announced. "We'll wait out the storm here, and hope it's not driving a massive tsunami before it."

Dakota knew what tsunamis were. She had learned about them back aboard the Diana. If one did come that was deep enough to reach the submarine, what would happen? She imagined the sub being rolled by the forces, getting swept along until it was dashed upon the bottom somewhere. Or maybe it would get sucked up to the surface somehow, and thrown onto land. That would be interesting, if the submarine became landlocked on, say, Quarantine Island. Of course, a wave that could do that, would wipe out the container yard.

"Would you like a tour of the submarine now?" Bronislav asked her.

"Okay."

"Are you feeling alright?"

Dakota shrugged. "Sure. Just nervous."

"About what?"

"Lots of things."

Bronislav nodded, not needing to ask any follow-up questions to understand. He was likely worried about the container yard, too.

"How deep can this thing go?" Dakota asked as a way of turning her mind to something else.

Bronislav told her what the sub was rated for, but she didn't have a great grasp of distances, and couldn't picture the answer in relation to anything.

"What happens if we try to go deeper than that?"

"The deeper you go, the greater the water pressure outside. If those pressures exceed what our hull was built to withstand, we get crushed like a tin can beneath a boot. The pressure would kill you before you could drown."

Dakota shivered as she thought about it. Not the best topic to redirect her mind toward.

"Come along." Bronislav headed in the direction of the sub's nose, walking with an easy confidence. He told another man, one of the Germans, that he had the helm while they were gone.

Dakota got to see everything on the ship. The torpedo tubes, empty missile silos, radar station, crew bunks, captain's quarters, kitchen, engines, all of it. Only the reactor was off limits, and that was because the radiation within would kill everyone on board should there be a mishap. It was monitored at all times.

"Why do we have so many supplies on board?" Dakota asked when she had seen the storerooms.

"It was decided that the submarine was the safest place for them," Bronislav told her. "There are other caches all about the container yard. We didn't want to put all our eggs in one basket, as the saying goes, but this is the largest. If everything gets wiped out, but the people survive, we'll still be able to feed them all for a couple of days."

A couple of days. That was not a lot. Those who had journeyed away from the container yard needed to make contact with a friendly group soon. They needed food. What would people start doing when they ran out? Nothing good, that was for sure. They might even need to abandon the container yard, which made Dakota's insides twist themselves up. In spite of the many deaths recently, she still saw the place as being far safer than anywhere else.

"Do you have any questions?" Bronislav asked after they had seen everything.

Dakota shook her head. She had too many. She was trying to mentally digest everything she had learned during the tour, to store it in her memory.

It was so quiet in the submarine. The engines had gone still, Dakota thought. No one spoke much, and when they did, it was in a whisper. There was no need to whisper, but in the silence, it came naturally. The metal around her sometimes popped and pinged, due to the pressure of the depths and the temperature changes in the water all around them. When the phone rang, a shrill jangle, Dakota thought she might jump out of her skin, it startled her so badly.

"Captain Bronislav," he answered, picking up the receiver with a casual speed and grace. Dakota had a memory, a very faint one, of her real mom answering the phone in the same manner. She couldn't make out the details of her mother's face, only that quick ease of doing something she had done many times before. Dakota could almost remember her voice, but couldn't be certain that it wasn't just her mind making something up to fill in that gap.

Bronislav said a few curt words in response to whoever was on the other end, then thanked the person and hung up.

"Come. I want you to hear something."

Hear something? Dakota's curiosity was piqued. What was there to hear that she couldn't hear already?

Bronislav brought her back to where the sonar technician was huddled away in his own little nook, wearing a huge pair of earphones on his head. Peter was there, and he had a wide smile on his face, which was something not often seen. Now Dakota was super curious.

"Here, sit down," the sonar man said, his voice thick with a Russian accent.

Dakota sat in the chair he had abandoned, and the headphones were placed over her ears. With those things on, it seemed like even her breathing became muffled.

"They're far off," the sonar man told her, his voice sounding quiet and flat. "You have to listen closely."

Dakota couldn't hear anything through the headphones except for her own pulse in her ears. She closed her eyes and focused. It took several seconds, but she thought she heard something. Her eyes scrunched even more tightly together as she listened. It was a rather haunting sound she was picking up. And it wasn't alone.

"Whales!" she suddenly cried out, realizing what the sound must be. When she looked to Bronislav, he smiled and nodded, confirming her thoughts. She listened for a while longer, their song travelling through the sea to her ears. She understood why Peter was smiling so much. There was a somewhat sad and eerie quality to the sound, but there was something magical about it as well.

After listening for another minute, Dakota pulled off the headphones and held them out to Peter.

"Do you want to listen some more?" she asked him.

"I have extra headsets," the sonar man told them. "You can both listen."

The headsets were brought down from an overhead storage. The sonar man took his seat back, but he gave Peter and Dakota a headset each and told them in what corner they could stand.

"Stay here," Bronislav ordered Dakota before her new headset could be plugged in. "I'll know where to find you if I need to."

Dakota gave him a thumbs up, which he seemed to find amusing. She and Peter stood huddled together, listening to the far away whales singing to one another.

***

Dakota thought she knew when the storm surge swept over them. The submarine floor seemed to rise slowly beneath her feet, and then drop away again. One of the twenty-something-year-olds said it felt the same as an earthquake. Dakota had to assume he was right, as she had never felt one herself.

Nothing else of interest really happened on the submarine. The whales had moved off, and the sub was rather stable, with a very gentle and continuous rocking. Dakota tried not to picture the fury that must be going on above them, but she did anyway.

"You should go to bed," Bronislav told her.

"I'm not tired," Dakota lied to him.

"I can see that you are. And it is very late. You've had a very long and busy day. Go to bed."

"I'm supposed to shadow you. I'm not going to sleep until you do," she challenged him.

Bronislav grinned. "Then it's a good thing that that is soon. I'm just waiting for the shift change to be completed."

Some of the submariners had gone straight to the bunks when they boarded. They would be monitoring the vital systems throughout the night. Dakota's body knew that it was very late, but she didn't actually know what time it was. Bronislav wore a watch, but he hadn't read out the time to anyone lately. When the shift officially changed, and he decided to get some sleep, Dakota learned that it was just shy of four in the morning. No wonder she was so beat!

There was only one bed in the captain's quarters, so Dakota had to sleep on the bunks with the rest of the crew. Because of all the training shadows on board, it was a little bit crowded, but not overly so. Not like it would have been for those who crossed over from Europe, or even for those who had fled the Black Box.

Dakota lay on the bunk above Peter's. He was already deep asleep, not even stirring when she climbed up past him. More than one person was snoring, and Dakota thought it would keep her awake, but was proven wrong. Her exhaustion and the gentle rocking of the submarine quickly sent her into a deep and dreamless slumber.

***

When she was shaken awake, Dakota's thought was that she hadn't fallen asleep at all. It hadn't seemed like enough time had passed. And perhaps not enough had. She didn't bother to ask the time, but considering that everyone was waking up, it was likely morning. Peter was the one shaking her.

"I'm awake," she mumbled as she propped herself up on her elbows.

"Bronislav is on the bridge. I figured you should be too," he mumbled, sounding apologetic for waking her.

"It's okay." She slid off her bunk, unable to tell if Peter understood that she was accepting his unspoken apology. Her clothes were rumpled, since she had slept in them, but there was nothing for her to change into. She used the tiny toilet stall when it was available, then followed the main group of people to the kitchen for her breakfast ration. It was disheartening how small it was. Without much sleep, she would have to rely on the food to sustain her, but it didn't look like that was going to be possible. Since the destruction of the Black Box, she had grown used to the feeling of hunger. There were times when that revelation was more awful than the hunger itself.

Bronislav was where Peter had said he would be. She sidled up beside him as he read through a report of some kind. The writing was very small and cramped, and Dakota guessed that the large dots separated various messages. Some were likely much older than others; paper had become rather scarce. The tiny letters went all the way to the margins, and there was barely a space between words. Bronislav squinted as he read. Maybe he needed glasses. They had a small pile of reading glasses stored away at the container yard somewhere. Maybe Dakota should suggest he look through them when they got back. Provided there was anything to go back to, reading glasses included.

When Bronislav was done with the report, he gave orders to his men before turning to Dakota.

"We're going up closer to the surface," he told her. "We have to check on the storm to determine whether we are to go back today."

"We might not go home today?" Dakota was under the impression that the sub trip would only be for a single night.

"The worst of the storm has likely passed over us, but the seas could remain rough for some time. Days even. The rains as well."

Days? Dakota hadn't considered that possibility. Surely Cameron had been informed, and so she wouldn't worry. Well, she'd worry, but she'd have something to latch onto, to convince herself that she was being silly.

Bronislav spoke on the phone and his voice echoed throughout the submarine from overhead speakers. An alarm sounded briefly, the same kind as when they were preparing to dive.

"You may want to hold onto something," Bronislav told her. "I suspect this will be a short yet rough journey."

Dakota went to the corner she had discovered the other day and held on to the bar there. Everyone standing, which was mostly shadows like herself, had found something to cling to. Bronislav reached a hand up and held onto a pipe above his head.

As they rose, the swaying of the submarine got worse. The deck beneath Dakota's feet moved in unexpected ways. They rolled, pitched, and yawed, never in the direction that she thought might be next. She had never been on a roller coaster, but imagined it was somewhat similar.

Bronislav was barking a continuous stream of orders. His first mate, the German he had left in charge during yesterday's tour, was relaying a constant stream of information back to him.

People around the bridge began to get green around the gills, even some of the experienced sailors. No one left their post, however. It seemed too dangerous to move, to try walking anywhere. Dakota was also beginning to get queasy.

When they reached the surface, Dakota could only tell because of a change in Bronislav's orders, and a change in the sounds the submarine made. It was raining hard out there; she could hear it hammering on the hull. That meant there was still a downpour at the container yard. She felt sorry for those left behind. Even if it turned out that everything remained safe and secure, they would have to travel through this weather in order to get food or use one of the toilets. At least they didn't have to worry about distilling seawater, as rain was usually safe to drink. It should also wash away anything that remained of that gross slime the zombies had left behind.

They spent some time on the surface, rolling with the waves, then the dive alarm sounded again and they began their descent. As soon as they reached calm enough waters, several people ran off to find somewhere to throw up. Dakota was determined to keep her meagre breakfast down, so she sat in one of the abandoned chairs, taking deep breaths.

"You would actually feel better if you threw up," Bronislav told her.

Dakota shook her head. It wasn't that she didn't believe that she'd feel better, it was just the best answer she could give that didn't involve opening her mouth.

"Don't throw up on the instruments."

Eventually the crewman whose seat she had taken returned, and she was forced to stand again. Her legs felt a little stronger than before she had sat down, but she wasn't feeling completely better yet.

"Why did we spend so much time on the surface?" Dakota asked, hoping to take her mind off how she felt.

"You weren't listening to what I was saying," Bronislav pointed out.

"It's hard to follow when I don't know the lingo."

"And when you feel sick."

"Yes, and when I feel sick. So, why?"

"I thought it best to run the air exchangers for a bit. Of course, our fresh air has now been spoiled by the reappearance of people's breakfasts, but better they spoil fresh air than stale."

Dakota nodded, not really sure if she agreed or not. It just seemed like the easiest answer.

"We'll be maintaining our position for a while. We won't be testing the waters above again until evening. Would you like me to start teaching you the lingo so that you can follow along next time?"

Dakota nodded again, although if next time was anything like this time, she wasn't sure she'd be able to follow along even when she knew the words. Perhaps agreeing to shadow Bronislav on the submarine had not been the best decision.

21: JAMES
8 DAYS AFTER THE BOMBING

Several booted feet entered James' field of vision. Many hands grabbed his limbs and hauled him off across the road. They didn't try to blindfold him at all, so James could see clearly that they brought him into the garage, the one his group had considered staying in instead of the post office. There were no windows for the attackers' lights to shine out.

Inside the garage, James was dropped onto the cement floor beside a lantern. The people who had carried him quickly dispersed into surrounding guard positions, but there was one who was already sitting on the other side of the light. James struggled upright, pulling the rag out of his mouth in the process. He noticed that they had allowed him to keep his knife.

"Sorry for that," the woman across the lantern from him spoke. "Without knowing who you are, we felt it safer getting one of you alone."

James looked around the space and counted six other people, the woman making it a total of seven. His group outnumbered them.

"Can you speak for your party?" the woman asked. "Or is there a leader we should be communicating with instead?"

"I can speak for them," James told her.

"Excellent. So who are you?"

"Travellers. We're trying to get to the Theatre." The Theatre was what Evans had called the place, but James hadn't a clue whether that was a moniker known to others.

"Oh? Are you now? And why are you trying to go there?" Maybe the woman knew where he was talking about, maybe she didn't.

"We were told it was the kind of place that we could go to."

"And who told you that?"

"A friend of ours. Goes by the name of Evans." James hoped to see some sign of recognition in the woman's facial expression. He saw nothing.

"And who is Evans?"

"Another traveller."

"Like yourselves?"

"Different. We come from a specific place; he calls nowhere home for long. He's been a lot of places; you may have seen him without learning his name. Six foot four, blond hair and beard, carries a big sword?"

Nothing from the woman. She either didn't know, or was very good at masking her reactions.

"My name is James, may I know yours?"

"Dinah."

"And are you a traveller as well?"

"No. Where is it you come from?"

"A place by the sea." That seemed like a safely vague enough answer to James. "We are hoping to connect with other communities, in order to trade."

"Why are you only doing this now? Why not before?"

"We lived on a ship before." James wasn't going to bother mentioning that they had lived on land for the past five years. Let her think their arrival was new.

"What happened to your ship?"

"An unfortunate encounter with pirates. Where are you from?"

"Not far. Not close." She was matching James' vague answers, although he knew it had to be relatively close, given the way the buildings here had been stripped. "What is it you are looking to trade for? And what are you offering?"

"I am only to discuss that with the leader of a community."

"And if that leader was a tyrannical dictator?"

James shrugged. "Everything has to be played by ear. Why? Are you led by a tyrannical dictator?"

Dinah made a scoffing sound, which was accompanied by a few snickers from the surrounding guards. Whoever they were led by, most definitely didn't fall into the tyrannical dictator category. That was good for James.

"We shouldn't be far from the Theatre. Surely you've heard of it? Are they led by a dictator, is that why you mentioned it?"

Dinah gave away nothing. "The people you travel with: there is someone injured among them?"

"Yes. Skip has had his hand crushed, but Aaron is our major concern. He was bitten on the ankle by an infected pig. We managed to remove the limb in time, but he is not doing well. We're worried about infections, and don't have the medicine needed to treat him ourselves. I was hoping that when we reached the Theatre, someone there would be able to help him." When it came to those who needed help, James didn't hold back any information. He wasn't going to gamble anyone's life in some weird attempt to make his group look stronger. Aaron was desperate, and they would take help where they could get it.

"You are concerned for your friend." It wasn't a question; Dinah was just stating a fact. "What do you have to offer for healthcare?"

"Are you offering healthcare? Because if you're not, all I need from you is a point in the right direction to the Theatre. Or your camp, if it's closer."

"How many guns does your group carry?" Dinah asked.

James kept his mouth shut on that one. They may outnumber the seven, but in the lamplight he could see pistols on their belts, and more than one rifle slung over a shoulder. In a fight, his group would lose.

"How do I know that we can trust you?" Dinah asked instead.

"How do I know that I can trust you?" James countered. "Neither of us can answer that question if we both refuse to bend. We are both in a difficult position. You don't want to lead hostiles to your home, and I don't want my people to be robbed or injured any more than they already are."

Dinah had nothing to say to that. Her arms were crossed and her finger tapped against her bicep as she thought. Or maybe as she waited. Waited for James to fill in the silence. He knew how to play that game too, but he wondered if he should.

"Would you trust me if I told you a little bit more about my community without telling you exactly where it is?" James decided.

"Maybe."

"Very well. We live in a shipping container yard." A dedicated person with time and a good map could eventually find them, but James trusted that there were a number of container yards along the stretch of sea within a reasonable distance of where they were. "We built a wall out of the containers to protect us. That wall was recently put to the test. We were first attacked by raiders, who attempted to uproot us from our home." It seemed best not to mention the Black Box, and instead bend the truth a little. Thanks to Chant's radio broadcast on the Day, everyone around the world had learned that the Marble Keystone Corporation had deliberately released the zombie virus into the population. James would not be treated kindly if they knew that anyone from his community, or that he personally, had any affiliation with them, whatsoever. "We managed to defeat the raiders, but at a great loss to our supplies and growing lands. While attempting to recover from them, we were attacked a second time. I don't know if you've ever encountered this horde of zombies before, but I actually hope you haven't. I have never seen so many in one place." James hadn't been there, but he had heard the stories and seen the photos the runners had carried with them. He had also seen the mess that was left behind. "Our walls are maybe sixteen feet high, but the zombies got over them. We were extremely fortunate to have survived. I have no words for that mass of dead flesh. Maybe you've seen their wake? A massive trail of guts, and blood, and bits of flesh, flattening everything in its path."

A guard at the edge of James' vision shifted uncomfortably. They had seen it then, or at least knew of it.

"Even now, we're still disposing of the ashes of the burned bodies."

"No one could have survived that horde," Dinah finally said. "I don't believe you."

"We had help. Runners, who had been tracking the mass, reached us first. They managed to warn us. We had hoped for the zombies to just go away if we stayed quiet behind our walls, but they didn't. The runners warned us of a smart zombie in the pack, the smartest one ever seen." Another lie, a smaller one, for James had watched Roy, a zombie who had taught other zombies to hurl dead children over the walls of a prison. "They also had some men outside. Those men were able to signal us the co-ordinates of the super smart thing, and we had skilled men and women who were able to get grenades to that point. Most of the fast zombies were clustered around the smart one, so we got most of them too. The group that gave us the co-ordinates were also able to set off fireworks, to lure away a large chunk of the zombies at the rear. With preparedness, discipline, and the sacrifice of too many, we were able to overcome the dead that came over our walls."

"Tell me the names of these so-called runners?" Dinah unexpectedly asked.

"Boss, Betty, Tommy, Mark, and Suzanne. They called the mass of dead the comet horde. Before I left, they were still living in my community, however they hadn't yet decided whether they wanted to stay or go somewhere else now that they didn't feel a need to track the zombies. They think that with the super smart one dead, the comet horde won't reform."

Finally, a twitch on Dinah's face. She must know the runners, or at least know of them. "Perhaps you're telling the truth," she said. "There are details in your story that would be hard to make up so quickly. And you also told me more than you probably would have liked. Your community's food supplies are low, and it's very likely your ammunition is as well. You're seeking aid from the Theatre, and not just for your man Aaron."

James knew it had been a risk to say so much. He didn't confirm for Dinah that she was right, but she was smart enough not to need him to.

They sat in silence for a few seconds before Dinah finally spoke again. "We're from the Theatre."

James breathed a sigh of relief. He had been hoping that this was the case, but had no way to be certain. "May we have an audience with your leader then?"

"If I allow it, you will have to tell them the entire truth." *Them,* so they were likely led by more than one person.

"I will. Every detail." Although he'd probably turn the Black Box into a normal bunker that they had stumbled across. No need to mention Keystone.

Dinah thought for another second, and then sighed. "I suppose anyone who can claim to have survived the comet horde as truthful sounding as you have deserves an audience. We'll take you to the Theatre once the sun comes up."

"Thank you. Thank you so much." James poured every ounce of sincerity that he could muster into his words. "I take it you've had a run-in with the comet horde?"

"We heard that they were coming, warned by the runners you talked about. Maybe one of our leaders even knows this Evans guy you mentioned, but we've all heard of Boss, Betty, Tommy, Mark, and Suzanne. With their warnings and plans, we were able to use portable sirens to redirect the horde away from us."

James nodded. "I just wish my home could have done the same."

"Perhaps they could have, if the runners hadn't seen an opportunity to kill the one they called Dean. They were obsessed with finding a way to destroy him."

James nodded again. He had heard about their obsession from Boyle, and could see it in the way they now appeared lost without their self-assigned purpose.

"You're free to return to your people." Dinah finally uncrossed her arms. "Explain to them what we have talked about. We will stay in here for the night while you stay over there. We will meet in the street at sun-up."

James agreed and rose to his feet. The guards who had been standing around him were a lot more relaxed now.

"You really survived against the comet horde?" one asked in a whisper as James made his way to the door, doing his very best not to limp as badly as he wanted to.

"I'm not yet sure we *have* survived," he responded, and then stepped outside.

When James returned to the post office, he found that everyone was awake. Katrina was pointing her rifle at him from behind the counter.

"Just me," James said, raising his hands.

"Where the hell have you been?" Katrina hissed, clearly pissed off. "Lindsay noticed you got up, and figured you had to take a piss. When you didn't come back, she woke the rest of us. We were just deciding if we needed to send out a fucking search party for you."

"I'm glad you're concerned, but I'm all right. Let me tell you what happened." James sat on the counter as he explained his abduction and the ensuing conversation. People were relieved to hear that they would be taken to the Theatre tomorrow. Caution remained, however, and a guard rotation was assigned for the rest of the night. James managed to get out of that one, because they didn't need everyone to take a shift, and they thought he deserved the rest after his negotiating. And James felt he needed that rest. He was finally tired, and when he lay down on his bedding, he was asleep almost instantly.

***

There wasn't much of a sunrise; the sky was heavy with clouds. A storm was coming, one that had already hit the container yard if James was right. He and his group nervously gathered up their things. Dinah and her friends were still inside the garage, but the door was open, and someone was clearly watching the post office. The horses were eased out, and Aaron was once more strapped to Spark's back. Aaron made almost no noise of complaint, which struck a cord of concern within James. The man was barely conscious.

James hauled himself up onto Soot's back as the people who claimed to be from the Theatre left the garage. He had considered the fact that Dinah could have been lying when she said that they were from the Theatre. She could have decided to use James' desire to go there to lure him and the others into a trap. But they had to risk it. For Aaron's sake, if not for those back home.

After brief introductions were made all around, they headed out. A clear division formed between the two groups, with Dinah and her people leading, and James with his following behind.

"You didn't tell us she was gorgeous."

"Huh?" James looked down at Katrina, who had spoken quietly beside him.

"Dinah," she gestured forward with her chin. "You said nothing about how fucking beautiful she is. You sure you were thinking with your head last night?"

"I honestly hadn't noticed." It made James sad that he was telling the truth. Ever since the Day, it was as if his brain had been completely rewired. The way he thought about things now, he no longer took into account how people looked. Maybe he should, because certain people thought differently based on the way they believed others saw them. He had accepted years ago that he would die without any sort of life partner. One night stands were fine, but he just couldn't commit himself to one person like so many others had. He spent too much time thinking about everyone, about what he needed to do for them. Some little thought, buried within his brain, believed that he would be considered selfish if he held one person above the others.

James was happy to see that they took the road he would have taken to get to the Theatre. But he was unhappy every time he looked up. The clouds were dark enough that he was surprised they weren't yet getting hit by rain. The wind was picking up as well, pushing against their backs. He hoped the Theatre was close, but worried it wasn't close enough. He was proven right, when the clouds finally broke, and a wall of water dropped on their heads.

Hunched over Soot's neck, James was soaked through in an instant, despite the tarp he had draped over himself. Everyone huddled and hunched their shoulders against the driving rain. It lashed at their backs, and people lifted their packs higher in order to protect their heads. Aaron seemed to be revived momentarily by the water, but his weakened body wouldn't be able to withstand much more without catching pneumonia.

Lightning cracked the sky overhead. For safety's sake, they could no longer stay in the open.

"Dinah!" James had to shout to be heard above the wind and rain, even though she wasn't that far ahead.

She dropped back in order to hear what he wanted.

"How much further?" Even at a close distance, he had to speak loudly. "We can't stay out here much longer!"

"Not close enough!" Dinah shouted back, half hidden beneath the hood of her thin, plastic poncho.

Shit.

They walked a little farther, reaching the fringes of a town. They came across an old Costco store and hurried into the shelter of its thick walls. The place was stripped bare. The Theatre must have sent out many people to gather it all.

They didn't go far into the store, merely passing the second layer of doors. There was plenty of space for the horses, but they stayed close to the humans and their light sources. It was disturbing that the light of their lanterns couldn't reach the ceiling. One of Dinah's people must have thought the same, as he set his flashlight down pointing straight up in order to make it visible. Two others walked off to penetrate the rest of the store's shadows and make sure it was as empty as it looked.

Ponchos, tarps, and rain slickers were all shucked off and laid out to dry. Aaron was pulled down from Spark's back, and then his sodden clothes were peeled off him. He was quickly patted down with a ragged towel Marissa had produced, and then bundled up in a sleeping bag. People didn't care much about decency as they stripped down to their underwear, laying their wet articles of clothing flat on the cement before searching for anything that might somehow still be dry in their packs. Items that were wet, were laid out with the clothes.

"Why do we keep getting soaked?" Skip mumbled.

After Lindsay had taken her boots off, she started walking on the spread of clothing, squeezing out whatever moisture she could.

Dinah's group had been carrying some wood, and so they were able to start a small fire. Aaron was placed closest to it, while the rest set up a rotation for who would get to sit beside the flames, usually with an article of clothing that needed drying the most. It wasn't James' turn, so he removed Soot's gear and began to brush the water off of him.

"Do you ride when the others don't because of your leg?" Dinah asked, coming up beside him. "I've noticed that you limp."

"It's my foot, actually. I got injured when those raiders I mentioned attacked."

"Are the raiders why you are so cautious?"

"We've always been cautious. They sent a child to us first. A little boy, alone and nearly starved. We took him in not knowing he was a spy for them."

Dinah frowned. "Some people have resorted to some terrible things."

James nodded in agreement. "I just hope that you're not one of them."

"And I hope the same of you. For all I know, you are one of the defeated raiders, who merely witnessed the comet horde from a distance. But you told us things hoping that we would learn to trust you, and so now we would like to return the favour. Your community needs food, and so I'm guessing you don't carry much with you. We do. We can provide lunch, and dinner if this storm continues until nightfall."

"Thank you. We very much appreciate it."

With the large, high ceiling they didn't have to worry much about the smoke, but Dinah's people were experts at maintaining the fire in such a way that it didn't produce much to begin with. Lunch was a tense affair; James' group didn't completely trust the food they were given. Everything had to be cut into pieces, with Dinah's group eating some of it to prove it wasn't drugged or poisoned. But the food was good. They had fruit and vegetables, and even bread. The protein they provided was salted and cured fish, and they had some spices to go with it. The Theatre was truly well off if they had this sort of bounty to share. James hoped that they were so well off, they would be willing to trade food to the container yard for very little in return. He still wasn't sure what he was going to offer them in exchange. He would have to see what was there, and what the container yard could possibly have to offer. Perhaps some of the medicine they had smuggled out of the Black Box.

The rain outside was relentless. It must have been a hurricane that had come in off the sea. It would have been worse for those back home. James was much farther inland, where the earth would have slowed and weakened the great storm. He hoped his trade delegation didn't turn out to be for nothing. He hoped he had a home to go back to.

"What are you thinking about?" Katrina asked, sidling up next to him where he stood looking out through the doors at the rain-lashed streets.

"Home."

Katrina nodded. "I'm sure they're all right. This would have crept up on them yesterday, right? People would have seen it coming and prepared for it."

James couldn't tell if she was trying to convince him, or herself.

A bolt of lightning snapped down from the sky, turning everything into the harsh white of light, and then the deep black of shadow. The resulting thunder came instantly due to the proximity of the lightning. It slammed into James' ears and shook the glass in the doors. Nature's most frequently used explosive. Despite knowing he was perfectly safe, it sent a jolt of primal fear through him. For a few seconds, the bright after-image remained as a ghostly glow over the terrain.

"I hope the lightning stops soon," Katrina said quietly after the rumble had passed. Was she speaking quietly, or had the thunder been so loud that it had left its own impression on James' ears, just as the lightning had on his eyes?

"Hard to say."

"Aaron needs more help than we can provide. If the lightning stops, we should press on, even if it's still raining like this."

James reluctantly agreed. He did not want to go out into that downpour again, but he would. The lightning wasn't the only danger the storm produced, but it was the deadliest. While Aaron had the highest chances of catching pneumonia, any of them could. There was also the wind to worry about. A strong enough gust could knock someone over, and they could land badly. Or even more troublesome would be the debris. While the people from the Theatre had done a very good job of clearing out the streets, even removing most signs, the streetlights still stood, as did many trees and several power poles. And debris could be carried from far away. Once the wind picked something up, there was no telling how far it would carry that object. Even something as small as a can with a sharp edge, could be deadly. No, James truly did not want to go out there.

When it was finally James' turn to sit by the fire, he brought Soot's blanket, the one that went under his saddle, with him to dry instead of any of his sodden clothes. Katrina had her turn at the same time and sat down next to him holding her wet pants. Aaron appeared to be asleep, but his breathing was harsh and laborious.

"Smells like wet horse," one of the Theatre men commented as he sat down to take a turn at the fire. His name was Lee, if James had caught it correctly.

"Focus on the scent of the fire," Katrina told him.

"I saw you laying out your things earlier," Lee turned to her. "Was that a lion pelt I saw?"

"It is," Katrina nodded.

"Where in God's name did you kill a lion?"

"On our way here."

James was glad she gave no clue as to the distance or direction.

"Were there more? What were they doing?" Lee continued to ask.

"There were others, and when I shot that one, she was killing one of our friends while the rest stalked us." Katrina's voice had a hard bite to it.

Lee fell silent, a momentary embarrassment crossing his features. "I'm sorry you lost your friend."

"We also lost another one to the pigs. Hopefully we won't lose a third." Katrina gestured to Aaron.

"When it's safe, we'll get your friend the treatment he needs," Lee told her in a promissory tone.

"Provided we trade for it," Katrina grumbled rather bitterly.

"I'm sure your lion pelt would be enough. No one at the Theatre has even seen one before; its rarity will make it fairly valuable."

A sharp hiss came from one of the other Theatre men who had overheard. The meaning was obvious: shut up.

Katrina nodded silently to Lee, thankful he had revealed the lion pelt's value so that she wouldn't let anyone rip her off. The way Lee nodded back, his words were not a slip of the tongue, but intentional. He didn't want her getting ripped off either.

Everyone had had a turn by the small fire, so James was able to sit there for longer, drying the horse blanket as best he could. Katrina slipped off, likely to go check on her lion pelt, to make sure no one was thinking of stealing it. Dinah ended up taking her spot next to the low flames.

"You care for your horse's comfort more than your own?" she wondered as she looked at James.

"He's an old horse, and he's been through a lot, most recently with me on his back. I figure he'll appreciate a dry blanket when we get going."

"It'll only get wet again. The rain isn't likely to stop soon."

"And so will my clothes."

"Would you be willing to tell me about the pigs that attacked you? How you defeated them?"

"Under normal circumstances, I would," James admitted. "But I need to hold onto everything that might have value right now, including stories like that one."

"I understand," Dinah nodded. "Could you at least tell me if you killed all the pigs? We've had an incident before where one hunted some people all the way home."

Wee, wee, wee, all the way home, James absurdly thought. "Yes, we killed all the pigs."

"Good. And the lions?"

"They're too far for you to worry about."

"I'd rather decide that for myself."

"And yet, you'll have to trust me on this one."

All afternoon, people drifted about in the Costco, occasionally sitting beside the fire. With a flashlight to guide his way, James took a walk through the large, empty building. Only the support posts remained, coming out of the darkness at him like tall and slender men. When he reached the far wall, he turned off his flashlight and looked back. The fire, the lamps, and the flashlights that moved about the group seemed so small and insignificant. They were a tiny island of light in an all consuming darkness. The darkness felt oppressive, and as James stood in it, with the rain hammering the roof far overhead and the thunder crashing, he began to shake. He allowed himself to become overwhelmed, to feel the grief of losing White and Jack, and all the others that had gone before them. He curled up into a ball on the floor, feeling that his body was going to rip itself apart if he didn't hold it all together. His tears were silent.

The moment didn't last long. James couldn't let it. With a few gasping breaths, he regained control and sat up. As he wiped at his face, he flicked his flashlight back on and shone it in a quick pattern around himself. Although the building had already been searched for threats, it was hard not to imagine something sneaking up on him. James got to his feet, then relieved himself against the far wall—which others had done based on the smell and the stains—and then limped back to the fire.

"Are you all right?" Katrina asked him, a frown touching her brows.

"Right as rain," James told her.

"Not this rain, I hope. We're thinking it's time for dinner."

"Sounds good."

Throughout the day, there were moments when it sounded like the lightning was moving off, but it had always come back before anyone could suggest they leave the Costco. While they were eating dinner, it moved off again, and a fair amount of time passed without a crash overhead.

"We should move," Katrina finally suggested.

"No," Dinah responded.

"Why not? The lightning's gone."

"It's too dangerous."

"We've dealt with worse than rain and wind."

"No. We're staying here for the night."

"The night?" This time it was Belle sounding outraged. "Aaron might not have that long!"

"And if we try to get to the Theatre now, perhaps none of us will make it," Dinah snapped. "It's far too dangerous in the dark. The weather will have stirred up any dead in the area, and we won't be able to see any of them. Our lights can only penetrate so far through the rain, and they would make us a target. Anything walking around out there, will come straight to us."

James saw the wisdom in her words, but he also saw Aaron's ghostly pale skin. "Give us directions. A tiny group of us will carry Aaron there, and the rest can follow when it's safe."

"No." Dinah remained firm.

"Why not?" Skip demanded. He wanted a doctor to look at his hand.

"No one returns to the Theatre at night. The gates will not be opened. If you try to enter, you will be killed. No, we *have* to stay here for the night."

There were further arguments, but they went nowhere. Dinah and the others stood firm, refusing to leave and refusing to say where the Theatre was. They would have to wait out the night.

Bedding was spread out. Earlier they had cautiously mingled during their stay in the empty building, but now the division between the two groups formed sharply once more. There was anger on both sides. One hated the stubbornness of the other, and the other hated the lack of understanding. The fire was allowed to die out.

***

James' sleep was fitful, for he partially woke every time someone had to take a piss in the night. His missing toes also itched on occasion. Whenever he cracked open his eyes, he was greeted by either total darkness, or the light of a carried flashlight making its way to the back wall. Eventually, a very soft, almost unseen, grey light drifted in through the front doors. It was still raining as morning came, but it was no longer torrential, and the thunder hadn't been heard for hours, not even in the distance.

While thinking of dozing for another hour, a sharp inhalation of breath brought James to full alert. As the sound turned into a harsh sob, everyone awoke. Lamps and flashlights blazed all around, finally pinpointing the source of the distressed sound. It was coming from Marissa.

"He's dead," she wailed as several people asked what was wrong. "Aaron is dead."

22: ONIDA
APPROXIMATELY 1 YEAR AGO

If she hadn't been constantly afraid of her people making an appearance, Onida would have quite enjoyed living with the Amish. She liked all the people she met during meals, and she didn't mind doing what work she could find, which was usually helping a group of women preserve part of that year's harvest. It was something she knew how to do, and was as good at it as someone could be. In return for her work, she was able to keep some of the preserves, as well as some of the fresh fruits and vegetables. Once, she helped bake bread. She wished she could talk more with the people she worked with, but she was always afraid of saying the wrong thing, or saying too much.

Shawn never liked the people. Often he hunted, bringing back whatever he could. He kept most of the meat for himself, but some of it he traded in exchange for having his preserved in salt while he did other things. Whenever he wasn't hunting, he was helping a work crew with construction. He spent more time working than Onida did, but she liked to think that was because she still needed to take care of the horses every day. Askuwheteau didn't seem to get any better with the rest, but then Onida rarely saw him anymore. He had been deemed well enough for the Amish to keep him, and so he had been moved into one of the barns where they kept their own horses.

A handful of times during their stay, someone came to find Onida in order to offer supplies in trade for what she and Shawn had put on display. Since Shawn was usually off hunting outside their fences, Onida had to manage all the trading herself. She thought that she was okay at it. She had sometimes spied on her elders when they were in trade negotiations with strangers. Of course, it helped that the Amish never seemed to try to swindle Onida. Their offerings always sounded reasonable, and Onida tended to accept them if she didn't think she could squeeze out just a little bit more.

While the food was always delicious, Onida thought she enjoyed the beds even more. Having a warm, soft place to lie down each night melted away the aches and pains she had developed during their travels. The guest lodge didn't provide much privacy between Shawn and Onida and the messenger boys who were also staying there, but the beds were worth it. Because there were so few visitors and so many bunks, Onida could have slept on a different bed every night, but she chose not to make an extra mess of the sheets for the Amish. Mask loved the bunkhouse, climbing up and down the beds every morning and evening. Onida didn't mind being woken up by the sound of his nails scratching against the wood as he went up or down, so long as it wasn't the middle of the night. The boys were less appreciative, but they were passive aggressive in their complaints, merely sighing heavily or pulling their pillows over their heads.

When Onida woke up after the third night, she was sad to know that they would be leaving that day. She was glad to be moving farther away from her former home, but wasn't looking forward to hours of riding, followed by nights in sleeping bags, and food rationing at all times. At least the weather was nice for their departure.

All morning, after breakfast in yet someone else's home, Onida and Shawn prepared the horses. A few last minute trades were bartered, and some of the Amish even gave them gifts. The gifts were not much, but every little bit helped. Straw men were bound with string, and dressed in clothing the Amish didn't want. Onida noticed that the clothing tended to be a very bright colouration, not the Amish way. Therefore it was still fairly decent quality. She wondered how much of it was donated by people who had decided to join the Amish, and how much was taken from stores in the nearest town, destined to become rags or other such things in time. The straw men were laid out along the ground, to be propped up on the horses when they left.

Lunch was a big affair. Paul informed them that they had to stay for the meal, and neither Shawn nor Onida objected. It meant not dipping into their rations until dinner, and that they would get to fill their stomachs with hot, fresh food one last time. The weather was pleasant enough for the big tables to be set up outside, just the way it was when they had arrived. Shawn was still uncomfortable, but not as much as he had been the first time. Mask was even given a tall stool and his own little plate beside Shawn's, although he didn't use either much, preferring Shawn's lap and plate. Onida ate as much food as she could, to the point where she was uncomfortably full.

When the meal was done, several of the Amish said a personal goodbye to Onida and Shawn. They were the ones who had shared their homes for various meals, as well as several of the people who had worked with Onida. She got the impression that people were really saying goodbye to her, and included Shawn only to be polite. The horses were then lined up in their trains. One was missing at the end of Onida's what with Askuwheteau being left behind. The two youths they were to accompany had their own horses.

"Are you sure you don't want us to lead some of your horses?" one of them asked. "Make the trains shorter?"

"We're sure," Shawn grumbled. He wasn't going to risk one of the boys taking off on them, and stealing some of their horses and supplies in the process.

The straw men were all mounted up and strapped down. Onida thought they looked ridiculous. Even with the wide-brimmed hats casting shadows, she had no idea how anyone could mistake them for real people.

As they rode to the gates, Jacob accompanied them on his beautiful mare. Onida thought that with rest and proper brushings, their horses no longer looked so shabby in comparison, but they still didn't look as good. They couldn't, not without their genetics being altered. Onida wondered if Askuwheteau would be bred with Jacob's mare at some point.

Jacob opened the gate for them and said a final farewell by wishing them luck, both with the bandits and whatever came afterward. Glancing back, Onida saw that he continued to sit astride his horse, watching as they headed out of sight.

"So do we have any sort of plan as to what we're going to do about these bandits?" Onida quietly asked Shawn. They were riding abreast of one another, with the boys currently ahead of them and the trains behind.

"You have to tell me something first." Shawn's response was unexpected.

"What?"

"Was your grandfather really sick?"

The question was so uncalled for that Onida bristled. But she also shivered.

"See, what I don't understand," Shawn went on, "is why he would ask you to kill him despite knowing what would likely happen. You say he was in pain, but was he really in that much? And why use a knife? It would have been a lot safer for you to have smothered him with a pillow. With no marks left behind, people would assume the illness finally got him. So be honest with me: was your grandfather really sick? Was it even your grandfather that you killed?"

Onida's mouth pressed into a tight line. Her eyes prickled with tears she didn't want to shed. She dug the fingernails of one hand into the back of the other in an attempt to prevent the moisture from leaving her eyes. Shawn saw all this and nodded. Apparently, it was enough of an answer for him.

"I have two plans, which I'll let you pick between. We can do what we were told to do, and accompany these messengers to where they're going. We will most likely run into the bandits, and we'll probably have to fight them. I'm confident I can get at least the three of us away, but I can't guarantee that either the messengers or our horses will escape." He was including Mask when he mentioned the three of them. "Or, before we get anywhere near where the bandits are supposedly camped, we ditch the messengers and go our own way."

"We made an agreement. The Amish gave us food and beds so that we'd accompany these boys."

"And there's no reason we have to honour that agreement. What can they possibly do about it now?"

"They could send word to any communities ahead of us, tell them what we did and make it impossible for us to receive help again."

"To do that, they would have to be able to get their messengers through. These boys are trying to go somewhat south and a lot west. We simply have to go south and east instead. So what will it be?"

Onida thought hard. The Amish had been so nice to her. But then Shawn was right; it wasn't like she was ever going to see them again. She looked at the boys riding ahead. They wouldn't be harmed if they just left them. The two messengers could just turn around and go back to the Amish, and wait for a better time.

"If we were to ditch them," Onida wasn't going to sugar coat her words. Ditching them is what it would be. "Where and when will it happen?"

"It's three days travel to the town they're trying to reach. It's no coincidence we were offered three nights. On the first night, while they sleep, we'll simply leave."

"What if they wake up?"

"What if they wake up? What can they do?"

"That one carries a rifle," Onida pointed out.

"Don't worry about that."

But Onida did worry about that.

"You have until tonight to decide."

Why is Shawn putting this decision on me? It didn't seem fair to Onida. But then, what had happened in her village wasn't fair. What had happened to

Shawn's home wasn't fair. Nothing was fair, but despite knowing this, Onida continued to imagine how things should be.

Onida wasn't going to make this decision in haste. As they rode, she kept quiet and pondered the situation. It helped that she could no longer ride so close to Shawn. Shortly after their conversation, they learned that the horses in their trains sometimes attempted to eat the straw men sitting on their neighbours, and so had to be separated. When they stopped for the night, no matter what Onida decided, figuring out how to keep the horses from eating the decoys would be troublesome.

The messengers usually rode ahead, but they had a tendency to wander. Sometimes they dropped behind, or rode on one side of a train or another. They didn't talk to each other much, and they didn't attempt any real conversation with either Shawn or Onida. It had been that way in the bunkhouse as well. Or at least it had become that way after their initial attempts on the first night hadn't borne much fruit. One thing the boys commented on during the ride, was how Shawn and Onida never stopped, not even to relieve themselves. Each messenger had to hop off their horse a few times, piss on a tree, and then mount up again and trot to make up for the distance that they had fallen behind. Onida hadn't realized it until they had said something, but thinking back, she discovered it was rare that she would have to empty her bladder while riding. Apparently her body had adapted to waiting until they stopped for their lunch break, or when they set up camp for the night.

Night had kept coming earlier, and it did so once more. They rode a little distance through the dark, seeking a good building in which to take shelter. The messenger boys ended up choosing for them, when they came across a vehicle dealership that they had stayed in before. There was a lot more glass than Onida would have liked, knowing that there were bandits somewhere out there. At least the horses could easily fit through the door that was once used to move display cars in and out. They remained outside because of the lack of space inside, but if there was an incident like the one with the wolves, it was nice to know that they could all be brought indoors in a hurry.

"What have you decided?" Shawn asked as, for once, he helped brush down the horses.

Onida glanced over her shoulder at the car dealership. It was all that glass that made her decide.

"We're going to leave," she told Shawn in the lowest whisper that he could hear. The messengers were nowhere nearby, but she still feared being overheard somehow.

Shawn nodded, and the decision was made. He left the horses to her to go off hunting again. It was difficult to manage the horses by herself when they kept wanting to eat each other's straw men, but Onida managed. She used the bumpers of several vehicles as hitching posts. They were lower than she would have liked, given all the flat tires sinking into the pavement. She chose vehicles that were in the middle of the lot, where a decorative island of greenery had overgrown and would provide the horses with fodder. In twos, she brought the horses over to a water-filled ditch so that they could drink, her ears sharply attuned to the darkness for any sign of danger. At no point did either boy offer to help, which made Onida feel better, more justified, in her decision.

Waiting was difficult. After she had settled the horses, Onida kept busy setting up her and Shawn's bedding, assembling a smokeless fire, and putting together their dinner. After all that was complete, however, and the plans had been carefully made, she had nothing with which to distract herself. She had to pretend to be asleep while waiting for the messengers to nod off. They were too far away for her to be able to determine that on her own, and therefore had to rely on Shawn, who was on watch duty, to tell her. She had to wait.

Several hours slipped by. Onida's arm hurt from the way she was lying on it. The pain was on purpose: it kept her awake. But she desperately wanted to roll over onto her other side. She was about to give in, to allow herself to be comfortable, when Shawn appeared in the weak moonlight and touched her shoulder. Onida needed no more than that to get up and go outside. Shawn could move a lot more silently than she could, and so he was going to pack up their bedding while she made ready the horses.

"What about them?" Shawn asked after placing their gear on the horses. He had pointed to the messengers' steeds.

"What about them?" Onida replied.

"We should take them."

"No." That had never been discussed as part of the plan.

"Why not?"

"They will need them to get back."

"They have legs. They can walk."

"We're not taking them," Onida insisted. "If you need an excuse, they might not get along with our horses. They might not take to being in trains."

"It's a waste," Shawn said as he mounted up.

Onida didn't bother to respond as she climbed up onto her own horse. She didn't bother to tell Shawn, but she didn't really want any more horses. She liked the herd they had, and while she missed Askuwheteau, she was glad to have one less horse to manage. Adding two strangers was not appealing to her.

They kept to a walk as they left the vehicle dealership, trying to guide their horses over patches of weeds and piles of leaves to keep the sound down. Once they were far enough away, Shawn wanted to trot, but Onida told him that they shouldn't. A walk was a fast enough pace, and the horses had rarely trotted while in their trains and so wouldn't be used to it. Besides, that seemed like a great way to lose their straw men.

Shawn seemed to sulk in the dark as they rode, but he didn't suggest they go faster a second time. Mask was more energetic than usual. Normally he slept during the day, either with Shawn or in a pouch on horseback. Travelling at night was strange, and the raccoon let them know it by grunting and moving around a lot. He had learned to safely move back and forth along a horse, but whenever he wanted to move from Shawn's horse to the one behind it and vice-versa, Onida had to ride up beside them to help. That night, she helped Mask several times. Onida didn't mind, because paying attention to his needs kept her distracted from the buildings all around them. She was used to the woods, and the foreign nature of the town they had entered put her on edge.

"We need to find a place to stop and rest. Somewhere the horses can fit inside," Shawn told her after they had ridden through the dark for several hours.

"We wouldn't be hard to track," Onida pointed out. They were undoubtedly leaving quite the trail of horse shit behind them.

"Which wouldn't be as much of a problem had we taken their horses. But I don't want to ride any longer. Look for a place."

So Onida scanned the structures in the dark, seeking a building that felt safe. All of them were far too small. She could tell that Shawn was becoming increasingly impatient the longer it took, and Onida guessed that he was about to lower his standards when they finally came across an adequate structure.

The horses fit easily through the office building's double doors, and there was plenty of room for them to spread out in the empty lobby. No longer needing the straw men, Onida and Shawn dismantled them, letting the horses nibble some of the straw. The clothing was then packed up with the rest into bags. Onida went to sleep on a cracked, faux leather couch in a sort of waiting area near a security counter. It was more comfortable than her bedding, but not as nice as the Amish beds had been.

***

They rode east after a couple of hours of sleep. By the time the messengers found where they had spent the night, they would be long gone. That's if the boys even bothered to look.

Another bridge burned, Onida thought. Once word spread, she would never be able to return north again. She'd never see the lands where she grew up, the place that had been her home for all sixteen years of her life. Good. She had no interest in going back there, and closing the way off behind her meant she could never be tempted later.

"Why do you continue to ride with me?" Onida asked Shawn when they made their short stop for a late lunch in the parking lot of a Walmart.

Shawn acted like he hadn't heard her.

"Because when I showed up, your house burned down," she went on. "You could have given me up to either my people or the Amish for a decent amount of supplies, and then rebuilt or even gone ahead on your own. I want to know why you're willing to stay with me."

Shawn shrugged. "Mask likes you."

Could that really be all it was? Shawn wasn't exactly all there in the head, so Onida couldn't be certain. Maybe he himself didn't know why he continued to bring Onida along.

"You don't need to tell me what you really did," Shawn said, seemingly out of the blue. "We're far enough south now that I don't think it should be a problem. You can keep the details to yourself."

Onida was tempted to tell him anyway. The words trembled on her lips and tongue, but ultimately she kept her mouth shut. As he had said, there was no need to tell him anymore. He seemed to have a rough idea anyway. She was going to keep the particulars of her secrets, just as he kept his.

When they mounted up once more, they headed south-east. Other than being more tired than usual, and checking over her shoulder more frequently, Onida passed the day as any other day before meeting the Amish. As the sun began to set, they searched for a place to stop for the night. Onida had a feeling that they were skirting around the edge of some city. The buildings remained relatively the same size and were evenly spaced. She wondered which one. Too many signs were rusted out or overgrown, making it difficult to read the words on them. She also didn't pay that much attention to them, as she had never had to before.

"Do you know if we've crossed the border?" Onida asked when they found a dilapidated factory to stop in for the night.

"We have," Shawn told her with absolute certainty.

"I don't remember passing a crossing."

"We had gone off road when we crossed." During their weaving around to avoid the radiation, they had travelled overland plenty of times instead of following the roads.

"Then how do you know when we crossed?"

"I just do." Shawn wasn't interested in her questions and went back outside to look for food.

The factory was large enough for all the horses to fit inside, so Onida let them wander about. There were large machines within the building, but they were all rusted and covered in cobwebs. Windows high up in the wall let in the fierce orange of a cloudy sunset, and filled the interior with sharp shadows. Onida used Shawn's crank light several times as she worked, saving the candles they had gotten from the Amish for when they were needed more.

It was a cold night in the factory. When Onida woke up the next morning, she could see her breath. Checking outside revealed a crisp layer of frost. After she mounted up, she wrapped a blanket around her shoulders.

"I had planned for us to keep heading south-east," Shawn said as he got up on his horse, Mask snuggled within his carry pouch. "But with this cold, perhaps we should head straight south."

"I wouldn't mind a faster route to warmer climates," Onida told him.

Shawn nodded and led them south, past more factories and warehouses. For some time now, the leaves had been changing colour. In the past, Onida saw it as beautiful, but this year, it was only a troublesome reminder of the coming winter. Having abandoned the messengers after promising to take care of them, Onida couldn't see her and Shawn being welcome to stay anywhere through the winter.

The morning was deceptively quiet. Usually there was a zombie or two not long after they headed out, drawn to the area by the sounds of the horses' hooves the previous evening. That morning, they didn't come across a single dead person. Onida shifted uneasily in her saddle. She didn't like any disruptions to the established routine, especially not so soon after what they had done. She couldn't help but think that some sort of retribution was coming.

Past the warehouses and the factories, they headed along a highway through a forested area. Fallen leaves skittered across the pavement, pushed along by a strong wind. The leaves still clinging to the branches rattled and hissed. Onida futilely tried to take comfort from the relaxed attitude of her horse, and the constant, never changing level of alertness in Shawn. But his alertness did change.

Up ahead, a man stepped out onto the road. He stood straight and tall and was clearly no zombie. In his hands, he carried a rather large assault rifle. Shawn came to a stop, his bow flashing into his hands, arrow nocked and drawn.

"It's all right," the man said, his voice far too calm for the situation. There was an obvious arrogance in everything he did, especially in the relaxed way he stood with the rifle's muzzle pointed toward the road. "You don't want to go shooting anyone." He moved one hand, flicking it to the side.

A patch of asphalt kicked up slightly ahead of Onida and Shawn's horses, the crack of the high powered rifle that fired the bullet reaching them a second later.

"It wouldn't be good for you," the man in the road continued.

Shawn loosened his bowstring, but he didn't return either arrow or bow to their places on his pack.

"Just remember that while we talk," the man went on, pointing to the bullet hole.

"What are we going to talk about?" Onida asked, doing her best to keep her voice from wavering.

The man grinned at her. "Road taxes."

"You're the bandits we had hoped to avoid," Shawn grumbled.

"Now who told you that we were bandits?" He put on a tone of false offence.

"The Amish," Shawn told him truthfully. "They wanted us to help them get a pair of messengers back to their own village."

The man leaned sideways and looked down the lines of horses. "I don't see no messengers."

"We reneged on the deal, with the intent of going around you."

This seemed to delight the man. "So you basically stole from the Amish in order to avoid us, and yet we bumped into one another anyway. Which, incidentally, means the road for those messengers is clear at the moment. I guess we should have left someone back there as well. But here we are."

"What do you want?" Shawn asked him.

"What do you got?" The man's voice dropped the humour in its tone, at last becoming completely serious.

"We have what we need to get south," Onida told him, trying to sound capable and sure of herself.

"What's south?" the man wondered.

"Hopefully a place to live," she told him.

"You don't even know where you're going?" The man sounded happy again. "Well ain't that a kicker. We don't yet know where we're going either."

"And yet, you tax the roads," Shawn pointed out.

"Wherever we are, we own it," the man informed him. "And whoever's there, we own them too, along with whatever they're carrying."

Shawn didn't raise his bow again, but he did pull back on the string. "No one owns me. Onida, watch our rear."

Onida slid around in her saddle to face backward and watch over their train of horses. She also placed her hand down by her waist, pretending she had a pistol there that didn't exist. Maybe the bandits would be fooled into thinking they were better armed than they actually were.

"You know you'd be dead before you could fire that little stick of yours," said the man whom Onida could no longer see.

"No, I wouldn't. I'm very fast. I may die, but so would you."

There was a silence, and Onida wished she could see more than just the faces of horses.

"You said you don't know where you're going," Onida finally spoke up to fill the void that had previously only been filled with tension. "Why don't you travel south before winter hits? We can all travel together. An exchange of supplies for added protection."

"Why should we trust you?" the bandit spoke to the back of her head. "You didn't follow through on your deal with the Amish."

"And we have no reason to trust you," Shawn retorted. "No reason to believe you won't try to kill us and steal our stuff the moment we let our guard down." His words were sharp, and partly aimed at Onida. He did not like her suggestion.

"I wanna go south." A new voice had spoken up, one that was distinctly feminine.

"Goddamnit, get back beyond the tree line, you daft woman," the first bandit shouted.

"I like the girl's suggestion," the woman went on. "They have enough horses for all of us. And I don't want to spend another winter starving and half-frozen. We should go south with them."

Another silence made it impossible for Onida to resist twisting at the waist and taking a look forward. The woman was just as well armed as the man. The two of them were staring each other down, a silent conversation happening between their eyes.

"We can't trust them," the man eventually insisted again.

"You didn't trust me when we first met. Or Mikey, for that matter. None of us really trusted one another until after we had all stuck together for a while and played by one another's rules."

"And if these two fuck us?"

"Then we're no poorer than we are right now, only maybe we'll be a little farther south."

Onida had to face backward again, worried about them using the distraction to pilfer their packs.

"We still don't have a reason to trust you," Shawn said.

"That's fair enough, we are bandits after all," the woman replied. "I suggest a set of rules."

"What rules?"

"During the day, we get to ride your horses, untethered from the others, and you get to carry our firearms on yours."

"What?" the man practically shouted, clearly disliking the idea.

"We try to take your horses and whatever supplies are on them, well then you just got yourself a stash of guns. You try to take off on us, well then we got horses and foodstuffs."

"What about at night?"

"We sleep in different camps. You and your horses in one place, us in another. We don't tell each other where those places are, we only set up a time and place to meet the next morning. You're too small in number to try finding and attacking us in the night, and we really don't want to hurt those horses none, which would be a huge risk if we came at you in the dark. Either party doesn't show up to the meeting place in the morning, then it means we decided not to go on together, and we're all right where we are now, just farther south."

Onida could see some holes in this plan. What was to stop their sniper from picking them off as they headed to the morning meeting spot? But then, what was stopping him from killing them right now? Maybe the bandits weren't actually all that ruthless, and just threatened harm to get what they wanted.

"I like this idea," Onida leaned over to whisper to Shawn. "Better climate probably means we're going to run into more people and more dead, and having better protection than just your bow would come in handy."

Shawn sat as still as a stone, mulling it over.

"We wouldn't have to worry about wolves," Onida added. It was a bit of a dirty trick to use his fear like that, but it got him thinking the way she wanted him to.

"Bring all your people out here," Shawn told the pair in the road. "I need to see them before I decide anything."

When the man blew a sharp whistle by placing two fingers between his lips, Onida glanced over her shoulder at him. He augmented the whistle with an arm gesture, which Onida bet was for the sniper's benefit. Considering the time delay between the bullet strike and the crack of the rifle, that person was a fair distance off.

As three men and one woman came out from the forest, two on either side of the train, Onida knew that Shawn had been right to have her turn around. She watched those people walk toward the others in the road, and turned back around in her saddle in order to face them all. Two other women came from ahead of them, so that there was a total of eight people, equally balanced between the genders and ranging in age from late twenties to early fifties. A mangy dog stood with them; a tattered rope acted as a collar and leash. The sniper was still likely making his or her way to them, and would bring the number up to nine. They waited for that to happen. Onida was surprised to discover that the sniper was around her age, maybe a little older: a pimply boy who was practically as thin as the massive rifle he carried, and nearly as short.

"So this is us," the man who first spoke made a gesture to encompass his band of bandits. "What do you think?"

Shawn took his time scrutinizing them. He studied every face, the posture in which they held themselves, and, most definitely, the weapons they carried. There were assault rifles, repeater rifles, semi-automatic pistols, revolvers, and, of course, the sniper rifle. Every one of them carried a gun, and a few had multiples.

Onida leaned over to Shawn in order to whisper to him. She couldn't tell if he wanted her opinion or not, but she gave it to him. "If they don't have any packs hidden away somewhere, they don't have much in the way of supplies. I don't even see a tent among them. Going south before this weather gets worse is very much in their interest. They need our horses."

Shawn continued to think for another minute after Onida returned to an upright position on her horse.

"We can't untether the horses," he finally said. "We don't have reins or saddles for the ones we're not riding. We'll still hold onto your guns, but this means that neither of us can run off from the other."

"That sounds all right to me," the woman spoke.

The man grunted and drew his people into a huddle. They had a long conversation between them. The horses were beginning to get annoyed with this unscheduled stop.

"All right," the man finally turned back around. "We have come to an arrangement. But one of you is going to have to help us mount those horses. We're not all experienced riders."

Onida ended up doing that job, as well as performing the task of gathering up their guns and finding room for them on her and Shawn's steeds. She led each bandit to a horse based on what they said their experience was, which was never much, if any, and helped them climb up onto the horses' backs amongst the packs. She told each bandit what his or her horse was named, and explained all the best ways to hold on. The dog would have to walk on his own, too large to be carried like Mask. Once done, Onida returned to her horse and swung her leg up and over the saddle.

"Do you think we're doing the right thing?" she whispered to Shawn after a glance over her shoulder.

Shawn's jaw clenched and unclenched, but otherwise he didn't answer. He knew only as much as Onida did.

And so they walked on. They continued south, no longer just the two of them, but now in a party of eleven people, fourteen horses, one dog, and one raccoon. Onida couldn't stop looking over her shoulder.

23: CLAIRE
8 DAYS AFTER THE BOMBING

There wasn't much time to worry about the mannequin with the grotesque smile. When they brought their supplies up from the parking garage, they dragged it with them to show the others, but also to ensure it wouldn't pop up someplace else. Rose noted that it had the number twelve carved into it, so it had come from the batch in front of the store. They then wanted to search the building for an intruder, but there was no time. The storm hit harder than they had expected, and if the mystery mannequin person were in the building, they would be trapped in there too.

"We gotta get this stuff above ground," Jon insisted as the roads outside became rivers.

They all agreed and began hauling. Everything they had gathered was dragged up the stairs to the third floor in order of priority. And not a moment too soon, for the parking garage began to fill with water rather quickly, as the nearby river flooded its banks, adding to the rain washed streets.

Once the ground floor, storage room, and parking garage had been cleared, they started on the apartments of the second storey. No one stayed to guard their stash; everyone scrambled to save what they could. If the intruder stole anything, they couldn't get far. Besides, the six of them staggered their runs up to that floor, so that nothing was left alone for very long.

Getting into the apartments wasn't easy. They used pry bars and the like to smash open the handle locks, but whenever a deadbolt was thrown, they had to stop and pick the damned thing. Claire was assigned the fourth apartment they got open to search on her own.

Following Jon's instructions, she went to every door in the apartment, closets included, and threw them open. She held her tire iron at the ready each time, in case a zombie came stumbling out at her. The rain lashing at the windows made it difficult to first check by listening. Claire also checked behind, under, and inside any furniture where a child could fit. Jon hadn't specifically told her to do this—he had only mentioned looking under beds—but Claire wanted to be thorough. There was no one dead in the apartment, zombie or otherwise. Claire worked as fast as she could, searching for the most important stuff first. She developed a rough idea of what was in there and where, and then proceeded to haul what she could up to the third floor. It was hard work climbing the stairs. She thought three floors up was overdoing it, that the second floor should have been adequate.

She couldn't remember ever having seen so much rain before. They had experienced a number of storms since moving back to land, as well as a handful that had almost capsized the Diana while out at sea, but this rain was relentless. Normally a downpour like this wouldn't last very long, a couple of minutes at most before becoming something lighter. But the water wasn't stopping. Even when she finished retrieving the most useful items from that first apartment and was ready to move onto the next, it just kept splashing down in great sheets. It wasn't easy to see anything out of the windows, to see beyond the storm. Claire realized she couldn't even see the road anymore. It was buried beneath a deep layer of water. As a burnt out car was slowly nudged down the street like a dead beetle, Claire thought that maybe being prudent by going up to the third floor wasn't such a bad idea.

It was dark in the hallways. It was pretty dark in the apartments too, but at least some of the grey storm light came in through the windows. In the hallways, and in the stairwell, there was nothing. With her hands full, Claire couldn't always hold her flashlight in the most optimal position, and so had to move carefully, using her feet to confirm where walls, doors, and steps were. Her flashlight could be recharged by shaking it, so she turned it off and did that whenever she could. The supplies were lit by a pair of solar charged lanterns, one by the stairwell door and one at the bend—the apartment building had a forty-five degree kink in the middle. Claire put down the bundle of blankets she was carrying and flicked off her light. Something caught her eye before she could start shaking it though, some movement. Turning back toward the bend, she flicked her flashlight back on. Maybe it was just one of the others, using the other stairwell? But then maybe it wasn't.

Claire moved at a jog, holding her tire iron high as she reached the turn. But there was nothing there. She had heard no running footsteps, and no doors opening or closing. She could easily see all the way to the stairwell door, and nothing stood between it and her. Still, knowing that someone had been following them earlier, Claire went to each apartment and tried the handle. They were all locked, as she had expected they would be. This place had been evacuated. People had had time to lock their doors. She also checked the stairwell, but couldn't see anything in there either.

"Claire?"

When she returned to the hallway, Rose was looking around the bend at her.

"What are you doin' over there?" she asked.

"I thought I saw something. I guess I didn't."

"Yeah, places like this can get pretty spooky." Rose's shoulders were bunched up in a way that suggested she wasn't just saying that to make Claire feel better.

"Especially with the storm and that mannequin."

Rose nodded. "Wanna head back down together?"

Claire agreed and they headed to the stairwell. Claire couldn't resist one last look over her shoulder, but she still saw nothing amiss. Soon, they would have to start piling up stuff around the bend, as the hallway was already getting rather full.

Reaching the second floor, Claire looked over the railing in the stairwell.

"The water's rising," she told Rose.

Rose, who had been about to exit the stairwell, turned around and joined her at the railing. "Yup. Ground floor's gettin' pretty flooded. We better hurry up, just in case. I'm not sure that this building isn't in a low spot."

Claire followed Rose out into the hall. "Have you ever seen rain like this?"

"No. This might be a once-in-every-twenty-years storm, or some crap like that. We haven't been here long enough to know. And with the sewers and whatever never being cleaned out, the floodin' only gets worse."

Claire could tell that Rose was trying to make the two of them feel better, but that she didn't really believe this kind of storm could come every twenty years. The blocked off storm sewers was definitely fact. Claire wondered about the animals in the area, where they went during something like this. Would the alligators get washed out to sea?

They left all the doors on the second floor open, so that they knew which places they had been through already.

"Will the foundations of the building hold?" Claire wondered as she approached the next apartment being unlocked.

"Don't know," Danny shrugged. "I don't see why it wouldn't."

"But what if it doesn't?"

"Then we won't have to worry about the weather for very much longer," Larson told her. It was the nicest way of saying that they would all be crushed or drowned. Claire actually preferred the former to the latter.

"Do you think the container yard is okay?"

No one answered Claire's question this time. They didn't want to think about it. Claire didn't want to either, but she couldn't help it. It was their home. The reason they were gathering all this stuff was so that they could bring it back there. Maybe the others couldn't stop thinking about it either, but none of them wanted to give voice to their concerns.

"Do you think we could catch any fish in that water?" Claire decided to change subjects with a gesture to the window once the apartment was opened.

"We could try, but it's unlikely we'd catch anything," Danny told her before moving on to the next door.

"We should try," Claire told them, as Rose took the recently opened apartment. "Our food stores are pretty meagre. We counted on proper hunting and foraging to feed ourselves."

"We're aware," Jon sighed, getting exasperated by her chatter. "We'll do what we can, but that won't be much until the rain stops."

Claire knew her questions were bothersome, but the storm had her freaked out. The mannequin too. Whenever she found herself near her friends, she wanted to talk, to hear their voices. She was told to search the next apartment they got open, which meant no more questions. No more talk.

In a bedroom, Claire found a corpse. It wasn't the mobile kind, just a dried-out human form in a fetal position on top of the blankets. Claire stepped closer to it, to make sure that it was indeed dead, and not just a deaf zombie waiting to spot movement, or maybe a person who liked to move mannequins dressed in some crazy disguise. Her prodding with the tire iron produced nothing, and closer inspection revealed that there were, in fact, two corpses. Curled up against the belly of the first was a shrivelled toddler. Claire could see no injuries to their heads. The pair of them must have died fairly early on, before the contagion went airborne and infected everyone with a dormant version of the virus. Claire wondered if they had simply starved, or dehydrated, or if the larger corpse had given them both something so that they'd sleep without ever waking. Whatever the case, it was sad. Claire didn't touch the blankets, but she raided the closet and dressers. It didn't matter how sad the scene was; she still had a job to do.

The apartment contained the same semi-useful stuff as the previous apartments Claire had cleared. She began carrying it in loads up to the third floor, always checking around the bend whenever she was up there. On one of her trips back down, she heard a grunt of frustration from one of the boys, along with what was likely a boot striking a door. She found that it was Larson, trying to get the final apartment open. Danny and Bryce, who'd been clearing out other places, had also heard and come out to see what was going on.

"I got the door unlocked but something's blocking it from the other side," Larson complained.

Danny walked over and placed his ear against the door. "Something's moving around in there."

"Our mannequin friend?" Claire worried.

"Doubtful. Whoever that is, they're quiet. This sounds like a zombie. It's on the other side of whatever is blocking this door."

"A zombie *inside* a barricade." Bryce sounded pleased about this although Claire didn't know why.

"What does that mean?" she asked.

"Only two reasons a zombie would be inside. Either they died of natural causes and the airborne shit turned them, or, they barricaded themselves inside after being bitten, either in a panic or because they didn't know what was going to happen," Bryce told her.

"So?"

"So, if it's the latter we might find some really good stuff in there," Larson said this time. "Could be someone who had been stockpiling canned goods when they got bitten. As long as they were stored well and haven't rusted, they might still be edible."

"Might also be some dried goods, or MRIs," Danny added. "Bryce, come over here. I think we can shove this open. On the count of three. One, two, three."

Bryce and Danny threw their shoulders into the door together. It didn't open, but it budged a little. Danny counted to three again, and they repeated the action. By the third strike, Jon showed up, and by the fourth, Rose came as well. The door had opened enough for them to see the back of a tall chest of drawers, but the weight suggested there was more than just that in the way. They couldn't get the door open much farther before it jammed completely.

"Hold on." Claire stepped up to the door as Danny and Bryce backed away from it, grateful to give their shoulders a break. "Someone give me a boost."

Jon obliged, bunching up on the floor so that Claire could use his back as a stool. She was high enough and thin enough to wedge her head through the opening above the drawers. Her flashlight rested on top of the dresser so that she had some light to see by.

"Yeah, the barricade's now braced against a wall," Claire told everyone. "It doesn't look like it can be easily broken by force either. There's a couch and then a pair of big lounging chairs."

"What about the zombie?" Larson asked.

"It's there too. He's on the living room side of the barricade. I think I can wiggle myself through to the hallway side."

"Are you sure you can do it safely?" Jon asked her from beneath her feet.

"Yeah. The zombie can't get over the barricade. There's some dining room chairs overturned on top of the couch, and the thing is definitely stupid."

"Do it," Danny told her.

Claire twisted so that she could shove her arms through the opening alongside her head. Two of the boys grabbed her legs to lift her higher as she wriggled through, grabbing onto whatever she could in order to pull herself forward. The dresser met a short length of wall beside the door, but once Claire was past that, she was able to drop down into the hallway. It was not a graceful fall, and she landed on her shoulder fairly hard.

"Claire? You okay?" Jon asked upon hearing the thump.

"Yeah, I'm alright. Gonna have one hell of a bruise later, though."

"Can you kill the zombie?" Larson asked.

"Not with my tire iron. I don't have enough reach."

"What about my sword?" Jon asked.

"That might do."

The sword immediately came sliding through the opening, safely enclosed in its scabbard. Even with it, Claire couldn't take out the zombie right away. She had to perch on the end of the couch, holding part of the pile of dining room chairs for balance. Several thrusts of the katana missed, or didn't penetrate deep enough. Claire carved up the zombie's face until finally a strike sank through enough flesh and bone to hit its glob of a brain. The zombie dropped to the floor, properly dead. Once it was down, Claire set to moving the dining room chairs so that she could slide the couch out from the middle of the barricade.

"Okay, push!"

The dresser squeaked as it dragged along the floor, and threatened to topple over.

"Stop," Claire told them once the opening appeared large enough for everyone to squeeze through. If the dresser fell over, it could jam itself against the big, heavy chairs, and Claire couldn't be certain she'd be able to move any of it on her own.

When Jon came through first, Claire handed him back his sword. He instantly went with it to check the rooms off the hallway behind her. Danny squeezed his way between the dresser and chairs to investigate the living room.

"Let me see your shoulder," Larson said when he came in.

They stood out of the way for Bryce and Rose, and Claire pulled her long sleeved shirt up around her neck, freeing the one arm with a wince and trying not to pull up her T-shirt at the same time. When she rolled up the short sleeve, they could both see that her shoulder was already changing colours. Larson gently prodded the area around the wound, causing gooseflesh to erupt across Claire's chest. While not exactly attracted to Larson, she had to admit that he was very good looking, and it wasn't often a handsome young man touched her skin in any way.

"Doesn't appear that anything's broken or dislocated," Larson informed her. "That's going to be one gnarly bruise."

"It already is." Claire thought she would have known if her injury had been worse, but then she could recall people hurt even more badly who had insisted they were fine. Claire was fairly certain she would never be one of those people, that she didn't have the mind and body separation needed for it, but then Larson didn't know that. Really, Claire couldn't know that either unless it actually happened. Those people claiming to be fine as they bled out probably also thought that something like that wouldn't happen to them. Claire shivered.

"You all right?" Larson had seen.

"Yeah, just not used to having my arm bare, is all." Claire rolled the short sleeve back down and then winced some more as she put her arm back into the long sleeve. "How's your finger doing, by the way?"

Larson held up a hand, his missing finger replaced by a strip of cloth that was more to hide the wound than to act as a bandage. "Haven't popped any stitches yet. Still itches like crazy sometimes."

There was some commotion going on in the kitchen, so Larson and Claire made their way in that direction, after Claire had picked up her pack that Jon had dropped by her feet.

"Check it out!" Rose crowed, proudly displaying a cupboard full of cans and dried goods.

"Nice!" Larson walked over to look at them, taking a can down to inspect it for rust.

Danny was taking even more cans out of another cupboard. "I don't think this guy evacuated. He must have stocked up before the infection reached here and thought he could ride it out or something. Claire, come over here. Turn around."

Claire complied. Her pack was slung over her good shoulder, but she attempted to lift it over the injured one as well when she felt Danny loading her down with goods. It hurt, but most of the bruise was on the outside of her arm and she thought she could tolerate it, as long as she kept the strap up high, near her neck. From where she stood, she had a view of a window. It didn't really look like rain out there anymore. More like some sort of fountain curtain, given the amount of water coming down. The view was terrifying. Once it felt like Danny was done filling her pack, Claire drifted over to the window for a proper look.

Trees were thrashing above the waterline, bending ridiculously low in the wind. Waves were being pushed up off the floodwaters; the crests were misting and blended in with the rain. Claire could barely see the closest structure, and nothing beyond it.

"Best not to focus on it," Jon spoke from behind her. He placed a hand on her good shoulder and turned her away from the window. "Focus on the task in front of us."

"We found another body in the bathtub," Bryce explained as he stood in the kitchen doorway, waiting to see if his pack would be needed. "I'm guessing the guy who owned this place knew her, and let her in when he really shouldn't have. She turned, he got bitten in the process of putting her down, then simply waited for the same thing to happen to him."

"You know it's a female because she was wearing a sundress?" Claire asked.

"Yeah. Dresses are the only way I know how to tell when the long dead are women, without getting too close. Why?" Bryce looked over at her.

"Because this woman really liked sundresses." Claire had spotted a cluster of framed photos on a table. In all of them were a rugged man and a woman who was always in a sundress. They looked like they were in love, but probably didn't live together given the utter lack of feminine clothing and personal effects.

"I guess that explains why he let her in," Bryce agreed, walking over for a closer look. "It must have been really hard at the start; knowing your loved ones were bitten and being unable to do anything for them."

"It's still really hard now," Claire told him.

"Yeah, of course, but back then people weren't used to it. Someone got hurt or sick, you just brought them to the hospital and the doctors made them better. They had more hope than we do now. These days, we know better. We know we can't do anything but give them the option of going out before they turn. It's still hard, but we're used to it."

"I'm not sure you'd say the same if it were Becky who had been bitten." Claire knew that Bryce had lost his parents on the Day, but he hadn't really had to see what happened to them. Claire, on the other hand, had had to watch as her mother, siblings, and friends were torn apart and drowned, only to reanimate and attack the person next to them. If it hadn't been for Jon and Lauren, she might never have learned to live with the pain.

"Maybe," Bryce reluctantly agreed. His voice then dropped to a whisper so that the others couldn't hear them. "You were asking about the container yard. What do you think? Do you think they're all right?"

Claire remembered that Becky was back at the yard. "They've ridden out storms before. You should know, you lived there through some of them."

"None of them were like this, though." Bryce's eyes flicked toward the window. "Not this bad."

"Maybe we're getting the worst of it. We're far enough west that they might not be getting the same amount of wind and rain that we are."

Without looking at her, Bryce took her hand within his and squeezed it. Claire squeezed back. Lauren, Abby, and Peter were all still at the container yard. Her second family. She had to believe that what she said to Bryce was true.

"Bryce?" Danny stuck his head out of the kitchen. "We need your pack. This guy had MREs too."

"Wow, this place is the mother load," Bryce replied as he turned toward the kitchen, his expression changing to one of more cheer and excitement. Claire now knew that that was false, that maybe everyone right now was wearing a sort of mask. But she understood that she should wear one too. They had to be a united front against their own fears.

"Jon? Why don't we try to move the barricade some more?" Claire suggested. "Make it easier to get in and out for multiple trips."

***

"You know, we might all just spend the rest of the night shittin' our guts out," Rose said as they laid out their bedding in a third floor apartment. The hallway outside was so full of things from lower down, that only a narrow path led through it. "Yet, I'm still gonna say that eatin' out of those cans was worth it."

They hadn't eaten much, maybe two-thirds of a can for each of them, because they wanted to save as much as they could to bring home. Claire had gotten a third of Jon's can, and a third of Danny's, and while she felt fine for the moment, neither of them had really tasted right. But there was food in her stomach. Blessed fuel to offset all the energy she had expended that day going up and down the stairs. Her legs felt like rubber, and she still had a headache, but it had lessened after eating. She always tried her best to ignore the aches and pains of her body, but as she lay on her bedding, she let them through. She actually preferred to think of them as opposed to her other options: the storm and whoever was leaving mannequins around.

Claire listened to Rose and Bryce talk about the food, with her eyes closed as she was about to drift off.

Thump.

Claire's eyes flew back open. Had she dreamed that? She looked over at the others. The conversation had stopped and all eyes were directed toward the ceiling. They had heard it too; Claire hadn't fallen asleep.

"Maybe a window up there has been left open," Larson suggested in a whisper, "and the wind finally managed to knock something over."

"That sounded like a fairly large something," Danny told him.

"Hence why it took so long," Larson retorted, sounding not at all confident about it.

They all continued to stare silently at the ceiling for another few seconds, but no other sounds were forthcoming.

Rose sighed. "We're goin' to go check it out, ain't we?"

Jon nodded. "We should. We know it's possible that someone else is running around in here, and I, for one, would really like to know if that's the case." He got up and headed for the door.

"One of us should stay here," Danny spoke up before Jon got very far. "The food is too important to leave unguarded."

"You volunteering?" Bryce had also gotten to his feet. "Want me to stay with you?"

"I'll be fine on my own," Danny told him. "I can lock the door behind you guys." They had chosen this apartment because they hadn't needed to break the lock in order to get inside. "You're welcome to stay if you want to, though."

Claire didn't want to stay. She wanted to see for herself what had caused that noise, just in case it was something Jon would be tempted to lie to her about later. It seemed that everyone but Danny also wanted to investigate first hand, since they all got up onto their feet and headed for the door.

"Check the peephole," Larson suggested before Jon could open the door.

Jon glanced through it, but shook his head. "It's pitch black out in the hallway. I can't see anything." He grabbed the handle and pulled open the door.

Jon had very fast and aggressive reflexes. His sword was out and slashing forward, before Claire even had time to register that there was a figure standing just outside the door. The blade didn't cut into any flesh, however, just plastic that clattered to the carpet.

In the light of Bryce's lantern, Claire could see Jon's face turn a furious red. He didn't even scream or curse at the mannequin this time, which she realized she would have preferred.

"It's the same one you guys brought up from the parkin' garage," Rose reported as she dragged the various pieces inside. "Someone put it back together." Now it had a rather large gash along its torso and painted face.

"Well, we can now be certain that someone else is in the building with us," Bryce commented.

"Let's go." Jon spoke through gritted teeth as he stepped out into the hallway.

Claire looked over her shoulder at Danny, who had followed the group in order to lock the door behind them. He understood her unspoken question and nodded that he would be fine on his own.

"We should split up," Jon instructed once they were out of the apartment. "Bryce, Larson, you take the far stairs. Rose, Claire, and I will take these." He pointed to the stairwell at the end of the hallway.

Bryce and Larson agreed, turning to disappear around the bend, between the stacks of stuff. Jon led the way to the closer stairwell, rage still pouring off him. Claire wondered whether the storm outside was stronger or weaker than the one broiling inside Jon.

When they entered the stairwell, Claire couldn't help but go to the railing and look down. Her flashlight illuminated the water below. Would it keep rising? Would it manage to reach the second floor? Would it somehow just keep coming, forcing them higher and higher up the building until there was nowhere left to go? Was God washing the world clean as she had apparently done before, leaving only an ark to continue on?

"See anyone?" Jon asked her.

"No." Claire didn't admit that she hadn't been looking for people. If there had been someone down that way, though, she figured she would have seen them. The water was dark and full of trash.

"Come on." Jon forged ahead up the stairs.

Claire followed after him and Rose, wondering again about the apartment building's foundations. How much water and debris could it withstand? It was silly, the building was solid, and yet Claire couldn't help but worry.

On the fourth floor, they didn't find much. Bryce and Larson shook their heads when asked if they had seen anything. The apartment above the one they were staying in was unlocked, but empty. A fair-sized bust made out of a solid chunk of wood lay on an ornate carpet in the weirdly rich apartment, so they guessed that that was what had made the thump. But there was nothing they could find that would suggest why it had fallen off its table, other than by human intervention.

"I don't think he meant to knock it over," Rose said, poking the bust with her toe. "I think he left in a hurry, which is why the door wasn't locked behind him."

"Could be a chick," Bryce said.

"It could be more than one person," Jon added. "None of us have actually *seen* anyone. We only know someone's around because of the damned mannequins."

"What if it's ghosts?" Larson's question was wholly unexpected, especially given the serious tone in which he asked it.

"Ghosts don't exist," Bryce said in an off-handed manner. It gave Claire the impression that this was something that had come up between the two of them before.

"There used to be a time when zombies didn't exist either," Larson retorted.

"And just how far do you think ghosts can travel?" Jon chimed in, his tone biting and annoyed. "We've been dealing with mannequins since before we reached this area. You think a ghost just decided that it was bored because there were no people around, and thought to take its plastic people and go find someone to haunt? Ghosts don't exist, and even if they did, this wouldn't be their work."

Of course that all made sense, but now that ghosts had been brought up, Claire found the little hairs on the back of her neck were standing up. The all-consuming darkness and constant lashing of rain at the windows didn't help.

"Let's get back to Danny," Jon told everyone, turning back toward the main hallway.

"Should we split up again?" Bryce asked once they were out of the lavishly furnished apartment.

"Yes." Jon headed back toward the stairs they had climbed, leaving the others to either follow or go the other way. They broke up into the same groups as before, with Rose and Claire keeping a few paces behind Jon until they entered the stairwell.

Before they could descend, all three of them heard two loud, banging doors, one following shortly after the other. Claire jumped in place, the sound unexpected, and it came from both above and below them.

"There's more than one," Jon grumbled. "You two go check upstairs. I'll go make sure that Danny is okay."

Rose immediately began to climb higher, following the glow of the camping light strapped around her forehead. Claire's legs were wiped, but the injection of adrenaline had her sticking close to Rose's back. She had the tire iron grasped tightly in both hands. Below, Jon's light disappeared onto the third floor as they reached the fifth.

Rose turned to Claire, holding up her hammer and her stump. She was silently asking the other girl to open the door. Claire swallowed the lump in her throat and took the lead position. She breathed deeply, grabbed the handle, and yanked the door open.

Rose was ready with the hammer poised over her head. The hallway beyond was empty.

"Look," Claire whispered, pointing to the base of the door. There was some sort of contraption there involving an egg timer and a padded stick with a spring on one end. Rose knelt down and pulled back the stick with the claw end of her hammer. When she let go, the spring pushed it back against the door. The resulting bang made Claire jump.

"Why would someone make this?" Rose whispered up to Claire.

Claire shook her head. How could she possibly know? This was likely the work of a person who left painted mannequins for them to find in startling places. She wanted to assume it was the work of the totally insane, but the device seemed almost too clever for that.

"Hey, turn off your light for a second," Rose said after standing up. She turned off her own light.

"What? Why?" Claire didn't like the idea of being in total darkness, not with some loony running around.

"Just do it," Rose insisted.

Claire grudgingly obliged. She expected to see nothing at all when the light went out, but she was wrong. Down the hall, there appeared to be a little point of faint, yellow-orange light. Claire shifted in place, moving her head to make sure it wasn't an illusion, some trick her mind was playing on her. That didn't seem to be the case, because the tiny light stayed put. She turned her flashlight back on after only a few seconds, despite the discovery.

"Come on." Rose led the way toward where they had seen the light, flicking on her headlamp in the process.

Claire thought that they should probably go back down, to find Jon and make sure everything was okay, but she couldn't leave Rose alone, and Rose seemed determined to investigate. The light was a peephole within one of the apartment doors. Something was shining through the tiny bubble of glass. Rose gestured with her stump for Claire to try the door. She shook her head for she didn't want to. Rose frowned, and gestured more angrily this time. When Claire still refused, Rose pushed down on the handle with her stump, hunching awkwardly with her hammer at the ready.

The door wasn't locked and pushed open too easily. The hydraulics had been removed. When the door swung all the way open, it crashed into the wall. Rose had used more force to open it than was necessary. Both Rose and Claire winced at the sound.

Inside the apartment, an oil lantern was burning on a table that must have been moved from somewhere else, for its placement didn't make much sense. Before Claire could suggest that they leave, that the lamp could have been set up to deliberately shine through the peephole and lure them in, Rose was off, stalking toward the bedrooms, hammer at the ready. Claire followed, wondering what she could say to stop her friend.

As Rose reached one bedroom with its door opened a crack, she gestured for Claire to go check out the wide open door beside it. Claire knew then that she couldn't convince Rose not to investigate, she could only help get it over with more quickly.

When Claire reached the entrance to the bedroom, she jumped inside her skin. Her flashlight landed on a figure standing across the room. Its bald head and lack of ears informed her that it was another mannequin. Claire would rather not go near it, but she knew she had to. She had to determine if it was one of the ones with carved numbers.

Halfway across the bedroom, the door behind Claire slammed shut. She screamed and whirled around, the tire iron held high as her flashlight clattered to the floor. She fully expected someone to be standing behind the door. But in the flashes of her dropping, and rolling flashlight, she saw no one. As she snatched the light back up off the floor, Rose burst into the room, with eyes wild and nostrils flared as she prepared for a fight.

"Where is he?" she screamed, her headlamp swinging this way and that as she checked the corners. Once she was all the way through the door, it slid off her shoulder and slammed behind her. Claire screamed again at the sound, although softer this time and Rose's voice joined hers.

With both their lights pointed at the door, they saw that some sort of spring-loaded hinge was attached to it. A pin lay on the floor nearby, attached to some fishing line that formed a tripwire Claire had activated as she crossed the room.

"This guy is sick," Rose gritted through her teeth. "He's tryin' to scare us on purpose."

"Trying?" Claire panted, her heart still racing in her throat. "I would say that he's succeeding."

Rose nodded, admitting that, she too, was frightened. She then went over to the mannequin and checked its head.

"Number nine," she informed Claire.

"I suggest we take it, and the oil lantern, and get the hell out of here," Claire advised. "This guy is playing games with us. Deliberately splitting us up and luring us out of the apartment where we have the food. I'm worried about Danny."

"Yeah," Rose nodded again, turning away from the mannequin. "Let's get back down there. And fuck the mannequin, we'll leave it here. He's probably got a bunch in this place anyway."

Back near the door, Claire exchanged her flashlight for the oil lantern. There wasn't much oil in it, but it would be more than enough to get back downstairs. Rose took a quick look in the kitchen, just in case there was any food left behind, but reported nothing.

Back out in the hallway, they walked quickly toward the stairwell, noting that the banging device was still attached to it. One right after the other, they scurried down the steps to the third floor where they came across Bryce and Larson.

"Hey, are you two okay?" Bryce asked, his posture and voice tense.

"Yeah, we're fine," Rose told him as she ushered the boys back toward the apartment. "What about Jon and Danny?"

"Freaked out, but okay. Whoever this person is, they've booby trapped some of the rooms."

"Yeah, we found that out for ourselves," Claire told him, raising the oil lantern for emphasis.

As they made their way between the gathered items in the hallway, Claire found herself tense and wary of the piles. Was it all the same as they had left it?

Had anything been moved? Could someone have carefully rearranged a few items and was now hiding right alongside them?

They reached the apartment without issue, and Jon let them inside. With the door safely locked behind them, they all swapped stories. Jon hadn't found any noise makers, so he had probably been chasing down the actual perpetrator, but he had seen no one. Bryce and Larson had a similar experience to Claire and Rose on their side of the building. They had been lured to a certain apartment by a sound and a light, but when they opened that apartment door, a mannequin had come swinging down from the ceiling, striking Larson as he went through.

"Seems we weren't the only ones busy today," Danny commented after Claire and Rose had explained what they had seen.

"All right, no one leaves this apartment again until it's time to go. Are we agreed? Unless there's a fire, we stay put until it's safe enough to go outside, then we head straight home. There's no point in searching anywhere else, as it's all going to be damaged by the flooding anyway."

"Sounds like a good plan to me," Bryce agreed.

Everyone else nodded.

"We'll keep a guard posted overnight, just in case the stranger tries to get in here," Danny said.

"You checked that all the windows are locked, right?" Claire asked, trying to sound less frightened than she was.

Danny nodded. "We did when we first decided to stay here. We searched the whole place, top to bottom, and it's empty and secure."

"I kinda hope the bastard tries to get in from outside," Rose commented. "Maybe he'll get swept away by the storm then."

"I'll take first shift," Jon volunteered. "The rest of you should try to get some sleep."

As Claire lay down on her sleeping mat, her mind and body were still humming. Sleep was such a foreign concept these days.

24: EVANS
9 DAYS AFTER THE BOMBING

"Evans, how nice to see you again," said Frannie as she took his hand into her warm ones. Evans had forgotten that about her, that her hands were always exceptionally warm.

"Hello Frannie, thanks for seeing us." Evans silently added, *and not shooting us.*

Walking into town, they had startled a great number of people. Lots of weapons were suddenly pointed in their direction, held in nervous hands.

"Well, you always bring such interesting things," Frannie joked, with a gesture to the people, camels, and horse that were assembled behind him. They had been confined in a large alley that had been turned into a pen of sorts. There was an entrance at either end, one which led into town and the other into the zombie corral.

"Now that you know it's me, can we talk inside somewhere? I'd rather not be out here when this storm breaks over our heads." The wind had picked up considerably. Most of the town's folk had retreated indoors by then. The booth-like shops Evans remembered seeing lining the main street last time he was here were all folded up and missing. In the corral behind him, no zombies were pressed up against the fence. They had all been brought to some indoor holding facility for safety. The idea of such a room for such a reason repulsed Evans.

"I suppose you'll want somewhere for all of them and the animals to stay as well," Frannie commented.

"Please."

"All right. Come along then." Frannie unlocked the gate.

Evans gestured for everyone to follow him out. Gerald led Moe and the silent ones urged their camels along. The animals were all very skittish, making sounds of displeasure as they remained outside in the wind. They knew the storm was about to hit them, and wanted to be indoors just as badly as the people did.

Frannie took them to a building that was familiar to Evans. It was the same tiny mall he had stayed in the last time he had visited the place. There wasn't much to it. It had an entrance on either end of a wide hallway, with four small shops lining one side, and one big store dominating the other. The big store served as their visitors' quarters, with bunks, and cots, and tents for privacy. Along its back wall, makeshift pens had been erected for either animals or the rare visiting zombie, which was apparently a thing here. Candles were all over the place. None were lit for there were no other visitors at the moment. Evans was glad to see that.

"Make yourselves at home. Light whatever candles you need," Frannie told Evans' party, gesturing around as they entered the space. "You're on your own for food at the moment, since everyone's closed up shop."

"We'll be alright," Evans said.

"You're going to come with me to my office, so that we can catch up," she spoke as she turned to him.

"Of course. Ang, Burt, Gerald? I'm just going to be across the hall for a minute. Moe and the camels can be kept at the back, and choose whatever beds you like."

Gerald frowned, but didn't argue. Evans guessed that he was assessing the place, trying to take in as much of the community as he could. If they accepted him, this was to be his new home.

Evans followed Frannie across the hall and into a former, tiny hair salon. Everything but the chairs and the mirrors had been removed. Frannie picked up a lantern on the reception desk, and used it to guide their way to the back. She kept an office there, in an emptied storage room, and used the chairs out front as waiting seats.

"Sit down," Frannie gestured to an empty desk chair as she sat in one on the other side of her scarred work surface. She flicked the switch on a lamp, and a pale yellow light shone across the desk, highlighting the agitated scratchings of people who had been sitting where Evans was now. He hadn't made any himself, but he had seen even Frannie pick at the wood on occasion. He didn't know much about what she dealt with on a day-to-day basis, and therefore held no judgements about any bad habits.

"What's powering the light?" Evans asked, the closest thing to small talk that he could manage: asking for tidbits of information that he would write down later.

"Did you notice the plywood plastered all over the place next door?"

"I did," Evans nodded.

"We have some infected in there. If we can get a bunch of them walking on these special treadmills that Winnie designed, we can power a few light bulbs here and there."

Evans felt his muscles tense, and had to force them to relax. Zombies in the building was never a pleasant thought, even though he knew that Frannie and her people had exceptional control over them. They had been handling and managing the dead for years, with no recent accidents. At least, no accidents that Evans knew about.

"Do people still call you the Zombie Farm, or have you managed to decide on a new name?" That had been a thing when Evans had last been there. He left while they were still deliberating on the new name. Thinking back, that had been over a year ago.

"Yeah, we're called Paddock now," Frannie told him. "We have a nice sign over the entrance on the other side of town; you should check it out once the storm's passed. Haven't gotten around to a second sign yet, where you came in. All the wood's been needed elsewhere."

Evans nodded.

"So, let's get to business, shall we?" Frannie decided. "What are you doing here? I know you're not very keen on Paddock, and you'd avoid us if you could. Just here to ride out the storm?"

"No, this was my destination."

"Go on." Frannie leaned back in her chair, clasping her hands behind her head.

"There's a kid with me—a teenager actually. He's like you guys: zombie friendly. The place where he lived was very unhappy when he brought a… an infected person within their walls." He had almost said 'a dead person' but caught himself. People at Paddock didn't consider the zombies to be dead, despite the lack of a pulse or a need for respiration. "He also attacked the person who had given away his secret, but try not to hold that against him too much. There were some crazy circumstances at the time, and everyone was wired weirdly. After a trial, Gerald was banished and I agreed to bring him here."

"That was kind of you."

Evans shrugged. "I was leaving anyway."

"So that's it? You just came to visit to drop off the kid?"

"Pretty much. That's if you'll take him."

"I'll interview him later. What about the others? Are any of them staying here?"

"We came across them along the way. There's a town of silent ones not terribly far from here. I'll point it out on a map for you."

"We know about them," Frannie told him. "We avoid them, and they keep to themselves. You're saying those people are from there?"

Evans nodded. "Didn't know they were there until it was too late. Spent a night in one of their prisons. The people with me, they helped Gerald and I escape. They didn't want to be there anymore. They asked that I take them to Bridges."

Frannie sighed heavily, placing her hands back down at her sides and leaning forward once more.

"What? What's wrong?"

"Bridges is gone."

"What do you mean? How?"

"Raiders. Infiltrated and took over the place. They cast everyone out and killed anyone who opposed them. The survivors made their way here. We eventually went to check things out, but by the time we reached the place, the raiders were gone. They burned Bridges to the ground, presumably after stripping it of everything valuable."

"When was this?"

"Maybe five or six months ago. The Bridges folks are still here, trying to decide whether they want to rebuild or not. We've offered to let them stay."

"Can I talk to them? I want to ask about the raiders." Evans was curious if they were the same band who had taken over the Black Box. It would be good to know if they had been taken out, or if there was another group still running around out there. Evans had liked Bridges. It was a nice little community on a fair sized island formed by a split in a river. He found himself hoping he had blown up the people who had destroyed it.

"Sure, but you'll have to wait until after the storm. As you can see, they no longer stay in our visitors' quarters. They've been moved into what would normally be permanent housing. So I heard you mention a Gerald twice? I'm guessing that's the kid. Where's he from, exactly?"

"A new place," Evans told her. "They haven't reached out to any other communities yet, at least as far as I know. I told them where various, friendly places are, however, so that they can make contact when they're ready. They might even try reaching out to Bridges, which will be a shame when they find what's left. They lived at sea until something like five years ago."

"I'm guessing they don't have a name yet?"

"Not yet." Evans knew that Paddock—formally the Zombie Farm, formally something worse—was a stickler for names. Here, they liked names that properly defined a place, like Bridges, which had three of them.

"What kind of place is it?"

"A shipping container yard. They've built a wall out of the containers, and use them for housing. Good people. Very smart, and care a lot for one another."

"What's their aggression like?"

"Hard to say. I met them under very strange circumstances. They can be forgiving, but they can also be brutal in their retaliation against attackers."

"For you to learn both of those things, it really must have been some strange circumstances." Frannie clearly wanted to know. "I'm guessing it's also related to Gerald attacking someone?"

Evans explained as best he could how his people had first attacked the container yard due to a misunderstanding. He tried to keep out details that would place where they were, not because he didn't trust Frannie, but because he didn't think the container yard was ready to receive unexpected visitors just yet. When he talked about the Black Box, he didn't use the name and spoke of it as though it were a nearby cave system, in part because he didn't know all that much about the place.

"So they were one community living as two?" Frannie asked for clarification.

"Yeah, I guess that would be a good way to describe it."

"Sounds like it worked out for them, having somewhere to fall back to. Perhaps we should consider supplying just such a place." Paddock didn't have nearly as many people, not if you didn't count the zombies. They couldn't split into a fully functioning second community, but they could find a place to use as a fall back point.

"Now that Bridges is gone, you should," Evans advised. Bridges and Paddock were a little less than three days walk apart, and so had a fairly strong relationship. It had worked out for the survivors of Bridges, but meant that Paddock could no longer do the same.

"What will you do, now that Bridges is gone? Where will you go when you leave here?"

"I don't know," Evans told her honestly. "I'll have to talk it over with the others, see where they would like to go."

Frannie nodded this time. "Do you plan to stop for long? Are you here to trade at all?"

"Depends. We'll have to wait out the storm for sure. I'm guessing by the end of it, you'll have decided whether Gerald is allowed to stay or not. I wouldn't mind trading some labour for supplies. I don't have much in the way of resources at the moment."

"I'm sure we can find something for you to do. This storm is definitely going to cause some damage."

Evans glanced up at the ceiling where they could hear the rain now pounding upon it. It had arrived and then steadily increased throughout their conversation.

"Not too much damage, I hope," Evans eventually said, turning away from the pressboard ceiling.

"We're never hit by the worst of it, so we should be alright. It's one of the reasons we chose this place."

Evans wondered who *was* getting hit by the worst of it, and what that must be like for them. He worried it might be people he knew.

"You can head back to your party now," Frannie decided. "You have to start making new plans. Can you send Gerald over?"

"Sure."

When Evans stood up, Frannie did as well. They shook hands across the desk.

"I'll let you know if I hear of any jobs you can do before the storm lets up," Frannie told him.

"Thanks."

"And Evans?"

"Yeah?"

"It's nice to see you again. I know our way of life makes you uncomfortable, but you should stop by here more often than you do."

"I'll think about it."

When Evans left the office, he took the lantern to light his way. As he crossed through the hair salon, he could see that Gerald and the silent ones had lit a number of candles in the visitors' centre. It appeared they had chosen to stay in one of the back corners, near the stables.

"Evans!" a voice cried out as he crossed the main hall.

Evans turned to see a stout little woman rushing at him. He had just enough time to register that it was Winnie, before she was jumping up, her hands on his shoulders to pull herself higher, so that she could give him a kiss on the cheek.

"How are you, Winnie?" Evans asked once she had both feet back on the floor.

"I didn't know you were here!"

"I only just arrived."

"How long are you staying? Same length as last time?" She held his hands while she spoke. Winnie was too affectionate for most people, and too energetic as well, but Evans had learned to accept that it was just who she was. They had travelled together many years ago, only a few months after the outbreak. They had come across the start of this place together, before it had been given any name at all, and Winnie had chosen to stay and help them build it.

"Not long, I'm afraid," Evans told her. "I'm just here to drop off a kid, wait out the storm, and hopefully pick up some supplies."

"Oh, poo." Winnie let go of his hands so that she could gently punch his arm.

"I hear you made treadmills that can produce power?"

"Yeah, not much, but that's better than nothing, right? I'm hoping I can improve their output. I was just about to go check on them, if you'd like to come."

Evans looked at the boarded up shop next to the hair salon. "I'd love to," he really wouldn't, "but Frannie needs to talk to that kid I mentioned I'm dropping off. Also I have to discuss some things with the party members that are leaving with me. We were supposed to be going to Bridges."

"Yeah, it's such a shame what happened there. Make sure you talk to the Bridges people before you go. Some of them might want to join you."

"I will."

"See you around!" Winnie bounced off toward the chunk of plywood that served as a door to the zombie generator house.

Evans was glad to be heading the other way. He'd like to talk to Winnie some more, learn what new things she had learned, but he'd wait until she was in her workshop in the store beside Frannie's hair salon office, where her hands could be kept busy with other things.

Before entering the visitors' centre, Evans looked down the hallway toward the glass doors. The sunlight had become a sheet of dull grey, as water splashed down from the sky. He watched for only a second, before heading off to find Gerald.

"Frannie wants to talk to you," he reported once the teenager was located. He was sitting on a camping cot across from Blue, having a conversation in sign.

Gerald sighed. "Now?"

"Yes, now. Here," he handed him the lantern. "She's in the back room of the hair salon."

"You're not coming with me?"

"No."

Gerald continued to hesitate, clearly preferring to keep his conversation with Blue going, as opposed to starting a new one with Frannie. Evans let his pack slide off his shoulders and thump onto the floor. When he removed his sword to drop alongside it, the sound of the sheath hitting the hard floor was loud enough to make Gerald jump. The kid glowered at Evans, but when Evans refused to break eye contact, he got up and started his journey toward the hair salon.

Evans claimed a bunk that appeared unoccupied, and picked up his stuff to place upon it. He noticed that Blue was watching him.

"Do you need something?" Evans asked.

Blue shook her head. It seemed that she was just studying him. It made Evans wonder what, if anything, Gerald had said to her about him. He didn't really care, so long as the teenager wasn't encouraging the girl to try to murder him in his sleep. He had had to worry about such things before, although given the nature of the silent ones, that threat seemed greater than usual. In the past, he had always woken up before the attack could take place, but would a silent one cause him to wake? He didn't know, and really hoped he wouldn't have to find out. There was no reason Evans could think of why Gerald or any of the others would want him dead, so he should be safe. But then why was Blue staring at him so much?

"You know that makes people uncomfortable," Evans finally told her. "When you stare like that?"

Despite flushing red, she didn't look all that embarrassed as she turned away from him. Maybe she was just odd. Unable to talk to her without a translator, Evans couldn't really get to know her as well as he had the others.

"Evans?" Ang called to him in a loud whisper.

"Yes?" Evans left his things on the bed in order to walk over to the stables where Ang and Dev were watering the camels. With the storm outside, there was no shortage of hydration.

"We don't know much about horses," Ang admitted to him.

Evans understood. "I'll take care of Moe."

"Can I assist?" Dev asked. "I would like to learn."

"Of course. Come on." Moe was being kept at the end of the line of camels, still wearing all his gear. Evans was annoyed that Gerald hadn't taken care of the horse. Still, it wasn't like he'd have to deal with the kid for very much longer. Evans wasn't yet sure if he was going to be pleased when Gerald was gone, or if he was actually going to end up missing him.

***

Their first night at Paddock passed without incident. Evans hadn't found time to talk with Gerald, as the teenager seemed to be avoiding him, but he didn't look upset. He didn't look happy, but he didn't look sad either. Evans guessed that his talk with Frannie had gone well, but that he was still judging the place for himself. Frannie had gone dashing across the street to where she lived without saying goodnight, so asking her how it went was out of the question.

The rain on the roof high overhead was really rather soothing. Evans didn't sleep well because part of his mind wouldn't let go of its worry about Blue, but just lying still and listening to the rain was enough for him. Only once did he get up from his bunk, and that was to go double check that the door to the zombie generator was secure. It was. He couldn't even open it when he tried; there was a large padlock that hadn't been there earlier. Winnie had probably locked the place up tight when she left, worried that someone in Evans' party might wander in there and slaughter what they found.

In the morning, Evans first went to check on Moe. He also took the opportunity to wash his face in the horse's trough. A system involving rain barrels and pipes bored through the walls kept the troughs full, and, with the storm, Evans wasn't worried about wasting any. He could hear that it was still raining, and decided he would check on the severity of the storm after breakfast. If it didn't look too bad, he could take a much needed shower in it.

Breakfast was a quiet affair, as Evans had no desire to start discussing the future yet, and Gerald was still asleep.

"If you need anything, I'm going to be just outside, cleaning off," Evans told Burt.

He gathered up the few spare clothes he had and brought them with him, heading toward the end of the stables. There, a metal tub sat empty behind a curtain, some soap perched on a ledge above it. Evans took the soap. From previous visits, he knew he could pull a small lever to divert some of the water from the horse troughs into the tub, but he preferred the rain. The tub was far too small for him.

Just as he reached the doors that led out to Paddock's main street, Frannie came bustling in.

"Oh, good morning," she greeted him as she pulled off her poncho and shook it out.

"Good morning."

"Sleep well?"

"No issues."

"I found a job for you to do this afternoon if you'd like."

"Sure. I'm free now if you want."

"No, no, take your shower, relax. I won't need you until this afternoon."

"All right. See you then."

While Frannie walked off toward her office, Evans stepped outside. The rain wasn't exactly warm, but it wasn't too cold. The wind from yesterday had died down somewhat, so that it was no longer raining sideways. Evans took off his boots and left them just under a sheltered overhang with his belt, knife, and the soap when it wasn't in use. Looking up and down the street as he scrubbed himself on the sidewalk, Evans spotted two others making use of nature's shower. One was washing like him, the other appeared to be scrubbing clothes against a washboard. He thought about walking over and asking if he could borrow the washboard, but eventually decided against it. He couldn't count on the person being someone he knew previously, and because he and his party had arrived just before the storm, not that many people had been able to get a good look at him. It was safer to remain close to the visitors' centre.

Winnie dashed over from the small two-storey apartment building across the street, wearing hip waders and carrying a large umbrella. She gave Evans a quick hello and stuck her tongue out at him for some reason, before heading inside. Another man, someone Evans hadn't really met but knew to be a doctor, entered the building a couple of minutes later, also coming from the small apartment. It seemed like the place to live if you had an office in the visitors' centre. Later on, three kids wearing bright yellow rain slickers went running by, laughing over some game. It seemed the storm could only halt life in this place for a short time. Evans wondered how long it would be before the shops sprang back up along the sidewalks.

Once he and his clothing were washed and rinsed, Evans went back inside. He didn't have a towel, so he just hung out near the entrance to keep from dripping on everything. Wearing only his underwear, Evans wrung out the rest of his clothes, and then laid them all flat on the tiled floor. He kept his stuff to one side of the large hallway so that he wouldn't be in the way, and watched the water follow the gentle slope toward the doors. The floor was probably just making his clothes dirty again, and it would take a while to dry them without the sun, but they shouldn't be as stiff with dirt, sweat, and grime as they had been.

When Evans was no longer dripping, he walked the length of the hallway, cinching his belt around his hips so that he could carry his knife with him. Outside of the rear doors, was a fenced-in parking lot filled with planters and plants. Secure tarps and perforated roofs protected the plants from the full brunt of the storm, while letting some of the water through. Evans knew that that had been one of Winnie's first contributions to the place. Just outside the doors, however, a few of the silent ones were washing themselves as Evans had been. It was the first time Evans had seen any of them without their rags on. Their skin practically glowed, ghostly pale beneath the overcast sky. Evans gave them their privacy and returned to his things.

He passed the time with exercise, and caught up with Winnie for a bit when she left her work space and wolf whistled at him. By the time lunch rolled around, his things were dry enough to move. He brought them back to his bed, and hung them from the railing of the unused bunk above his. Gerald was finally both awake and alone. Perhaps Blue was one of the ones showering out back.

"So how'd your talk with Frannie go?" Evans asked him as he rooted through his pack for something to munch on.

"Okay, I guess," Gerald shrugged.

"Do you like her?"

"She wasn't mean, if that's what you meant."

"What do you think of this place so far?"

Gerald shrugged again. It was strange for Evans to be the one trying to hold up the conversation.

"Well, if Frannie says you can stay, then you're staying. I'm not taking you anywhere else."

"What if I want to go with the silent ones?"

"Given your head space, this is the best place for you. Besides, I'm not quite sure where the silent ones are going."

"What do you mean? I thought you were taking to them to that place in your notebook."

"That place apparently doesn't exist anymore. I'm going to have a sit down with them to discuss their options."

"They could stay here."

"They could, if they wanted to." Evans didn't think they would. They could have chosen this place while looking through Evans' notebook, but they hadn't. They had chosen Bridges instead for a reason.

After eating, Evans donned a damp shirt and a damp pair of pants. He didn't bother with socks before putting his boots on. While not exactly comfortable in the damp clothes, Evans didn't really care. He was used to feeling uncomfortable.

"Enjoy your shower?" Frannie asked when Evans stepped into her office. She had a notebook open in front of her and was studying a cramped series of numbers and words. She had plenty of notebooks, mostly unused, piled all over the office, yet she still wrote as small as she could all the things she needed to keep track of. She was prepared for the long haul in this place, knowing that someone else would eventually have her job, and that she wouldn't be the one writing in every notebook.

"It was refreshing," Evans told her as he sat down. "What's the job you have for me?"

"Feeding time requires two people," Frannie said, gesturing to the wall beside her with one hand while continuing to study the notebook in front of her.

Evans' eyes flicked toward the wall. It was the one with the zombie generator on the other side.

"Not even Winnie's allowed to do it alone," Frannie continued, "and her usual partner isn't coming in today."

"Can't it wait?"

"No, we don't want them to starve and rot."

"Why not ask Gerald to do it?"

"Because I don't yet trust Gerald." Frannie finally raised her head. "But I trust you to do this job. I know you dislike it, so I'm willing to offer you more rations than I probably should in exchange."

"I suppose you're too busy to do it, and the doctor simply won't?"

"You got it."

"Can I bring Gerald along with me anyway? He should probably see it."

"By all means."

"I'll have to tell the silent ones what's going on as well."

"Go ahead. As long as they don't go breaking in there and commit a slaughter, I don't care what they know."

Evans drummed his fingers against the desktop once. "Fine. I'll do it."

"Thank you." Frannie's head lowered back to her notebook. "Go get Gerald, tell the silent ones, whatever it is you need to do, then go find Winnie in her workshop."

Evans grudgingly got up and left the office. If this was the kind of work he was going to be given, he definitely wasn't going to stay any longer than was necessary.

The silent ones had returned from their shower. Less concerned about dripping, they hung their rags to dry over the rails of unused beds, and over unused tents throughout the large space. They must have had a second set of clothing packed upon the camels that they hadn't washed, because Evans could barely tell which of them were the ones who had washed up. Only damp hair gave them away, yet some were wearing their hoods again, so Evans couldn't be certain.

"Good, you're all together," Evans said as he found a place to sit among them all.

The statement drew the attention of all the silent ones, who gathered even closer together.

"You read my notebook right? I assume you chose not to come here because I noted that this place was zombie friendly?"

"That's right," Burt nodded, answering for everyone.

"Okay. You should know that in that room across the hall," Evans pointed to the one all boarded up, "there are a bunch of zombies being kept."

Several of the silent ones shifted uneasily.

"I know, it makes me uncomfortable too, but I can assure you that they are well contained. In fact, I'm about to go inspect them myself, to make sure of this fact." No reason to tell them that he would actually be assisting in feeding them. "I just thought you all should know so that you won't be frightened if you hear anything." Evans bet that some of them were already frightened now. "When

I'm done, we're going to need to have another conversation as well, so I'd like to ask you all to stay close by. Is that all right?"

A few of the silent ones nodded, a couple gave a non-committal grunt. Evans bet they were all going to wait right where they were for him.

"Gerald?" Evans stood up and sought him out. "You're coming with me."

Gerald sighed. "Why?"

"Because you want to get to know this place better, right? So come take a look at what they do. See if you approve."

Gerald muttered something under his breath, but got up to follow.

"I didn't want to say this to the silent ones," Evans spoke quietly once they entered the hallway and headed to Winnie's workshop, "but I'm actually going to be helping feed the zombies, not just checking out their restraints."

"They feed the zombies here?" Gerald sounded genuinely surprised.

"Did you not feed yours?"

Gerald clenched and unclenched his hands at his sides. "I wanted to, but our food was always rationed, and I was never able to catch anything outside the wall."

"Other than your dead friend."

Gerald clenched his jaw this time. Evans couldn't tell, but he thought the kid might have been embarrassed. Because he captured a zombie, or because he couldn't feed it?

"By the way, they don't like to refer to the zombies as dead here," Evans said just as they reached Winnie's door. "They're merely infected."

Gerald nodded.

Evans pulled open the glass door and stepped through. Inside, a variety of tools lined the walls, and a scattering of workbenches were covered in all sorts of junk. Evans noticed that there were a number of power tools, including a large band saw, a table saw, and a drill press among others. A series of rechargeable batteries sat in a row, their chargers all hooked up to a much larger set of car batteries.

"Winnie," Evans called out to where she was huddled over something in the back corner. A dim light bulb glowed there, similar to the one in Frannie's office. It was likely also on the zombie generator. Evans wondered if the doctor had one too, or if three light bulbs were one too many. Elsewhere there were candles, and lights sitting next to more car batteries that were currently off.

"Evans!" Winnie turned and smiled at him. "Just give me a minute to finish up what I'm doing here, and we'll get to work. Feel free to look around, but try not to touch anything." She turned away again.

Evans had hoped for more than a minute, but he did take up her offer to look at things. Trying to discern what her various projects were distracted him from his coming task. He came across plans for a windmill. Not the kind that generated energy, but the old kind that was actually used for milling. Other than that, Evans failed to identify what any of the pieces were going to be used for. Of course, some of the things around the workshop might just be what they looked like, since Winnie surely repaired things for the people around here.

"Okay," Winnie spun around on her stool and then hopped up onto her feet. "Let's get to work, shall we?" When she spotted Gerald, she scurried over to him with her hand held out. "Hello! You must be Gerald. I'm Winnie, it's a pleasure to meet you."

"Hi." Gerald shook her hand and then took a quick step back, unused to Winnie's forward nature.

"I used to travel with Evans too," Winnie told Gerald as she led the way out of the workshop and toward the boarded up storefront, picking up a sealed, yellow bucket along the way. She also donned a headlamp, and handed over a pair each for Evans and Gerald to wear. Evans noticed that most, if not all, of the silent ones had gathered along the windows across the hallway to watch. He doubted they would see anything, but he knew he would do the same in their position.

"Yeah? Did he also once tie you up and leave you alone in a gas station?" Gerald grumbled.

"You turned out fine." Evans normally wouldn't bother with a reply, but with Winnie there, one felt necessary. "I came back just like I said I would, and I hadn't been gone for long."

"No, he never tied me up," Winnie answered Gerald's question as she unlocked the door. "He did once push me off a cliff though. There was a river at the bottom, and it was our only means of escape. I was too scared to jump, so Evans gave me a good shove. Man, that water was cold! You remember that, Evans?"

"I remember."

When the door swung open, Evans saw that there was soundproofing material on the backside, just like the room where the silent ones kept their camels. He expected to be greeted by haunting moans, but it was eerily lacking in zombie sounds within the room beyond. The only noise he could hear was a whirring. It wasn't really one sound, though, it was several overlapping. Winnie stepped through and urged Evans and Gerald to follow her. When they did, she shut the door behind them.

"Usually we don't bother to close it behind us, but I figure the rest of your party will appreciate it." The sound of Winnie's voice made some of the whirring increase in speed. It was also accompanied by a thumping. "One or two will sometimes scream when we feed them."

"You have smart zombies in here?" Evans felt a lump form in his throat. Only the smarter zombies screamed, and only they could run, which was the thumping he heard. He couldn't see any of them yet, for the store had been filled with plywood walls. He was in a small corridor that spanned the front of the place. Two other hallways branched off the corridor to his left and right, following the walls to the back of the store. Several tools, all on telescopic poles, waited in a corner.

"Of course. They're much better for producing energy. Come on, I'll introduce you."

Evans didn't want to be introduced, but he stayed near Winnie. He wished he had his sword, but all he had with him at that moment was his knife. The sword he had deliberately left behind so as to resist the temptation to use it.

Winnie brought him around the corner nearest the tools. The hallway extended all the way to the back of the store. On one side was the store's outer wall, and along the other were a series of plywood stalls, similar to the horse stalls at the back of the visitors' centre. Cabling snaked its way out of the front of each stall, and disappeared around a corner at the far end.

"This is Sheppard," Winnie said, standing in front of the first opening and gesturing inside. "Sheppard, this is Evans and Gerald."

Evans slowly stepped into view. The bottom of the pen was taken up by a modified treadmill. On it, feet donning sneakers and ankle braces, pushed against the surface, trying to run forward. The zombie was wearing a bright blue jump suit, its wrists strapped to its waist, which was held in place by a pair of rods connected to the sides of the pen. A bar at the same height crossed the front of the pen, most likely to remind people not to get too close, but it had also been painted with the name Sheppard. The thing's head was being held, but not as rigidly as its waist. The blue bike helmet looked absurd on the zombie. A chain connected it to the back of the pen. Also attached to the helmet was a leather facemask, strapped tightly across the zombie's mouth and chin. Nothing covered its eyes, that were still far too human, and staring right at Evans.

"How..." Evans tried to swallow the lump in his throat, his mouth dry. He kept one hand wrapped firmly around the hilt of his knife. "How long has he been dead?"

"You know we don't say they're dead here," Winnie reminded him. "But a few months now. Sheppard got bitten while out exploring one day. He volunteered for this job, provided he turned into a smart one. Would rather keep contributing than be set loose out in the paddock. You all right, Evans?"

Evans was thinking about the wave after wave of zombies that had come at him during the attack of the mega horde. He remembered falling off a container, remembered thinking he was dead as he landed among them. He lost his mind for a while after that, only dreadful flashes of the dead remaining in his memory.

"I'm okay," he eventually answered. "Let's just get this over with."

The yellow bucket was revealed to be full of bloodless, half-rotted meat, and bits of animals that no one wanted. Some of it was placed on a sort of spoon on a rod, which Evans was supposed to hold out to the zombie. Winnie used another tool to unlatch the mouth guard. The zombie immediately screamed at them.

"Push the food closer," Winnie encouraged Evans, her rod tool still in hand for the far end remained hooked to the facemask. "He won't scream if he's eating."

Evans moved the food closer. The zombie latched on, repeatedly biting at the meat and metal. It wasn't so much eating, as it was attacking. But the pieces that went into its mouth were swallowed, and it ate more than it dropped. Evans then noticed that just behind the treadmill, there was a little pile of shrivelled, mouldy meat from what the zombie had dropped in the past. It seemed the smell wasn't only coming from the walking corpses.

When Winnie decided that the thing had eaten enough, she told Evans to withdraw the spoon tool. She then reattached the facemask in place, which was a little more difficult than removing it had been.

"There. Easy, right?"

While it had been physically easy, it certainly wasn't emotionally easy. All of Evans' inner warning bells were going off, and his system was flooded with adrenaline.

"Tito is next."

Evans helped feed three more zombies. They were all named. Most of them had been found out in the wild and so their names had been assigned. Some were in worse condition than others, but they were all smart, and Evans had a hard time looking at them. Unfortunately, the nature of the task meant looking at their faces, since he had to see where he was holding the spoon.

"Can I try feeding the next one?" Gerald asked.

"Sure, I don't see why not," Winnie said.

Evans was more than happy to hand off his duty. Gerald didn't seem to mind the task at all, and often asked questions, like where each zombie had come from. He learned about how they occasionally misted the zombies to keep them from drying out too much, especially their eyes, and how they were working out a schedule for cleaning out the back of the pens where the mess always gathered. Winnie was also thinking of training them to pedal modified exercise bikes, which would be more space efficient. Gerald took over Evans' work, so that Evans had only to follow them around, often avoiding looking into the pens. The hairs on the back of his neck would not lie flat. He didn't care if Winnie told Frannie that Gerald did most of the work, and if she cut down the number of rations she was going to give him because of it; he just wanted to get out of there. But he wasn't about to leave Winnie alone with Gerald.

When the task was finally completed, Evans was grateful to step out into the fresher air of the main hallway, taking a deep breath as Winnie locked the door.

"I like you, kid," Winnie patted Gerald on the shoulder. "I hope you stay." She then headed back toward her workshop.

"Are you all right?" Gerald actually asked Evans.

"Do you care?"

"I care when your reputation is my best in to this place. I don't want you to wig out and kill their friends."

"So you're saying you want to stay here?"

Gerald shrugged. "I guess so. I mean, I don't know much about their day-to-day stuff, but they seem okay. No worse than the container yard."

Evans was relieved to hear it. He did not want to have to bring Gerald to another place like this one. He never wanted to see another room like that one ever again. Outside, the rain continued to wash the streets.

IV: By the Sea

It was dark and noisy inside the container. Riley sat on the floor with Hope wrapped up in her arms. Cameron and Brunt were trying to keep a pair of cows calm. The chickens were free to run around, although they had all seemed to finally find a place to settle. One of them was against Riley's side, and Hope had reached out a few times to pet the hen. If she turned on the flashlight, Riley might be able to identify the fowl, but she didn't. It wasn't worth draining the batteries for even a second. Along with the cackling of the chickens who hadn't gone to sleep, there was the occasional lowing of a cow, and the ceaseless rain drumming overhead. It was too loud to make out Hope's breathing, but Riley could feel her daughter's side beneath her hand, the gentle rise and fall indicating that she was asleep. Maybe she'd stay asleep for more than three hours this time. A sharp odour indicated that one of the cows had just taken another piss. Not as bad as their fresh shit, or that of the chickens, but still pungent.

Riley wondered if they would all survive. How many of those who had decided not to flee to the upper level of the wall were now dead? Drowned in their homes, or swept away if they had decided to evacuate too late. Some might still be alive. Their containers weren't water tight, but if the water level remained low enough, they'd still have plenty of air. Last anyone checked, the water hadn't risen higher than the first containers. Not yet anyway. If it somehow did, those still below should be able to get out through their emergency hatches.

If it hadn't been for Josh, more of them would be dead. He had looked out into the storm and seen that the water level had spilled over the end of the U-dock, which, while lower than the rest of the container yard, wasn't vastly lower. Riley was the first person he found after noticing it. His girlfriend, Anne, was fighting through the storm to find Boyle, who had returned early from a scavenger trip just before the storm hit. Riley didn't wait for Boyle. She immediately took charge and began barking orders as though she were back in Leighton's ER. Whether people agreed they needed to flee upward or not, they nevertheless helped out. The ramp they had built earlier for the exodus of envoys and scavengers was quickly located and placed against the wall. Animals, stubborn and complaining, were hauled up the slick, water washed metal, sometimes having to be pushed by a crowd as they lay on their sides. The animals were all crowded into the upper containers, shoved in wherever there was room among the supplies stored there. People and whatever food stores had remained then filled in the rest of the spaces. Some people chose to remain a level down, hoping their homes would protect them. Riley thought they were idiots, but she didn't want them to be wrong.

She silently cursed Bronislav. Why hadn't he brought Hope with him? Surely she was as capable as Dakota. Younger, maybe, and certainly headstrong at times, but surely as capable. This was unfair to Bronislav, she knew, but it gave her anger a focus. Something that wasn't a storm, a natural occurrence in nature.

Abby and Lauren were in the container across the way, along with Josh, Anne, Robin, Quincy, Freya, and anyone who still had wounds that needed monitoring. The crowd of people must keep them occupied, but Riley knew that Abby and Lauren would be frightened every time they got a second to think. Not for themselves, but for Peter in the submarine, and Jon and Claire who were God-knows-where. They probably prayed a lot, as they actually believed in God, unlike Riley. Robin's cat, Splatter, would be terrified. Riley hadn't seen the feline get carried into the container, but she was sure it was in there. Robin would never have left him behind, and Freya was the kind of person who could catch and hold a cat in any situation. And she would for Robin.

Riley's mind kept going every which way, unable to touch down on anything for long. The one thought it kept coming back to was that Mathias had drowned. He had been attacked by a shark, but something told her that he had drowned. Misha had seen him get pulled under, and never saw him come back up again. Mathias had drowned and it seemed that same fate might be awaiting Riley and Hope. A whole family drowned.

Hope took a sharp intake of breath as she awoke, maybe from a bad dream, and then coughed from the stink. The sound woke up the sleeping hen beside them, and she clucked for a bit. Hope soothed the chicken with gentle pats.

It was at least another ten minutes before Brunt spoke up.

"I'm going to open the door for a bit, check on the water level and get us some fresh air, if no one objects."

"I want some fresh air," Hope whispered to her mom. Even though it was just Cameron and Brunt in there with them, she had taken to only whispering things to her mother. Perhaps she also couldn't stop thinking about the time her father had disappeared beneath the sea.

"Okay." Riley flicked on the flashlight, illuminating her sister. Cameron looked exhausted. It was hard to say with any certainty how long they had been in there, but she had been on her feet virtually the whole time, and at no point had she slept. Dakota was in the submarine, where it was likely safer, but that meant that she wasn't here where Cameron could see her and ask how she was feeling. Instead, she had the cows to care for.

When Riley attempted to stand up, Hope clung to her, wanting to be lifted and carried.

"I can't carry you and the flashlight," she said. Really, she couldn't carry Hope at all. Her chest was still healing after her surgery, and she had to be careful. Her barking orders outside had almost been too much, and her chest had hurt by the time she sat down in the container.

Hope knew this was the real reason, since she got up on her own without complaining, or suggesting that she herself hold the flashlight. She was a bright girl, bright enough to have been let aboard the submarine.

Together, they met with Brunt by the container's doors.

"Door one, where I have to fight the wind to keep it open," Brunt said, pointing to one of the two doors. "Or door two, where I have to fight the wind to keep it from opening too far?" He pointed to the other.

"Fight to keep it open," Riley told him. The other door would let in more air, but this one was safer.

Brunt moved the latches, and threw his shoulder against the metal sheet. The wind howled around the corrugated panel, attempting to push it closed once more. Rain slammed down on Brunt as he braced himself, hooking one foot against the door that was still latched just in case the wind changed direction. It did that frequently and without warning.

Riley kept out of the worst of the rain and shone her flashlight through the opening. It was grey out there. Must be daylight, but the middle of the day? Morning? Evening? She had no sense of time, especially when she drifted in and out of sleep.

"The water level is half way up the first row of containers," Riley reported.

"Let's fill all the water buckets," Brunt told her. "The wind feels stronger and we should avoid opening this door again for a while."

Hope helped Riley hand the buckets to Brunt. He held them out in the rain, letting them fill. The rain was safe enough to drink, although the higher the water got, the more they worried about a salty spray filling their buckets. Hope took the filled buckets from Brunt and carefully placed them farther inside. They were too heavy for Riley to carry in any situation other than an emergency due to her healing surgical scars. Then again, if this wasn't an emergency, what was?

Once the last bucket was filled, Brunt ducked back inside, slamming the door shut behind him and throwing the latches.

"What happens if the water reaches us?" Hope whispered as Brunt wrung out his clothes. "Will we have to retreat to the top of the container?"

"Out into the storm? We'll be swept right off by the wind," Brunt had heard her and commented in a jovial tone.

"Isn't that why we have rope?" Hope's worry caused her volume to rise a few notches. "Will the animals have to remain trapped inside, all alone?"

"The water won't get that high," Riley reassured her daughter, convincing herself that the imagined scenario was impossible.

"I could hold onto a chicken," Hope continued. "I wouldn't even mind if she pecked."

"We're staying right here, don't you worry," Cameron told her.

If the water did reach them, they likely wouldn't know it until it was too late. The water pressure below would already be making it impossible for those who stayed to open their doors. Hopefully they all had a high space to retreat to, like a bunk bed or a solid shelving unit, and weren't forced to swim until the water level retreated. Unlike them, the container Riley's family currently occupied didn't have an escape hatch.

"Cameron, why don't you sit down for a bit. Hope and I can take care of the cows for a little while," Riley suggested. Taking care of the cows wasn't difficult; it generally just involved petting their noses the way they liked to help keep them calm. Cameron had milked them relatively recently—at least Riley thought she had—and so they should be good on that front for a while.

"Yeah, that would be great. Thanks." Brunt had responded for Cameron. She protested weakly, but Brunt led her away from the cows as Riley and Hope took over. By the time she sat down, Cameron was out like a light. Riley switched her flashlight back off once everyone appeared settled. The cows provided a good distraction. Not just for Hope, but for Riley as well.

Some of the chickens were clucking and fluttering about, having been disturbed by the light and the air. Riley listened to them in the dark, her hands gently stroking the warm, soft muzzle before her. She preferred to listen to them, rather than trying to make out the sounds of waves lapping at the container walls below.

SECTION 5:
HATE

25: ONIDA
LESS THAN 1 YEAR AGO

It didn't take long for Onida and Shawn to end up on friendly terms with the bandits. One unexpected snowstorm was all it took. A midday blizzard had forced them to rapidly seek shelter. There was no time to hand back the guns, to split up, to make a meeting point for when the storm ended. Hell, they couldn't even see the area around them clearly enough to pick a spot they could find later. Instead, they all found themselves in the same grocery store, brushing piles of snowflakes off themselves and the horses. The dog had almost become lost in the snow, but managed to find its way to its owner's calling and then screaming voice. There was no food to be had. All the shelves had been picked clean of sustenance a long time ago. Even the pet food was all gone. Only a few cleaning chemicals and some cooking utensils remained. They had built a small fire using the old wooden fruit crates, and then added what wooden shelving they could find to chop up. The bandits had both a good splitting axe and a hatchet. Once the fire was going and the horses were settled, they had no choice but to talk. Well, the bandits did most of the talking, while Onida and Shawn listened. Even with Onida chiming in infrequently, they all pretty much knew one another once the sun came up the next morning to reveal that the snowstorm had moved on. They hadn't killed each other in the night, no one had even tried, and though Shawn still carried all the guns, he didn't tell Onida to ride backward to keep an eye on everyone. They stopped splitting up at night, and eventually Shawn and Onida slept at the same time. By the time a week had passed, everyone was properly armed with their own guns. Onida had been given an extra revolver she hadn't yet fired, and Shawn now carried a rifle. Not everyone had a saddle though.

"Man, does my ass hurt," complained Axel during a lunch stop. The group didn't travel as far each day as Shawn and Onida had managed on their own due to the need for prolonged stops, but neither of them complained. Despite slower progress, the journey was more pleasant. Shawn's only issue seemed to be his dislike of the dog.

"We really gotta find some saddles soon," Mikey complained. He always looked mildly ridiculous. He was a short guy with a face full of pimples: a teenager who carried around a gun about as big as he was. Onida hadn't seen him shoot since the time he had hit the pavement ahead of her, but had heard stories about his firearm proficiency. Apparently he had been shooting since he was a little kid, even before the infection spread. If the world had remained normal, he'd probably be some sort of Olympic hopeful by now. Onida wasn't even sure she could handle the revolver she'd been offered, and couldn't remember ever having seen the Olympics.

It was halfway through their break when Ronnie jumped to her feet. "Everyone shut up," she hissed.

They all fell silent, listening for whatever she thought she had heard. Onida saw Shawn out of the corner of her eye as he drew his bow. He was probably thinking about wolves.

"Do you hear that?" Ronnie was flicking her fingers in time with something. "I think I hear hoof beats."

Onida looked to their horses, but they were all standing still, cropping the yellowed grass. The snow that had been dumped on them that one day had since melted away. The mornings usually brought frost, but they hadn't had another real snowfall since. The sky sprinkled a few flakes on occasion, but they rarely survived the trip all the way to the ground.

"You're right," nodded Dom, the leader of the bandits who had been the one to step in front of them on the road. "Ronnie, Helen, go check it out and report back."

The two women, one of whom was his wife and who had convinced him that travelling south was a good idea, dashed off toward the sound. Onida could hear the hooves now too. They were on a different street, but drawing closer. They were coming from the south, so it was likely that they had no idea that the bandits were there.

It didn't take long for Ronnie and Helen to come back.

"Just two of them, on two horses," Helen reported.

"Excellent," Dom beamed. "What do you say folks, time to go to work?"

Mikey immediately got up and headed off, not needing to be told what to do.

"Onida, Shawn, are you going to come with us?" Helen asked. It was nice, and weirdly unexpected that she did.

"Onida, you should go with them," Shawn told her. "I'll stay here to watch the horses." He had slackened his bow, but still had it ready in case some unfortunate appeared.

"Good idea," Dom agreed. "Onida knows horses. She'll be able to tell us if their saddles are any good."

Following the bandits toward the hastily decided ambush point, Onida felt her heart hammering in her chest. They were in a suburban area, where the winding road allowed some of them to get to the other side of the street without being seen by the travellers.

"Stay close to me," Gatsby whispered, leading her over to a house where someone with mobility issues must have once lived. A small elevator was attached to the side of the porch, and by crouching down, the two of them could hide within the metal box. It was carpeted by mushy, wet leaves.

Jammed together within the enclosed space, Onida and Gatsby listened to the approach of hooves. The horses stopped a short distance from their hiding place. Onida took a quick peek over the edge. There were definitely only two of them. It was an old woman and a young man, making almost a weird parody of herself and Shawn. Dom stood in the road in front of them. He gave the pair roughly the same speech as he had given Shawn and her, accompanied by a shot from Mikey's rifle hitting the pavement. Onida didn't know where he was hiding, but it sounded closer than when she had been stopped.

"Do the saddles look good?" Gatsby whispered to Onida.

Onida briefly poked her head up again. "Hard to say when they're sitting on them, but I doubt they'd be using saddles that are falling apart."

Gatsby raised a quick thumbs up over the side of the box. Presumably Dom was looking for it.

"Now, if you would be so kind as to dismount," Dom told the travellers. "This can go smoothly and painlessly."

"Fuck you!" the young man shouted.

Dom sighed loudly. This seemed to be a signal, as Gatsby crept out of the box, drawing Onida along with him.

"For that, I'm going to take your saddles and reins," Dom told the young man. "Use language like that again, and I may take your horses next. Do you want that?"

The old woman was the first to notice that they were surrounded, which caused a startled gasp to escape her.

"Let's just give them what they want." Onida was now close enough to hear her speak quietly to the young man. "It's not worth it."

The young man scowled at her. He definitely thought that what they were carrying was worth it, but when she eased herself down, he followed suit.

"Step back from the horses," Dom instructed, gesturing to the space beside him.

The dog, a wiry mutt with the mismatched name of Butter, was on his rope leash again. A quiet command from Harper had him barking and snapping at the travellers, straining against the rope as if he wanted to kill the pair. Harper had admitted to Onida that if the rope ever broke, Butter wouldn't do anything. He'd probably get scared and cower behind Harper's legs. The travellers didn't know that, however, and so kept a wary distance from the dog.

Half of the bandits stood in guard positions around the old woman and the young man, while the rest of them picked over the horses' goods. It was all so pre-orchestrated, that nothing had had to be discussed beforehand.

"Take the reins," Gatsby hissed at Onida.

It took her a second to realize that he meant for her to remove the horses' reins, and not make some attempt to take charge.

Onida whispered soothing words to the horses as she did what she was told. She wondered what she must look like to the travellers. The bandits all wore blue jeans and fierce expressions, while she was all in leather pelts and confusion.

The horses were well behaved, and Onida hoped that meant they wouldn't be difficult to ride bareback. The saddles and saddlebags were removed as one unit, and quickly carried off out of sight between two buildings. Onida stood between the horses, each of her hands clasping a hank of mane. The reins hung off her arms. She didn't know what she was supposed to do next. When Gatsby had run off, helping to carry one of the saddles, had she been supposed to follow?

"Take your backpacks off, please," Dom said to the travellers, who hesitated. "Make this easy, and I might just let you keep one of them."

They both slipped out of their packs. The young man threw his on the ground in disgust.

Dom *tsked* at him. "Must not be anything very important in there if you're going to treat it like that. I'll just take it off your hands." He picked up the backpack and opened it up to rummage through the contents. Helen did the same with the old woman's bag. When they were done, the woman's bag was handed back to her, but the young man's was handed to Axel, who ran off with it.

"All right. Back up on your horses." Dom stepped off to one side, a symbolic gesture that the road was now open.

Onida didn't know what to do when the two travellers walked toward her and the horses. Should she run away? Should she not let them get too close? What was she supposed to do?

"Can you ride bareback?" she ended up asking the old woman in a soft voice.

"I've been riding bareback since before you were born." Her voice wasn't sharp, even though she had every right to bite, but instead was resigned. This probably wasn't the first time she had been robbed on the road. "Give me a boost though, my strength's not what it once was."

Onida knew it could have been a ploy, that she might be about to get kicked in the face, but she cupped her hands. The woman did not kick her, merely used her as a step, and swung her leg easily over her horse's back. She looked quite at home up there, Onida noticed. The young man, on the other hand, struggled for a bit as he got up on his own, and didn't look at all confident in his seat. He knew where to hold, so he had clearly ridden bareback before, but he definitely wasn't sure of himself.

Dom gestured for Onida to follow him. All bandits who were left melted away between the houses, going off in different directions so as not to give away their camp's location. Following Dom between two houses, Onida took one last look over her shoulder. She saw that the woman and man weren't proceeding forward in the direction that they had been going, but instead had turned around and were returning the way they had come.

"They likely came from a community and will head back to it," Dom explained.

Onida couldn't tell if he had seen her looking over her shoulder, or if he had intended to explain anyway.

"People travelling between two communities are always the best ones to hit. Knowing they have somewhere to go, somewhere to resupply, makes them more agreeable. Tends to mean we can't linger in the area long, because lots of communities will send out parties to hunt us down, but they're great one-offs. What do you think?"

"Think?" Onida wasn't sure what he meant.

"About taking their stuff. What did you think about it? What did you feel? Are you going to throw up? Because Ronnie threw up the first time we stole supplies from someone. Of course, back then, there was a lot less food to go around, because only the smart ones, the long time thinkers, had started to grow stuff."

"Oh. Um..." What *did* Onida think of their highway robbery? The only thing she really felt was that she was glad it wasn't her. "Nothing," she eventually answered. "I don't really feel anything about it."

Dom momentarily turned around to look at her as they walked a circuitous route back to their camp. He didn't seem to believe her, but Onida didn't know what else to say. What did he expect of her? For her to complain? To tell him that he was wrong to do what they had done? Onida had felt worse about going back on her word to the Amish. When she didn't say anything more, Dom drummed his fingers against his assault rifle and faced forward once more. Maybe he had expected to have to justify his existence. He might have had a speech lined up, and could even be disappointed that he wasn't going to get to say it. Or perhaps he was still assessing Onida's character, and found her to be a curiosity. Maybe he didn't have a type classification for her yet. It could be that she didn't fit into any of his preconceived boxes.

When they finally made it back to camp, Onida was glad to see that nothing had happened to it while they were gone. Knowing that Shawn was alone with all the horses and their gear, had been like having a tiny itch in the back of her mind. It had been hard not to think about how they had left the Amish in the night.

Most of the others were back already. Only Mikey was still out there somewhere. Their lunch stop had wound up taking much longer than usual.

"We should get going as quickly as possible," Shawn grunted. "We want to be somewhere else by nightfall."

Dom was in agreement, so they didn't bother to decide which horses were going to wear the stolen tack, and instead just loaded it up on some of the packhorses.

"Who's going to get the new saddles?" asked Julian as he scrambled up onto his horse.

"Whoever Onida thinks should get them," Dom answered.

Onida suddenly found that all eyes were on her. Every one of them was begging to be chosen, and she knew that that night, she was going to be harassed with offers, and maybe even threatened.

"I'm going to put the saddles on whichever horse they fit best," she decided then and there.

A strange combination of disappointment and hope went through the bandits. Disappointment that they would be unlikely to bribe her, but hopeful that their horse might be the one of correct size.

"It's going to be like finding fucking Cinderella," Anita cackled. She never laughed, just cackled, like some witch from a fairy tale. Her voice always sounded rough and broken. Apparently she had been a heavy smoker before the outbreak, and still scrounged everywhere for cigarettes. According to her, she hadn't quit like so many others, she had just been forced to take an extended break.

Mikey showed up a minute later and climbed up onto his horse. Once he was settled, they were ready to go.

"Was anyone hurt?" Shawn asked as they began walking.

"No." Unlike Dom, Onida knew exactly what he was asking about. He could see that no one in their party had been hurt, and was asking about the people who had been robbed.

"Someone will be."

Onida nodded. As long as it wasn't her, that would be all right.

***

They eventually did manage to get saddles and reins for everyone. Most of them were procured by stealing from people on the road. One set of tack was stolen in a not-so-daring heist when they stopped for the night in a tiny town with a population of less than one hundred. Another set they had actually obtained legally. They had stumbled across a large group of travellers. Both groups were well armed and of equal strength. Instead of fighting, they formed a shaky alliance over lunch, and bartered some of their goods. The other group had recently lost a man, and were therefore willing to trade the saddle and reins from his horse in exchange for a random assortment of food, blankets, and a few bullets.

Onida learned the ways of the bandits. Whenever a stick-up was to take place, Shawn always remained behind, guarding their camp. Onida could have done the same, but she regularly didn't. It wasn't that she enjoyed stealing from others. It was more that if something happened, she wanted to be there. Fewer than a handful of times someone got hurt, and it was never one of the bandits. They knew what they were doing. No one was killed, but legs and arms had been cut, or stabbed, and even shot. One man who tried to resist broke his wrist when Gatsby knocked him over. Onida would always apologize to those people, the ones who had been hurt. She didn't know why. Dom liked that she did. He thought it drove home their point about not really wanting to hurt them, that the injured person would have been fine had they just co-operated. According to Dom's way of thinking, it was the victim's fault. Onida didn't see it that way, but she didn't do anything to stop it. Most of the food she ate was acquired through robbery.

It got warmer as they headed south, and eventually they stopped finding frost every morning. They started wandering farther east for a while, and then back toward the west. With no destination in mind, it didn't matter which way they went, as long as the weather didn't start getting colder again. Sometimes they would camp out in one place for over a week, taxing a well travelled, yet undefended, road for as long as they dared. Often it was messengers they were sticking up, who usually co-operated. They understood that the hazard came with the job. It was amusing for all the bandits the day they held up a chuck wagon. Dom clearly liked the idea that everything seemed to have gone back to the old western days, including his profession. The main differences they had to worry about were fully automatic weapons and high-powered rifles like Mikey's.

Onida loved it all, but she especially took pleasure in the different places they went. They had stopped once at the Grand Canyon. At least, everyone assumed it was the Grand Canyon. They didn't have a map, and didn't come across a spot with any signs, but it was certainly a big hole in the ground. Another time, they were crossing along the top of some high hills with sheer cliffs for sides. Out over the cliffs, there was a majestic view of some great, grassy plains. A tribe was out there. They probably weren't all indigenous people, but they certainly lived that lifestyle based on what Onida could see of their tents. They had many horses, but Mikey pointed out something that didn't quite belong with the herd. By using the scope of his rifle, everyone had been able to look at the elephant in the crowd. The animal was huge, with great tusks that had been decorated with paints and feathers. A small figure sat astride the elephant's back. From their distance, it was impossible to determine if the person was controlling the elephant's wandering movements, or was just sitting up there for the hell of it. For a while, Julian and Axel argued over whether the elephant had once been a zoo animal or a circus animal. It was an argument to which they would never learn the answer, because they all agreed not to meet the tribe.

Occasionally they stayed in communities for a little while, and sometimes they avoided them. They especially avoided anywhere near the places where they taxed the roads. There were a lot more people in the world than Onida had imagined. Fewer of them had died during the outbreak than she had been led to believe. She supposed that was because she lived in the north, where the winters were bitterly cold, and radiation had poisoned large swaths of land. It had been easier for people to survive in the south.

Plenty of zombies roamed the warmer climates. It seemed like the bandits came across at least one zombie a day. Sometimes a small pack of them would be found wandering along a road, or a handful would be seen caught in some brambles. They were trapped inside buildings, in caves, in mud. Once the bandits saw three being swept down a river, trapped in the branches of a dead tree. Another time, there was a forest of them, strung up by the ankles, still wriggling and snapping at passers-by. A community of people must have done it, but the bandits never came across the perpetrators. It was possible that they were dead and gone. In one community, the bandits heard the story of a great horde, called the comet horde. Apparently it was so large, it swept away whole towns in the night, and trampled forests flat. A bunch of the bandits didn't believe the story, but Onida wasn't so sure. They had come across areas where the land had been strangely cleared, and while there was no slime trail like the one described to them, that could just be because it had rained enough times since its passage for the gunk to be cleared away.

It was the best winter of Onida's life. Spring was not to be the same.

It started when Hurit broke her leg. All the bandits had become rather good at riding, and Ronnie was no exception. She had been riding Hurit to check the nearby roads, when the horse's hoof went straight down an animal's den. With a sharp cry, Hurit went down, throwing Ronnie from the saddle. Ronnie said later that she had heard the snap of bone before she even hit the ground, and heard it many more times in her dreams. Ronnie got lucky in that she escaped with only cuts, scrapes, and bruises. Her bones remained intact. It took several hours for the others to find them, because Ronnie wouldn't leave Hurit alone. Even if the horse could somehow have gotten up, her foreleg was still stuck fast in the animal den. Onida would never forget finding them: Hurit lying on the ground, with her head in Ronnie's lap, tears still streaming down the woman's face.

"You can help her, right?" Ronnie had pleaded with Onida. "You can do something?"

But Onida could do nothing. It wasn't just a break, but a compound fracture; Hurit's bones had pierced through her skin. Still, Onida tried her best. With everyone's help, they managed to get the saddle off, and carefully dug out the hole some more so that Hurit's hoof could come free. The horse screamed whenever the injured leg was touched.

"We need to set it," Shawn said, indifferent, as he seemed to be to all the horses. Onida wondered how he would react if it were Nixkamich, the horse he rode every day.

"I'll need your help," Onida admitted. "I've never had to set a bone before."

"I have." Shawn did not elaborate on when he had had to do that. He seemed to have the most medical knowledge of everyone, so the others just stood around and waited for orders. Ronnie continued to hold Hurit's head in her lap, speaking soothing words and stroking her nose the way she liked.

Shawn explained what was going to happen, and why it was going to be very difficult without any sedatives. The bandits held Hurit down, and tied ropes to her legs to try to prevent her from kicking. Onida helped with the actual setting of the bones.

Hurit's scream was so human-like that everyone shuddered. Harper had to throw up afterwards.

They bound up the leg as best they could, using what bandages they had and making splints out of whatever was available. A sort of sling was made in the hopes they could get Hurit to keep her weight off it for a little while.

"You'll likely never be able to ride her again," Onida had to tell Ronnie.

Ronnie just nodded and sniffled and wiped at her runny nose.

With all of them working together, they managed to get Hurit up onto three legs. It would be too difficult to head back to where they had been camping, so they just made a new camp where they were. Everyone took turns, in pairs, staying by Hurit's side to help her hobble whenever she wanted to move. She didn't move much. The horse was clearly exhausted and in a lot of pain.

She survived for two nights, but everyone could see that the injury had become infected. They had no medicine with which to help the horse.

"What if we tried amputating the leg?" Ronnie suggested.

Onida just shook her head. "There's no reason she wouldn't just end up with another infection, if the pain and shock didn't kill her first."

"She's in so much pain."

Onida could only nod in agreement.

Later that day, Hurit lay down on the ground rather heavily. Onida could see that she was giving up. She explained to Ronnie the only thing they could do for her.

"Would we do the same to one of us? Wouldn't we try something else?" Ronnie spoke through her tears.

"We'd ask that person what they wanted. Hurit can't speak to us in the normal ways, but I can hear her. She's suffering and she wants it to stop."

Ronnie finally agreed. Onida gathered up the other horses, that they'd been keeping at a bit of a distance, and walked them further away with the help of Mikey, Gatsby, and Harper. Ronnie stayed with Hurit. Onida never asked whether she was the one to pull the trigger, or if someone else had had to do it. Ronnie certainly hadn't stayed to watch the butchery afterward, however. That was mostly done by Shawn, but they had all agreed not to waste the meat. Even Hurit's hair was kept, and her flesh made into a pelt. A new camp was set up a little distance away, but all the meat was cooked where Hurit was put down.

This helped Ronnie and even Onida pretend that it had come from some different animal.

The horses continued to cause problems throughout the spring, as the mares went into heat. The males got aggressive with one another, and they knew that if any of the females got pregnant, they wouldn't be able to ride her or pack too many supplies onto her back. Despite their best efforts, Onida became fairly certain that two of the mares were carrying foals.

"How long until the babies are born?" Shawn asked her.

"Eleven months."

A few members of their group didn't believe her, but she assured them that she was telling the truth. They now had only as many horses to ride as they did people, and they still had to watch out for the horses trying to mate late. This potential problem resolved itself somewhat.

"Son of a bitch!" Axel screamed as they hauled him into the barn, blood pouring out of his gut. A robbery had finally gone terribly wrong as Shawn had suspected one would, and a bullet was now lodged somewhere within Axel.

Shawn had Onida act as his nurse, while the others stayed outside in defensive positions. Mikey had blown away the shooter and probably some others. They didn't know how many were left, or if they had been followed. Apparently the people around here knew what to do about bandits, and knew to lay their trap immediately after a stick-up was reported. The bandits shouldn't have lingered in the area, but they had no way of knowing that.

"Are you hurt?" Shawn asked Onida as he stripped off Axel's shirt.

"No, all the blood is his."

The horses snorted in their stalls, displeased with the smell. The barn was proving itself to be an excellent place for them to have made camp, and hopefully would continue to do so, until at least they had dealt with Axel's problem. Mikey hadn't yet returned, presumably having spent more bullets holding back their attackers, and then run off in some other direction to make it harder for them to find this place.

Axel howled as Shawn inspected the wound, trying to wash it out with well water from the pump.

"No exit wound. The bullet's still in there somewhere," Shawn reported.

"Can you get it out?" Onida wondered.

"With what? My fingers? Besides, I don't know where it is."

"Can't you just follow the hole?" Onida tried to use her hands and fingers to mime an example of reaching straight down into the wound, while Axel cried and wriggled on the floor in front of her.

"The bullet might not be there," Shawn tried to explain. "It could've curved along its path into his body due to the resistance of muscles and organs, or maybe it bounced off a bone. Depending on where it ended up, his own body might have pushed it somewhere, or even all the jostling around you guys did with him by carrying him back. I have no way of knowing where the bullet is."

"Jesus," Axel whined as he listened to all of this. "Get it out of me, man, it hurts so much!"

Shawn sighed. He tried to find the bullet by moving his hands all over Axel's torso to see if it could be felt just beneath the skin somewhere.

"Stop moving," he repeatedly hissed at Axel as he worked. Overhead, Mask watched from the barn's rafters, pacing back and forth as though trying to find a better viewing angle.

When the bullet was not located, Shawn washed his hands a second time and then stuck one of his fingers into the wound. Axel screamed, but Shawn ignored it, merely shaking his head as he withdrew the appendage.

"I couldn't feel it. There's no way to find the bullet without an x-ray."

"Maybe... maybe just leave it in then," Axel panted. "You know, and my body will just push it out when it's ready. Like a splinter. It'll just come out on its own." He was clearly delirious.

"Can he survive with the bullet inside of him?"

Shawn shrugged. "It's not impossible. It would be a lot better if we had antibiotics, because it's likely to give him an infection."

In the end, it wasn't the bullet still lodged in his body that killed Axel, but the blood he lost. They couldn't tell how badly he was bleeding internally, and even if they could, they could do nothing about it. Axel was being buried outside the barn when Mikey finally returned, limping on a twisted ankle but otherwise all right.

It wasn't terribly long after they had left Axel behind beneath the dirt, that they were hit by a storm the likes of which none of them had ever experienced before. A tornado ripped through the area, throwing dirt and debris every which way. They managed to avoid getting hit by it directly, but it was a near miss. None of them got away without at minimum some sort of superficial wound, mostly because the small church in which they had been forced to shelter had plenty of stained-glass windows to smash out. Only a single piece of glass remained hanging from one window like a jagged blue tooth. Some of the horses had been cut up fairly badly, needing stitches. One of the pregnant horses miscarried, induced most likely by fear.

Not knowing where they were in relation to tornado alley, they headed west in the hopes of moving away from any more cyclones. This was an unfortunate mistake. They ended up spending a god awful amount of the summer trying to find their way back out of a desert they had mistakenly wandered into. Everyone survived, horses, raccoon, and dog included, but they were all rail-thin and crisped by the sun by the time they returned to greener pastures and better foraging.

"This is why I didn't want to stay north for the winter," Helen had grumbled a thousand times. "Same hunger, only you freeze instead of burn." They all got sick of hearing it and just learned to ignore her.

They stuck to the green fields for a long time after that, recovering from their misadventure. They foraged and hunted and held up travellers, eventually getting back up to a somewhat healthy weight. By then, Onida had learned to handle the revolver she had been given, as well as a compound bow they had stolen. She often went hunting with Shawn, who taught her everything he knew. She couldn't help but feel a little proud that she was the only one he would allow to accompany him on a hunt. But even after their many months together, Onida still couldn't be certain of Shawn's motives at any given moment. The only thing she truly understood about him was his fear of wolves, which, she had learned, also included coyotes, to a lesser extent.

"I've never seen the ocean," Mikey admitted one lovely night while they camped out beneath a clear sky, absolutely loaded with stars. There wasn't even a moon to dim the shine of those small points of light, and every time Onida moved away from the fire to pee or check on the horses, she was amazed all over again.

"Really? Never?" Dom was honestly surprised by this fact.

"I haven't seen one either," Anita added. "I've always lived in the middle somewhere. Even with you guys, we've never travelled far enough in one direction to reach an ocean."

"I've only seen the Arctic Sea," Onida decided to mention, for no particular reason. She was happily rubbing Mask's back and belly as he wriggled around on the dirt beside her.

"That's not a proper ocean," Julian told her. "Too much ice."

There wasn't really that much in the summer, at least not during the one in which she had seen it, but Onida didn't bother to correct him.

"That settles it then," Dom slapped his hands against his thighs. "We're going to go find us an ocean. I mean, it's a big body of water ain't it? People like to live next to water, so there should be some good opportunities for us."

And just like that, they began to head south-east again the next morning, in the search of an ocean.

26: MISHA
9 DAYS AFTER THE BOMBING

The puppies had been born safely within the cramped nesting upon the cart. Misha had stayed up all night with Trigger, making sure she had enough clean water and that there were no complications. He also had to monitor the rising floodwaters. By the time morning came, it had nearly reached the level they had camped out on. The others were moving what gear they could up to the offices. Misha continued to sit on the cart, watching Trigger suckle her pups and making sure there were no follow-up issues.

"What are you going to name them?" Sherlock asked. He was not helping to move anything because no one wanted him to. Instead, he sat on the stairs, high enough to watch what Misha was doing.

"I'm going to wait until they're a little older before I name them," Misha told him. He wanted to make sure the puppies were healthy and were going to survive before he gave them names. For now, he mentally separated them by gender and colouring.

"What are the sexes?" Sherlock asked next.

"Two males, three females."

"And do you know which dog is the father?"

"I'm not certain." He had been guessing that it was either Guard or Stock, and definitely knew it wasn't Barrel because he was too low in the pack hierarchy, but now he wasn't so sure. The variety of colours in the coats was making him think that it could have actually been Bullet who had done the deed. It didn't seem possible, given that Bullet tended to spend every minute by Misha's side.

Not during meals, Misha reminded himself. All the dogs but Rifle were kept out of the community centre during meal times. They weren't let in until afterward to lick up the scraps. There was no reason it couldn't have happened then, even if it seemed to Misha that Bullet always waited patiently at the door for him. He would have to wait until the pups got bigger to say for certain, when they were no longer floppy little blobs. Both Guard and Stock had very different builds from the other dogs, and if either of those presented in the pups at all, Misha would know.

"Water's still rising," Crichton called out. He had gone over to the stairs leading down to the door to check. "It's started to slop over onto this level."

Misha raised his head and could see that he was right. The light coming through the high windows was weak and grey, but Misha was at an angle to the water that caused it to shine. It was lapping over the edge of the floor, growing a puddle.

Everything that had been put down on the marble slabs had already been moved up to the offices. Only the supplies they had gathered on the cart remained. The items that could be moved, which excluded the planted vegetables, were being brought up as well.

"Ki-Nam, do you think you could let my dogs out the next time you're up there?" Misha asked as the man came back down the stairs to get another load.

"I can do it," Sherlock volunteered, jumping up onto his feet. He disappeared up the stairs before Misha could tell him that he would rather have anyone else do it.

The dogs all came rushing down the steps, creating their own flood of fur. Misha had shut them up in an office once he was certain that Trigger was giving birth, as he wanted them completely out of the way. Now, they wanted to find Misha, but instead were greeted by the new scent of babies. They gathered around the cart and sniffed at it. Trigger growled at Powder, the one dog tall enough to stick her head over the side, and then again at Spring when she hopped up onto the driver's board.

"Go on. Leave her be." Misha made shooing gestures at the two dogs, but Trigger's growling had actually been enough to keep Powder back and to make Spring hop back down onto the floor.

Rifle was the last one down the stairs; he hadn't run like the others. He stopped and sniffed in the direction of the cart before he reached the bottom, then turned around and went to lie down on the landing. Misha could just see his nose and the tips of his paws from where he sat on the cart. He had felt especially bad closing the door on the German shepherd, and wondered if Rifle was upset with him for doing so.

It wasn't much longer before the entire floor was covered in water. Misha could hear his dogs moving around in it, the shallow pond splashing around their feet. The horses had different opinions about the water. Thumper seemed to enjoy kicking at it, sending sprays out ahead of him, whereas Potato had a rather sullen look. Perhaps he knew that the water was likely to keep rising, and that Thumper wasn't going to be able to enjoy it for much longer. If the water got too high, the horses would have to climb the stairs, which would be no easy task given the relation of hoof size to step width. The tight landing might also cause some difficulty.

"How are the puppies?" Crichton asked, standing in water that was already ankle deep. He was grabbing the last of the supplies that they could move off the cart. The wood they had left in the dance studio had likely already floated away.

"Healthy, as near as I can tell. Trigger seems to be doing all right too."

"I once had a dog who whelped. If you think Trigger will let me near, would you like me to take a look at them?"

The offer surprised Misha. He wasn't used to hearing Crichton mention anything about his life before the Day. He had never before mentioned having owned a dog at any point in his life. In Misha's mind, he had always been on some military base, barking orders, or at a mercenary compound, doing the same. While it should have been obvious that Crichton would have had some sort of life outside of that, it had never occurred to Misha. He felt his face flush with embarrassment, but hid it by turning toward Trigger.

"I have a feeling she's not going to let anyone near but me right now, but we can certainly try later." Even Misha had to be careful with Trigger and her pups. She hadn't growled or nipped at him, but when he was checking over the puppies for any obvious developmental issues and confirming their genders, she had constantly licked his hands, as if trying to passive-aggressively tell him to put her pup down.

"Here, why don't you carry this upstairs and stretch your legs a bit?" Crichton held out the pack he had picked up off the cart. "I'll watch her and call you if anything seems amiss."

Misha did have to pee. "All right. Thanks."

He hopped down into the water, his feet immediately becoming soaked through his boots. When he carried the pack up the steps, he stopped to sit with Rifle for a bit on the landing.

"I'm sorry, *bratishka*," he whispered into the dog's fur as he scratched his ears and gave him a gentle, if not somewhat awkward, hug. "You know why I had to do it, right?"

Rifle groaned and rolled to one side so that Misha could scratch his belly, which caused Rifle's tail to thump against the landing.

He could have stayed there the rest of the day, but he told Crichton he'd take the pack upstairs and he still had to piss, so he had to get back up. Rifle didn't seem to mind.

When Misha turned, he found Sherlock watching him from the very top of the stairs.

"What?" Misha asked, thinking he must want or need something.

"Nothing." Sherlock shook his head and turned away, disappearing into the shadowy hallway. Misha found it strange that Sherlock was walking around without a light, although his own solar charged lantern wasn't being used much. He had to turn it on sparingly, given there was no way to recharge it until the storm passed.

Carrying the pack up, Misha went through the first open door where the supplies were being stored. There were windows in there, and the gear was stashed as far from them as possible, just in case the glass broke. Watching the rain lash against the panes, Misha could see why the others worried when they chose to move everything in there. Misha tried not to worry about it; Crichton knew what he was doing. But it was hard not to worry about the water. What if it kept rising? What if it reached the next level, the offices, then what would they do? There were no more stairs to climb. They'd have to break a window and swim. How could he carry the pups in that event? Could the horses swim well enough to survive? Could his dogs? Could he?

Misha flinched when a cold nose brushed his hand. He looked down to find Bullet's pale eyes staring up at him. Bullet never worried about the future. Misha wished he could be more like him.

Heading all the way to the end of the hall, Misha found a restroom. The toilets didn't work anymore, but he had had to pass through two doors to get inside, so it was a good place to take a piss without the smell infecting the whole building. Someone else had already had the same idea, Misha realized, spying their urine in the bowl. Misha realized he could have just relieved himself in the floodwaters, but he had already made his choice.

Stepping back out into the hallway afterward, Misha wondered where Sherlock had gone. He had come down this way, but Misha hadn't gone past him. Was he in one of the offices with the closed doors? Angela was in one of them, getting some shut eye, so maybe Sherlock was doing the same. Because of the incident with Rifle, Misha felt better knowing where the transgender stranger was at all times. On his way back to the staircase, he searched in offices for him, but only succeeded in disturbing Angela. There was a second hallway that branched off the first; maybe he had gone down that way? There wasn't anything there other than the dead elevators. Misha checked anyway, but still had no luck.

"Have you seen Sherlock?" Misha asked Crichton once he was downstairs and in the water again.

"How recently?" Crichton wondered.

Misha shrugged and didn't bother to answer. It had only been a few minutes.

They heard a large splash, and both of them quickly turned to see where it had come from. It was Guard. He had wandered over near the entrance steps and hadn't realized that there was a drop beneath the surface. The big dog spluttered and thrashed until he found his footing, pulling himself out of the water, soaking wet. That's when Misha spotted Sherlock, not far away, looking around behind the teller windows. A tension he hadn't noticed building up in his shoulders loosened.

Misha climbed up onto the cart's driving board and sat near Trigger. Bullet stayed nearby, but one by one, the other dogs began to go upstairs. They were no longer entertained by the water. The horses weren't either, but they didn't have much of a choice. They stood near the cart, the closest thing to home at the moment, and whinnied in complaint whenever Trigger growled at them. Crichton retreated upstairs, and so did Ki-Nam and Harry, having explored what they could on the main level. They were trying to find everything that could be burned in order to start boiling some water. A wooden flagpole removed from the wall appeared to be all that they had found.

The water had risen to about mid-shin height, Misha noticed when Sherlock came back from around the teller windows. The doors prevented the large debris from coming in, and the bank no longer contained anything for the water to pick up. The silt got through, however. The water was a muddy swirl, and Misha knew why Guard hadn't been able to see the steps. From his perch on the driving board, he couldn't even make out the pattern of the marble floor.

"You should take off your boots and let your feet dry out." Sherlock had wandered over, making barely a splash as he walked. His own boots hung via their laces around his neck, the ends of his socks poking out of them.

"You should be careful. You could rip your foot open on something beneath the surface," Misha warned him. Why he cared if Sherlock injured himself, he had no idea. But he did take his advice and stripped off his wet footwear. It was certainly more comfortable that way.

"There's probably sharks swimming in the water out there right now." It seemed that Sherlock wanted to make conversation. "It's definitely deep enough."

Misha tried to show no reaction to his words, but apparently Sherlock had picked up on something anyway.

"You don't like sharks? I find them fascinating."

"One of my best friends was killed by a shark."

"Oh? I'd say that's a good reason to dislike sharks. Most people tend to not like them because they don't understand them. It's the same with the zombies. They're less scary once you know about them, how to avoid them, and, when you can't do that, how to safely take them out."

"Are you saying you like the zombies?" Misha didn't even try to hide his disgust.

"No, I wouldn't say I like them. I have a certain fascination with them, like I do with sharks, but I avoid them whenever possible. Why take the risk, right?" Sherlock walked some more, disappearing and reappearing around the large bank's support posts, disguised to look like old colonnade pillars.

"Why do you keep moving around? Why can't you just stay put somewhere?" Misha finally asked.

Sherlock considered the question. "Things rarely work out well for me if I stay in one place for too long."

"I meant, why don't you sit down and stop sloshing around?" Misha thought sloshing was too loud a word. Sherlock kept rather quiet in the water.

"I know, and that's what I meant too. People don't like me very much, but even when I'm alone, something bad eventually happens. A zombie comes, or an alligator, or a pack of coyotes. Lots of times bugs crawled over my skin. Tree branches break, roofs collapse, and buildings flood." Sherlock gestured around himself. "I haven't found a place yet that seems to want me, so I feel better when I keep moving."

"Well it bothers me. Go pace upstairs, or else sit down for a while."

Misha had been hoping he'd go upstairs, but instead he sat on the steps again, a little higher than last time, for the water was continuing to rise. He sat too close to Rifle, which put Misha on edge. Then again, if he went all the way upstairs, he would be too close to most of his pack. Either Misha had to be bothered by his walking around in the water, or by him being too close to his dogs. There was no winning.

A whine made Misha look down at the water again. Bullet was still standing there, but the water was now reaching his chest. He was concerned, but he also wanted to stay near Misha. After checking on Trigger, Misha let Bullet hop up onto the driving board with him, but made sure he stayed on the far end so that the new mother wouldn't get snappy.

"That harness was originally Rifle's, right?" Sherlock asked. "It looks like it's supposed to fit a bigger dog, and it looks about as old."

"Why do you keep hanging around and talking to me?" Misha finally asked, exasperated.

"You don't like me because I tried to take your dog, and I understand that," Sherlock answered. "Angela detests me because she thinks I'm one of those raiders, which I'm not, and Crichton is very difficult to read. I can't tell what he thinks of me."

"Then go hang around Harry or Ki-Nam."

"Ki-Nam frightens me. There's something dangerous about him that I can't quite put my finger on. I get the impression that if he were told to kill me, he could do it without feeling a thing."

"And Harry?"

Sherlock shrugged. "Harry's... boring."

"So you'd rather hang around someone you *know* doesn't like you?"

"Yes. You're far more interesting."

Misha sighed. No wonder this guy kept getting kicked out of communities.

"Who's the most interesting person you know?" Sherlock asked, unable to keep his mouth shut for very long.

"I don't know." It wasn't something Misha had ever thought about before. He was pretty sure most people didn't rate their colleagues on their interest level.

"Think about it," Sherlock encouraged him.

Misha didn't spend a long time thinking, hoping to end this line of enquiry faster.

"I guess it would be Freya," he decided.

"Freya? Who's that, what's she like? Tell me what makes her interesting."

"She's mute, and could probably rip your head off with her bare hands."

"Is she your friend?"

"I guess. Probably more of an acquaintance. We don't exactly hang out."

"I don't think you hang out with anyone. Other than your dogs."

"I have friends," Misha bristled.

"I didn't say you didn't. I just don't think you're the kind of person to 'hang out' with anyone. Who's your best friend?"

"Rifle."

"Your best *human* friend?"

"What does it matter to you?" Misha tried to keep from snapping. He could see that his tension was transferring to Trigger.

Sherlock shrugged. "It doesn't. I just wanted to know more about you."

"And how does asking me about people you don't even know do that?"

"By the way you look when you answer."

"I imagine I look pretty hostile due to the one who's asking."

Sherlock actually grinned, although why, Misha had no idea. "So who is your best human friend?"

"If I tell you, will you stop asking me questions and leave me alone?"

"Sure. For a while at least. I can't leave you alone forever in this confined place."

"I'd probably say that Danny is my best friend."

Misha expected another question, but he was wrong. Sherlock did what he said he would do, and left Misha alone. He went upstairs where Misha could no longer be certain of his exact whereabouts or what he was up to. That lack of knowledge didn't improve Misha's mood.

He leaned over and gently patted Trigger on the head. Below him, the water continued to creep upward.

***

They were forced to remain in the bank for the rest of the day, and the following night. Much to Misha's relief, the water stopped rising before reaching the cart's axles, which was the determinate height he had chosen to move Trigger and the puppies. During the night, the water level began to go back down, which the horses were pleased about. Misha slept, cramped, on the driving board, after shooing Bullet off. He and Rifle stayed on the landing of the staircase, eager to receive ear scratches whenever Misha popped upstairs for food, or drinkable water, or to relieve himself. He chose not to piss in the floodwater, figuring it was dirty enough without him adding to it. Misha learned during that time that horse shit floated. He didn't think Sherlock would be walking around barefoot in the water after that.

The clouds must have been thinner the next day; more grey light managed to reach inside the bank. When Misha woke up, he saw that the water had retreated to below the level of the main floor, leaving behind a film of muck. It wasn't as bad as the zombie slime, but Misha still didn't like having to step on it when he put his booted feet down.

After stretching, he walked over to the stairs leading up from the entrance. It was drizzling outside, nowhere near the crashing destruction that had frightened him. The water level was about half way up the steps, and Misha thought he could see it lowering. One of the doors at the bottom of the wide staircase was blocked by a car that must have been lifted up and pushed against the glass. If the bank's doors weren't as strong as they were, they likely would have broken.

Retreating upstairs to find some breakfast, Misha first had to stop and say good morning to his pack. All of them but Trigger had gathered on the landing in the night, creating an impassable carpet of fur until Misha woke them and moved them out of the way. Finally making it the rest of the way up, he discovered that all the humans, Sherlock included, were awake and sitting around in the office where they had stored the supplies.

"The water's receding," Misha said as he sat beside Crichton and accepted the tiny meal he was offered. The dogs followed him into the room and proceeded to beg, by sitting or lying down near someone and staring at them with sad, watery eyes. Misha found himself flanked by Rifle and Bullet, the latter wedging between Misha and Crichton.

"We saw," Harry said, responding to Misha with a gesture toward the window. "I think it might recede enough for us to head out at some point today."

"Good," Crichton nodded.

"What are you going to do with me?" Sherlock immediately asked. "I doubt there's any sort of trail left I can follow for you out there."

"You can leave whenever you want, and go wherever you want," Crichton told him, much to Angela's annoyance.

"Okay." Sherlock gave no indication about what he might do.

The morning passed slowly. After remaining cooped up for so long, Misha was energized and ready to go, but the water was not so accommodating. Trigger and the puppies were doing fine. The new mom even stood up and stretched for a while, leaving her pups alone in the nest for a few seconds while she paced the length of the driving board. She also relieved herself on the pile of dirt in which the crops they had saved were growing.

Walking around the main floor was still a bit dangerous without the water. The mud and tiny pools it had left behind made the marble really slippery in places. Still, Misha explored, feeling a need to move. He looked around in all the same places that Sherlock had already been. Bullet followed him into every corner, his feet becoming covered in slime. The exploration worked out in the dog's favour when he pulled a slimy, rotten stick out of the muck, and proceeded to carry it with pride. When Misha finally made his way back to the cart, the other dogs all wanted Bullet's stick, and so a game of chase-me started up, shot through with interruptions of tug-of-war. Misha enjoyed watching them play. He was glad that they weren't so hungry that they didn't have the energy for it.

They decided to leave when the water was low enough. They were hoping to reach at least the halfway point back to the container yard, home, before the sun set. It's where they would have been before the storm, if Misha hadn't decided to have Sherlock follow the trail of the raiders.

The first job was to get the doors open, the ones that didn't have a car pressed against them. A lot of mud had built up around the base of the doors, and so it took a bit of effort to move them. Once open, however, the mud then oozed around and helped hold them open. The horses were carefully walked down the steps, which was a lot harder for them than going up had been. Getting the cart down was even more of a challenge. Misha emptied one of the packs, filled it with padding, and placed the tiny pups inside so that they were out of harm's way if the cart lost control. Trigger whined and licked his hands the entire time he held them to his chest. Crichton insisted he not put the puppies in danger by helping with the cart, so Misha could stand aside and watch, relatively guilt free. Sherlock actually helped with all the moving, even though he said he wasn't going to come with them. The pack the puppies were in was needed to transport supplies, so Misha settled them back in the nest on the cart once more. The chopped wood had been used to block in Trigger's nest, and to secure a rain tarp over it. While the others retrieved the gear from the office, Misha got his dogs ready. Because Trigger would be in the cart, he was going to be the one to drive it, with Rifle joining him on the driving board. Spring, Barrel, and Stock would ride upon the cart as well, since the water was uncomfortably high for them; they would tire quickly in it. Bullet and Slide should have probably also been on the cart, the water reaching their bellies, but it was already crowded enough, and they were strong dogs. They could handle walking through the water, especially if they didn't end up travelling far. Being such large dogs, Guard and Powder were fine with the depth. Trigger was unhappy about sharing her ride, but Misha made sure the other dogs gave her space, while also issuing firm *lie down* and *stay* commands so that they would stay in place.

"That's the last of it," Crichton announced, checking one last time that everything on the cart was properly secured. "Let's head out."

Sherlock walked with them to the end of the block, and then went his own way. There were only a few goodbyes exchanged, and neither he nor Angela acknowledged their departure from one another. Misha couldn't help but wonder where he was going to go.

Everything looked so different. Windows had been smashed, roofs had collapsed, trees broken, and of course, there was debris everywhere. The storm had created sudden and violent change, sending everything into disarray.

It was slow moving. Not only was there some water resistance to deal with, but debris constantly got in the way. They had to wind their way around cars and trees, and even pieces of buildings. They always managed to find a route for the cart to follow, but it was nowhere near a straight line. It didn't help that it was still raining, reducing visibility. Misha was soaked to the bone.

They travelled along a very gradual uphill route, so that eventually the water was low enough for even Spring to make her way through it. Only Rifle remained on the cart with Trigger and the pups. The dogs were all quite happy about the aftermath. The storm had brought a fair number of fish ashore, which had died or become trapped in puddles. Certain land animals had also failed to escape. Their corpses became part of the garbage. There was plenty of meat for the pack to chow down on as they travelled. Crichton was even kind enough to grab a few fish for Misha to give to Trigger and Rifle.

When Ki-Nam called for them to stop, he did so abruptly. His head was swivelling about, having sensed something he couldn't be sure of.

"Sniff check," Misha commanded the dogs nearest to him. "Go on. Sniff check."

While being told to sniff check generally meant sniffing the people near them for signs of infection, Misha hadn't taught them a command for sniffing around the area; they tended to do that anyway. By ordering a sniff check though, the dogs became alert, and began to specifically check for the scent of zombies. It was Spring who found something. Her high-pitched yapping flew out of her body as she raced away from the tangles of a fallen tree just ahead of Ki-Nam.

Drawn by the bout of barking, a zombie crawled out from the branches. Twigs peppered its dead skin so that it appeared similar to an upright porcupine. Misha tested the breeze. They were upwind from the mess, which was why the dogs hadn't been able to scent anything ahead of time. The dogs gathered near the cart, all of them silent now. They waited for Ki-Nam to take out the dead thing, but instead, the man retreated.

"There's more," he hissed. "A lot more."

A chorus had started up, loud enough to be heard over the rainfall. The moaning and groaning of the dead. There was a lot of gargling, as most of their lungs had filled with water. The sound came from everywhere. Misha wanted to give Spring the benefit of the doubt, by assuming she had barked in surprise, because it was possible that the little dog may have just killed them all.

They came from around the corners and insides of buildings. They crawled out from under cars, rising up out of the low water. They ripped free of the trash that hid them, trailing seaweed, and torn strips of thin plastic, and muddy leaves. They were everywhere, all around them. There was no way for the travellers to circle up defensively around the cart: there weren't enough of them.

"Misha, get out of here," Crichton ordered.

"What?"

"Get the cart out of here before it's too late. We need to get those supplies back home. Run, before they close off your escape. We'll catch up."

Misha couldn't allow himself to think, only to follow the command. He wheeled the horses around and snapped the reins. Thumper and Potato needed no urging; they were more than glad to get the hell out of there. A sharp whistle drew the dogs with them, but Misha had no idea if they would be able to keep up, especially if they reached deeper water. But as long as they started running, they should be all right.

The horses crashed through the water, weaving together around obstacles already passed once before. Misha had to focus, to find the largest openings through which to guide the horses. Rifle whined beside him, bouncing around on the driving board where he had no purchase. Misha couldn't offer him any aid or comfort, forced to trust that he wasn't yet too old to keep holding on.

He looked back only once, and only over his shoulder at where Trigger and the puppies had been resting beneath the tarp. Trigger was on her feet, her legs splayed as she braced herself over top of her babies, who bounced about in the nesting. The tarp half hung over the side, as some of the wood had jostled enough to let it loose. Misha didn't want to look back any farther. He didn't want to see his dogs falling behind, or the humans as a horde of the dead closed in around them.

The way back was eventually blocked by more of the dead, a soggy mass that had been unknowingly gathering behind them. A handful had barnacles clinging to them and they could barely stand or move. These were zombies dredged up from the bottom of the ocean, the ones that had wandered in and never wandered back out again. How many had once been part of the comet horde? How many had been jostled over the sides of the bridge on their way to the container yard, or had been pushed over the edge into the river once they got there? The number was probably a large one, and the current had carried them out, safely away from the container yard. And now the storm had brought them back.

Misha guided the cart through unknown territory. He had no idea if he had walked these streets before, as none of them looked the same. He just kept searching for the next opening, and the next opening, with the horses panting as they built up a lather.

It wasn't until he had stopped seeing zombies for several minutes that Misha finally brought the horses to a slow walk. Their muscles jumped and jittered beneath their harnesses, and their snorts came out hard and loud. When was the last time that they had eaten more than the small handfuls of grain Ki-Nam had offered inside the bank?

Misha looked all about, attempting to orient himself. But the clouds hid the sun's exact location, and nothing looked right. Casting all about, Misha couldn't see any of his dogs that weren't on the cart. How long had he been driving the horses? How far had he gone?

Patting Rifle's head, Misha comforted himself with the knowledge that he wasn't alone. His *bratishka* was with him, as were Trigger, her puppies, Thumper, and Potato. He was not alone. But he was hopelessly lost, and night was coming.

27: CLAIRE
9 DAYS AFTER THE BOMBING

Drifting in and out of a series of dreams and nightmares had Claire even more exhausted the next morning than just staying up late would have. But by now, she was used to feeling that way. In the soft grey light that marked the daytime, she reviewed her dreams. They were all completely different, involving fantastic landscapes, and friendly people. She then reviewed her nightmares. There were a lot of mannequins and narrow hallways in those.

"You awake?" Rose whispered, lying only inches away.

Claire nodded and turned her head to face her.

Rose slowly signed that she hadn't been able to sleep either. Claire signed back that she had had nightmares about the mannequins, and Rose nodded, because she had had them too.

Larson padded past them. His bare feet were muted further by the apartment's area rug. He was moving from the front door, where he had probably been peering through the peephole, to the balcony door, where he could look out through the windows. Rose and Claire both tracked him with their eyes, and he nodded to acknowledge that he saw that they were awake.

Claire wondered if Jon, Bryce, and Danny were awake too, or if they were managing to stay asleep. The start of the night had been the worst, when their mystery visitor created some more loud sounds to try to lure them out, including knocking more things over in the apartment above them. But after about an hour of no one stepping outside, whoever it was had given up and fallen silent. Maybe Claire was wrong, and maybe that had been the worst time, wondering what their stalker was up to. Claire bet whoever it was had slept just fine last night.

Rose asked her what was the first thing she wanted to do when they got home. Claire told her that she wanted to bathe and then sleep until next year. Rose agreed that that sounded like a great idea. They signed back and forth for a bit, silently talking about the things they missed about home, both the container yard and the now destroyed Black Box. Their clothing whispered as their arms moved, which was enough to rouse Danny to sit up. After signing to them and Larson, he went outside onto the balcony to pee. The bathroom was rank with the scent of urine, so Claire was happy to see that the wind had slackened enough that they could go outside. She and Rose would probably go out together, taking turns holding onto one another while they sat on the railing and peed over the side. She told Rose this, and Rose nodded in agreement.

When Danny came back in, Bryce and Jon were up, so there was no more need for sign language. The guys all took turns relieving themselves outside, and then clustered in the kitchen to give the girls what privacy they could.

The air was damp but fresh, smelling strongly of salt and mud. It was still raining, but it was almost like a heavy mist now. Looking over the edge, Claire could see that the water had risen only an inch or two, if at all, in the night. It had certainly slowed its upward climb. Maybe it would finally start to recede. Maybe it already had. Claire certainly hoped so.

"That's a lot of water," Rose said, looking over the side with her and giving a low whistle. "We must be in a really low spot or something." All the houses were drowning. The skeletal branches the trees managed to thrust up above the water line, were mostly stripped of leaves by the wind, but still standing.

"Too bad we didn't think to investigate up on a hill. You don't think we're in a bowl do you? That the water won't recede from here?"

"Naw, it'll recede. If we were in a bowl, this area probably would've been flooded long before we came to look around."

They worked together to safely empty their bladders, and in Rose's case, her bowels.

"After this, we're friends for life," Rose said once she had pulled her pants up, now wet both inside and out from the rain. "Neither of us can risk a fallin' out, because we've seen too much." She laughed and Claire couldn't help but laugh with her.

They both stopped laughing when the head of a mannequin, with its neck tied to a rope, came swinging at them from above. They both squawked as it narrowly missed striking them. After the back swing, it started to retreat upward.

Claire and Rose both grabbed hold of the railing and twisted around to look up. The mannequin head was being swiftly withdrawn to the balcony two storeys above.

"You motherfucker!" Rose screamed.

Claire was tempted to run up there and finally confront the person, but she knew that they would be gone before she could reach them.

"I'm gonna kill your ass!" Rose kept shouting as the head disappeared and the boys came to investigate. "You hear me? You're dead! I'm gonna crush your puny little brain beneath my boots!"

"What's going on?" Jon demanded to know.

Claire briefly explained while Rose threw some more insults skyward. When she was done, they all retreated back indoors.

"I really hate that guy," Rose fumed, shaking the water off herself.

"Could be a girl," Bryce mentioned.

"Fuck that," Rose snapped. "No girl would be that stupid. This is definitely some male bullshit."

No one thought it was worth it to argue with Rose, and therefore let her continue to rant and rave until she was out of steam. She ended by sitting down in a huff; the rocking chair she had chosen creaked from the force of it. It didn't take long for Rose to start rocking back and forth, the motion helping to calm her.

The smallest manageable breakfast was passed around. Since they didn't plan on going anywhere, or doing anything, they shouldn't need to eat much. Claire was still hungry when she finished, and it hadn't done much to offset her exhaustion. Once the adrenaline had worn off from the flying mannequin head, she was even more tired. Despite the light, and everyone else awake nearby, she actually managed to take a brief nap. In fact, she thought it was because of those things that she was able to relax.

When she next awoke, she felt a little better, but could tell that not much time had passed. Her mouth felt scuzzy, so she retrieved her toothbrush and cautiously went outside to brush. She looked up, down, and to both the left and the right, grateful not to spot anyone hanging over a balcony railing, watching her. She brushed her teeth quickly and then retreated back into the apartment.

It was fairly silent inside. No one was talking; they were all just sitting around, not even fidgeting with anything. Rose wasn't even rocking in the chair anymore. If it weren't for the rain outside, and the rise and fall of their breathing, Claire could believe that time had frozen in this moment. All the seating was taken, so Claire stretched out on her sleeping mat once more. She wasn't there long before Jon moved, sitting upright on the couch and looking about the room.

"We should go explore some more," he said.

"And what? Set off more booby traps?" Danny sighed.

"Yeah," Jon actually agreed. "Every time we find his shit, we dismantle it, keep the good parts for ourselves, and chuck what we don't want out into the storm. Two of us stay here to guard our stuff, and the other four stick together out there. We never allow ourselves to be lured away from one another, and we prepare for surprises."

"Sounds better than sittin' around here all day." Rose nodded. "Besides, I'd love to steal that prick's toys. Teach him not to fuck with people. Maybe I'll even get to punch him in the face."

"So? Are there at least four of us willing to go exploring? We might even find some more food."

"I'll go," Claire decided. She had to admit that she didn't like the idea of just sitting around the apartment all day. That would definitely lead to her going stir crazy.

Rose was very enthusiastic about the idea, but Claire was a little surprised when Danny also volunteered.

"Bryce? Larson? You guys good staying here by yourselves?" Jon asked them.

"Yeah, we'll be fine," Bryce nodded.

"Just knock when you get back, and we'll check the peephole," Larson added. "Unless you're worried about being coerced or something?"

"We should all be together so you'll see us all at once. But just in case, if someone does get separated or taken or something, we'll flip you off to let you know we're there of our own accord," Jon decided.

"Sounds good."

Claire got up, making sure her knife was still secure in its sheath, and located her tire iron. Not having to bring their packs meant they were ready to go fairly quickly. Rose didn't bother with her prosthetic, feeling the quarters were too tight for it to be of much use.

"We'll check the second floor again and work our way up?" Jon wondered once they were out in the hallway.

"Why not," Danny shrugged, as the locks snapped behind them.

It was unsettling walking down the stairs, getting close to the water. When they reached the second floor, Claire looked over the railing at the water. It was uncomfortably closer than the last time she had been down there.

On the second floor, the doors were all closed.

"We definitely left these open," Danny commented.

They walked along the corridor, testing each door to see if it was still unlocked. Their 'friend' had been there, and might still be hiding in one of the apartments. None of the doors were locked, however, and nothing rushed out when they were opened. Despite having searched these apartments already, they agreed to give them another once over.

When they searched the apartments, they quickly settled into a pattern. All four of them would stick together as they went into each room, making sure they were clear of both the dead and traps. They even opened closets while standing only a few feet from one another. Then, two of them would perform a more thorough search, while the other two stood by the doorway and watched the hall for anyone moving about. They tried to keep up a constant chatter among themselves, so that they could always hear and ascertain that the other pair was fine. There was very little that they had missed during the first search, although they still found the occasionally overlooked or hidden item. Even good stuff, such as medicine, batteries, rope, tape, lighter fluid, matches, and candles. It was a shame to leave all the toilet paper behind. Eventually they accumulated more than they could carry in their pockets, so they took a backpack from one apartment to stuff it all into.

"I'm surprised we missed this much and that it's still here," Jon commented as he and Claire watched the hallway. They were halfway along, standing at the dogleg so that they could see down to both stairwell doors. They rotated who did what job. Claire preferred searching the apartments.

"Of course we overlooked things, we were rushing yesterday. But why are you surprised it's still here?"

"We left the doors unlocked all night. I figured our friend with the mannequins would have come in here and taken all this stuff when he closed the doors."

"Probably too crazy to take what's actually useful," Rose called out from inside the apartment. "Probably too busy fuckin' a hole he cut into one of his plastic people. Gettin' off on the idea of scarin' us some more."

Claire scrunched up her face. She'd rather not have had that mental image. "Gross."

"Rose, you're truly disgusting sometimes," Danny muttered, almost too quietly for Claire to make out.

Although she preferred it when it was her turn to search an apartment, Claire still didn't enjoy it. Even though all the rooms and closets were searched first as a group, she kept expecting some sort of surprise booby trap in one of the cupboards or drawers. Every time she opened one, her body tensed, ready to spring away from something being launched out of the confined space. She noticed that the others tended to do the same, even Danny, who hadn't yet experienced one of the tricks. Strangely, the more times something wasn't found, the more tense Claire became. Even though she told herself that it was silly, she couldn't help but think that when they did come across something, it was going to be so much worse. Like pressure building up with the passage of time.

The second floor turned out to be empty of traps, and everyone was fidgety.

"Maybe he thought just closing the doors was enough to freak us out," Danny suggested. "And he could have worried about the water rising up to this level, so he didn't want to waste time on anything elaborate."

"That's a good point." Jon did a poor job of hiding the fact that he was nervous.

"God, look at us," Rose laughed, sounding a tiny bit forced. "All jittery like some scared kids in a haunted house. It's not even dark out." She gestured to the diffused light that entered the hallway from the apartments. They had made sure all the curtains were wide open, so as to provide the most light.

"We should check out the third floor now," Claire said, trying to sound tough. She didn't feel tough.

"Hey, remember that four poster bed?" Danny suddenly changed topics as he pointed toward an open apartment door.

"What about it?" Jon asked him.

"It's the kind of bed where those posts can be unscrewed by hand. I checked. I think they're long enough that we can use them to jam the stairwell doors shut from the outside."

"Why would we do that?" Rose asked the question, and Claire was glad that she wasn't the only one confused by the suggestion.

"Well, if the mannequin man *is* on this floor, we'll have trapped him. If he isn't, then he'll have to move the bedposts to get to this floor, and we'll be able to tell if he's done that."

"I like that idea. We should do it." Jon didn't wait for the girls to agree, he just started walking toward the apartment with the four poster bed. Neither Claire nor Rose had any objections to the plan, however, and so followed closely behind him with Danny.

Danny had been right about the bedposts being easy to unscrew. They each took a corner and twisted it loose. The decorative knob on top wasn't even secured there, it just slid out of a slot. The posts were carried to the nearest stairwell, and once the door was shut, they tested to see if the size was good.

"Perfect fit," Danny grinned.

It wasn't exactly perfect to begin with, but the metal screw on the bottom of the post could be adjusted until it was. Once the bedpost was wedged between the door and the concrete lip at the edge of the stairs, they tried the door. It couldn't be opened. Maybe if someone on the far side threw themselves into it the right way, the post would slip and that person could escape, but Claire liked having it there. She liked knowing that she could look down from the higher levels and see if the man with the mannequins had entered a floor they had already checked. Looking over the railing now, she saw that the water level had lowered while they had been searching, revealing a couple of the previously submerged steps. Claire found herself thinking about the two dead bodies she had found, the adult curled around the toddler. She had warned the others before they went in there again, and was glad to see that they remained unmolested by the mannequin man. She wished she could protect their final resting place with more than just bedposts.

"Now we gotta go around to the other side." Jon led the way back up to what Claire considered their floor. They had unlocked some but not all the doors up there before settling into their chosen apartment for the night. As they moved to the other stairwell, they tested the handles, confirming the doors they had unlocked remained that way, and the ones they hadn't were still bolted.

"Guys?" Rose spoke to stop them. "I don't remember us unlocking this one." She pushed open the door to the apartment beside the one Bryce and Larson were protecting.

"That's because we didn't unlock it," Danny confirmed. "Shouldn't be surprised though. Of course our visitor would want to linger right next door."

"We'll put another bed post down, and then come back." Jon turned to keep walking.

They had to use their flashlights again, and in the dim lighting, Claire almost didn't see it.

"Stop!" she shouted, but it was too late. Jon's foot hit the fishing line that had been strung across the hallway, down near the carpet. They all heard the sound of a heavy spring letting loose. A large stack of blankets next to Jon was pushed from behind, the ceiling-high pile engulfing him in a mess of flapping fabric. As he was buried beneath the mass, Claire could see that a piece of plywood had been placed between the wall and the blankets, the spring having pushed on that to make sure the whole tower toppled at once.

"Jon? You all right?" Danny didn't sound very concerned.

Several muffled yet distinct curses could be heard from beneath the blankets. Jon struggled to find his way out from beneath the heap, so Danny helped him. Rose and Claire simply kept out of the way.

"I saw the trip line just before you hit it," Claire said as Jon appeared, his hair sticking out in wild tufts, making the scar along the side of his head more readily visible.

"Yeah," Jon grumbled in response. "But that was not there when we left. We walked this way when we headed out and I very much doubt we would have all managed to miss it."

"You guys okay out there?" Bryce called through the door before Jon had even finished talking.

"We're all right," Rose called back. "Just a blanket avalanche. No one's hurt."

Claire thought that maybe Jon's pride had been wounded just a little.

"So we know our visitor is still running about and laying traps for us," Danny commented. "He gave us some fishing line, though."

They ended up heading down to brace the other second floor door before totally dismantling the trap. When they did get to it, Jon took great joy in whipping the spring out into the storm, hurling it off the balcony of the first apartment they went into. The fishing line they pocketed, and the plywood they left in a living room after placing a heavy chest of drawers on top of it. The man laying the traps would have a hard time moving it off on his own. Even though there were plenty of bookshelves with thin wooden backings that he could pry off pretty easily if he wanted to, it made everyone feel better knowing he couldn't reuse this particular find.

***

They didn't come across much in the way of either supplies or traps in the third floor apartments, not even in the one they had found unlocked. They did, however, come across plenty of things left behind by the man with the mannequins that weren't really traps. Pens arranged on a carpet saying hello. A bunch of balloons scattered about on a bathroom floor. A mannequin posed at a table, as though it were enjoying a lovely meal. Claire hated it when she would open a cupboard or a drawer, and there would be a rubber rat, or rubber snake, or a mannequin's head or hands sitting inside. It freaked her out every time. Occasionally they heard some loud banging, possibly the perpetrator or possibly one of his devices. But when they ascended to the fourth floor, and found more traps involving springs, tripwires, and carefully balanced objects, Claire began to realize something.

"None of it's real," she said, after a closet door had been opened, and a mannequin propped against the inside had fallen out.

"What?" Rose turned to her, misunderstanding as she panted and tried to lower her heart rate. She had been the one to open the closet door.

"Everything he's done. It's not real. There's no real danger. Fake rats, fake snakes, fake bugs, fake body parts. He's never tried to actually hurt us. No real dead bodies, which we've found a number of around here. No actual rats or snakes that could bite us. The only times we get hurt are when we don't move out of the way of something swinging at us, and even then, the worst it would cause would be a bruise. When the blankets were shoved on top of Jon, that trap could have easily been set up elsewhere, behind something like a wardrobe that could crush a person. Or when those pens were balanced on the door and toppled onto Rose. Those could have been razor blades. But no, this guy chose items that weren't dangerous. He doesn't want to hurt us, he's just trying to scare us."

"You mean like those old haunted houses at the carnivals?" Rose wondered.

"I never got to go to one of those," Claire admitted. "But yeah, I think so."

"She's right," Danny agreed. "Not once has this person put us in real danger."

"So?" Jon snapped. He had picked up the mannequin in order to throw it outside. "What does it matter that he hasn't tried to hurt us yet? Doesn't mean that he won't step up his game. And it's not like that knowledge can allow us to lower our guard. If we do that, and we come across a real zombie hanging around in one of these rooms, we're dead."

Claire pursed her lips, unable to articulate the point she wanted to make. She knew that they were going to continue to be startled by everything, or creeped out by the words and tableaus they came across, but she thought that maybe they didn't have to be so angry at this stranger. Specifically Jon, who sometimes lashed out at whatever they found. Rose seemed merely prone to cursing, but Claire worried that Jon was going to end up doing something rash. She also worried that if she said that to him, he would only get more upset, especially that it came from her, his adopted little sister. She ended up keeping quiet and they finished checking all the rooms.

The next two apartments they managed to get through without incident, both of them untouched by the stranger. In the next apartment, however, they were all brought to an immediate halt upon entering the living room. Slopped across the floor in a dark red liquid were the words *HELP HIM*.

"You don't think that's blood do you?" Rose asked, her voice strangely hushed.

Danny approached it and knelt down a little way away from the lettering. He bent at the waist and sniffed at the red glop that Claire was hoping was just paint.

"It smells like blood," Danny informed them. He gingerly touched it with one gloved finger. "Fairly fresh too."

"Bryce and Larson," Jon whispered as he turned back toward the door, ready to rush downstairs.

"Wait! It might just be animal blood," Claire said as she followed him out into the hallway.

They weren't far from a stairwell, but when they both exited the apartment and glanced toward the dogleg, they saw a figure disappearing around it.

"Son of a bitch!" Jon took off running after it.

"Jon! Wait! We're supposed to stick together!" Claire yelled, running after him and hoping that Rose and Danny could catch up.

Every time her boots hit the threadbare carpet of the hallway, Claire's thoughts thumped inside her head. Was it just animal blood, like she had hoped? Or had something happened to Bryce or Larson? Who was the *him* in the message? Did it mean anything, or was it just to scare them?

Jon crashed through the door into the stairwell. Claire was so close behind him that she didn't even touch it as she passed through the opening. However she rammed into the back of Jon when he came to a sudden halt. He grabbed the railing and kept them both from toppling over it, but quickly took off again, running up the stairs this time, where they could hear someone else's feet pounding on the concrete.

Claire climbed after him, occasionally bounding up two steps at a time. They didn't get far before she heard the stairwell door crash open again behind them, this time by Danny and Rose, who didn't need to stop to check which way to go.

On every floor, Claire kept expecting them to come across another door swinging shut, which would send them racing down another hallway. Every time they didn't, her body gave a tiny scream as it was forced up more stairs. She was fit and full of adrenaline, but it was still a lot of steps.

The beams of everyone's flashlights bounced all about the stairwell. The steps ahead of her flickered in and out of the darkness; the light in her hand pumped up and down with the motion of her arm. Long shadows were thrown by the railings, twitching and flashing and distorting perspective. Claire trusted the rhythmic motion of running, and that building codes ensured that the steps were all the same.

When they passed the top floor, Claire thought she had miscounted. She thought that somehow they had missed the stranger leaving the stairwell. She imagined that he was a spirit who had vanished into thin air. But another door crashed open ahead of them, this one leading outside into the grey light. Jon didn't even hesitate to run out onto the roof, and so neither did Claire.

The rain hit her like a wet blanket. Her clothes were immediately soaked through, and her hair plastered to her head. She flicked off her flashlight, grateful for its waterproof housing, and stuffed it into a pocket. She wanted to have both hands free for her tire iron.

Rivulets of rain gathered and washed down her face, dripping off her brow line and obscuring her vision, but she saw him. She saw the stranger, the visitor, the man with the mannequins. He had scrambled over an air conditioning unit and stood on the edge of the roof, looking back at them. Finally seeing him had brought even Jon to a halt, allowing Danny and Rose to cluster up behind them.

It was still possible that the man was actually a woman, since Claire couldn't see any of his details. Wrapped around his arms, his legs, and his torso were shells of plastic with absurd, sculpted muscles. Only the joints were unprotected by the flesh coloured armour, connected by a black fabric. This man was so into mannequins that he had turned himself into one. His true face was covered by one made of plastic. Dark eyes with bright whites, the only real, fleshy parts of the man that were visible, stared back at them. Was that hatred? Curiosity? Indifference? Claire couldn't tell based solely on those orbs. The fit was so tight, that she couldn't even identify the colour of his skin. He wasn't blinking.

Jon started to draw his sword, but was startled out of it before it cleared the scabbard.

"I'm gonna crush your puny little brain beneath my boots!" The voice came from the mannequin man, but it was a near perfect imitation of Rose.

Claire involuntarily took a step back.

"Son of a bitch!" This time the mannequin man used Jon's voice. If it weren't for the muffling, and slight imperfection of it, Claire would have thought that the man had recorded them.

"Wait! It might just be animal blood." Claire's own voice came out next.

"Fuck this." Jon spoke for himself, fully drawing his sword this time.

The mannequin man said nothing of his own. He crouched, and grabbed up a rope that snaked between his feet and hung over the side of the building. Claire hadn't been able to see it due to the air conditioner. Just as Jon made to climb over, the mannequin man hopped off the side of the building.

Claire joined the others in approaching the edge, and looking over the side. The mannequin man was already two floors down, sliding with ease along the rope, right at the outside edge of the dogleg, so that he was passing between balconies.

"Fuck this guy," Jon muttered. He swung his sword at the taut rope tied to the base of the air conditioner. There was no time for anyone to stop him. His blade bit clean through.

Claire watched the mannequin man drop. She couldn't tell if he panicked or not. He didn't try to grab onto any of the balconies. Instead, he tucked in his limbs and allowed himself to fall. They all watched the splash as he hit the floodwaters.

"If the impact didn't kill him, he'll drown," Jon said. His cold and emotionless tone regarding this fact made Claire's stomach shrivel up. "Come on, let's go back down. We have to check on Bryce and Larson."

Claire couldn't move. She just kept staring over the side, waiting to see if the mannequin man was going to pop back up, either alive and swimming, or dead and floating with the storm debris.

"Claire?" Jon had already climbed back over the air conditioning unit, and Rose was halfway across.

"We'll catch up," Danny told him. He had begun to untie what remained of the rope. "I dropped the backpack of stuff we gathered just inside the stairwell door, there. Grab it on your way down."

Jon and Rose both left without a word.

"Claire? Are you all right?" Danny gently placed his hand on her shoulder. The pressure of it slowly guided her away from the edge. "Do you need to sit down?"

"I can't believe he did that," Claire exhaled a breath she hadn't realized she'd been holding.

Danny brought her over to the air conditioner where they could sit down together. Claire's pants were already drenched, so she didn't notice the additional water soaking the seat of them.

"He murdered him," Claire finally used the word she didn't want to. "No warning. No negotiating. He just killed him."

"I know." Danny agreed and Claire waited for a *but*, but none was forthcoming.

"Could you have done that?" Claire asked him.

"If I was in the same headspace as Jon, yeah."

"Without trying to talk to him?"

"Did he look like the kind of man you could talk to? Jon did what he did to protect us. For all we know, that blood came from either Bryce or Larson. Even if it didn't, our visitor might have been working himself up to actually hurt us."

"He just wanted to scare us."

"And hurting one of us would scare the others. It could have easily escalated to that point."

"And it might not have."

"How do you think Jon would feel if he hadn't cut the rope? If he let him get away, and then that guy came back and hurt someone? Hurt you? He wasn't going to take that chance."

"It still doesn't seem right."

"I know. And maybe it wasn't. But the world's not exactly right anymore."

Claire heaved a sigh that was almost a sob.

"Come on. We should get back inside." Danny stood up.

Claire nodded and climbed over the air conditioner with him.

"When we get home, you should ask to be assigned to container checking duty."

"Why?" Claire thought this was a sudden change of topic.

"You're good at keeping an eye out for danger, and you're good at searching through and organizing things, but you shouldn't be a scavenger, Claire."

"Why not?" Claire was too exhausted to get angry. The adrenaline had worn off, and her legs now felt like rubber. She was glad they only had to go down the stairs, but knew to be careful in case the water dripping off everyone had made the steps slippery.

"Because this is the kind of shit you have to deal with out here." Danny gestured to the edge of the roof. "Not everything makes sense, awful stuff happens all the time, and you have to look straight at it. You have to make snap decisions, right or wrong. You've been doing great, but I can tell you're not sleeping well because of it. Over time, you would. You would change. And I don't think you should change."

The raw sincerity in his voice stunned Claire into silence. She didn't know how to respond to that. It seemed that Danny didn't expect a response. As they walked downstairs together, Claire wondered how scavenging had changed him.

"How's your shoulder?" she eventually asked once they reached their floor.

"Starts hurting if I use that arm too much," he admitted, his other hand moving to rub at the injury. "But it's been getting a little better each day. I was hoping it would be back to normal by the time we got home, but it might take a little longer than that."

They entered the apartment and discovered that Bryce and Larson were totally fine. They hadn't had any difficulty guarding the stuff. The only thing that had happened for them, was hearing them when the blankets had toppled over on Jon.

"We should continue to search the apartments we haven't gotten to yet," Jon spoke before Claire could even sit down. "It would be a shame to miss something."

Rose got to her feet, ready to start again.

"I would like to stay here," Claire admitted.

"Sure, we still need someone to guard the stuff." Did Jon know how she felt just then? Or did he just think that she was tired?

"I'll stay with her," Larson volunteered.

Claire had kind of been hoping that maybe Danny would stick around, but it was not to be. He went with Jon, Rose, and Bryce to see if any more food could be located.

"Rose told us what happened," Larson said once the others had departed and he had locked the door behind them. "You okay?"

"I'll be fine." Claire immediately wondered if she had just told a lie.

28: JAMES
10 DAYS AFTER THE BOMBING

Chaos briefly erupted in the Costco. James could barely stop a brawl from breaking out, and he failed to prevent Vin from punching one of Dinah's people. At least with Skip's injured hand, he couldn't start swinging, because he was the kind of person most likely to cause an all out war. After being hit by the flailing limbs of one of his own people, James finally managed to calm them down and back them off. Dinah did the same with her group.

"They're murderers, James," Marissa hiccuped, sad and angry at the same time.

"They didn't murder Aaron," James told her and everyone else.

"We should have left yesterday!" Lindsay yelled at the others over James' shoulder.

"Aaron would still be alive if it weren't for you!" Skip added.

"Guys, calm down." James held out his hands, trying to ease the tension. He didn't want to get hit again. "Aaron was in a bad way."

"Murderers!" Marissa screamed before he could finish.

"Marissa, please. They're not murderers. Aaron was bitten by a zombie pig, and had to have his leg amputated. They weren't a part of any of that."

"They could have helped," Marissa's voice dropped to a hushed breath.

"They did what they could. They had no medicine on them."

"We should have left yesterday," Skip snapped. "We could have gotten him medicine at the Theatre place."

"Maybe," James shrugged. "Maybe not. Maybe we would have just been shot, or maybe Aaron would have died en route, out in the rain. I think he was too far gone. I don't think any medicine would have made a difference by the time we got there."

"He's right," Lucy agreed. "Aaron wasn't going to make it. Let's face it, we all saw him. We all knew he was going to die. We just wanted to hope, is all."

"Bullshit, I didn't know he was going to die," Vin turned on her.

"Guys, please." James made another gesture for calm. "The fact is, we have a body to bury. And those people over there are still our best hope for our friends and family back home. We can't go fighting them. We need them."

Lindsay threw up her hands, aggravated, and stormed off towards the entrance to be alone. The rest also turned away from James, to take their grief and grievances elsewhere. As long as it wasn't toward the Theatre group, James didn't care where they went. Only Marissa stuck around.

"Where are we going to bury him?" she asked James.

"We could find a place outside. Or we can ask Dinah if there's a graveyard at the Theatre where we can lay him to rest. What do you think?"

Marissa's expression became conflicted, and James knew why. A graveyard did sound a lot better than some random strip of earth beside a road, but when that graveyard belonged to the people she had accused of murdering Aaron...?

"We have time to think about it. Why don't I go ask Dinah if they even have a graveyard first? Then, if they do, we'll ask the others what they think."

"Okay."

Marissa remained rooted in place as James went to talk to the Theatre group. In the dim light, Dinah's people looked pissed off, not appreciating being called murderers. But like James' people, they hung back, letting Dinah meet James halfway between the groups for a quiet conversation.

"You know what we have to do, right?" Dinah said, gesturing toward where Aaron lay motionless. Motionless for now, at least.

"I know. I'll do it myself in a second, but I have to ask you something first."

"What? It better not be some veiled accusation, because we did nothing to your man. We were going to help him."

"I know. I know that. What I wanted to ask was if the Theatre has a graveyard we might be allowed to bury him in. We might decide to bury him somewhere else, but I have to ask if that's an option."

Dinah sighed, releasing the tension from her body. "Yeah, we have a graveyard. You can definitely bury your man there if that's what you want."

"I'll tell the others and let them decide."

"Now can you please handle the body before it becomes a problem?"

"Yeah, of course."

James walked over to Aaron and knelt down beside him. Holding the head firmly against the floor, he checked for any signs of life that may have been missed. There were none; he was clearly dead.

"What are you doing?" Marissa asked, shuffling closer.

"Just making sure. I'm going to have to stab him now. Do you want to watch or…?"

"I understand. Go ahead."

She stuck around as James drew out his knife. Aaron's skull was still pretty hard, so he grabbed a crowbar someone had left lying nearby to use as a hammer against the end of the blade's handle.

"Need some help?" Marissa asked.

"If you don't mind."

Marissa knelt down and held the knife steady so that James could get a good swing at it. If he could succeed on the first try, that would be better for everyone. The crack of bone and clang of metal striking metal were the only sounds in the Costco.

"They said we can bury him in their graveyard if we'd like," James told Marissa after the deed was done and he had cleaned off his blade. "Why don't you go tell the others?"

"Okay."

James carefully wrapped up Aaron by himself. It wasn't difficult. His sleeping bag, which no one would want to use after this, became his body bag. James used the man's pillowcase as a shroud for his face, and secured it all with some rope.

"Need any help?" Dinah asked, keeping a safe distance.

"I'm all right." It wasn't exactly easy to roll Aaron's body back and forth to get the rope around him, but James wanted to do it himself. After the way they had left White and Jack to be eaten by animals, he felt he *had* to do it himself.

Breakfast was sombre, and James found that he couldn't eat much. He wasn't sure if the others could, as he focused solely on his own meal. It was the only way to smother the grief. He couldn't let it rise up; he needed to focus on the task ahead: figuring out what they could possibly offer in trade to the people at the Theatre.

"Have you decided where you want to bury your friend?" Dinah came over and asked after eating with her own people.

"They would like to bury him in your cemetery, provided they don't take issue with it once they see it."

"Okay. Are you ready to get going? It's safe enough and bright enough out there."

The rain was more like a heavy mist, soft and all consuming. James sat astride Soot, bundled up against the damp as best he could beneath a tarp around his shoulders, but every part of him that was exposed was going to be soaked through by the time they reached their destination. Beside him, Aaron was slung over Spark's back and tied on like luggage. The drenched pillowcase turned semi-transparent, revealing the shadowy outline of his dark hair, while gravity drew blood out of the head wound and formed stains.

Dinah and her people led the way. It was nice to see that they didn't feel the need to surround James and his people as they travelled, and they didn't mind having their backs turned toward them. Dinah had convinced her people to trust James' despite that morning's hostilities.

The walk was dreary. No one felt up to talking, providing no distraction from the grey landscape all around. James tried to stay vigilant, to keep an eye out for danger, but there was something about travelling with Dinah's people that gave him a sense of security. These were their lands after all, and they clearly patrolled them.

By the time Dinah's people stopped, James was pretty much in a daze. It was the same state he used to drift into during long car trips. He didn't realize until just then that he used to call it zombie driving. If zombies could drive, they would have had a lot more problems over the years.

"The Theatre isn't far," Dinah spoke loudly enough for everyone to hear. "But this is our cemetery."

It was a large empty patch of ground between two buildings. James didn't think it had always been a cemetery, but there were headstones now, some of them large with crosses or angels on top. The ones James studied were very old and worn down by decades of weather. They were also crowded quite closely together.

"Why isn't it closer to where you live?" Marissa asked.

"People don't like having the dead too near." It wasn't Dinah who answered, but someone James thought was named Gabe. "Some people don't want to visit, so we decided to choose a spot that was out of the way.

Somewhere where visiting is a choice. Would you like me to help you find a spot for your friend?"

"Where'd you get the headstones?" Katrina asked.

"Some we made. Most are from another cemetery, a very old one," Gabe admitted. "All the identifying markers had been worn off. We cleaned them up, and chiselled the names of our own dead onto them."

"So you stole them?" Katrina raised an eyebrow.

"Did you steal Aaron's pack, that I notice is being carried with you? Did you steal that pelt from the lion? We use what is no longer needed by others. And it's not like we left the old graves unmarked; we just put smaller rocks in their place." Gabe motioned toward the wall of a neighbouring building where a pile of large, smooth stones had been piled. "You can pick whichever rock you'd like to use as a marker. We'll have someone chisel Aaron's name into it, and anything else you might want it to say, once the weather is good."

James stayed on his horse during the burial. A spot was chosen near the road, as close to the shipping container yard as it could get. It turned out that the Theatre people buried their dead in a sort of upright fetal position, so as to save space. They planned to live here a long time, and were thinking ahead about the many people who would die of natural causes over the years. No one from the container yard minded, especially when it meant digging a smaller hole. Shovels and a pickaxe were retrieved from inside one of the neighbouring buildings, and people from both places took turns digging.

"How do your people normally handle the dead?" Dinah asked James, having drifted over to where he watched. "What are your funeral rites?"

"We would bury our dead beneath our farms. Crops were our headstones."

"No markers? No names?"

"The names were all written down. I think the plan was to build a memorial for them all once we were finally comfortably settled, but those names are gone now." They would have been lost during the attack on the Black Box.

"How many names can you personally remember?"

"Too many." James had missed the worst of it, but he knew that during the container yard clean up after the zombie attack, plenty of people had been burned instead of buried. There just wasn't time. Had anyone written down their names?

Aaron was planted in the muddy ground, his hole partly filled with water. The dirt was pushed back on top of him without much ceremony. One of the stones was chosen and plunked down on top.

"We should include White and Jack when we tell them what to write on the stone." It was an unexpected idea from Skip, but everyone agreed that it was a good one. They had died coming to this place, so they should be honoured here as well.

Three people had died on the journey to the Theatre. James wondered how the hell he was supposed to go on, to go farther. There were two other communities their group was meant to visit, one of them to be reached by Katrina and him alone. At that moment, it didn't seem possible.

Vin, as the most religious of their party, spoke a few words over the grave. Nothing personal was said. No one thought there was time to mourn just yet.

Once Vin was finished, they merely gathered up anything they had put down and started walking once more.

Dinah hadn't been lying when she said that the Theatre was near. They walked a few blocks, following a zigzag of roads between old shops and restaurants. When it suddenly opened up, they knew that they were there.

A massive parking lot dominated the space in front of the large movie theatre. About a third of the way across from where the visitors had arrived was a cobbled together wall. James now understood why they had stripped everything they could from all the nearby buildings. Shelves, couches, fencing, cars, even flat screen TVs had been wedged together and stacked to form the twenty-foot high barricade. It swept all the way across the arch shaped parking lot, and James assumed it continued on behind the building where it took a sharp bend out of sight. Guards stood, sat, or walked along the wall at regular intervals, all of them huddled beneath ponchos and rain slickers. Past them, James could make out the top of the movie theatre, where greenery lined the upper edge; it seemed they grew something on the roof. But past the theatre was a sight James hadn't expected: a massive windmill. It barely turned, for the air was quite still, but James could imagine it slashing through the storm last night. There were no other windmills in sight, as James would have expected of a wind farm.

"Was that already here?" he couldn't help but ask.

"No," Dinah told him. "We found the parts on some trucks, I think. Or in a warehouse? I can't remember. Took us years to figure out how to assemble it here and hook it up to some batteries. Come on." She and her people started across the empty section of the parking lot.

James was amazed at what they had done here. They must have lived in this one place since the beginning, or at least close to. As they approached the wall, he could see the problems with it, namely that it was scalable by anyone or anything smart enough, but it was still impressive. Whoever had designed it had done a good job, managing to work in everything that couldn't be used elsewhere.

"We've got travellers hoping to trade," Dinah called up to a guard on the wall. "Nine people with two horses. They've never been here before."

James failed to see where the door was. The hodgepodge of stuff didn't have any obvious openings.

"All right, give us a minute," the guard called down.

Dinah turned to James and his group. "This is as far as I take you."

"What?"

"You'll be escorted inside. Don't worry, no one will take any of your things. Just follow them, and they'll make sure you talk to the right people."

"Why aren't you coming with us?" Katrina asked before James could.

"Not our time. We still have a job to complete out here. You'll be fine. By escorting you this far, I've vouched for you. Just don't do anything stupid."

Dinah and her group waited with them until an opening was revealed. A chunk of plywood, a large stop sign, and a free standing car door swung upward like a hatch. The opening wasn't square, and was just large enough for the horses to fit through, as long as James dismounted first. A man stepped out through the opening to greet them. He didn't have a rifle with him like those on the wall, and wore a smile as bright as his thin, yellow poncho.

"Hi, hello!" he said, offering his hand to Katrina, the first person he came to. "I'm Reggie, I'll be your liaison while you stay with us. What's your name?"

"Katrina."

"Katrina, it's nice to meet you." Reggie went around and introduced himself to everyone. He repeated every name once he was told what it was. James had met someone who used that trick before. He bet Reggie would never forget their names the entire time that they were there.

"James," he said when it was his turn. He came last, because he had to climb off of Soot's back first.

"James, so glad you're here."

"Can I get a doctor to take a look at my hand?" Skip asked.

"Certainly, Skip. But let's get you inside and settled first. I'm sure you'd all like to get out of this rain, and how does a hot meal sound?"

It sounded great to everyone.

James led Soot through the opening, studying the hidden hinge, and how it was opened using a winch on the other side of the wall, a little like an upside down drawbridge. Just inside the wall, platforms had been built for the guards to stand on, using the same inconsistency of materials. It didn't always look safe.

Once they were all through and the door swung shut behind them, Reggie led the way across the rest of the parking lot. Neat rows of planters were interspersed with camping tents of all sizes and colours. Despite the weather, a fair number of people moved about. Most were tending to the plants, repairing any damage that had been done to them by the storm. Others were repairing and shoring up sections of the wall, which James had been right about when he thought it went past the side of the theatre and beyond. A handful of people ran about, their exact purpose unknown, but James guessed that they were delivering items and messages. Through a few tent openings that were thrown aside as someone entered or exited, James could see more exotic plants being grown, including some mushrooms. Evans had claimed this was a large population centre, but right now, the place seemed too big for the number of people James saw.

Reggie first led them toward the entrance of the theatre, but then started to guide them around the side of it.

"We'll get your horses set up and comfortable in the stables first, and then we'll see to you folks. Sound good?"

No one answered, still taking everything in with a dose of caution.

The building was large. From what James could see, the central structure was a cylinder, with two wings extruding from either side. As they followed along the edge of one wing, they passed a crude structure that James thought might have housed some gas generators at one time. He thought this because the generators were still clustered outside the shelter that had been constructed from the massive, fabric posters that must have once hung on the side of the theatre. The generators were rusting heaps, that helped to keep the sun-bleached posters in place during windstorms, and had been butchered for parts. People must now live under the posters if bedding inside was any indication. James couldn't see it being a pleasant place when there was any wind, what with the open ends of the structure.

As they rounded the side of the theatre, they came upon other small structures. Some were sheds, the assemble-yourself kind that used to be sold at hardware stores. Others were made out of repurposed materials. At least a couple of the structures housed chickens based on the noise coming from them. James couldn't determine all of the sheds' functions. People popped in and out of a few of them, but they were quick, always sliding through a minimal sized opening that they blocked with their bodies.

Around the back of the theatre, the structures, tents, and planters gave way to trees. A massive orchard prevented James from seeing just how far the wall stretched; he was guessing it encircled the base of the windmill, which was still a fair distance off. This place was huge.

"Here we are," Reggie said as they approached a long, low structure built against the inside of the wall. "Several of our horses are out with a few of our roaming parties right now, so there should be plenty of space for your two."

They all crowded in through the doorway, taking shelter from the rain beneath the roof made of aluminium sheets bolted together. In a few spots along the walkway, the rain was dripping through into buckets. Stalls flanked one side, most of them empty, but a few were housing horses at the farthest end. Above the stalls, and beneath the sloped roof, was a loft full of hay. At least one person was asleep up there, with his arm hanging over the edge, oblivious to the sounds of new people entering the space.

"Hi, Oleg," Reggie said as a gruff man who *had* heard them came out of one of the occupied stalls. "We have guests, and they have horses. Think you can see to them?"

"Of course," Oleg nodded. "Just put them in these first two and I'll see that they're fed, watered, and brushed down. What are your beasts' names?"

"Soot and Spark," James told the man who smelled like horse. "Soot here is old and mostly deaf, Spark is rather rambunctious."

Oleg gave a curt nod of understanding. "Don't worry about them. They'll be fine as long as you're staying here. We'll even exercise them if they need it, and feel free to visit any time."

"Thanks, Oleg," Reggie told him.

James and Katrina walked the horses into neighbouring stalls. The others helped to remove the gear the horses were carrying, dividing it all up among them. Before heading back out, James gave Soot's chest a scratch, and hoped he had somehow conveyed to the horse that they would be back. As he passed back out into the rain, one last look over his shoulder revealed to James that Oleg was giving some hay to both horses, who munched on it eagerly. They would be fine. Probably.

Reggie guided them toward the centre of the theatre's backside, where the closest entrance was located beside a third protuberance jutting out from the center cylinder. This last boxy structure was a lot shorter than the other two wings. Some of the glass within the doors had been shattered and replaced by plastic sheeting. As they stepped through, James noted that there were security gates still intact. He figured that those had probably saved these people a number of times before their wall was built.

The sound inside struck James before he even looked around. The theatre was crowded with human voices; this is where all the people were. It was well lit, with strings of lights hanging from nearly every surface that would support them. The main section of the building, the cylinder, was a large, high-ceilinged circular space inside, with a concession stand circling the center and a private party space up above it, but everywhere James looked, there were people. Men and women sat on stools behind the concession ring, assembling bullets and chatting with one another. Two mobs were gathered at the walls on either side, one in front of what used to be a pizza place, and the other where hot dogs and fries had once been cooked; steam and the mouth-watering aroma of cooking food rose from both. A woman with a rifle patrolled along the edge of the party space, looking down on everyone. Voices indicated that there were others up there with her, unseen. Around toward the front, in what used to be the arcade centre based on the signage, were dozens of mattresses and heaps of blankets. Some of them were occupied, with people sleeping through the buzz of activity, while others were neatly made. And everywhere, people bustled back and forth. James couldn't see the other half of the space past the central concession ring, but he guessed it would be just as chaotic.

"Is the whole theatre like this?" James asked Reggie, having to raise his voice to compete with the din.

"Like what?"

"Crowded."

"More or less, yes," Reggie shrugged.

Glancing over at his companions, James could see a couple of mouths hanging open. They were just as impressed and overwhelmed as he was. But they hadn't yet had the same thought as him. They hadn't discovered what they had to offer in trade.

"Let's get you settled." Reggie moved off, gesturing for them to follow.

***

James appreciated that they had been put somewhere quiet. The IMAX screen at the back of the theatre was the one auditorium that hadn't been converted into living space, according to Reggie. There was a pit down below the massive screen where they let visitors camp out, understanding that they needed some private space for themselves. When Reggie had gone off to get them some food, James explored the auditorium. His foot was feeling up to a bit more walking.

Reggie had explained that on the first of every month, they showed movies in there. All month long, a vote was held to decide which films they would watch, as their scavenging had resulted in the accumulation of a vast collection. They played movies from nine a.m. to nine p.m., thanks to being able to rig up some DVD and Blu-ray players to the projector. They even had a couple of VCRs. They didn't use the auditorium's impressive sound system, however. It was just too loud, and required too much power while running everything else. Instead, a lot of small computer speakers were strung all about, clustered between chairs, so that they could keep the volume low and still allow everyone to hear just fine. James was impressed by the level of engineering that had gone into just this one room, and it was only so they could watch movies on a big screen once a month. They must have some smart people with a lot of time on their hands in this place.

When Reggie returned, he was accompanied by several people bearing trays of hot meals, and a doctor carrying a black medical bag who introduced himself as Dr. Dilton. They gathered in the pit after clanging down the metal steps that clearly hadn't been part of the auditorium's original design.

"You guys are the best, thank you!" Samson sounded like he had seen the face of God as he was handed a hamburger. An actual hamburger, with a bun and tomatoes and lettuce and cheese. There was a buttered baked potato on the side as opposed to fries, but not one person complained. They were also given the option of water, apple juice, or milk to drink. It all seemed too good to be true, but when James took that first bite, nothing else mattered. It was good. It was the best burger he had ever eaten in his whole life. Not only was nothing stale, but the bread was clearly fresh, the meat was juicy, and the lettuce was crisp. He didn't even notice that there were no condiments. It seemed that ketchup was still beyond these people's grasp.

Skip ate one-handed while the doctor took a look at his injury. His left hand was a discoloured and swollen puff, but Dilton thought there was a chance he wouldn't have to lose it provided the bones could be correctly set. Once Skip's hand had been injected with a numbing agent, the doctor set to work, draining off some of the built-up fluid and attempting to set the bones.

"What is that you gave him?" James asked, watching as a loopy smile spread across Skip's face. He still winced occasionally—the numbing agent not totally effective—but it was doing its job well enough to keep him from full on flinching.

"A cocaine solution," Dilton answered.

"Seriously?" Marissa's eyebrows shot toward her hairline.

"If it works, we use it. We grow coca plants on the roof, along with marijuana, peyote, and poppies. Don't worry about your friend becoming addicted. I should only need to give him this one dose, and there's no way for him to find any more in this place. The roof is heavily guarded and if you try to go up there, you will be shot."

"Yo, we should grow coca plants when we get home," Skip suggested.

James thought it wasn't a bad idea. They used to grow their own marijuana and poppies in the Black Box, but they would first have to find a way to protect both the plants and the final product like the people here did. Just having alcohol available to the public had caused some avoidable issues in the past, and while they didn't restrict the smoking of pot, anything harder would be considered too dangerous.

It seemed that Dr. Dilton had been forewarned about the state of Skip's hand, because he even had the materials in his bag to create some sort of plaster cast once he reset the bones.

"You work awfully fast," Lindsay commented. They had all finished their meals and were watching with interest.

"I've dealt with plenty of crush injuries, especially to hands. I've gotten good at patching them up." He looked Skip in the face. "That doesn't mean this will heal perfectly. It will still hurt for some time, especially when you try to move it after the cast comes off. It'll likely cause you some pain your entire life."

"Will I be able to predict when it's going to rain?" Skip wondered.

"You might." Another syringe was withdrawn from the bag and loaded with something new.

"What's that?" James asked.

"Penicillin."

"You guys know how to make penicillin?"

"Isn't it just bread mould?" Vin wondered.

"You have to mix it with a few chemicals," James told him.

"Correct," Dilton agreed. "And we keep a very careful watch on our supplies. Your friend's hand is very clearly infected, otherwise I might not have given him any."

"What if I were allergic to penicillin?" Skip said as he was given a fluff of cotton to hold against the needle puncture.

"Then I'm sorry." Dilton shrugged. "*Are* you allergic?"

"I don't think I am."

"Then you'll be fine." Dilton packed up his bag once more and stood up. "I'll come check on you in another hour, and then we'll decide if anything else is needed after that." He left as briskly as he had worked.

"This thing is heavy," Skip commented, lifting and lowering his injured hand.

"Leave it alone," James told him before turning to Reggie, who continued to hang around. "When can we talk to someone about a trade?"

"For small, personal items, feel free to talk to anyone. For anything larger, we'll have to wait until the council has finished their meeting and are free to speak with you. What is it you're looking for?"

"I'd rather only speak about that with the people authorized to trade with us," James told him, closely watching his reaction.

Reggie didn't seem to mind or take any offence. "Of course. It's still going to be a little while before they're free. Would you like a tour of our home in the meantime?"

James hadn't been expecting that, but he certainly wasn't going to refuse. Skip wasn't in any shape to go walking around, so he stayed put, and Marissa agreed to keep him company. James didn't have to tell anyone that they shouldn't allow themselves to be alone in this place, not before they knew the people here better.

Reggie was an excellent tour guide, willing and able to answer all their questions. It was a little eerie how readily he trusted James and his friends. When James questioned him about it, Reggie explained that Dinah would never have brought them here if she thought that they were dangerous. Reggie trusted Dinah's opinion, but it made James question Dinah. Things had gotten rather hostile that morning, and yet she still brought them here, knowing how much weight that carried. When had she decided that they were okay? This place hadn't even disarmed them, although there were plenty of people wearing police hats walking about, and James bet they were all really good shots.

During their tour, they learned that along with the windmill, the Theatre produced their power with solar panels around the base of the windmill and on the roof. They also had modified exercise bikes that someone was always using housed within all but the IMAX's projector booths. They were all hooked up to a variety of large, rechargeable batteries.

The auditoriums were crowded with living spaces. The seats had been removed and several of them turned into quasi beds. Clustered around the living spaces, that were separated by hanging sheets, were looms, spinning wheels, wash tubs, and even stone grinding wheels for milling grain into flour.

They learned that the sheds out back had various uses, from animal pens, to a couple of small blacksmiths, to a smokehouse. They had nearly every animal that James could think of a use for: cows, goats, sheep, pigs, rabbits, chickens, alpacas, donkeys, horses, dogs, cats, rabbits, even a trained falcon and several bee hives. Any plant that they had discovered was edible, they found a way to grow.

People had been living at the Theatre since the beginning, which gave them plenty of time to figure out what worked and what didn't. They had been attacked on occasion, by both the living and the dead, but nothing had yet come along that had put them into the kind of crushed state the container yard was currently suffering. The fact was, they had so many people, that they could lose a few dozen and not be impacted. On rainy days like this one, they had trouble keeping everyone occupied. A fair number of teams like Dinah's were always kept outside the wall on a rotating basis. They were on the lookout for people like James and his group, guarded against anything that might be considered a threat, hunted wild animals, and fished in various rivers and lakes they knew about. In fact, as a by-product of keeping everyone busy, they were able to have flushable toilets, which was probably the best part of the tour for everyone. The Theatre had redirected the pipes so that they emptied into the storm sewers, which were larger and easier for people to keep clear of any jams. Another team had the sole job of keeping buckets filled with water so that the toilets could be flushed. There was pretty much always a line for the bathroom, but it was definitely worth it.

"What the hell are we going to offer these people?" Katrina asked James, her normal speaking voice as good as a whisper within the din. "I doubt my lion pelt will get much."

"Don't worry about it. I have an idea." James might have told her more, but Reggie started going off on their election process and he wanted to hear. It seemed they held an election every year, for half the council seats, so that each council member got a minimum of two years, and there were always people with at least a year's experience. The weird part was that no one was allowed to campaign for themselves. It had to be done entirely by unrelated people who thought you could do the job. To get caught aiding your own election or re-election meant an immediate expulsion from the council if you already held a seat, and you were barred from ever being elected. When James asked about the rule, Reggie explained that in the first few years, they were already seeing corruption involving the elections, so they hoped the new rule would nip that in the bud.

"So much for the American way," Lucy had commented.

"If you think this is still America, you're wrong," Reggie told her. "There are no countries anymore. Everyone has to govern themselves in whatever way works best. How do you handle elections?"

"We don't," James admitted, which caused Lucy to blush. "We have people who have been leading us since the beginning. They've done a good job of it so far; not too many people have complained."

Reggie nodded. "That's why Vee keeps getting re-elected. She showed up here in the earlier days and took charge of what she found. She's personally kept a lot of people alive, and is the only member of the council to have always been on it. Not many people have ever had a problem with her."

Hearing that, James hoped he would get a chance to talk to her about the trade. He understood people like that given how closely he had worked with Crichton and the others over the years.

"Have you ever been on the council?" Belle asked Reggie.

"I was up for election one year," he nodded. "But I think those campaigning for me eventually picked up on the fact that I wasn't really interested in the position."

The tour continued with them learning about the Theatre's attempts to install a monetary system, which still needed work. They would always have food to feed everyone, but they were trying to find a balanced way to reward those who performed the harder and/or more dangerous tasks. They had procured a lot of cash from various bank vaults, and it didn't have much use as anything else.

After the tour ended, James and his troop returned to their auditorium and explained everything they had seen to Marissa and Skip, both of whom had already discovered the flushable toilets when they had needed to venture out and use them. James' foot had started to bother him again, but after resting for a while, it felt better by the time Reggie said that they could meet the council.

They climbed the dead escalator that led up to the party centre above the middle of the main space. A section of it was taken up by a large table. Plastic storage boxes were piled everywhere else, each one labelled with a name in dry erase marker. James spotted Dinah's among them and figured they each held the personal effects of those outside the wall, the things they didn't or couldn't bring with them. There were a lot. The eight council members sat near the table in office chairs, all of them wheeled around so that they could face the same direction. People moved freely up and down the escalator and around the space, as a bridge on either side of the raised platform led to the various projectionists' booths. Those returning from the exercise bikes looked exhausted. The policewoman James had spotted from below continued to circle around the perimeter.

"Welcome to the Theatre," one of the council members said once they had gathered. The floor and sides of the raised platform did a decent job of muffling the din below, but it was far from inaudible.

Reggie introduced James and the others to the council members. James specifically noted which one was Vee; the black woman sat to one side, watching them with a cool, impassive expression.

"Talking to all of you at once might get a little confusing. Do you have someone who can represent all of you?" asked Jorge, who had been the one to welcome them. Perhaps he was their speaker.

James felt someone literally push him forward. He suspected it had been Katrina.

"So, what brings you here?" Jorge asked.

"We're a community hoping to expand our network, and we're looking to trade," James told him.

"Did you happen to stumble across us, or did someone let you know where we were?"

"Evans told us where to find you. I don't know if any of you remember him. Tall guy, big sword, looks like a Viking?"

"I remember him," Vee said with a slow nod. "So he's still alive, is he?"

"Last time I saw him, he was." Although the last time James had seen him, Evans had been bleeding pretty badly from a gash on his arm, and James himself had just lost some of his toes.

"What is it you're hoping to get from us?" Jorge asked next.

"Food. Whatever food you can spare. I also think it would be great if some of your engineers could take a look at our place, to see if they have any advice for improvements. And while our system of leadership and how we deal with crime has worked so far, having someone come who could explain your legal system would be pretty great too."

The council members shifted somewhat, a few glancing at one another. Vee's expression changed subtly to one of curiosity.

"That's a tall order," Jorge informed him. "Where exactly do you come from, and what do you have to offer that you think is worthy of such an exchange?"

"I offer you more living space and stronger walls," James told the council, looking each one in the eye. "We come from a shipping container yard. We've been using them for both protection and housing for years now. You could certainly use more housing, and no offence, but your wall looks like it could use some shoring up in places. It also doesn't look that hard to climb. Replace the bad sections with containers, and now not only is your wall stronger, but you can have people living inside of them, safe from elements, and private."

James could see that his offer had intrigued the council, despite their attempts to hide it. It had probably been a long time since they had been offered something they could actually use.

"Why wouldn't we just go find our own containers?" Vee spoke up.

"You could do that. We're probably the closest though, and we can teach you how to move them around and modify them so that they lock on the inside instead of the outside."

"You have a very high opinion of your containers," said the man who was introduced as Qaletaqa.

"As we should." Katrina stepped up beside James. "I've personally lived in one for something over four years now. I have a bed, some shelving for anything I want, and a desk for whatever work I decide to do in there. And that's with a roommate. How many of your people here can say the same? As for secure? It hasn't even been two weeks since we were attacked. First, a party of raiders and then the biggest zombie horde you'll ever see. But we're still standing."

"Ever meet a man named Boss? Or Tommy, Mark, Suzanne, or Betty?" Lindsay spoke up from behind them, knowing that they had because of James' conversation with Dinah.

"The runners," James added. "Going around and warning people of what they called the comet horde."

"They've been here before," Vee confirmed.

"Well that comet horde broke upon our wall," Katrina told her, not without pride. "I gotta say, I like your place here with its electricity, and its flush toilets, and all its food, but I would not want to live here. I wouldn't feel safe."

"If we were to accept your trade, how would we get some of your containers here?" Jorge asked.

"You managed to bring a windmill over here," James gestured in its general direction. "Based on the remains of the gas generators I saw outside, I don't think you did that until the gas ran out. I think you got a big flat bed trailer from somewhere, and brought it here using a team of horses."

A small smile touched Vee's lips. "You do a lot of extrapolating," she commented.

"When I see something, I want to understand it. Even if we don't trade anything today, I'll be heading home with knowledge that we might be able to put to use."

"Do you plan to offer this trade to anyone else?" asked a woman named Sly.

"If it seems like the best offer. We have a number of groups visiting various communities. Some of us here are supposed to move on, to visit places Evans called White Fang, and the Dale."

"We don't recommend that," Jorge shook his head. "White Fang has been overtaken by a particularly vile group of people, and everyone from the Dale is dead. Some sort of plague burned through everyone there, and not the kind that walks."

James was a little ashamed of the relief that washed over him. He wouldn't have to travel farther. Once he was done here, he could go back home.

"How many containers do you have to offer?" Jorge asked.

"We've never counted how many we have," James admitted. "We live in a large yard, maybe taking up a quarter to a third of it. There are still plenty of untouched containers. There's also a smaller yard not far from us that we haven't even had a chance to look through yet."

"What's in these containers?"

James shrugged. "It's a surprise every time. Rotten food, medical supplies, clothing, engine parts, cars, mattresses, toys, literally anything that someone would ship across the ocean might be in one."

"How long would it take us to travel there?" Vee wondered.

"It took us around a week to get here," James told her. "But we ran into several problems that could be avoided with a large group."

"What kind of problems?"

"Some zombie pigs, although we killed them so they should no longer be an issue. And lions."

"Lions?" Qaletaqa frowned.

"Yeah, African lions," Katrina told him. "Must have survived from a zoo. I killed the one that killed our friend White if you want to see the pelt."

"In a large group, especially one as well armed as you all seem to be, the lions should pose no threat." At least James thought they wouldn't. He couldn't claim to be an expert on the mind of a lion.

"How many friends did you lose on your way here?" Vee asked.

"Three. Jack was killed by the pigs, and Aaron died of his wounds after we had to amputate his leg following that same attack. One of your parties outside the wall, the one led by Dinah, was with us when he died. We had hoped to get him here before that, but we were too late. She let us bury him in your graveyard."

"You didn't mention that," Reggie spoke for the first time since making introductions. "Let me know what you want the headstone to say, and I'll see that a carver heads out there."

"Thank you."

"We'll have to deliberate upon your proposal," Jorge decided. "And you'll need to show us on a map where you reside. You know where we live, but we don't know where you live."

"That's fine." James thought of Dinah trusting them, and so decided he should return that trust. Seemed like a fair trade.

"Go back to your camp. Reggie will inform you when we have made a decision."

James thanked them for listening, and walked back to the auditorium with the others. Reggie made sure they had everything they needed, and then went to find a carver once they had written on a white board what they wanted the headstone to read.

"That was clever, offering the containers," Lucy commented.

"Looked to me like privacy was sorely needed around here," James shrugged.

"Do you think they'll accept the trade?" Samson wondered.

"We can hope."

29: EVANS
10 DAYS AFTER THE BOMBING

Evans sat with the silent ones, who were living up to the name he had given them. They were waiting for him to speak, but he wasn't sure how to start.

"I have bad news," he decided to begin with.

The silent ones had no reaction to this proclamation. It seemed they accepted bad news as a matter of course.

"The place you wanted to go to, Bridges, doesn't exist anymore."

This stirred them up a bit. A few of them turned to look at one another. They continued to sit there, expecting Evans to have more to say, but he didn't. That was it.

"We don't want to stay here," Ang spoke up after about a minute.

"Then we have to decide where it is that you want to go."

"Wherever is closest," Burt said this time. "There was another place, west of Bridges, wasn't there?"

"Far west of Bridges," Evans nodded. "If it still stands. It would take us a long time to get there, much longer than our journey here." And while Evans wouldn't say it, he found it difficult to imagine the silent ones living in the Theatre. With its crowding, they might not even be willing to take in new people.

"Are you sure there is nowhere closer?" Ang pressed. "Some place we may have overlooked in your journal?"

There was a place that Evans hadn't yet taken the time to write about. But he had just come from there; did he really want to go back so soon? He looked at the silent ones gathered before him, and saw the desperation in their eyes. They were more than ready to settle down, but they couldn't in a place that let zombies roam so close, a place that tried to control the dead, no matter how successful they were with it. Evans understood the need to not be here.

"I guess there's one place," he finally sighed.

"Where? What's it like?" asked Patterson, squeezing the hands of her two children.

"It's in a shipping container yard, by some sort of large ocean inlet, or something. I didn't spend that much time in the surrounding area."

"And do they allow zombies?" Ang questioned.

"No. In fact, Gerald is from that place, and he was kicked out for bringing one in. I was bringing him here as a sort of payment for a debt I owed." Evans hadn't wanted to tell the silent ones that, especially not Blue, who had gotten along so well with Gerald. He could see it immediately changed their opinion of him, which was an unfair thing of him to do while Gerald was off getting a tour of the place. Then again, Evans supposed that if Gerald would no longer be travelling with them, it wouldn't matter.

"If you just came from there, then surely it is still standing," Dev insisted.

Evans shrugged. "I can't say anything for sure. There was some trouble with raiders that should have been resolved, maybe not. They were also in the midst of a supply problem when I left, and like I said, they're by the sea. The storm will have hit them harder than it hit us."

A quiet moment of contemplation settled among the silent ones. A few of them turned to one another and used their sign language so that Evans couldn't follow what was being said. He saw a few frowns, and a few gestures that seemed to be making some sort of definitive point, but otherwise he couldn't understand any of it.

Finally, Burt turned back to Evans. "We want to go to this place by the sea, the shipping container yard."

"Whichever place we decide on may have been destroyed," Ang expanded. "We might as well go to the one that's closest."

Evans nodded. He suspected that some of his former party members would be pissed to see him return after he had abandoned them the way he had, but he had dealt with that sort of situation before. He needed to think about what was best for the children, Iris and Oz, as well as the old folk, Elmore, Patrick, and Janet. If the container yard could get back on its feet after what it had been through, it was certainly capable of protecting them.

"We're going to need all the supplies we can get," Evans told the silent ones. "And I'm going to need to see a map." The quickest route back was actually not the one he had taken to get here.

The silent ones immediately got moving, glad to have a task. A map was quickly produced from their gear for Evans to pore over. Ang placed himself at Evans' side so that he could see where they were going. The rest of the silent ones dispersed in teams, ready to find jobs that would earn them what they needed. It seemed they could get over their stand-offish nature if it meant something positive for them in the end.

"Where's the town you used to live in?" Evans asked Ang, trying to get his bearings among the squiggly lines.

Ang pointed it out, and Evans was able to work out where Paddock was from there. He then worked backward until he found the container yard. Evans had travelled in a vaguely fish hook shaped route. By heading directly from the Paddock to the container yard, they should be able to shave off a few days' worth of travel. That was the hope, anyway.

"I'm going to go talk to the survivors from Bridges," Evans told Ang. "They may want to come with us."

Ang tagged along as Evans first went to see Frannie to fill her in. It seemed she already knew about the recently planned departure, since the silent ones had gone to her first in their quest for jobs.

"It hasn't stopped raining yet," Frannie pointed out.

"It's light enough that you sent Gerald out on a tour with someone," Evans countered.

"Fair point. I've already given all the names and locations of people who might need an extra hand to your friends. You'll have to go around to find whatever jobs they haven't scooped up."

"Not looking for a job just yet." Evans hoped, for their sakes, that none of the silent ones ended up with a job like the one he had done earlier that day. "I was thinking that now might be a good time for me to talk to the people who came from Bridges."

Frannie agreed that Evans should talk with them. She didn't have time to accompany him and Ang, but she gave them the address where they were staying as well as a glass paperweight. Apparently the paperweight was proof that Evans had been sent by Frannie, should they prove mistrustful when he arrived. The silent ones had been given a couple as well before they went job hunting.

It was still raining, but it had slackened off even more since Evans had taken his shower that morning. As he and Ang made their way along the street, they passed a few of the silent ones helping some people set up their shops. While it would probably be too late to open their trade market by the time they were done, the sellers would be ready to start bright and early the next morning. Evans was glad, for they were going to make use of the market.

The people from Bridges occupied two houses near the centre of town, where they were away from any zombie corrals. Evans didn't know if they had a leader, and if they did, which house that person might be in, so he just chose to knock on the door of the nearest one. It was swung open by a man, and then partly closed again when he failed to recognize the men outside.

"Sorry to bother you." Evans held up the paperweight. "My name is Evans, and this is Ang. Frannie sent us to talk to you. You're from Bridges, right?"

"Yeah. What do you want?" It seemed the paperweight did not bestow all that much trust.

"I've been to Bridges a couple of times. It was a good place, and I'm sorry about what happened to your friends and home."

"Thanks." The man relaxed a tiny bit. Not a lot, but even a little was progress. Evans could hear people whispering somewhere behind him, likely wondering what was going on.

"Some of you might know me, but I wouldn't be able to say who. Frannie didn't tell me who survived. I'm here to offer you another place to go. May we come in? I don't want to open the map out here and risk getting it wet."

"One minute." The door closed, and Evans could just make out the muffled sounds of a hurried conference occurring on the other side. When the door opened next, both Evans and Ang were ignored. A different man exited and went to the second house. When he came back a couple of minutes later, he was accompanied by several people.

"Evans!" one of them called out. "It's been a while."

Evans recognized the face, but blanked out on the name.

"Paul," the man offered helpfully along with his hand to shake.

"Right, Paul, sorry. I can't remember you living in Bridges."

"I didn't, not until a few months before the raiders came."

"I'm sorry for your loss."

"Harder on the others than on me." Paul motioned with his head to those around him. "Come on, we should all go inside instead of standing out here in the rain."

The man at the door reluctantly let Evans and Ang enter with everyone else from next door. They gathered in the living room; a few bedrolls were moved out of the way so that people could sit on the floor. Evans hung around near the entrance, wanting to intrude as little as possible, and not wanting to drip all over their things.

"Talk," the man who opened the door said to Evans.

"Well, as I mentioned, I'm here to offer you a different place to go. A community to live in that isn't here."

"Is it a new community?" asked a woman.

"They've been around for five years, give or take."

"What are they called?" another woman asked.

"They haven't reached out to other communities yet, so I don't think they have any sort of formal name like this place does. I just think of them as the container yard."

"Where is it?" asked Paul, who was standing closest to Evans and Ang.

Evans reached under his clothes to take out the map he had brought. It was already folded to reveal the necessary locations.

"Here's Paddock," he said, pointing it out on the map to Paul. "And here's the container yard." He let Paul take the map and show it around to the others. "They had some hard times recently, and I can't imagine this storm having made it any better. I'm bringing Ang and his people there, and you're welcome to join us. We'll have to bring as much food as we can, and be prepared to work hard, but they have shelter, and they don't allow zombies in." Evans hoped they were still there, and that they had room. He knew that plenty of people had died during the zombie attack, but then they had that crowd come over from the Black Box, as well as Evans' surviving party members. They hadn't sorted out their population before Evans left, and now here he was assuming that they could take on more.

"How long has it been since you were there?" asked a man.

"I don't know, more than a week, but I haven't been keeping track."

"A lot can happen in a week," someone muttered.

"That's true," he nodded, acknowledging the mutterer's comment. "That's the other reason we need to gather as many supplies as we can. If the container yard is gone, then we're going to move on to the next nearest community, most likely the Theatre. My friend here," at this he motioned to Ang, "and his people have no desire to live in Paddock. I'm going to find them another place to live, even if it isn't the quickest to get to. You may stay here if you like, obviously, or wait until some other time to travel, but a larger group is a safer group."

There were some whispers, as several people leaned over to their neighbours to share a word.

"You don't have to make your decision right away," Evans added when he saw some combative expressions. "Take your time. The earliest we can leave is tomorrow, and that's provided we gather everything we need. Ang and I are going to go find some work for ourselves. You can come find one of us once you've made your decision."

Paul attempted to hand the map back before Evans left.

"Hold onto it," he insisted. "It might help with your deliberations."

Paul nodded his thanks and turned back to the group of survivors from Bridges. Once Evans was outside and as he was closing the door behind him, he could hear the conversation rising in volume.

"Are there jobs we can do once the sun goes down?" Ang asked as they headed away from the pair of houses. "Because the light's not going to last much longer."

He was right. The afternoon was drawing late, and there wasn't a lot of time left before the sun would disappear for the night. "We'll have to find out. Let's go see what your people have found to do."

Back on the main street, it didn't take long for Ang to find work helping some people set up their stalls. Evans could have helped, but he first wanted to see what the rest of the silent ones were up to. He was worried about them being exploited in some way, despite the fact that they had proven quite capable of taking care of themselves. Instead, he found Gerald.

"I want to come with you," the teenager said.

"You can't."

"Blue said that you found some other place that they can go. I want to go with the silent ones."

"You *can't*," Evans stated again.

"What happened at the container yard happened because I didn't have any friends. Blue's my friend. If I go with her, the same thing isn't going to happen. I don't *need* to live in a place like this. I don't have to be where-"

"Gerald," Evans caught him off guard with a sharp tone. "You can't come. I'm taking them to the container yard."

Gerald's jaw flexed and relaxed, flexed and relaxed. The container yard was the one place he couldn't argue about. He was banished from there, forever. It didn't matter that Blue was his friend. Nothing would convince the people who had kicked him out that he wouldn't end up just doing the same thing all over again. That he wouldn't put people in danger again.

"You have to take us somewhere else," Gerald finally said.

"No, I don't. I don't have to take *you* anywhere. The silent ones are going to the container yard, and you're staying here. End of discussion." Evans attempted to walk away.

"I'll just follow you," Gerald called after him.

With a sigh, Evans turned back around. "Really? You're going to make me tie you up before we leave?"

There was already a small distance between them, but Gerald increased it with a step backward. "You would have to catch me first to do that."

Gerald wasn't allowing himself to be bullied, so Evans switched to a softer tone. "The silent ones want to go to the container yard. They're the ones who made the decision. If you think you can change their minds, go ahead and talk to them. I don't recommend lying to them about anything though, because you know I'm going to ask them what you said. Hell, talk to Blue, ask her to stay here if you want her to. Maybe she's not as put off by the zombies as the rest of them."

Gerald's expression twisted and Evans got the impression that he had already asked her to stay with him. She must have shot him down for one reason or another. It was most likely because of the zombies.

"I'll take the silent ones wherever they want to go. It's up to them whether or not we go to the container yard." It was the only hope that Evans could give to Gerald, even though he knew the kid wouldn't be able to change their minds. They didn't know him well enough to be willing to travel farther just so that he could come. Once they learned that he had been exiled, they would want him around even less. If Blue loved him, maybe he stood a chance, but that seemed unlikely.

It didn't look like Gerald had anything else to say, so Evans moved on. He located all of the silent ones, and found them doing various jobs, mostly repair work after the storm. Evans helped out for a little bit in a tomato garden that had sustained damage to its plants. He helped upright and replant those that could be saved, and was paid with nearly ripened tomatoes whose plants had been too severely damaged. He didn't get many, as the work didn't last very long before the light left them.

Back in the visitors' centre, he dropped off his tomatoes with what the silent ones had gathered, and then went to talk to Frannie. He had hoped that maybe the people from Bridges had come by with an answer while he was gone.

"Sorry, haven't seen any of them today," Frannie told Evans when he asked.

Evans relayed what he had talked to them about, returning her paperweight in the process. The paperweights that the silent ones had been given were already neatly lined up on her desk.

"How soon were you thinking of leaving?" Frannie asked him.

"As soon as I think we have enough supplies. I'm hoping that we can be out by tomorrow afternoon, the next day at the latest."

"I'll see what I can do to get you what you need. I may want to send some emissaries with you to meet these people. Perhaps we can set up a trade route like we used to have with Bridges."

"They're farther away than Bridges."

"And everyone other than the silent ones are farther away than that. No reason not to make friends."

Evans nodded. Frannie asked him a few questions about what things had looked like outside, and then they parted. The silent ones had all returned by then and were making dinner. They prepared enough for both Evans and Gerald, while using a minimal amount of supplies. Gerald refused to be near or even look at Evans. He spent dinner sulking off by himself. If he had tried to convince the silent ones already, it looked like he had failed. Sometimes Evans pitied the kid. Living here would be good for him, though. He was bound to make another friend, someone who understood what it must have been like for him to grow up with a rotating set of protectors. Unlike the container yard, the people here hadn't been together since the beginning. There was a lot more variety when it came to their personal survival stories.

After eating, Evans changed into drier clothes and lay down on his bunk. He wanted to be as rested as possible for whatever tomorrow brought, and he didn't think he was going to sleep well. While this place would be good for Gerald, the kid clearly didn't see that yet, and Evans worried about him doing something stupid in the middle of the night. He kept both his sword and his knife within easy reach.

***

"Evans, wake up."

His eyes opened easily, the dream he was having about a tiger instantly melting away, so that only the stripes remained in his mind.

"Frannie? What time is it?"

"Sunrise. I have a job for you and whoever you consider the most able-bodied of the silent ones."

Evans sat up. "What kind of job?"

"You do it, and I'll make sure you get all the supplies you need."

"That's not very reassuring."

Frannie nodded. "The job can be dangerous, but I need two more people."

"To do what?"

"It's easier if I show you."

Evans looked around. Most of the silent ones were already up; only the oldest and the youngest were still sleeping on their bunks. Those awake watched Evans and Frannie with interest.

"Where's Gerald?" Evans wondered.

"I have him doing another task," Frannie told him. "Related, but different."

"All right, just give me a minute." Evans had to piss, and then wolf down some breakfast before he was ready to go. Dev volunteered to assist when Evans told the silent ones that Frannie had a potentially dangerous job for them to do. Frannie had left while Evans was getting ready, but he and Dev met up with her just outside the visitor centre. Still overcast, it had at least stopped raining.

"This way." Frannie led them toward the edge of town. They walked down the main street which looked very different now that the stalls were set up. Evans eyed the various wares, which people grew or made themselves, and then traded with other families and the occasional visitor. With Bridges gone, outsider sales had probably decreased dramatically.

Following Frannie, they left town, passing between a field for farm animals, and a field for zombies. Reaching the end of the fences, they then turned to continue following the border of the zombies' paddock. Evans had a sinking feeling.

Up ahead, a group of people were gathered alongside the fence, and it was pretty clear that that was where they were going. Frannie waved, and those waiting waved back.

"Mind handing me your sword and knife?" Frannie turned and asked before they reached the group. "You too, Dev. Hand over any weapons you're carrying."

"Why?" Evans questioned, although he handed her his sword. His knife took a little more work, as he had to free the sheath from his belt.

"Because I don't want you accidentally killing anyone."

Dev looked at Evans, his face lined with concern. Evans nodded to him, trying to appear confident that everything would be okay when he didn't feel

311

even remotely certain. Dev reluctantly withdrew a set of throwing knives from various places within his rags and handed them to Frannie.

"Thank you." Frannie carefully stored the knives with Evans' in a backpack she carried, and slung the sword over her shoulder.

"Thanks for helping," a man from the waiting group said as they reached them. "Here, take these."

Evans was handed a heavy SWAT shield, all black metal with a small window, and Dev was handed a lighter, mostly transparent riot shield with the word POLICE emblazoned across the middle of it. Next to where they had gathered, a section of the fence was flat on the ground, where the rain had washed away the dirt around the posts in a muddy stream.

"They haven't noticed us yet," the man who handed Evans the shield said with a nod toward the field. "But they will once we start working."

A woman waved a hammer to emphasize this.

"We don't think any escaped," Frannie told Evans. "We have teams out looking, however, just in case. Gerald's helping with that. We let them out of their indoor holding yesterday, not realizing how weakened this section of the fence was. It was standing during last night's checks. The indoor holding is still being cleaned while some vital repairs are being made to a few support posts, so we can't put them back in there while we do this."

"Which means we're supposed to stop them from getting to the people fixing the fence." Evans had been able to put it together, especially with all the other shield bearers standing around. Most of them had riot shields like Dev's, but a few of the larger individuals carried the heavy SWAT shields like Evans had been given.

"You got it." Frannie nodded.

"You two are with me. Come on." The man who had handed over the shields guided them and the other shield bearers over the downed fence.

"I'm beginning to regret volunteering," Dev whispered to Evans.

"You're going to regret it even more when the zombies come at us and you remember that you're unarmed and not allowed to kill any of them."

Dev's face paled as the man directed them into position, creating an arc that covered the opening.

"Just think of the supplies we're going to get," Evans advised Dev. "We're going to get enough that we can leave for the container yard this afternoon."

Dev nodded, not picking up on the fact that Evans was talking mostly to buck himself up as opposed to his compatriot. He couldn't stop thinking about the battle with the comet horde, only this time he had no sword, only a shield.

The man instructed them how to stand, with the shields overlapping. "It's not hard," he specifically told Evans and Dev who had never done this before. The others acted like they had. "They're slow and weak, so it doesn't take much to hold them back. And remember that their hands are tied to their waists, so they can't reach for you. Just hold your ground and you'll be fine."

"What if one falls over?" Evans asked. "Are they any good at crawling?"

"That's rarely ever happened, but if it does, just shout and I'll come over and handle it."

"What's your name?" Dev asked.

"Wells."

After Wells had gone to double check that everyone was in position, Evans glanced over and could see Dev's lips moving, although he wasn't making a sound. At first he mistook it for a prayer, but then noticed that Dev was repeating just one word: Wells' name. Evans didn't think either of them would have trouble remembering his name if they should need him, but let Dev do what he needed to do.

Behind them, the fence repairs began. Evans twisted his head around a few times, watching their progress. The first thing they did was remove what had fallen over. This required separating it from what still stood, which wasn't a silent process. The first zombie was drawn over, and began bumping into the shields off to Evans' right. He was able to see snippets of the workers shoring up the mud with rocks, and driving the posts back into the ground before a zombie came for him.

The dried out corpse crashed into his shield, tripping itself as it tried to bite him. The thing's jaws snapped above the barrier, which Evans had to hold sideways in order to properly overlap with his neighbours. Wells had been right that the things couldn't push against the shields with much force, but this provided little comfort. Evans didn't know how these people could stand to be near such rotting husks, even if they once belonged to loved ones. He had to resist pushing the corpse over and stomping repeatedly on its head. That urge died down as more and more zombies found their way over, drawn by the groaning and the snapping of the first arrivals. Usually the things hung around near town, where they sometimes saw people, but one by one, they were crossing the field. Once there was a layer of them, Evans no longer wanted to move his shield in any way, afraid of compromising the barrier.

"Real nice place you brought us to," Dev commented beside him.

"Certainly has some interesting sights," Evans tried to joke back, but he didn't feel very jovial. He had to watch the zombies in case they surged at one point more than the others, or in case they fell down. He was constantly afraid of his grip slipping, of the shield dropping low enough for teeth to reach him. The shield was heavy and Evans found himself sweating. It was a cold sweat, drawn out more by fear than exertion at that point, but the longer this took, the weaker his arms were going to become. The gash on his left forearm, which was now a scar, began to itch as though it knew further injuries were coming.

"Fence is fixed!" came Frannie's call from somewhere behind him. It couldn't have come too soon.

"What do we do now, Wells?" Evans raised his voice over the moaning. "Climb over the fence?" It was only chest high, so Evans thought it shouldn't be too difficult to hop over.

"Too dangerous for the last few men who won't have anyone to protect their asses. We're going to walk to the nearest gate."

"Did he say walk?" Dev asked Evans, his eyebrows crawling up his forehead.

"He said walk."

Wells commanded everyone from his position at the centre of the arch. The first thing they did was pull in closer so that they were all shoulder to shoulder, which allowed Evans and everyone else to turn their shields the right way up. While his legs were still exposed, Evans could now keep the zombie's teeth from snapping over the top, and instead had them pressed against the little window. Once the group was as tight as it could get, and all the shields were locked together, they started to move. Wells bellowed like the slave master on a ship, smacking his hand on a garbage can lid to keep time in place of a drum. The huddle moved as one, pushing its way along the fence. Evans, being near the top of the arch, had to step sideways on the beat. He thought it was a good position, because he didn't need to walk backwards and risk tripping and falling over, or push his way into the zombies which carried the risk of knocking *them* over. Wells had probably stuck him and Dev where he had for that very reason.

They inched along the fence one small step at a time. Evans could hear Frannie and the rest of the fence repair crew making a lot of noise down in the opposite direction they were headed, luring away what zombies they could. Evans didn't dare look around, but if he had to guess, most of the dead continued to follow the shields. Movement tended to lure them as much as sound did.

The gate wasn't terribly far—there was one at the nearest corner—but it still took several minutes to reach it. Evans' left arm had developed a slight tremble from carrying the heavy shield for so long, and he understood why Frannie wanted the most able-bodied of the silent ones.

At the corner, they cleared the zombies away and turned their half circle arch, into a quarter circle. Wells opened the gate and instructed everyone in what to do. One by one, people were pulled from the arch, their neighbours quickly sliding together to close the gap. Dev got to go before Evans. When it was Evans' turn, he dropped back like he had been told, getting out of the way as fast as he could so that his neighbours had ample room to close in. He didn't need much encouragement to move quickly. Once outside the gate, he dropped the heavy shield on the ground with a *splop* of mud. He hung around and waited until everyone made it out of the corral, the last man slipping through the gate and dragging it shut behind him. The zombies all piled up along the fence, snapping their teeth.

"How you doing?" Frannie asked Evans and Dev once she walked over.

"I could use some water," Dev admitted.

"Me too." Frannie was grinning. "Why don't we go get something to drink, and then we'll gather up those supplies you need for your journey? Sound good?"

Evans nodded, too tired and shaken to reply in any other way.

Frannie took them back to the main street, stopping only once at a rain barrel so they could refresh themselves. She stuck with them the whole time they walked as Evans explained what he thought they would need, and then she made sure that he got it from various traders. Everyone at Paddock knew who Frannie was, and only a few tried to argue when she asked them to hand something over.

"I'm sending an emissary team with you," Frannie told him. "Just three people, so it shouldn't be much of an extra burden on you."

"Do you think three is enough for them to get back here safely?"

"Should be. They're all experienced travellers, and the world's not as dangerous as it was a couple of years ago. We all know how to handle both the infected and road bandits these days. You could have made it here by yourself."

Evans remembered the barn with the rattlesnakes and knew that that wasn't the case.

Paul found them while they were still picking out supplies.

"Hey Paul," Frannie greeted him. "Have you guys made up your mind?"

"Some of us are going," Paul told her and Evans. "The rest want to go, but they want to hear that the place is safe first. Would that be all right?"

"I don't mind. That okay with you, Evans?"

"They'll have to find the way on their own," Evans warned Paul.

"They believe they can do it."

"I take it you're coming with me?"

"If you'll have me and the others," Paul nodded. "When were you thinking of leaving?"

"I was hoping within a few hours."

"Oh."

"Why? What's up?"

"Can you wait until tomorrow morning? It'll give us all time to make sure we're properly packed up, and for people to say goodbye. Some might even change their minds about travelling with you."

Evans didn't need to mull it over. "Sure, we can wait." It would give him more time to make sure they were well supplied and packed up, and he did prefer leaving places in the morning, so that they would have the most light. Besides, after that shield job he was feeling pretty tired.

"Great, I'll let the others know." Paul ran off.

"So you're going back to the place you came from, huh?" Frannie commented. "This must be some kind of record for you, shortest time between visits to one place."

Evans shrugged. "Might be." He was almost positive it would be.

"I know you don't like it here, so I don't expect you to visit much, but maybe you could try sending a letter sometime?"

Evans laughed. "Not sure the postal service is running."

"Not in the traditional sense, but we've had visitors carrying letters before. A lot more make it to their destinations than you'd think. I have a pretty good correspondence going on with the leaders of a few other communities."

"Yeah?"

"It's good to keep in touch."

"Maybe I'll write a letter then." Evans doubted he would. He wasn't the letter writing sort.

"So, back to supplying your trip. Do those camels need anything?"

Evans redirected the question to Dev, who had been following quietly a few steps behind. During Dev's reply, Evans mentally composed his goodbye to Winnie, who would be upset if he just disappeared on her. He hated goodbyes. He also wondered what the hell he was going to tell Gerald. The kid wasn't exactly the most stable individual. Evans thought through various places where he could tie him up for a few hours to prevent him from following the party. But as Gerald had said, Evans would have to catch him first.

30: DAKOTA
11 DAYS AFTER THE BOMBING

Three nights had passed on the submarine. Dakota had gotten used to the sounds it made, as well as the motions. She still turned green every time they surfaced, but she was proud of herself for never having thrown up. Bronislav thought she was just being foolishly stubborn.

By the time they rose to the surface that morning, Dakota could follow along with Bronislav's orders, knowing which ones were directed at whom. It would take a lot more lessons for her to learn *why* certain orders were given, but the captain had promised that he would continue her training after they went home. He was going to set aside at least one day a week to give her personal lessons, and perhaps more once everything was settled.

Before they even reached the surface, Dakota knew they would finally be heading home. She could feel that the water, although still rough, was calmer than it had been, and Bronislav's orders were different from the other times they had surfaced. No one turned green, and the engines began pushing them home.

A hollow bong echoed through the sub.

"What was that?" Dakota wondered.

"We hit something. There's a lot of debris in the water." Bronislav ordered the hatch opened and some men to go out on deck. They were given poles to push what debris they could out of the way, and shouted when there was something they would have to go around. The engines were slowed so that they wouldn't strike anything too hard.

Dakota listened carefully to the shouts coming down from the men above, especially when they identified some of the debris. She feared that they would come across a shipping container, but it seemed to be pieces of old boats, houses, and trees that kept scraping along their sides. These were all things that could be smashed and broken, unlike the containers.

Bronislav took a look for himself a few times, peering through the periscope.

"What's it look like?" Dakota asked.

"The water level is still high," he informed her. "It doesn't help that the tide is in. I can see empty spaces where a few houses once stood, and those still standing have been heavily damaged."

"Can you see home?"

"Not yet. I'll let you know when I do." He didn't watch the whole time, but checked periodically. Dakota wanted to take a peek herself, but she wasn't going to without Bronislav's permission.

It took a lot longer getting home than it did going out to sea. Dakota kept bouncing on the balls of her feet. She was eager to get back on land, and to see Cameron. She missed Brunt, and Hope, and a bunch of others. While she hadn't gotten claustrophobic like a few of the other shadows had, she was looking forward to the open air and having the sky above her. Even just having the hatch open was nice.

"I can see Animal Island," Bronislav reported.

"And?"

"Look for yourself."

Dakota quickly took his place at the periscope. It took her a few seconds to register what she was looking at. Animal Island was tiny. When Bronislav had reported high water levels, she hadn't expected this.

"The shack's gone," she noted.

"I'm surprised it hadn't washed away before this."

"The chicken coops and fences and things are all gone too."

"We can rebuild it all, and better this time." Bronislav placed his hand on her shoulder, and Dakota knew to step back to her out-of-the-way corner.

"We're seeing pieces of Bitch Bridge!" someone from up above shouted down the hatch. "Should we try to grab them?"

Bronislav ordered them not to risk their safety for them. They could gather the pieces later, when they were actually ready to repair the bridge.

"How much stuff do you think we'll need to fix?" Dakota asked.

Bronislav didn't answer.

Dakota scratched absently at her arms. If they could see Animal Island, surely they could see the container yard by now? Dakota knew that, based on the direction Bronislav was pointing the periscope, he was looking right at it. His silence made her dig her fingernails into her elbows.

"Take a look," he finally said, his expression betraying nothing as he stepped away.

Dakota nearly banged her face into the periscope in her hurry to look through it. For a second her heart sank, as she thought she was looking at floating containers, but then it leapt back up when she realized the effect was caused by the water level being high enough to cover the rocky shore. The waves splashed up across the pavement and puddles were everywhere, but the containers were where they were supposed to be, at least the ones she could see. Even better, people were walking among them, with a few watching the submarine go past.

"They're okay!" Dakota couldn't stop herself from shouting.

She wanted to wave, but was able to resist, knowing that she couldn't be seen. Instead she turned to Bronislav with a big smile on her face. Other people on the bridge were now grinning, but Bronislav's face remained still.

"What's wrong?" Dakota glanced through the periscope again, but when she saw nothing different, she turned back to Bronislav.

"We know that *some* people are okay. Not everyone," Bronislav answered her, dampening the mood. "While it's a good sign to see that the storm was survivable, we have no idea what the conditions are like. That row of containers hasn't moved, but we can't see the ones beyond it. We don't know if our remaining supplies have survived. Living through the storm is one thing. Continuing to live after it is another."

Dakota absorbed this, turning the words over in her mind. She was no longer ecstatic, but she found she was still very happy. They could have come home to a lot worse.

The U-shaped dock was underwater, but they found they could tie up alongside the cement wall beyond it just fine. Some men would have to stay on board, ready to move the submarine as the water level dropped, but most were ready to get off and find out what the damage was. When Dakota climbed to the top of the conning tower and out of the hatch, she noticed one thing that was missing right away: they had parked where the toilets once stood. Some of the submariners helped her cross from the submarine to solid ground, where she continued to feel the rolling waves beneath her. She had felt this effect before, after spending years on the Diana. She had sea legs.

"Dakota!" Cameron was running toward her, a bright smile on her face.

"Cameron!" Dakota would have run to meet her had the woman not closed the distance so fast. She was swept up in a hug so hard that it knocked the hat off her head. "How are you? Are you okay? What was it like in the submarine?"

"I'm good, I'm okay. And the submarine was fine. I got queasy a few times when we rose to check out how rough the water was at the surface, but other than that, it was mostly just smelly."

Cameron let go to look her over and then gave her another hug. Dakota hugged her back, feeling overwhelmed and grateful to have found someone who cared that much for her. On the Diana, her caretaker never would have been so concerned. She barely would have given Dakota a second thought.

"Here's your hat, kiddo."

Dakota was released and turned to find that Brunt had picked up her hat for her. He gave her a brief, one-armed hug, and then plunked her hat down on her head.

"How are you guys? How's everything here? I noticed we lost our toilets."

"And Bitch Bridge, but you probably saw that too," Cameron said. "Everything else is still standing. The empty containers we hadn't finished modifying got moved around, but none got pulled out into deep water. We're still checking inside people's homes. Just about all of them leaked, so there's a lot of water damage to deal with."

"Did anyone die?" Dakota knew that if she didn't ask directly, she wouldn't be given an answer.

"A few," Brunt told her when Cameron kept her lips pursed. "Most of us retreated to the upper containers on the wall, but some stayed below."

"How did they die?"

"You don't need to know," Cameron insisted.

There was a brief stare down between her and Dakota, but Brunt broke the silence.

"A few drowned in their containers," he explained, much to Cameron's obvious annoyance. "From what I've seen and heard, it was mostly elderly people who didn't have anything to climb up on. The others we assume also drowned but can't be sure. They haven't turned up."

"Washed away, I guess." Dakota wondered if any of them were people she knew. If any were kids, then it was likely. "Any zombies?"

"We have to be really careful opening the containers." This time it was Cameron speaking up. "Those who died inside them have already turned. Luckily, no zombies were washed in here, or at least none were left behind when the water receded."

"Well, I'm ready to help. What can I do?" Dakota offered.

"There may be no zombies, but there's still a lot of debris lying around. The kids are gathering it up if you want to help them."

"On it. You two get back to what you were doing." Before Dakota could run off, Cameron gave her another hug.

"I'm just glad you're all right," she told her.

"I'm glad you're okay too," Dakota said back. "But we really should be helping."

"Of course. Go on."

Dakota ran off toward a bramble of branches piled up along the base of the wall. There were scraps of mostly unidentifiable detritus everywhere. Soggy, mushy paper was plastered against the sides of the containers, shreds of plastic bags gathered in the corners, and leaves and mud turned the pavement into a splotchy carpet. All of it would have to be picked up and moved somewhere else. Dakota wondered if any of it was hiding a rat, and was glad when she saw Robin's cat, Splatter, sitting halfway down a row, cleaning his paws. Animals wandered everywhere; they had been moved from Animal Island. Pigs rooted about in the litter, while cows stood in a clump, looking dull and bored. There were no chickens anywhere, so Dakota guessed that they had been corralled into one location, kept safe from Splatter and the other cats who might be tempted to have a go at them. While a few dogs trotted about here and there, sniffing at everything, Dakota didn't see any of Misha's. She wondered where the away teams had hidden from the storm.

Approaching the heap of dead and dying wood, Dakota started by breaking off the small branches that she could snap with her hands. By scraping her boots along the pavement, she made a relatively clear spot in the mud and leaves and piled the broken sticks there. They would make good kindling once dried out, and after the huge pile of bodies they had had to burn, they needed to refill their fuel stores. Without gloves, Dakota's hands eventually began to hurt, and she was going to need an axe or something once she got to breaking down the larger branches. She paused in her task to go look for what she needed.

Heading toward her home container, Dakota distracted herself from thinking about the fact that it had likely flooded by studying the debris and the people cleaning it up. A bunch of kids had a wheelbarrow and were scooping up the muck by hand and dumping it in. Dakota stopped momentarily to check that they were all wearing gloves, and moved on when she saw that they were. With the bits of housing mixed in, there were bound to be nails and screws and glass about, not to mention insulation. Dakota didn't have any experience with insulation herself, but Brunt had told her never to touch anything that looked like it with her bare skin. There was definitely some insulation mixed into the crap.

When Dakota spotted a stop sign with the post still attached, she picked it up and peeled the leaves off the metal bar. The very bottom of it had bent and twisted to the point of breaking off. Placing the flat edge of the top of the sign against the ground, Dakota pushed it ahead of her like a snow shovel, clearing the slop ahead of her as she walked. It didn't work great, because a lot of leaves and a thin, watery layer of mud often remained, but it pushed the larger stuff out of the way, creating an easier walking path. Might be good for messengers to have a path to run down. Maybe she should tell someone to work on that, or abandon the branches and start doing it herself.

Dakota's container had been checked already, as evidenced by the doors standing wide open. All the containers in the area had their doors open, because it was the best way to let everyone know that they had been cleared. After putting down her stop sign, Dakota stepped inside. The floor was a puddle and everything lower than the bottom bunk was drenched, including the ends of her blankets that hung over the side. She had expected worse and was happy to find that her mattress remained dry. The place smelled of damp metal. Luckily, Dakota's gloves were stored on a shelf above the water line. She put them on, trying not to look around at the damage. They needed to clean up space outside before they could start drying anything out in the sun; the sun that was still hiding behind clouds and not being very helpful.

"Hey, you're back."

Dakota was startled as she stepped back outside. "Elijah! You're okay." She immediately felt stupid for feeling so happy to see him.

"Not for the storm's lack of trying," he joked. "How was it on the submarine? I heard you were on it."

"Cramped, and smelly, and constantly moving. Not too bad. How was it here?"

"Same, minus the movement. I was in one of those containers up on the wall with something like twenty other people and a pile of tires."

"I like the smell of tires." Dakota mentally slapped herself. *I like the smell of tires?* She wanted to go back inside and crawl under the blankets.

"What are you up to right now?" Elijah asked, ignoring her tire comment, for better or worse.

"I was breaking up some branches, but needed to grab some gloves. I gotta go find a hatchet or a saw or something as well."

"I know someone with a hatchet who's not using it. I can ask him to let you borrow it if you want."

"You're not too busy?"

"Naw, I just finished helping to push a container back in place."

"One of the empty containers?"

"No, one of these," he gestured to the homes around them. "None came out of line, but the line didn't stay completely straight."

Dakota looked at the homes but it was hard to see if they were lined up when all the doors were opened to differing degrees. She thought of the big chains attached to the rebar at the ends of the rows, and was awed that the water had still moved them.

"Where are those branches you were breaking down?" Elijah asked. "I'll bring the hatchet to you once I find the man who has it."

"Over there, against the wall," Dakota pointed in the direction. She was a little bummed that she wouldn't be going with Elijah to get the hatchet, but that would be a waste of time when she could be doing her job. Bronislav had trusted her to shadow him on the submarine, and she couldn't let him down by slacking off now.

"Great, I should find you in a few minutes."

"See you then."

As soon as Elijah was headed off in the opposite direction, Dakota rolled her eyes at herself. Every encounter with Elijah always left her feeling like a silly, stupid girl. She wondered who she could talk to about it. Not Cameron, for sure. And Hope wouldn't know anything. She needed someone older, with experience. Maybe Robin? She didn't know Robin all that well, but Dakota knew that she and Jon had dated on and off a bunch of times when they lived on the Diana. Maybe she would have some good advice.

The stop sign scraped along the ground as Dakota walked and thought. When she reached the branches, she set to work breaking them apart once more. It was easier with her gloves on. Just as she was getting to the point where she could no longer use just her hands, feet, and knees, and was thinking that Elijah had forgotten about her, he showed up with the hatchet.

"Sorry, I got shanghaied into helping move an aluminium boat to the water. Still floats."

Dakota said it was fine, and then, with a fluttering in her stomach, accepted his follow up offer to help. They didn't talk much while they worked. Dakota held the branches still and Elijah swung the hatchet at them.

"Some of these will definitely need a saw, or at least a bigger axe," Elijah commented, and Dakota agreed.

"Do you want to get some lunch?" Dakota asked after they had worked themselves into a sweat. She had no idea what time it was, but was feeling hungry.

"That sounds like a great idea. Maybe afterward we can find that saw."

Dakota liked that he had said *we*.

In the community centre, the walls dripped with moisture, but someone had gone around and righted everything, as well as dried off all the seats. Watery but hot stew was being served and Dakota took as much as she was allowed. The table where she sat had some puddles here and there along its surface, but she didn't mind. Her gloves and sleeves were already damp from working with the wet wood.

"Did they move the medical beds to the upper containers?" Dakota asked Elijah when she noted their absence.

"Yeah, I think so. I wasn't really involved with that."

If asked, Dakota would have sworn that Elijah was embarrassed by that fact. She didn't think anything embarrassed him; she thought she owned that entire domain when it came to their interactions.

"Dakota!"

She suddenly found herself sitting up much straighter at the sound of Bronislav's voice.

"Yes, sir?" she turned in her seat to face him as he strode over.

"I have a job for you," he told her, then looked over at Elijah. "What's your name again?"

"Elijah, sir."

"Elijah, you can help too."

"What's the job?" Dakota asked.

"I'm sending the kids who have been trained over the wall. I want the debris between the containers cleared away so that our people can reach us when they get home. Once that's done, I'll likely have you start checking the contents of the containers that are accessible. You don't need to empty them out, just record what kind of items they hold, and immediately report on any food that might still be even remotely edible."

"That sounds like a job that's going to take more than just the afternoon," Dakota noted.

"Then you'll take several days to do it. Go report to the wall. I've already sent a number of candidates to gather there."

Dakota lifted the bowl to her lips and slurped down the remaining dregs of her stew. She had thought she was going to have to train a lot longer before being given a task on the other side of the wall. But in emergency situations things changed, and this was an emergency. Still, it worried her. Bronislav must be really concerned about the food situation. As she returned her bowl to the wash-up pile, she realized that maybe the stew wasn't watery because it had been poorly made and in a hurry as she first assumed. Bronislav would never admit to her, a fifteen-year-old, just how badly off they really were, but she could see the signs for herself once she looked.

Moving back toward the wall, Dakota walked faster. She was suddenly so worried for the container yard, for herself even, that she didn't even think about the fact that Elijah was walking with her.

***

A single ladder was lowered on the far side of the wall. If they needed to retreat, they would have to climb single file. Not a comforting thought. At least Freya was watching over them from the wall. There was no one else on guard duty, no one but her, while the crisis was being dealt with. As Dakota crossed the empty patch toward the container maze, she looked back over her shoulder. Freya stood silhouetted against the grey sky, standing on top of the second row of containers so that she could see farther. In her hand was a golf club, which she could bang against a container like a warning bell if she spotted danger. Everyone was on alert for that sound.

There were seven of them heading out into the containers, and at eighteen, Elijah was the oldest of them. Three of the teenagers Dakota had learned to sling with were part of the group, and the last two were a sixteen and seventeen-year-old who Dakota knew only in passing. She had been given a rough map of the container maze and led the way alongside Elijah. Behind them, the others surrounded a plastic wagon full of the gear they might need: axes, saws, shovels, and rope. Later, they would bring cans of spray paint to label the containers they had checked as well as a ladder to reach the higher ones, but Dakota didn't think they would get to that before nightfall, no matter how much she wished they would.

They moved slowly between the containers, worried about running into a stray zombie, or even a small herd that may have washed up. Then they started using the square-headed shovels to scoop debris out of the way.

"I don't know why we have to do this," Maui complained about shovelling. "People can just walk over it."

"Because some of them have carts," Dakota told him. "We need to make sure that the carts can get through when they get home, especially because they're the ones most likely to have food with them." She was being a little more snappy than she meant to be, but that was the fear coming out of her. She was both afraid about the food situation and of what they might come across outside. Those people who had washed away? No one had yet looked for them beyond the wall. They might easily come across the corpse of a friend, or worse, the zombie version of them.

They slowly worked their way through the maze, scraping a path through the mush, hauling away the larger items, and cutting through branches. The route Dakota originally chose for them to follow had to be scrapped when they found that a container on the second level—presumably an empty one—had fallen at a crooked angle, blocking the way through. Everyone took turns being the lookout, both at the rear of the group and at the front, while the other five worked. Dakota assumed that the others felt the same way she did whenever she got to be a lookout: relief. While more stressful in terms of responsibility, it was a much easier job to do physically. Sometimes one of them would grumble about the work, but no one gave up. They all understood the trust that had been conferred upon their shoulders, that they were being given a chance to prove themselves, especially the fifteen-year-olds.

As they neared the end of the day and the end of the maze, Josephine ordered them to stop with a terse whisper.

"I think I hear something coming," she told everyone.

They quickly gathered in a group behind Elijah, the only one of them carrying a rifle. Dakota put a stone in her sling, glad that Freya had made them take a few of the potential projectiles. She may not have great aim when it came to slinging, but it could also be used like a bludgeon if anything came close.

Muscles tense, they listened to the mush of feet travelling over debris that hadn't yet been cleared and the scrape of pavement underneath. Dakota's mouth was dry. She had killed her first zombie only a few days ago, and that was in a safe, relatively controlled environment. Nor was it someone she knew, which this could very well be. Her hand tightened around the sling.

A dog walked around the corner ahead.

"Barrel!" Dakota practically cried with relief. It was one of Misha's dogs. His stubby little tail wagged as he trotted over to Dakota. Right behind him came Crichton, Harry, and Angela with Spring. The terrier dog saw Barrel getting affection and ran over to receive the same.

"What are you kids doing out here?" Crichton asked as he and the others approached.

"We're clearing a path for you and everyone else who returns, sir," Dakota told him, standing upright as the dogs went to receive pats and scratches from the other teenagers.

"Who told you to do that?"

"Bronislav."

"Aren't you too young to be outside the wall?"

"He's been training us since you left."

Crichton's expression didn't change, but Dakota was certain he was going to have some words with Bronislav about this.

Dakota grew concerned when she didn't see more people and dogs round the corner. "Where's Misha?"

"And Ki-Nam," Elijah added.

"After the storm, we ran into a large pack of zombies," Crichton spoke more to Elijah than to Dakota. "Misha took off with the cart, as I ordered. The rest of us escaped, but we somehow got separated from Ki-Nam."

"I'm sorry," Harry added, placing a hand on Elijah's shoulder.

"He's dead?" Elijah frowned, trying to process.

"We can't say for certain, but it didn't look good."

"But you didn't see it. It's possible he's alive," Elijah insisted.

"It is possible, yes," Harry reluctantly agreed.

"But then where's Misha? And his other dogs? You have Spring and Barrel with you, but what about the others?" Dakota demanded to know.

"There was no time to set up a meeting point," Crichton told her. "He has to find his own way back. His dogs ran off to follow him, although I can't say whether they found him or not. These two came and found us eventually. What about here? Were there many casualties? Do you know?"

"Not many," Elijah informed him. "Bronislav and Boyle would know."

"Boyle's already back? Well, why don't you accompany us back home?" Crichton recommended.

"No, sir," Dakota immediately refused. "We were given a job to clear the route, and I intend to finish. When Misha returns with the cart, we want it to be easy for him to get to the wall. Besides, some of the pathways are completely blocked, and seeing a cleaned up area will let everyone know which way to go."

"All right, finish your work then." Crichton nodded to all of them, and proceeded to use their path. The dogs were quick to follow after him, as was Angela. Harry lingered for a minute.

"Can you tell me if Elizabeth and Adam are all right?" he asked Dakota about his wife and adopted son.

"I haven't seen them, but no one told me that they weren't okay," she responded. "I think Cameron would have mentioned it if something had happened."

"Thank you." He then followed the other adults.

"Who are Elizabeth and Adam, and why would you have been told if something had happened?" Elijah asked as they set back to work.

"Adam's a friend of mine. Sort of. He's kind of a booger, but he's a friend of my friend. Elizabeth is his mom."

"Okay," Elijah nodded.

"Hey, I'm sure your friend Ki-Nam is okay," Dakota told him. "He probably found Misha and is helping to bring the cart back."

"That's a nice thought." But clearly Elijah wasn't certain he could believe it.

Dakota left him alone, wondering if he thought she was naïve for hoping for the best. She told herself that Misha was fine, that most of his other dogs would have come back if something had happened to him. This was their home after all. And like Harry said, no one had actually seen what happened to Ki-Nam; who's to say he didn't escape? He could literally show up at any moment, having fallen only a couple of minutes behind the others.

Dakota and her crew continued to clear away the debris. They were almost done. The end of the maze was in sight down the corridor on which they were working.

"I'm going to go roll this tire out there," Dakota informed the others, gesturing to the end of the maze with her head.

"Be careful," Mike warned her.

"I'll keep an eye out, don't worry." She rolled the tire down the way, and looked all around her as she reached the end. No zombies and no people were anywhere in sight. She did notice some footprints in some mud not far away, though. Maybe they belonged to Crichton? He might have gone to check a different route into the maze only to discover that it was blocked, or maybe Ki-Nam had returned and gone that way. Dakota walked over to the opening, wondering if another container could have fallen over. As she neared the entrance, the little hairs on the back of her neck stood up. She couldn't say why, but she suddenly knew that these footprints didn't belong to anyone she knew. She stopped just before the corner and thought about it. If it had been Crichton, or Harry, or Angela, why weren't there footprints coming back out? And if Ki-Nam had been that close behind them, he would have seen the others and called out at some point.

Dakota turned, intending to go back for help. It was then that a pair of arms whipped around the corner, one clamping across Dakota's face, the other around her chest. She had no time to scream before her mouth was covered, and she was yanked backward so quickly that her hat flew off her head. Her nostrils flared as she breathed rapidly through her nose, filling her lungs with a rotten scent. She imagined a zombie about to chop down on the back of her head, but instead the point of a knife pricked the underside of her chin.

"Don't go squirming now," foul breath accompanied the whisper in her ear. "Wouldn't want to cut that pretty skin of yours."

Dakota stayed perfectly still, petrified. No one knew she was over here. No one had taught her what to do if grabbed from behind and held at knifepoint. Her jaw hurt from the pressure of the hand clamped around it. The back of her head was being pressed into the man's upper chest.

"Dakota?" Elijah called out, looking for her.

Dakota wanted to scream, to tell him to go get help, but she couldn't move. The man shifted around, holding her like a shield, keeping her body between him and the end of the row of containers in case Elijah showed up. And Elijah did, drawn by her hat, which sat on the ground.

"Put her down," Elijah commanded, raising his rifle.

The man took a step back between the containers instead, dragging Dakota after him.

"I said, put her down!"

Another step back.

Dakota's eyes widened. A zombie was coming up behind Elijah, moving silently as all his focus lay on her. She couldn't make a sound, she was barely taking in enough air to breathe. She couldn't warn him.

Elijah spun at the last moment, maybe sensing something, or maybe understanding that there was a reason why Dakota was looking past him. But the zombie wasn't a zombie. Instead of opening its jaws and lunging, it raised a rifle of its own and bashed the butt of it into Elijah's head. His legs gave out and he collapsed into a heap.

"Two for the price of one," the man whispered in her ear. "What do you think? Can we get the other five? Let's find out."

V: WIND AND WATER

Shannon ran down the path, even though her mom hated it when she did that. Her mom always imagined Shannon slipping one day and tumbling off the cliff. It had happened to others, but not for a very long time. Ever since, they had made a rule that restricted all drug and alcohol use to a single cave, which they then weren't allowed to leave until they were sober, the number of falls had dramatically decreased. Besides, Shannon wasn't afraid of falling. The river was deep here, and she was certain she could swim to one of the shore points before reaching the rapids. People could survive the fall, and this was the kind of situation that required running.

"There are people," she panted as she reached the central cave, which was more like a large divot taken out of the cliffside. "There are people coming."

"Coming *here*?" Horace shot to his feet.

"They're following the unseen path."

"Who is it?" Chuck asked.

"I don't know. I didn't recognize any of them."

"Then how can they be following the unseen path?" Horace frowned.

"That's what makes it so exciting!" Shannon loved it when visitors came, especially when they brought new people. But new people on their own? That was unheard of.

"Did they see you?" Chuck wondered.

"No, I spotted them well in advance from the stone tree. They haven't yet come out of the hills."

"We should go meet them," Horace decided. "Better to greet them in the field than down here."

"I want to come," Shannon immediately volunteered.

"No, you wait here and tell the others when they return from fishing."

"But I saw them first," Shannon pouted.

"And you have chores you've been avoiding all morning. Don't think your mother didn't tell me."

Shannon groaned but knew she couldn't fight this one. She helped Horace to his feet and watched as he and Chuck went up the path. As soon as they disappeared over the lip, she darted through a tunnel that took her down lower on the cliffs. She popped out of the dark again near the bridge.

"I need to cross," she told Verne, who was currently working this side.

"Your mom was looking for you," he told her as he lowered his half of the wood and rope bridge. On the far side, Paris spotted the movement and began to lower the other half.

Shannon rolled her eyes. "I know. I was at the stone tree, watching for herds. Saw people instead."

"People?"

"Yeah, three of them, following the unseen path. All strangers." Before Verne could ask any more, Shannon zipped across the bridge. She used to be scared of the way it bounced in the middle where the two pieces met, but after years of crossing it nearly every day, she now trusted it.

On the far side, she threw Paris a quick hello and ran off into the warren of tunnels and cliffside paths that would bring her to her home. She and her mom lived in a bubble-shaped scoop that had a tiny hole down low, forming a little window to the outside. Mom said that a long time ago, water had created their bubble, swirling around and around until the window was formed, and the water could escape. Shannon didn't know if that was right, but she believed her mom. She had seen what water could do to rocks. Wind too, which had helped carve the paths and caves so many years ago that it was hard to comprehend.

Shannon got to work on her chores right away. She swept the curved floor, so that all the dust and sand gathered at the bottom of the bowl shape. There she left it; they were letting the sand slowly form a flat spot for them. Next, she peeled off the duvet covers, sheets, and pillowcases so that they could be washed. She ran with them through the warren until she emerged at the nearest shore point. News was already spreading about new people coming. Shannon picked her way across the rocks, finding an empty spot among the washers. Farther up the river, she could see the fishing platforms making their slow way back, drifting from catch point to catch point along the sheer walls. Rocky paddled back and forth between them in a kayak, making sure no one missed a point. The fishing platforms would never survive the rapids and weren't easy to manoeuvre. They had lost a couple when the current had caught them. While Shannon hurriedly scrubbed at the bedclothes, she watched Rocky working his powerful arms. They were going to get married some day, Shannon was certain of it. She just had to wait until she was eighteen.

Deciding that the sheets were clean enough after only about half the time she should have spent on them, Shannon hauled the sodden mass around. She brought them to a path that received a decent amount of light during the day and draped them over the wooden rails that had been built specifically for laundry. When Shannon ran back to the bridge, her shirt was damp but she didn't care.

"I want to cross," she told Paris.

"You and all these other people," Paris told her, gesturing to the crowd Shannon had pushed past. "Everyone has to wait."

Looking up and across the gorge, Shannon could tell that there was a gathering in the central cave. The new people had said something to Horace and Chuck that had convinced them to bring them here. Who were they? Shannon was desperate to know, but until they were certain the newcomers could be trusted, the home warren on this side of the river was to be cut off. Dropping her eyes, Shannon watched the fishing platforms coming in and got an idea. She pushed her way back through the people waiting for the bridge to be lowered, and then ran down to a shore point.

"Rocky! Rocky, don't get out yet!" she called to him.

Curious as to why he was being yelled at, Rocky paddled over to Shannon. "What's going on?"

"New people, up in the central cave. They won't lower the bridge. Can you take me across?"

Rocky knew how much she enjoyed meeting new people. "All right, hop in."

Shannon giggled as she awkwardly climbed onto his lap. He sighed and rolled his eyes, but was smiling too. He was also waiting for her to turn eighteen. They had one more year to go. Shannon knew she was lucky to find someone willing to wait until she was old enough for courting. Rocky was already twenty, and plenty of single young women had made passes at him. Single young men too: Rocky was the kind of guy that appealed to just about everyone.

"We might get in trouble for this," Rocky told her as he pushed them across the river, fighting against the current that wanted to sweep them into the rapids with its hungry jagged rocks.

"I need to cross the river and they wouldn't lower the bridge. Just tell people it was an emergency."

"Yeah? The emergency of you wanting to meet the new people?"

"You know, I saw them first. I was out in the stone tree looking for herds. The only reason I didn't get to go out to meet them was because I had to do my chores."

"Should have done those first thing in the morning."

"But then I wouldn't have seen them following the unseen path."

"They were following the path?" Rocky wondered as they bumped into a shore point on the opposite side of the river and Shannon scrambled out.

"Exciting, isn't it? Thanks for the ride." Shannon reached back and squeezed his hand. They weren't supposed to have any physical contact, but she thought people would be too distracted to notice. She then turned and bounded up the cliffside through its tunnels and along its paths.

In the central cave, plenty of dwellers had gathered to see and greet the new people. Weaving through them, Shannon heard Evans' name mentioned. She had liked Evans, and was glad to hear that his name wasn't being mentioned as a dead man. Apparently he had sent the newcomers, from a community that wanted to reach out to others.

Shannon finally made her way to the front of the crowd. The three strangers were sitting on a log bench, drinking water. Tired, dirty, and blasted by the sun, they looked ready to fall asleep for seven years.

"We started out with six of us," one of the men was saying. "Three of our friends died along the way."

"I'm so sorry," Horace sympathized.

Shannon listened to the story of zombies, and wild dogs, and an accident in the hills. One of the men did most of the talking, while the other man and the woman merely drank their water and ate the fish when it was offered. Eventually Horace's interview was complete and Shannon saw her opening.

"Hi, I'm Shannon," she said, stepping forward and offering her hand.

"I'm Lenny," the speaker introduced himself. "This is Shaidi and Winchester."

"I'm sorry about your friends, but I'm glad you made it."

"We're glad to be here," Lenny agreed.

"I'm the one who first spotted you following the unseen trail. Did Evans tell you about it?"

Lenny nodded as he ate some fish. "Even knowing about it, it's hard to spot."

"Hence the name," Shannon joked. The unseen trail was a series of carefully chosen and placed rocks that led to the top of the cliff path. Anyone who didn't know what to look for, wouldn't recognize it. "So you came from beside the sea?"

"We did."

"Shannon!" her mom barked. "Come over here."

"Oops, I think I'm in trouble." Shannon grinned. "If you need anything, ask for me. I know everything about this place and would love to hear about yours."

"Thank you, I think we're all right for now."

"Shannon!"

"Coming, Mom!" Shannon turned and walked over to the woman, who started berating her for this and that. Chores, Rocky, running along the paths and through the tunnels. There was always something for Shannon's mom to get upset about. Shannon just listened for a while and then began the process of soothing her with promises they both knew wouldn't last a week. Especially with newcomers. Shannon was eager to hear all they had to say. While she loved living on the cliffs and had no desire to leave, that didn't mean she couldn't also love hearing about far away places and how the people there lived.

SECTION 6:
HOMECOMING

31: CLAIRE
9 DAYS AFTER THE BOMBING

The water might have been low enough for them to leave by nightfall, but no one wanted to go out into the dark. Claire had managed to nap for an hour or so while guarding the room with Larson, but it hadn't been a restful sleep. Her dreams were disturbed, full of rats and silent screams. She was still exhausted that night, but she wasn't looking forward to sleeping.

When the others returned from scavenging, they reported nothing about the mannequin man. A few more of his traps had been found, but there was nothing to indicate that he had survived the fall. Nothing new appeared in places they had already been, and there were no strange sounds.

Claire volunteered to take the first night shift. While the others slept, she sat by the window, occasionally getting up to peer into the dark hallway through the peephole. She found herself strangely hoping to hear a thump in the apartment upstairs. Apparently the silence was worse than the strange noises.

After trading off with Rose, she fell asleep within minutes. This time she had no dreams, and didn't wake up until Danny began to gently shake her shoulder.

"Come on, time to get up," he spoke softly.

"What's going on?" Claire whispered, and not entirely on purpose as her voice took a little longer to wake up.

"We're heading out soon. I thought you'd want some time to pack and eat."

"Oh. Okay, thanks."

When she went out to pee over the balcony, Rose silently accompanied her. Claire wanted to ask her what was wrong, for she was usually so much more talkative in the mornings, but was afraid of the answer. She didn't want to hear that the others were worried about her. Maybe they weren't; maybe it was just a quiet morning, but still. She couldn't help but think about what Danny had said about her not being cut out to be a scavenger. Not yet, anyway. Did he mention these thoughts to the others while they had been searching the rooms? What kind of conversation might she have managed to sleep through that morning?

Everyone's bag was stuffed to the gills, and everyone's pockets were overflowing when it was time to leave. The laundry sack they had found, and a few other bags, were also crammed full and were either hung down people's chests or tucked under an arm. The water hadn't completely drained away yet, so they had wrapped everything in plastic bags and tape. It was also still raining, so Claire draped her poncho over herself, hoping to at least keep her head dry.

As they reached the ground floor, they had to slow down, taking one careful step at a time since they couldn't see what lurked below the water level. Some floating wooden ornaments clacked together as Claire stepped into their midst.

"Warmer than I thought it'd be," Rose commented as she slid deeper just ahead of Claire.

"Hurricanes draw their power from warm water," Bryce spoke up from the back of the line.

"Is that true?" Rose didn't know.

"According to the Discovery channel it is," Danny told her from just behind Claire.

"You still remember what you learned from the Discovery channel?" Jon asked.

"Some of it."

"Okay, but I learned it from actually paying attention in class on the Diana," Bryce said.

"I rarely paid attention," Larson admitted from his place ahead of Bryce.

"That's because you knew I would always help you with your homework," Bryce ribbed him.

By the time Claire stepped off the last step, the water reached her lower ribs. She held her arms up out of the water instinctively, but she knew that she would have to lower them soon when they tired. At least it turned out that her backpack was slightly buoyant, taking a little bit of the weight off her shoulders, unlike the messenger bag slung across her.

"We should have built a raft for our stuff," Danny commented as they moved out of the stairwell. He carried the awkward laundry sack, sometimes by hugging it and at other times by throwing it over a shoulder.

"Too late now," Jon told him, slogging his way forward, toward the grey light, after turning off his flashlight.

When Claire looked ahead, she saw that most of a rather large tree had been uprooted and smashed through the front doors. Jon found a way through by breaking some branches and ducking under others to head out into the rain.

Once outside the apartment building, they no longer needed to walk in a straight line but continued to do so anyway. Despite Jon's warnings, Claire often found herself banging her shins against mysterious submerged objects. Everyone tripped a few times, dunking themselves in the muddy water before being able to get their feet back under them. Several times they had to pull one another back upright. Claire was disappointed that she hadn't been able to keep at least her head dry.

There was a current that frequently caused something unseen to brush against Claire's legs. Each time, her heart jumped, as she wondered whether it might be a zombie, or an alligator, or something else with teeth.

The ground was not level. Sunken detritus resulted in a lot of up and down, and during the low points, Claire was more swimming than walking. Stuff that was floating bumped into them. Claire hoped none of it would turn out to be the mannequin man.

"How do you know where we're goin'?" Rose asked Jon.

"Well, we need to go east, so I'm walking east. You got a better idea?" He grunted as he pushed a floating mattress to one side.

"No."

After about an hour of walking, they changed positions. Jon dropped back to the rear of the line, and Rose began leading the way, pushing aside debris and calling back warnings when she came across suspect footing. Another hour later and it was Claire's turn. It was hard work being the lead. Some of the floating debris was difficult to shove aside, which included stuff just beneath the surface that snarled around her legs. She just kept heading east, occasionally referring to the compass that Jon had given her to make sure that she hadn't wandered off course. That hour felt longer than the others, and she was extremely grateful when it was her turn to drop back, allowing Danny to take charge. Walking was easiest at the back of the line and she wished she could stay there all day.

After Larson's turn was over, they agreed to a short lunch break. There was a mound of collapsed housing they could sit on. No one spoke during the break. They were all drenched and sullen, despite their trip being rather successful, all things considered. They were bringing home a fairly large number of MREs, which should feed everyone for a day. At least, Claire was hoping they were carrying that much. She had never been in charge of food rationing, and so wasn't entirely sure. She should probably learn more about it.

When they got moving again, Bryce led the way, followed by Jon. They noticed that either the water level had been lowering all day or they had finally begun to reach higher ground. Claire didn't have to half swim, as the flood water sloshed around her upper thighs, although it made some of the debris a little more frustrating to move. Once the water reached only to her knees it was much easier. They had definitely gone up a gradual rise, and Claire breathed a sigh of relief as the buildings around them were more intact.

The shallower water actually enabled the area to smell worse. More rot and decay were exposed, including dead animals trapped in the wreckage. Everyone kept a sharp eye out for movement, wary of zombies and rats. Claire startled when she saw a mannequin sticking out through a car window, but it hadn't been placed there deliberately. A clothing store nearby had had all of its windows broken, and sodden clothes were scattered about along with their various displays. They passed several more mannequins in that area, most of them in pieces.

Claire was starving, but no one called for them to stop again until the sun began to sink. They found a restaurant with an apartment above it and made their way inside. Stepping around tables and chairs and broken dishes, they eventually found their way up. Everyone found a place for their bedding, and then they hung their clothes off whatever was available.

"I don't think my feet will ever be dry again," Claire commented once she peeled off her socks. Her feet were pale and wrinkled, and she rubbed them as she sat inside her sleeping bag, wearing only her underwear and a sports bra. Her hands, having spent all day in drenched gloves, weren't any better.

"I hear that," Rose agreed.

Food was passed around but it was barely enough to stop Claire's stomach from growling. It was strange to be carrying so much food, and to be so hungry at the same time. Unlike their departure from the container yard, there was nothing to forage while they walked. No overrun gardens to find, no wild berries to pick; they weren't even going to stumble across a nest of eggs. The water had swept it all away.

"My legs are going to die tomorrow," Larson lamented from where he and his sleeping bag were sprawled.

"It won't be too bad," Jon commented, perhaps to lift Larson's spirits, but also maybe to lift his own. "They'll hurt when we start out, but the exercise will soon loosen them up again."

"Or they'll seize and I'll face plant into a tire," Larson quipped.

"Yeah, or that."

Hearing Jon joke with Larson was strange for Claire, who, throughout the day, kept remembering the way he had cut the mannequin man's rope with zero hesitation. She understood that she was struggling to reconcile the boy she knew with the man he now was. Danny's words had haunted her all day, *I don't think you should change.* They were sweet, but she couldn't help but wonder if he meant more by them. Was he worried that she would become like Jon? Did he think that what Jon had done was wrong, but he didn't want to say anything because of Jon's anger? Her thoughts whirled around and around, fading away only once her exhausted body dragged her mind down into sleep.

***

Claire had no idea what woke her. Maybe it was a dream, but she couldn't recall having one. She was asleep one minute, and awake the next, sitting up with her heart racing. The apartment was pitch black; there wasn't even moonlight lining the curtains. She strained her ears in the dark, listening for anything that might have drawn her from slumber. The others were breathing gently on either side of her, and the wind rustled something outside. They hadn't posted a guard, no longer believing that they needed one as they had on that first night. That first night when they had woken up to mannequins outside the window.

Snatching up her flashlight, Claire brought the beam to life. She thrust the light into every corner. No rats, no zombies, and, most importantly, no mannequins. The door was still locked, and the furniture they had placed in front of it hadn't moved. She next shone her light on Rose to her left, and then on the boys to her right. They were all present, and all breathing. Bryce mumbled something in his sleep and rolled away from the light.

Still not satisfied, Claire slipped out of her sleeping bag and went to the window, turning her flashlight off as she grabbed the curtains. There was nothing to see outside. It was just as dark out there as it was within. A faint patch of clouds could be seen, but that was it. Everything else was black nothingness. Still, Claire continued to stand there, her eyes adjusting. She wasn't sure whether she hoped to hear something moving around out there or not.

For several minutes she stood at the window without hearing or seeing anything out of the ordinary. The sudden energy she had been shocked with upon waking wore off, and she was left feeling weary. Not just tired, but exhausted with everything. She wished she could just teleport home. She wished that home was still the Black Box. She didn't want to be out here anymore.

To make her way back to her sleeping bag, Claire flicked her flashlight back on. As the beam passed over Jon again, he blinked and squinted, coming awake.

What's wrong? he asked in sign. He probably couldn't even make out who he was talking to.

Claire settled into her sleeping bag before turning the light so that they could make out one another in the dark. She told him about her sudden awakening, and about how she couldn't find anything wrong.

Jon told her that that happened sometimes. It was good that she had checked, but it could have just been her subconscious producing imaginary danger. He told her to go back to sleep.

After turning out the light, there was no difference between Claire's eyes being open and when they were shut.

I don't think you should change, Danny's words echoed in her head. Claire thought it was too late for that.

***

When Claire next awoke around dawn, Jon wasn't in his sleeping bag. She spotted him already dressed and standing by the window, peering through a crack in the curtains. When she whispered his name, he turned and smiled, but it was the false kind. His eyes had dark pouches under them. Had he gone back to sleep after Claire had accidentally woken him? Or had he stayed up all night, maintaining a guard position all on his own?

The others mumbled and groaned as they woke up. Everyone had stiff legs, Claire included.

"We'll probably be able to get home today," Jon told them as he divvied up their morning meal. "So long as nothing holds us up. Also, it stopped raining."

Larson and Bryce cheered weakly at this news, both of them still groggy with sleep. It had been dark when Claire had taken off her clothes the previous night, and now she felt a little embarrassed as she sat bundled in her sleeping bag. Most of the boys couldn't care less as they walked around in their boxers, leisurely gathering up their clothes. Rose was even less inhibited as she lounged in her undies on top of her sleeping bag. Only Bryce seemed remotely modest, grabbing his pants and shirt and putting them on as quickly as he could.

"Here." After pulling on his cargo pants, Danny had gathered Claire's clothes and handed them to her.

"Thanks." She wriggled around inside her sleeping bag as she pulled on her jeans, the fabric still damp and clingy in places. Her shirt was only a little drier. No one wanted to put their socks on, choosing to hang around barefoot until they were ready to go. Rose was the last to get dressed, not bothering to put on a scrap until after she had eaten and taken a piss. This place had no balcony, and so they had just used the bathtub.

"We have enough water to make it back, right?" Bryce thought out loud as they were rolling up their bedding and wrapping it in plastic once more.

"Our containers are pretty much all full, so I should think so," Danny said.

The previous day, they had simply opened their mouths and looked up when they were thirsty, drinking the rain.

Once the bedding was all packed, everyone grudgingly pulled on their socks and boots.

"It's squishy," Rose complained as she waited for Danny and Larson to move the furniture away from the door.

"Pretty sure there are still puddles in mine," Bryce added.

"Just think about getting home before nightfall. Then you can put on fresh socks and a dry pair of shoes or something," Jon advised, forgetting that most people had given up their extra footwear to the people who came from the Black Box. Claire couldn't forget, having walked with all those barefoot individuals. She had been one of the lucky ones, able to put on her boots before leaving.

As they left the apartment, Claire couldn't help but study the door, and the walls, and the stairs, wondering if there was anything different from when they had entered. As they crossed the restaurant, she argued with herself as to whether the tables and chairs were in the same positions or not. Even outside, she kept expecting to come across something strange. She kept expecting a message from the mannequin man.

The water was only ankle deep in the worst spots, often trapped in large puddles. There were areas where they got to walk on what was just wet pavement, no splashing at all. Still, they formed the same line as the day before, only now they didn't need to change who was leading. Nothing needed to be pushed out of the way; they just walked around anything too big to easily step over.

Claire checked for signs of the mannequin man as they walked, but what could be considered a sign? Unless it was an obviously written message, there was no way to know if that couch in the middle of the street was deposited there by the storm or not. Or that cracked and half broken bust against the tree branches. Anything that might be even remotely connected to their time in the apartment building, Claire was suspicious of. None of it was ever definitive. She found herself wishing that if Jon *had* to kill the mannequin man, he had done it in such a way that produced a body. It would certainly have put her mind at ease knowing for certain that he was dead. Even knowing he was still alive would be better than this uncertain dread. She felt like there was a ghost among them, a real one. She wondered if the mannequin man's body had become a zombie.

They trudged forward all day. Conversations were most often started with someone complaining about their feet or legs. They didn't talk about anything important. They told stories from their past, humorous anecdotes that might not have always been completely true. No one talked about home. No one voiced what the first thing they would do when they got there would be. The more destruction they came across outside, the more they feared what had happened back there. No one wanted to get their hopes too high, only to have them smashed to pieces.

Claire wondered what they would do if they found that home didn't exist anymore. She couldn't say what the others might do, but she knew that she would sit down and cry and probably never stop. If the container yard was gone, then that would just be too much. It would break her in the way that she had seen others broken, in the way that repairs weren't possible. She remembered living in the motel after the Day and before they made their way to the Diana. She remembered that there were people who had stayed in their rooms the entire time, refusing to come out. Others had done their best to feed them, to coax them back to life. Had they been saved? Claire didn't know. She didn't know if any of them had eventually been lured out, or if they had all made it onto the convoy vehicles. Had some of them stayed behind? Were they still there, curled up on the beds, hollowed out husks like that mother and child in the apartment? Claire didn't know, and she was never going to ask someone who might.

At lunch, they stopped only long enough to eat. Claire's shoulders hurt from the weight of her bag, especially the bruised one, but all she could do was resettle the weight when they got back up to keep moving. She kept trying to shift the messenger bag to her bruised shoulder only to have to move it back a minute later.

As the afternoon dragged on, Claire's whole body hurt. Her back got stiff, her head thumped from an imbalance of food versus work, and her guts cramped up. Still, she walked. Everyone kept walking, not once recommending they stop. If someone had to go to the bathroom, they stepped aside and went, then caught up again once finished. It was easier to keep moving, to allow momentum to carry them forward, step after step. Despite them not discussing it, Claire kept thinking of home. She kept picturing the container she had been given to share with Abby and Lauren and Peter before she left, once the rats were officially cleared out. Most of all, she thought of the bunk bed she would be sharing with Peter. She imagined collapsing down on the mattress, her head hitting the pillow.

"Hey." Danny shook her backpack, startling her eyes back open. "You started to drift sideways there."

"Sorry."

Neither of them acknowledged how tired they both were.

They finally broke their single file rank in order to buddy up at Danny's suggestion: Jon and Rose, Danny and Claire, and Bryce and Larson. They were to keep one another engaged, and make sure no one fell behind. Claire held Danny's hand in case she started to drift again. He didn't seem to mind, and would squeeze her hand whenever her eyes were shut for too long.

Sometimes they saw animals, not many, but mostly what they spotted were birds. No one tried to hit them with sling stones. The birds were far more alert than the humans were as they picked through the trash for morsels. A couple of times someone spotted a mammal, but then it was gone in a flash, too quick to be identified. Small lizards were occasionally spotted clinging to the sides of buildings. So far, none of the animals tried to kill them as they trudged on.

Their next break should have been for dinner, but Jon thought that if anyone sat down, he wouldn't be able to get them back up again. Instead, he passed around the food while they walked, and they ate while moving.

Claire had begun to see familiar buildings. At least, she thought they were familiar. She hadn't seen all that much of what was around the container yard, and couldn't be certain they were backtracking their original route.

"Are we getting close?" Claire asked Danny, the first time someone acknowledged the distance.

"Yes, we're getting close," he answered.

"The sun has nearly set," Claire noticed.

Danny nodded. "We'll have to walk through the dark for a bit, but we'll get home. We won't have to find somewhere else to sleep."

"Good. I don't want to sleep anywhere else."

"Neither do I."

Jon grunted what sounded like an agreement, but no one else even acknowledged their brief conversation.

When it became dark, the containers still weren't in sight, but Claire was certain that she knew where they were. They clicked on their lights and kept them pointed at the ground. It made a somewhat obvious puddle of light as they walked, but they couldn't navigate the storm-smashed streets without them. Besides, they were close enough to home that no one minded.

When the container maze at last came into view, Claire's legs nearly gave up right there. She was more than ready for this trip to end.

It didn't take them long to find that a path had been cleared through the glop in the container maze. They immediately took to following it.

"First the zombie slush, and now this," Rose commented.

"I prefer this," Bryce spoke up.

The atmosphere had become lighter once they entered the maze. Everyone was walking a little more upright, with a little more energy. They were almost there.

Once they exited the maze and began to cross the open space to the wall, Claire almost felt like she could run. Instead, she had to come to an abrupt halt.

"Stop right there!" someone shouted from the wall.

The fear and anger in the voice had all six travellers shooting their hands up into the air, deliberately pointing their lights down onto their own faces.

"We're returning scavengers!" Jon shouted. "It's Jon, Rose, Danny, Claire, Bryce, and Larson!"

"Walk slowly toward the wall!"

They obeyed, spreading out to walk side by side, making sure they were all visible. Claire felt a lump in her throat. Was it always like this when a scavenger team returned after dark?

"Thank fuck," someone said as they approached. "All right, you can put your arms down. Get up here."

They found a ladder waiting for them and scrambled up. As Claire hauled herself over the top, she saw someone climbing up from the inside. Once a light reached him, she recognized Bronislav. Crichton followed right behind him.

"Did you see anyone else out there?" Bronislav immediately questioned them.

"What do you mean?" Danny asked.

"Out there, in or near the maze. Did you see anyone?"

"No," Jon shook his head. Claire could see the same concern in his eyes that was no doubt inhabiting hers. "Why? What's happened?"

"Two teenagers have been kidnapped," Crichton informed them. "Dakota and Elijah."

Claire didn't recognize the second name, but she certainly knew the first. Dakota had lived in the motel with her, and was friends with Peter. Claire had played with or teased her countless times as they grew up.

"What do you mean, kidnapped?" Danny's voice had gone cold. "When? How?"

"A couple of hours ago," Crichton informed him. "They were part of a team that was clearing the path through the container maze. The other five heard the commotion, saw what was happening, and managed to make it back here safely. There were at least two men, disguised as zombies. There could be more, for all we know."

Jon's pack thumped down onto the wall. He was turning around to go back out there, to start searching.

"We already have a team looking for them," Bronislav stopped him with a heavy hand on his shoulder. "You'll only get in their way, and perhaps even get killed."

"Besides, you're all clearly exhausted," Crichton added. "We should get your supplies to the community centre, and then you should all rest."

"What were they even doing out there?" Bryce was actually angry. Dakota was also friends with his little sister, Becky.

"I sent them out," Bronislav admitted. "I had been training the younger ones, especially the teenagers, ever since the exodus. I was going to have them begin digging up those rocks alongside the container yard, have them start preparing the soil for farming. But clearing a path through the maze needed to be done, and they were capable."

"I saw them not long before the kidnapping happened," Crichton added. "They knew what they were doing, but unfortunately, so did the kidnappers. This could have happened to anyone."

Jon's hands were trembling, his rage keeping him upright. He clearly wanted to start searching for himself right away.

"You're no good to them right now," Danny spoke to his friend in a quiet tone. "In the morning I'll come with you."

"As soon as the sun rises." Jon didn't state it as a question.

"As soon as the sun rises," Danny agreed.

Crichton picked up Jon's pack and they headed down off the wall. As Claire made her way with the others to the community centre, she felt hollowed out. The elation of finally being home had evaporated in an instant.

Too tired to empty her pack of even her personal items, Claire left it with the messenger bag for others to manage, then turned and went to find her container. Lauren found her first.

"Claire!" She ran over, her arms wide. "I heard that someone had come back, and I prayed that it was you."

Claire allowed herself to be swept up in a crushing hug, her face becoming buried in the woman's wild red hair.

"What is it? What's wrong?" Lauren asked, completely overflowing with concern. "You're shaking. It's not Jon is it?"

"Jon's fine. I'm just so tired." Claire began to cry. She let the tears flow as Lauren held her, making soothing sounds as she stroked her adopted daughter's much straighter hair.

"Come on. Let's get you to bed. The lower mattresses got soaked so you'll have to share the top bunk with Peter, is that okay?"

Claire nodded as she clung to Lauren's side. "I heard about what happened to Dakota."

"People are out looking for her. She'll be found and returned home safely, don't you worry."

Claire desperately wanted to believe that.

When they reached their container, Abby squeaked with delight at seeing Claire, who was then passed from one set of loving arms to the next. She was fussed over and allowed it, letting them help her get off her wet gear, especially her boots and socks.

"Sorry about the smell," Lauren said as she located a dry pair of pyjamas for Claire to wear. "Turns out this box wasn't completely waterproof."

"Doesn't smell much different from where I've been," Claire pointed out. Everything carried a damp scent to the point where she no longer noticed it.

When Claire finally climbed up to the top bunk, Peter was there, squished up against the wall to give her room.

"Hey, buddy," Claire said as she wriggled herself in under the blankets beside him. "I've missed you."

Apparently he had missed her as well, because the moment she got comfortable he latched himself onto her side. She had been wrong. Not everything smelled damp. Peter's hair was clean and good.

Abby and Lauren performed some last minute tasks before getting ready for bed. They planned to sleep on a tarp on top of their double bed. They kept peeking up at Claire as they moved around, worried about what she may have gone through or that they might be keeping her up. But Claire wasn't bothered at all. She was in a bed with her arms around her little brother and had fallen deeply asleep.

32: DAKOTA
11 DAYS AFTER THE BOMBING

Dakota had planned to run and fight like hell the moment the knife blade was removed from her throat, but she didn't get the chance. The man who held her was very fast. The blade left her neck, but the butt of the dagger was then immediately crashed into her skull. She wasn't knocked completely unconscious like Elijah had been, but she was stunned. Her body went limp on her, long enough for the man to gag and hog tie her on the ground. A clump of wet stuffing beneath her oozed water into her clothes, soaking her body underneath.

As the man who had grabbed her moved away, she could see that he was dressed like a zombie, just like the other man. She knew she should be watching them, but it was hard to tear her eyes away from Elijah. He wasn't moving.

"The others ran off," one of the men grunted to the other. "Probably heard this one shouting." He nudged Elijah with the toe of his boot.

"They're going to get reinforcements. Pick him up; we should get out of here and back to the others."

Dakota was hauled off the ground and slung over a man's shoulder like she was a pack. Her joints screamed as they were pulled, and her breathing turned rapid. She wriggled around, trying to do something, anything.

"I'd stop that if I were you," the man carrying her spoke. "All that will get you is a pair of popped shoulders."

He probably wasn't lying, so Dakota went still. She would need her arms in their sockets if she was going to fight her way free later. Instead, she focused on where they were going. Dakota had never been out here before, so she needed to pay attention if she hoped to find her way back. The container maze glowed orange in the sunset, the alleyways within it deepening their shadows. As the containers faded from sight around the corner of a building, Dakota could hear the alarm. The others had already made it back to the wall, and Freya was hammering on the container, warning everybody. They wouldn't just let Elijah and Dakota be taken. She knew this. They would send people after them. She would fight until they found her.

It got dark and still they walked. Dakota could barely see anything, but she still tried to figure out where they were. It was hard, especially since she had to focus on keeping her breathing slow and even. She feared something was going to pop despite her holding still. With every footstep she was jostled, and she imagined her tendons creaking and groaning like the hull of the submarine.

She wished Misha had made it back. He and his dogs would be able to track her, using the scent from her hat, which had been left behind. Maybe Barrel and Spring could do it? Would they understand a complicated command like that, given by someone who wasn't their master? Dakota knew that Spring was good at catching rats, so maybe she could be equally good at finding people. Maybe one of the other dogs from the container yard could follow the scent trail? It was a hope to hold onto.

The pain was too much to fall asleep, but Dakota had the awful feeling that she had passed out from it for a little while. She had definitely stopped paying attention to where they were going for a length of time she couldn't determine. She wanted to curse, but the gag prevented it.

She wondered how the men who had taken her could see where they were headed. They didn't have any sort of light source, and yet they hadn't tripped over anything or walked into any walls. When they finally entered a building, the only way Dakota could tell was when the air went still and stale, and the quiet shuffle of feet took on a bit of an echo. Whatever building they were in was dark, until a door was opened and a flood of light spilled forth. Dakota blinked, her eyes unaccustomed to the bright, and then she was dumped in a corner, facing the wall. Elijah was placed beside her, bound more loosely than she was but still unconscious. She was very worried about him. Having spent so much time around Cameron and Riley, she knew that being hit unconscious for even a few seconds was dangerous, and Elijah had been out for many minutes. It might have even been an hour for all Dakota knew. He could have brain damage. He could be a vegetable.

"Only two?" a voice asked from somewhere behind Dakota.

"There were five more, but they ran off. That one warned them."

"And you let them escape?" Anger simmered in the voice. "They'll have warned the whole community by now."

"What were we supposed to do? Run them down? They were fast kids, and they weren't unarmed. That one was carrying a rifle, the other had this bag of rocks, and they both had knives. So what was I supposed to do? Shoot the ones running away? It's not like I had a silencer."

"They'll be looking for us now."

"Settle down," a new voice calmed. "They can't find us. And besides, a search party means a small group of people outside that wall of theirs. They'll be easy to pick off."

Dakota's heart jumped. She hadn't imagined that these people would attack the search party. She had to escape, and if she was going to do that, she needed to know what was going on. She needed to see more than a dusty baseboard. Using mostly her thighs, she was able to start squirming herself around. For the first time in her life, she wished for smaller breasts, as they kept getting painfully crushed beneath her. She bit down hard on the gag to push through the pain until she had turned enough to see the room without having to crane her neck.

The first thing she made note of was the light bulb hooked up to a car battery. It wasn't shaded at all, just a bright point of light, like a small star. The next thing she looked for, she didn't find. There were no windows in that room, meaning the light couldn't be seen from outside. She should have expected that. Finally looking at the people around the light, she realized there were more than she had anticipated. Along with the two men, still half dressed as zombies, there were at least a dozen others. They were all so quiet, so still, that she had had no idea. It was possible that there were even more she couldn't see, hidden behind the others or behind the boxes in the room, or maybe even guarding outside somewhere. Studying the collection of men and women, Dakota was able to determine how her captors had moved so easily through the night: a pair of night vision goggles sat on the floor beside them. If Dakota did manage to escape, stealing those would be a great help to her, and a hindrance to them. Of course, there were a lot more steps to figure out first.

"The girl is looking at us," the calming man spoke. Dakota hadn't even seen him glance over at her; they all seemed to be ignoring her and Elijah.

One of the false zombies got up and spun her back around to face the wall. She then had a blindfold tied over her eyes. For the first time, she wondered what these people planned to do with her. Was she going to be tortured? Was she bait or a bargaining chip to be used against those at the container yard? Was she going to be eaten? Her muscles contracted with fear. Was she going to be raped?

Her captors weren't talking. There were no plans for her to overhear. They must have decided everything in advanced. Her breath started to come in short, rapid bursts. She couldn't get enough air around the gag. She was suffocating.

Someone in the room sighed, and then a knee was placed on her back.

"Scream if you want. No one other than us will hear you," a stream of hot breath whispered in her ear as the gag was removed.

Dakota refused to scream. She was terrified, but she refused to let these bastards know it, whoever they were.

"Check that the other one isn't dead," requested a voice not yet heard before.

"Still has a pulse," was reported from beside Dakota.

So Elijah was still breathing. That was something.

"How hard did you hit him?"

"Pretty hard. He had this rifle."

"We'll find a use for him, even if he never wakes up," the calm voice insisted. Dakota was beginning to think that that one was the leader.

She sensed more than physically felt when the person who had removed her gag went away. Blindfolded, she carefully scooted herself sideways until she bumped into Elijah. The warmth of his skin was reassuring, and if she bent her head toward him, she could make out his breathing.

What was she supposed to do next? She knew the location of one door, but not if there was a second. She had no idea how to get out of her bindings. With the blindfold on, she could no longer even be certain when the light was turned off, when her captors decided to sleep. Maybe it wouldn't be turned off. Maybe the reason they were so quiet was because some of them were already sleeping. It seemed logical that they would take shifts, especially now that they had hostages. It all seemed so hopeless that Dakota wanted to cry.

And then she felt it; a gentle pressure against her arm. It slackened off, and then eased on again. Elijah was pressing his arm against hers. He was awake! Dakota returned the pressure, hoping she was being slow and casual enough for it to go unnoticed by the gathering behind her.

When Elijah next pressed his arm against her, he did so in a sort of pattern. It took Dakota a minute, but she eventually realized that he was using Morse code. Bronislav had taught her some on the submarine, but she hadn't been able to memorize the whole thing during that time, not with everything else he had been teaching her about bulk heads and bilge pumps and ballast. She only knew how to signal SOS, and there wasn't much she could say with only two letters.

"No," she dared to whisper as quietly as she could, hoping that Elijah understood that she meant she didn't understand. She then sniffled loudly, hoping that if anyone had heard anything, they would have just put it down to her crying.

Elijah stopped using Morse. He pressed his arm against hers one last, lingering time, and then stopped all together. He had understood.

The fact that Elijah was awake was a great development. Dakota felt a flood of relief at not being alone. She wondered how long he had been awake. Was it just recently, or had he been deliberately faking it for a while? If he could keep faking it, that might be good for them. But this also meant that it was up to Dakota to learn more about their situation, and the only way she could think to do that was to talk to their captors. What could she possibly say?

"What happens when I have to pee?" she finally spoke after a lot of thought.

"No one here cares if you piss your pants," came the reply.

"I'm here, and I care," Dakota retorted. This got no answer, so she went on. "What do you plan to do with us?" Silence. "Will we be fed at all?" Beyond her first question, no one would answer her. Maybe she just needed to think of the right question? But what could that be?

While Dakota thought, she wriggled around a little bit, trying to find a position that was even remotely more comfortable. The bindings had dug into her wrists, which weren't protected by any clothing like her ankles were. She wondered if she was bleeding.

"Do I have to stay like this the whole time? It hurts." Dakota didn't need to fake the whine that invaded her voice. She felt weak for doing it.

No one voiced an answer, but someone did kneel down beside her. She flinched at the touch of their knees against her arm and side. But then the bindings were removed. Her arms and legs flopped free. A series of pins and needles shot all through her limbs, the pain rendering her helpless. Her legs were tied back together first, both around the ankles and the thighs. Her wrists were then bound to her own belt loops, although the rope was a little looser this time so that it wasn't digging in. A single rope was used for her hands, with the knot tied together at the small of her back where she had no hope of reaching it.

When the person left her side, Dakota relaxed her muscles. Freya had taught her that if she was going to be tied up, to flex all her muscles, so that when she went limp later, the bindings would be looser. They were definitely looser around her thighs, but that wasn't much help. She pulled at her hands, but that only hurt her wrists some more.

"Am I allowed to roll onto my back?" Dakota asked. When she didn't get an answer, she thought that meant that it would be okay. Leveraging with her toes, she managed to roll her body over, briefly crushing her arm. The knot at her back was uncomfortable, but she still felt better than she had on her stomach. The motion had moved her away from Elijah, so she wriggled until she was back beside him. She realized that she would be able to sit up if she wanted to, could even prop herself up against the wall, but for now she wanted to just lie on her back and think. The uncomfortable knot should help keep her from falling asleep. But she was wrong about that. With the adrenaline worn off, and dinner missed, her body was wiped out. It had no fuel to sustain itself. Within the dark confines of the blindfold, Dakota didn't have a choice when it came to drifting off.

***

There was no passage of time within the dark confines of the blindfold, but something had happened while Dakota was out. She could hear the flurry of activity within the room, and Elijah was once more pressing his arm against hers. She pressed back, letting him know that she was awake. She then raised herself up into a sitting position in order to better listen to what was going on.

No one was speaking, not in a voice that Dakota could make out. There was some whispering, but it was all too low and too distant for the words to reach her. She had to see what was going on.

Scooting back down onto her back, she started to rub her head against the ridge of the baseboard, trying to get it to push up on the blindfold. A couple of times it moved up only to fall back into place again, but she eventually managed to get it to stay up enough for her to peer beneath the fringe of the fabric. Lying with her head on a slight angle, her eyes pointed downward, Dakota was able to somewhat see. The exposed light bulb was still glowing brightly. Bodies scurried about here and there, gathering things up. Several people were leaving through the door. Dakota wished she could see what was out there, but the door swung the wrong way, blocking her limited view. The last six bunched together, had a brief, whispered conversation, and then three of them left with the others, so only three of them remained. Dakota peered around the room, but didn't think there was anyone else. Only three people were left to watch over them. That was certainly better odds if Dakota could figure out what to do.

"What's going on?" she asked, figuring they had already seen her sit up and knew that she was awake.

One of the three strode over and grabbed her by her shirt. Dakota squealed as she was hoisted partly off the floor.

"If those fucks come in here, you die first," the man with rotten teeth hissed at her. He then released her shirt. She winced as her head bounced off the floor.

Those fucks? Dakota's heart hammered against her rib cage. Surely he must have been referring to a search party, right? People were looking for her and they were close. Closer than these people thought they would get. It had to be that, didn't it? Who else could the man be referring to?

Dakota's mind whirled. If she and Elijah were going to escape on their own, now was the best chance they were ever going to get. But how were they going to do that?

Think, Dakota commanded herself. *What would Freya do?* She'd probably take things one step at a time. Break down the problem into smaller parts. What was the first thing Dakota needed? To be free of her bonds. So how could she go about doing that?

With her limited field of vision, Dakota scanned the area for anything sharp, but there was nothing near the corner where she and Elijah were located. A woman sat near them, a bit to the left, her back to them as she watched the door. The man with the bad teeth was sitting on a mouldy cardboard box across the room, sharpening a knife with an awful *scrape, scrape, scrape.* The third man couldn't be seen, so Dakota guessed there was a way around the shelving laden with more boxes off to her right. None of them were directly watching the captives.

Scooting over to Elijah, she stuck out her hand like an awkward flipper and grabbed the highest point on his arm that she could reach. Shifting away from him, she tried to roll Elijah onto his side, which was easier said than done.

"Hey, what are you doing over there?" the man with rotten teeth had reacted to the movement.

"Making sure he gets some blood flow into his hands and feet." Dakota impressed herself with how quickly she had come up with an excuse. "I saw how you had him tied up earlier. Gravity will have been draining the blood from his limbs."

"Your friend's never going to wake up, so I don't know why you're bothering."

"Shut up!" Dakota dug out her fright, hoping that it overlaid her voice more than her anger did. She wanted them to keep thinking that she and Elijah were completely helpless. Which for all she knew, they were.

The man watched Dakota struggle for a while, and then returned to sharpening his knife. Dakota patted Elijah twice, trying to tell him to help her. Whether he did or not, she couldn't tell, but he ended up awkwardly on his side, with most of his left arm trapped underneath him. Dakota sat still for a while, watching the man with the bad teeth. When she was certain he was paying more attention to his knife than he was to them, she used her hand to locate the knot holding Elijah's wrists and ankles together. Her fingers explored the rope, sussing out what kind of knot it was. In that moment she was very grateful for Brunt's teachings. She might not have always remembered the names of knots, but her fingers were attuned to mapping out the curves and she was able to figure out how the rope was twisted and threaded around itself. She found the first coil she needed to pull on and began tugging at it with her fingers. She wished she could use more than just her left hand. The knot was tight, but Dakota was determined.

When the first twist was freed, Dakota felt her chest swell. She checked on the man again, but he still wasn't paying attention. Before she could pull free the next loop, easier now with that little bit of looseness, he finished with his knife and put it away. Dakota froze once more, a dread of certainty that she would now be caught making the blood pump hard and loud in her ears. But the man didn't care about her or Elijah. He leaned back on the boxes and closed his eyes. Completely out of everyone's line of sight, Dakota worked faster.

When Elijah's bindings sprang free, Dakota had to bite her tongue to keep from cheering. He rolled slowly back onto his stomach, lowering his limbs and no doubt feeling the painful tingles that Dakota had experienced. He had no blindfold and was quite capable of seeing the people around the room. As Dakota watched, he pushed himself up into a crouch, lifting his feet high when he moved them to prevent any scraping on the concrete floor. She stayed still to do the same, and so could no longer see Elijah's face when he stood up. Their escape was in his hands now. She wished she knew what he had been trying to tell her in Morse.

Elijah's feet moved with slow, deliberate strides toward their nearest captor: the woman sitting on the box facing the door. Dakota could see Elijah's plan just before he executed it and wanted to tell him not to do it, but to say anything now would give him even less of a chance than he already had.

On the back of the woman's belt was a k-bar knife. Elijah's hand reached for it. He hesitated for only a second, when his hand was mere inches away. And then he grabbed it and all hell broke loose.

Elijah was fast. So fast that Dakota briefly wondered if he had done this before. The knife was up and out of the holster and into the woman's neck before she could even turn around or cry out. Blood sprayed across the room as a major artery was sliced open, some of it landing on the bare light bulb with a sizzle, and turning half the room red.

The man with the bad teeth had opened his eyes and jumped up from his boxes, taking in everything at a glance before rushing at Elijah. But there was a third man. Dakota didn't know if Elijah had seen that a third person had stayed behind, that he was just beyond the shelves somewhere.

As the man with bad teeth roared at Elijah, Dakota rolled about until she was on her knees and then up on her feet. At multiple times during this action she nearly lost her balance, which would probably have been the end for both her and Elijah. But she got upright, and as the third man came around the shelving unit, Dakota sprang, throwing her whole body. Both men were too far away for Dakota to hit either of them, but the light bulb wasn't.

There was a crack, a pop, and then a searing pain lanced through Dakota's side as the glass broke and tore through her shirt and her flesh. By the time she hit the ground, the whole room had been plunged into darkness. It didn't matter how well her blindfold was on now: no one could see anything.

Someone tripped over Dakota's prone form. Was it Elijah or one of the men? She couldn't tell. There was too much animalistic shouting bouncing off the walls. If Elijah was one of those voices, she couldn't identify it.

It didn't matter who it was, Dakota rolled in the opposite direction, her hand crunching over more glass and getting cut up. She ignored the pain and kept going until she hit a wall. Only it wasn't a wall, it was the shelving unit laden with boxes. There, she struggled against her bonds to no avail. Feeling the flare of pain from the cuts on her hand, she wished she had thought to grab some of the glass as she passed over it. Maybe there was some stuck in her, but she had no way of knowing for certain and couldn't pull it out even if there was. Not with her hands tied to her sides.

Despite the dark, a struggle was still going on. Boots scraped over the floor, as an occasional flesh on flesh smack indicted a fist had landed. The roars had mostly died down into a rough panting. Who was winning? Not wanting to really think about what it would mean for her, Dakota knew she couldn't count on Elijah coming out on top of this. Pushing boxes aside, she attempted to make a gap between them, some sort of opening that she might be able to hide in. She didn't know what else to do. At least, not until she heard a clatter of metal on concrete down near her feet. Dakota thought she knew what that sound was. Spinning around, she wormed herself toward it. Her head found the object first with a sharp prick. She twisted her body about until her right hand was able to grab the knife. Whose knife was it? Who had been disarmed? The fight had fallen quiet. Were people dead? Were they all dead? Or had they just broken apart from one another? Were they circling in the dark, waiting for the other to give away his position?

Dakota flipped the knife around, nicking her arm with the blade in the process, and proceeded to saw at the ropes. The knife was quite sharp; maybe it was the one belonging to the man with the bad teeth. Her wrist finally sprang free of her waist, the left one still trapped by the weaving of the rope around her belt loops. She ignored that wrist for now, taking the knife to her legs. She sawed through the rope around her thighs first, and her ankles second.

Then the door opened. Light entered the space, and Dakota found herself springing away, hiding off in a corner that was still dark. She pulled the blindfold off her head, awkwardly for she refused to put down the knife.

Whoever had opened the door was silhouetted for a moment. The person was hunched over and canted sideways, injured. Was it Elijah, or the third man? They both had similar builds, similar enough that Dakota couldn't tell them apart from that short glimpse. The door swung shut as the person who had opened it was tackled to the floor.

Dakota didn't know what to do. Try to help? Open the door again so that there was some light? Hide? She remembered that her left hand was still bound and set to work freeing it. When she finished, the room had fallen silent again. The struggle had paused.

Seconds ticked by, how many Dakota couldn't count. She had to do something.

"Elijah?" she called out, quickly moving out of the corner she had been in to prevent herself from becoming a target.

There was no answer.

"Elijah?" she tried again, more afraid. He might not have been answering for fear of giving himself away, or he might be dead.

A hand lashed out of the darkness, grabbing the front of her shirt. She couldn't know who it was, not for certain, but that foul breath was telling enough for Dakota. She slashed out with the knife, again and again, aiming for where she thought the face was and where she knew the arm must be.

A man cried out, a rough sound. Dakota took that as encouragement, and kept slashing, even when the hand let go, even when the figure tried to retreat. She pursued the retreating form, often swiping at nothing but air. When the man fell, she nearly tripped over him. Instead she deliberately dropped to her knees, plunging the knife down again. The response was a solid grunt as loud as her impact. She pulled back the knife and stabbed again. She stabbed again. She stabbed again. Her hands became hot and slick with unseen blood. She had no idea what she was hitting. Something with bones that deflected, and meat that absorbed. Dakota didn't notice that she was screaming, or crying, or that the figure beneath her had gone still. Not until her arms were too exhausted to continue. One last plunge of the blade, and then she sat there, panting, hands still wrapped so tightly around the handle that they hurt.

The door opened again. Pale light flooded the room. Whoever had opened the door wisely kept to one side of it, hiding in the shadows. The light fell directly on Dakota this time; there was no hiding from it for her. She looked down at the back of a man. Where his lower back met his ribcage was now a bloody mess, the wounds overlapping into one carved-up mass. His arm, thrown to one side at an awkward angle, was red with gashes. His face, twisted sideways, bore smaller injuries, and for a span of time faster than the eyes can blink, Dakota thought it was Elijah, before the planes dissolved into those of the man with bad teeth.

"Dakota?" a voice spoke from the dark. "Are you all right?"

"Elijah?" She searched for him. A figure stumbled out from behind the door. Adrenaline still hammering through her veins, she raised the bloody knife, ready to defend herself.

"It's just me," Elijah said, raising a hand. The door stayed opened as he moved away from it this time.

Dakota shot to her feet, and almost immediately lost her balance. She tripped more than walked to meet Elijah halfway. They collapsed into each other's arms, leaning on one another to keep from falling. Over his shoulder, Dakota could see the legs of the woman's body holding the door open. The large pool of blood surrounding her was smeared everywhere. On the other side, the light just reached a hand, the fingers partly curled and prone. It must have been the third man, but Dakota didn't get a good look before she and Elijah made their way out the door. She didn't look back at the man she had killed, not once.

They were in a factory, and Dakota had assumed the light was dim because it was early morning, but once they pushed outside, she learned that was only an effect caused by the dirty glass. There were still plenty of clouds in the sky, but the sun was finally peeking through here and there, making tiny blue patches and sun beams.

"Are you injured?" Dakota asked as they made their way away from the factory. Neither of them seemed to know which direction they were going, but for now, away was all they needed.

"I think I have a cracked rib or two," Elijah told her. He had his arm thrown across her shoulders, while she had both her arms wrapped around his waist, the knife still clutched in one hand.

"We need to hide somewhere," Dakota told him.

They didn't pick any of the buildings, but instead crawled into the back of a work van. It lay on its side, pushed there by the storm, and had water puddled along the floor that used to be a wall. The broken windshield and front windows let in enough light for Dakota to see by as she inspected Elijah. While his ribs were paining him the most, he also had a pretty bad cut on his right leg, and his left arm hung strangely.

"Your shoulder's popped out," Dakota determined. "I don't know how to put it back in." She helped Elijah turn his shirt into a sling. His torso had a massive bruise forming along its right side.

Not caring about what she looked like in her bra, Dakota stripped off her shirt and used it to wrap up Elijah's leg. The front of the shirt was so thoroughly soaked with blood already, she was careful to place the back of the shirt to his injury. She used the floodwater to rinse off her hands and face a little once she was done.

"We have to keep moving," Elijah groaned as he pushed off the wall he was leaning against, which was the van's former roof.

Dakota agreed, and helped him hobble out and then down the street. She continued to keep hold of the knife in one hand, not wanting to risk losing it by trying to tuck it in somewhere. Neither of them could determine which way the container yard lay, so they simply picked a direction and walked.

"Are there paperclips holding your bra together?" Elijah asked as he limped.

"Yeah, the last time I got to pick a new one, they had my cup size but not my band size. I keep meaning to get it adjusted."

"That's clever. The paperclips."

"Thanks."

"I once had to use tape as a belt."

"You didn't have any string or rope or anything?"

"Nope. Just tape. Those pants were huge on me."

"How'd you lose the pants that fit you?"

"I was climbing over a fence and they got snagged. I was hanging upside down for a bit. There were zombies coming, and I thought it would be faster to just drop out of my pants than it would be to try to free them."

"Probably a good decision."

"Probably."

They shuffled on in silence for another block.

"I forgot to ask if you're okay," Elijah eventually said.

"I'm all right. My wrists are pretty sore from the bindings, but I wasn't in a fight like you were." She had a couple of cuts from the broken light bulb and from finding the knife, but they were superficial and had already stopped bleeding.

"I meant up here." He tried to tap his head with his bad arm and failed.

"I'm okay."

"You had only just killed your first zombie a few days ago."

Dakota knew what he was really saying: she had never killed a living man before. "I'm okay," she repeated.

"Well, if you need to talk, I'm here. Some people take that kind of thing pretty hard."

"How about we get back home before we start worrying about my mental health, yeah?"

Elijah chuckled, which turned into a groan because of his ribs. "Yeah, that sounds like a good plan."

As they walked, Dakota took comfort in the warmth of his skin against hers. She planned to have a talk with Bronislav and Freya once they got back to the container yard. Their lessons definitely needed to cover a few more things.

33: MISHA
11 DAYS AFTER THE BOMBING

The scream built up in Misha's chest but he didn't dare let it escape. He couldn't trust that there weren't zombies lying in wait for him outside. Although it wasn't like he was exactly silent. Cart axles creaked and the horses snorted and stomped.

"Okay, stop. Stop." Misha told Thumper and Potato. "Take a break."

As the sun had set, Misha had been forced to find a place to stop for the night. The area he had found himself in had been hit fairly hard, and the water was still relatively high, making it incredibly difficult for Misha to open any doors on his own. He ended up having to choose a retail shop that had had its double doors smashed off. The place used to be a comic book store, one that also sold books, movies, and merchandise. All of it had been churned into a colourful soup by waters that had almost reached the ceiling at some point. Misha had spent the night in there checking on Trigger and her puppies, making sure Rifle wasn't injured, and finding food for the horses. He got a little bit of shut eye here and there, sleeping on the counter, but thoughts of threats and his other dogs often kept him awake. Several of them had found him during the night. Bullet and Slide had been the first two, followed by Guard and Powder. As the sun rose, Stock finally came floundering in, exhausted from having swum a good portion of the way there. So far there had been no sign of Spring or Barrel.

When Misha decided to leave, he quickly learned that that was easier said than done. Because the doors had been smashed in, plenty of mud had accumulated inside the store: enough that the cart had become stuck fast in it overnight.

Knowing he would have to dig the cart out and that it could take a while, Misha untethered Thumper and Potato once more. If an attack came while he was working, he wanted the animals to be able to escape. Kneeling down in the muck, he set to work with his hands. Layers of comics, so wet they were barely holding together, came up with the mud. Misha used them to build sort of a wall to help prevent the slop from backsliding into the space he was working. As he scraped away gunk, certain smells were released. This was not a good, clean mud like there'd be at a sandy beach, but something that smelled as sick as it felt. It was akin to sewage, and it coated Misha's arms up to his elbows, filled his gloves, seeped through his pants, and oozed down into his boots.

Rifle watched him work from the driving board above, whereas Bullet tried to help without knowing what he was doing. He dug, but in random places where it wasn't really helpful. A couple of times he stuck his nose into Misha's hole, but Misha pushed him away. He worried that if the dog started to dig there, he might actually make it worse rather than better. Trigger was lying in the cart with her puppies, while the rest of the dogs wandered about, some of them outside the shop hunting for a morsel to chow down on.

Misha spent a few hours digging, having to pause every now and again when Slide came over to warn him of a zombie outside. Every time she did that, he worried he'd find a small horde out there, but two was the most he ever saw at once. They all dropped like empty sacks when Misha's machete met their craniums.

When the trenches in front of the tires looked to be of an adequate size, Misha gathered up a handful of DVD cases, took out the disks, and placed the opened cases in front of the tires so that they had something to grab onto. He also decided to help himself to a Hylian Shield backpack and stuff it full of soggy Hogwarts house scarves. The material looked like it could be useful once cleaned. After adding the backpack to the cart, Misha rounded up Thumper and Potato again.

"All right, guys, this time we're going to do it." Misha went to the back of the cart, preparing to push. "Go!"

The cart moved far more easily and quickly than Misha had expected. With his boots in the mud, his feet stuck fast as the cart rolled away from him. He fell forward and landed in the mire face first. When he came up sputtering, he barely had time to wipe clear his eyes, because the horses were still moving, heading slow and straight, right out the doors. Misha ran after them as best he was able, scrambling up onto the driving board once they were outside. He let the horses walk until they reached a section of pavement where the cart wouldn't get stuck again, and then brought them to a halt. Coated in slimy mud from head to foot, Misha just sat there for a minute. But then Rifle nudged him with his nose, getting some of the muck on himself.

"No, you don't want this on you," Misha told his friend as he climbed back down. "I can't pet you right now." The other dogs had it all over their feet and legs, and in Guard's case, his belly, but Misha wouldn't pet them either. If they decided to roll and get extra dirty, he couldn't stop them, but he wasn't going to deliberately make the mess worse.

Locating some nearby trapped storm water, Misha used it to rinse off his face and hands. The water wasn't clean, but it was cleaner than he was. When he was done, he stuffed his gloves into a side pocket of his pants, which was probably also filled with muck. His boots squished as he walked. To prevent the mud from drying over his joints, Misha walked with the horses. Some dogs trotted ahead, and some dogs lagged behind, but they all kept fairly close. Misha's head was always swivelling for danger. The fact that Spring and Barrel weren't there caused constant stress as his canine headcount was always two short. He didn't know where they were, and he couldn't waste time worrying about them. His priority was to get back home, which was where the dogs were likely to go anyway if they couldn't find him. Provided nothing had happened to them.

What Misha had to worry about was finding his own way back home. He didn't actually know where he was. How far north? How far to the east or west? He hadn't been able to pay attention while fleeing, focused as he was on spotting the best route through which to guide the horses. He knew that if he headed south, he'd eventually reach water, but where was he in relation to the bay? If he was on the east side, he might come across the Black Box again. If he was north of the bay, then there were likely a bunch of zombies to the south of him. If he was to the west, then that was good, but was he to the west? Not knowing, he thought he should head in that direction until he was certain he had gone far enough. It might mean looping back around, but it felt like the safest option to Misha.

It was both easier and more difficult to walk that day than it had been the previous one. The water had retreated, revealing obstacles it had previously hidden, but it had also left things behind that had previously been floating and were no longer simple to push out of the way. Misha worried about food, often stopping whenever they came across greenery he thought the horses might want to eat. The dogs were still finding dead animals in the wreckage, and Misha had to find a few to give to Rifle and Trigger. He wasn't interested in consuming any of it himself, as he couldn't separate what was rotten and what wasn't. He did keep an eye out for anything that looked like it had died relatively recently, but so far, he hadn't had any luck. What he did find to eat, however, was a small scattering of coconuts the storm had likely brought in. The first one he tried proved edible, so he made sure to gather up the rest.

It was well into the afternoon when he spotted Powder standing still up ahead, her head and ears perked up. Misha stopped the horses, wondering if they would be forced to flee from more zombies, but then Powder's tail swished back and forth, a slow metronome, like she wasn't sure. If it were zombies, her tail would have remained still, or even tucked up under her.

"What is it, Powder? What do you hear?" Misha asked, encouraging her to go find it.

She looked back at him when he spoke, but remained rooted in place. She whined a little, uncertain what to do.

"Crichton, is that you?" Misha risked calling out in a slightly louder tone of voice. "Harry? Ki-Nam? Angela?" But he got no response. He figured Powder would only wag her tail if it was someone she knew, or food, and since she wasn't eating, it wasn't the latter.

Misha checked the area, making sure there wasn't one of his friends lying injured nearby, but he couldn't find anyone. He had his dogs search too, but they came up with nothing. Collecting the horses, Misha walked for another block before stopping again.

"Sherlock? Are you following me?"

"Guilty," a soft voice called from one of the rooftops.

Misha groaned and ran a hand over his head, forgetting how much mud was drying in his hair and regretting it instantly.

"Come down here," Misha ordered.

He stood there, waiting in the street, until Sherlock appeared and walked over to him.

"For how long have you been following me?" Misha demanded.

"Not long. Powder noticed me almost right away," Sherlock told him. "So, in a way, I haven't really been following you; you just happened to stumble into the area in which I am. Why are you here anyway? Where are the others?"

"We got separated by a horde of zombies," Misha told him. He grudgingly admitted to himself that he was happy to see the man. He loved his dogs, but another human voice provided a kind of comfort that they could not. "I don't suppose you've seen any of them?"

"No, sorry."

"You wouldn't happen to know where we are, would you?"

"Like, on a map? Nope. Why, are you lost?"

"I got turned around a little." Misha didn't want to admit that yes, he was lost. "I'm not quite sure where my home is in relation to this spot."

"You think it's west? Because you're heading west."

"I know I'm heading west." Misha had to bite back a snap. "And no, it's south, but I need to make sure I'm far enough west that I've passed the bay, or else I might run into the zombies again."

"I don't know about a bay. I haven't been in this area long, so I can't help you with that. Sorry."

"Well, I have to keep going." Misha started walking once more, bringing the horses and cart with him. Sherlock kept pace beside him, which Misha kind of figured he might. He had tried to steal Rifle because he was lonely, after all. The thought still sparked a coal of anger in Misha's gut, but he understood loneliness, and supposed that meant he might be able to one day forgive Sherlock. Maybe.

They walked in silence for nearly an hour before Misha next said anything.

"If you saw any indication that a person had passed through the area, you'd point it out to me, right?"

Sherlock nodded. "I haven't seen any tracks, not even from animals that aren't your own."

"When did you last eat?"

"I found some prickly pear this morning. Wasn't very good."

Misha grabbed one of the coconuts he had found and handed it over. Sherlock stared at the hairy fruit while he walked for nearly a minute. When he turned to Misha, he held it out toward him.

"I don't know how to open one of these," he admitted.

Misha brought the cart to a stop in order to show him how to crack it open, as well as how to separate the meat from the shell in order to eat it.

"I think I preferred this morning's cactus." Sherlock made a face as he sliced off pieces of coconut meat while they walked.

Before night fell, Misha had finally turned them south. Sherlock pointed out a furniture store that had doors large enough for the cart to fit through, so they spent the last of the light clearing away the debris in front of it. The furniture inside was no longer arranged in its nice display locations; instead it was heaped all over, mostly near a window that had broken. With Sherlock's help, Misha was able to manoeuvre some of the furniture in order to block off the opening, working carefully so as not to break the other windows that had cracked. Some holes in the padded furniture suggested mice or even rats made their homes there, but the dogs failed to locate any that were still alive.

"What do you think of this lamp?" Sherlock asked after they had checked out the place and confirmed that it was secure.

"It's a lamp," Misha responded. He had never been one for interior decorating.

"I like it," Sherlock told him. "I like abstract things like this. It's not supposed to look like anything real, and yet it can still evoke feelings."

"Uh huh." Misha didn't care. He wasn't one for art, either. "Why are you still following me?"

"I'd say I was walking with you as opposed to following you."

"Okay, then why are you still walking with me?"

Sherlock shrugged. "I like your dogs."

"But you walked with me, not my dogs."

Sherlock grinned as Misha turned his own word specificity against him. "Maybe I like you because I like your dogs."

"I wanted to kill you."

"But you didn't. You didn't even try."

"You know I'm heading back to my community, right?"

"I know." Sherlock took a deep breath and let it out slowly. "I think I might like to go there with you. If you'll let me."

"I thought you didn't like communities?"

"Maybe yours won't be as bad as I first thought."

"What if I decided not to let you?"

"What if I decided to just start wandering around until I found it?"

"I could tell them not to let you in."

"And I bet they would listen, but I don't think you would do that."

He was right. Misha had no interest in banning Sherlock. What would be the point? Besides, he clearly had certain skills that they could make use of.

Misha found a rope hammock still suspended between its display posts over in the patio furniture section. It was damp like everything else, but given the amount of mud Misha was covered in, he didn't mind. He let Sherlock borrow a tarp from the gear on the cart, which he used to cover a soggy, mouldy mattress on which he had chosen to sleep.

The night was long and not filled with much sleep. Even though Misha had decided to bring Sherlock back to the container yard, he still didn't completely trust him, not enough to let his guard down. He kept his dogs close, and every time he awoke from strange dreams, he shone his light over at the dark lump that was Sherlock. He knew he woke him up a few times doing that, but it didn't stop him.

One of the times he checked, Sherlock wasn't there.

"Turn the light off," Sherlock hissed from nearby.

Misha immediately obeyed. He rolled out of the hammock, then he and Sherlock located each other in the dark.

"Zombies outside," Sherlock whispered.

Misha didn't know how he could tell, given the darkness, but he believed him. His dogs and the horses might have all been asleep, but if any were awake, they were keeping quiet and still, scenting the threat. Straining his ears, Misha heard a faint scuffing in the direction of the broken window. Creeping slowly along on his fingers and toes, placing every limb deliberately, he made his way toward the window. By huddling against the furniture they had placed there, he could hear the sounds more distinctly. There were definitely awkward, shuffling footsteps making their way past. Some were even close enough for a rattling, wheezing, unneeded breathing to be heard. Sherlock had made his way over as well, just as silently as Misha had. They sat together and listened as the unknown number of zombies shambled by. Misha's heart hammered in his throat the whole time, dreading that his light might have been seen and that the dead would try to get in. But they had gotten lucky. The things outside kept walking, and left the living in peace.

After deciding that they had moved on far enough, when he hadn't been able to hear them for several minutes, Misha made his way back to his hammock. This time, when he awoke from sleep, he didn't check on Sherlock. He actually slept better for it.

***

When morning came, Sherlock scavenged the immediate area for food while Misha got the horses ready. Thumper and Potato could definitely use a good brushing down, but that would have to wait until they got home. Misha wondered if the cranes had been reinstalled, or if they would need to lay down the ramps again.

"Found some berries," Sherlock announced once Misha exited the furniture store with the cart.

They split the berries between them and shared a coconut. It wasn't much of a breakfast. They hung around the area for a little bit, searching for anything else to eat, while letting the dogs forage. Rifle enjoyed stretching his legs, and even Trigger left her puppies for a little bit to get in a quick run, and gobble down something dead and rank smelling. Misha had Sherlock show him where he had found the berries, which had been attached to an uprooted bush. He carried the foliage back to the horses to see if they would nibble on it.

When they got moving, they headed south as much as the streets would allow, keeping up a constant search for anything to eat. Sherlock spotted a few tracks in the mud, most of them belonging to the dead.

"How do you know it's the dead and not those people who pretend to be?" Misha asked him.

"Well for starters, that one's walking on the side of its ankle near as I can figure," Sherlock told him, pointing to a distinct drag mark. "Not something a living person is generally willing to do. The fakers can never quite imitate the slow shuffle of the dead; they tend to want to move a little quicker and a little less painfully. Also, they leave less of themselves behind." Sherlock scrunched his face and pointed out a coil of black intestines that had become snagged on a branch in the street. The dog pack shied away from it as they walked past.

They also finally began to see signs of animal life here and there. Nothing worth trying to track down and catch, but it was nice to see that it wasn't just them and the dead moving about. A few song birds even darted overhead.

"We have to keep an eye out for alligators," Misha warned Sherlock, not knowing if he had ever had to deal with an infected one before.

"What's the worst animal you've ever seen infected?" Sherlock asked him.

"Alligators," Misha replied, not knowing what could possibly be worse. "You?"

"You mean other than humans?" Sherlock joked.

"Yes," Misha answered seriously.

"I saw a silver back gorilla once. They go full zombie, in case you didn't know. I guess it had been a zoo animal. It was still terrifyingly strong."

Sherlock sounded more sad than frightened as he described it. "It bit a guy, someone I never knew, and took out a whole chunk of his ribcage. Ripped his arm off afterward like it was nothing."

"I'm glad I don't live near any gorillas then," Misha commented.

"Yeah. At least, as far as you know, you don't. I'm not sure if the gorilla I saw was ever put down or not."

"Well then we'll keep an eye out for gorillas as well as alligators."

"Hey, was that a joke?" Sherlock smiled, teasing him.

Misha didn't give him the satisfaction of a response.

They continuously foraged for food while they walked. Sherlock knew what meat was still safe for them to eat, provided they could cook it over a fire. Even though they shouldn't be out there another night, Misha told him to gather it anyway. The container yard could do with whatever food they brought back. Sherlock actually got Misha talking for a little while, explaining what life was like at the container yard. Misha was careful not to describe their defences other than the wall—and even that in not much detail—just in case. But he talked about how they were assigned jobs suited to their skills and preferences, how they made lights for the containers, and how everyone tended to eat at the community centre. Sherlock occasionally had questions, some of which Misha answered, and some of which he did not.

Up ahead, Slide stood in the same posture that she had adopted in the little container yard when she had smelled the zombies. Misha brought Sherlock and the horses to a halt, and gestured for him to remain quiet.

"Stay here," he whispered.

Misha hurried over to Slide, who was at the head of the dogs. The rest of the pack, seeing Misha's crouched way of walking, knew that something was up and gathered silently behind him. Slide stayed where she was, nose pointed forward, as Misha made his way past her. Most of the dogs hung back, but Bullet stuck close to his side, his head low and his ears pulled back.

Ahead, a dump truck on flat tires blocked half the road. Misha pressed himself up against it and peered around the side with Bullet standing right behind him.

There were six zombies staggering around in a clear spot up ahead. Not enough to cause too much concern when there were two people to take them out. He and Sherlock shouldn't have to go around.

A tap on his shoulder made Misha flinch. Sherlock was behind him, or rather behind Bullet. He didn't know sign language, but he was still able to make enough gestures to let Misha know that he wanted to look around the corner too. Misha let him. When he was done, they hurried back to the cart.

"You should have stayed with the horses," Misha snapped at Sherlock in a quiet voice.

"They knew to stay put," Sherlock defended himself.

"It's not them wandering off on their own that I'm worried about. What do you have in terms of weapons for taking out a zombie?"

"We should leave those ones alone," Sherlock suggested.

"Why? There's only six of them."

"How closely did you look at them?"

Misha shrugged. He didn't know what Sherlock was getting at.

"Well I looked closely. They're fairly fresh, but what's worse, is that they all have bite marks."

"So?"

"I've never seen one of the really scary zombies without a bite mark. You know, the ones that can run and stuff?"

"I've seen slow zombies with bite marks."

"Yeah, but do you want to risk it? What if all six of them are the scary kind? The fast kind? The odds for us aren't so good then. Even two would be bad. And I think they might all be the scary kind. The way they were moving was a little more fluid than the others."

"They were staggering."

"And they weren't staggering as badly as others," Sherlock insisted. "We should go around."

Misha looked at the nearest intersection. It wasn't like the streets were so littered that they were trapped going this one way, and it shouldn't add too much time to go around. He wished he knew what the street layout was like in this area. If it were a grid, great, barely anything would change, but if the street they took started to loop away from where they wanted to go, it wasn't so good. Still, if Sherlock was right about the zombies being the smarter kind, it would be a lot safer to avoid them. He did notice things that Misha didn't, so he decided to trust the other man's judgement.

"All right, we'll go around," Misha told him. "I'm going to drive the cart; go sit on the back to watch our rear."

Sherlock looked relieved as he went to do what he was told. Misha quietly called his dog pack to him and instructed them to follow closely. Bullet would certainly understand what that meant, but some of the other dogs were a little finicky about whether they followed that order or not. Misha would just have to hope they did.

He climbed up onto the driving board, where Rifle changed positions in order to place his head on Misha's lap. Looking back to make sure Trigger and her puppies were comfortably settled, he also checked that Sherlock was seated well enough that he wasn't about to fall off. Satisfied, Misha flicked the reins, and Thumper and Potato responded instantly. He guided them around the nearest corner, away from the garbage truck and the zombies up ahead. If those zombies were the smart kind, and they heard the horses' hooves on the pavement, then Misha and Sherlock could have a problem, which was why Misha wanted to be on the cart. If the horses needed to run, he didn't want them leaving without him.

Constantly glancing over his shoulder, Misha kept expecting to see the zombies chasing after them, and was always pleased when he saw that they weren't. His pack was also obeying his order for the time being, all of them clumped together and trotting along behind the cart. Maybe having Sherlock back there helped keep them on task.

The road took them farther west than Misha would have liked, but they did come across another road that went south again before he got too worried. Based on how long they had travelled south already, they were definitely west of the bay. Without knowing how far north he had been, he decided that it would be safer to just keep travelling south until he reached the sea, and then follow that home. When they crossed over a river, he thought that they must be close. It might have even been the river that dumped into the bay where the container yard was, but Misha wasn't going to risk following it without knowing for certain. The ocean was a certainty.

"Hey, can we walk again?" Sherlock asked from the back. "I think I might be getting motion sickness sitting backwards like this."

Given the scavenging opportunities, Misha didn't mind slowing down. He hopped off the driving board. Rifle whined until he was lifted down as well. Apparently he felt like walking too. Seeing Misha back on foot, the rest of the dogs scattered, going back to their search for edibles in the area. Bullet stuck by Misha and Rifle though, even after he was given the release command.

Misha knew they were nearing the ocean when the buildings began to be more spread out, and the shops and houses disappeared. Here, there were factories and warehouses, and, eventually, the sound of waves. The smell of salt reached them shortly before they saw the expanse of water from between the buildings. As they approached the shore road, Misha could see all the debris floating around against the rocks, and a few stray pieces bobbing about farther out.

"Give me a second, I'm going to wash off a bit. Guard the horses," Misha told Sherlock.

This time Sherlock stayed put as Misha climbed over the barrier at the side of the road and crawled down the rocks to the water. He pushed the pieces of a shattered boat around, using the wood to move away the seaweed and scummy foam until he had a spot of clear water. He dunked his head under and scrubbed his hair. The mud dried in it had been getting rather itchy. The rest of him he left muddy. Bullet had followed him down across the rocks, and then back up, where Rifle was standing and waiting. Sherlock hadn't left the horses this time.

"Feel better?" Sherlock asked.

"Less itchy," Misha told him.

"Which sounds like an improvement, so yes, you feel better."

They followed the shore road, having to wind around from lane to lane, as the debris tended to be spread out more. Misha worried about getting a flat tire, despite the fact that the cart had already rolled through worse areas. He felt that if he was going to get a flat, it would be close to home, but not close enough to get help easily.

"Hey, what's that?" Sherlock spoke. His voice then dropped to a whisper. "There are people down by the water."

It took Misha a few seconds to spot them even after being told where they were. Two figures were huddled down among the rocks, trying to hide behind some debris and almost succeeding. Had they heard the horses coming and that's why they had hidden? Or were they hiding from something else? Were they strangers, or some of the others from whom he had become separated? Misha made a choice and hoped he wasn't going to regret it.

"Bullet," he whispered, causing the Australian shepherd's ears to perk up. "Sniff check. Go sniff check." He pointed down at the people.

Bullet understood and wormed his way under the barrier beside the road. Misha readied his rifle, although without any bullets, it was just a prop. If those people down there decided to hurt his dog, there was very little he could do about it.

As Bullet neared the pair, Misha felt his throat tighten. It relaxed in an instant when the dog's tail began to wag. Not slowly either, but a very rapid and happy swish. Misha instantly vaulted the barrier and hurried down the rocks, moving faster than he safely should.

One of the figures, the one petting Bullet, heard him scrambling along and looked up. Because she wasn't wearing her hat, it took Misha a moment to recognize her.

"Dakota?"

"Misha!" She shot to her feet and rushed up to meet him, nearly breaking her ankle in the process.

Misha wasn't one for hugs, but the shock of seeing her out there, without a shirt no less, stunned him long enough for her to wrap her arms around him. Feeling her whole body tremble, he returned the hug, hoping to provide a little comfort.

"What happened?" Misha finally asked, pulling back so that he could get a better look at her. Her bra and pants were stained with blood, and she had some pretty bad abrasions on her wrists. "Who's that?" Bullet was sitting with the other person, a male who looked familiar but Misha wasn't certain.

"Elijah. He's hurt. I'm pretty sure his shoulder has popped out." Dakota then spilled the whole story in a rush, and not completely in order; she was jumping back and forth between parts. But Misha got the gist of it. She and Elijah had been kidnapped and then escaped. They didn't know where they were and had kept moving until they ended up by the sea, where they had needed to take a break.

"Come on, let's get the two of you up to the road." Misha made his way over to Elijah in order to help him up the rocks. Dakota went to his other side to help as well, being careful not to touch his arm.

"Who's that?" she asked, looking up to the road.

"Sherlock. I got separated from my team and he's been helping me find my way home." Misha didn't want to get into the whole bit about how he had tried to steal Rifle.

The dogs were very excited to see Dakota and got in the way as they helped Elijah to the cart.

"I saw your team. Most of them. Ki-Nam is still missing, but Crichton, Harry, and Angela made it back," Dakota told him. "Spring and Barrel were with them."

A weight lifted off Misha's heart.

Elijah groaned in pain, but they got him up and seated on the driving board.

"You didn't see them, did you?" Dakota asked. "The people who kidnapped me?"

"No," Misha shook his head. "But based on what you said, about the zombie disguises, they came from the Black Box."

"Something made them leave the factory. Only three of them remained to guard Elijah and me," Dakota's voice started to crack. "I'm worried that they're going after the search team that will have been sent out to look for us. Misha, we have to warn them."

"I don't know how," Misha admitted.

"I could find them," Sherlock spoke up, unusually hesitant. Maybe he didn't want the new people to hear his voice and learn that he had female genetics.

"How?" Misha asked him.

"Well, maybe not the search party, but I could find the kidnappers. I can follow her trail back to where they ran from, and then follow the kidnappers from there. You'll at least be able to learn if they've found the search party or not."

"We can't bring the cart with us. And Elijah needs a doctor." Misha had watched dislocated shoulders being popped back in, but he wasn't about to go trying it himself. Besides, his leg wound likely needed stitches.

"I can drive the cart," Dakota offered. "Just point the way."

"This road will take you home," Misha said, pointing east. "But *can* you drive the cart?"

"It's one road. I get the horses walking, and they take us home."

The horses were really good at finding their way. The road, while covered in small debris, didn't look like it was blocked with any large stuff that would stop them.

"Please, Misha, if someone gets hurt because of me..." Dakota shivered as her eyes filled with tears.

Misha sighed. "All right. Sherlock and I will go look for the search party. We'll warn them. But you're to go straight back to the container yard, you got it? You tell everyone what happened to you, and explain where I've gone. Understand? You warn them that the people are the remains of the Black Box raiders."

"I understand."

Misha didn't know if anyone in the search party was one of his good friends, but he could easily see a few of them volunteering. Brunt was likely to be part of the group, and Cameron too. He couldn't say no to helping them.

"Puppies," Dakota gasped once she joined Elijah on the driving board and saw Trigger behind her.

"You have to take care of them," Misha told her. "Try to guide the horses along the clearest path so that there's fewer bumps and less risk of damage to the tires. You don't want to get a flat." He gave Dakota a tutorial on driving the pair of horses, who wanted to go home just as much as the humans did, and so shouldn't be difficult to handle.

"I get it, Misha, I can do it," Dakota eventually became exasperated with his constant, repetitive instructions. "Please, go find the others. Tell them that we're okay and that they can go back home."

"All right." Misha turned to his dog pack. "Rifle, come here. You're going home with them too."

But Rifle refused to come. When Misha walked toward him, the German shepherd moved away.

"*Bratishka*, what are you doing?" Misha sighed.

"I think he knows you're trying to make him leave," Sherlock suggested. "He doesn't want to."

Misha groaned. They didn't have time for this. "Fine, you can come. Dakota, get going."

He didn't have to ask her twice. She flapped the reins and the horses got moving at a gentle pace. Before they got out of earshot, Misha heard Elijah say to Dakota, "Hey, I've finally seen the ocean," which made Dakota laugh for some reason. Misha really hoped that they would be all right. He also wished that he could be heading home with them, but the thought that Cameron might end up with those same abrasions spurred him to remain away.

Once the cart was a good distance off, Rifle walked over and leaned against Misha as if nothing had happened. Misha rolled his eyes, but bent down to scratch his ears and told him that he was a good boy even though he hadn't been. The thought that the old dog, his best friend, might get hurt during this made Misha feel queasy.

"All right, *Sherlock*," Misha said as he stood back up. "Which way do we go?"

34: ONIDA
8 DAYS AFTER THE BOMBING

Onida and the others had been skirting around the edge of a city when a massive storm hit them. They had found a bus depot in which to ride it out; the inside was big enough for the horses to walk around freely. It had flooded, but there was a raised section that had stayed dry and could fit everyone comfortably. The horses didn't seem to mind the water, but the humans wanted to be dry, at least while sleeping. Onida and Shawn sloshed around in it, however, since they hoped the flood would have forced some animals out of their homes to make for good hunting. Other than an opossum, they hadn't had any luck. Onida suffered persistently wet feet, since she kept checking on the horses, making sure that they were all right. She especially focused on Nuna, who was miraculously still pregnant after all they'd been through, and Nixkamich, who was fighting off a minor infection. The infection finally looked like it was starting to get better, but Onida constantly feared a sudden reversal.

During the worst of the storm, they sat huddled around a small fire that sent its smoke pooling up against the high ceiling. Ronnie had the largest section of Hurit's pelt draped across her legs, her hands stroking the fur of her former horse. She often did this when she was nervous, and Onida had to admit that she felt the same. She kept remembering the tornado, with its screaming winds mingling with those of the horses, and the church's stained glass windows bursting inward with a flurry of colour and sound. They were all silently glad that the raised section of the bus depot wasn't near any windows.

All night, the fire was kept alive. They had gathered plenty of wood before settling in, yet most of it was wet and needed to be dried next to the fire before being thrown on it. Some of it burned fast, like the broken pallets, but the downed hardwood burned slower. Wood was wood, however, and there was always someone awake to feed the flames. Whenever Onida stirred in the night, and cracked open her eyes, she took comfort from the glow.

The storm lasted a long time, almost long enough for them to worry about the water level rising to the height of their platform. They spent a second night in the bus depot, with the fire burning much smaller and lower as they attempted to conserve fuel. Shawn had gone out for more, but the wood he brought back wasn't just wet, it was completely soaked through. Mask looked upset with his decision to accompany Shawn: the raccoon's fur was drenched and plastered to his skin. To warm up, he snuggled with Onida, the only dry person willing to hold his sodden body. The horses were displeased with the water by then, and Onida worried about their hooves and skin, as well as the depth becoming too much for them. The raised section was up a ramp, so after convincing everyone to move their stuff, she brought the horses up to dry out a little. They would have to go back into the water at night, however, due to the lack of space.

Finally the storm began to slacken off after the second night, and everyone agreed to move on. It was still raining, but not nearly as hard as it had been. The horses made ripples as they walked, but they went slowly to reduce kicking up spray on themselves and the others.

"Are we still heading toward an ocean?" Mikey wondered.

"We must be," Dom answered. "It's not like we've changed directions in a while."

"We could have gotten turned around," Harper pointed out. Butter, the dog, was sitting awkwardly on Harper's horse with her in order to keep out of the floating debris. He did not look happy about being draped over Harper's lap like a dead thing. Shawn seemed pleased with how easy it was to keep his distance, though. Even after all that time, he didn't like being near the dog. His fear of canines ran deep.

"We're heading south, we'll reach an ocean," Dom told her, twisting around in his saddle to do so.

"What if we end up walking through Mexico?" Helen wondered, her voice dreamy as she spoke mostly to herself. "What are those little countries between Mexico and South America? We could walk through them. Head through the jungles. End up all the way down at the bottom of the point, close to Antarctica."

"Yeah, that wouldn't happen," Gatsby informed her. "I think we'd notice the border. And even if we somehow didn't and kept wandering, there's the Panama Channel."

"Canal," Julian corrected him. "It's called the Panama Canal. It's not a channel."

"Whatever. We're not going anywhere near Antarctica is what I'm getting at."

"Do you think there are zombies in Antarctica?" Anita asked.

"Why would there be zombies?" Gatsby retorted. "There's no people."

"They could walk underwater until they popped up on the ice," Helen said, rather matter-of-factly. "Or float. And there's people in Antarctica. There's scientists there."

"Doubt that there are anymore," Dom grumbled.

"Maybe penguins can be infected," Anita theorized. "There could be just a whole army of zombie penguins waddling around on the ice."

"No, penguins are too cute!" Harper mock-complained. "Don't make me think of them all gross."

"More like *in* the ice," Mikey added. "Anything dead down there will have become a Popsicle."

"God, I miss Popsicles," Helen sighed. "They were the best in the summer."

"My mom would always give me one after a trip to the local pool," Dom agreed.

"I liked Freezies better," Ronnie chimed in.

"God, I hated frozen treats," Harper spoke up with a hint of disgust. "They were always melting. So messy."

"Wait, are you saying that you don't like ice cream?" Mikey said, aghast.

"Nope, never have," Harper affirmed.

"You're crazy," Dom decided.

"Yeah, it's worked out for me. I'm not the one pining for anything right now." Harper was quite pleased with her retort.

"What about your kids? Did they eat ice cream?" Anita asked. Harper was the only person that Onida knew for certain had once had children, because she was the only one who was able to talk about them for even short periods of time.

"You think I could stop them?" Harper laughed. "They loved the stuff. It felt like every day I was scrubbing melted chocolate stains out of the carpet."

"So what did you have on a hot day then?" Gatsby asked, curious.

"Lemonade."

"That's it?" Ronnie scoffed.

"It was really good lemonade," Harper defended her past self. "Freshly made, and incredibly cold. Our taps could pump out water so cold that it hurt your teeth."

"I miss running water," Helen sighed again.

The conversation continued this way for a while, with people randomly chiming in, changing topics, and occasionally trying to one-up one another. Only Onida and Shawn kept quiet. Onida never knew what she could possibly add to the conversation, and when she had tried in the past, she often couldn't get a word in edgeways, or by the time she did, the conversation had moved on from what she had wanted to say. She did enjoy listening, though, learning random titbits about her companions. Shawn just had no interest in talking, and it was impossible to tell if he was even listening to those who were.

"Shut up," Shawn eventually called out. "Zombies ahead."

There was a cluster of them trapped by a tree that had been uprooted. It was possible that the zombies posed no threat, but they decided to go around anyway. More could be lurking underwater, and they didn't want the horses receiving any unexpected bites to their ankles. Besides, it wasn't like they were in a rush to get anywhere. Before the storm, they had even had an unexpected little boon to their food supplies, having come across some good foraging as well as a group of travellers to rob. The travellers hadn't had much to steal but any little bit helped them. The travellers had been an easy target too, as none of them carried a gun with any bullets in it. Onida and her group hoped to find more like them.

After going around the trapped cluster of zombies, they ran into a few more of the dead things. They had never run into a group of zombies so large that they felt the need to flee. Instead, they took turns riding up to them and putting them down. The horses didn't like getting close, but they trusted their riders. Onida had gotten skilled enough to be able to ride past at a run, leaning over the side of her saddle, and lopping off heads with a sharp sickle as she went by. She liked showing off the skill whenever it was her turn, because the others always seemed so impressed. Shawn always just used his bow, retrieving his arrow afterward.

As night fell, they found themselves in an area full of low houses. Several of the houses had collapsed, so no one trusted spending the night inside one of the ones still standing. Instead, they set up their tents on a roof that had been dislodged and deposited in the middle of the street, after testing it for stability. The surface was uneven, and they needed to spread out across it to distribute their weight, but at least it kept them out of the standing water.

Onida checked all the horses, lifting their feet up to properly inspect them. She worried about all the time they had spent in the wet, but there was nowhere dry enough for them to stand. They couldn't even get up on the roof without the risk of their weight snapping through it. Their hooves were all coated in mud, making it difficult to check on their condition, but Onida was determined to inspect each one. Several of the other riders found some greenery with which to feed the horses while Onida worked.

"We should have doubled back and gone a different way after that storm," Dom complained as he sat on the roof. "This area has been decimated; there's not going to be much for us to find."

"We're close to the ocean," Gatsby told him. "That was an ocean storm."

"How would you know?" Dom challenged him.

"The affected area can't be *that* large, can it?" Mikey said before Gatsby could respond. "We've already been travelling through it for a day, so we might as well keep going."

"I'm saying we should have turned around when we left the bus depot," Dom insisted.

"Well we didn't, and saying we should have doesn't do us any good now, does it?" Helen was clearly feeling snippy. She never liked having to sleep on an angle.

Dom kept any further remarks about what they should have done to himself.

They spent the night sleeping in shifts, always keeping a close eye on the horses. It was very dark and hard to see them, but they had been hobbled and any movement was accompanied by the sloshing of water. Onida kept awake during her shift by playing with Mask with her fingers, in the same way one might play with a cat. He had learned not to bite hard, but Onida knew she was going to wake up the next morning with a couple of scratches from his teeth and claws. She didn't care; her hands were often marked up by him.

When the morning came, it revealed patches of wet pavement and marshy, overgrown lawns. A dead rat was floating belly up in a puddle formed at the end of a driveway. Butter ate the thing with a crunch and snap of bones.

Onida checked on the horses' hooves once more. She took the time to wipe the mud off their legs, and insisted that they give the horses a break in order to dry out, especially since it had finally stopped raining. The others didn't mind. They were in no rush, and instead picked through the wreckage around them. Shawn went hunting, but instead of coming back with fresh meat, he had found only firewood he intended to dry out. He had it bundled up in leather in case it started raining again.

It was after lunch when they moved on. Onida had suggested they walk with their horses instead of riding them, and everyone agreed. The horses had also filled themselves on the long, soggy grass, which Onida was happy about when she saw they were entering a more developed area. The buildings crowded the sides of the streets, leaving little room for greenery. The plants that still clung to their small patches were mostly buried under garbage.

"Man, that stinks," Dom commented. "I'll be glad when we leave here and don't have to smell all this trash anymore."

"Dom, you are trash," Ronnie teased him. "I don't think you'll ever escape the smell."

"The dead fish are what's getting to me," Mikey added, waving his hand in front of his face.

"We're definitely near the ocean," Gatsby spoke up. "Why else would there be fish? I *told* you it was an ocean storm."

"Yeah, but you didn't know that. You just got lucky," Dom decided.

"Fuck you, I know shit," Gatsby retorted.

They didn't reach the ocean that day, because Onida had had them stop for so long in the morning, but they suspected they were getting rather close. The number of dead fish had been slowly increasing. Mask loved it, sometimes unable to decide which carcass to eat first. They came across a few zombies that day, but they were easily killed, and had posed no threat.

When the sun started to sink once more, they located a warehouse in which to spend the night. There was nothing in the warehouse besides a bunch of rotten pallets, some cardboard boxes that had fallen apart and all but fused with the floor, and a heap of plastic bags in a corner. The place had probably been abandoned since even before the outbreak of the zombie virus.

Once they had set up their tents, the doors were closed so that the horses could roam freely inside. Mask managed to find a way to climb up to the rafters above, and scared some pigeons that had been taking shelter up there. Shawn managed to shoot down two before they all escaped through a broken window. Onida had fired an arrow as well, but she had missed. The pigeons were cooked and eaten that night. Everyone got just a sliver of meat off the small bodies. Shawn carefully placed the best feathers in a supply of them he kept for making arrows. The cook fire had been as small as they could make it, and then they let it die out once it had served its use. Shawn's crank lamp was passed around, so that everyone could take a turn keeping it lit as they stayed up a little longer and talked about inconsequential things. When Onida finally crawled into the tent she shared with Shawn and Mask, she fell asleep in an instant.

***

Onida started the next day feeling great. She knew they were going to see the ocean that day and she found herself looking forward to it. She was actually excited to see the sea.

Having woken up before the others, she prepared breakfast for everyone, and then exercised Butter by repeatedly throwing his ball across the warehouse. As everyone else got up, one by one, they also seemed to have an uncommon energy. They had been travelling for a long time just to see an ocean, and now they were nearly there. No one had asked what would come next. They could come to a decision on that later.

The conversation at breakfast was light, mostly full of pleasant reminiscing of things that had happened after the infection had broken out. While they often reminisced about times before that on their travels, there was always a dark cloud of loss hanging over the words. Talking about the good memories that came after kept the mood lighter.

The horses were deemed fit to ride, but everyone decided to walk that morning anyway. They had enjoyed stretching their legs, and wouldn't mind doing some more of the same. Onida threw her saddle and all her gear over her horse's back, and spoke soft words to her. She had been riding Nadie since the beginning, and so considered her extra special. She gave her special horse scratches and kisses while she waited for the others, who were always slower about packing up.

The sun was poking through the clouds in places when they left. Not where they were, but in the distance, sunbeams lit up the sky. Onida smiled at the sight of them. Today was going to be a good day.

Shawn and Onida were in the lead, as they always were. They walked just ahead of their horses, guiding them through the debris. Behind them, all the others walked in a staggered pattern, sometimes side by side, and sometimes alone.

Onida was just starting to think that she could hear the ocean, when suddenly a group of zombies walked out ahead of them to bar their path. That wasn't typical zombie behaviour, and a cold trickle rolled down Onida's spine.

"Turn around," Shawn hissed. "Turn around, go back."

But there was no time. The zombies had rifles, and raised them to their shoulders. With a crack, one fired. Onida felt a bullet rip past her.

Nadie, who had carried Onida so far, screamed with her last breath. The bullet had punctured through her chest, and into her heart. She collapsed sideways, dead a second later. More shots split the air, and Shawn's horse went down as well, and then another bullet took out Nixkamich, who had been following as a packhorse. Onida faintly registered that in order to hit Nixkamich, there would have to be other shooters, not just the ones in front of them. And since when did zombies fire rifles?

"Get out of here!" Shawn shouted as he slammed into Onida. He kept running, dragging her with him, both of them collapsing through the smashed window of a bar.

"Sorry about your horses!" a voice taunted. "But it seemed only fair!"

Fair? Who was speaking? Onida didn't recognize the voice. One of the zombies? Her mind struggled to make sense of what was going on.

"Show yourselves!" Dom shouted back. He had been near the back of the line and wouldn't have seen the zombies with the rifles.

"We still have your little friends! Would you like to see them? One of them doesn't look like he's doing so well."

Onida had no idea what the taunting was about. As Shawn pulled her upright, she saw Nadie again, lying in the street. She was dead. How could she be dead? All the horses were dead. How could all the horses be dead, just like that? She had taken care of them for so long, they couldn't just all die!

"Come on!" Shawn hissed in her ear, dragging her toward the back of the bar. She felt his hands grab at her waist and startled, but a second later he had pulled her revolver free and held it out before him. His rifle had been left back on his horse, along with just about everything else. He wore only his hunting rig, his bow and arrows on his back, with Mask in his pouch, a scrunched-up ball of terror. Onida had nothing, her own bow still on Nadie's saddle, likely snapped in two with the way she had fallen. She couldn't recall where she had last put her sickle, but it wasn't on her.

Shawn pulled her through the dark, into a kitchen that could only be navigated by its faint reflective surfaces, and painful collisions. When he let go,

Onida continued to follow Shawn, no longer listening to the voices out on the street. Her panic had returned, humming through her very skin as she trusted the man ahead of her to get them out of this.

The back door squealed as it was forced open. The revolver roared before Onida even had a chance to see who Shawn was shooting. He fired twice, and once Onida's eyes had readjusted to the light, she saw a man on the ground, choking on his own blood. One bullet had punched his gut, while the other had torn open his throat. This one was definitely no zombie.

As they fled down the alley, Shawn fired every bullet from the revolver. He killed a woman guarding the end of the passage, and winged a sniper up on a roof.

"Someone go around and cut them off!" Onida heard an unfamiliar female shouting nearby. "Don't let them get back home!"

Home? Onida thought, just one more point of confusion among many. *They didn't have a home, so how could they be cut off from it?*

Shawn and Onida didn't stop running. They changed directions often, hoping to lose anyone that might be following them. They wove around dead cars, and hurdled fallen branches. Onida skidded a few times on sodden trash, but she always kept to her feet. She was good at running, always had been.

When they slowed, it was because Shawn was out of breath. His lungs heaved as he staggered, and as he walked, he threw up. Onida went to his pouch and drew out Mask, holding his bundled form to her chest. She spoke words that were meant to calm him, hoping that they would calm her too.

"What just happened?" Onida asked Shawn once his breathing seemed to be under control again.

"I don't know," he admitted with a shake of his shaggy head.

"Would you like to hold Mask?"

Shawn held up the revolver, which he refused to put down even though Onida knew that it was now empty. Onida continued to cradle Mask, who began to relax as they kept walking.

"Did those zombies shoot at us?" Onida couldn't keep the question inside.

Shawn shook his head. "They weren't zombies and they weren't shooting at us. They were people wearing rotten skins, and they deliberately aimed at the horses."

Onida had considered the horses as part of the us, but she didn't point that out. She was horrified by the idea of living people wearing the skins of dead people. Why would anyone do that?

"If it makes you feel better," Shawn said, "they will likely become ill from the rot." It was uncommon for him to say anything of comfort, so Onida nodded despite the words not making her feel even remotely better.

They had just left the others. They had abandoned Dom, Helen, Gatsby, Julian, Ronnie, Mikey, Anita, and Harper like it was nothing. They had run from the dead carcasses of their loyal horses, and all the supplies they had been carrying. They hadn't lingered for even a second, to find out what was going on.

Onida had no idea which direction they were headed. They wandered about in what felt like circles. She attempted to slow her heart rate, but every unexpected sound had it hammering.

As they headed down a narrow alley, Mask began to squirm and grunt. Onida carefully put him down, and the raccoon headed backwards a short way, and then started to climb a fire escape. Before Onida could suggest they follow him, a man appeared at the end of the alleyway, not far off. So did a large pack of dogs.

Onida froze a few feet behind Shawn. She could see his hand trembling, and she thought she heard the word *you* escape from his lips, but couldn't be certain.

The skinny man at the end of the alleyway broke the startled standstill by raising his hands. Sound started to escape his mouth, but Shawn was too wired, too frightened. He raised the empty gun before any words could escape. He shouldn't have done that.

The dogs reacted, charging at Shawn. The empty revolver clicked several times as he tried to fire at them. He was too frightened to think of drawing his bow. He was too scared to run, but Onida was not.

She took off. She ran away from Shawn just as his screams pierced the air. The dogs were barking and growling as they bit into him, but Onida didn't look back. Maybe Shawn always knew that this would be the way he died. Maybe that was why he was so afraid of canines. But Onida was afraid of everything, so what did that say about her own end?

She ran. She ran, and she ran, and she ran. It didn't matter where she was going, as long as it was away from there. Her legs were pumping, her feet slapped against the pavement. She remembered this. She remembered running for her life, only now she was dodging storm debris as opposed to the trappings of the forest. She didn't even have a backpack with her this time. She had nothing but the clothes she wore.

She ran. It was what she was destined to do.

35: EVANS
12 DAYS AFTER THE BOMBING

The sun rose in a splash of yellow against the lingering clouds. Evans had woken up early to give their provisions another once over, and to search for Gerald. The kid was nowhere to be found. Not even Blue knew where he had gotten to, answering Evans' enquiry with a shrug and a shake of her head. He didn't need to know sign language to understand that much.

"Keep an eye out for him," he told Frannie, as he performed a quick search of places where he might be in town.

He ended up saying the same thing to his travelling party once they were ready to go. "He's not allowed where we're going, but he may try to follow us," he added.

With eleven silent ones, six people from Bridges, and Frannie's three emissaries joining Evans, that put the party at twenty-one. As for non-humans, there were seven camels, two horses, five rather ornery mules, and a disabled hawk that one of the Bridges people had been taking care of for several years. Since there weren't enough ungulates for everyone to ride, Evans stayed on foot with the majority, having Moe carry a few more supply packs instead.

"They better like us, given how much food we're bringing them," one of the emissaries, who had introduced himself as Mac, said to Evans as a few last minute goodbyes were exchanged.

"Given the size of our party, we're carrying less than you think," Evans responded. "Especially since you and two others will be making the return journey." Not knowing if the container yard still existed, Evans had done his best to procure enough supplies to make it to the Theatre, should they need to continue. They were also carrying some seeds, which, if everything went according to plan, the container yard people would pay for by returning the same number of seeds from their future crops.

"Everyone ready?" Evans called down the line once it looked like the goodbyes were complete. He spotted Winnie standing off to one side, her eyes shimmering, but she refused to cry. Evans had told her that he hated saying goodbye, and so she was doing her best not to get emotional about his short visit. Once everyone behind him had given a thumbs up as he had instructed earlier, Evans started walking.

Frannie accompanied them to the edge of town, where a guard had resumed his post after the storm. She said nothing as they departed, merely stopping on her border and watching the rest of the party pass.

Once they had officially left the town behind, Evans sent ahead the man he had chosen to be their scout. He usually liked to send at least two people, but this man was mounted on the only other horse and seemed very capable of taking care of himself. When Luke had first told Evans that he carried a lance, Evans had pictured some cheap, mock jousting thing, or maybe a wooden spear, but it turned out that what Luke carried was as real as Evans' sword. He rode with ease, the long piece of metal resting in a cup on his horse's saddle and against his shoulder. The sharp, pointed end glinted in the light. Luke had come with the people of Bridges, but Evans suspected he hadn't always lived there. He wore a bulletproof vest, a military combat helmet, metal grieves that protected his lower legs, and leather bracers on his arms. Even his horse was partly armoured with what Evans suspected was some sort of light plastic, that had been wrapped in leather to reduce any noise. The horse seemed particularly well trained and so Evans thought of it as the second man to make himself feel more comfortable about not having another human accompany Luke. The fully loaded repeater rifle on the back of Luke's saddle also helped.

Evans drifted up and down the line as they walked, talking with the people from Bridges and the emissaries in order to get a better idea of their various skill sets and experience. Most of the people from Bridges had travelled long distances before their journey between their ruined home and Paddock. It seemed that the ones willing to venture out were those who had arrived at Bridges after it had been established. They had been newcomers once before. Paddock's emissaries were also well travelled, having reached out to other communities in the past. Evans decided that the party was a good group of people to travel with. The only children were the two silent ones, and while little kids were often a liability, these two naturally kept quiet, and always stuck to the middle of the pack with their mom. They seemed to have no curiosity about their surroundings, even when they stopped, which kept them out of trouble.

They made decent time that morning, and Luke didn't report any dangers. He had found them a patch of rock that was relatively flat and mostly dry, and suggested they break there for lunch. Evans agreed. While they were stopped, he had everyone check each others' feet for hot spots, not wanting any of them to end up with unnecessary blisters. He instructed two of the people from Bridges on better ways to tie up their boots based on their individual foot shapes.

"Being straight laced is not for everyone," he told them. This drew a chuckle from the older of the two.

When they got walking again, Evans found himself drawn toward the mules. He knew a lot about mules, more than he knew about horses, because he had travelled with several in the past. But he drifted over to them because he didn't know much about hawks. The bird of prey sat with its talons wrapped around a padded bar that stuck up from a mule's supply packs. Its legs appeared to be tied down, but its eyes scanned their surroundings with razor sharpness.

"I thought they usually wore some sort of hood thing," Evans commented to Erin, the owner of the bird.

"She has one, but I only put it on her at night, or if she's becoming particularly distressed. I'd rather have her eyes looking out for danger, wouldn't you?"

"Can you tell when she spots something that we would need to know about?"

Erin wiggled her hand in the air. "Sometimes, but not always. I have to watch her body language."

"What kind of hawk is she?"

"Falcon, actually. A gyrfalcon."

"I heard she was disabled." Evans couldn't see anything physically wrong with the predator.

"I found her with a busted wing. I might have been able to set it right with the proper equipment, but since the uprising, I haven't exactly had access to that kind of stuff."

Evans had heard many names for the time when zombies spread around the globe, and assumed that the uprising was Erin's. "Did you work with birds before then?"

"I did, I was a falconer."

"You could make a living at that?"

"Surprisingly, you could. People hired me to bring my birds to airports to clear away the pest birds. Sometimes I was hired to help clear away the pigeons from a certain building downtown, although that's a losing battle. I would also bring my birds to conservation areas or schools to put on presentations."

"What happened to your birds?"

"I released them. I didn't know if I was going to survive, and I wanted to give them a fighting chance. I was rather lonely until I met Sheila, here. Never did get along with people much when I didn't have a bird nearby to talk about." She grinned at Evans, pointing out that they were currently talking because of the bird.

"What does she eat?" Evans wanted to make sure they had food for the falcon on their journey, and needed to know what to look out for.

"Just about anything," Erin answered. "Other birds, mostly. If she could fly, ground birds would be her preferred target, but small mammals would do in a pinch."

"What's the best way to feed her, since she can't fly?"

"I usually hunt a small animal for her, then toss the carcass her way once I've put her down in a safe location. She'll pounce on it and feed herself."

"I'll let the others know to keep an eye out for small animals that you can feed her."

"Thanks."

Evans drifted away, walking up the line to tell everyone exactly what he said he would. He lingered for a little longer beside Blue.

"Any sign?" he asked her.

Blue shook her head. She had been given a special task to keep an eye out for Gerald. He figured that if the kid were following anyone, it would be her, and so it stood to reason that she was the most likely to spot him. He might *want* to be seen by her. Evans had convinced Blue that locating him was for Gerald's own safety. He had been exiled from the place they were going to, and he didn't know what they did there to people who attempted to return. Evans didn't want Gerald to get hurt, and neither did Blue.

"Well, let me know the moment you see anything." It was possible that Gerald wasn't following them. He might have stayed back at Paddock like he was supposed to, disappearing before everyone left in order to avoid a potentially painful goodbye. Evans could understand that impulse. But he didn't think that's what Gerald had done. He was a teenager after all, and teenagers were prone to do whatever they decided was best, even if everyone else told them that it really wasn't. Evans knew about that impulse as well.

With such a large group, it was harder to find a place in which to stop for the night. They were crossing a lot of undeveloped land, which was both a positive and a negative. There was a greater distance between buildings whenever they decided to continue on to the next one, but the buildings they came across were often large barns. They found a massive pig farm, which put everyone on immediate alert, but it seemed that none of the animals were still around. The barn they had been housed in was empty of all but a faint, lingering smell. They searched the place, end to end, just in case, but nothing squealed or rushed out at them. The structure was solid, and they were able to lock the doors from the inside, which made them all feel a lot safer. Just because they hadn't run into any undead pigs outside, didn't mean that it wasn't still a possibility. Evans wondered if Gerald was out there somewhere. If he was, hopefully the kid could find himself a safe place to shelter for the night.

As Evans picked a spot to lie down, he was grateful for the packed dirt floor. He wondered if Sheila ate snakes. Erin hadn't mentioned them when she talked about the falcon's diet. The bird of prey probably knew better than to mess with a rattler.

***

Evans was awoken the next morning by a restless Moe. It was early in the morning, too early based on Evans' internal clock. The ugly horse was apparently dissatisfied with his current accommodations. Worried that maybe a rat was in there bothering him, Evans got up to look. But no, the horse was alone.

Looking down the row, Evans saw that only Kathy was awake, the last guard of the nightshift. He almost didn't see her; her small form and rags made her disappear against the pens where she sat. If she hadn't waved in acknowledgement, he might have assumed she was patrolling outside. Using gestures that weren't sign language but were hopefully understood anyway, Evans attempted to communicate to Kathy that he was going to bring Moe outside and take a look around. Whether Kathy fully understood or not, she waved in acknowledgement again. After changing his position to gather Moe's lead, Evans struggled to find Kathy a second time, despite now having an idea where she was. Even the rest of the silent ones, who were all asleep, were hard to make out as human figures. If anyone *had* come upon them in the night, they would likely have been in for a surprise.

Moe seemed happy once he and Evans were outside, and quickly set to work cropping the grass. He must have just been hungry. Evans guided Moe in a slow circle around the outside of the pig barn. He studied the grass for any movement of undead pigs, but he also searched for where Gerald might have spent the night. There was a lot of open terrain around the pig barn, not conducive to providing shelter. The safest place that was not inside the barn, was on top of it, but there was no way Gerald had the skill to get up there without the sound-sensitive silent ones hearing him. A group could spend the night in the grass after flattening out a large clear spot, but Gerald would be on his own. Where would Evans go if he were by himself and trying to follow the party? A small stand of straggly trees presented the best option. If there was no indoor shelter, then up off the ground was where you'd want to be.

With Moe in tow, Evans made his way toward the trees. Whenever he wasn't checking for danger around him, he scanned the branches.

Ah, there you are, Evans thought to himself as he picked out a suspicious bump within a large fork in a tree. As he approached, he kept expecting Gerald to stir, but the kid was fast asleep.

"Good morning, Gerald," Evans softly called up once he stood directly beneath the tree.

Gerald flinched and nearly toppled from his perch, managing to grab a branch and steady his balance at the last moment.

"Comfortable?" Evans asked him.

Gerald looked down at him with a sullen expression.

"Trees don't make the best sleeping spots," Evans went on. "Too much fear of falling out of them, but they make do in a pinch."

"I'm not going back," Gerald told him, loosening the straps of his pack. He had used the bag to secure himself to the tree, which was clever. If Gerald *had* fallen over in the middle of the night, he would have ended up hanging by his armpits, his neck and head scraping painfully along the bark as he and the pack changed places. Still, he wouldn't have fallen.

"I know you're not going back," Evans spoke up to him. "I can't force you, and I'm not going to waste a day trying."

Gerald's mouth moved. He had clearly planned on an argument. "So I can come with you, then?" he eventually decided to say.

"You're still not allowed in the container yard."

"I want a new trial. I've changed."

"Whether you have or not, I don't think they'll care. You tried to strangle an old woman."

"That was after the battle, after all those zombies came. Everyone was kind of out of their mind then."

"You tried to strangle her because she told people about the zombie you had somehow smuggled over the wall, which got it killed. I don't think your defence is going to hold any water."

Gerald sat in the tree, pouting, his pack now held tightly against his chest and stomach. "It's my decision."

"And it's my decision as to whether you can travel with the party or not."

"I'm going to keep following you."

"I know, and I'm tempted to continue letting you stay at a distance. Maybe being on your own out here will teach you something important."

"The others will let me walk with you guys." His tone was becoming that of a petulant child.

"Will they? You were banished from the place where they are hoping to live. How hard do you think it would be for me to convince them that treating you as a hostile would be in their best interest? I wouldn't even have to convince all of them, just a few would be enough to force you to keep your distance."

Gerald's face turned a sickly pale. He clearly hadn't considered that.

SOCIAL INSTINCT

"So how was your night up there?" Evans asked. "Bet you didn't sleep well. Hear any strange noises in the night? Feel anything creeping along your skin?"

The way Gerald turned his head away, Evans knew it had been a bad night. Of course it had been. Evans knew what it was like to be out there alone. He had learned how to take care of himself after years of travel, but even then, the first night after leaving a party, he always struggled to sleep.

"Your body is going to be sluggish today," Evans continued. "You're a teenager, so it won't be as bad, but travelling will be hard, especially alone, and especially while trying to follow a group without them noticing. You'll be less alert, and it will be easy for danger to slip your notice. Tomorrow, after you fail to sleep well a second time, it'll be gruelling. There will be times when the only thing you can focus on is putting one foot in front of the other. Even if you spot the danger before it reaches you, your reaction time will be slowed. You may even misinterpret the danger, thinking it's less severe than it really is. Or more severe, and end up wasting more energy that you don't really have to waste. Your muscles will ache, and your head will throb, and your guts will get all twisted up. Tell me, Gerald, does any of this sound worth it to you?"

Gerald was refusing to look at him, but Evans could see the tear rolling down his cheek.

"Do you think Blue is worth it? You barely know her. You've travelled together for a few days, which is a lot different than living in proximity for weeks. She barely even knows what life is like outside of the silent ones. She's going to go through some things, internally, and that may change the person you believe she is. Hell, on the flip side, she barely even knows who you are. At least she had the wherewithal to realize that. She knew better than to stay with you in Paddock. She knew that you weren't worth it. So come on, Gerald, tell me. Is all of this worth it?" Evans was unconcerned about going too far or saying too much. He was actually hoping to eviscerate Gerald with his words, and knew that the kid's exhaustion would help him in that matter. "Answer me, Gerald!"

Gerald flinched and nearly lost his grip on his pack. He finally turned to Evans. "What do you want me to do?" he screamed down at him. "What am I supposed to do, huh? You want me to go back to Paddock? You want to me go by myself?" Anything else he might have said got strangled by sobbing.

"Well, I want you to come down from that tree, for starters," Evans told him, his voice becoming gentle.

He waited patiently as Gerald put on his pack and began to make his way down. When his foot slipped, Evans moved forward to help, but Gerald barked over his shoulder at him.

"I can do it!" He dropped the last few feet, stumbling as he landed. Up close, Evans could see the dark bags under his red and puffy eyes.

"I don't want you travelling back to Paddock by yourself," Evans told Gerald, letting the kid take hold of Moe. The ugly horse seemed to provide him with a modicum of comfort. "I also can't spare anyone going with you. What I would like to do, is have you travel with us, but you cannot go to the container yard. I don't even want them to know that you're in the area, because I promised

378

them that I would take you away. Once we get close, we'll find a safe spot for you stay for a few days. And you *will* stay there. I don't expect Frannie's emissaries to stay for very long. When they leave, they will pick you up, and you can travel back to Paddock with them."

Gerald snuffled and wiped at his nose. "Will you be coming with us?"

"I don't know, but I honestly doubt it. Once I'm certain that the silent ones have settled in, I'm likely going to accompany some people from the container yard to a colony I think they should get acquainted with, if they haven't already. I'm also thinking about trying to find a way to get the silent ones still remaining in their town on board with some sort of trade agreement, but I haven't quite figured out how to do that yet. I don't know exactly what I'll be doing, but it very likely won't involve going back to Paddock."

"Okay," Gerald snuffled again, and nodded.

"While we travel, you try to avoid talking to the others. Even Blue. You say goodbye to her. Understood?"

Gerald nodded.

"Make friends with Paddock's emissaries. And you *can* make friends with them, Gerald."

While Gerald nodded again, it was impossible to tell if the words were sinking in anymore.

"Come on, let's get back. The others are probably already halfway through breakfast by now."

Gerald led Moe toward the pig barn. Evans followed a few steps behind. He didn't want Gerald to see him. He didn't want the kid to notice that his hands had started shaking. What he had just done to Gerald had reminded him far too much of his own father, a man who had graduated from abuse to butchery. A man whose voice could be heard through the walls, and taught Evans to be quiet and still. A man he had had to kill in order to save his own life at just thirteen years of age, although he hadn't been able to save his mother. Evans knew that that man still lived within his bones, a dark shadow that followed him no matter how far he travelled. And it had kept him alive more often than Evans cared to admit.

***

Gerald kept his word that first day. He didn't make any attempt to communicate with the silent ones other than when necessary. He also didn't speak to the people from Bridges, unless they spoke to him first. Even then, he kept his answers short and polite. Although he stayed near the emissaries, especially Mac, he hadn't yet attempted to strike up a proper conversation with any of them. He mainly just moped along, probably too tired to do much else. Evans let him ride on Moe's back for a little while after their lunch break.

That night, they were still in farm country, but the barn they came upon was in no condition to shelter them. Thankfully, the farmhouse was, sort of. The main floor quickly became quite cramped with Moe, Luke's horse, the camels, and the mules spreading out through the living room and kitchen. With all the people upstairs, there wasn't much space left there either. Evans made sure that Gerald's bedding was placed in a corner, and that only Mac and the other two emissaries were near him. He then went back downstairs to take the first watch.

The best part about travelling with a party as large as theirs, was that they had enough adults so that everyone had to take only a short shift, and only every other night. Gerald would be able to sleep the whole night through, and be more productive tomorrow.

They headed out bright and early, and hadn't gone far before they found themselves in what was once a cornfield. The plants had survived through the years, overgrowing their once neat rows. Several other plants had also invaded their space. The stalks were tall, which was worrisome due to the lack of sight lines, but they pressed through them anyway. With Luke on his horse up ahead, Gerald on top of Moe at the back, and some silent ones on camels in the middle, they had a good number of lookouts to scan the field for signs of movement. As an added bonus, they found some corn that was still edible. Much of it had been eaten by birds or beasts, or become over-ripe, so they gathered it up in order to separate the good from the bad during their lunch break.

At the far end of the field, a large number of crows flapped and cawed around them. They were angry that the humans were walking through their territory, but they were smart enough not to try attacking. Maybe if a person had been on their own, they'd have had a problem, but the birds were far too cautious around so many people and ungulates. Sheila, the falcon, probably frightened them too. Evans had once been told that a flock of crows was called a murder. As a rule, he wasn't superstitious, but something about large gatherings of crows always put him on edge.

Gerald finally started a few conversations with the three emissaries as they walked. So far it looked like he was getting along best with Malala, although she was probably the farthest from him in age. It appeared to Evans that Malala was willing to take Gerald under her wing, which he thought would be great for the kid if he allowed it.

When night came once more, they had reached what was either a small settlement, or the fringes of a bigger one. The gas station with the garage attached to it was their best bet for the number of people, and so they piled inside. The security doors across the main entrance had been twisted and broken by scavengers at some point, but the bars over the windows were still intact, even across the window that had had the glass shattered out of it. Evans noticed that the amount of destruction was slowly increasing as they headed toward the sea. He knew the coastal area would have been hit harder by that storm. Evans helped get the garage door open from the inside, and then closed it again after the animals were led within. Not having to take a guard shift that night, Evans found himself a corner and went straight to sleep after eating dinner.

The next morning, Evans stepped outside and was greeted by sunlight. Not just a couple of beams peeking through the clouds here and there, but full sunlight. There was finally more blue sky than there were clouds, and Evans' mood was immediately elevated by that fact. He had been sunburned many times and would likely die of skin cancer if he lived long enough, but Evans always preferred the sunny days.

It seemed the sun had everyone's spirits up. There was more talk during breakfast, and the two children played patty cake with their mother, which was an uncommonly noisy game for them. Mac told some jokes, which had several people in stitches, including Gerald, and Paul showed everyone how he could pop his own shoulders in and out. Evans had seen the trick during their previous time travelling together, but he enjoyed watching the fascinated, disgusted, and horrified expressions of the others as they watched. It was actually a handy trick, because he could have his hands clasped behind his back, and bring them up over his head so that they were then in front of him. Probably wasn't good for the joints, but it could certainly help if he were ever snatched by somebody.

Other than the happier mood, the day was going like the others. Luke rode on ahead, while Gerald watched the rear with Malala. The kid and Evans took turns walking Moe, and today was Evans' turn. The horse kept bumping his nose against Evans' shoulder, but Evans had no idea why. He suspected the horse wanted something from him, but he couldn't figure out what it was. He had certainly eaten enough. What more could he need?

It was shortly after their lunch break when the day was disrupted.

Luke had gone on ahead while everyone else finished packing up, as he always did, but just before they started walking, he came thundering back.

"I spotted some people up ahead," he explained.

"How many? What did they look like?" Evans asked him.

"I saw four, and they had a bunch of dogs with them. They looked exhausted, based on the way they were walking."

"Gerald, Ang, I want you to come with me. Luke, can you lead us to where you spotted them?"

"Of course." Luke dismounted in order to walk at their pace, but he held onto his horse's reins and brought it along.

They didn't have to cover much distance, as Luke had known better than to scout too far ahead. They climbed a rise that overlooked a stretch of highway littered with dead cars. The debris-covered swath of asphalt carved a clear path, allowing them to see a fair distance in either direction. Luke pointed out the figures making their way along it. They weren't moving fast, which was likely why Luke thought that they were exhausted. And they did seem to have a number of dogs moving around them. The dogs twigged in Evans' mind, and made him realize that the figures were coming from the general direction of the container yard. Evans slid off his pack and pulled out his binoculars. After staring at the figures for several seconds, he handed them off to Gerald.

"Recognize any of them?" he asked the kid.

Gerald peered through the binoculars for about as long as Evans had. "Yes. Three of them I've seen around the container yard. I don't know the fourth."

"All right, wait here, I'm going to go down and talk to them."

"Are you sure it's a good idea to go alone?" Luke questioned.

Evans wasn't sure, but didn't answer. "Gerald, whatever happens, you keep well out of sight."

Gerald grunted in annoyance, but he also nodded.

Evans made his way down the hill, and then started along the highway. He drew his sword and held it in the air above his head. They might recognize him by his sword, but even if they didn't, they could spot him coming more easily and be less surprised. As Evans walked, he slowly turned the sword, actually hoping to flash some light off it in their direction. Bad things happened when you came upon a person unaware.

Once Evans was close enough to see the four people over the top of a cluster of sedans, he put his sword away, his shoulder aching slightly from the effort of keeping it aloft so long. Some of the dogs reached him first, and Evans thought he remembered a few of them, especially the big and lanky Great Dane. He was glad to see that the dogs knew him too, as they were wagging their tails when they came up to him.

"Evans? Is that you?" one of the travellers called out, completely surprised.

"It's me, Danny," Evans answered. He didn't know if Danny would be happy to see him, given that Evans had once kidnapped him.

"What the hell are you doing out here?" he asked. The smile on his face made Evans feel better about their chance encounter. "Nice getup," he then added, referring to the fact that Evans was wearing some of the rags that the silent ones had given him.

"I think I should be the one asking that question. Hello, Misha."

Misha responded with a faint nod of his head. He had been carrying one of his dogs, a German shepherd, and had only just put it down.

"I don't know if you ever met Jon," Danny went on, pointing to one of his companions.

"I remember seeing you around," Evans spoke to Jon. "You were one of the people who threw the grenades over the wall. I'm sorry to say that I don't recognize the fourth member of your party at all."

"This is Sherlock. He's fairly new to us as well," Danny told him.

"So why are you out here?" Evans asked now that the pleasantries were done with.

"We're tracking someone," Jon spoke this time. "A small group."

"Tell me what happened."

Evans listened to the story split between Jon and Danny, with Sherlock and Misha adding a few bits and corrections here and there. They started by telling him the condition of the container yard after the hurricane, and he was glad to hear that it was still standing. He then learned how some of the raiders had survived the explosion that Evans had helped set off, and that they had eventually found their way to the container yard, and snatched two teenagers. Evans didn't know the girl, but he tensed up when he heard that the other had been Elijah. The story took some unexpected turns from there. Elijah and Dakota had managed to escape on their own when most of the raiders had left, presumably because they had spotted the search party. Based on what Misha and Sherlock had seen, it was not the search party, but a completely separate group of travellers, that no one had seen before.

"You all right, Misha? You look paler than normal," Evans observed.

"My dogs killed someone. I don't know if it was one of the raiders, or just one of the travellers who managed to escape and thought that *I* was one of the raiders." Not knowing was clearly eating at him.

"There was a girl, too, who got away," Sherlock added.

Danny and Jon went on to explain how they had left to help the search party early in the morning, before anyone at the container yard knew that Elijah and

Dakota had escaped. Like Misha and Sherlock, they were eventually drawn to the gunfire that had passed between the raiders and the travellers. When they got there, they found a bunch of dead bodies, including a number of horses. The travellers all seemed to be dead, but some of the raiders had survived. That was who they were now tracking down.

"You've been tracking them for three days? Why?" Evans thought that seemed a little excessive.

"Sherlock is aptly named," Danny told him. "He can tell that the raiders have someone who's not going along willingly."

"Someone from your search party?"

"No, we found them and they're all accounted for. We left them trying to decide the best way to get the dead horses to the container yard. No reason to waste good meat."

"We think it might be one of the travellers," Jon said.

"You've been tracking the remaining raiders for three days because they have someone you don't know?" Evans struggled to wrap his mind around it.

"If we let those fuckers go again, who's to say they won't just come back?" Jon's voice was filled with anger, which explained why he was hunting them down. The way Danny looked at Jon, he was probably just making sure that his friend didn't get hurt.

"The travellers might have been friends," Misha spoke in a quiet voice. "We sent some people to a number of the colonies you told us about. The travellers might have been from one of them, coming to meet us. We owe it to them to find out."

Evans suspected that rescuing this unknown person was Misha's way of making up for what his dogs had done to the stranger.

"All right, your turn," Danny said to Evans. "What brings you to this spot?"

Evans told them about the silent ones and the people from Bridges, as well as Paddock's emissaries. His story was a lot less convoluted than theirs.

"We're not far behind the raiders," Jon told Evans. "We think we'll be able to catch them before the end of the day. We thought maybe you were one of them at first. Problem is, we don't have much in the way of firepower. If you and your party are willing to help us, I guarantee that they'll be accepted into the container yard."

"It's my in as well," Sherlock mentioned. "Although I have to say, all this tracking has been kind of fun. In an exhausting, starving kind of way." There was something strange about Sherlock's voice, but Evans didn't comment on it.

"It's not my decision," Evans told Jon. "But I'll ask the group and see what they decide upon."

"Well make it quick. We don't want to let them get any farther ahead than they already are."

Evans did make it quick, running back to where the others were waiting up on the hill. He was surprised to find the whole party had gathered behind the rise. It made it a lot easier and quicker to fill them all in between his panting. The silent ones and the people from Bridges both held conversations amongst themselves to decide: the silent ones with a flurry of gestures, and the Bridges people whispering in a huddle.

"We'll stay back with any supplies you don't want to bring too close," Mac offered. "We're just emissaries. We're not going to go sticking our necks out before we know these people. We'll also watch over the kids if they need watching."

The silent ones had not discussed it for long. "We'll help," Burt voiced their decision. "We don't mind killing people for our new community."

It was a little disconcerting for him to put it like that, but Evans thanked them. The people from Bridges took longer, eventually deciding against getting directly involved.

"That's all right." Evans understood completely. "We should have more people guarding the supplies anyway. I only ask that you let your future friends from the container yard use some of your guns."

The people from Bridges accepted this. Paul actually looked glad that he had something to offer other than himself. He had likely been pushing for them to help, but had been outvoted.

The whole party moved over the rise and found the small group from the container yard. Even Gerald came, although Evans made him wear his silent one rags with the hood up.

"The silent ones all offer their help," Evans told the foursome once they had been located. They had continued to walk along the highway while the discussions occurred. "Those from Bridges offer whatever supplies you need, but they and the emissaries from Paddock are going to stay behind and guard our supplies."

"Fair enough," Danny nodded.

"Even Sherlock couldn't pin down their numbers. Are you sure there's enough of us?" Jon asked Danny.

"There's more than enough of us," Ang answered him instead, with a cold confidence that reminded Evans of the way they had appeared around him and Gerald when they first met.

"Let's get going then," Evans recommended. "Sherlock was it? Lead the way."

***

Jon was right about them not being far behind. By leaving back the camels and mules, the party could actually travel faster than it had been. At Evans' insistence, Misha had also been left back with those who weren't going to fight. He clearly hadn't been eating enough during his journey, especially if he had been carrying that old dog half the time. Evans knew the look, and made him and his dogs stay with the others. Misha didn't put up much of a fight about it, he just made Evans promise that he would do whatever he could to save whoever it was that had been snatched. Evans didn't mind making that promise.

They had come to a town when Sherlock slowed.

"What's wrong?" Jon immediately asked him. "You didn't lose the trail, did you?"

"No, it's just that I think we're getting really close. I'm worried about turning a corner and being on top of them." Sherlock had whispered, which made everyone start being cautious about the sounds they were making, except for the silent ones, who did that naturally.

"They'll be looking for a place to spend the night," Danny observed, gesturing toward the sky.

"I've been in this town before," Sherlock told them. "There's a square with a courthouse up ahead. A group of this size might find the building's large, open rooms appealing. It matches up with the other places they've been staying."

"Let's get over there then," Jon urged.

Sherlock led the way, taking an unconventional route. They ended up climbing up onto a long building and travelling across the roof, passing over a strip of stores below. They then crossed a small bridge made out of a very heavy plank to pass over an alley. Evans had been uncertain about this route, but discovered that it had been for the best when they came upon the square at the end of it. Across from them, the group of raiders were prying off a board that had been nailed over the doors of the courthouse.

"Idiots don't realize that the window to the left isn't locked," Sherlock pointed out with a grin. "There's no need to ruin that perfectly good barricade."

"Why was it boarded up to begin with?" Danny whispered. "Are there zombies inside?"

"No," Sherlock shook his head. "If we had travelled at street level, you might have noticed that just about everywhere around here is boarded up. It's just what this town did when they evacuated."

"Anyone see the captive?" Ang asked in a voice that almost couldn't be heard.

Evans couldn't see anyone struggling, and the majority were clumped together too tightly for him to look for bindings, even with his binoculars. But wait…

"Fuck, it's Ki-Nam," Evans hissed.

"People back home thought he was dead," Jon told him. "He was with Crichton but got separated during an attack of the dead. I guess these fucks found him before he could make his way back."

"Which one is Ki-Nam?" Ang asked, his voice in Evans' ear.

Evans handed over his binoculars in order to point him out more effectively. Ang didn't have much time to spot him before the raiders had pried the last board off the doors and swung them open. The whole group crowded through the opening together.

"How do we rescue him?" Danny wondered.

"You wait here. We'll handle this," Ang told him.

"What do you mean?" Danny looked at him, confused.

"Wait here." Ang and the rest of the silent ones turned around and found their way off the roof.

"Evans," Jon turned to him. "What the fuck? Most of them didn't even take guns."

"Just let them do this." Evans knew there was no way to stop them now anyway.

"We should spread out around the courthouse," Danny suggested. "Make sure we have any escape routes covered."

Sherlock agreed to take him and Jon to good positions from which they could watch, while Evans remained where he was, with a rifle borrowed from Paul in his hands. Being careful not to let the setting sun reflect off the binoculars, he peered through them again at the courthouse. Through some of the windows, he could see a couple of the raiders exploring. He guessed that Ki-Nam was in the room on the far left of the building, for he saw the most movement over there.

Searching for the silent ones, he saw nothing.

The orange of evening faded into the purple of night. A few lights flashed about inside, but never for long. The raiders were confident, but also cautious. Evans hadn't seen any evidence of them dressed up like zombies, as Sherlock had said they were wont to do.

One of the courthouse doors opened, and two men carrying assault rifles stepped out. There was a small flash as a lighter was briefly lit. Evans wondered whether these men had actually managed to find cigarettes, or if they were smoking something else they had found. Either way, they were careful to keep the glowing cherry hidden behind their hands.

As Evans watched, something he couldn't hear distracted the two men. They both looked to the left, which was not the direction of the danger. From the sharp shadows cast by the moonlight, a pair of silent ones emerged on their right. It was over before Evans even really knew what was happening. The two men collapsed, a black puddle of blood growing around them. From the left, a third silent one appeared and all three slipped through the doors. Evans had no way of knowing who they were, only that one wasn't Kathy. Due to her size, she was the only one Evans would be able to identify from a distance. If he could spot her.

There was no way to know for sure what was going on within the building, but Evans could certainly imagine it. While he had only seen three go in, he imagined that the others had found their own routes inside. Now, whenever a light disappeared, Evans didn't think it was because the owner had turned it back off.

There was only a single sound that reached him. At one point, a startled cry made its way across the square to Evans' ears. It sounded like French to him, but he couldn't be certain. There was nothing after that.

A tense few minutes later, the doors to the courthouse opened. The silent ones all exited with a very confused looking Ki-Nam in their midst.

"Did you get them all?" Jon's voice drifted from a building somewhere to Evan's right. There was awe in his voice.

One of the silent ones raised a pale hand with its thumb up. They believed they had gotten them all, and Evans had no reason to doubt them.

"Ki-Nam, are you all right?" Evans called from his rooftop.

"Evans? That you?" Ki-Nam responded, surprised. "Yes, I'm okay, nothing broken. You've made some interesting friends."

"Wait there, I'll come down to you."

The silent ones gathered in the square, around the dried-up fountain. As Evans turned away from the edge of the roof to find his way down, he wondered where Gerald was. The silent ones would have left him behind while they worked.

Evans climbed down a ladder hanging off the side of the building, having to drop the last few feet to reach the alley below. He had just turned to head toward the square, when a shape rushed out at him from a doorway. Evans pulled in his stomach and twisted as the moon glinted off metal headed for his gut. His shirt ripped. There was no time to grab his sword, so he swung with the rifle butt and missed, the stock whooshing through the air above his attacker's head. Sharp pain bit into Evans' leg, just above the knee as his attacker's blade became buried there. Evans cried out and toppled sideways.

As his attacker pounced again, Evans raised the rifle to defend himself. Instead, the full bodyweight of the person landed on the gun, which was then pressed down into Evans' throat. In an instant, he could barely breath.

Struggling to lift the person off him, or throw him to one side, Evans finally looked up at the face of his assailant. It was Gerald. The kid loomed over him with a crazed look as he leaned all of his weight down onto the rifle, and counterbalanced Evans' attempts to buck him off. Evans had pushed him too far. He should have known better. He should have known that if Gerald was willing to strangle an old lady over a zombie, he'd attack Evans over... over what? What he had said? Blue? Taking him from his home? It didn't matter now. Spots were filling Evans' vision. His pack was working against him, caught on something to his right. The knife was still in Evans' left leg, making his leg all but useless. Every attempt to use it sent a jolt of paralyzing pain up his whole body.

"Die already," Gerald spat in his face.

And then suddenly the pressure on Evans' throat was gone. Gerald's face disappeared as his head was ripped back. Too far back. His head had been nearly cleaved off, and Evans soon found himself drenched in the kid's blood. As Gerald's body fell off him, Evans was finally free to sit up. His breath wheezed, and he coughed, his throat feeling like fire. His face was hot from the blood, and he set to wiping it away from his eyes.

"Are you okay?"

Evans had expected a silent one, but instead he heard the voice of Jon. Once Evans could see, he watched as Jon wiped clean the blade of his katana.

"Are you okay?" he asked again.

Evans nodded. "That's Gerald," he wheezed. "He's not a silent one. He's dressed like them, but he's not one of them. He's crazy."

"Don't try to speak. Come on, let's get you some help." Jon assisted Evans to his feet.

The knife continued to protrude from Evans' leg as they hobbled into the square, but Evans didn't care to pull it out.

"What the hell happened?" Danny asked when he spotted them.

"Gerald," Evans puffed.

"Who?"

"I'll explain."

"Later," Jon insisted. "Let's patch you up first."

Evans was dumped onto the grass, and packs were thrown down beside him, as people found water and first aid supplies. Ki-Nam knelt down on his left.

"You've made some terrifying friends," he spoke in a low voice to Evans as he started wiping at his face with a wet rag. There was a look of fright in his eyes that Evans didn't think he had ever seen before. Ki-Nam was normally so stoic.

"Yes," was all Evans answered.

As the knife was extracted, and the wound cleaned and stitched, Evans's eyes sought out Blue. He wanted to say that he was sorry about what had happened to her friend. Maybe it was the pain talking, but he wanted to apologize for Jon's brutal actions, as if the silent ones hadn't just done the same to more than a dozen others. But he couldn't find Blue. He couldn't tell which one was her. All he saw were shadows.

36: JAMES
11 DAYS AFTER THE BOMBING

It was the day after making his offer that James finally heard back from the council. They had accepted his trade: food for a shipping container. Supplies were going to be loaded up onto the flatbed truck, and exchanged for one, unopened container. Whatever was in the container, whether it be useful or not, would belong to the Theatre.

"I can agree to that, provided you throw in some seeds from your medical plants."

The council shook on the deal, with all parties knowing they were likely to make many more in the future, should it all work out.

James had expected to be busy with preparations after the agreement, but instead he found himself somewhat bored. The Theatre didn't need his help getting ready. He had pointed out the container yard on a map the other day, and apparently that was all they required of him. He walked around and watched the hive of activity, until his foot started to hurt too much. He ended up back in the IMAX theatre, sitting down with the others.

"Do you know when we're expected to head out?" Skip asked him. Only he and Marissa were in there with him, the rest of the group off exploring, or making use of the flush toilets while they could.

"I was told tomorrow morning," James answered.

Skip nodded. "I won't be coming then."

James frowned. "Why not?"

Skip raised his injured hand. "Dr. Dilton doesn't recommend travel for a few days. I mean, I still could, but I don't really want to."

"Do you want to join this community?"

"Maybe," Skip shrugged. "But really, I'm just tired. Tired of walking and sleeping in different places every night. I need a longer rest before making my way back."

"Well, it's up to you, if it's all right with the people here."

"Reggie said it's fine. He probably likes the idea of one of us remaining behind while a bunch of them go out to our place."

"Two of us," Marissa added. "When Skip told me he planned to stay, I volunteered to stay with him."

James nodded. "All right then. You have until tomorrow if you change your mind. And make sure you tell the others."

The two of them returned his nod.

James took off his boots and his socks and checked his foot. It still jarred him to see the absence where his two left most toes were supposed to be, and the mess of angry scars that wrapped around the area. He knew he had been lucky not to lose the whole foot without anyone having to tell him that. He washed both his feet and then left them out to air dry, as he lay stretched out on his bedroll. It was all too easy to imagine ending up like Aaron, having a limb lopped off to save his life, only to die from an infection after the procedure. James' foot had sometimes been red and puffy during the journey, but that had always just been from irritation. All the wounds were closed up now, and he should be safe from an infection claiming the rest of him.

The day passed slowly, with members of the group wandering in and out. Skip and Marissa explained to each of them their decision to stay. Belle was the only one to offer up any sort of protest, saying she would miss them, but neither Skip nor Marissa were swayed. No one offered to join them in remaining behind. James bet they felt like him: this place was nice, but it just wasn't home.

Knowing they would be leaving the next day, James had hoped to get a full night's rest, but instead found his mind unable to let go of consciousness. He lay still, hoping that at least his body would be rested, but his mind kept bouncing around, thinking about everything that could happen on the journey home. What if there were more pigs? What if the lions weren't intimidated by their larger numbers? A trailer was not something that could be easily stowed away inside a building for the night. They would need to have guards outside with the supplies. What if the lions came then?

James eventually fell asleep, but the morning came too soon after. There were no windows in the theatre, no way of knowing just what hour it was, but Reggie came to wake them when it was time to get ready.

"Will you be coming with us?" James asked their guide as he packed up his gear. While he would have liked to have left sooner, at least his clothes had had ample time to dry out.

"Me? Oh no, I'm staying here." Reggie sounded honestly quite surprised by the question.

"Not a traveller, huh?" James commented.

"No. No, I'm not a traveller," Reggie agreed. "Besides, with Skip and Marissa remaining here, they'll need someone around who they feel comfortable questioning."

"So you'll take care of them?"

"Of course."

"How long are they allowed to stay?"

"I don't know. Depends on how long they want to stay. They may be required to do some work to pay for their keep, but it's unlikely to be very manual labour. You might have noticed that we barely have enough jobs to keep everyone occupied as it is, and we wouldn't want to put unnecessary strain on Skip's injured hand."

"Thank you."

"I'm just doing my job."

"I have to ask. Were you like, a hotel concierge or something before all this happened?"

Reggie merely smiled in response.

Once they were packed up, everyone said their goodbyes to Skip and Marissa. Even though they might see each other again, maybe even in just a few weeks, it was a rather solemn moment, since they all knew just what kinds of things could happen between now and then.

Reggie first led them all to breakfast, which was a meal larger than James' stomach was able to manage. He actually couldn't eat it all, and he struggled to remember the last time he had felt so stuffed. Reggie's breakfast was much smaller, and when this was pointed out, he said that they were given a large meal as was customary for everyone before they travelled outside the wall. Knowing that food would be tightly rationed, the Theatre liked to send people off with full stomachs.

"Or bursting ones," Samson quipped.

The scraps were gathered up by someone who had been waiting off to one side. The leftovers would be taken to the animals, so James didn't feel like he was actually wasting anything. In fact, if he had known beforehand, he might have eaten a little less.

Reggie led them outside, and then across the parking lot toward the wall.

"Where's my horse?" James asked.

"Already saddled and waiting beyond the barrier for you," Reggie told him. "Both of them are."

James looked around for any last minute preparations, but couldn't see any. "Are they all waiting on us?"

"I don't know. They might still be arranging a few last minute items on the trailer."

It seemed that the folks from the Theatre had gotten up extra early to get ready, and had allowed James and the others to sleep in. It caused an odd twist of guilt and embarrassment to roll through James' gut. Or maybe that was just his body trying to remember how to digest so much food all at once.

They passed through the hidden door and found their new travelling companions outside. James was surprised to spot Dinah and her team, and wondered who had decided to pull them off their patrol. He also saw that Vee was coming with them. She sat at the head of the large, modified flatbed trailer, looking mighty impressive with the team of draft horses before her, replacing what would normally be a long haul truck. On the trailer behind her, a large heap of boxes and bags had been secured, and a few tarps were still being strapped down over the lot of them. If there was food filling everything that James saw, the container yard should be able to survive until their crops grew in, even though they hadn't even started planting yet. They would have to keep rationing, and he didn't know how much of the food was of a kind that could keep for a long time, but it was an uplifting sight nevertheless.

"These fellas have been waiting for you," spoke an unfamiliar voice from the direction James hadn't been looking. He turned and saw a man walking two horses toward him. Soot and Spark had been cleaned up so nicely that for a brief second, James had failed to recognize them. Soot had no such problem with him, and trotted the last few steps, placing his head on James' shoulder when he reached him.

"Hey, boy," James said to Soot as he gave him a scratch. "Did you enjoy your stay here?" He then searched for the man who had handed the horses off, but he had already left to do some other task.

"It's like they've been to the spa," Katrina joked as she looked over Spark. "Someone even buffed their hooves."

James didn't think they had actually been buffed, but a farrier had certainly been at them. They remained barefoot, but their hooves had been properly trimmed, and cleaned as thoroughly as the rest of them. James ran his hand down Soot's neck, feeling how soft and clean his coat was. It certainly wasn't going to last with the journey ahead.

Katrina hoisted herself up onto Spark's saddle.

"You're going to ride today?" James commented, still looking over Soot's saddlebags.

"There's a lot of people walking, and a lot of people riding," Katrina commented as she cast her gaze about the area. "I can ride without feeling guilty, so I'm going to do it."

James scrambled up onto Soot. He had sometimes felt guilty about riding when the others had walked, but with his foot, it had been necessary. Even with other riders around, and more people on foot, James felt a little bit of guilt as he sat above them. He wondered if Katrina was being honest, or if she had some other sort of reason for wanting to ride.

James guided Soot around to say hello to Vee.

"I didn't realize you were coming," he told her.

"It's been a while since I've seen somewhere new. I decided I should stretch my legs. Besides, Reggie mentioned you wouldn't mind having someone explain our legal system to your people. I thought who better to do that than me?" She was smiling and looked quite eager to get underway. It really must have been a long time since she had gone out, because James didn't think anyone should be that happy leaving the safety of their walls.

After clarifying a few points regarding the route they were taking, James then rode along the trailer to which Dinah was helping to secure the last of the tarps. He noticed then that Katrina was deliberately following him, and thought he knew why she had chosen to ride: to make sure James wasn't alone, or singled out among them.

"I didn't expect to see you again so soon," James said, drawing Dinah's attention away from her work.

"The council figured you'd feel more comfortable if the party included people you already knew," Dinah explained her presence. "Given what happened to your friend while we were together, I wasn't so sure you'd want to see my team again, but I do the job I'm asked to do."

"I can't speak for the others, but I'm glad you're here."

"I prefer familiar faces to all these strange ones," Katrina added.

This led to Dinah pointing out who the important people were. Vee, as the only council member making the trip, was in charge of the whole operation. If she said something, they were all to obey. Along with Dinah's, there were three other teams, each of them consisting of six to eight people, and each with its own leader. Of the four teams, two were on foot, and two were on horseback. There were also another five people who, like Vee, didn't normally leave the Theatre, although they had made several trips to other colonies in the past. There were two doctors, two engineers, and a woman with a head for numbers, who was going to keep track of everyone's supplies as they travelled.

"Quite the group. We're going to have trouble finding places to sleep at night," James noted.

"Most of us will be sleeping right here," Dinah commented, gesturing to an empty space on the trailer between the supplies and the edge of it. "And when the ground is dry, more of us will be sleeping underneath. Of course, you're welcome to spend the night wherever you please."

James would decide that with the others whenever they stopped.

All the team leaders Dinah had pointed out, as well as herself, eventually reported to Vee that they were ready to go. After James checked with his own group, making sure no one wanted to change their mind at the last minute and stay behind with Skip and Marissa, he reported the same.

"Let's get this train moving then!" Vee shouted. She snapped the reins and set the team of draft horses to walking. James had thought that she had been sitting up there in order to watch the preparations; he hadn't actually expected her to be the one to drive the trailer. Commanding a large team of horses like that took skill, and he had to admit that he was a little impressed. He could ride one horse just fine, and knew how to drive a small team of two, but he didn't think he'd even have the courage to sit in Vee's place. He was beginning to see why she was so well respected.

The people from the Theatre had clearly planned in advance the order in which they would travel. One of the teams with horses rode out ahead, acting as their vanguard, while the second team brought up the rear. The two teams on foot, which included Dinah's, walked on either side of the flatbed trailer. While Vee drove at the front, the doctors, engineers, and supply woman, all sat along its length. There was no obvious gap for James and his people to fill in, so they were free to walk wherever they wanted. They started by grouping near Dinah's team, since they knew them and none of the others.

Throughout the day, the people who had been riding on the trailer swapped places with some of the people from the teams who had been walking. Their break for lunch didn't last long. The draft horses weren't even set free of the traces, and instead were fed and watered from bags. Other than bugs and birds, James hadn't yet spotted anything that moved aside from them. He wondered if that were true for the vanguard. He also wondered if they were accumulating a trail of the dead behind them. If they were, they'd find out when they stopped for the night.

That stop came before sunset, giving everyone ample time to prepare before it got dark. There was no finding a good, sizeable shelter; they just stopped in the middle of the road. The horses were freed of their traces, and left to wander in a makeshift corral that consisted of ropes hung between the trailer and a nearby house. James removed Soot's tack and let him join the other animals. Katrina did the same for Spark.

"Guard duty will be split into six shifts," Vee gave the order from the trailer bed as dinner was handed out. "Karl, your team will take the first shift. Dinah, you have the second, while my team will take the third." Based on the shifting of feet, James hadn't been the only one who hadn't thought of Vee and the group on the trailer as another team. "Djimon, your team covers the fourth shift. Scarlet, you have the fifth shift, while James, I'm trusting your people to cover the sixth."

James was glad to hear that his group wasn't being left out of the protection duties. He didn't want anyone from the Theatre to feel resentment toward them, or to think that they weren't pulling their weight. Besides, he had already started thinking about where he would post guards the moment they had stopped. The house nearby had a second storey, which would be a good vantage point from which to view the street, so he'd probably post Katrina up there. Everyone else he'd position around and on the trailer, while maybe taking a post among the horses for himself. Where he was going to position himself ultimately depended on how his foot felt when he woke up.

People spread out their bedrolls along the trailer bed, beside the supplies, as Dinah had said they would. Others set up beneath the trailer, while still others camped out on the house's porch. James and his group went inside the house, spreading out in the living room. They all agreed that they felt safer indoors and liked having a little bit of separation between them and the people who were still strangers.

James slept well, which surprised him, and he felt rested when Scarlet woke him. His foot felt good, so he stood among the horses after walking a patrol around an invisible perimeter. There were a couple of dead zombies lying about that hadn't been there when they had stopped, so everyone knew to be on the alert for them. Scarlet hadn't mentioned her team taking any out so they could have been dispatched by the first team, but she had looked exhausted as she crawled to her bed underneath the trailer and might not have thought to say anything. James couldn't tell just how recently the dead had been put down, so he went into full alert assuming that more could be in the very immediate vicinity. But there weren't. The end of the night passed without issue, and the others began to wake with the sun.

After a cold breakfast, the horses were saddled up once more, the draft horses harnessed, and then they set out. This time, James rode apart from his people, deliberately taking some time to get to know more of the people they were travelling with. He started with Djimon, whose team flanked the other side of the trailer from Dinah's. Katrina shadowed him, thereby inadvertently getting to know a few more people. By the end of their second day of travel, most of James' group had begun to socialize with the others. The only people they hadn't really been able to converse with were the ones in the vanguard. At least, not until they stopped for dinner.

The following day was more hectic. The travellers came across a fair sized herd of zombies shortly before their lunch break. There weren't enough zombies for them to consider redirecting, but enough that they had to close ranks around the trailer and carve their way through the dead. Due to their proximity, lunch occurred late and was interrupted by more zombies as some stragglers from the herd they passed through caught up. No one was hurt, but by the time they stopped for the night, everyone was a lot more tired than they had been the previous two nights. The guard shifts at night remained the same. This time everyone was a lot more vigilant, and the previous shift wouldn't leave their posts until their replacements were in position.

For nearly a week, James and what remained of his group from the container yard travelled with the people from the Theatre. They came across more zombies, had to deal with two aggressive alligators, and once stumbled upon a nest of rats. Miraculously, no one got killed. One of the Theatre people, however, fell off his horse when it reared. He got away with only a broken rib, and was well taken care of by the two doctors they had with them.

Knowing that the pedestrian bridge was out, James was glad to see the other bridge they had chosen to cross was still standing, especially when considering that the amount of damage they passed through got worse every day. The vanguard now rode even farther ahead, as the trailer frequently caught up to them whenever they had to stop to clear a path for it. After crossing the bridge, James kept a sharp eye out for the lions, especially along rooftops. Not once did he see a flash of tawny fur. He hoped that meant that they had moved on, or maybe had gotten washed away by the storm.

It wasn't until then that James finally registered that he would be home soon.

***

"I'm going to ride ahead," James told Vee one day when they had stopped for lunch. "We're almost there, and I think I should give everyone an advance warning." What he didn't say, was that he was worried about the place still being there. Not just because of the storm, but because he knew that food supplies had been running low and the place might have needed to be abandoned in an attempt to find something to eat.

"Very well," Vee told him. She then leaned toward him in a conspiratorial manner and whispered, "Does my hair look all right? I find first impressions can be rather important when two leaders meet."

James had learned while travelling with her that she had an odd, and sometimes intense sense of humour, and that her remark had been a joke. "You look fine and fierce," James informed her.

Vee gave him one of her sharp smiles before he rode off. Katrina immediately caught up with him.

"Can't wait to get home either?" James asked her as Soot and Spark trotted side by side for a few blocks before slowing to a walk.

Katrina shrugged. "I could probably wait. I just figured that you shouldn't be alone in case something bad has happened there."

"Thanks."

"So when we get back, I assume you're going to become the container yard's Reggie? Making sure everyone from the Theatre has what they need?"

"Are you kidding? The Theatre is going to be making sure that our people have what they need. They're the ones with the food, after all."

"We're very fortunate that they're so well off."

"We're fortunate that they were willing to help us," James countered.

"What would we have done if they had refused?"

James shrugged. "Come back empty handed, I guess. Or moved on to the next place."

"The place we were supposed to go is dead. And the other one was taken over by assholes."

"If the Theatre had refused to help us, would you have believed what they said about those places?"

"I guess not. I'm glad we didn't have to go to the Dale. Could you imagine adding weeks more to this trip?"

"I can, but I'm also glad we didn't have to go any farther. I felt relieved when they told us what had happened."

"Me too. I'm surprised how willingly the council believed us. If I were them, I would have thought we were just trying to weasel some supplies out of them."

"I think it's because of the people we lost along the way," James told her. "Dinah saw what happened to Aaron, and if we were lying about Jack and White, we probably wouldn't have thought to mention lions. Besides, look at us. I don't know if you've noticed, but we're basically all loosely held together bones."

"I've noticed," Katrina sighed.

They led their horses between some buildings and could finally see the structure that marked the very end of the massive cement pad that made up the entirety of the shipping container yard, not just the part they lived in. That building had already been half falling apart, with a large section of roof caved in, so James wasn't overly surprised to find that it was now mostly flat, with only a few deeply rooted support posts left rising up into the air. Still, it caused his jaw to clench with nervousness.

As they approached the container maze, James realized that they were going to have a bit of a problem. The trailer was definitely not going to be able to navigate the sharp turns within. Either they could try to bring it around the side, where the terrain was very rough and rocky, or they would have to park at the end of the maze and everyone would have to haul the supplies through it by hand.

The clipping of the horses' hooves echoed among the containers as they rode between them. They didn't make it very far through the maze before a stone came whizzing out of the corridor ahead, striking a container with a *bong*.

"Friendlies!" James shouted, trying to settle a startled Soot. "We're returning from a community visit! Friendlies!"

"Fuck," Katrina hissed as Spark nearly reared under her. He backed up a ways before Katrina could get him under control.

"It's James Brenner and Katrina!" James called out, not realizing until that moment that he didn't know Katrina's last name. He didn't know a lot of people's surnames; there wasn't much need for them.

Freya stepped around the corner with her sling swinging and murder in her eyes. James instinctively threw his hands in the air, dropping Soot's reins and hoping the horse didn't dump him.

"Just me," James said. "And Katrina. We're back."

Freya registered who they were and relaxed, which allowed James to do the same.

"What are you doing out here?" James asked the fierce woman.

Guarding the children like I should have been, she answered in sign. She didn't offer any further explanation, leaving James somewhat confused.

Guiding Soot around the corner, James was at least able to figure out what children she was referring to. Dakota, Maui, one of the new kids James knew to be Elijah, and two others whose names he couldn't quite recall, were standing in a group. They had clearly been ready to fight or flee depending on what had happened with Freya.

"What are you all doing out here?" James asked as he neared.

"Looking inside containers and using a code to mark what's in them," Dakota explained, gesturing to the wagon of spray paint just behind them. Looking at the containers farther along, James saw the ones with doors that could be reached had all been marked with various symbols and colours. "We're looking for any food that might have lasted. MREs and junk." When Dakota readjusted the hat on her head, James picked up on the faint, healing injuries on her wrists. Elijah was also sporting a few cuts and bruises, and one of his arms moved stiffly. *Something* had definitely happened here.

"Well, you probably won't need to do that for much longer. I come bearing many gifts," James told her.

All the children and Freya eyed the rather meagre supplies on his horse.

"I made us some friends," James explained. "They brought a lot of food for us. Unfortunately they're not going to be able to fit down here, so I think I need to find some people to go to them. Is Bronislav still around? And are Crichton and Boyle back?" Really, James was wondering if they were still alive.

"Yeah, they should all be around somewhere. I suggest looking for either Boyle or Crichton," Dakota said.

"What's wrong with Bronislav?"

"He's… fallen from favour," Dakota told him without explanation. Maybe she had learned that from Freya.

"James?" Katrina spoke up. "I'm going to head back to the edge of the maze. If Vee and her people show up, we don't want any of them trying to find their way through here only to be greeted by Freya's rocks."

"Probably a good idea."

As Katrina turned back, James forged on ahead alone, leaving Freya and the children to their work. He would get the full story from Crichton.

Crossing the open distance between the maze and the wall, James rode with his hands in the air, the reins clutched in one of them. Soot was walking a little faster than his normal pace, knowing that home was just ahead. James was surprised to see that there were no ladders lowered in case Freya and the kids had to return in a hurry.

"Hello, Misha," James greeted him as he approached the nearest wall guard. "I guess if you're back, then I wasn't lied to when I was told Crichton should be around."

"He's here somewhere," Misha confirmed. Two of his dogs had been lifted up onto the wall with him. From Soot's back, James could just make out one that was sleeping, while the other was staring over the edge, its nose wiggling in James' direction. The dog's eyes were the same ghostly pale blue as Misha's. There was also a second person up there with Misha, someone whom James didn't recognize in the slightest.

"Who's that?" James wondered.

Misha glanced over his shoulder. "Sherlock. He's new. Crichton said he has to stick with me while he learns the ropes."

"Hi," Sherlock waved.

"Hey. I'm James."

"Nice to meet you, James."

"So can I have a ladder, or what?" James asked Misha.

"You'll have to go around to the short side," Misha gestured in its direction. "All the ladders are over there right now."

"All right. Thanks. Is there someone there who can watch Soot? I'm not seeing any cranes."

"The cranes are over there right now as well. And if they're busy, there should be someone able to watch Soot."

"Thanks."

"I'll let them know that you're coming." Misha took off at a jog along the wall, followed by Sherlock. Both dogs then chased the pair, after the one who had been asleep jolted awake. James saw that it was Rifle, the only dog whose name he knew.

James followed along the wall at a more sedate pace, wondering what would require all the ladders and the cranes to be over by the short side of the wall. Maybe they were finally finishing the second layer over there. But why would that require all the ladders?

As soon as James turned the corner he knew. The terrible soil beside that section of the yard was being worked. Every teenager and several children were moving rocks and turning over the rough ground. Horses were harnessed to a boulder that needed moving. They were attempting to prepare the land for planting, a difficult task to say the least. Several adults were helping as well. Along the wall, the number of guards had been doubled, bolstering those that had lined up on foot along the edge of the plot. Every single ladder was here, because if they needed to scramble over the wall, they needed as many routes as possible.

"Hey, what's going on here?" James looked up and asked the nearest wall guard. He saw that it was Claire.

"Planting, what's it look like?" Claire told him.

"No, I can see that. I meant there." James pointed down the length of the wall to where the cranes were set up. He assumed they were over here for the horses, but now that he was looking at the area more closely, something else was going on.

"Oh, that," Claire laughed. "Yeah, the storm actually shifted some of the containers down in the water. Harry's organizing a crew to fix it. He's also going to put a new container in there, one with doors on either end that can only be opened from our side of the wall. We're going to finally have a door, no more ladders! If you hurry, you can probably get in through the opening before they plug it up."

"Thanks, Claire. By the way, do you know where Crichton is?"

"I don't see him out here, so he's probably organizing dinner in the community centre."

James kicked Soot into a trot. The old horse didn't mind at all. It seemed the animal had been given a shot of energy by being back in familiar surroundings.

Claire hadn't been lying about a door being installed. The container was lined up with the opening in the container wall and logs were being laid down to roll it forward. James and Soot squirted through before it was blocked off. A handful of people greeted him, recognizing that he had just returned.

Entering from this side of the container yard was unusual. Having lived at the Black Box, James was used to visiting by boat, and arriving at the dock which was at the opposite end of where he was. Except for the work crews, he entered a patch of the yard that was empty. It used to hold containers that had been partly modified for living, but now those were all gone. James wondered if that was because they were now in use somewhere else, or, since they had been empty, they had been moved by the floodwaters and were now sunk in the sea somewhere.

As he rode Soot along just above the rocky shore, James saw that some things were still being dried out. A string of mattresses were lined up in the sun; a handful of elderly people were methodically stepping on them in an attempt to squeeze out the deep moisture. James recognized that one woman was Nessie, with her bird hopping on the mattress in imitation of the people. It lightened James' heart to see her up and helping with the work, because when he had left, she had still been recovering in the community centre after being shot and then strangled. If she still lived, surely everyone who had remained here had.

His good mood turned to confusion when he thought he saw some camels walking along one of the container streets. There were plenty of animals around, including those that were normally kept on Animal Island. It seemed that Bitch Bridge was gone, and for all James knew, their fleet of small boats was too. He didn't recall there ever being camels over there, however.

Confusion eventually gave way to a sinking feeling. As he neared the community centre, he saw an array of pelts on stretchers just outside of it. He thought maybe some cows had been sacrificed to feed everyone, until he realized that the pelts had once belonged to horses. Had they really gotten so desperate for food, that the horses were being eaten? He had seen the two outside pulling the boulder, but no others. He was fairly certain that all the horses had been sent out, ridden by people who were supposed to travel to far away places like him, or pulling carts to communities likely to help without much in the way of an immediate trade. Had they come back already? James stroked Soot's neck. They could eat the camels before he would let anyone kill his horse, no matter how old and deaf he was.

Dismounting outside the community centre, James then took the time to remove Soot's gear. With Katrina waiting out there for the Theatre group, he didn't feel too rushed. After letting Soot wander off, he stepped inside the building.

And nearly crashed directly into someone.

"James!"

"Evans?" This was even more confusing than the camels. James didn't think he'd ever see Evans again after the attack on the Black Box.

"How's the foot?" the man asked him. Last Evans would have seen of James, his foot had been a bloody and mangled mess.

"Lost two toes," James told him. "How's your... I don't remember you injuring your leg."

"Yeah, that's fairly recent." Evans had a bandage wrapped around his leg just above the knee, and seemed to be getting around by using his sword within its scabbard as a cane.

"Are you sure you should be walking on it?"

Evans chuckled. "Probably not. But I don't do well staying cooped up in one place for too long, injured or not. I need to walk, even if it's just around your place. Don't tell that doctor of yours that you saw me, or I'm afraid I might end up with more injuries."

James stepped aside to let him pass. "Which doctor? We have more than one."

"Riley. She can be rather fierce."

"I've heard. Enjoy your walk. You'll have to tell me the whole story some time."

"I will." Evans hobbled out into the sunlight.

It wasn't difficult to find Crichton inside. He was orchestrating a group of people who were dividing what food there was into equal portions of two different sizes: one for adults and one for kids.

"Crichton," James called to get his attention.

Crichton turned and was clearly surprised to see him. "James. We didn't expect you back for a long while yet."

"White Fang and the Dale are no good," James said by way of explanation. "Are you really eating the horses?"

"Not our horses," Crichton told him. "I still don't fully understand what happened myself, but apparently we no longer need to worry about any surviving raiders from the Black Box showing up here."

"Tell me everything."

"You first," Crichton insisted.

So James went through the whole story, not skipping any details when it came to the deaths of White, Jack, and Aaron. He did try to condense everything he saw at the Theatre however, figuring that could all be drawn out later.

"You should have started with the fact that people are waiting out there. Let's go meet them." Crichton called for someone else to take over, and then walked with James outside. "You said they brought food? How much?"

"A lot. At least enough to fill half a container, possibly more."

The smile that crossed Crichton's face was one of genuine relief. "Scavengers can't find much since the hurricane hit, and while Evans and the people that came with him brought some food, and we found those dead horses, we didn't think we'd last much longer. We've already killed one of the cows that couldn't produce milk anymore. There are only so many animals to slaughter around here, and many mouths to feed with them. We're even struggling to feed the animals. Most of them are doing their best to survive on washed up seaweed."

"Well, once you see what Vee and her people brought, you won't have to worry so much. We've even been given some seeds, for when that land is ready."

"So you think we'll be all right?" It was the only time James could recall hearing doubt from Crichton.

James was happy to answer without any. "I think we'll be just fine."

THE END

CHECK OUT OTHER GREAT ZOMBIE NOVELS

Z BURBIA
by Jake Bible

Whispering Pines is a classic, quiet, private American subdivision on the edge of Asheville, NC, set in the pristine Blue Ridge Mountains. Which is good since the zombie apocalypse has come to Western North Carolina and really put suburban living to the test!

Surrounded by a sea of the undead, the residents of Whispering Pines have adapted their bucolic life of block parties to scavenging parties, common area groundskeeping to immediate area warfare, neighborhood beautification to neighborhood fortification.

But, even in the best of times, suburban living has its ups and downs what with nosy neighbors, a strict Home Owners' Association, and a property management company that believes the words "strict interpretation" are holy words when applied to the HOA covenants. Now with the zombie apocalypse upon them even those innocuous, daily irritations quickly become dramatic struggles for personal identity, family security, and straight up survival.

ZOMBIE RULES
by David Achord

Zach Gunderson's life sucked and then the zombie apocalypse began.

Rick, an aging Vietnam veteran, alcoholic, and prepper, convinces Zach that the apocalypse is on the horizon. The two of them take refuge at a remote farm. As the zombie plague rages, they face a terrifying fight for survival.

They soon learn however that the walking dead are not the only monsters.

CHECK OUT OTHER GREAT ZOMBIE NOVELS

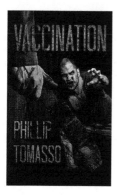

VACCINATION
by Phillip Tomasso

What if the H7N9 vaccination wasn't just a preventative measure against swine flu?

It seemed like the flu came out of nowhere and yet, in no time at all the government manufactured a vaccination. Were lab workers diligent, or could the virus itself have been man-made? Chase McKinney works as a dispatcher at 9-1-1. Taking emergency calls, it becomes immediately obvious that the entire city is infected with the walking dead. His first goal is to reach and save his two children.

Could the walls built by the U.S.A. to keep out illegal aliens, and the fact the Mexican government could not afford to vaccinate their citizens against the flu, make the southern border the only plausible destination for safety?

ZOMBIE, INC
by Chris Dougherty

"WELCOME! To Zombie, Inc. The United Five State Republic's leading manufacturer of zombie defense systems! In business since 2027, Zombie, Inc. puts YOU first. YOUR safety is our MAIN GOAL! Our many home defense options - from Ze Fence® to Ze Popper® to Ze Shed® - fit every need and every budget. Use Scan Code "TELL ME MORE!" for your FREE, in-home*, no obligation consultation! *Schedule your appointment with the confidence that you will NEVER HAVE TO LEAVE YOUR HOME! It isn't safe out there and we know it better than most! Our sales staff is FULLY TRAINED to handle any and all adversarial encounters with the living and the undead". Twenty-five years after the deadly plague, the United Five State Republic's most successful company, Zombie, Inc., is in trouble. Will a simple case of dwindling supply and lessening demand be the end of them or will Zombie, Inc. find a way, however unpalatable, to survive?

CHECK OUT OTHER GREAT ZOMBIE NOVELS

RUN
by Rich Restucci

The dead have risen, and they are hungry.

Slow and plodding, they are Legion. The undead hunt the living. Stop and they will catch you. Hide and they will find you. If you have a heartbeat you do the only thing you can: You run.

Survivors escape to an island stronghold: A cop and his daughter, a computer nerd, a garbage man with a piece of rebar, and an escapee from a mental hospital with a life-saving secret. After reaching Alcatraz, the ever expanding group of survivors realize that the infected are not the only threat.

Caught between the viciousness of the undead, and the heartlessness of the living, what choice is there? Run.

THE DEAD WALK THE EARTH
by Luke Duffy

As the flames of war threaten to engulf the globe, a new threat emerges.

A 'deadly flu', the like of which no one has ever seen or imagined, relentlessly spreads, gripping the world by the throat and slowly squeezing the life from humanity.

Eight soldiers, accustomed to operating below the radar, carrying out the dirty work of a modern democracy, become trapped within the carnage of a new and terrifying world.

Deniable and completely expendable. That is how their government considers them, and as the dead begin to walk, Stan and his men must fight to survive.

Made in the USA
San Bernardino, CA
16 June 2019